If Where You're Going Isn't Home

Book 2

Of the World

Max Zimmer

the stuff of Big Love pyrotechnics; this is the real, compelling, and revealing look into the demands of the faith as Shake and his young friends take their first steps into adulthood. But the great craft of this book is that it neither demonizes nor sanctifies its characters. And it neither demonizes nor sanctifies the Mormon church and faith. Zimmer presents his wonderful, quirky, and often hilarious cast with affection for all their foibles and strengths."

— *Rolf Yngve, novelist,* Any Watch They Keep, *San Diego*

"Zimmer's writing is rich and full of detail. Zimmer . . . has an incredible talent for making his readers feel part of his stories."

— *Deseret News*

"Shake's observations reveal the absurdity of fundamentalist logic, the deep-seated racism in Mormon history, and the extraordinary way music can transport us to a different time, mindset, or spiritual state."

— *Kirkus Reviews*

"That Zimmer has tackled Shake's journey as a trilogy is commendable. He has captured the nuances of not only the essence of jazz, which becomes central to Shake's inner life, but also the era of the fifties from the perspective of a young boy thrust into a religious community during an era of societal change throughout America. This is a novel for those who appreciate a lyrical quest for truth, a story filled with images and sounds, and a boy who longs for the world of Miles Davis."

— *Dana Bishop Smith, Association for Mormon Letters*

"Other authors create a world and then expect me to believe in it. What makes Zimmer unique is that he writes his story and uses my world to tell it. I didn't want the book to end."

— *John Murray, artist and novelist, New Jersey*

"I wanted to read sections again — slowly — just because the writing is so good I wanted to live in them. Zimmer's detail is unrivaled. Shake's story so perfectly shows the unresolvable nature of inhumanity."

— *Nikolaus Tea, musician and poet,* Red Bandana, *Vermont*

"As a musician, I felt that the pulse of music in Shake's life, as well as his whole world as created by Zimmer, were so compelling — so real, I forgot I was reading fiction. There's such delight in the details, it was impossible to look away."

— *Fred Simpson, poet and musician, New York*

THE STORY AND ITS MAKING

Of the World follows *Journey* as the second book of the trilogy *If Where You're Going Isn't Home*, a story that chronicles ten years in the growth of a boy to manhood. *Journey* brings him four years from the age of almost twelve to almost sixteen, where *Of the World* picks his story up and takes it through his nineteenth birthday. The third book, *Instrument of the Lord*, takes his story the distance to the age of twenty-two.

The genesis of what has evolved into this project is a love story I wrote in the summer of 1978. The story haunted me for several years. What I eventually came to recognize was that its psychic and dramatic setting – what it was like to grow up Mormon in America – had never been put on the map of our collective consciousness in a universal way that readers everywhere, from all walks of life, all religions, all cultures, could reach and experience from the familiar territory of their own lives. To create that setting, I put the original story aside, and began where the story needed to begin – with a boy at the beginning of his duty to his father's faith and his dream to play jazz trumpet. His story – the three-book chronicle of his ten-year odyssey – has been in the making now for more than two decades. It is a story still guided and informed by the beacon of that love story that gave it life that summer.

If Where You're Going Isn't Home

Book 2

Of the World

Cover photograph of moonrise over a desert highway adapted and used by permission of Suncruiser Publishing at www.suncruisermedia.com.

Cover executed by Kevin Young

The religious teachings and customs portrayed in this book are accurate. Based on actual experience, verified by research, they are true to the doctrine and authentic in rendering the culture of the Mormon Church as taught, practiced, and lived in Utah in the early 1960s.

Occasional scriptures cited in this work are taken from the Book of Mormon and the Doctrine and Covenants. Both books are official scripture of the Church of Jesus Christ of Latter-Day Saints.

The author is grateful to the writers, composers, and performers of the following songs, lyrics from which are cited in this book.

"Summertime" by George Gershwin and DuBose Heyward
"Sometimes I Feel Like a Motherless Child" performed by Louis Armstrong
"All the Things You Are" by Jerome Kern and Oscar Hammerstein II
"My Funny Valentine" by Richard Rogers and Lorenz Hart
"Teen Angel" by Jean Dinning and Red Surrey
"When Sunny Gets Blue" by Jack Segal and Marvin Fisher
"Embraceable You" by George and Ira Gershwin
"Since I Fell for You" by Buddy Johnson

State Street still runs straight and almost endless through the long heart of Salt Lake City. As anywhere, most all of the clubs where you could once hear jazz and dance are gone, like most of Route 40 West through the desert towns of Nevada and across the Sierras into California. They are brought back to life in these pages because without them Shake Tauffler's story could not be continued.

ISBN 978-0-9854481-5-8

"Shall I tell you the law of God in regard to the African race? If the white man who belongs to the chosen seed mixes his blood with the seed of Cain, the penalty, under the law of God, is death on the spot. This will always be so."

Brigham Young
Journal of Discourses

———————

Yes, sometimes I feel like a motherless child.

Why?

Why? Cuz nothin ever happens.

Nothin?

Well, nothin good.

So what's good?

You know, to have a ball, man.

You sick?

No.

Hungry?

No, man! I just had myself a whole mess of black eyed peas and rice!

See what I mean?

I did! I am a long ways from home! But things could be worse, sure could.

Louis Armstrong
Sometimes I Feel Like a Motherless Child

———————

In 1978, through divine revelation, the Mormon Church acknowledged that Negro men were finally fit to bear the Priesthood. In the meantime, generations of children had been taught to believe that the Negro race was a cursed and inferior race, and that it wasn't wrong to believe this way, but necessary, a necessary matter of their faith in the word of God.

FOR MY MOTHER AND FATHER

Contents

PART 1

MOTHERLESS CHILD

LOUIE ARMSTRONG. Lester Young.

All of them. The gallery of their framed and autographed photos arranged on the wall that Mr. Selby's staircase climbs from the living room where he teaches trumpet to the rooms upstairs. Along the way you've heard there's something wrong with them. Sometimes in the questions your father answers like you've asked him something else. And sometimes just this sense, at church, there among your father's army, this sense of something silent shared, not shared like knowing two plus two is four, but more like this rock hard silent understanding at the heart of some necessary mystery.

Cootie Williams. Charlie Parker. Coleman Hawkins.

There's the lesson you know is coming down the road where you'll hear how the story goes from its beginning to what its end will someday be. The official version. The version you'll accept as the word of God. The closest anyone's come to saying anything about it for real is your buddy Yenchik. There was the speech in the General Priesthood Session where the Second Counselor to the President of the Church talked in these broken angry rambling pieces Yenchik had to show you how to fit together. If they talk about Cain, he said, they mean niggers. Or who gets to have the Priesthood and who don't. They mean niggers. Or not everyone being equal or from the same estate or having the same intelligence. They mean niggers. Or passing the Priesthood from father to son. They mean niggers. Because if one nigger got it, pretty soon they'd all have it, because they're all related.

John Coltrane. Red Garland.

He didn't mean the word niggers bad. He was just telling you. Cain. The first of them. Who all the rest of them came from. Fence Sitters. Spirits who didn't fight in some big war in Heaven before Adam or Eve or anyone came to Earth. Spirits who sat on some fence instead. You've remembered the fence you sat on in La Sal, the weathered gray velvet of the top log, you and Jimmy Dennison and David White watching the cowboys cut cattle into the chute, the sheepherders cut sheep, calves get branded, and every Saturday morning waiting with your carved spears while a steer got shot and then hung upside down and gutted.

Ahmad Jamal. Art Farmer.

Their albums. Albums Mr. Selby lets you take home in your leather pouch to set on your portable record player in the garage. Albums you learn how to play along with. In the ceiling of the closed garage the bare bulb is frosted with smoking dust. Its reflected light is a thin spear of bright fire along the gold brass pipe out toward the dented bell of your trumpet. Dizzy Gillespie. Bud Powell. Some reason deep in their bones why they can't have the Priesthood. Why you could have its power starting when you first turned twelve and they could live to be a thousand and still not be close to having it. The men who taught you everything you know about the way you play.

Sometimes you've wondered if you're one of them. A white nigger. A white nigger kid with his white nigger band. Eddie and Jimmy and Robbie. If that's what your father sees when he comes home from work and finds you standing there.

Clifford Brown. Sonny Rollins.

There was the photo Blackwell showed you in National Geographic magazine. The Negro girl with the high school face and the big bundle on her head and her naked breasts out there for anyone to look at. You could tell she was high school because if her breasts were white they were the breasts you imagined high school breasts would look like.

Who her mother was.

Motherless Child. A slave song. Your father's favorite song.

Dexter Gordon. Thelonius Monk.

Men you've never met except in the stories Mr. Selby tells you. Men who were always there. Before you heard that sound on the radio in the cattle truck. Before Mr. Hinkle. Before Mrs. Harding. Sometimes you've wondered if they were there through that secret winter in the sandpit in the hills behind your house, when you had to play alone through all the questions, when all the questions tore through you like wind and went away unanswered. Giants in the sky around you watching over you. If they took the shapes of clouds. If the hard bright points of the early stars as the sunset lost its color into night were their eyes or the diamond rings some of them wore in Mr. Selby's photos. If you could have seen them in the constellations. But you didn't know them then. That they were even there for you to look for. Before Mr. Selby. Sometimes when he's in the kitchen getting milk and cookies, when he's in the bathroom, you'll stand in front of the wall and look at them. Duke Ellington. Count Basie. In the end they're men you only know through sound, like someone blind, the sound the needle lifts off the grooves of their albums. Men you play along with deep inside their songs. Men from whose solos you lift and give flight to your own. Not so they know. But there you are. There where they stand like giants around you and back a step or two away to give your solos room to fly.

Eubie Blake. Fats Waller. Eric Dolphy.

Fence Sitters. Sometimes shame makes you look away from the blind way they look at you out of the sightless eyes of their photos. Sometimes shame makes you glad you're blind yourself while you play along with them in the garage. Roy Eldridge. Stanley Turrentine. Buck Clayton. They came to Earth with skin that looked like it had been baked pitch brown in the ovens of Hell. They came to Earth as Negroes. So they could be recognized. So you'd know who they were. So you could pity them. So you wouldn't give them the Priesthood by mistake. So you wouldn't lie down with one of their girls, or marry one, because if you did, even by accident, you'd be struck dead on the spot. She only had to have one drop of negro blood to draw down lightning.

Wayne Shorter. Clark Terry. Ornette Coleman.

All of them. Spirits who came to Earth as Negroes. Negroes who came to America as slaves to sing their slave songs. The pretty Negro girl in the National Geographic magazine. You could look at the photo of her face, and even touch the photo where her breasts were, but you couldn't see or touch her real ones.

Oscar Peterson. Cannonball Adderley.

Somewhere along the way you've heard they're not responsible enough to know how to handle the sacred power of the Priesthood. You've wondered what that means. You've wondered what they'd do with it. Drive it like a runaway train off a railroad bridge across a canyon. Set fire to their houses or make their heads explode. You've heard the time will come when God will decide they've finally proven they're responsible enough. You've wondered when. What they'll need to do to prove themselves. If all of them will become responsible together, at the same time, in the same hour or day or year, like a kind of graduation. If you can touch a Negro girl then and not be killed. All you know for sure is that when that time arrives, when God decides, he'll tell the Prophet of the Church through a revelation.

Miles Davis.

In a few weeks, when you turn sixteen, your father will advance you from the rank of Teacher to the rank of Priest. Your new power will authorize you to bestow the Aaronic Priesthood on those who are worthy of its power. You'll have your buddies there to help you. They'll all be Priests this summer too. You'll have one of them hold his trumpet. In a vacant classroom you'll move back the metal folding chairs and leave one chair standing in the clearing in the center. You'll have him sit down. You'll take your place behind him. Keller and West and Doby and Jasperson and Lilly and Yenchik will form the rest of the circle around him the way your father's friends did you. You'll put your hands on his head and look for traction on his short thick hair, and your buddies will stack their hands on top of yours, and then, unable to see the proud black unforgiving fierceness concentrated in his face, you'll be ready to do the ordaining prayer the way your father did for you.

You start with his name.

"Miles Dewey Davis the Third."

Because that's what Mr. Selby said his whole name was.

CHAPTER 2

SUMMERTIME. For your last time through the song you stick the silver mute back in the bell of your trumpet and bring them home, back to the melody they recognize, back to the bleachers in the gym, back to where they can whisper and hum the words they know. Fish are jumpin. Robbie's back to brushing on his snares. Jimmy's back to laying down the uptempo pace of the bass line. Eddie's back to playing under you with the taste of lemonade still in his sax. You're sending the line of the melody out again, the way you started, no big deal, nothing serious, just the easy muted liquid breeze of just another summer day. And your momma's good lookin. Home from the vast and wild place where dusk fell and they could start to hear the gentle questioning in the cries that animals make at night. Home, to this April afternoon in this town called Bountiful, this town you started calling home four years ago when Manny and Hidalgo moved your family here, home to this high school gym. You and your band. Four tenth grade punks. Four white nigger kids. Hush little baby don't you cry.

And when the last note dies and you bring your trumpet down the gym itself is dead. Nothing. They never came along with you. Through the song, your solo anyway, they sat here wondering where you'd gone. Behind you, you can feel the air go out of Eddie's heart, Jimmy getting pissed the way he does when he doesn't know what else to do, and Robbie wondering what the fuck.

"Wait," Jimmy says, quiet behind you.

Nothing. In the cold dead shaming calm of the gym it's time to go. Where the four of you make the long walk from the center of the basketball court across the slick striped hardwood and out the distant door at the end of the gym. You know what you did. Miles. You played him. You can feel like him. His gleaming black defiance concentrated in your white face. Just go. You step up to the microphone and hear your voice come down from the speakers flat and blank and tuneless on the student body of Bountiful High.

"Thank you."

And when you turn around to tell your band it's time to go you hear a whoop. One quick sharp startling whoop from back of you that makes Robbie jump like he goosed himself and take a crazy look out past you. And then both sides of the gym explode. Clapping and whistling and hollering so wild you look at both ends of the court to see who made the basket. And then at your band again. Eddie looking scared. Jimmy bashful looking down at his bass guitar like he doesn't know where else to look. Robbie grinning from behind his cymbals like he had it coming all along. Across the floor behind them the other bank of bleachers is thick and furious with hands. The noise keeps coming. This constant rain off the high steel beams of the rafters and the banked hillsides of the bleachers crashing down around the four of you while it dawns on you that you need to face them.

"I told you," you hear Jimmy, loud this time.

You can't look up. Because your heart is in your face and you don't know what you look like. Because they'd see your heart there in your face where you can feel it beat so hard and wild you can't get your mouth to cover your teeth. You don't look up but you raise your trumpet and take the microphone for real this time. Eddie Meservy on sax. Jimmy Hepworth on bass. Robbie Fox on drums. Thank you again. Thank you. And look toward the door at the end of the gym.

You don't know what draws your eyes his way. Something you feel, maybe hear, like a vague uncertain distant sound that has something like your name in it, a presence you sense alone in the dark. But there he is, against the wall by the door like he just stepped in to stand there and wait for you to leave, an old man, tall, distinguished, his hair white, a white shirt and dark tie and smooth dark suit. In the racket of the gym he couldn't look more out of place. Around him there's this pool of stillness that holds all the noise at bay, an insistent stillness that reaches you across the gym to surround you too, to where the gym goes slowly quiet, where it's only you and him.

You can't look at him straight on. Not without him drifting off your line of sight like something elusive floating on the surface of your eye. You can't make out his face at first. And when you finally can there is no face. It rivets you. In the place framed by his white hair and his ears and the collar of his shirt, in the place where there should be a mouth and nose and eyes set into the skin and bone of a face, there's just this place, blurred, vacant of anything except for the way it radiates this raw congested scorn. It holds you there. You smell shit. Mothball dust and the stale shit kids would leave in the decomposing upstairs rooms of the big abandoned house with the roof half gone when you pedaled down the long dirt road that ran out of La Sal. It wants you to smell shit. The dust stale mothball smell of old shit where his face should be.

"Hey. Shake."

"Yeah. Okay."

The noise again. The bleachers going empty. The reflex to point him out to Jimmy. But you know that you're the only one who sees him. And then he's gone if he was ever even there.

Who he was. If he was real. If what you smelled was from the place where he should have had a face or from a fart that Eddie cut when the gym came crashing down. You'd just played Summertime. A song you got off Miles. Maybe what you saw was what Miles would have seen in the face of a distinguished looking white haired man in a distinguished suit. Maybe the smell is what he wanted Miles to smell. Since then, you haven't really seen him, just his image, the elusive ghost flash of his image as it cuts through what you happen to be doing. And then it's gone, and nothing's changed, but when you start to think he maybe wasn't real, the smell is there to tell you.

"It's not five four," says Eddie. "It's ten eight."

"Jesus!" Jimmy hollers.

Everyone ducks, looks at the ceiling, then waits for the hard crack of thunder outside to let go of Robbie's house and roll away. Even in the basement you can hear the roar and whip of rain and wind from the cloudburst going on upstairs around the house.

"It's five four," Robbie says. "That's why it's called Take Five. You don't hear anyone calling it Take Ten, do you?"

"You're a drummer. You can play it that way. But look at how it's built. On eighths. I'm playing eighth notes. Jimmy and Shake too. Think about it."

Your band. Robbie half Mexican from his mother, half Mormon from his father, his hair black like his mother's, curly like his father's, his arms and legs and head all jumps and rolls and angles when he's moving like he's always rapping drums and whacking cymbals. Eddie not Mormon from either side, not anything really, just this tall loose flabby guy from out of nowhere with oily dark brown hair and black Paul Desmond glasses and this big slack face with this endless window shade of a bottom lip that looks like you could roll it down forever before you had to let it whip back up. Jimmy born Mormon, up in Pocatello, but before he turned old enough to baptize, his mother and father moved south from Idaho to Utah, to West Bountiful where the freight trains sound their long horns, and then from there they never went to church again. And you, from Switzerland, when your father and all your aunts and uncles followed your grandfather here twelve years ago. You were four years old on the Queen Elizabeth.

"Five four, ten eight," says Robbie. "What's the difference."

Eddie won't let go.

"I bet Morello's playing ten eight on his drum solo," he says.

"Okay," says Robbie. "What were you playing in the gym?"

"Ten eight."

"I was playing five four. You notice anything?"

Eddie stares at him.

"I didn't think so," Robbie says. "So it don't friggin' matter."

"But look at it. It's all eighth notes."

"It's not some algebra problem," says Jimmy. "It's a frickin' song."

"All I'm saying is we oughta know what we're playing."

"All I'm sayin' is it's a frickin' song," Jimmy says.

In the basement of Robbie's house his drums and cymbals take up one whole corner of the room. The rest of the room is furnished with mismatched stuff his family got tired of having in the living room upstairs. An early American sofa upholstered with faded sunflowers the size of plates, the cushions flattened, red towels on the armrests to hide the stuffing breaking through the holes, Jimmy in the near corner, flipping through a magazine, his knees together to hold the neck of his Fender bass, its sunburst flame gold body resting on his shoes. Eddie deep in the far corner, his sax on the cushion by his leg, curled there like a brass cat. Robbie in the big upholstered armchair, one leg tossed over an armrest, an arm tossed over the other one. Space age end tables, their black paint chipped, scarred with blistered circles left from drinks. On one of them stands a driftwood lamp. Three music stands hold the charts you've been working on. The gleaming barrels of Robbie's drums are swirls of marbled white and turquoise. You on the bench with your back to the keyboard of the old upright piano, the ivories missing off some of the stained keys, some dead, some stuck, the strings so out of tune that Chopsticks comes off sounding like drowning animals crying.

"You find that song?" Robbie asks you.

"Motherless Child? No."

"You could check Hinkle's place. If he doesn't have it, he'll at least know it."

You look at Robbie. How he sees Mr. Hinkle any time he wants, for sticks, for skins, for cymbals, even for drums. How Eddie does for pads and reeds and Jimmy does for strings.

"I got a lesson when I leave here," you say. "I'll ask Mr. Selby."

"We still need a name," says Eddie.

"God," says Jimmy. "Here we go with the name thing."

"You didn't feel stupid when the student body vice president asks who we are in front of the whole school?" And then he says, "I mean stupider than usual?"

"It's cool we don't have a name," says Jimmy.

"We're the band that played Summertime," says Eddie. "That's what everyone calls us. The Band that Played Summertime. That's not right. We played Scrapple from the Apple. We played Take Five. But nobody says that. Oh. You're the band that played Take Five. Ever."

"I thought it was Take Ten," says Robbie.

Another crack of thunder rocks the house. The fluorescent lights in the ceiling flicker, go out, come back. You're done practicing. Just waiting for the storm to rain itself out before you wipe down your bike and head for Mr. Selby's.

Eddie's still going.

"You seen the way chicks like Margo Swenson smile at Shake. Like you're not there. You could be standing right in front of him. She'd see right through you."

He's right. The way kids have started seeing you since the assembly. Even jocks and their chicks. You can't remember what it was like, being invisible, the same way you can't look in a mirror and remember what it was like to look in one before you had a band.

"She doesn't even know my name," you say.

"Summertime," says Eddie. "Ain't that enough?"

"I'd like to see through those sweaters she wears," says Jimmy.

"I know," says Eddie, "I can stand there and look at her boobs all I want. She doesn't even care. Like I'm a friggin' teddy bear or hamster."

"You can bitch about anything," says Jimmy.

"No. I'm just saying. While she's smiling away at Shake. We need a name just so we'll all be equal."

"Okay," says Jimmy. "The Eddie Meservy Band."

"That's not what I'm saying."

"The First Vision Quartet," Robbie says, not looking your way, just grinning.

It's enough to make Eddie finally smile.

"The Mormon Tabernacle Jazz Quartet," he says.

"The Wives of Brigham Young," says Jimmy. "We could dress like 'em."

"We could be the Angel Moroni Band," says Eddie. "With Shake's horn."

"Yeah," says Robbie. "We could put Shake up on that other spire. Paint him gold. Let him and Moroni duke it out."

"Shake'd blow that angel off his bowling ball," says Jimmy.

Your band. Just you Mormon when the banter turns that way. When Robbie starts going after Joseph Smith or Jimmy after all the women

Brigham Young could pick from when he went to bed at night. When they start coming after you with the easy and teasing resentment you get from a few of the guys in your auto mechanics class who aren't Mormon either. It doesn't come up much. And when it does you don't get mad. More like restless, the twitching walk of a seagull at the edge of taking off, the nervous skitter of flame on a puddle of gasoline. Because you know what they mean. The way they get looked at by some of the Mormon kids in school.

"The Fence Sitters," Robbie says. "We could do Al Jolson faces."

"Shake'd have to stay white," says Jimmy.

"Why?" says Robbie.

"Cuz he'd lose the Priesthood if he didn't," says Jimmy.

And now they're taking looks at you. To see how they've rattled you. If they've taken it too far. You're thinking the faceless man in the gym again. Who he was. What he was there for. He shows up in your head the way he did that first time. Like he just stepped out of some dark place way back in your head to where he's barely in the light. Where you can smell his dust stale dirty smell, a smell that leaves you dirty, a dead smell from the place where he should have had a face. He wasn't there for Miles. You've figured that out. He was there for who you thought you were, soaking up all the applause like a summer cloudburst, thinking you had it coming.

Around the house the wind and rain are letting up and the thunder moving on. Outside, if you could see them, the clouds would be lifting off the foothills up the flanks of the mountains, the sky out west would be blue again, the roads puddled, the asphalt steaming.

"What do you guys think boobs would sound like?" you say.

"Boobs?" says Robbie.

"Like Margo Swenson's. If they made sound."

"Not like anything," Eddie says. "They're not built for sound."

"Come on," you say. "It's not a biology test."

"How do you come up with this stuff?" says Jimmy.

"Eddie brought 'em up," you say.

"Yeah," says Eddie. "But not like that."

"Just all the time," says Robbie.

"Maybe if you took Rosita down," says Eddie. "I wouldn't always be reminded."

On the knotty pine wall across the room from the sofa, two album covers hang on either side of a life-sized velvet portrait in a battered red frame, a soiled portrait of a dark-haired Mexican woman, the ruffled top of her white blouse pulled halfway down her pale gold arms, her neck and shoulders and chest naked well down into the valley between the rising pale gold flesh of her boobs. Robbie found her one night outside a diner on Redwood Road, and brought her home, and tried to clean her up, and hung her on the wall and gave her the name Rosita. On the album covers hung on either side are photos of two of Robbie's favorite drummers. Max Roach and Joe Morello.

"How would you even play 'em?" Jimmy says.

"Like bongos," says Robbie.

"That figures," Eddie says. "For a drummer."

"Bongos is too easy," says Jimmy.

"Maybe with your mouth," says Eddie. "They got mouthpieces."

"Maybe squeeze 'em," says Robbie. "Like those clown horns. Think of it. A whole choir. Just honking away."

"Bagpipes," says Jimmy.

"Bagpipes," says Eddie. "I'd never go near 'em if they sounded that ugly."

"Yeah," says Robbie. "Like you could ever get near 'em anyway."

"Yeah?" says Eddie. "Closest you'll ever get is your sister's dolls."

"No jokes about my sister," Robbie says.

"I said her dolls."

"Her dolls either."

"I still think we need chords," Eddie finally says.

"Here we go again," says Jimmy.

"We already got chords," says Robbie.

And then Eddie's looking at you. But you like it clean too, simple, the way it is, just Jimmy's bass to anchor you, without the guitar or piano Eddie keeps saying you need, just the four of you. It amazes you how all the squabbling goes away when the four of you just settle in and play. When Eddie shuts his mouth and puts his endless lip to work.

You need to go. You wonder if he'll be out there waiting, across the road, watching from a yard or field somewhere while you wipe down the seat of your bike with your teeshirt, put it on again, lash your trumpet to the rack behind it, head for Mr. Selby's, your skin cool where the wind draws water off the wet spots of your teeshirt. Waiting out the rain has made you late already.

"Sorry," you tell Eddie. "I like it this way too."

CHAPTER 3

HIS AUNT DIED. And so you went without last week's lesson while
he went back to New York to help take care of closing down her life
the way the man came from Chicago on a train for Mrs. Harding. Today
he's back. Now, while he gets the oatmeal cookies you smelled all
through your lesson, brings them out and sets them on the slab of the
typewriter tray that pulls out of his big desk, you wheel his round piano
stool across the wooden floor of the living room he uses as his studio.
You watch him pour your glasses halfway full with milk, set the bottle
down, pick up a glass and a cookie, sit down in his big upholstered office chair. Across the top of the desk, out the picture window, there's
the shade of the roofed porch, the handlebars and seat of your bike
leaned up against the outside wall.

"So," he says. "How's everything else?"

"Okay. How was your trip?"

"Know what?" he says. "I've got an old family." He smiles. "They all
got old on me."

You smile back. Look down to hide how it feels to have him talk to
you like this. Till a year or two ago you always used to be scared that the
next lesson you came here for would be your last one.

"How's the band?" he says.

"Good. Better all the time."

"I like hearing that."

"I need to find a song," you say.

"Uh oh. Not something you heard in a cattle truck."

"No." You both laugh remembering Mr. Hinkle. "I got a name this
time. Sometimes I Feel Like a Motherless Child."

"Sure," he says. "Why?"

"To learn it."

"Know anything about it?"

"It's a slave song."

"You know what a slave song is?"

"A song slaves used to sing."

"They'd sing in the fields," he says. "Call and response like we just did. They'd do it to pace their work. Spirituals came from them. Gospel and blues. And somewhere in there jazz."

"It sounds sad. Just the name."

"I know," he says. "They used to sell children right out of the arms of their mothers."

"I heard that."

This quiet smile rises into the field of his trimmed white beard and into the finely ledged skin around his gray eyes while he reaches out and fiddles for a second with the different sized ball bearings he keeps in a little bowl on his desk. It's his story look, the look he gets when you're about to hear some story, about New York where he was born and where he played, about some band he played in, one of the musicians whose photos hang framed on the wall behind you, some other place he played.

"I was in New Orleans once. Funerals can be pretty festive there. Like parades. Music. Costumes. But solemn. It was this gray afternoon. One came down the street. I had a room on the second floor of this old hotel in the Quarter. I could hear it coming a ways off. Dixieland. Gospel. I went out on the balcony to watch. There were some instruments up front. Some men had the coffin on their shoulders. Lots of people walking along behind them."

Mr. Selby picks up one of the big ball bearings, one that reminds you of the steelies you sometimes used to play marbles with, looks at it, puts it back.

"Just before they got to me they all went quiet. No instruments. A woman started singing Motherless Child. She went right past below me singing. I'd heard it before. I'd even played it. But this was something. Before I knew it, I was standing on that rickety old balcony crying. I don't know why. I just was. I didn't even try to stop myself."

While he reaches for another cookie you see your little brother Roy at your grandfather's funeral a couple of months ago, in his sport coat and bow tie, standing alone against the wall of the room where the casket was, silently and helplessly bawling while the noise and crowd and organ music of the viewing went on around him. His open mouth. His unprotected face.

"I'd never heard a more naked song," Mr. Selby finally says. "It's one of the rare blues spirituals. How'd you come up with it?"

"My dad said it's his favorite."

Now he looks at you.

"You want to play it for him?"

In the garage. When he gets home from work, pulls the Chevy station wagon in on its exhaust, gets out, comes around the back, heads for the door into the house. For three years now you've stood there, back where the yard tools are, your portable record player on the workbench with one of Mr. Selby's albums on the black plate of the turntable, your trumpet in your hand. The glancing look he's thrown your way for three years now. Welcome home, Papa. Yes, son. Wanting to play for him. Not knowing how to ask. Not having time to work it out before he takes his briefcase through the door. This time you won't ask. Just play.

"Yeah. For Father's Day."

You watch Mr. Selby's face.

"What do you think he'll do?" he says.

"I don't know," you say.

"He tell you why it's his favorite?"

"No."

A slave song. A song about being motherless when it was his father who died. A negro spiritual when he was born and raised in Switzerland. When he knows how the Church expects him to look at them. When he doesn't even know a Negro.

"Have you ever played for him?"

"No."

"He's never heard you."

"By accident maybe."

"He's never asked."

"No."

"Then he's got a real treat in store. Here's something for you. If you know Summertime, you know Motherless Child."

"How come?"

"Gershwin based Summertime on Motherless Child. He pretty much used the same harmonic theme."

"He did?"

"Yes. I've got a Louie Armstrong recording. Pretty basic. Leaves lots of room to do what you want with it."

"Does he sing it?"

"He does both. We'll take a look. Before we do, though, I'd like to know if you've been to pay our mutual friend at the music store a visit."

An album called Louis and the Good Book. In the afternoon heat of the closed garage you set the album over the post on the turntable of your portable record player, switch it on, let the needle down where the song starts. Motherless Child. While you tie your bandana around your head to keep the sweat out of your eyes you listen to it. Mr. Selby was right. There's not much there. A gospel choir, Louie playing trumpet, then singing, then having a bantering conversation with someone, like someone interviewing him, one of the choir guys maybe, a voice out of the dark of the album.

Yes, sometimes I feel like a motherless child.

Why?

Why? Cuz nothin ever happens.

Nothin?

Well, nothin good.

So what's good?

You know, to have a ball, man.

You sick?

No.

Hungry?

No, man! I just had myself a whole mess of black eyed peas and rice!

See what I mean?

I did! I am a long ways from home! But things could be worse, sure could.

Even with the choir, the clowning little conversation, you hear the grief break through Louie's permanent smile, and from the words and the melody you can tell how the song could make Mr. Selby stand on a balcony in New Orleans and cry. Standing there listening, its simple twelve bars, its changes, its substitutions, its modal harmonies, you recognize Summertime. Just a different melody and words and phrasings laid across the same slow deep river of the changes. One song can come from the other. Hush little baby don't you cry. Turn the song around to the start again and do motherless child this time.

Your daddy's rich like a motherless child.

Sometimes I feel like your momma's good lookin.

You take the needle off the album and put the tone arm on its hook. You can't remember more grief in a simple song. You wonder where your father was when he heard it. Who was singing it. If he started crying out of nowhere too. If he changed motherless child to fatherless and that was how he could cry for his father dying. You pick up your trumpet, find the key, start playing through it.

Behind you the door from the house pulls open. You figure it's your kid brother Roy, come out to stand there and listen like he always does, the matching red bandana you got him tied around his head. You keep playing. Your notes ring bright and sad and long and clear off the walls. You take the melody out past Louie's version where it feels like it wants you to go. You come back around to get to some of the quieter stuff you heard Louie play. And then you bring your trumpet down because you need to hear him play it again.

"Hey," you say, taking the tone arm off its hook to set the needle back on the record again. "Know that one?"

"No, Shakli."

Your mother, the startling ring of her Swiss accent where you expected Roy's bashful but proud small voice, standing by the closed door in a yellow blouse and gardening jeans, too far back from the throw of light from the overhead bulb to where you could read her face under the straw brim of her sun hat. You stand there holding the tone arm off the record.

"I thought you were Roy."

"Your mother can hear it too," she says.

"This one."

"Yes."

You set the needle. While she listens you watch the record circle and the arm wobble as it comes around and around to a small warp in the grooved black plastic. Close your eyes when Louie says in his hoarse heartbreaking voice he just had himself a whole mess of black eyed peas and rice. When it ends you set the tone arm on its hook and turn the player off.

"Why are you playing such an unhappy song?" your mother says. "Are you unhappy about something?"

"No. I just wanted to learn it."

"Did your teacher give it to you? Is that another one of his records?"

"I asked him for it."

"You aren't a long way from home, Shakli. You have a home. A good home." And then she says, "You have a mother too."

You can hear it coming. The complaining helpless little singsong uptick in her voice.

"I know I do," you say. "It's just a song."

"You should play happier ones."

Her piano upstairs. The upright piano she brought all the way from Switzerland. And then stood in every living room in every place you lived before you came and lived here. The way she tried to teach you and Karl and Molly. Her Broadway songs. Songs you've softly played along with, down here in the garage, to her playing and singing upstairs. Your kid brother Roy her only student now.

"You play sad ones too," you say. "Having to love one man till you die." And then you say, "I know you're not thinking about Papa. You just like the song."

"And why do you like a song about a child without a mother?"

"I'm learning it for him."

"Your father?" she says, "Why?"

"For Father's Day. To surprise him."

"Why would you want to play such a song for him? He has a home too."

You stare at her. You figured for sure she'd know his favorite song. For sure he would have told her.

"He told me he likes it," you say.

She comes forward to where the light can reach her upturned face and you can see the wounded almost owlish look of her curiosity there.

"He likes it?" she says. "Did he tell you why?"

"No." And then you say, "It's a surprise. Please don't say anything."

"Yes, Shakli. It is a surprise to me too."

"So let's keep it that way."

"I'd like to know why he likes a song about being far away from his good home."

"Please don't ask him," you say. "It's just a song."

"Why couldn't he ask his wife to learn and play it?"

"He didn't ask me either. I told him I would."

"I would have told him no. He doesn't need a song like that."

"Promise not to say anything before Father's Day. Please."

"I don't know, Shakli," she says. "It's a long time for something so important."

"Please."

"Why don't you ask him for me? Why he likes such a song! Pfui!"

"Please, Mama."

She turns back to the reason that drew her down here. Grabs her bucket and the long-stemmed screwdriver whose forked steel end she uses to reach down and snap the deep roots of crabgrass and dandelion weeds. You wait till she's gone. Think back to the day you brought your trumpet home. The mysterious smoke-sweet history of the worn blue velvet in the case. It was yours. Nothing else mattered. You should have been ready for her to turn the quiet air of the Saturday afternoon in the house explosive with her rage. Ready for her to make your father drive you back to Mr. Hinkle's for a refund. You take Louie's record off the turntable, slip it into its paper sleeve and then into its jacket, then into the leather pouch you made to carry Mr. Selby's records back and forth. You'll have to practice at Robbie's now, leave the album there, hope she lets it rest, hope she forgets. Father's Day. You wish it could be tomorrow. Wish you could clear all the stuff between now and then away. Driver's Ed. Mother's Day. Tenth grade ending. Clear everything out of your way and get to Father's Day before your mother does.

With Louie's album tucked in your leather pouch you ride down the long road through the abandoned fields to Robbie's. In his basement you play it for your band.

"Shit," says Jimmy.

"So what do you think?" you say.

"That's one sad song," says Robbie. "Jesus. Break your heart."

"Yeah," says Jimmy. "Other than making you want to put a gun in your ear, it's just straight minor blues. Goes melodic for that second verse. Real simple. But shit it's sad."

"That's the way I'd like to play it," you say. "Simple."

"Those black eyed peas and rice sound good," says Robbie.

"Not much of a melody," says Eddie. "But there's some cool modal stuff in there."

"I think that's the idea," says Jimmy. "It just kind of moans. Like sad people." And then he says, "Man. You can hear Louie smiling. That's where it's really sad."

"You can come into it right from Summertime," Eddie says. "Same changes."

"Yeah," says Jimmy. "I heard that too."

"Just a turn in the melody and you're there. From your daddy's rich right into like a motherless child. Your daddy's rich like a motherless child."

And then he's picking up his sax and doing what you did. Playing the notes of your daddy's rich into the melody of like a motherless child.

"You gonna have somebody sing it?" Robbie says.

"No."

"Too bad," says Jimmy. "It's got cool words."

"He already knows them."

"Then have him sing along."

"I'm thinking of doing that conversation, though. Where him and that guy are talking."

"About those peas and rice?" says Robbie.

"Yeah."

"This is about slaves, right?" says Eddie.

"Jesus, Eddie," says Robbie. "It's a spiritual. What do you think it's about?"

Eddie ignores him. Looks at you and says, "You gonna do your face with black shoe polish? Put on a curly black mophead wig and a nanny dress like the kids in that assembly did?"

The chorus of maybe forty kids on stage, mouths and eyes like big white holes in the black masks of their painted faces, singing Camptown Races and Dem Bones. You wondered why they didn't use brown shoe polish.

"Why? What?"

"What I'm saying is you're white," he says. "You do that conversation, it's gonna look like you're makin' fun of 'em."

The photo Lupe gave you right after Mrs. Harding died. The photo you were stupid enough to hang on your wall where your mother could find it. In the photograph Mrs. Harding wasn't the fragile trembling white haired woman whose big yard you tended for money to buy your trumpet. She was dark haired and young and beautiful. A band of negro men dressed in their tuxedos surrounded her. Musicians who played the songs she sang so long ago back in Chicago. You could play like them. Sing their songs. Just not talk like them like you're one of them. You look back at Eddie.

"You're right."

"You talking about black eyed peas and rice," says Eddie.

"Yeah," you say. "I get it."

"Not cuz you're Mormon or anything. Just cuz you're white."

"I said I know."

"The trouble is you need chords for all the modal stuff," he says. "That's why they got the choir there. All the harmonies."

"We'll get a harp player," says Jimmy.

"You guys wanna mess with it a little?" you say.

"Sure," says Robbie.

"Yeah," Jimmy says.

"Need to hear it again?"

"Later maybe."

"You wanna go first?" you ask Eddie.

"Sure," says Eddie. "Wanna try coming in from Summertime?"

CHAPTER 4

BUD POWELL. Sonny Rollins. Thelonius Monk. Wayne Shorter. You can play like them. Just never think you're one of them.

You watch your mother and father for any sign she's gone after him in her nasty ridiculing way for the song you were stupid enough to think he would have told her was his favorite. All you see and hear is the usual stuff. He's a sucker for the Church. Needs to lose weight. Can't drive without her constant terrified direction and her hand braced on the dashboard for a stop sign still two blocks ahead. Looks for ways to call him clumsy or a coward. Says no instantaneously, out of instinct, to everything he brings up doing, leaving it to the rest of you to change her mind. You wonder what it does to him. If it deforms or disfigures him inside somehow. There are always sores on his husky forearms, sores like spider bites or punctures from the thorns of his rosebushes, and he picks them till they bleed and then picks at the scabs the blood leaves till they bleed some more. You wonder if the way she mocks him in front of the five of you works like a kind of poison that eats like acid through his skin. If this is a way to poison someone you're supposed to love. If she can keep her mouth shut.

That spring, along with Robbie and Jimmy and Eddie, along with West and Keller and Doby and your other buddies from church, along with your auto mechanics buddies Porter and Quigley and Snook, along with every other sophomore looking to turn sixteen, you take Driver's Ed from Brother Clark, the man who taught your Priesthood class when you and your buddies were Deacons, the massive hairless man in the hide-colored suit who sat behind the little table at the front of the classroom. You remember the level way he took you through the logic of everything he taught you. The fake police department. The level way he would answer the questions Strand would try to trip him up with.

How some of the older Deacons called him Pear Head because of the way his face came down and bellied out around his chin.

You never once saw the knot of his tie. But you always knew that teaching Driver's Ed was his real job. He uses a 53 Pontiac with a brake pedal on the passenger floor. This big wallowing boat of a Pontiac with a stickshift on the steering column and a clutch pedal you can't reach unless you pull the big bench forward to where Brother Clark has his huge round knees against the dashboard in the passenger seat.

He doesn't wear a suit or tie. Just a short sleeved shirt where his forearms are big and white and hairless and shiny with sweat. Two other kids take turns with you when you go out. This tall giraffe of a girl from your English class named Evelyn Lundquist. This wicked greaser kid named Hazelik with a high stack of scalloped black hair.

With its endless hood the Pontiac's like being back in your father's old Buick, except that you're in the driver's seat, on a cushion to get you high enough to look over the steering wheel. Brother Clark rides next to you, a clipboard on his knees, big green sunglasses on his gleaming face, a pencil in the fingers of his left hand. The steering wheel is the size of a bike wheel. The way the Pontiac sags and lifts and wanders makes it feel like you're driving on water. Starting out from stop signs, from lights, from changing drivers, before you catch on to the clutch, you start out bucking, and the bucking puts your feet into the pedals, making the Pontiac buck harder, to where Brother Clark has to put his hand on the dashboard to keep from pitching back and forth. When he pitches forward you can see the ventilated cushion he sits on. How wet the back of his shirt is. Sometimes the bucking gets so bad he reaches for the key and turns the engine off and uses the brake on his side of the floor.

"Just put the clutch down," he says calmly. "Put the clutch back down when it starts to buck like that."

The pencil's there, in his left hand, in case you grab the steering wheel from inside the rim to get a better pull on it, in case he needs to reach across and whack you on the fingers.

"Never take the wheel from the inside. If you lose your grip, and the wheel spins, one of those spokes can whip around and break your hand or snap your wrist."

And the pencil's there in case you go to make a left and then start to turn the wheel while you're still waiting for a car to come the other way. From the back seat, from behind Brother Clark's head, you watch his pencil dart out like a lizard's tongue and whack Evelyn Lundquist's fingers, watch her yank her hand off the wheel and wave it in the air like she's shaking fire off it.

"Oww."

"Always keep your wheels straight while you're waiting. Don't start turning till you're clear to make the whole turn. Say someone hits you from behind. Hard enough to push you forward. With the wheels cocked into the turn, which way will you go? Straight?"

"No."

"No. You'll be turned right into the path of the car you're waiting for. So now you've got a rear end collision and a head on collision. You keep the wheels straight, if you're hit, that's the way you'll go. Straight."

At the end of Driver's Ed Brother Clark signs a form that lets you get your learner's permit. You can drive now with a licensed driver in the passenger seat. A driver like your father. West goes apeshit. He can't stop taking his permit out of his wallet just to stare at it like it's something out of Escapade or Playboy.

"Look at this thing," he says, putting it in Doby's face. "Just look at it."

"Yeah, West, I know," says Doby. "I got one too."

Your church buddies. Four years now. All your voices changed. West with his hair cut more like Tony Curtis. Keller with a little Zorro moustache because someone said he looked like Errol Flynn with freckles. Doby still using Brylcreem to scallop his dark brown hair in waves and fenders. Yenchik with his curly hair grown out in this wild orange sagebrush nobody can talk him into taming. Four years now since he peed in the deep pool of the font in the basement of the Temple where all of you were baptized for the dead. Jasperson getting closer, still not always getting it, still ready to let you know when you've stepped on his sense of reverence. Strand still the same cool guy who sits in back of class and keeps your teachers scared they'll stumble.

It's after Priesthood class. You're hanging out outside, by the double glass doors off the back of the churchhouse, you and West and Doby and Yenchik and Keller and Jasperson, watching families tumble out of station wagons in the parking lot for Sunday School, the way you've done for four years now since all of you were Deacons. Jasperson stands a few feet off like he always does in case one of you says something that could bring lightning down out of a cloudless sky.

"Another week, my old man comes home, all he's gonna do is go riding with me. I'm gonna be drivin' the lug nuts off his Caddy."

Out in the parking lot, Paul Hunt and his Hawaiian wife are getting out of a new white Corvette convertible, their sunglasses on, slick and beautiful and smooth as a couple out of a fancy magazine. Brother Hunt. When you turn sixteen in June and get made a Priest he'll be your Priesthood teacher. West and Lilly and Keller and Jasperson are already there. West looks at his permit again. Making sure the writing that says he can drive hasn't faded off the paper. Then says to you, "Polk teach you how to hotwire cars yet?"

You smile. "Naw."

He turns and squints across the parking lot again in the morning sun just breaking the crest of the foothills.

"If I was a Chevy guy," he says, "I'd hotwire that little Corvette and be gone. He'd never miss it. Hell, it's just a demo anyway. They'd just give him another one."

"I'd rather hotwire his old lady," Keller says.

"Jeez, Keller," Jasperson says. "Nice talk for a Priest. Especially at church."

"I'm not at church. I'm outside. See this? It's called grass."

"You're close enough," says Jasperson.

"Bet Shake could take her away from Hunt," says Yenchik.

"How?"

"Just play Summertime. She'd wet her garmies."

"She'd follow you anywhere," says West.

"Yeah," says Doby. "She'd have to be deaf not to. That was cool."

You never looked at your trumpet that way. There was Carla, in the music room that last day of school two years ago, the way she said she never liked the color of her hair, then took your trumpet and set it on the shelf next to her glasses, and then came back and kissed you. Danny Boy. But that was the closest you came.

"Thanks."

West still has the dark green lenses of his black sunglasses trained on the parking lot. "Me and Janice and that little Vette and the top down. Just on some highway. Across the desert. Headed for Reno maybe."

"What would you do there?" says Doby. "They don't let kids gamble."

"Maybe just keep going," says West. Then he says, "Don't call me a kid."

You watch the doors on your father's Chevy wagon open and your family come out. When you go inside for Sunday School, your mother will be at the organ, playing some sleepy prelude. Motherless Child. If you don't think about it then maybe she won't either. If you can keep it out of your head then maybe you can keep it out of hers. If you could forget the name and words and even the melody then maybe it wouldn't be there to find when she goes snooping through your head. If you could stay away. If you could stay till Father's Day in Robbie's basement. And then you know you're thinking crazy.

"Janice likes blueberry pancakes," you tell West. "You could get her breakfast."

"Nah. She likes apple turnovers now."

CHAPTER 5

"HEY! TAUFFLER!"

You're crossing the parking lot behind the high school headed for your auto mechanics class. Quigley comes loping your way through the cars. With each lope, the fenders of his black hair flap up off the sides of his head like a crow's wings, trying to lift his big head off his neck. He's got a brown hat in his hand.

"What's up?" you say when he gets to you, breathing hard, his rough face lunatic.

"Polk told me to bring his truck into the shop," he says, raking his fenders back across his ears. "Figured we'd take a quick ride. Come on. We only got a coupla minutes."

"You're nuts."

And then he's got you by the shoulder, pushing and pulling you into trotting across the parking lot, to where Polk's pickup must be parked.

"Hey! You're nuts! We can't!"

A big pale blue stepside Chevy pickup jacked high on its fat tires so you know it's four wheel drive.

"Put this hat on," Quigley says. "You'll look older. Like you got a license."

It's one of those brown felt FBI hats with a small brim all the way around and two big dents in top. The dents are stained with old hair oil. "What for?"

"It's Polk's," says Quigley. "If anyone sees us, they'll think you're him. Come on, man."

You pop the passenger door, push a couple of parts catalogs and a small paper bag out of the way, climb up. Quigley's already cranking the starter. The engine grabs. Quigley revs it. The cab twists sideways from the torque.

"Shit," you say. "He's put his money where his mouth is."

"Yeah. Put the fuckin' hat on, man."

"We're gonna catch hell."

"We gotta get caught first. Okay. The gearshift."

"That short one's the transfer case."

Quigley gets it in gear and starts idling out of the parking lot.

"Where we going?"

Quigley looks across. "You look like Frank Sinatra in that fuckin' thing."

He turns the big high-riding rumbling pickup left out of the parking lot onto the long straight road that rises up the climbing slope of the valley into the foothills. You roll your window down. Sure enough. From the tall side mirror on your door it's Frank Sinatra looking back at you. Quigley takes it easy long enough to get out of earshot of the school. You can feel the nervous loping of the engine restless to get going.

"Okay," he says. "Here we go."

He brings the truck to a standstill. Shifts the floor lever into first. Moves his foot off the brake to the gas and starts bringing up the revs while the truck starts rolling backward. The engine sounds like something ready to come through the shaking hood when Quigley dumps the clutch. The nose of the truck comes up. Your head bangs off the rear window. The back tires break the asphalt screaming and the rear end starts to drift around the side. Quigley saws the wheel to keep it straight. The tires start finding traction. Quigley slams it into second and breaks them free again. And then third. The road starts to blur. In the wind you almost lose Mr. Polk's hat. In the yard of an old house on Quigley's side of the road, before you're past her, you catch the petrified wide-mouth look on the old face of a white haired woman watering her grass with a hose. From there you just hang on till Quigley finally brings it down. You look at the speedometer. Thirty never felt slower.

"Holy shit," he says.

"How fast?"

"We busted a hundred," he says.

"You're crazy."

"Wonder if we gave that old lady a heart attack."

"Just what we need," you say. "Her to die."

Quigley takes a long look at the rear view mirror.

"Looks like we're good," he says. "Nobody's after us."

"Yeah. So why not let's turn around and get it back."

"You don't wanna drive?"

"I'm not even supposed to be here," you say.

"Yeah. Fine."

On the way down the long hill you pass the old woman with the garden hose again. This time she just looks furious. You smile and touch the brim of Mr. Polk's hat. Farther down the road you see two patches of black on the asphalt on the other side. Quigley slows down.

"That's where I hit second," he says.

And farther on down the two long snakes of rubber from when he dumped the clutch on first.

"Crap almighty," he says. "Must be a hundred feet."

"There's two of 'em," you say. "He's got the rear end locked."

"That or limited slip. Holy shit."

He takes the truck the long way round the parking lot and drops you off around the corner of the shop.

"Wait. Where'd you get his hat?"

"His office. On that wood chair in the corner."

"Which way'd he have it?"

"I don't know. Hell. He probably don't either."

When you get the hat back in the chair, when you get to the shop, the truck is standing in the open center of the varnished concrete floor. Mr. Polk's got the hood up. You can see the shimmer of heat off the engine. You can hear the ticking of wounded metal cooling. Quigley's standing there so innocent he looks like the little Coppertone girl not knowing her butt's half naked. Mr. Polk touches a rear tire, yanks his hand off, comes back to where Quigley's standing. The rest of the guys are hanging back and giving Quigley all the room to stand there on his own.

"Tell me again," you hear Mr. Polk say. "See if you can look at me this time."

CHAPTER 6

ONE NIGHT in May, just shy of Mother's Day, after he washes the supper dishes, he puts his tie and suit back on to go Ward Teaching to the Soderstroms. You get in your Sunday clothes to go with him the way you've done four nights a month for almost two years now, since he ordained you a Teacher, the way Billy Hess and Brother Jeppson used to come visit your family, the way Gene Minette and Brother Horton come by now, once a month, to see how all of you are doing, make sure you're following the commandments, teach your family a lesson on how to love and respect each other, on testimony, on paying your tithing, on keeping the Word of Wisdom. For almost two years your father and you have had your own four families. The Talbots and Binghams and Beckwiths and Soderstroms.

He has you drive. Brother Soderstrom's big white Freightliner truck is parked next to the house with its tall grill and high fenders and ghost headlights facing the street. It dwarfs the little house. You hand your father the key to the wagon. He knocks on their door. Brother Soderstrom lets you in. Their little living room is thick with the smell of fish. Sister Soderstrom rounds up their little girl and their two little boys while Brother Soderstrom brings in the usual chair for you from the kitchen. They arrange their kids around themselves on the sofa the way they always do, obedient and prepared, like your father's a photographer here to take their portrait. It makes you nervous here because you're here to look around inside their family. The Soderstroms are nice but there's always this fatigue in the way they talk and this hollow submission in their faces like you could walk out the door with their oblong coffee table and they'd let you go. Your father sits on the edge of the easy chair. You hear him ask the Soderstroms how they're doing. Listen to Brother Soderstrom say they're doing fine. Hear your father ask if there's anything they need help with. Watch Sister Soderstrom start fidgeting with her little girl's hair. Watch Brother Soderstrom glance at his wife before you realize he's fishing for a way to answer your father's question.

"No," he finally says. "Nothing I can think of. We're doing okay. Aren't we, Shirley."

"If that's what you call it, Fred."

Sister Soderstrom keeps running her fingers through the same place in her daughter's hair like she's a cat. Their boys sit on the rug in their diapers and rubber pants and look at your father and you.

"Let's not get into that, Shirley."

"He asked, Fred. I don't see why we can't be honest about it."

"That's okay, honey. We'll work it out."

Sister Soderstrom takes her fingers out of her little girl's hair and puts her hand on the armrest at the end of the sofa.

"Tell him, Fred. Maybe it's time we asked for some help."

"We'll work it out, Shirley."

Sister Soderstrom turns to your father.

"Fred lost his job. He can't find work."

"Shirley—"

"No, Fred. I'm sorry." She looks at your father again. "Fred hasn't had work in four months. The truck's broke. And it was spotty before that, with other repairs it needed. We can't afford to fix it this time. He's trying to sell it."

"We'll just keep praying about it, Shirley. Asking the Lord."

"We can't ask the Lord, Fred. Not the way we've gotten behind."

"Shirley."

"Fred. Listen to me. We need help."

"I've got a couple of people interested, Shirley. You know that. I talked to Consolidated too. We're just about to turn the corner."

Four months, you're thinking, you've sat here not knowing a thing.

"He wants to take out a loan," she tells your father. "To catch up on our tithing."

"A loan's the only way, Shirley. We still owe on last year's. For Pete's sake. We can't even get our Temple Recommends renewed."

"I'm not saying I'm against the loan, Fred. I'm just being honest."

"Listen, Shirley. Another week or two and we'll be okay. Let's drop this. Let's get to the lesson."

Sister Soderstrom looks at your father head on in a way you've never seen anyone look at him. Not with any kind of look. Just plain. The way she might look at a rock or something she's got in a frying pan. On the edge of the sofa she's got her knees together under her dress. One hand on her little girl's back to keep her quiet.

"Tell me something, Brother Tauffler. Why is it ten percent? Why not eight or seven? Or four? Or twelve or thirteen?"

Your father looks at her. He hasn't known either. "I don't know," he says, "All I know is that tithing is defined as ten percent. That's what the Church expects."

"I don't care about definitions. I know what the Church expects. But why does my faith in Joseph Smith depend on dollars? On one out of every ten dollars? If I give a dollar less than ten percent, my faith in Joseph Smith isn't good enough?"

"Shirley—"

"No, Fred." Not taking her eyes off your father. "These kids here? They're ours, but they're God's too, and it's our duty to God to feed them, keep them healthy, make sure they've got clothes, a roof over their heads."

"Honey—"

"Let me be!" And then back to your father. "So tell me. I know we're supposed to pay our tithing first. Before our house payment, Fred's truck payment, groceries, doctor bills, everything. And if we do that, then God will help us cover the rest. Well, we tried that for a while. God just took too long. We've got three kids to feed. His kids."

Brother Soderstrom is looking down at his hands. Your father sits there looking back at Sister Soderstrom with this anguish trapped in his face. Even you know what's happening. The public suicide of Sister Soderstrom's testimony. You don't say the kind of stuff she's said. You know that. And then, like she knows it too, she starts to cry, so quietly that the only way you can tell is the way her eyes go red and her cheeks turn wet in the light from the floor lamp next to your father's chair.

"I'm sorry," she says. "I'm so sorry."

"Mommy?"

"It's okay." She reaches down and sweeps her daughter up while Brother Soderstrom heaves himself over and puts his arm around her. One of her diapered boys starts spanking the rug.

"I'm sorry," your father says. "I didn't know."

You know what a loan is. Money you borrow from a bank to buy something. Like a house or a car. Like your father did the Chevy wagon and West keeps talking about doing since he passed Driver's Ed. You've never heard of a loan where you borrow money just to turn around and give it to someone else. Where you get it from the bank so you can hand it to the Church.

Outside again, heading for the wagon, your father offers you the key.

"That's okay. Thanks."

In the wagon, following the headlights home in the dusk from the Soderstroms where your father left a long prayer on the coffee table, you want to know if the Church can't just give them a Temple Recommend now, and wait until Brother Soderstrom's got a job again. If the

Church can't wipe out the tithing they owe and then let them start out fresh. But you know from the busy way your father's back teeth are clacking not to bother him. And you know the rule yourself. Pay your tithing first. Trust the rest to God. Settle your tithing up at the end of every year with Bishop Byrne so you can keep your Temple Recommend. If the Soderstroms had kept up their tithing they wouldn't be in trouble. If they'd had enough faith to go ahead and pay it God would have looked out for them. He would have blessed them tenfold. He would have opened a way for Brother Soderstrom to fix his truck or find another job by now.

"So," your father says. "Mother's Day is this Sunday. We have to plan something nice. I don't want your mother to cook."

"Like a barbecue?"

"I was thinking of taking her out."

"You and her?"

"No. The whole family. Maybe to Harman's."

The restaurant in Salt Lake that does Kentucky Fried Chicken.

"Sounds good to me." Wondering what Brother Soderstrom plans on doing for Sister Soderstrom on Mother's Day.

"Then let's plan on it," he says. "Right after Sunday School. We'll surprise her."

"How do we keep her from cooking dinner?"

"I hadn't thought of that," your father says. "What do you suggest?"

But you're thinking of the Soderstroms. Of your money in the bank. Tithed already, it feels clean, all yours.

"I could give them some money," you say.

"Give who money?"

"The Soderstroms."

"Yes," your father says. "That's very generous."

"I mean it."

"Yes." And then he says, "You know whose name is on your savings account."

"She wouldn't have to know."

"You can't withdraw anything without her signature."

"I can't?"

"You weren't old enough when we opened the account."

You sit back, watch houses go past outside, the houses of your neighbors, where the last of the sunset chases you up the hill in this dull red moving gash across the repeating sheets of iron that are their picture windows.

"You're not going to tell on her, are you?"

"Who?" your father says.

"Sister Soderstrom. What she said about tithing."

"Of course not," he says. And then he says, "That poor woman."

But your mind is back on your mother by then.

"We'll tell her we're doing a barbecue," you say. "That way she won't plan on cooking anything."

"Who?"

"Mama. For Mother's Day."

"By golly," your father says. "I knew I could count on you."

At home he gets out of his suit into his slacks and short sleeved shirt and heads downstairs for his makeshift den in the furnace room. You change too and start wrapping up what's left of your homework. It isn't long before you can hear the clack of the keys on his big electric Royal typewriter, their usual pattern, rushed while he types some sentence out, then silent while he phrases out the next one in his head, then rushed again, the slam of the heavy carriage as it returns for another line. His Sunday School lesson. A letter to a Church Authority. You don't know. Behind you the door to your room opens.

"Oh, Shakli! Come! Hurry! I need your help with the oven!"

She's standing there in her bathrobe but you can tell from her hair she hasn't been to bed yet. Since you started taking auto mechanics instead of band, learned how to use tools, learned how to take a repair job one step at a time, you've been the one who fixes things around the house. In the kitchen you take a look. The door to the oven won't stay closed. A hinge is loose. The place where it bolts to the door is hidden behind a metal liner. You have to take the door off the oven, and then the metal liner off the inside of the door, to get to it. You ask her to spread out a dirty towel on the kitchen table. She does it like a housegirl, obedient and hurried, hoping she arranges it the way you meant her to. You fetch a couple of screwdrivers and a crescent wrench. You watch the springs that load the hinges when you take the door off. Lay the door face down on the towel. Use a Phillips screwdriver to remove the screws along the four sides of the liner. Use a regular screwdriver to work the liner free. Inside, when you pull back the insulation, there's the mounting plate for the hinge, and the screws that came loose are lying there. She sits at the table and watches while you work. She gasps when the hinge almost bites your hand.

"Shakli! Be careful! Maybe we should call a repairman!"

"I've got it."

Your mother frets while you screw the hinge on and the metal liner back in place. In her flannel nightgown, a nightgown that will be soaking wet by morning, Molly wanders in, then wanders out again when your mother doesn't look at her. She holds the door while you bolt its hinges back to the face of the oven. It gets you nervous working this close to her. You get the hinges tight and back away.

"Try it now," you say.

She pulls it open and closes it. At first she acts like she doesn't trust it to work. And then she acts like it's a miracle that it does.

"Oh, Shakli! Thank you!"

"You're welcome."

"I could never ask your father to do that." In her little laugh you can hear scorn along with pity for your father's way with tools.

"Sure you could."

"Oh, Shakli," she says, like it's a sad secret between the two of you. "If only you knew. Let me make you something! Would you like some ice cream and frozen raspberries? A sandwich? What would you like? Tell me!"

"Can I just talk to you?"

"Of course. But let me make you something! Aren't you hungry? A little snackli for my Shakli?" she says playfully.

"No. I just want to ask you something."

"What is it?"

"Can we talk in the dining room?"

"Of course."

Your mother turns on the small chandelier. You take chairs across the table. You can hear your father typing through the floor. Molly wanders in again.

"Mama?" she says.

"Not now, sweetheart. Your brother and I are having a talk."

You look at Molly's hands to see if she's carrying anything Karl got hold of. A doll with its hair ripped off or its feet turned into stumps of melted plastic with a candle flame. But her hands are empty when she turns to go back where she came from. Your mother strokes the surface of the table like she's smoothing a tablecloth you can't see. She looks at you.

"So, Shakli. What is it? What do you need to ask your mother?"

You search her face. If you can use the oven to get her to keep her promise. But all you can see is her question.

"Never mind," you say, thinking how close you came. "It's okay."

Last time you were here, a day before the assembly, the door was locked. Through the glass of the recessed door you could see the long fluorescent tubes that hung from the high ceiling low into the long room. They were dark. The dull ghost glint of the brass instruments and the glass counter came from light through the window displays on either side of the door in whose recess you stood. Instruments still hung in the window displays on silver wire so thin you had to look for it to see it. Your silhouette was on the glass. The back half of the store was black. You couldn't see the door to his shop in back where he taught you how to take apart your trumpet and reassemble it. You couldn't see light around the edges to tell you if he was in there with some other kid, showing him how to take apart some other instrument, some other kid who'd done yardwork to pay for it. On the tall window of the door, the reflected ghost of Main Street behind you, the backward letters of Roy Price Chevrolet on the showroom building across the street, your silhouette took up more of the glass than you remembered, and the silver letters of his name were positioned lower than they were four years ago.

Hinkle Music.

Where everything started.

You'd grown.

You were two months shy of turning twelve. Fresh off the cattle truck that moved your family here, Manny driving and Hidalgo riding shotgun, you between them on a stack of gunny sacks so you could see the road and the old green Buick that carried your family from La Sal here to Bountiful, to the new house on the circle of new houses, at the edge where the town ended and the foothills began for real above the orchards. There was the wild field of weeds off the back yard. There was the long gout of the sandpit just up beyond the crest of the first ridge into the foothills.

Your first time to this door four years ago you didn't know about the sandpit. You were three days new to this town. There was the tall old lanky man in the button-up sweater vest and green tie behind the counter. He asked you what you wanted. You had a sound off the radio of the cattle truck. You wanted the instrument that made it. That could take the breath of a voice and make it a bird made out of the sound of steel. He played you don't remember how many instruments for you. Told you what they were and showed you how you played them. The standup bass you thought was a violin for a giant. The deep throb of its strings made your chest pulse and then your heart race because it had been there too, that throb, on the radio, mixed in with the sound you were looking for. Jazz, he said, when you told him. It's probably jazz we're looking for. You remembered the word then from Hidalgo saying it in the truck. Sheepherder music. Mexican jazz. The man played the foghorn of a sousaphone just for fun. And then the simple horn he lifted off the wall whose sound took you back to the high huge endless sky out through the windshield as Manny brought the old truck whose trailer held everything your family owned down off Soldier Summit.

It was called a trumpet.

His name was Mr. Hinkle. Like the store. He offered you a used one. You made a payment every Saturday for six long weeks you thought would never end out of the money Mrs. Harding paid you for her yard. Then came the Saturday you finally paid it off and got to take it home. Maybe an hour later you were back to ask for your money back while your father waited for you outside, in the Buick, reading a book on the steering wheel. You remember trying to lie to Mr. Hinkle. Him looking out front and seeing your father waiting. Then going out to shake your father's hand and tell him a lie of his own. You remember standing there, watching in shame, for making Mr. Hinkle lie, for your father believing him, for breaking something it took two grown men to fix. You remember thinking Mr. Hinkle would never want you in his store again. Thinking it till Mr. Selby wised you up. Told you how Mr. Hinkle always asked about you.

Four years.

What he'll say.

What you'll tell him.

The trumpet he sold you back then was his. You didn't know that then. Now you do. If you should let him know. In the recessed doorway to his store, you draw breath, let it out, turn the knob, crack the door, take your case and step inside.

The same long room with the wood floor flanked along the right wall by the long glass counter. The instruments under the glass and hung on the walls. The music racks. In the back wall of the store the door to the shop where he taught you how to clean and oil the trumpet before he let you take it home. You close the front door behind you and the dry shoe polish smell of the room rushes forward to immerse you. He's leaning on the counter next to the register, a notebook open on the glass, a pencil in his hand the way he wrote down your payment every Saturday. He raises his head, lifts a pair of glasses off his eyes, looks to see who's come in, brings himself up straight, folds his glasses closed and lays them down. And then for a minute looks you over. You stand there. The ghost of the bashful kid you were four years ago with a hurt knee and scabbed hands. The sudden past of this place.

"Well," he finally says. "What sound are we looking for today?"

The half kidding look in his eyes. The way he's still here, a silver necktie and button-up sweater vest and shirt with its sleeves rolled up to just above his elbows, an old man keeping his instruments dusted. You look away, at the floor, then at the wall where the ghost of the brand new student trumpet hangs, before you look back. This time there's a grin whose corners still pull up and back and make folds of his gray cheeks. He lays his pencil in the crease of his notebook and closes it.

"You look good," he says. "Grown up some."

"You look good too," you say. And then you say, "You've still got that bassoon."

He turns and raises his head to the long dark polished shaft of the instrument where it hangs on the wall behind him.

"Looks like I do," he says. "Your voice changed too."

"Yeah."

"Let me put the sign out," he finally says. "Then we'll go in back and catch up."

CHAPTER 7

QUIGLEY TAKES the heat himself for taking Mr. Polk's truck for a joyride up the road into the foothills. It was his idea. It was him who talked you into going. It was him who told you to wear Mr. Polk's hat. Still. It wasn't him in the passenger seat. Or him who looked like Frank Sinatra. It was you. So you go see Mr. Polk on your own, after school, when his pickup in the parking lot lets you know that he's still there. When you get to his office he's on the phone with a pencil in his other hand.

"Come in," he says.

You stand in front of his desk. With his head down you can see through the standing hair of his flattop down to his white scalp. Posters from speed equipment manufacturers are tacked to the wall behind him. Iskenderian. Edelbrock. A poster from Weiand has a big gleaming supercharger with two ribbed barrels and the long snout of its pulley shaft. One from Giovannoni Cams has a drawing of a dark haired woman with her skirt blown back off her naked legs, her feet bare, her blouse off her shoulder. She's riding a camshaft bareback like a horse. On his desk there's a polished piston standing on its head with an inscription that lets you know it's some kind of trophy. His hat's in the chair in the corner. Just not the way you put it there. Quigley's out in the shop, doing his punishment, cleaning the windows and scrubbing grease and oil off the big floor and every other job Mr. Polk put on his list, singing and whistling while he works because it's better than having Mr. Polk report him to the cops, better than losing his permit for a year. Mr. Polk talks to his black receiver, scribbles down something on his desk pad calendar, hangs up and waits for you to tell him why you're standing here.

"I was in on it."

"On what?"

"What Quigley did. With your truck."

"Tell me about it."

"I went along."

"You went along. You drive it too?"

"No." And then for a minute you don't know how to tell him the next part. "Quigley needed someone who looked old enough to have a license."

"You?"

"I know," you say. And then you say, "That's why I took your hat."

"You did what?"

"We figured I'd look older if a cop saw us." And then you say the rest of it. "We figured they'd think I was you."

He brings up his hand and rests his chin on his knuckles and smiles at you like you're some monkey picking its balls in a cage at Hogle Zoo.

"So you impersonated an auto shop teacher."

"I guess so. Yeah."

"So tell me why I'd be a passenger in my own truck. Like I'm teaching Driver's Ed."

"I guess we didn't think of that."

He looks past you. The smile leaves his face. You turn around. Porter and Snook are in the doorway. Porter in his black engineer boots with the sleeves of his short sleeved shirt cuffed up across his biceps. Snook with his thick blond crewcut and hairy Popeye forearms. They give you looks like you do them. Like what the hell they're doing here.

"Come in, gentlemen. Sorry I don't have any chairs."

You move over to make room in front of the desk. Mr. Polk just sits there watching while Snook and Porter wait each other out for which one has to talk.

"That thing Quigley did with your truck," Snook says.

"You mean steal it," says Mr. Polk.

Snook looks at Porter. Porter looks at the floor.

"Yeah," says Snook. "We were there. We were part of that."

And now you look down.

"You mean you went along for the joyride."

"Yeah."

"Four of you," he says. "The cab was big enough. You sit on each other's laps?"

Four guys. Next to you, you can almost hear Snook doing the arithmetic, catching on to what you're doing here.

"Yeah," Porter says.

Mr. Polk looks back and forth across the three of you.

"So what'd you think, Porter?" he says.

"Of what?"

"My truck."

"It's cool." Porter shrugs and starts to flash his quick reflexive grin before he catches on that Mr. Polk's not being friendly.

"It could use more power," says Mr. Polk.

"Yeah," says Porter. "But what couldn't."

"No such thing as too much power," says Snook.

"You like the way I mounted the tachometer?"

"Yeah."

In a big hole he drilled in the middle of the dashboard. But they can't hear what you're thinking no matter how loud you're thinking it in their direction.

"Only thing I don't like is the automatic tranny," Mr. Polk says.

"You could convert it over," says Snook. "I know a guy who did."

Stickshift, you're hollering, in your head. Stickshift. Stickshift. And then you're thinking it was in the shop. His truck. All class long. They could have looked if they were planning on doing this.

"Okay," says Mr. Polk. "I want one of you boys to tell me what Tauffler here was wearing that he usually doesn't wear."

Both of them look you up and down while you stand there. In the chair, you're thinking, in the corner. Look in the fucking chair.

Snook shrugs. "Nothing."

"Like what he's got on now," says Porter.

"No, that's not right. He tells me he was wearing something he's never worn before and won't ever wear again. What was it?"

From the way Porter starts going red you can tell he's catching on that he's been had. Snook just stands there in his crewcut looking grim now.

"I didn't notice," he says.

"Tell you what," Mr. Polk saying. "I think you're all lying to me. Especially that part about my hat. I think you're here to help your buddy Quigley out."

"That was it," Snook says. "He had a hat on. I remember now. That was yours?"

Mr. Polk just looks at him.

"You were already in the shop," he says. "When your buddy Quigley brought my truck back."

Snook glances up at the poster of the woman riding the Giovannoni camshaft and then down at his shoes.

"Okay," says Mr. Polk. "I don't much take to being lied to. But I like guys who stand by their friends. So go ahead. Help him out. He's got a long list to work off. Now it's your list too."

CHAPTER 8

"THINK I've got it."

Standing across from each other in the living room Mr. Selby uses for a studio, you've just played through Motherless Child together, trading the lead back and forth, trading the backup harmonic shading. He's wearing a tie the way he always does, all year round, his shirt sleeves short or long, sometimes with a sweater vest when you can't see the fish or the parrot painted on them. This time it's a pink and orange lizard on a blue rock.

"Down cold," he says.

"Thanks."

"You still don't know why it's his favorite song."

That Saturday in the garage when you were cleaning up from opening the yard for spring and the shovel fell and hit him in the head and then fell again and he threw it at the wall and went on a swearing streak in Swiss. You wondering if this was how he cried for his father dying. Him breathing hard and calming down and asking you about your trumpet for the first time. You asking for his favorite song so you could play it. Him telling you. And then slipping away from you again, out of your reach, before he would tell you how it went.

"No. I want him to forget he told me anything."

"For the surprise," says Mr. Selby.

"Yeah."

You've been watching them. There's been the usual stuff. He's fat, can't drive without her hand on the dashboard, never stays home unless it's for the Church. Nothing about his song. You could tell if it was. Mr. Selby crosses the room to the low shelf where your open trumpet cases sit, takes out his handkerchief, blows the spit valve into it, twists the mouthpiece out, lays his trumpet in its case.

"My dad passed away around fifteen years ago." Closing the lid, snapping the latches, turning around. "I know what your dad's going through. It's not easy."

In the quiet left in the wake of your playing, the lesson over, you can smell the peanut butter cookies he baked before you got here.

"What's it like?"

He looks at you. Maybe thinking if telling you what it's like to have your father die is something he should tell you. He folds his arms and leans against the low shelf where your cases are.

"Tell me what your grandfather was like."

"He was pretty famous. I mean in the Church." And then you say, "In Europe during the war he kept the Church together. He translated the Book of Mormon into German."

"Sounds like an important man."

"Yeah."

"A busy man."

"I guess."

"Were you close to him?"

Him being dead the one time you remember touching him. The one time you saw his eyes without his glasses. And they were closed.

"Not really."

"Remember the difference between a note and a tone?"

"Yeah."

"What do you remember?"

You wonder if he's kidding, asking if you remember something in your ears and fingers, in your blood. What he's looking for.

"How a note has all these tones," you say. "Depending on what's around it. The song. What key. What the motion is."

"Let's take your dad. Let's make him a note and put him in some different songs and see what kinds of tones we come up with for him."

"Okay."

"In one song, he's your dad, right?"

"I guess."

"No guess. In the song where he's a father, he's your dad."

"Okay."

"In that song, his job is to keep a roof over your head, feed you, make sure you've got clothes, help you do your homework. That's one of his tones. Listen for it. Does it want to go out? Stay home? Is it the root tone?"

"Yeah. Maybe."

"In another song he's a husband. That's the song with just him and your mom in it. Just the two of them. Same note. Different tone."

"Okay."

"The guy who fell in love with her, proposed to her, hoped she'd want him. A tone that wants to resolve, maybe. Look for home too. Or adventure."

"Yeah."

"Didn't you tell me he had some church job?"

"He teaches Sunday School."

"So in that song he becomes another tone. A teacher."

"Okay."

"What does he do for a living?"

"He's a bookkeeper."

"Okay. What does he dream about?"

"He wanted to be a history professor."

"So there's a dream song. And maybe in that song he's a stay out tone. Chasing his dream. A tone that doesn't want to go home where he's a father and a husband and a teacher and everything else."

"What are you saying?"

Mr. Selby looks at you. Takes his time. "Here's another song," he finally says. "You're not in it. None of your family is. The song where he's just a son. A son like you."

You look down at your trumpet. The thin tooled brass pipes. The valves. The bruises in the old lacquer. The gold flare of the dented bell.

"I'm not trying to be clever," Mr. Selby says. "You asked me what it was like."

"I know."

Mr. Selby stands up and walks a couple of steps away from the shelf and then stops and looks at the floor.

"When my dad died I felt like a little kid again. I was a grown man. Like your dad. But all I could think about was being my dad's kid. His son. The son he was raising. To be a son, though, you need a father. So when he died, that song where I was a son was gone for me. And for a while nothing else mattered. None of the other songs. I'd look in the mirror and all I'd see is the son I'd been. Just this kid. No dad. On his own now."

When he looks up at you his gray eyes are steady. In the clearing his beard leaves for his mouth there's the line of a quiet smile.

"I was a note again," he says. "Just a note. A naked note. Lost. The most naked and lost I'd ever felt in my life."

"Did you cry when he died?"

"Yes. I did."

"I don't think my dad did."

"Maybe he just didn't cry in front of you."

"I hope so."

"He's got a new song now."

"What?"

"The song of a son who lost his dad. A son who longs to be young himself, your age, when he remembers his dad. When he had his dad around. What tone do you hear?"

"A sad one. Minor. Blues."

"Maybe a little dissonant. Maybe a little confused. A little lost. Not sure of himself. Ambivalent. Not sure where to go next."

The way he looked at you in the garage once he calmed back down, caught his breath, apologized for swearing. Like lightning gone off, thunder still rocketing around inside his head, this wild stare like he knew he was supposed to know you but was still too blinded by the lightning to make you out.

"Yeah."

"That's who you'll be playing for when you play Motherless Child. Okay?"

"Yeah."

"Okay then. Let's have some cookies while you can tell me all about your visit with our old friend Mr. Hinkle."

CHAPTER 9

DOWN AT the churchhouse on Mother's Day they have to open the massive folding doors across the back of the chapel and set rows of folding chairs out on the hardwood floor of the gym to catch the spill of all the mothers. In the lobby stand racks and racks of cup-sized flower pots with limp little red geraniums in them. After Sunday School, on their way out, you and Doby and Yenchik and the other Teachers will hand them out to all the mothers. The rest of your church buddies, Lilly and West and Keller and Jasperson and Strand, have moved on. They've turned sixteen. They've been to an empty classroom down the hall to sit in a chair in a circle of standing men to be advanced to the rank of Priest. Their new power lets them sit at the Sacrament Table, tear slices of Wonder Bread into scraps to signify the flesh of Christ, then bless the bread and then the water trays and hand them to the Deacons. For now they're new at it. Still caught in the change. Waiting for you and Doby and Yenchik before they can feel like it's permanent. It's why West and Keller are in the Sacrament Room with you, hanging out while the three of you do your job as Teachers, getting the Sacrament ready, racking paper thimbles in the holes of the water trays and running them under the tap.

You slant the water tray you just filled to level off the water in the little cups. West takes a look out the open door below the organ pipes.

"Man. Hope you got enough Sacrament."

"How come all these mothers turn up on Mother's Day?" says Keller. "Where the hell do they come from?"

"Maybe they came for their geraniums."

"That slice looks stale," West says to Yenchik. "You can't put that on a tray."

Yenchik grabs the slice. Tests it with his thumb. Then rips it in half with his teeth.

"Come on," says West.

"You ain't blessed it yet," says Yenchik. "It's still just bread."

"So when you getting your Pontiac?" says Doby.

"Soon as school's out," says West.

"Why not before?"

"My dad wants to see my grades."

"Your grades? You're hosed."

"Up yours, Keller. Don't call me for a ride."

"Where you gonna keep it?" Yenchik says.

"The garage."

"I thought your mom had her beauty parlor there."

"It only takes up half of it."

"Where's your old man gonna park?" says Doby.

"He's on the road most all the time. When he's home I'll use the driveway."

"You got it figured out," you say.

"Yeah," says West. "Since I was twelve."

You finish filling the water trays. Pull two fresh white heavy folded tablecloths off the closet shelf. At the front of the chapel you and Doby spread one of them across the Sacrament Table. Smooth it out. Leave the other tablecloth to cover the bread and water trays once you bring them out and line them up. Under the high vault of the chapel the racket is fresh and exuberant as rain with the sun shining. With the back wall opened it echoes back from the big gym. Across the chapel, with just her black hair visible above the console of the organ, your mother plays Brahms while Yenchik hauls bread and water trays down from the Sacrament Room.

"Hope we put enough trays together," says Doby.

"Yeah."

"You doing anything for your mom?" he says.

"My dad wants to take us out to Harman's Kentucky Fried."

"Now I'm hungry."

"Have West reject another slice of bread."

"Too bad they don't use fried chicken for the Sacrament."

"It'd never make it out of the Sacrament Room. Not with Yenchik."

"Yeah," says Doby. "They'd be passing trays of bones around."

Your mother rides home from Sunday School with her baby geranium in her lap and a quiet smile on her face in the afterglow of playing the organ and having her motherhood honored. In the back seat you wonder when your father plans on springing the surprise. He steers the Chevy wagon out of the parking lot and up the hill and along the street to your circle, eases it across the hump of the curb down your driveway, stops where all of you are looking at the closed door of the garage.

"So," he announces, his voice big. "Who has to go to the bathroom before we take your mother out for Mother's Day?"

In the front seat, your mother turns and stares at him across Maggie's little head, at the big way he's smiling into the rear view mirror where you can see his eyes.

"I thought we were having a barbecue, Harold."

You can hear it. The wondering high fretful voice of a girl with the lightning-riddled underside of a slow black cloud behind her. Your father can hear it too. The twitch in the skin of his jaw when his back teeth start clacking.

"Surprise, Mama," you say. "Happy Mother's Day."

"Where we going?" says Karl.

Your father glances around. "Harman's Restaurant."

"Kentucky Fried?" says Karl.

"Yes."

"No, Harold." Fussing and nervous now. "Let's just have a nice time at home."

"We'll have a nice time at the restaurant. Now. Who has to use the bathroom? Come! We have a reservation!"

"I do," says Molly.

"Me too," says Roy.

"We are not going," your mother says. "Children, someone open the door. Come inside. We will have a nice afternoon at home."

"Let's go, Mama!"

"Yeah! Come on! Finger lickin' good!"

"We'll have fun, Mama!"

"So," she says. "We are not going. You can go if you like. You can leave your mother home on Mother's Day."

"Come on," you say. "You'll enjoy it."

"No, Shakli, I won't enjoy it. I don't want to go. Please don't make me."

And now she has her hand flat on the dashboard like she always does when she sees a stop sign or a red light coming, like she's scared, scared like your father's going a hundred miles an hour with the closed garage door smack in front of her, scared like he's going to put it in reverse and take her anyway, like by pushing on the dashboard she could hold the wagon back from going up the driveway in reverse.

"Nobody's going to make you," your father says. "Why don't you want to go?"

"I don't have to give you a reason! We can go on Father's Day if you have to have your fried chicken! I'm going in the house! Children, come with me!"

You've already got the door open to let Roy and Molly out. Now you close it to keep the neighbors from hearing her. But for a long time there's nothing to hear. Just a family to look at. A family sitting in their driveway in their station wagon.

"Okay," your father finally says. "Who would like Kentucky Fried Chicken?"

"Me!"

"I do!"

"Me!"

"Then let's make a deal," he says. "I'll go get a bucket and some mashed potatoes and gravy. We can eat in the dining room. How's that, Mother?"

"You should have told me," she says, sharp, but her hand off the dashboard. "I could have cooked something."

"You don't have to cook anything. Now get out, everybody. I'll be back soon."

"I'm coming with you."

In the rearview mirror he looks back at you. All you can see are his eyes and the weary defeat in the heavy congested skin around them.

"If you like," he says.

CHAPTER 10

YOU MOVE to the front seat. With your father driving you thread through town and then head south on Highway 89 past the Cudahy Stock Yards and the Phillips 66 Refinery. Soon you're in Salt Lake, on State Street, in the takeout room in back of Harman's Restaurant, waiting for your order. Soon you're headed back, a red and white bucket on the floor between your Sunday shoes, a bag of mashed potatoes and gravy and string beans and biscuits in your lap, the smell of eleven secret herbs and spices in your nose. Back in the driveway you pull the garage door up. For a second, with the engine of the wagon idling behind you, you can see what you'll look like to your father, standing back there, deep in the garage, your trumpet in your hand, what he's seen a million times when he's come home from work. What he'll see the Friday before Father's Day.

A fresh white tablecloth on the dining room table. Cloth napkins. A china plate embossed with a silver ring and painted with gray and lavender flowers and a set of silverware arranged where every chair but the eighth chair stands. Without changing, your father puts his apron on, takes all the chicken out of the bucket, arranges the pieces in a steel bowl. You find glass bowls for the beans and the mashed potatoes and gravy and a platter for the biscuits. Molly wanders in, and Maggie, and Roy, and then your mother, and finally Karl, all in their regular clothes. Your mother uses her knuckles to test the heat of the chicken and mashed potatoes and beans and biscuits.

"Oh, Harold, it's cold. Let me heat it up first. Now that my oven is fixed! Now that my little mechanic has fixed it! Yes, children! This is more like it! At home with my children on Mother's Day!"

When the bowls have been passed around, instead of your mother's food, a breaded thigh and a wing from Harmon's restaurant are on your plate, soft chopped string beans, and a muddy pile of mashed potatoes and gravy. Your father blesses food that was cooked by strangers in red and white striped paper hats. Everyone starts eating. In his street clothes, a short sleeved shirt that exposes his short stout forearms and the one or two sores they always have, he takes a sheet of paper off the buffet behind him. You know what it is. His usual tribute to your mother on her birthday and on Mother's Day. Half of the tribute is his. The other half is quotes he's found in his books about the miracle of mothers. Your mother sees it coming too.

"Oh, Harold, please. We are all eating. We can't let it get cold again."

"Keep on eating," your father says. "Everybody. I have something to read to you. To remind you all what we're celebrating today."

He starts off. Across the table, Molly keeps her braided head close to her plate while she listens to your father crown your mother the world champion of motherhood and give her every virtue in the encyclopedia. You look at the small bone of the chicken wing you've stripped. When you reach for your tumbler of cider you look at your mother. Impatience and ridicule crawl under the restless skin of her face. Your father finally gets to the part where he crowns her the best cook in the world.

"Yes, Harold," she says, a complaining laugh she passes around the faces at the table. "If I am such a good cook, then why did you want to go to a chicken restaurant?"

"It was my idea," you say.

She looks at you. "What was your idea?"

"Taking you out for Mother's Day."

"Yes, Shakli," she says, this confused and cross-eyed little smile like she can't quite see you. "That is nice. But your father didn't have to agree with it."

"It's over," you say. "We're home the way you wanted."

"Yes, Shakli. That is how you talk to your mother on Mother's Day."

"Then let Papa finish."

"It's all right, son," your father says. "Come. Let's all enjoy our meal together."

He folds the sheet he typed his tribute on. Reaches around to lay it on the buffet. Picks the thigh off his plate. Your mother watches him. Her lips are stitched so tight her mouth looks like a lizard's mouth.

"Yes," she says. "In your motherless home."

"Don't," you say.

Your father raises the heavy lids of his eyes to look at her.

"Why would you like a song like that?" she says sharply.

"A song like what, Mother?"

"Don't," you tell her.

"A song about a motherless child. What is wrong with you? You have a good home. You aren't a child. Do you sing it just so that you can feel sorry for yourself?"

Your father stares at her.

"Yes! You can tell your son that you don't have a home! You can tell him that you don't have a mother!! What is he supposed to think? That he doesn't have a mother either? That he's far away from home?"

You put your napkin next to your plate and back your chair away and get up. In the garage the screwdrivers and wrench are where you left them. In the kitchen the oven's still hot from heating the dinner you and your father brought home.

"What are you doing!" Grabbing your arm, your shoulder, her fingernails raking your hand. "My oven!"

You whip around. What she sees in your face backs her off.

"Stay away from me."

"Help me! Harold! Father!"

You go back to work while your family gathers in the doorway from the dining room. You can't keep your hands from shaking.

"What's going on?" your father yells.

"He's destroying my oven!"

"Stay away from me."

"Come now," your father says. "Let's be reasonable."

"Karl! Bring the rugbeater! I'll show him!"

You turn your head to stare your brother down where he's standing behind the counter.

"Don't be stupid," you tell him.

"Don't listen to him! Help me! Father! He is your son! Make him stop!"

"That's enough!" your father says. "Come! Let's get back to dinner!"

"Help me! Somebody call the police!"

"You promised me."

"I promised nothing!"

You ease the last hinge off. Lay the oven door on the kitchen table. Take out the liner screws and slip the liner out and go after the screws to the hinges.

"Stop him!"

"You don't want to touch me."

You leave the hinges and screws and tools in the shell of the door. Turn to her.

"Now you can call a repairman," you tell her.

"Yah!" she says. "Out of your savings account!"

You look for Roy. His scared round bewildered face there behind the counter.

"It's okay," you tell him. "I'll be back."

"Yah! Go! Find out what it is like to be far away from home! To be motherless!"

In your mind you were on your bike already, your trumpet lashed to the rack behind the seat, flying down the long hill that would take you out of here, out of this Mother's Day neighborhood with a geranium in every living room, letting the wind go through you, leaving behind all the names of everything the way you've always done, going till you were nameless yourself. But now you can't look away from your brother's face. Out of his helpless face he looks back at you like he can count on you to fix this. The way you were thinking of having him wear his bandana and do the talking part, the black eyed peas and rice part, until Eddie wised you up. How close you came. How he'd have wanted to wear his gloves, the gloves whose fingertips you cut off for him, to go with his bandana. In the dizzy stench of the Colonel's eleven secret herbs and spices you look at the rest of them, Molly and Maggie and Karl and most of all your father, all of you breathing the same Kentucky Fried Chicken air. You ride out the urge to puke. Your arms relax. Your hands go still. You pick up the tools.

"Just go eat," you say. "I'll fix this."

PART 2

BOYS OF SUMMER

CHAPTER 11

THE AFTERNOON a couple of years ago toward the end of March when you were pedaling home from Mr. Selby's house on the hard dirt path that ran along Orchard Drive. You remember the sun still stingy from winter, the air just warm enough to let you ride barehanded, warm and still enough to where you could smell the dust of winter rising from the dry dirt and gray grass and the asphalt where the grit from the sanding trucks had collected along the curb. The smell of early spring. Out past the wrists of your corduroy jacket your knuckles were red from the air where your hands held the handlebar grips. Your schoolbooks rode in the basket between your hands, their spines forward, to keep the wind from blowing back their pages. Your trumpet case was lashed with clothesline rope to the rack behind your seat.

You remember hearing it first. The flat bark and whining howl of an engine you'd never heard before coming up the road behind you. Looking up when it went by. And whatever you used to think whenever you thought of a car, whatever you used to picture when you heard or said the word, was gone. In its place was this.

On a road you'd taken home from school for almost two years now, a road where you'd watched a Jeep full of high school jocks go tumbling over when it tried too quick to turn around and come gunning after you for flipping them a double bird, the little car looked so out of place you didn't know what to do with it. Like nothing you'd ever seen before. A little red car whose roof and fenders and rear end were pulled in round and smooth and close and low around its wheels like the shell of half an apple. Whose red roof became its red body and then its red body went smooth into its red fenders and then its fenders and sides just came around and wrapped smooth around the bottom. Even the bumper was red where it curved around the rear. No fins or scoops or chrome or fancy taillights. Just plain. Like it was made from one clean curved and rounded surface.

It looked defiant. It didn't have anything to do with a Pontiac or Buick or Chevy or Ford or any other car. It didn't belong. It didn't want to. It wanted to just keep going. It made you feel this sudden defiant feeling you knew you shouldn't feel, for not belonging either, for wanting to keep on going too, for wanting a car you should never have thought of ever having. Your bike slipped and stumbled off a hard ridge in the packed dirt. You put down your foot to catch yourself. Stood there and watched it keep going down the road. And then it was gone. Before you knew it. Gone where the road disappeared through the late winter trunks of the trees. And then you couldn't believe you'd stopped and let it go.

You got back on the pedals. Stood on them hard. Stayed off the seat to let your bike ride loose and your legs absorb the holes and ridges in the dirt. Your schoolbooks chattered in the wirework of the basket. Your trumpet case slammed against its harness. You jumped the curb and used the street. Pedaled harder. Flew past houses. Shot through crossings. Your legs burned. Your face itched. And suddenly there was Safeway. Where your father took your mother grocery shopping. You swerved into the parking lot. Went up and down each row. Nothing but the cars and pickup trucks and wagons your neighbors drove. You went around back where the truck docks were. A man in a white smock smeared with blood was leaning against a faded gray Plymouth smoking a cigarette. He watched you pedal past him. By the time you left the lot you felt stupid. Stupid for having thought that someone with a car like that would ever go to Safeway. Would ever go shopping for cereal or mayonnaise the way your mother and your neighbors did. By the time you left the lot you knew there would never be another car you'd dream of owning.

You were thirteen then. You didn't know who made it. Now you do. A company called Porsche.

School lets out. Now, looking at sixteen, you're through working in Old Man Tuttle's fields and Charlie Bangerter's orchards for their miser pay. Karl starts working for them. You get a dishwasher job at Servus Drug on Main Street where they've got a soda fountain and some booths and then a banquet room for private parties down the back stairs in the basement. Guys you know come in, guys from school, sometimes in their letter jackets, sometimes with their girlfriends, girls you know too, and sometimes when you come out and go behind the counter to grab a tub of dishes you can hear them pause just quick enough to take you in, a kid in a teeshirt and apron with his belly wet, a kid they don't recognize unless they remember Summertime, doing his job. On Saturday mornings you clean up the party the night before down in the banquet room, most of it glasses, glasses with lipstick, with waterlogged slices of lemon and lime in bronze-colored fluid you know was booze. Sometimes one of the waitresses comes back to the kitchen, lights up a cigarette from a pack she keeps in her apron, and stands there smoking, sometimes quiet, sometimes talking to the cook, sometimes to you, smoke from her mouth and nose like punctuation marks the way the sheepherders and cowboys did on the porch of the bunkhouse. You wonder if someone deaf could read what she was saying just from the smoke. At home your mother quarrels with herself about the reek of cigarettes in your teeshirts.

Your buddies get jobs for the summer too. West pumping gas at Steed's Texaco. Jasperson helping his big brother Andy deliver cinderblocks. Keller bagging groceries at Albertson's. Doby mowing the cemetery, clipping grass around people's headstones, cleaning up dead flowers. Lilly sorting mail in the office where his mother works. Your birthday comes up along with your turn to be ordained a Priest. You go for another interview with Bishop Byrne to make sure you're responsible enough. There's the big lie everyone has to tell. Have you molested yourself. Easy. All you do is lock the look in place and tell him no. The look with all the hard confidence of steel. The look of human steel.

He takes you through the duties of a Priest. In his office, the curtains drawn on the window against the deep gold halo of the setting sun, he sits across his desk from you, his big hands flecked and his coveralls spattered from painting someone's house that day. You feel immersed again in the enormous kindness of his homely strength. You keep wanting to tell him about the Soderstroms. How they need help. How they could use a break from paying tithing. You figure it's your job. You don't know how. You might get Sister Soderstrom in trouble. You never find a way or place to do it. A day later your father takes you to the State Fairgrounds for your driving test. That Saturday, for the first time, you drive your mother to Safeway to do her grocery shopping. At the churchhouse the next morning your father ordains you to the rank of Priest.

For the third time now you make the trip down the hall to a classroom with your father and his friends, hear him call himself and his friends the Elders of Israel, and feel your head lift on its own when the weight of their hands comes off your neck. For the first time now you wear a real tie, a hanging striped cloth sword, instead of a bow tie clipped to your collar. And an hour later, in Sunday School, you sit behind the Sacrament Table up in the front corner of the chapel, facing the congregation, a vantage point you've never had before. Keller's there on the bench with you.

"This is weird," you whisper.

"What?" says Keller.

"Looking at everybody."

Among the cobblestone heads of the congregation you've singled people out. Earl and Nicky Bird. The Allers. Elder Jensen. Susan Lake. The Clarks. Your father.

"Yeah," says Keller. "They can all look back at you too."

"You can't even talk up here."

"Yeah. You just gotta learn how not to move your lips."

You remember last Halloween. Keller's talking from behind the fanged and bloody ventriloquist mouth of his mask. Woody Stone answering the door and asking if you guys weren't getting a little old for this.

"You should just wear that vampire mask."

"You could wear that spaghetti strainer over your face. Like those masks hockey players wear."

"Want some gum?"

"Why? My breath bad?"

"Kind of."

In front of you the trays of bread and water are lined in rows under the spread of a white tablecloth. Keller lifts the edge of the cloth to make sure the two-sided card is there where you can read the blessings for the bread and then the water. On a shelf below the card is the microphone you'll use. You find where the Soderstroms are out in the congregation so you'll know where not to look. During the opening service, down in his lap where the table hides what he's doing, Keller pulls out his Chinese handcuffs and plays at sticking his fingers in the ends until they grab. Up at the podium, one of the Cleverly twins is giving a two-and-a-half minute talk, his amplified voice warbling and high with terror. Keller pulls out a puzzle where you slide little tiles around inside an interlocking pad to get all their numbers in order. He can't get two of them from being backward. You tap his leg, hold out your hand, and he gives it to you. A minute later you hand it back to him.

"Crap. How'd you do that?"

While Of These Emblems We Partake. Your mother starts playing the slow dirge of the Sacrament hymn on the subdued and grieving organ. Sister Lake, the redheaded chorister, starts using her white baton to lead the congregation through the verses. You and Keller get up, fold the cloth back off the bread trays, start shredding slices of Wonder Bread into pieces, your fingers nibbling through them fast as you can make them, turning slices into piles you'd throw to seagulls. The fourth verse ends. The smack and thump of hymn books being shut and dropped into their racks goes traveling around the chapel. Keller's two trays ahead of you. Your mother keeps playing through the hymn, soft, without the congregation, while you and Keller finish breaking bread in the last of the trays and sit back down. Your mother ends the hymn. Keller pulls a footstool out from underneath the table, plants his knees on it, takes out the microphone, reads the blessing for the bread.

"Oh God, the Eternal Father, we ask thee in the name of thy Son, Jesus Christ, to bless and sanctify this bread to the souls of all those who partake of it, that they may eat in remembrance of the body of thy Son, and witness unto thee, O God, the Eternal Father, that they are willing to take upon them the name of thy Son, and always remember him and keep his commandments which he has given them; that they may always have his Spirit with them. Amen."

You listen to Keller's voice come off the speakers in the rafters and you're suddenly thinking your band. Eddie and Robbie and Jimmy. What they're doing while you're here. A cold shadow cuts across your stomach and leaves it raw. Maybe fear. Because they're out there and you're not. You don't know. When Keller's done with the blessing you both get up. Your mother starts playing the Sacrament hymn again, slow and repeating, while the Deacons come filing out of their benches and line up in front of you. You hand Karl his tray. The scowl on his face could be taken for solemn reverence by anyone who hadn't seen him break the legs and arms off one of his sister Molly's dolls or set fire to her paper Christmas angels. Your mother keeps playing while the Deacons go off to pass bread around the congregation. You and Keller stand at the table and wait for them.

"What kind of car you think you'll get?"

It surprises you how easy you can say it with your lips not moving.

"I hope a Sprite," he says.

"What's that?"

"An Austin Healey. It's got these headlights that stick up off the hood like eyeballs. And this smiley little grill. It's cool." And then he says, "How about you?"

"You heard of a Porsche?"

"No."

"It's hard to describe. You gotta see it."

"That what you're getting?"

"When I'm rich maybe."

"So what kinda car you getting for now?" Keller whispers.

"I don't know."

The Deacons start wandering back, hand you their trays of picked-over bread, go back to their benches. You and Keller cover the bread trays and fold the cloth off the water trays. Your mother stops playing. It's your turn to kneel. Turn the card over to where the blessing for the water is. Talk into the microphone and hear your voice come off the high vault of the rafters reciting the blessing you memorized for your father.

The Deacons file up again. You pick up a water tray. Karl reaches out for it with his scowling face intent on taking its handle from your hand. And then he goes, following another Deacon off, and what you feel is quick and familiar and incomprehensible as ever. What you felt when you stood with him in the room with the baptismal font the day you first explored the churchhouse. When you got him off the hill away from the cave where the rattler had snaked along your shoe. This restless wilderness of feelings you can't name. Fear maybe. Mostly this longing to know.

CHAPTER 12

As SUMMER COMES on your buddies start getting cars. West gets his yellow 57 Pontiac. Lilly is driving a beige 56 Renault Dauphine before the end of June. Somewhere in July, Keller gets a dark green Sprite whose close-set headlights stand up off its little hood like the blind eyes of a toy frog. Jasperson's father gets a Plymouth for the family and gives Jasperson the family Rambler. When July ends, Yenchik's got a 40 Ford, a big red whale-fendered coupe someone already started to customize. You get to share the fever, what it feels like, owning something that big and real, fenders, engine, wheels, dashboard, radio, upholstery, instruments, brakes, the way they smell, everything all at once. The last time you came this close to owning something big was when they retired Rex the workhorse and gave him to you down in La Sal.

You get to ride in all of them.

"Feel that?" says Yenchik. "Look. Look at my hands. See that?"

You're headed up Highway 89 through all the orchard towns that run along the foothills north of Bountiful. Centerville. Farmington. Kaysville. Yenchik's hands are shaking holding the wheel. You can feel it too. In the seat and the floor and where you've got your passenger arm on the window sill. The steady tremor. Like you're riding a washboard instead of the flat cement out the windshield.

"Yeah. I feel it."

"It only happens around this speed. Sixty five. Watch."

Yenchik floors the pedal. The Ford hunkers down and bulls forward up through seventy toward eighty. Sure enough. The washboard feel of the highway goes smooth and then vanishes for good.

"Yeah. I see."

"So what the fuck's wrong? You know?"

"Your engine's about to let go."

"Let go?"

"Explode. Send the pistons through the hood. The rods out through the oil pan."

"You shitting me?"

He takes his foot off the gas.

"No! Don't slow down! Whatever you do! Don't let it get down there again!"

"So what do I do?" Yenchik hollers. "Spend the rest of my life doing eighty?"

"No. Just listen, man, cuz you gotta do this right."

"What?"

"Just listen. Take your cigarette lighter. Push it in. Get it hot."

"Okay," he says, when it pops back out. "Now what?"

"How should I know? I don't smoke."

"You cocksucker." And then says, "Can I slow down now?"

"Yeah."

The speed drops down and picks up the tremor again.

"So what's wrong?" says Yenchik. "You even know?"

"Probably a tire out of balance."

"How do you fix that?"

"Steed's got a balance machine. Take it when West's there."

You get to ride in Porter's red 53 Mercury Monterey. You get to ride in Snook's pale blue 55 Chevy. You get to ride in Quigley's malevolent flat black 52 Hudson.

"Somebody's already chopped the roof," he says.

"Yeah," you say, from the passenger seat. "Makes it feel like a submarine in here."

"How many submarines you been in?"

"Zero."

"I figured."

"How'd they lower it?"

"I think channeled it," Quigley says. "I gotta look."

You get to ride in Eddie's gray 53 Volkswagen. You get to ride on the back of Jimmy's used Indian motorcycle. In August, Robbie's father gets a new van for his plumbing business, and gives Robbie the old panel truck to cart his drums around. And his band. And open the possibility for playing somewhere else besides his basement or the high school gym. You get to ride in the passenger seat.

"So now we just need gigs," says Robbie. "Somewhere to go."

"Where do we look?" says Jimmy. "Who'd even hire us?"

"My dad said we should try hospitals," Robbie says. "And old folks homes."

"What's an old folks home?" says Jimmy.

"Where old people live who can't take care of themselves," you say.

"They have homes for that?"

"Yeah."

"Like houses?"

"Yeah. Where they live. All together."

"So we'd be playing for sick old people," says Eddie.

"That's right," says Robbie. "And doing it for free."

The warning in Robbie's voice lets Eddie know he'd be cool to just drop it.

"Sign me up," you say.

"Yeah," says Jimmy. "Me too."

"What about night clubs?" says Eddie. "Where we'd get paid?"

"We'd need underage cards," says Robbie. "And we'd need to audition too."

"Underage cards?" says Jimmy.

"Yeah. You need one if you're not twenty-one."

"Is that some kind of Mormon liquor law?"

"I don't know. We can't get 'em anyway. We ain't old enough yet."

"How old you gotta be?"

"Eighteen? Dunno. Older than us."

"That doesn't make sense," says Eddie. "They're called underage cards but you gotta be old enough to get one. So underage is bullshit. What's the point?"

"To keep five year olds like you from getting in," says Robbie.

"So how do we get into hospitals and old folks homes?" says Jimmy.

"I'll talk to my old man," Robbie says.

"I'll ask the Professor," you say.

You've had the hunger too. The only car you'd ever want if you could name and paint it has the name Porsche and the color red. Other than that you don't have anything particular in mind. Just their permission to buy one with some of the money you've banked. One Saturday morning in July, your license to drive still burning in your pocket, you catch them at the kitchen table while your brothers and sisters watch cartoons downstairs.

"I'd like to get a car."

Your mother lets out a small moaning cry, claps her hand up to her mouth, looks at your father like you've punched her in the face.

"I've got money."

"Sit down," your father says.

"I'm okay here."

"You know what your money's for," your father says.

"Yeah. My mission. My friends are going on missions too. They're all getting cars."

"Look at it logically."

"I am. All my friends who are going on missions are getting cars. I'd like to get one too."

"That's just my point. All your friends are getting cars. That means that you can have a ride whenever you need one. But you don't have to bother with all the headaches of owning a car. You should feel fortunate. Instead you're standing here complaining."

Your mother recovers. "Yes, Shakli. Just buying a car is only the beginning. Then you have insurance and gasoline and tires."

"All my friends do too. They can afford it. Just like I can."

"Yes, Shakli. But they are different."

"Different how? How are my friends different from me?"

"Oh, Shakli, I don't know." Timid and fretful the way she always gets at the helpless edge of saying something ugly.

"Because they don't know me like you do. That's it, right?"

"Ach! What a terrible thing to say! Shame on you!"

"Then tell me how they're different."

"Your friends don't have your intelligence." Your father there to rescue her. There to head you off. "They don't have parents who tell them what's best for them."

Like the brine flies that blanket the sand of the beach at the Great Salt Lake, flies that lift and then fall in a rolling black wave as you wade through them, you wait for the swarm of rage in your head to come to rest again.

"What if I want to go somewhere myself?"

"Where would you want to go, Shakli?"

"I don't know. Maybe a date."

"Oh, Shakli."

"Then you can borrow the station wagon," your father says.

"What if you're using it? What if you have to go to the office?"

"We'll just have to arrange it ahead of time."

"So I'm just supposed to mooch off my friends."

"You can help them buy gas."

"What could you even afford, Shakli? Besides an old junker?"

"I could fix it up myself. I take auto mechanics."

"Auto mechanics," she says, like you're kidding. "And where would you keep it?"

"I was thinking the extra space in the garage."

"Harold. Please put a stop to this."

"When you can afford a decent car, you can keep it in the garage," your father says. "After your mission. We'll make room. We'll even help you."

"I could keep it in the driveway. Or out in front. Out of the way."

"Yah. Where all of our neighbors would have to look at it."

"Then in the field. Out back."

"That field doesn't belong to us," your father says.

"It doesn't belong to anybody. Nobody uses it for anything but junk."

"And you want to put one more piece of junk out there."

You watch your mother's face take quiet triumph in her cleverness.

"So the answer's no," you say.

"Don't act so disappointed," your father says. "By golly. We've said it before. You're going on a mission. That's your first priority."

You look at your father.

"What if I just went out and got one?" you say.

"Without asking us?"

"I've already asked."

"Then without our permission?"

"Yeah."

"Then you could go live in it."

How you tested the oven door when you got it bolted back in place and then couldn't stay for a plate of Kentucky Fried no matter how bad you wanted to stay with Roy. How you said you'd be back and then got on your bike and left. And kept pedaling until you'd outrun everything. The pungent stench of the Colonel's eleven secret herbs and spices. The man in the suit and the dust stale smell of shit where his face should be. The name of your father's favorite song while your hands put the door together. This is it. Their answer no matter how much you want it the other way. Bumming rides the next three years. What your buddies and other guys will come to think when they turn the key and look across the car and there you are. Or see you at the borrowed wheel of your father's wagon. The hurt in your throat from wanting it the other way and the answer raw and sore down in the bottom of your gut despite the way you saw this turning out.

"I figured," you say.

"You figured what?" your father says.

"You'd say no."

"So why did you even ask?"

"I wanted you to say it."

"So!" In his chair your father explodes. "Enough! Now get off your high horse!"

CHAPTER 13

THE CHEVY wagon your father offers to share with you suits him the way it came from the dealer. Stock. Run of the mill. You know there's no way to argue him out of leaving it that way. No spinner hubcaps. No steering wheel knob. No pine tree air freshener. No steelpack muffler. You and your buddies feel different. Just having a car is missing the point. You need to make it yours. West wants to turn the Pontiac into a car he can reliably score with. Lilly has his hands full just keeping his smoking old Renault running. Yenchik wants power. Keller wants to take his Bugeye racing. All Robbie wants is the name of his father's plumbing business off the doors of the panel truck.

And so you go to work. When you're not practicing, not doing what you've started calling sessions with the band, not washing dishes down at Servus Drug, you're helping your buddies make their cars their own. Without your own to work on you're the one guy who can work on everyone else's car. With almost a year of auto mechanics you're one of the guys they come to. The other is West. You and West strip every piece of chrome off his 57 Pontiac and cart them to a plating shop. You don't like working on the Renault because it couldn't get out of the way of a marching band and nothing Lilly does leaves it anything more than stock. But you help him replace the generator, the water pump, the ignition coil, the fuel pump, the brake lines, all the hoses. You and Yenchik install an Edelbrock manifold and three two-barrel Holley carburetors on the flathead engine of his 40 Ford. You help Keller put the engine for his Sprite together once the racing parts start coming in the mail.

West files a claim for the theft of a set of spinner hubcaps he never had. State Farm honors the claim. He buys himself a brand new set from Western Auto. You talk about what to do, now that he's got a set for real, to keep someone from really swiping them.

"I could get those locks," he says.

"What locks?"

"Those ones you put on the valve stems."

"Yeah. They're kind of heavy though."

"So?"

"You'd have to balance your wheels again."

"Yeah," he says. "Right."

"You could do what this guy from auto mechanics did."

"What?"

"See how your spokes are hollow in back?"

"Yeah?"

"He's got the same thing. He stuck some putty in there. Regular window putty. And then he stuck some razor blades in the putty. So if someone grabs the spokes to yank 'em off, guess what happens."

West sits there thinking for a minute.

"Jesus H. Christ," he says. "That's sick."

"He'd had two sets swiped. He'd had it. He knows a guy who did the same thing with his hood. Along the front. After his chrome rocker arm covers and air cleaner got swiped."

"Who is this guy?"

"I can't say. He doesn't want anyone to know."

"Then how come you know?"

"We're buddies."

"What's he drive?"

"I can't tell you."

"So introduce me."

"Then you'd know who he is."

"You just want him all to yourself."

"You wanna do the razor blade thing or not?"

West thinks for a minute. In one of the bays at Steed's he looks back and forth along the length of the Pontiac.

"There's this other way I heard," he finally says.

"What?"

"Scratch your initials in back. Then get the word around that you registered them with the cops."

You help West bolt his chromed parts back in place when you get them back from the plating shop. Robbie take his father's shelves off the inside walls of his panel truck. Use steel wool and turpentine to take Fox Plumbing and the telephone number and plumbing license number off the doors where his father had them painted on in red.

"Whaddaya think?" says Robbie. "Should we put the name of the band on there?"

"We'd have to get a name first."

"Forget it."

Nobody but Eddie is ready to name the band. And he can't come up with one. So you leave the doors blank and the gray paint dulled where you steel wooled it. You and Eddie don't do anything to his Volkswagen except adjust the clutch. You and Jimmy put a tall set of handlebars on his Indian and leather tassels out the ends of his handlegrips.

At Steed's Texaco you learn that there are bottles of Olympia in the old round refrigerator back in the parts room by the bathroom door. You listen to Elvis and Buddy Holly and the Everly Brothers and the Pretenders and the Kingston Trio when the hammering of the compressor isn't drowning out the radio. You bolt shackles into the A-frames of his front suspension and drop the nose of the Pontiac down a couple of inches. You help Keller get his engine tuned and running again. Help Yenchik and West swap out their mufflers with Smitty steelpacks that are open throats for the brutal explosive stuff going on inside their engines.

At Steed's Texaco, you and West bring the Pontiac down off the hoist one night, lock up, head down Main Street where the noise gets the big black picture windows of the store fronts shivering in the street lights, relish the mean triumph of making something work.

"These fuckers are loud."

"Yeah."

"You sure they're legal?"

"Yeah."

"Listen to that."

"Leave it in second. Back off the gas."

"Holy shit. Like a semi."

And you drive. At least your buddies do. And from their passenger seats you can feel the change. You on your bike. You thought you were somebody. Thought you were going somewhere. This is what it looked like, passing you back then, a kid on a bike, making his way from one telephone pole to the next, roads whose shoulders you used to pedal at a pace where you could smell the creosote and see gouts in the wood from the cleats where men had climbed them. Distances you used to think would take you too far from home. Places where you had to turn around to have the daylight and strength left in your legs to make it home again. Places like Lagoon, the amusement park off Highway 89 up by Farmington, where you watched the distant cars of the roller coaster from across the back road fields before the sun turned the rails in the trestles to looping arcs of gleaming gold and it was time to go. The place where the tracks cut through the road when you ride with Robbie out to West Bountiful to pick up Jimmy.

You used to make it this far.

You don't tell Robbie. Or Keller or West or Yenchik. Or Porter or

Snook. You just ride with them. Ride for the first time to places like Clearfield and Kaysville and Layton without your father or Scoutmaster Haycock or some other grownup at the wheel. Cruise Main Street with the radio going and the high school crowd on the sidewalk out in front of Wally's Burger Bar and Servus Drug and Pace's Dairy Ann. Hammer up and down Highway 89. Pull off and hang out with the high school crowd around the Frostop in the yellow light of its parking lot off the highway. Hit roadside cafes along the orchard towns north toward Ogden or south toward North Salt Lake and look for tunes on their jukeboxes. Let girls get their casual ganders from the sidewalks and from other cars while you're out riding with Yenchik in his 40 Ford.

"She wants you, man."

"Yeah. Sure."

"Her friggin' tongue was hangin' out."

"She was lookin' for you. I just got in the way."

"Naw. She was lookin' at you."

"Come on. I'm just the passenger."

"You sure?"

"Slow down. Let her get another look. I'll duck down. I'll prove it."

Chapter 14

Passenger. To guys who pull up in their souped-up cars along the passenger side of the Pontiac or Ford or Hudson and take a look at you and then look past you for West or Yenchik or Quigley. To guys at the Frostop and Wally's Burger Bar who come around for a look at the Pontiac or the Chevy. It doesn't matter much what you did to make the car what it is. It isn't yours. Or how black you got your hands. It wasn't your grease. Passenger. A ghost rider to guys who talk about chopped roofs and channeled floors and frenched taillights and louvered hoods and shaved handles, lowering and raking and flaming, boring and stroking their engines, metal flake and fish scale in their paint jobs, lakers along their rocker panels, scavenger exhaust pipes with flared tips hung under their rear axles.

You learn quick to come off like the kind of passenger who's got a car himself. Who left it home to go out cruising with his buddy. This easy sprawl with your passenger arm out the passenger window and your left arm up along the backrest. Not like some wide-eyed zoo-faced tourist. Not like you're being done some favor you can't repay. Like you're cool being driven around because there's a set of keys in your pocket too. Keys to the little red Porsche. At the Frostop one night, there's a skinny kid off the front of a lowered maroon Buick, wearing this long sleeved shirt with the sleeves down to his wrists, his glasses in his hand, doubled over, chucking stuff up, a guy behind him in levis and a teeshirt, trying to steer him away from the Buick.

"What's wrong with him?"

"Just his first smoke."

"That'll do it."

"Yeah. I think it was a Kool."

"Who is he?"

"Some kid."

"Poor pity the bastard who's gotta drive him home."

"I think the guy with the Buick."

"He just left."

"What is that stuff, anyway?"

"I saw him eatin' looked like a taco a while ago."

No way to argue your father out of leaving the wagon stock. No spinners. No steering wheel knob. You know without having to ask him. And so all you bother asking is if you can use it. He has a hard time saying no. He has to keep proving to you his reasoning that you don't need a car of your own.

"Are you staying home tonight?"

"Yes. What is it?"

A half-typed page in the carriage of his big typewriter. The electric motor humming and ready to go again as soon as you're done with what you're here for.

"Okay if I borrow the car?"

"Where were you planning on going?"

"Just down to meet some friends at the Frostop."

"What do you plan on doing there?"

"Just spend time with my friends."

"When can we expect you home?"

"I don't know. Before ten."

"Ask your mother. If she says yes, it's fine with me."

Rarely where you say you're going. Mostly to drive. In the driver's seat of your father's station wagon you still feel like a passenger. But you learn how to disconnect the speedometer cable. How to read the gas gauge to put enough back in to have the needle cover where you told him you were going. You drive past Wally's Burger Bar and Servus Drug on Main Street. You drive past the Frostop where the cars are parked nose first like chromed and painted cattle feeding with their rear ends faced out toward the highway. You keep going. A couple of faces look out, but by then you're looking forward, not knowing from the dead speedometer how fast you're going, chasing the music on the radio from the one station on the night dial that plays jazz.

You and Robbie take the front seat out of a pickup truck at a junk-yard, bring it back to his house, drill holes in the floor of the panel truck behind the two front seats, bolt the junkyard seat in place. All four of you can ride now. There's still enough room in back for his drums, Jimmy's amplifier, the rest of your instruments. You and Robbie hang speakers in back in the holes where his father's shelves came out. Run wires up to a fader knob you mount in the dash. Switch the radio on, crank the volume, turn the fader knob toward the back speakers, listen to sound come rising out of the dark steel chamber behind the seats, the radio voice of Big Daddy Hesterman so huge it sounds like he's back there himself.

"Wow."

"Yeah."

Robbie turns the tuning dial across to the jazz station. A huge sax floods forward from the deep back of the truck, blasts you from behind almost like wind, kicks little metal rattles off around the cab.

"Yeah," says Robbie. "Now we're talkin' lollipops."

"Man."

"You know what we need now?"

"What?"

"A radio that'll play what we want."

"Like requests?"

"No. More 'n that. Say you wanna hear a Miles tune. Or Eddie a Bird one. We could just push a button or something, and it'd play it."

"How?"

"I dunno. They could have this big radio station, with a thousand record players, ready to go."

When you first moved here, started hearing music on the radio, thinking the singers and bands were actually at the radio station before you caught on to things and found out they were only playing records. And then it felt like they were cheating. Like they could get in trouble for pretending.

"You'd never hear new stuff that way. Just stuff you already knew."

"Maybe we could rig up a record player somewhere in here." Robbie looking around the cab from the driver's seat.

"The needle'd go crazy."

"Yeah. We'd have to park to play it."

The panel truck. Nobody looks past you for the driver. Nobody bothers trying. Robbie cares as much about paint and chrome as he does about Teddy Roosevelt's head on Mount Rushmore. What he cares about is what can go in back, behind the seat, in the dark chamber that amplifies every bump or joint in the road with this orchestra of quivering steel walls and suspension pieces crying to be lubricated. His drums. And where his drums can take him. And where his drums can take him depends on where his panel truck can take his drums. You start talking gigs. Places you could play besides the high school gym. Mr. Selby tells you you're right to try some old folks homes. You've seen a couple from the roads you've pedaled. Old people watching you go past from chairs on the roofed porches of big houses.

"Not for pay necessarily," he says. "Just to show them a good time. And get in some practice in front of a real audience."

"What kind of stuff would we play?"

"Remember where they came from," he says. "The music they grew up with. Thirties and forties. Standards. Stuff you already know. We'll look through some charts."

Thinking it over. Playing for old folks.

"Most of those folks have families. Kids and grandkids. They'll talk about you. They'll get word out. This hot young jazz band. Take it from there."

In bed, on nights when the room is hot and the air stifling, when you're lying there without covers on the white slab of your mattress, when it's even too hot for your pillow, you calm the nervous jittering in your legs by taking a road somewhere in the little red Porsche. A road you patch together from pictures on your father's calendars and other scraps of roads in your head. Your trumpet in the passenger seat. Some clothes and music in back. Everything you own. On the mattress next to your head, on your transistor radio, you've got jazz playing, turned down in the sleeping house to where the instruments approach the sound of insects but still hold some resonance as music, the resonance of an engine, the motion of the song the road you keep leaving behind you, the road whose hills and turns and open stretches are the song and where it takes you. You go to sleep not knowing how far you'll have gone or where you'll be by the time you wake up in the morning.

One day Jimmy's father tells you he talked to someone out at the Tooele Army Depot about playing at a club there in the desert. He gives you a guy's name and address on the inside of a matchbook. You and Robbie take the panel truck one afternoon and head south toward Salt Lake and then west.

"Ever notice how long Eddie lets his fingernails get?"

"Yeah."

"Got any idea why?"

"Pick his nose?"

"He only needs one for that."

"We oughta ask him some day."

"Go ahead."

"Maybe it's some superstitious thing."

"At least he doesn't bite 'em."

"Maybe he wishes he played guitar."

You head west out past the airport. West past the ruined pier and buildings of Saltair on the shore of the Great Salt Lake. West through the pinchpoint of land between where the black mountains come down and almost meet the shoreline and where the smokestack looms high and huge and menacing up above the long black rubbled wall of mine tailings that follows the highway west. And then you're free of the valley. At the threshold of the desert. Desert out across Skull Valley and then the Salt Flats all the way west to Wendover and then across Nevada if you wanted to. The wind through the cab is crazy and hot and savage. Robbie turns the radio up. Wake Up Little Susie. You bring your trumpet out and slip the mouthpiece in. Robbie looks over. His hair like a black tornado all over his face but you can see him grin.

The tired-looking guy who runs the club at the Army Depot doesn't even ask you to audition. Just tells you to come back in a couple of years when you don't look so much like Mouseketeers. But you get your first gig at an old folks home in Centerville. It doesn't pay. Not even Eddie cares. The night you show up, stop out in the road to make sure the number's right, you don't tell Jimmy and Eddie and Robbie the way you used to pedal past this place. A few old people watch you from the broad porch. You wonder if any of them will remember you from riding by. You figure not. There's a big room off the back with windows around three sides, a ping pong table they've folded up and leaned against the wall, some couches and cushioned chairs, some rows of folding chairs, shelves of magazines and table games, a door where you help Robbie bring his drums in from the panel truck. The manager shows you where to set up. Shows you an outlet for Jimmy. Drops the blinds in the windows behind you to block the yellow fire of the low sun from out over Antelope Island.

"I gotta tell ya," he says. He's a thin guy with slick black hair, around your father's age, the skin of his temples pitted. "They're real excited. All they've talked about for days."

"Cool," says Jimmy.

Robbie sets out his rug and then his drums on top of it. Eddie and you start warming up your horns. The manager leaves and closes the door. When it opens again they start coming in. Some with walkers and canes. Some in wheelchairs. Some on their own power. Some in robes and slippers. A couple of men in suits. Some ladies in dresses and lipstick. All of them have the white hair Mrs. Harding did. Women who work there get them settled and then go back and stand along the wall behind them. Across the empty floor in front of you they sit there and look at you. Some of the women are smiling like you're their grandkids. Under the fluorescent lighting recessed in the ceiling tiles their faces are stained with the pale red bath of sunset through the blinds behind you and the windows in the side walls. The manager welcomes them to Ballroom Night at Roseland. Some women, radiant with some memory, smile at the name. Eddie and you take a look at each other. Ballroom

Night. While everyone claps you get why they're all pushed back to open as much of the old wood floor as possible. And then the manager's gone and Robbie's counting down. The Way You Look Tonight.

Do Nothin' Till You Hear from Me. April in Paris. Red Sails in the Sunset. Satin Doll. Take the A Train. Over the Rainbow. Stormy Weather. You start out playing straight ahead. Keeping the solos mild. Not knowing how far to take them. They know the songs. They know the words. Some of them clap for the solos. They come to the front of the room and dance right there in front of you. They make requests. Sweet Georgia Brown. In a Sentimental Mood. Love Walked In. They sit in their chairs and couches and sing. They sing to each other while they're dancing. They ask if they can take the microphone and sing. Amazing Grace. Don't Get Around Much Anymore. When the Saints Come Marchin' In. The windows go dark while you play, and turn to mirrors, and leave everyone dancing and singing in colorless fluorescent light as harsh and bloodless as a captured flash of lightning. The manager turns on some lamps and shuts off the lights in the ceiling. Even the music goes suddenly hushed and easy. Autumn in New York. When Sunny Gets Blue. I Loves You Porgy. After dancing slow, cheek to cheek, from the eloquence of memory, some of them come up, reach for your hand, want to put coins in it. Quarters and half dollars. The first time it happens you look at the manager. From the side of the room he nods like you should take it.

At the end of the summer, when school starts again, the only other guy who doesn't have a car is Doby. He uses his mother's 59 Impala. Retired from teaching, she hardly uses it, and lets him do whatever he wants to it. So it's close enough to having one. You help him replace the factory mufflers with Smitty steelpacks the way you did West and Yenchik. You help him bolt a necking knob, a swiveling ball of plastic the size of a baby's fist with a red heart encased inside it, to the steering wheel. You help him install a hula dancer with a pair of eyehooks for a pelvis on the deck behind the back seat. You help him wire her ruby eyes to the brakelights.

CHAPTER 15

LINDA BOWEN. She's a sophomore. She's pretty. Just not in a way that makes her popular. A quiet smile kind of pretty. Her open brown eyes and the taper of her oval face remind you of a deer. It's the way she dresses and does her hair that makes it hard to see at first. Like the daughter of a pioneer. Clothes with the old-fashioned look of hand-me-downs from a sister ten years older. Long brown hair that's waved in a way you've seen in old issues of Life Magazine. Strands pulled back off her temples and tied with a thin ribbon she matches to some color in her blouse.

You never see her with a guy. Just always the same two girls. One of them is one of the school's more unusual girls, this tall, big-boned girl with a face as flat and blank as a full moon hubcap and this huge unapologetic Mona Lisa hairdo. You've never seen her talk. Linda's other friend plays cello. You've seen her in the music room with her knees spread wide to give her cello the belly room it needs. You figure Linda's shy. So asking her out is like trying something new in secret. Like using a vacant warehouse to see if you can jitterbug. You know that if she turns you down she'll keep it to herself. She won't go making fun of you for thinking she'd go out with you.

"Who?" West wants to know.

"Linda Bowen. She's a sophomore."

"What's she look like?" says Doby.

"She's cute. Long brown hair. Nice face." And then you say, "She dresses kind of weird. No big deal."

You're in West's garage. Doby has the white plastic cover off the dome light in the ceiling of his mother's 59 Impala. West has the inside of the cover painted red with a spray can. You're waiting for it to dry.

"She got tits?" says West.

"Jesus," Doby says.

"I'll ask her," you say. "You know Bob West? He wants to know if you've got tits."

"I still can't place her," Doby says.

"You know that chick with the Mona Lisa hair?" you tell him.

"No," says West. "You're not taking her out."

"No. Not her. The girl she hangs out with."

"The kinda short one?" Doby says. "Old fashioned looking?"

"Yeah. That's her."

"Yeah." And then he says, "Yeah. She's not bad."

"She wouldn't be bad if someone clued her in," says West.

"Where you taking her?" says Doby.

"The State Fair."

On Tuesday you track her around at lunch. She's with her Mona Lisa friend. You watch her from the table you're at with Robbie and Jimmy across the cafeteria. Watch her try to eat a Sloppy Joe without having it fall apart. Watch her take her tray and dishes back. Watch her have to get out of the way of a couple of football guys who are deaf and dumb and blind to anything that isn't blond and in a sweater. One of them is Tingey, a guy you're coaching through algebra, and you figure right then he's flunking algebra without knowing why. You tell Robbie and Jimmy you'll see them later. You run your own tray back and follow her down the hall.

And suddenly you're scared. In picking her, you figured you'd made this easy, but for the way your Sloppy Joe keeps reaching up your throat, you might as well have picked the Homecoming Queen. At least with the Homecoming Queen you'd get exactly what you see. A standard blonde with a standard cheerleader smile and standard sweater. And exactly what you'd get if you tried to ask her out. You could even have your comeback ready. I figured you'd be stupid enough to say no. With Linda there's no telling. Everything that made this easy now makes it hard. Everything that made her simple now makes her complicated. The pioneer-looking dress. The old-fashioned hairdo. The wisp of the ribbon. The way she's shy. You wish your trumpet could talk. You wish you were wearing clothes yourself that looked like they were handed down. But then you'd need an older brother who could hand them down to you.

Down the stairs. Out through the front door into the sunlight down the broad front steps. They're headed for the flagpole out in the big front sloping lawn. Lunch is ticking off. But they amble along like time is something that only cops or parents or janitors have to think about. They mosey around the flagpole twice. Kids start coming past you up the steps. Linda and the Mona Lisa start to sleepwalk back. You know by now they won't be splitting up until they have to. You go from being scared to being mad. Mad at her Mona Lisa friend. In the lobby you watch them reach the hall, touch hands, finally head off in opposite directions. You follow Linda. Watch her move quietly through a river of hurrying kids without leaving a ripple. And then you're not afraid or angry anymore. Just someone with something to do and not enough time to do it. You're there when she reaches the door of her class. Mrs. Whitaker's room. English.

"Hi."

"Hi."

"My name's Shake."

"I know. I'm Linda."

"Could I talk to you?"

The bell rings. You watch her look into her classroom.

"Just for a minute."

"Okay."

You step into a calm eddy against a bank of gray steel lockers. Suddenly this close, this face to face with her, an animal in the woods.

"If you're not busy Saturday after next, you want to go to the fair?"

"Saturday after next?"

"Yeah."

"The State Fair?"

"Yeah." And then you say, "Or somewhere else if you want. You know. Lagoon. Or a movie."

"The fair would be neat."

"They've got rides and animals and all kinds of stuff." You can't help yourself. "We could get something to eat afterwards."

"I'd love to go. What time?"

"Three-thirty?"

"Sure. I'll be ready."

She turns away from you. Slips through the door. You've got a class too. But he's there, just back from where she was, the old man in the dark suit, the gleaming sleek black shoes, the white hair, the perfect knot of his tie, the dust stale stink, the congestion of scorn where his face should be. You're used to him by now. To what he would tell you if he had a mouth. Mrs. Whitaker comes to the door and reaches for the knob. She smiles, not an inkling that she smells him, pulls the door closed, leaves you out in the hall with him. It's you and him when you look where his face should be. You know what he sees. What he wants you to know. The way you fooled her into thinking you were someone who was worth it. This time you stare him down. Get a fix on where his eyes would be in the faceless intensity of scorn and stare him down.

You see her in the classroom, at her desk, thinking possibly of a week from Saturday, possibly of you, while she smiles, opens up her notebook, hands her homework forward.

Go fuck yourself, you tell him. She said yes.

And then he's gone. Because without a mouth he can't answer you. Gone to where long ranks of lockers and their combination locks line the vacant hall.

"Where's she live?"

"Shit."

"What?"

"I forgot to ask her."

"Just call her," Doby says.

And while you realize you didn't get her number either, West picks up the plastic bowl of the dome light cover by its rim, touches the paint inside.

"It's dry. Here."

Doby takes the cover, gets in the driver's seat, closes the door, leans back, reaches his arms up over his head, snaps the cover back in place.

"Get the garage door," West says. "I'll get the light."

You pull the door down. West kills the light. The garage goes black.

"Hey, dipshit," you hear West say. "Open the damn car door."

You hear Doby unlatch the door. Suddenly the interior of the Impala is flushed this soft erotic ghostlike pink.

"Holy shit," says Doby.

He reaches out to touch what looks like the pink ghost of the Impala's dashboard. He looks around to where you and West are hunkered down on the passenger side looking in. The light makes his face look sunburned and ravaged by desert wind.

"Passion a la mode," says West.

"Cool," says Doby.

"What's your mom gonna say?" you say.

"She'll never know. She doesn't drive at night."

"So who you gonna try it out on?" says West.

"Dunno," says Doby. "I'll find somebody."

"Okay," says West. "All you need now's a little Elsha, the right music, a little breathing in her ear. Once you figure out who."

"If you take her to a drive in," you say, "make sure you dirty up the right side of your windshield."

"Fuck you," says West. But he laughs.

"What?" says Doby.

"That's what West did one night," you say. "So she'd have to scoot over to watch the movie through his side. Tell Doby how that worked out."

"Fine for a while," says West. "Then I guess I got grabby. She went and got a cup of water and some napkins and cleaned her side off."

"Shit. All those people watching."

"Hey. I got my windshield cleaned. About all she was good for anyway."

"When you take her out?" Doby asks you.

"Yeah?"

"Ask her what the deal is with her friend."

"Mona Lisa? You mean if she'll go out with you?"

"No. Just what the deal is. You turd."

At school you track Linda down again for her number and address. Her Mona Lisa friend stands next to her with this quiet approving Mona Lisa smile. You tell Doby her smile's nice and her teeth are small. You ask your father if you can borrow the wagon. You think about a place to eat once you've done the fair. A place that's a step or two up from the Frostop or the Dairy Queen. A place where you can sit and get waited on. Not a fancy place where the lights are low and the tables small and couples can cozy up. Not a place that could say to her that you're after something more. And not a place where anyone you know hangs out. Just the two of you. So Servus Drug is out. But you want a place with booths. A place where you can sit across the surface of a booth from her. Where you can let her know that all you want is company. You decide on Lee's Café and Restaurant on Highway 89. You've never been there. You don't know why. It's just one of those places where nobody goes. From the highway, through the windows, you can see its booths.

That Saturday you wash and wax the wagon, suck popcorn out of the cracks of the carpet and seats with the hose of your mother's Electrolux, polish your Sunday shoes. Then, since the box is out and your fingers are black already, you do the shoes your family plans to wear to church tomorrow. You put the shoeshine box away and scrub the polish off your fingers. By three o'clock you're ready. Dressed in slacks, your sport jacket, your shoes, your wallet filled with money you've earned at Servus Drug. You find your mother and father at the dining room table going through mail. Your mother's face is already raised in your direction. Your father's opening an envelope. You're wondering if there's too much Elsha coming off your face.

"Okay," you say. "Here goes."

Your father's little leather case that holds his keys is on the table. You wait for him to reach for it. Your mother gives you a smile as watery as the drinks you clean up Monday mornings in the basement party room at Servus Drug.

"You look very nice," she says. "You are a handsome young man."

"Thanks."

"Is she Mormon, Shakli? From a good family?"

"Yes."

"Your father has something to tell you."

"What's that?"

Your father mutters something. You see a quick wave of agitation pass across the back and shoulders of his short sleeved shirt. You round the table to where he can look at you.

"Tell him, Harold. You are his father."

"Tell me what?"

"Tell him," she says. "Don't be a coward. He is your son."

Your father sends the envelope skidding across the table.

"I'm not a coward, Mother!"

"It's okay," you say.

"It's nothing, son." Your father turns his red and bedeviled face up to you. "Just have a good time. Take good care of the car. And remember who you are."

"Ten o'clock," your mother says. "Tell him not a minute later."

Your father turns to her. "He is standing right here, Mother. Don't you think he can hear you? By golly, aren't you speaking English? Does he need me to interpret it for him?"

"That's very nice, Harold, to talk to your wife like that."

"I'll be home on time."

And then you don't know what to do. You watch your father reach for the envelope.

"I need the keys," you say.

Your father reaches across the table for the leather case. You can feel your fingers move while he works the key to the wagon off its little hook.

And then finally it's in your hand.

"Thanks." And then you say, "I'll remember who I am."

CHAPTER 16

THE NUMBER Linda gave you is next to the front door of a small red brick house with the windows and roof trimmed in dark green. The concrete driveway is empty all the way back to a small shed off the side. The yard's a well-kept layout of flowers and shrubs and grass that rises to the house. A curving path of red bricks leads from the curb to the steps of a small brick porch. A storybook house. You're there ten minutes ahead of when you should be. You've heard it isn't cool to show up early. You keep driving. But something has changed just seeing it. Sunlight comes off the gleaming hood in spears through the windshield so bright you have to squint to see the street. The houses take on the sacred look of churches. The yards hold up the manicured jewels of their shrubs and flowers in this quiet but fierce display of early autumn. Water from a turning sprinkler skitters and dances off the hot invisible griddle of the sunlight. You smell cut grass and lawnmower engine exhaust. Your face burns. You know why. It's someone else's neighborhood, this neighborhood where you've brought your father's wagon, where your hands are on the steering wheel like they've reached into this neighborhood for Linda.

Her mother answers the door. She's plump and not as tall as Linda. The way her hair is shaped around her open face reminds you of Annette Funicello. But when she smiles at you it's Linda's smile.

"You must be Shake."

The way she says it. Clear of anything you can recognize as trouble.

"Are you Mrs. Bowen?"

"Yes."

"I'm here for Linda."

"Of course you are."

She takes your arm and guides you into the living room where you stand on soft red carpet. The house is storybook on the inside too. The living room like the inside of a jewelry box with a picture window where sunlight comes through and gets caught in the glass and crystal. The furniture some European style named for some king or country. A vase of red and white carnations on the coffee table. The sofa and armchairs covered in this red and cream and yellow flowered cloth that looks like velvet. Small ornate frames with photographs cover the end tables and the mantel over the fireplace. You ransack your brain for the name of the furniture. King Louie maybe.

"Linda? Shake's here!" She calls it gentle to an archway to a room with a dining table. Then turns to you again. "So you're off to the big fair?"

"Yes. And then some dinner." And then you say, "She'll be back before ten."

"Sounds like you've planned a wonderful afternoon and evening."

"I hope so."

"Linda's very excited."

"Me too."

"She tells me you play the trumpet."

"She does?"

"She says she heard your band. You played Summertime."

"Oh. I'm sorry. I forgot."

"One of my favorite Gershwin tunes."

And then Linda's in the archway. Her mother hurries over, adjusts her hair without changing anything, leads her back your way. Linda looks up at you from her lowered face and smiles.

"Hi."

"Hi. Hope my mom didn't bore you to death."

"Oh, honey," her mother says. "You didn't give me time to bore him."

She's wearing a high-collared blouse like you've seen pilgrim women wear in movies. A striped beige skirt. A light brown mohair sweater across her shoulders without her arms in it. A white ribbon holds her hair back off her forehead.

It dawns on you that this is for you.

"You look great," you say.

"Thanks. So do you."

"You have a nice home, Mrs. Bowen."

"Why, thank you, Shake."

"I don't know what style your furniture's called, but it's beautiful." And then you say, "It feels really good in here."

"Thank you. Handsome young men have better things to keep in their heads than furniture, but thank you for noticing."

You look at Linda again. "Are you ready?"

"Do you think I'll need this sweater?"

"We can always leave it in the car." You turn to her smiling mother.

"Thanks, Mrs. Bowen."

"You kids just have fun."

On the drive to the fairgrounds you understand how wrong you were about what this would be like. Nothing's had anything to do with this. Nothing from looking at Playboys at Servus Drug. Nothing from Blackwell. Nothing from Scoutmaster Haycock's wife. Nothing from playing jazz. Nothing from painting the dome light of Doby's Impala red. Nothing from hearing that Elsha would take a girl's sweater right over her head. Nothing from Robbie and Eddie and Jimmy. Nothing from Rosita. Nothing from Mr. Selby. Nothing from church. Just this life there next to you. You head south on Highway 89 toward Salt Lake. You pass the Cudahy stock yards and Phillips 66 refinery. When the stink of sulfur floods the wind of the open wagon you hope she knows it's the refinery. Her life. You want to know everything about it. All kinds of stuff you know you can't bring up. What her handwriting's like. What brand of toothpaste. What tv shows. What records. What movies. What cereal. How soggy she lets it get. What kind of stuff is taped to her refrigerator door. How late she stays up. What kinds of fibs she tells her father. Everything but what the deal is with her Mona Lisa friend.

"For Science? Prows."

"I had him last year."

"He's really hard."

"I know. All the homework. How about History?"

"Briscoe. He's so fun. He makes us act things out. I got to be Eleanor Roosevelt."

"I missed him. I had Holbrook."

"You should really take Briscoe if you can."

"You like Mrs. Whitaker?"

"She's so sweet. But she's strict."

You go from there. You learn that she came to hear you play this summer in Liberty Park. That her father sells appliances at Sears. That he's on a bowling team. That her favorite singer is Buddy Holly. That she wishes she could ice skate. That she's got a cat named Moonlight. That she doesn't have a sister. An older brother named Lyle and a little one named Frankie. Soon you're headed down Second West past Wasatch Springs. She learns who your brothers and sisters are. That your father's a bookkeeper. That your mother's the Ward Organist. That you lived on a ranch where you had a horse named Rex and a dog named Rufus. Who Miles Davis is. Soon you find that she's slid across the seat to where she's close enough for you to know what her perfume's like. Soon you're turning into the parking lot for the fairgrounds where you took your driving test three months ago. The banners for the fair are faded. They hang without moving in the air. You hope she doesn't notice how they're shabby. She leaves her sweater on the seat. You lock the doors. She hooks her hand in your arm. Crossing the gravel lot toward the sun-bleached banners the easy weight of her hand makes you feel like you're wearing a tuxedo. You can already smell the animals.

The second Porsche you've ever seen comes nosing slowly out between two rows of cars. This time dark green. This time a man and a woman through the windshield as it approaches and idles past where you could reach out and touch it. You turn to watch it go. Linda follows your arm around and stands there waiting while it reaches the street and then turns right and accelerates.

"Do you know those people?" she asks.

All you can do is imagine them and where they're going.

"No," you say. "I just like the car."

"What kind is it?"

"It's called a Porsche."

"I've never seen one. It was cute."

"It's from Germany."

You do the livestock first. Chickens and goats and pigs and geese and llamas and ponies and even some beehives. Then the arts and crafts pavilion where you look at quilts, dolls, homemade animals with button eyes, paintings of people and flowers and fruits and birds and mountains, birdfeeders made out of popsicle sticks, scarves, coffee mugs with names and slogans, tables of belts and trinkets and tools and baubles and jewelry. She only takes her hand off your arm to pet the goats. Feel the coarse fur of a llama. Pick up a necklace with a plastic heart for a pendant.

"You want it?"

She puts it back down.

"I've got one. My brother Lyle made me one in shop."

"I made one too."

"He's graduated. He's getting ready for his mission."

"Where's he going?"

"Kentucky."

"I'm going on one too."

She takes your arm again and you hit the rides. The tilt-a-whirl. The hammer. The haunted house. The house of mirrors. The roller coaster. The funhouse. The bumper cars. The merry-go-round. The whip. Her hair is everywhere. In the bumper cars it recoils like it's alive when someone hits her from behind. In the whip, with her body up against yours with more centrifugal force than you could ever hold her with, it lashes across your face, looks for your mouth. You catch a hot dog and then take in the weirder side of things. The World's Largest Snake. The Bearded Lady. The Fat Man. The World's Smallest Woman. The Tattooed Man. Exhibits of pre-fab houses, water heaters, sprinkler systems, swimming pools, yard furniture, miracle pots and pans and knives. You throw hardballs at bowling pins and shoot air rifles at metal ducks. Win her a bright pink monkey. Hear them announce a demolition derby. Stay for the first two heats. In the smoke and dust you go back to the wagon for her sweater. You watch the sun go down from one last ride on the Ferris wheel where she sits up against you on her own and pretends she can pluck the black leaves of the trees out of the red sky. You leave the fairgrounds just before nine o'clock.

Lee's Cafe and Restaurant. The entrance is toward the back. You climb the steps and hold the glass door open. There's a cigarette machine in the entrance. A small bar and small round tables in a shadowed room whose carpet looks like it came from a theater. Fifty years of old tobacco in the air. A place where people come to sit and smoke and drink and maybe talk each other into dirty things. A place where you might play a trumpet. You want to get out. But the place is empty and there's already a waitress coming your way with menus.

"Two?"

"Yeah."

"The restaurant's closed. The café up front's still open."

You look at Linda. She nods and shrugs.

"Where the booths are?" you say.

"Yes."

The café part is this bright and shiny room at the other end of the place with turquoise booths, small kitchen tables and chairs out on the floor, a counter with turquoise stools on chrome-plated posts. Everything's clean. The lighting is everywhere. An elephant couldn't leave a shadow. You feel okay again. The waitress gives you a booth. You let Linda choose a side and take the side across from her. On the wall right next to you is a window and a drawn back curtain. You open the menu and look for the most expensive thing. It's the hot roast beef sandwich with mashed potatoes and dressing and gravy.

"You should try the hot roast beef sandwich," you say.

"That's okay."

"You sure?"

"Yeah. Just a cheeseburger and cherry coke. No onions."

You tell the waitress you want the same thing. She takes the menus and leaves you and Linda there with your placemats and utensils.

"Can I ask you something?" Linda says.

"Sure."

"You're so far away. Can I come sit on your side?"

And so you let her in against the window where the curtain is. Reach across and slide her placemat over. And then you sit there side by side and talk, and toy with your knives and forks and napkins, and when things go quiet sometimes, you look at the empty side of the booth or past her out the window. Side by side is the way you've spent the day. In the Chevy wagon. Walking. In the whip. In the bleachers for the demolition derby. On the Ferris wheel. And now here. Where the afternoon has turned into this journey into evening. This journey you've made side by side. Through the window, past the profile of her face, down and across the highway, you can see the crowd in the yellow light around the Frostop. Yenchik's Ford. Quigley's Hudson. Porter's red Mercury. West's Pontiac. Snook's Chevy. You watch Linda look at the back of her hand and stretch her fingers out. And then out of nowhere you're riding a bus. You and her. At night on a Greyhound bus whose only destination is where it happens to be on any highway. Where the moon bathes the desert out through the window and fires the sleeping edge of her forehead and nose and mouth. She's got the window. You the aisle. Guarding her. You look at her hand for a minute too. The waitress brings your cherry cokes and cheeseburgers.

Buddy Holly comes on the radio on the ride home to her house. Raining in My Heart. She starts to sing along. Her voice is barely more than a hum with the lyrics barely there. You turn it down a touch to hear her better. You know them too. You and your buddies sing along with the windows open and the radio so loud the song comes in shreds through the cavitating speakers. You want to join in. But she sings it this private way, to herself, even though she's turned your way on the bench, looking at you while she sings. You get to her house. There's a car in the driveway now. Too dark off the side of the house to see what it is. Two bright lantern-looking porch lights frame the front door. You draw the wagon up to the curb and listen to her sing until the song is over.
"You can sing."
"Thank you. You can play trumpet."
"You saying a duet?"
"Maybe."
You walk her up to her porch at five to ten. In the light cast by the porch lanterns, she looks up at you, smiles, takes your hand. The skin of her forehead is flushed and gleaming. The tendrils of hair where her scalp begins are limp like a child's but so intensely clear and magnified in the light that you can almost see into their follicles. In her hazel-colored eyes you can see that the browns and greens aren't blended, but torn, membranes suspended like swirls of marble in an amber-colored

liquid. It amazes you that she can look through them at you. Through the membranes, through her eyes, you sense all the little things each day of her life is made of. What would taste good for breakfast. What she'll wear. What color ribbon. You can see where she's made the beginning of a place for you. If not a place then the possibility of a place. A place for you in what she thinks about. A place that has your name. A name she may idly write in the margin of her notebook while she listens to Mrs. Whitaker read to the class. The thousands of filaments of her mohair sweater shimmer in the light. She has her bright pink monkey cradled in her arm.

"He's asleep," you say.

She looks down.

"Yeah." Her laugh soft. "With his eyes wide open."

"He needs eyelids."

"I'll see if Mom can make him some."

"I really had a good time."

"Me too."

"I'm glad."

"I'd like to do it again."

When she says it you can smell the phantom trace of her cheeseburger on her warm breath.

"Me too," you say.

You pull away from her house. You watch the rearview mirror until you see the lanterns on her porch go dark. You realize that every time you touched it was her idea. You wonder if you might have been too shy. If she was hoping for something more. If you hurt her feelings. You remember the Porsche you saw. Imagine it for the first time with someone in the passenger seat. Linda. Her voice. The weatherman says clear today. You turn the radio off and start singing the song you listened to her sing.

CHAPTER 17

THE PORCHLIGHT'S ON for you when you round the corner at the top of the hill and look down the street to where your house is. You pull the wagon in the garage, bring down the door in the well of exhaust behind it, go into the house through the basement. In the stairwell you can hear the clacking of your father's typewriter through the wall from the furnace room. You think of the clacking of tappets under the rocker arm covers of West's V8. The engine that drives the house. Your father doing what he loves to do. Writing a letter to someone in the Church. Typing his Sunday School lesson for the morning. Things are okay. Things are what they've always been. Up the stairs you can see the light from the living room. You reach the top and find your mother standing between the piano and the sofa. Her hair is crazy. In her desolate and broken face is the sense that something horrible and irreversible has happened while your father's been typing away. She's wearing her pink bathrobe. Wearing it backward with the belt untied so that its ends are tails and the back of her robe hangs open. The evening is still in your blood like a stupor you suddenly know you have to shake.

"What's the matter?"

"Yes, Shakli. How was it?"

"Fun."

"Did you meet her parents?"

"Yeah. Her mom. What's wrong?"

"Is she a nice lady?"

"Yeah. What's the matter?"

"You promised us you would be home by ten."

Her voice is small, melancholy, exhausted, reaching you like a song that had to travel from another neighborhood. You can hear the strain in it. You watch her move toward the sofa and put out a hand for the backrest for support. Fear begins to work your stomach.

"It's only a quarter after."

"Yes, Shakli. Only a quarter after."

She's wearing this watery almost innocent smile. The smile of someone wounded but still capable of being kind. The insanely tranquil smile
you've seen saints wear in paintings of their executions. A smile you've
seen her direct at your father but never at you. Not like this. You hear
the typewriter stop. Wait for the creak of the office chair to tell you he's
coming upstairs. She's hiding her hand at her side in the folds of her
robe but you can still see what she's holding. The whisk broom from
the kitchen. Her way of beating you when you were young comes back.
The bamboo rugbeater she never used on rugs. The welts that looked
like pretzels in your skin. But it's not the broom that makes you sick.
The broom's just pain. It's her face and hair and robe on backward with
the dangling ends of the thin pink belt around her knees. Through the
floor, from the furnace room, you hear your father go after the keys of
his typewriter again.

"I'm sorry I'm late."

"Yes, Shakli. You are sorry. What did you do?"

She starts to move toward you. You move around the front of the
sofa, around the coffee table, to keep her on the other side.

"We went to the fair. Then to eat. Like I said we would."

"And that took until after ten o'clock?"

She keeps her voice so weary she barely gives what she says the
strength to be a question. She matches you step for step along her side
of the sofa.

"We were at the fair until dark."

"Yes, Shakli. Tell me what you did at the fair in the dark."

"We rode the Ferris wheel. To see the sunset. Then we left."

You watch her gather strength. Watch her smile stay put but her lips
take on the tight stitched look that lets you know she's done with being
kind and ready for business.

"And you were alone with her on the Ferris wheel."

"There were other people there."

"Yes. I can imagine what kind of people."

"She's a nice girl." Your voice starts going tight and high and reckless knowing where she's going now.

"A nice girl doesn't stay at a fair after dark, Shakli. A nice girl doesn't
go to a café."

"I couldn't afford a restaurant."

"Then maybe you should wait until you have the money to date a
nice girl."

"I do. I have to save it for my mission."

"Seven hours! Pfui! What do you do with a girl for seven hours?"

"You said ten o'clock was okay."

"Did you have a good time?"

"Yeah. We did."

And now her smile is gone. Gone with the songlike Billie Holiday exhaustion in her voice. Gone like smoke that comes up through the wrinkles when a wad of paper breaks suddenly into flame.

"Did you like her little breasts?"

"What?"

"Did it feel good to touch them? Hah?"

"I didn't touch them! You're crazy!"

"Don't lie to me! I am your mother!"

"I didn't! You're nuts!"

The typewriter goes quiet again. You hear yourself begging in your head. For the chair to creak. For him to come upstairs. You watch her come around the far end of the sofa. See her bring out the broom. You stand there. Let her come till she's close enough to where you see broken red filaments of blood in the whites around her eyes. Faint stains of yellow along the cracks between her bare white teeth.

"Tell me the truth! Tell me how you played with her! Tell me how good it felt!"

"I didn't! I swear!"

"Yah! You also promised to be home at ten! You liar!"

She raises the broom. For the instant you see it airborne it looks like a club with a mohawk haircut. It comes down on your head and then against your ear before you can grab her wrist. She struggles to free her hand. She glares at you with such open and focused hate you can feel it cut through you like this sharp and searing hail of ice and fire together.

"Stop! Please!"

"Did it make you feel good? Did it make you feel like a man? A big man?"

"Don't say that!"

"Did it make you feel good to fool her mother?"

"I didn't fool anyone! Her mom liked me!"

"Yah! Because you fooled her!"

"How did I fool her? Jesus Christ!"

"You got her to let you take her daughter out!"

"You're crazy!"

"Let go of me! Let me go!"

She tries to pry your fingers off her wrist. Her nails bite the skin of your knuckles. The shoulder of her robe slips off her arm. Without looking, without wanting to, you can see her naked shoulder, the heavy blue-veined bag of her naked breast, her naked hip and leg. You keep your eyes on her face.

"Promise not to hit me!"

"Let me go! You are hurting me! Harold! Harold! Help!"

"Promise!"

You watch her face compose itself again around this loathing you can feel inside you. "I promise. Now let me go."

You let her go. Keep your arm in the air for the broom. But she lowers it and steps back. Pushes her robe back up her arm and shoulder. Much of the rage has left her face. You watch her try to pull what's left of it together. You think of a woman picking up something she's spilled, like bottlecaps or oranges, off a sidewalk. You feel crazy. Something down inside you starts losing hold. Something so deep you can feel its roots start losing their grip in the muscles of your legs. You don't dare look away. You don't dare wipe away the points of spit she left on your face.

"Yes. I know how you fooled them." Her voice is still a snarl. "Look at you. It makes me sick to even look at you standing there. In your Sunday jacket. Fooling good people!"

"I didn't fool anybody!"

"They don't know you like we do! They don't know what you are!"

"What? You keep saying that! What am I?"

"Yah!" She gathers breath again. "I'll tell you! A rape artist! That's what you are! A fucking beast! Yah! A fucking beast!"

She rakes her eyes across your face to make sure you've understood. And then she's gone. You hear her hang the broom on the nail in the kitchen. Go down the hall and close her bedroom door. And then you don't hear anything but what she called you. Knowing she never swears. Knowing she meant what she said. A fucking beast. A beast that fucks. A beast that's a beast because it fucks. You listen for your father. Beg for the groan of his chair, for his shoes on the stairs the way you've always heard them, for him to come into the living room and tell you it's all right. You look around for anything to let you know what happened here was nothing close to sane. Blood on the walls. Her little Hummel figurines torn off the shelf of the mantel and shattered all over the flagstone hearth of the fireplace. The sofa smeared with shit and cushions ripped to pieces. The carpet splashed with vomit. Her piano busted open like a walnut. But the room looks like it always does. All it gives you back is how it's furnished. Blank. Blank as a vampire's mirror. Blank as the silence from the den downstairs. Blank and savage and ready for company. Everything in place. You the one thing wrong. The one thing out of place. The one thing blood and shit and vomit. You stand there shivering from heat and cold together. A boulder fills your throat and ears. The boulder of this long and crude and moaning howl that can't stop begging him to come and tell you none of this is you. You can hear it in your head but can't get it to move.

At first it startles you, sharp and hard through the carpet, explosive little pocks of keys on paper. You know he heard. You've been downstairs yourself and heard your mother's ranting travel through the floor like it's a drumskin. The keystrokes start out measured. A word or two at a time. It makes you cold and sick and hollow when you realize what he's doing. Testing the attitude upstairs. Pecking his way through the minefield of the house. Seeing if he can get away with getting back to work. It chills you. And then shame floods your face. Shame like the heat from a suddenly opened furnace door for thinking he'd come upstairs for you. You look down. Your shoes wear dust from the fairgrounds. The key still in your hand. You hear his keystrokes lose their hesitation. Start taking on purpose again.

And suddenly you can't stay here. Suddenly you're hammering down the stairs. You hear the clacking stop. In your head you can see him with his fingers pulled back off the keys like they've electrocuted him. You don't care. In the garage you yank the big door up. The springs shriek and the door bangs quivering up into its cradle. You're already in the wagon, at the wheel, stabbing for the keyhole, the door closed, when the light comes on and you hear your name.

"Shake!"

You crank the engine. Slot the gearshift into reverse. Look around in case he's stupid enough to be behind you. You catch a trace of Linda when you turn your head. Enough to smell. Not enough to trust. He's coming toward the passenger door. You step on the gas to take the door away from him. Halfway up the driveway you pull out the headlight switch. And there he is, your father, caught, blinded, bringing up his arm to shield his eyes and look for you behind the windshield.

"Shake!"

You swing the wagon out into the circle. In the driveway, out of the headlights now, your father is faceless, black, the silhouette of a stocky man in a short sleeved shirt against the light from the empty garage. Go fuck yourself. You're screaming. Go fuck your shoes. Go fuck your church. Go fuck your wife. The boulder finally moves. You start to cry. Because you don't know what you mean. Because this is where you live. Because you're leaving Karl and Molly and Roy and Maggie here while the house explodes. Because what you can smell of Linda is soft and sweet and dead. Because the back tires of your father's station wagon are leaving howling lines of rubber on the pavement of this placid circle. Because you don't know where to go this time of night if where you're going isn't home.

PART 3

VALENTINE'S DAY

COLEMAN HAWKINS. Lester Young. Bud Powell. John Coltrane. Sonny Rollins. Clifford Brown.

The Great War in Heaven. Like everything else they keep sitting you down and teaching you, in Sunday School, in Priesthood, in Sacrament Meeting, it's stuff you've heard a thousand times, stuff they keep repeating, stuff they keep embellishing with detail. Sometimes with mothering love whose touch you want to recoil from. Sometimes with righteous pounding anger from the Sacrament Meeting pulpit that lights this blazing bewildering fire in your head and chest. Again and again, from different teachers, until it builds to the range and weight of an overcast sky made out of iron, a heavy iron sky as far as you can see no matter which way you turn to look for sunlight.

Eubie Blake. Stanley Turrentine. Wayne Shorter. Cannonball Adderley. Roy Eldridge. Fats Waller. Charles Mingus.

You and the other Priests sit on gray steel folding chairs scattered across the brown linoleum floor of a small classroom with bare white walls and a fluorescent light box recessed in the acoustic tiles of the ceiling. Toward the front corner there's the single tall and narrow window every classroom up and down the long hall of the churchhouse has. On the front wall, behind a small table on steel legs, hangs the blackboard you've seen your Priesthood and Sunday School teachers use in every classroom you've spent Sunday mornings in for more than four years now. Brother Rodgers the telephone lineman. Elder Jensen the returned missionary. Brother George the welder. Brother Hess the auctioneer for the Cudahy stockyards. Bird the hairdresser who does dead people's hair. The only teacher who never used it once was Brother Clark. Out the window the sun has yet to crest the high shoulders of the mountains. The parking lot and the orchards that rise behind it still lie hushed in morning shadow.

At the front of the room, where he stands behind the table, Brother Hunt is a big good-looking guy with sandy brush-cut hair who moves with the smooth unhurried casual style of the quarterback and golf captain and homecoming king he was back when he played for Bountiful High. Up close, under his dark blue blazer, he looks built like a Roman statue of a golfer. On his mission in Southern California he baptized hundreds of people. And then he spent the Army in Hawaii where he married and brought home the most beautiful woman in the congregation. Now he's going to college at Weber State to be a coach. At night and on weekends he sells Corvettes at Roy Price Chevrolet across the street from Hinkle Music. He's always got a demo. You figure it's even Steven between him and the dealership. He gets to drive a new Corvette wherever he goes. They get to use his good-looking face and his beautiful Hawaiian wife for advertising. When they come driving into the parking lot for church, sunglasses on, they look like a live tv commercial. She teaches second grade at Tolman Elementary. Every girl in the congregation is in love with him and wishes his wife was dead.

Which is why you and West and Keller and Doby and Yenchik look at his voice as the equalizing hand of God at work. It's the last voice you'd expect. This high-pitched straining voice that comes out whining and underpowered like it's always working overtime. Like a lawnmower engine under the hood of a Corvette.

"God was ready to create and populate the Earth with his billions of spirit children. He had to send us to Earth so that we could take on the earthly mortal bodies we'd need in order to have our virtue tested, be baptized, and make our covenants in the Temple. He also sent us here to test our faith in him. He wanted to know which of us he could trust to return and live with him. He needed a plan to do that. A Plan of Salvation. And that was where he had a problem. Jasperson."

"He wanted all of us to pass."

"That's right. He loved all his children. He didn't want any of us to fail. Well, that's not how tests work. So he had a problem. What did he do? Lilly."

"He called in his favorite sons. Jesus and Lucifer. And asked them each to write a plan and bring it back to him."

"That's right. Lucifer came back with a plan where he'd rule the Earth with an iron fist. Force everyone to be obedient. Bring all of us back the way God wanted. Jesus saw it different. Force wasn't the answer. Force wouldn't test us. Show God who we truly were. He'd never know who he could trust. Now the plan Jesus put forth was to send us here with the freedom to choose. Good or evil. Accept or reject God. Jasperson."

"Free agency."

"Yes. The risk was that God would end up losing some of us. But he'd know for sure that those who came back to him could be trusted. Now," he says. "Jesus also had an ace in the hole. Any of you know what it was?"

Jasperson looks at his thumbs.

"Atonement," says Brother Hunt. "Those of us who failed his test could atone for failing it. Jesus would see to that by paying for our sins ahead of time. I think it's obvious whose plan God chose. What happened then? West."

"Was that when Lucifer went nuts and started the war in Heaven?"

"He was a sore loser. He rebelled. A third of God's spirit children rebelled along with him. The other two thirds sided with Jesus. And they went to war. Two big armies. I think it's obvious—"

"Jesus," Keller says.

"—who lost. God punished Lucifer and his hosts by banishing them from Heaven for eternity. They'd never get to come to Earth to take on mortal bodies. They'd never know what anything felt or tasted like. What a kiss was. They were condemned to roam the Earth forever but never experience its physical pleasures and responsibilities."

"Like driving," says West.

Brother Hunt smiles. "Playing football."

"Swimming," Lilly says.

"Mowing the yard," says Jasperson.

Brother Hunt keeps going. "The spirits who fought with Jesus? They got to come to Earth and take on mortal bodies. Bodies that would become immortal when they were resurrected. Like God's body. Bodies that would make it possible for them to be gods themselves."

Brother Hunt takes a glance out the window where the sun is just breaking the thin line of white gold fire it leaves along the ridge of the mountains.

"So those were the damned children and the rewarded children," he says. "The hosts of Lucifer and the hosts of Jesus. But there was a third group there."

"Niggers," says Yenchik.

Brother Hunt brings his head around and stares at Yenchik hard. "We don't call them that," he says.

"That's who you mean," says Yenchik.

"That's not what we call them."

"Fence Sitters then," says Yenchik.

"I wouldn't call them that either. But let's face facts. That's what they did. Sat on the fence while the rest of us did battle."

"So there was a fence in heaven," says Keller.

"No. There wasn't an actual fence. That's just a figure of speech."

"A figure of speech for what?" says Keller.

"For being indecisive. They couldn't decide which side to fight for. Or they had trouble fighting as hard as the rest of us."

"So they were wishy washy," says Yenchik.

"Well, maybe some of them."

"So they were cowards."

Ever since Yenchik got his 40 Ford, and the two of you tri-powered it, and then locked the rear axle, he's come alive. Grown into his skin. Learned what it is that makes him Yenchik. Developed this voice as big and deep and startling as the sousaphone Mr. Hinkle played. Gone after it like a bloodhound when something hasn't added up the way he needs things added up. When it comes to Negroes he's always known. How they add up. How they fit together. Now Brother Hunt gives Yenchik a long look. Like Yenchik's the one who can't be added up.

"I can't say they were cowards," he says. "Maybe confused. Maybe they didn't know what was at stake. Maybe their hearts weren't in it. Maybe they weren't as dedicated. Maybe they lacked conviction. I don't know. I can't speculate. All we know is what the gospel tells us. They weren't as valiant as the rest of us."

"Were they lazy?" Yenchik says.

"I can't say that either."

"Weak?"

Here in Priesthood class, with all the other Priests, the rest of you sit back and let Yenchik go. Let him sink his teeth in. After years of carrying his dopey weight in class while he sat there half the time so logy he couldn't tell you where he was. Then all of a sudden he got his Ford, and started being here, and looking for a reason why, and needing the things he was being taught to start adding up.

"Again, that's not for me to say. We just need to take the Lord's word that they were less valiant."

"What does valiant mean?"

Under the cloth of Brother Hunt's gray slacks his fingers are moving like he's turning some coin around and around.

"Determined to fight," he says. "Courageous. Fearless. Ready to give it their all."

"I don't get it," says Yenchik.

"Don't get what?"

"How they get from there to having black skin."

Inside his pockets Brother Hunt's fingers stop moving.

"From where?"

"From not being valiant."

All along you've had questions. How spirits fight a war. How they fought if they were spirits. What you were like as a warrior. How you fought without fists and hands and arms. What kind of weapons you used. You've looked at Doby and Keller and Yenchik and West and tried to see them as spirits fighting the hosts of Lucifer for everything they were worth. Karl and Molly and Roy and Maggie. Even Manny and Hidalgo. For years you've let the questions ride to where now they're the questions only children ask. Not worth asking. Except for Yenchik. Yenchik's just discovered questions. And he's figured out that jocks and coaches are as easy to play as ukuleles. Brother Hunt stands there and contemplates Yenchik. And then his fingers start fiddling around again inside his pocket.

"From not being valiant to having black skin," he says. "That's what you're asking."

"Yeah. How you get from one to the other."

"Okay," says Brother Hunt. "Let's try this. I give three kids a test. The first kid gets a hundred. That's an A, right?"

"Yeah." Yenchik probably still wondering what it's like to get an A on anything.

"The second kid gets zero. That's an F."

"Okay."

"Let's say the third kid gets sixty. What should I give him? An A too?"

"No."

"An F?"

"No."

"Then what?"

"Something in between. Like a C."

"Good. Now take the war in heaven. The kid who chose to fight on the side of Jesus got the A. He got to come to earth. Get a mortal body. The right to bear the Priesthood. The kid who chose to fight with Lucifer got the F. He got thrown out of heaven. That leaves the kid who got the C. What should he get?"

"A black skin."

"Forget that for a minute. Stay with me here."

"Okay."

"Does he deserve as much as the kid who got the A?"

"No." Yenchik going along with him.

"But he deserves more than the kid who got the F."

"Yeah."

"Okay. So he gets some of the blessings of the kid who got the A. But not all of them. He gets to come to Earth and take on a physical body. But he doesn't deserve to get the Priesthood. That sound fair?"

"So Negroes all got Cs in the war in Heaven."

You know what Yenchik's doing. Keeping Brother Hunt just out of reach of figuring out he's being played. Tightening a ukulele string to just before it breaks.

"Okay," says Brother Hunt. "You could say that."

"And everyone else on earth got an A. Or they wouldn't be here."

"You could say that too."

"Chinese. Eskimos. Mexicans."

"Yes."

"Indians."

"Apparently so."

"Arabs. Mongoloids."

"I think you mean Mongolians. I'm not sure about Arabs. They may have negro blood in them."

"How about Hitler? He got an A. He could of had the Priesthood."

"Hitler's a special case. I'm not sure he could ever be forgiven."

"How about Joe Louis? He's pretty valiant."

"Who?"

"The Brown Bomber. The heavyweight champ."

"Oh. Okay. How about him?"

"He beat that Nazi boxer. That Nazi was white. He must've been pretty valiant in the war in Heaven. But Joe Louis beat him."

"We don't know that. That's between him and God."

Brother Hunt gives Yenchik this look he probably gives every scruffy kid who wanders into the showroom to hang around the Corvette on the floor and ask all kinds of questions when it's obvious he doesn't have the cash to even put air in the tires. This get outta here smiling look. But Yenchik's not done yet.

"Were the Negroes Negroes before they got Cs?"

"No."

"What were they before then?"

"They were spirit children. Just like the rest of us."

"Were they Negroes before they were born?"

"No. They didn't have bodies. They didn't have skin."

"So why did God make them Negroes?"

"Well, first off, it was part of God's way of giving them a C. Second, God wanted to give the rest of us a way to recognize them."

"So when do they turn into Negroes?"

"When?"

"Yeah."

"When they're conceived. They inherit it from Cain. They all come to Earth through the lineage of Cain."

"Cain was a Negro?"

"He was after he killed his brother Abel. That's one of the ways God punished him. He marked him with a black skin. So that we could recognize him. He became the father of an inferior race because of what he did. You've heard of the mark of Cain."

"So all the Negroes come from Cain?"

"No. They come through Cain. They're known in the gospel as the seed of Cain."

"How come they need to be marked?"

Brother Hunt gives Yenchik this look again like he wants him out of the dealership but he's starting to think that there's maybe a chance that Yenchik's father might be the richest man in town. Yenchik's father the machinist. Not rich by a mile.

"So we won't give them the Priesthood by mistake," he says. "Or mingle with them. So we won't marry one by accident and curse our own children in the process."

"What curse?"

"The curse of not being worthy of the Priesthood."

"You mean if I marry some negro chick, and we have a kid, my kid's gonna be cursed because of her?"

"Not because of her. Because of what she is. She's a conduit for those spirits who sat on the fence and were cursed by God. It doesn't matter if it's half white or almost all white. If there's a drop of negro blood in your kid, it's going to bear the curse."

"One drop."

"That's not my opinion. That's what the leaders of the Church have told us. Apostle Mark E. Peterson, for one."

"So I could only have Fence Sitters for kids."

Brother Hunt sizes Yenchik up again for the chance that if he kicked him out of the dealership his father might be loaded.

"They wouldn't be entitled to the Priesthood." And then he says, "I get the feeling you aren't taking this as seriously as you need to."

"No. I am."

"You know what Brigham Young had to say about intermarriage?"

"No."

"I'll tell you. If the white man who belongs to the chosen seed mixes his blood with the seed of Cain, then the penalty under the law of God is death on the spot."

Yenchik sits there for a minute.

"Will he be excommunicated too?"

"He'll be dead," says Brother Hunt. "That's bad enough."

"I thought getting excommunicated was worse."

"You're right. My mistake."

"Can Negroes be baptized?"

"Of course. They can have all the blessings of any other member who doesn't hold the Priesthood."

"They just can't get to the Celestial Kingdom."

"They can. They can inherit the lower degree of the Celestial King-dom. They'll just be there as servants."

"Like slaves?"

Brother Hunt's face goes hard. Yenchik's come too close to breaking the ukulele string.

"No. Not like slaves." You can hear the high thin whining strain in the overworked lawnmower engine of Brother Hunt's voice. "Slavery's a sin in the eyes of God. You can't buy and sell his children. There's a huge difference between a servant and a slave."

Jasperson raises his hand. Brother Hunt gives Yenchik a minute longer.

"Go ahead, Jasperson."

"Do you know any Negroes?"

"Sure. I did anyway. In the army. I had a few of them for friends. One of my commanding officers was one."

"Did he order you around?"

"Of course he did. He was a captain."

"How are we supposed to act around them?"

Brother Hunt's fingers get busy again with something in his pocket.

"You don't know any?' he says.

"No," says Jasperson.

"None in school?"

"There's one. But I don't know him."

"Like you'd act around anyone else. You need to understand this. The Church doesn't bear Negroes any animosity. Neither should you. They're God's children. Don't judge them, or belittle them, or think you're better than they are. If anything, you should pity them, for the rights and blessings they threw away in the pre-existence."

And now he takes his left hand out of his pocket and looks at the silver watch on his wrist. And then he takes his right hand out of his other pocket empty, and puts his hands together like he's about to crack his knuckles.

"Any last questions?"

Back in the corner Strand puts his hand up.

"Go ahead," says Brother Hunt.

"Doesn't it say that one day they'll get the Priesthood?"

"Yes. We're told that. It won't be for a long time. But one day they'll have proven to God they're worthy. That they're responsible enough for its power."

"But they'll always be Negroes," says Strand.

"Well . . . yes."

"They'll always be Fence Sitters. Or whatever. Even after they get the Priesthood."

Brother Hunt looks at Strand different than he did at Yenchik. Like Strand could whip out a checkbook and write out a check on a Corvette fender for the full sticker price.

"They made a decision in the pre-existence," he says. "It was the wrong one. But that's too bad. I've got a few things in my past I'd like to do over. Some passes I'd like to have another shot at. Receivers I missed. Interceptions. Hooked shots. Stupid mistakes. But I can't. Same as we can't go back and fight the war in heaven over."

Errol Garner. Shorty Rogers. McCoy Tyner. The beauty of the gospel. Its logic this elaborate equation that describes everything in the universe and provides the answer to everything that was, everything that is, everything that will be. Its insistence on being the pure and simple truth. Like two plus two is four. No matter how it makes you feel. Because in the face of its logic the way it makes you feel is meaningless. You may want two plus two to come out three. Or six. Or maybe thirty. But four is what it is. You can prove it with toothpicks, pencils, the stainless steel cups you drink milk from, pennies, the headlights of two cars at the Frostop. There's nothing to wonder about or question.

Why Negroes can't have the Priesthood doesn't work that way. You can't take two Negroes, add two more, and suddenly have the answer to why they can't be Deacons or Teachers or Priests. All you'll prove is that two Negroes plus two Negroes is four Negroes. What you have to do instead is take the story that Negroes are spirits who didn't fight as hard as you or Roy or Molly did. Take it as gospel truth. Then it makes sense. Then its logic is there as clear as their skin is black. And that's where they tell you to stop. Don't question it. Just believe it. Give all the logic of the gospel the foundation of your faith. Because that's how it holds together, the equation that will answer everything in all its harmony, in the fullness of time, as long as you accept its fundamental truth, that all its logic and the gray majesty of its iron sky rests on the bedrock of your faith. If it doesn't make sense, it's you. If it doesn't feel clean, it's you. If it scares you, makes you sick, it's you. If it doesn't hold together, if it comes tumbling down, it's because your testimony isn't rock, but sand. Two Negroes plus two Negroes will always be four Negroes. Four Negroes without the Priesthood. It's the way it is. The way you've heard for years and not known what to do with. Now you know as much as you ever will. Now you know the logic behind the shame, looking at them, on Mr. Selby's wall and on their album covers.

In the dark back seat of Robbie's panel truck you can hear Robbie's drums behind you shiver inside their cases with the roughness of whatever road you're on. It's a sound you're used to. On the ride home from an old folks home, a party at an Elks or Moose Lodge in one of the orchard towns, the Officers Club at Fort Douglas. Miles Davis. You can play his songs. You can work through his arrangements. You can figure out his solos. You can look at photos of him on album covers but not look his photos in the eye. Tonight it's Jimmy's turn to ride up front. Eddie's in the back seat next to you.

"I'm tellin' ya," he says. "Ellington didn't write it."

Everyone has to talk loud to hear above the noise of the engine and the howl of the old transmission and the radio.

"Fuck he didn't," says Robbie from the driver's seat in front of you. "It was his signature tune. He played it every night."

"He didn't write it," Eddie says. "Billy Strayhorn did."

"You're fulla shit. Ellington wrote it."

"He arranged it. Okay? He just arranged it. Billy Strayhorn wrote it."

"Who the hell's Billy Strayhorn?" says Jimmy.

"Jesus," Eddie says. "You don't know who Billy Strayhorn is. What a surprise."

"How come it's got Ellington's name all over it?" says Robbie.

"Cuz you're just looking at his arrangement. Billy Strayhorn wrote it." And then he says, "They called him Sweet Pea."

"They oughta call you Encyclopedia," says Jimmy. "Encyclopedia Eddie."

"You don't even know what the A Train is."

"Yeah I do."

"What?"

"It's the train you take to get to the B Train."

"You know what? You're not worth it. You don't know shit."

"You know too much shit."

"The A Train's a subway train," says Eddie. "It goes to Harlem."

"Like I just said," Jimmy says.

Stuff they keep repeating. Stuff they've told you to trust so long it's like your skin and bones and organs. Miles. Dizzy. Louie Armstrong. Clifford Brown. You know how they breathe. Know what their tongues and lips and throats are doing. Know what's inside them from their music. Know how they're playing, not just with the song, but with anyone listening. Fence Sitters. Seed of Cain. Sometimes like tonight, cruising home on Highway 89, it's there, foul and sick, this turning dirty ball of mud in your stomach. You listen to the shiver of Robbie's drums keep time with the joints in the concrete of the highway. Headlights come the other way and torch the dirty windshield, and in their brief blaze, you can see the faces of the guys in your band, your all white nigger band, except for the half of Robbie that's Mexican.

"You know where the word news comes from?" says Eddie.

"Nope," says Robbie.

"Take a guess. Go ahead."

"Cuz it ain't olds," says Jimmy.

And then Robbie and Jimmy are cackling away up in front, and Robbie's reaching over and slapping Jimmy on the shoulder, and Eddie's pissed, waiting for them to finish.

"Cuz it comes from north and east and west and south," he says.

Nobody says anything. In the pale light from the instruments and the backwash of the headlights, Jimmy's looking out the windshield, but you can tell he's grinning.

"Get it?" says Eddie. "The initials?"

Nobody says anything.

"Cuz it comes from all over," Eddie says. "That's why."

CHAPTER 19

"SO?" says Doby. "How'd it go?"

Off the side door of the churchhouse you're watching the Soderstroms get out of their faded green old Chevrolet in the parking lot behind the churchhouse. They've got their coats on for the late October cold. Sister Soderstrom reaches back inside to pull her kids out of the back seat.

"What?"

"The big first date."

"It went okay."

"You get any skin?" says West.

You smile off across the lot.

"What'd you do?" says Keller.

"The fair. I told you. Looked at animals. Went on rides. Had a burger afterwards."

"Where at?"

You don't want to tell them. Want to keep what it was like all for yourself.

"Some place on the way home. I can't remember."

"What car'd you use?" says Yenchik. "Your old man's wagon?"

"Yeah."

"You coulda put an air mattress in the back," says West.

This time, still smiling, you turn and look at him, at your face on the lenses of his slick black sunglasses. "You got a mind like a camel's asshole."

"Just kidding."

"Wish I'd known," says Yenchik. "You coulda borrowed mine."

"It probably woulda scared her," you say. "But that's cool. Thanks."

"You get a good night kiss?"

"Wasn't looking for one."

"You even hold hands?"

The way she kept taking your arm that night. The way every time you touched it was her idea. The way she wanted to sit on your side of the booth. Next to you, in the window seat in the night bus, where you could keep her safe.

"Yeah. Some."

"You taking her out again?"

"I don't know yet."

"Doesn't sound like it went so hot."

"It went fine." And then you say, "I like her."

Bishop Byrne retires from being bishop. Like Rodgers, Clark, Bird, he becomes another man out in the crowd. The only place you've ever seen him sit is on the podium. Now, from the Sacrament Table, it's weird to see him sitting out in the congregation, next to his wife Lucinda, holding a hymn book open with her, belting out the Sacrament Hymn. In the meantime, the office of bishop went looking, and found Lloyd Wacker. The high school football coach. Coach Wacker. Out of nowhere. Bishop Wacker. Along with his coaching job, he sells used Fords part time, and sometimes, going down Main Street on Saturday, you've seen him out on the lot of Larson Ford, trying to peddle some guy or some couple a car. Your bishop. Nobody gets it.

"Maybe he'll make everyone start wearing helmets to church," says Doby.

You picture hundreds of football helmets singing Onward Christian Soldiers.

"It wasn't that funny," says West.

"Maybe he'll make everyone start going to his games."

"Maybe he'll make Brother Clark start doing calisthenics."

"Maybe he'll make everyone buy a Ford," says West.

Nobody gets it. But everyone goes along. His coaching job goes all the way back to the football players in the Jeep. The guy with the Everly Brothers hair. The gorilla guy. The redheaded guy with the broken bottle teeth. The dentist guy. They used to play for him. They used to take his orders. You wonder if he knows about it. If they went bawling to him when you rolled their Jeep with your finger on Orchard Drive. It scared you when you started high school. That they'd look for you. But it only took your first few days to learn that they were gone. You remember passing Coach Wacker in the hall one day, back when you were a sophomore, giving him your church smile, telling him hello. Remember the way your face burned when he looked at you and kept on going. Remember thinking you'd broken some rule you didn't know about, crossed some line, like not letting on that you knew him, from church, from passing the Sacrament to him. Like a bridge between two places where one side wasn't supposed to know about the other side. Or that there even was a bridge.

On a Thursday night in December, the soil crisp and the moon hard and high and bright up through the bare-knuckled branches of the fruit trees, you walk down through the orchards to the churchhouse for your annual interview. Bishop Wacker is doing all the Priests tonight. It's the first time you'll be interviewed by him. The first time you'll be by yourself with the coach of the football team. In the cold moonlight of the parking lot, Jasperson's old Rambler, Doby's Impala, West's Pontiac, and Keller's bugeye Sprite are clustered together where the sidewalk leads to the back door. Seeing them, you can feel their engine and body parts, their grease in your hands despite the gloves you're wearing.

Inside, in the lobby, the bishop's office up the hall, West and Doby are teasing Jasperson about the one big lie that all of you are here to tell. Sure, there are the little ones, where maybe you've tried a beer or smoke since the last time you were interviewed, but the big lie is the killer. Where you have to keep the look of human steel in place. The first time you'll be telling it to Bishop Wacker.

"Come on," West says. "We're your buddies."

"Yeah," says Doby. "You can tell us."

"There's nothing to tell," says Jasperson.

"You can't even find it, can you," says West.

"Yeah? How am I supposed to go to the bathroom if I can't find it?"

"Use a microscope," says West.

"Or maybe diapers," Doby says.

"Come on," says Jasperson. "You're in church."

"You seen Yenchik?" you say.

"He's gone already."

"You guys all waiting?"

"Yeah," says West. "You're after me."

You're thinking about the lie West has to tell, about getting into Madeline Porter's bra, when the door down the hall opens, light floods the dark floor, Keller comes walking out of the bishop's office.

"You're next," Doby says to Jasperson.

Keller and Jasperson pass each other in the hall. Keller looks relieved but not quite sure of things. You think of the Mason jar he was using to store his sperm in case he ran out before he got a wife. Of the way he got bored one day and dyed it blue with ink from a fountain pen.

"How'd it go?"

"Weird," says Keller. "He's Coach Wacker. I got him for gym."

"You do okay?" you say.

"I guess."

"Whaddaya mean?" says West.

"Having your gym teacher ask you if you jack off. It's creepy."

"He said that?"

"No. Same thing, though."

"How'd he say it?"

"Abuse yourself."

"Abuse yourself?"

"Yeah. If I abused myself."

"How'd you know that's what he was talking about?"

"Cuz he'd already asked me everything else."

"Maybe he meant—"

"He meant did I jack off. Jesus, West. I can tell when somebody's asking me if I jack off."

"Up yours," says West.

"He wanted to know if you're as queer as you look," says Keller.

"Fuck you," says West.

"Easy," you say. "Full moon tonight."

"Fuck you too," says Keller.

"Hey, man. You're in church."

"I don't care. I already got interviewed."

Doby. And then West. Strand comes in but he's after you. Bishop Wacker is sitting behind the big wood desk he inherited from Bishop Byrne when your turn comes up. His head still tan from football season, the hair he's got left still streaked from the sun, he's wearing a beige jacket that lies open across the turtleshell of his coach's gut under his pale blue shirt. You take the chair across the desk from him. His name-plate's right in front of you, white letters etched into walnut-looking plastic, in a little wood bracket on his desk. Bishop Lloyd Wacker. From the parking lot, through the closed window behind him, you hear West fire up the Pontiac and drive away quietly, at an idle.

Bishop Wacker moves some papers around, picks up a pencil to fiddle with, leans back, starts asking questions. How's your dad? Your mom? Been good to them? Paid all your tithing this year? Paid your fast offering every month? Obeyed the commandments? Articles of Faith? Smoked? Tried alcohol? He looks bored with the questions. Bored with you, with your answers, the way he looks bored up on the podium, bored at school. Maybe because you're not there to buy a Ford or run a touchdown. Maybe because he knows that all of you are full of shit. But you're pretty much ready, pretty much bored yourself, because it isn't long before you've gathered that there's really nothing spiritual going on between the two of you. Both of you are there just to get it over with.

"How's your attendance at meetings been?"

"I haven't missed any."

"Not one? Priesthood? Sacrament Meeting?"

"Nope."

"Done your ward teaching every month?"

"Yep."

You think of how hard your father works at any job they give him. How much restless vigor he puts into making everyone he sees on Sunday feel like a million bucks. How red and haggard he looks afterward, in a short sleeved shirt, back home at the kitchen table. You've never seen Wacker do much of anything except stand around and talk to Brother Hunt. You miss Bishop Byrne. The way he always started a meeting out by thanking your mother for playing the prelude. The way you felt when he interviewed you. The way he made you feel like him and God both understood how hard it was to leave your pud alone.

"Are you dating anyone?" Bishop Wacker's saying.

"Yeah. Here and there."

"Keeping your hands to yourself?"

"Yes."

When he gets around to asking if you've abused yourself, you look him in the eye and tell him no, then wait for him to wrap things up and let you go. But he doesn't. He fiddles some more with the pencil, then tosses it onto his desk, looks at you.

"I saw you play at that assembly last spring."

It never occurred to you he'd be there. Now it comes to you that he wouldn't be anywhere else. You look for his face in the bleachers where you remember the jocks all sitting.

"People tell me you're pretty good," he says.

"Thanks."

"What kind of example do you think you're setting?"

"Example?"

"For the other kids in school."

"I don't know."

"You think what you play is what you'd call wholesome music?"

"Jazz?"

"Negroes play that, don't they?"

"Bill Evans is white." You see that the name doesn't register. "Dave Brubeck. Chet Baker."

"You know what I'm saying."

"No."

"Is jazz something you'd be proud to play in front of your mom?"

"Proud?"

"Let me put it this way. I'm not qualified to say if you have any talent or not, but if you do, where do you think it comes from?"

This answer's easy. "From God."

"You're darn right it does. It's a gift. And there's only one reason God gives anyone a gift. To further his work."

"Okay."

"You use it for anything else, it means he pretty much wasted it on you."

"Okay."

"All I've seen you do so far is use it to make yourself popular around school."

"Okay." Your face goes hot. You wonder if it tortures him to be a coach and have a name like Lloyd.

"I'd say it's probably a good way to get girls, too."

"Not why I play it."

"You're sure."

"Yeah."

"Absolutely positive."

"Yes."

"Well, I'm not convinced. But then I'm not the Lord. I can't see into your heart."

"I don't play it for that." You hear your voice rise, get insistent, start to shed its requisite humility. You look at his nameplate to calm yourself down.

"You don't seem to do much else with it."

"What do you mean?"

"Take your mother. She's got a real gift for the organ. But you don't see her out playing jazz, do you?"

Your mother at the keyboard of a tired old grand piano, a cigarette half gone in a glass ashtray, Miles explaining a set of changes to her. Wacker leans forward. Puts his thick tanned hands on the desk. The cuffs of his jacket pull back to where you can see his wrist hairs curled around the big silver band of his watch.

"You want me to play in church," you say, "just say when."

"I don't think a trumpet's appropriate for the House of the Lord."

"Neither is a football."

It's out without you knowing it was coming. Wacker doesn't move. But from his face you can tell he's not as bored as he was just a minute ago.

"How many Individual Achievement Awards do you have?"

"Four."

"One for every year so far?"

"Yeah."

"Maybe that's enough."

"What do you mean?"

"You don't sound like you're too interested in getting any more."

"You saying you won't give me one?"

"Let me tell you something about football, bright guy. Football builds character. It teaches teamwork. Makes men out of boys."

"I know."

"It's played out in the open. In broad daylight. In front of hundreds of people. People who can bring their families. Not like jazz."

"I can play on the football field too. Just say when."

"You're not gonna play on any football field. Not mine, anyway."

"Then tell me where."

"That's up to you. First thing you should do is work on some humility. Lose that smart mouth. After that, do what I tell my boys to do. Never forget where your gift came from. Ask the Lord for guidance. He'll let you know what to do with it."

You think of his football players, strutting the halls in their letter jackets on their fake bowed cowboy legs, happy as pigs in shit to be themselves, and you know that he's lying or that his players think he's full of crap.

"Okay."

"I'll be keeping an eye on you."

"Okay."

"Send the next guy in. And don't let that trumpet go to your head."

"Yeah," you say. And then you say, "Can I just ask you one thing?"

"What."

"How come Lloyd has two Ls?"

He studies you for a long time. "Where you're concerned, I'm Bishop Wacker. Don't forget that."

"So you don't know either."

"What I do know, son, is your dad's telephone number."

After the State Fair you stop practicing in the garage. Stop using your father's vacant parking space for a stage. Start using the hillside again above the sandpit. Where you can play without the mute and not run the risk of ruining your mother's nap or having her warbling Broadway voice and underwater piano playing distract you. Without the smell of your father's engine. You know you'll be running into winter soon. But the hillside is where you belong. Like you've been away. Like this is where it started and all you've done is bring it back here.

After school when you're not down at Robbie's practicing. And sometimes after supper. Take your case, make the climb up past the sandpit, then the hill above the sandpit through the scrub oak and yellow weeds, listen for the hollow scratch of hard dry leaves on rock, reach the place where the small piece of hill has fallen away and made a level place to stand, the small dirt stage that overlooks the valley out toward Antelope Island and the Great Salt Lake. Your lungs are charged from the climb. Ready to play. They can't order you down off the hill this time. They can't shut you in the garage. They can go to hell. As winter sets in, and leaves the valley puddled white with snow, you wear your parka with the zipper hood, your Freddie the Freeloader gloves, your open galoshes again. At night, when there's not enough moonlight, you take along your Boy Scout flashlight to flush the rattlesnakes out.

CHAPTER 20

GARMENTS. The underwear you'll start to wear once you've been through the Temple and then wear the rest of your life. Short sleeved and short legged long johns. The winter ones made out of thin underwear cotton. The summer ones made out of rayon or nylon or some other cooler cloth. The funny symbolic buttonholes over your nipples and navel and one of the knees. Right angles and arrowheads. The big gash that starts in your crotch and comes up around your butt and ends where your back starts. The gash you can open wide to where everything's out in the open when you sit down on the toilet. The button halfway up to keep the gash closed when you're not using it, the button whose shape you can see, smack in the middle of someone's butt, through a woman's skirt and a man's pants when they're tight. The one button matched to the one buttonhole that works.

You wear them the rest of your life because they're a shield against the Devil and his evil spirits. The symbolic buttonholes are for covenants you make with God your first time through the temple ceremony. You wear them next to your skin. Your mother wears her bras and girdles over them. The only times you're allowed to go without them are when you go swimming, or shower or take a bath, or change them. From everything you and your buddies can gather, taking them off to have sex, to make babies, is optional. Your mother hangs hers and your father's on the clothesline by their shoulders where they dry in the sunlight and move in the breeze like ghosts without heads, like skins, like the fresh washed skins of your mother and father hung out to dry in the sunlight of the back yard.

Your father still heads back to work at night to do whatever it is he does there when he's got the office to himself. When your mother asks if he can't spend the night with his family at home he stares at her and tells her his family's the reason he has to go back. Or there's someone in the hospital to visit. Before he leaves he puts his apron on, puts his big portable radio on the windowsill above the sink, washes up the dinner dishes with the big indignant voice of Garner Ted Armstrong in his face.

You've asked if you could do them. Stood there, your hands and fingers itching to be useful, looking for an opening. You could hear what you thought was anger in the way the dishes banged. Sense fury in the rinse water. But he never let go of the washcloth long enough to let you even wipe the table down. If you went for the broom to sweep the floor he acted like you were throwing his rhythm off. If you stood around he acted like you were in the way.

"So. Put that broom back."

"I just wanna sweep the floor." You've gone toward the back door and stabbed the broom into the corner. He's reached around you and grabbed the handle.

"So. Let me have it."

"Just let me sweep."

"Come, come. I have to finish here."

"Why can't I help?"

"You have better things to do."

"Why can't you let me do the dishes for once?"

"Because I enjoy doing them," he's said. "It's the only break I have."

And so you've come to let him have the job. You and then Karl. You know you're supposed to feel relieved, off the hook, lucky not to have to do them. What you've felt instead is nervous. That you haven't done enough to wrestle things away from him the way he wants you to. That you've let him down again to where he's had to put his apron on and pay some price for you. This nervous hunger even after he wipes down the sink and hangs his apron up and takes his radio back down to his den and heads back to his office.

Now you can see it work on Molly. See her hang around the kitchen table, around the door, out of his way, unsure of herself, looking for her own way into his impenetrable confiscation of the kitchen. She senses his silent fury too. You can see her face confused, hear hope mixed with fear in her voice, feel the fragile thing she's putting into your father's lathering hands.

"Daddy, I can do the dishes."

"Oh, I can manage."

"Please?"

"I can have them done in no time."

"Can I dry them?"

"Go see if you can help your mother."

"She's just watching tv."

"Maybe she would like some company."

At least you've got the family shoes to shine, the yard to mow, the sidewalk and gutter to trim, the fence you built last spring to separate the yard in back from the field behind it, stuff you know how to fix around the house. She's got nothing. Nothing aside from handing clothespins to her mother when she hangs the laundry. And half the time her mother just reaches into the clothespin bag herself. So she hangs around behind your industrious father while the unforgiving voice of Garner Ted Armstrong makes the portable radio on the windowsill sound as big as an auditorium.

One night, while you're at the table looking through a Life magazine, Molly lunges for the washcloth and tries to grab a plate. He grabs her hand and yanks the washcloth back. She stumbles back against the counter. You look up at the wet slap of water and soap hitting the linoleum.

"See?" he says. "See what happens?"

"I'm sorry." She looks down at the floor and then back up at him. "I'll clean it up."

"Not on your life," he says. "Now go see your mother."

He turns his back on her and goes after the dishes again. You watch her stand behind him, look around with a hunger you remember while her face wrestles with her failure, and suddenly you can't stop yourself from sending the magazine across the table off the edge. Your father lifts his head from the sink and looks at you across the counter.

"Why can't you let her help?" you say.

"Why don't you mind your business?"

"Why do you have to hog the dishes all the time?" Shouting to make yourself heard over Garner Ted Armstrong.

"So! That's enough now! I don't hog the dishes!"

"Just give her a chance! Jesus Christ!"

"That's very nice talk for a Priesthood bearer!"

"Well, you're a High Priest, and you're here doing the god damned dishes!"

"Who are you to talk to me like that!" He's got his thick wet hands out of the water and on the countertop. You look down to cool off and collect yourself.

"Listen. I'll show her how. I'll do them with her. That way you can get to your stuff sooner."

"My stuff?"

"You know. The office. The den. That's all. Then you can be done sooner."

"I'm sorry. I need the kitchen clean first."

"Come on. I clean the kitchen all day at Servus Drug."

"Then let me have the same pleasure."

"Just let Molly help," you say. "Can't you see how she just wants to help you?"

"Oh?" This fierce derision in his smile. "Now you're an expert on raising my children? You need to get off your high horse!"

"Please don't fight," Molly cries. "Please."

You look at her where she's backed against the refrigerator door. The fear in her face sets lightning off inside your head. You look back at your father.

"See what you've done?" he says. "Are you proud of yourself now? Everything was going fine—"

"How the fucking hell proud are you!"

You're already up from the table. Already taken Molly by the wrist to get her out of there. For a second you've got him cold. See fear in his broad face. But then he starts laughing, big and loud and hearty, and you can hear his back teeth clacking. "So, Molly!" Shouting so you can hear him from the hallway over the bawling orchestral voice of Garner Ted Armstrong. "That's the kind of example your oldest brother sets for you!"

Negroes can't wear them. Not the men on Mr. Selby's wall or on the covers of his albums. Without the Priesthood they can't go to the Temple to make their covenants with God. Without the covenants the symbols of the buttonholes mean nothing. Negro women can't wear them because no one of the seed of Cain is allowed inside the Temple. Sometimes you wonder what would happen if a Negro put them on. If they'd burst into flame and the cloth fuse like burning tar to their cursed skin.

In the heat of summer, at night, your mother takes them off when she goes to bed and sleeps without them. She keeps the bedroom windows open and the door to her bedroom open too, for the hot air to circulate, and she lies on top of the bed uncovered, the covers tossed aside, the light on her nightstand on while she reads the paper that came that afternoon or some book or magazine. From your own dark room, your own windows open, through your own open door and a short way down the dark hallway, through her open door, starting from the foot of her bed, you can see everything. Everything Blackwell always wanted to see. See it as long as you want, as long as she keeps the light on, as long as it takes your father to end things at the office and make the drive back home.

In your father's station wagon, in your sport jacket and slacks and Sunday shoes, the windows down, the radio still set to the station Linda sang to, you drove that night back into Salt Lake, past West High on Second West, picked up North Temple, headed west past the fair-grounds where the Ferris wheel was dark. You took North Temple out past the lights of the airport where it turned into the highway. You took the highway out past the Kennecott Copper smelter and the long black ridge of tailings. You put the pedal to the floor and watched the needle climb and then waver just above 120. You drove through the dark of Skull Valley. You felt the cracks and pits and expansion joints of the concrete come up through the tires. You followed the headlights along the blurred onrush of the highway out across the desert past the Salt Flats. You scanned the radio looking for anything – a voice or song or advertisement – that would settle down the pounding in your blood. Fucking beast. Rape artist. You wondered how far you'd have to drive to outrun her names for you. Wendover. Elko. Halfway across Nevada. Maybe all the way to Reno before you could turn around.

You got to the neon spangled border town of Wendover. In your fa-ther's wagon you cruised the main drag on the Nevada side where the whorehouses and casinos drew cars with Utah plates. You stopped at an all night Texaco station. A geezer with his teeth out and the bottom half of his face collapsed ran three bucks of gas into your tank and looked you up and down while you stood there in your Sunday clothes and let him think away. You looked back. You put his face where the faceless man in the suit should have had his face.

You'd come far enough.

Calm again, you rolled the windows up and headed back east, east into the darkness you'd come from, back to follow your headlights across the lifeless desert, the brine dirt on either side ghost white in the moonlight. You found a call-in show on the radio. You listened to a woman from somewhere in the black American night talk with the voice of a mourning child about her husband dead from emphysema. People who called in after her used the same slow mournful voice to tell hospital stories of their own. They were calling from Idaho Falls. From Amarillo. From Flagstaff. From Omaha. From Rock Springs. Other American cities. The guy who was taking their calls was a guy with the gentlest voice you'd ever heard. It was like medicine made from warm honey. His name was Herb. Everyone who called him used his name. He knew everyone who called.

"Hi, Herb. This is Nancy from Topeka."

"Hi, Nancy. Nice to have you back. Nice to hear your voice."

"Well, I'm back, but not with the best news, I'm afraid."

"Why don't you share it with us anyway."

"Well, if you say so, Herb. It just won't be very pleasant."

"Maybe we can change that."

"Oh, I don't think so. Just so everybody understands."

"We'll all understand, Nancy. That's why we're here."

In your head you were driving the Porsche by then. The green one you'd seen and almost touched at the fair that afternoon. Closed inside its shell, inside the closed hand of its body and roof, you held its needle at 75. Coming back across Skull Valley you saw the dark give way to the haze of lights of Salt Lake City rising in the distance. Like a ghost ship rising out of the ocean of night they rose from out of nowhere. The lights of an American city. You thought of Temple Square. You thought of her next to you in the passenger seat. You thought of her asleep in her bed in the house on whose front porch you'd said goodnight to her. Fucking beast. Rape artist. Night opened up inside you, black and vast and raw and hollow, and you started to cry again as the lights began to give the city the form and shape of the only place in America you could call your home.

After the State Fair you start bringing Mr. Selby's albums over to Robbie's house to play them in his basement. Where you and Eddie chase and test each other around the line of the melody. Where the motion of the song lets you sharp and flat the tone, sour and sweeten it, lose and rescue it, Robbie's ride pattern always underneath you, Jimmy's bass line laying out the road ahead. Where you play farther and farther away, for longer and longer, and then come home to the melody for just a phrase, just a note, at the right place, to let them know it's been there all along. Where you take a song so far away you get to where you just stop playing, let it disappear like a kite on infinite string, just let Jimmy and Robbie keep things moving, leave it out there till Robbie and Eddie and Jimmy start thinking that it's maybe gone forever, then bring it back again from someplace sudden, behind or under them or sometimes right in front of them, from where they never expect it to reappear.

"Hot damn. Son of a bitch. Holy fuckin' moly."

"Jesus. You had me scared there."

"You had Rosita scared."

"Where'd you get those changes from?"

"That's what we're talkin' about. That's what we're after."

"Bet you can't do it again."

"Let's see. Let's go."

Listening to Mr. Selby's albums, and the albums you and Robbie and Eddie and Jimmy have started buying on your own, it starts to dawn on the rest of you that Eddie was right, back when he was bugging you about needing chords.

"See? There's always a piano. Or a guitar sometimes."

"Yeah. I know. I'm not deaf."

"Well, we need one."

"Hardly anywhere we play has got one."

"Yeah. What're we gonna do? Haul one around in the truck?"

"Yeah. Sure."

"What about a guitar?"

"That'd work. Know anybody?"

"Nobody at school. They're all rock 'n roll guys."

"I know this kid from West High."

"Who?"

"Santos somebody."

"Santos? Mexican?"

"No, moron. He's Danish."

"Up yours."

"Ya know, Eddie, when you learn how to take a fuckin' joke is when I'll get tired of playing with you."

"Well, I'm tired of you already."

"He play jazz?" you say.

"Yeah."

"He got a car?" says Jimmy.

"I'll find out."

"Cuz he'll need one. To get here from West High."

Linda. On the winter hillside you play sometimes to the long white scar left across the sky by a jet plane as it bleeds into the cold sunset. Sometimes to the stars. Sometimes to the afternoon, to the roofs of your neighbor's houses tiny and flat and gray down the hillside and across the long gout of the sandpit below you, out across the valley west toward the desert. You've got Jimmy and Robbie in your head, keeping things moving, and you've got Eddie there too, and nothing but sky out in front of you, sky where you can send the sound out like a hawk, send it north and south along the valley and west, send it out so far you can let it disappear from sight, because you know you can bring it back. Always bring it back.

CHAPTER 21

AT THE SUPPER TABLE one night that January your father makes a grand announcement. He's got a new job. In the accounting office of the Deseret Press, the press owned by the Church, the press that puts out all the books the General Authorities write, the books that fill his shelves in the furnace room, the books he builds his lessons from. He works for the Church now. Your mother's glad because he won't come home stinking of cigarette smoke. There's spaghetti and a breaded pork chop on everyone's melmac plate. Apple cider in everyone's steel cup. And then he makes a second announcement. He bought a family package of season tickets to the Utah Symphony. It won't just be him and your mother going on Fridays to the concerts at the Tabernacle. It'll be all of you who want to. Right down to Maggie. Lola, your mother's parakeet, chirps and scuttles and hops around in its wire cage on the washing machine.

"Oh, Harold." Your mother with her whimpering complaining nervous laugh. "Maybe for Shakli and Karli. Not the whole family. We don't have money to throw away."

"I didn't throw money away. It was just as cheap for the whole family as buying two more tickets for the boys."

"Yes, Harold." Your mother looking around the table for someone who wants to join her in her judgment that your father's lying.

"Fridays?" you say.

"Yes. Every two or three Fridays. I have a full schedule for the rest of the season."

"Yeah. I'll go. Thanks."

"Me too," says Karl.

"When's the next one?" you say.

"A week from this Friday," your father says. In your mother's face you see it register how she resents the way he knows.

"I'll go."

"They're playing the Eroica. We'll go to Snelgrove's afterward for ice cream."

Your mother turns to Molly with this heartbreak smile and reaches up and strokes her head.

For the first time you don't stay home and babysit. Doris Stone, younger than you but older than Molly, comes from across the circle. In your Sunday outfits, your sport jackets and ties and slacks, you and Karl ride in the back seat, your mother and father up in front, your father in a suit and overcoat, your mother in lipstick and rouge and a dark red dress under her long brown winter coat whose dark fur collar forms a nest for her head. People are pouring into Temple Square through the main gates. You pass the Handcart Pioneers sculpture. You're twice the size now of the young kid still pushing his father's handcart. You pass the Seagull Monument. The pool around its base is this shimmer of turquoise copper with all the pennies on the bottom. Off to the right the dark monolith of the Temple rises to its lighted elaborate spires where the Angel Moroni stands in his spotlight blowing his long gold horn. Girls your age in high-heeled shoes and flexed calves walk in the borrowed grown-up likeness of their mothers. Guys your age are mostly rich nerd-looking kids whose mean and vacant eyes tell you they're on the make.

You're proud when you look at your mother and father. They look like they belong here. There isn't a woman as classy and beautiful as your mother or with her European poise. There are doors all around the oval base of the Tabernacle, doors where dressed-up people stand in waiting clusters, where old people are taking tickets, where small signs give sets of numbers, numbers that match the rows of benches inside. Your father leads you to one of the forward doors. On the way around, a man hurrying, pulling a woman along by her hand, crosses so close in front of your mother she draws back startled. "I'm sorry," she says, in her church voice, her Swiss accent. The man throws a look back over his shoulder just long enough to look for who apologized. You watch his eyes find your mother. "That's okay," he says, and he's already turned around again when he says it.

That's okay. If you can take off after him, dump his woman on her ass, tell him that's okay, slug him in the gut, tell him that's okay, kick him in the nuts while he stands there doubled over, tell him that's okay. But you're on Temple Square on Utah Symphony night. You don't know how things work. And then he's gone.

"You see what that fucker did?" you tell Karl.

"Yeah. Asshole."

"Think you'd know him again?"

"Yeah. Probably."

A white haired man takes your father's tickets, holds them under a penlight, peers at them, nods, peels four programs off the batch in his arm, lets the four of you inside. You take one last look around before you follow Karl in. Row 27. Close to the front. Your mother mutters something to your father with this pained look in her complaining face. From the way your father's face goes sullen and bedeviled you figure it's something about how expensive it must be this close up front.

You've been here before. With your father to hear the Mormon Tabernacle Choir rehearse. You've heard the deep and powerful engine of its collective hum in person. Heard the gold smokestacks of the organ pipes give off their monstrous sound to the ministering fingers of the white haired man hunched over the racks of keyboards. Your father told you his name was Alexander Schreiner. Told you the organ had more than eleven thousand pipes. That there were over three hundred men and women in the choir. That there was a waiting list to get in. Now you impart this information to Karl.

"This is where they do General Conference. That's where the pulpit usually is. See all those seats up there? Like theater seats? They're for the Tabernacle Choir. There's three hundred of 'em. Women over there. Men over there."

"Why can't they sit together?"

"Cuz they have different parts. Tenor, alto, soprano. That's how they group them."

"The organ looks bigger in pictures."

"Wait'll you hear it. It's got more than eleven thousand pipes."

"Where are they? Behind the big ones?"

"Yeah. You know the radio show Papa listens to when he makes us breakfast on Sunday morning? The Spoken Word?"

"Yeah. The crossroads of the west."

"They do that from here. Live."

Tonight there's no organist or choir. The rows of seats that rise in an amphitheater from behind the podium have their velvet seats folded up against their backrests. There are tiered black platforms around the podium, folding chairs, music stands, cellos and other big instruments scattered around, the small conductor platform, a black grand piano just off the side. In back, on the last and highest tier, stand the gleaming copper vats of the kettle drums. Heads and arms hang out over the balcony. Under the huge dome of the high ceiling the trapped gabbling of people talking and coughing ricochets around like a thousand demon spirits in some crazy shrieking search for a way out.

"Hey," says Karl.

"What?"

"How do they change the light bulbs way up there?"

You look a hundred feet straight up at the chandeliers and the smaller lights built like recessed stars into the domed sky of the ceiling.

"I don't know. It's gotta be one tall ladder."

"Maybe like a fire truck ladder."

You open your program. Advertisements. Small portraits and biographies of different men and women. One of the conductor, Maurice Abravanel, a happy-looking man with thick glasses and gray hair off the sides of his head, a name you've heard around the house. The guest pianist. A younger guy with a Russian name. The stuff they'll be playing. All Beethoven. The Egmont Overture, Piano Concerto Number Four, and the Eroica, Beethoven's third symphony.

Musicians start coming out, through doors below the choir seats, carrying their instruments, violins, violas, cellos, flutes, trombones, different horns. You remember Mr. Hinkle and all the instruments he played. All of them are white. All of them wear black. The men in tuxedos whose bow ties make their faces look like wedding presents. The women in long sleek dresses with sleeves down their arms to their wrists. They find their chairs, start tuning their instruments, their lunatic tuning joining the racket of voices chasing itself around the dome of the ceiling.

You stand up and look around one last time. One last time for the guy who took your mother's apology like he had it coming. Like she owed him one.

"There's an intermission," you tell Karl.

"What's that?"

"Like a break. A long one. Where you can go outside."

"You wanna go look for him?"

"Yeah."

Up on the platform a fat man with a violin raps his music stand with his bow. The orchestra goes quiet. And then the audience in this long deflating hush. And then a man in a long tuxedo comes striding out. From the horns of gray hair off his head and the tiny explosions of light off his glasses you recognize Maurice Abravanel. Everyone stands and applauds. On his way through the orchestra he stops and shakes hands with the fat violinist. At his platform, he does a deep bow, waves a couple of times like he's going instead of coming, steps up to his music stand, picks up his baton, lifts both arms to his waiting orchestra. This skinny guy with this crazy red hair behind the kettle drums has a pair of tufted drumsticks ready in his hands.

She sits in the second row, to the left of the conductor, a violin tucked up under her chin. Only her arms move, her slender arms raised in their sleek sleeves to her violin, and her fingers, and you try to separate the strike and pull of her bow from all the other violins. Her posture in her sleek black gown on her folding chair. Her strict attentive face. Her long brown hair. You check out the guys with the trumpets. They're busy playing their fixed arrangements, taking their cues from Maestro Abravanel, turning the pages that hold their trapped notes captive. You come back to the girl with the violin. Carla. The girl who used to bring her violin case to History in seventh grade. Who told you about the music room. Told you she never liked the color of her hair. Took her glasses off and kissed you the last day of school when you played Danny Boy with her. And then moved to Saudi Arabia. The brown-haired girl on stage. It's not her. It just feels like her. It just feels like you could walk up to her and pick up where you left off. Walk up and kiss her like you'd never stopped.

When they're done with the pounding end of the Egmont Overture, with everyone applauding, she lowers her violin, smiles at the violinist next to her whose music stand she shares. She can't be much older than you. Maybe three years. It doesn't matter. For the night you're in love the way you were with Linda. Wondering what her life is like. Maurice Abravanel takes bows like crazy. Steps off the platform, reaches for the fat violinist, draws him to his feet, has him take some bows himself. She sits there smiling, unnoticed except by you, part of the scenery.

You sit through the Piano Concerto Number Four, watching the orchestra, the Russian guy at the keyboard, Maurice Abravanel, the red-headed guy with the kettle drums. The music doesn't much interest you. You can hear where it's going, what it's made of, well enough to play along with it, but it's your father's music. Your eyes keep coming back to the face of the girl with the violin. Carla. It's like you're cheating the way you're using her to remember Carla. Sometimes, when she's not playing, when she takes a look out over the audience, her eyes look like they're coming in your direction. You look away before they get there.

The concerto comes in for a landing, Maurice Abravanel crazy, boxing and dancing and swordfighting, everyone in the orchestra his partner or opponent, fighting back hard, the Russian pounding the keyboard, the violins insane, the redheaded guy whacking the kettle drums. And suddenly it's over. Maurice Abravanel collapses like someone hit him in the nuts, and the audience is standing, applauding like there's no tomorrow, eager to let the Russian pianist know how incredible he was, how welcome he is to be here, how grateful they are that he thought enough of them to come all the way from civilization to the Crossroads of the West.

The applause won't let him go. Won't let him stop bowing. Finally he just stands there, shaking his shaggy head, laughing, and when he finally turns and starts heading back through the orchestra, they've got him bowing again, and when he raises his arm to wave goodbye, the applause rolls off the audience like an ocean wave and sends him through the door. He has to come back twice. And then finally, with nobody left to applaud, the musicians getting up, milling around, heading for the doors they entered through, things putter out and die. And then it's intermission.

"So," your father says. You're both still standing. "That was something."

You look for something to say. And then recognize he was talking to himself. The palms of your hands are burning. The girl in the second row of violins is reaching down, hooking her slim black shoes over her heels while she's got her head turned, talking to the guy next to her. You hadn't noticed she was playing barefoot.

"Let's go find him," Karl says.

"Okay."

It doesn't take long. A couple of times around the Tabernacle, and then the promenade that cuts all the way through Temple Square from the gate on North Temple to the opposite gate on South Temple, and there he is, standing next to the pool around the Seagull Monument, talking to the woman he was hauling along.

"That's him," says Karl.

His face is underlit by the copper-tinged turquoise light off the rippling water of the pool so that the light on his face looks like water itself and gives his face the dappled gloss of a stream bed. The woman stands next to him with her back to the pool. He looks like a rich guy the way he did the first time. Smooth hair. Expensive-looking overcoat that makes you feel shabby in your gray and brown striped sport jacket and hooded parka. The relaxed tan of a guy who plays golf. Someone who could buy a Porsche tomorrow. Easy and sure of himself while he tells the woman the most important stuff in the world. What he had for lunch on Tuesday. Which one of his shoes he ties first. The kind of guy who'd stand there, watch your father hunt for ways to compliment him until his nose bled, think he had all of it coming while he looked at your father like some ass-kissing clown with an accent he'd never want on his golf course. Piano Concerto Number Four is this rage in your head that raises the hair off your neck. He's got his left hand moving like what he's saying about his snow tires or his favorite brand of applesauce is worth painting in the air. A wedding band shines in the light. Perfect.

"Let's push him in," says Karl.

"I got something better."

"What?"

"You'll see. Don't do anything. Just look sad."

"Sad?"

"Yeah. Like an orphan or something."

"Why?"

"Just do it. Your name's Charlie."

"Want me to limp?"

"Limp?"

"Like Tiny Tim."

"No. Just look sad. Ready?"

"Yeah."

And then you walk up to him. Put on the look as good as you've ever done.

"Excuse me."

He doesn't have far to turn because you're standing pretty much in front of him. You let him size you up in your cheap parka and your barely combed hair and your tie with the painted parrot you bought to see what the deal with Mr. Selby was.

"Sure."

"You know what time it is?"

"Sure."

He brings up his arm and pushes back his sleeves and looks at this thin slick silver watch. You can sense his wife smiling, standing there next to you, like her husband's benevolent act is one more reason to love him.

"It's eight thirty two," he says.

"You sure?"

"Am I sure?" Just the trace of wariness in the corners of his mouth. But he looks at his watch again anyway. "Yeah. Eight thirty two."

"Doesn't sound right," you say.

"No? Okay. Look for yourself."

And then he's got his watch in your face. You look at it close. The faint green delicate points and lines of lighted radium. The tiny chiseled word Omega. When you look back up you keep your face innocent and shy.

"That doesn't say eight thirty two."

You let him look at you hard and close. And then he looks at his watch again.

"Eight thirty three, then. Sorry."

"It doesn't say that either."

"What?"

"I'm just asking you to stop lying to me and my brother. We're not stupid."

He gives you this hard little curious smile. "What is this, boys? Some kind of bet? Some kind of holdup? I'm lying to you?"

"Well, when I ask you the time, and you tell me it's eight thirty three, and I know what the real time is, yeah. You're lying to me."

"Okay," he says. "I give up. What's the real time?"

You can sense Karl standing there, next to you, looking as sad as a kid with polio, and you hope he can hold it for what's coming, or if he loses it, for the light off the pool to be too tricky for them to notice.

"Time for you to leave our mom alone."

"What?"

"You heard me. Stay away from our mom."

"What—"

"I mean it. Please just leave her alone."

And now you can tell his wife's not smiling.

"Listen, kid. I don't know who you are, or what you think you're doing—"

"Look. I'm just asking. I can't beat you up or hurt you or anything. Please just stay away from her. She's our mom."

"I don't know your mom from Adam. I'm sorry. I'm a married man. You boys have the wrong guy."

"Yeah. I know. Just stay away from her. She's our mom. She's got three other kids besides us. We were pretty happy till you came along. We just wanna be happy again."

You stand there and watch his face go solemn.

"It's not me, son. I swear."

You don't say anything. Just hold his look for a minute.

"Let's go, Charlie."

You take Karl by the arm, turn him around, walk away with him. Halfway around the Tabernacle you look back. Nobody's come after you.

"He's doing something with Mama?"

"I just made that up."

"Something nasty, you mean?"

"Yeah. But I never said it."

"Holy fuck."

He says it more with a kind of evil wonder than he does with admiration. Like a trick he'd like to learn to do himself.

"I do okay?"

"Yeah."

You come around the far side of the Tabernacle. From the gowns and tuxedos under their coats you can tell that some of the people scattered around the door and out across the sidewalk and grass are from the orchestra. The violinist you're in love with isn't around.

"When this is over, we'll tell Papa and Mama we'll meet them at the car."

"How come?" says Karl.

"I don't want that guy seeing us with Mama."

"Yeah. Okay."

The Eroica. The program says four movements. An opening movement in allegro con brio, a funeral march in adagio, a scherzo in allegro vivace, and the finale in allegro molto. Except for the second movement it looks like a pounder all the way through. Back on the Row 27 bench, while you wait for intermission to end, your father tells you the story behind it.

"Beethoven wrote it originally for Napoleon for leading the French Revolution." He's got his head turned, so he can talk through the other noise right into your ear, and you can feel the warm pulse of his breath. "Then, when Napoleon declared himself Emperor, Beethoven saw that he wasn't a hero after all. Just another man who thought he was higher and mightier than other men. Another tyrant. Beethoven became furious. He took Napoleon's name off the symphony and changed it to Eroica."

"Who's Eroica?"

"What?"

And he turns his head so you're talking now into his ear.

"Who's Eroica?"

"Nobody. It just a word for heroic. The heroic symphony."

It starts from out of nowhere with two huge chords. You settle in and let it go. The trumpet players are back, the red headed guy with the kettle drums, the brown haired girl with the violin in the second row. This time you notice that her feet are bare. When you glance across at your mother her face is fixed on the orchestra. Her smile is light, nervous, the muscles under the skin of her thin cheeks tense with some restless annoyance she's working hard to keep to herself. Your father's face is radiant, lit almost like a paper lantern from inside, his smile trained on the orchestra. You wonder what he thinks when he gets to the guys with the trumpets.

Sometimes when it comes along you play to the distant horns of the long afternoon freight through West Bountiful. You can still see the locomotive from the time you were there two summers ago with Blackwell and he finally taught you what it meant to jack off. Your nails and pennies were waiting in the sun along the rails. Stealing around the bend like the dark square head of an iron snake, suspended just above the rails, afloat in a shimmering and furious mirage of heat and diesel smoke, the naked power of the locomotive in your stomach and legs where you were pressed against the trembling bank of the roadbed, the single eye of its headlight blazing in the afternoon sun. Two stories high, rocking side to side, thundering down on you, its steel wheels whistling in the rails, the hammering roar of the diesels, the shuddering bank of the roadbed. The wheels turning your pennies into faceless wafers and your nails into toy swords and sending them jumping into the two feet of air beneath the hurtling blur of the undercarriage.

You can still see the engineer. The open mouth and bared teeth and lunatic rage. The continuous raging blare of the horns. The punishing detonation of power and sound you didn't know was possible. The piercing stink of creosote and the taste of salt and oil off the gravel in your mouth. Sometimes, hearing its long hoarse whistle and watching it snake in the distance along the naked brine-soaked marshlands of the lake, you play to the engineer. Play all around him. Dare him to find you. Dare him to catch you. And then put it right in front of him, right in his raging face, and play. Play like a lunatic. Play as fast and hard and lunatic as you can around the steady blaring of his horns. Play your own defiant rage back into his raging face. Your own black rage into his raging face and into the raging blare of his horns. Motherless Child. Your own black negro slave song face.

CHAPTER 22

SANTOS SANTILLANES. He's got an old gray 52 Jimmy pickup truck he calls Dumbo because the fenders come off the front end like Dumbo's ears. The gears whine like crying sirens through the bare steel floor into the steel and glass can of the cab. He always shows up at Robbie's house like he's going to church. White long-sleeved shirt. Slacks because his mother won't let him out of the house in levis. Shiny black shoes because he can't wear sneakers either. Sometimes a sweater vest like Mr. Selby wears. His short thick black hair always has this fresh combed look like his mother just did it with spit and a stiff brush. He's on the short side, compact, polite and behaved the way he moves and looks and talks. He's got just the edge of the accent that Manny and Hidalgo and the sheepherders at the ranch had. Just enough to make you remember the porch of the bunkhouse and Hidalgo playing his big guitar and the smell of cigarette smoke. He's Catholic. He shows up with a banged up brown and gold hollow body Gibson and a Fender amp and a stool.

At first, you and Eddie and Jimmy are dubious, maybe even scared, because here's this Mexican kid from West High, and here's this band you've put together, and here's this way you've come to play, and you're supposed to open up and make room for this kid who comes in looking like he's headed for the Air Force. He puts down his gear, shakes everyone's hand, and before he does anything else asks Robbie where the bathroom is.

"Where'd you find him?" Eddie saying while he's gone. "The friggin' Debate Club?"

"Just wait," Robbie saying.

"No mariachi shit for me," Jimmy saying.

And then he's back, hooking up his cords, and Robbie's showing him where an outlet is, and he's got his Gibson out, using a tuning fork to tune it, whacking it on the seat of his stool between his legs, holding his ear to it while he tunes one of his strings, then putting it up to tune the rest of them.

"Okay." Looking up when he's done. "What do you want to hear?"

"Anything," says Robbie.

"Don't you guys need to see if I can do your stuff?"

"We'll get to that."

"Okay."

Sheepherder music. From out of nowhere. As soon as you hear it you get it. When he plays it's just his hands and arms that move. The rest of him is still. Like all that matters, all he cares about, is what his hands are making the strings of his Gibson do. What he says is what his father told him. Like my pops says, he says, if you're bopping, you ain't playing. Soon he's teaching Jimmy and Robbie all these rhythms, these pulsing latin rhythms with names like rumba, salsa, cascara, merengue, cumbia, mambo, rhythms from Cuba, Africa, Brazil, rhythms you can lay on top of one another to where Robbie's got everything going and Jimmy's hitting strings in whole new times and places. Rhythmic patterns called claves. Claw vays is how he says to say it. And then you're learning how to lay the rhythms under the stuff you're already playing. Standards. Ballads. Blues and bebop. All of it can ride the same layered percussive interplay of rhythms.

He brings in records by guys you've never heard before. Guitarists like Tal Farlow and Charlie Christian and Tiny Grimes and Herb Ellis and Charlie Byrd. Latin guys like Tito Puente and Django Reinhardt and Mongo Santamaria with harmonic moves you never knew were out there. Grinning and charged and exuberant rhythms. Rhythms you can hear in Charlie Parker, in Miles, in Coltrane, now that you know what they are and what to listen for. Next to Santos, his focused composure on his stool, Robbie stops throwing his hair around like a pom pom, starts to calm down too, keep his head and shoulders still. He gets it. Gets that all you move is what it takes to play.

"You need a cowbell, dude," Santos tells Robbie. "And some sticks. I'll bring some."

The sticks are called claves too. Short hard sticks you crack together in one of the clave beats. And he brings a set of conga drums. You take the sticks and let Eddie have the congas. Sometimes Robbie's mother comes downstairs, dancing in her pedal pushers, taking her bandana off to throw her long black hair around, arms high, clapping and sashaying. On the wall Rosita goes on smiling.

"Let's slow it down some," you say.

Because you've been hearing the coming and going trace of some deep familiar thing you can't get hold of.

"Sure."

Robbie starts off again with a more patient cadence on the rim of his snare. Brings in a slower ride pattern on his high hat. Jimmy comes in with a fatter less hurried bass. Eddie listens for a few measures, gets it, starts slapping the congas.

"Yeah. Just relax it. Just easy."

Robbie and Jimmy start off again. Eddie comes in. And there it is. The endless and huge and lazy and haunting rhythm of the desert. Soldier Summit. Southern Utah. Nevada. All the immense raw wilderness of land and sky from the back seat of your father's Buick and out the windshield of the cattle truck. Santos sits there nodding for a minute.

"That it?" says Robbie.

"Yeah."

Santos stops nodding and brings in his guitar. The music of the desert. The slow and easy polyrhythmic cadence underneath you. Imagining a vast black desert bird, high and slow and distant, its wings stretched out, unhurried and alone, you bring your trumpet in.

One day toward the end of January Mr. Frank tracks you down and asks you to play again for school. Not an assembly this time, but a concert, not in the gym but in the auditorium, at night instead of in the afternoon. Open to families. Scheduled for February. Other acts are performing. He tells you he's giving you time for two songs. You talk it over. Figure you'll have more time to stretch, show your stuff, let your solos go, if you just do one. Especially with Santos in the band now.

Mr. Frank likes the idea of one long open song. He doesn't like the idea of having Santos play. It's a school concert and Santos doesn't go to Bountiful. Robbie tells him your band doesn't know how to play without a guitar anymore.

"It'd be like going back to fifth grade," says Eddie.

From behind his thick glasses Mr. Frank gives Eddie the furious look you remember him giving kids back in band before he told you to switch to auto mechanics.

"I'm serious. You should hear what we're doing now."

"What about one of our guitar players?" says Mr. Frank.

"Who?" says Robbie.

"There's a couple you could use," he says. And then for a minute looks stumped. "Jeff Eccles, for one."

The four of you stand there and look at the stuff on his desk. The dirty pipe he takes out on the loading dock to smoke lies on its side in a saucer.

"Okay," he abruptly says. "You're right. Let me know what you plan on playing. I'll need a name for you guys too."

"The band?" says Jimmy.

Mr. Frank shakes his head of thinning electrocuted looking hair. "You guys have been playing nameless for how long now. Yes. A name. For the program."

You ask him how long. He says two weeks. After a short squabble the choice of song is easy. My Funny Valentine. You check with Mr. Frank to make sure nobody else is doing it. You decide to start it out as a straight ahead ballad, then take it latin, then take it crazy, then bring it back again when everyone's had their turn.

The name of the band is tough. So tough you let it go till the night before the last day down in Robbie's basement.

"You thought of anything?" Jimmy asks from his usual corner of the couch.

"Nothing that works," you say.

"How about you, Eddie?" says Jimmy.

"Nope," says Eddie, flipping through an issue of Downbeat over in the other corner of the couch.

You love it here. The way it smells when you first get here before you get used to it. The way Robbie lives here. The way he can come down here anytime he wants and stay for as long as he wants and do what he wants while he's here. The way his mother brings cookies and koolaid down that you and Eddie can't have till you're done playing. The way she'll stay sometimes. The way his father comes down sometimes and listens with his head bopping and his foot going. You wonder what it would be like to live here. Sleep on the old couch. Wake up to Rosita. The driftwood lamp and music stands and Robbie's drums. The sound of his family upstairs and the smell of coffee having traveled through the house.

Jimmy looks across the room at the sheet-draped armchair. "Robbie?"

"Ditto," Robbie says.

"Ditto?"

"Yeah. What Eddie said."

"Okay," says Jimmy. "So we got Ditto. Any other ideas?"

"Maybe the Fabulous Five," says Eddie.

"Jesus, Eddie," you say.

"Then you think of one," says Eddie.

"How about the Eddie Meservy Quintet."

"I hate my last name," Eddie says.

"The Jimmy Hepworth Quintet."

"No way," says Jimmy. "I don't want my name up there."

"How about Robbie?" says Eddie. "He's got a cool name."

"The Robbie Fox Quintet."

"You can't name a band after a drummer," Jimmy says.

"Oh yeah?" says Robbie. "Art Blakey?"

Eddie and Jimmy and Santos treat the room like just another place. A place where they can come and go the same way Robbie does.

"The Santos Santillanes Quintet," says Jimmy.

"It's not my school," says Santos.

"Nobody at Bountiful could pronounce it anyway," says Eddie.

"We gotta come up with a name," says Robbie.

"Jesus hates me, this I know." Everyone looks at Eddie, singing the song to himself, over in his corner of the couch. Catching the attention he's getting, he hesitates, but when he finishes the line, he hasn't looked up from the magazine. "For the Bible tells me so."

Robbie's the first to react. Picks up his sticks, sits up, starts laying a beat on his snares and cymbals. By the time you've got your trumpet up to play along, Eddie's bawling out the chorus.

"Yes, Jesus hates me! Yes, Jesus hates me! Yes, Jesus hates me! The Bible tells me so!"

You going off on a lunatic riff, Robbie bringing it crashing in for this wild landing, Santos grinning. Jimmy just shaking his head when you're done.

"You guys oughta be put to sleep," he says.

"Eddie," says Robbie. "I'm proud of you, man."

"What was that?" Santos says. "Some Mormon thing?"

"Just this song for kids," says Jimmy.

"We oughta play it instead of Valentine," you say.

"Yeah," says Robbie. "We wouldn't need no fuckin' name."

They don't know you like we do. The line you used to give your mother opportunities to use on you. You've heard her start using it on Molly now. Somehow Karl sidestepped it. Maybe learned from watching you how not to give her ways to use it. But Molly gets it hard. Just keeps walking into it. When she tells your mother her one friend Loretta can't understand why she can't come to their backyard picnic. Yah, sweetheart. They don't know you like we do. When she tells your mother her teacher read a poem of hers to the class. Yah. The regretful mocking nervous little laugh you used to get. If only your teacher knew you like we do. When she comes home with her knees scabbed and the palms of her hands raw because some girl knocked her down on the playground. What did you do to her to make her do that? Nothing. You had to do something. No. She just came up and did it. They took her to the principal's office. Yah. There must have been something. They just don't know you like we do. And then when you've heard enough.

"What do you know that they don't know?"

"Oh, Shakli."

"No. Tell her. What do you know? Come on. Don't tell her crap just for the sound of it. Look at her."

"Yah, Shakli. We will wait till your father gets home."

"You know what I know? You don't know crap."

"Yah, Shakli. I wonder sometimes why you and your sister had to be even born. How God could hate me so much."

When you used to get away, when you had to get on your bike and go because that was the only way you could stop the way all the stuff inside you wouldn't stop exploding, the road where Robbie lives was one of those roads you'd find, one of those roads you didn't want to end, one of those roads whose name you didn't want to know. An old road out on the flat floor of the valley, paved but not striped or curbed, maybe a road through farms once, now just a road through the rubbled and gray and unused land it divides. The neighborhood where Robbie lives is barely a neighborhood. Not mapped out like yours, where the yards are locked together like the matched pieces of a jigsaw puzzle along the streets, each piece a yard and a house, the pieces jointed tight enough so that no dirt shows through the joints between them except where there are flowerbeds. And even there the dirt's not real, not the dirt that was always there, but topsoil, brought in and raked in a layer out over the real dirt. In Robbie's neighborhood the dirt is real. Now you know the name of the road. Now you know the inside of Robbie's house. Now you know who lives here.

"Maybe we just oughta talk about what we want a name to do," says Jimmy.

"Make us look like assholes," Robbie says. "Like those nerds that do the Kingston Trio stuff."

"Yeah," says Eddie. "The Troubadours. They gonna play?"

"Probably," says Jimmy. "Except they can't play."

"Three chords," says Robbie.

"Sorenson doesn't play anything," Jimmy says. "Just stands there and sings with this come fuck me grin."

"Yeah," Robbie says. "Isn't he supposed to be the guy with the banjo?"

"Yeah," you say.

"It gets him chicks," says Eddie.

"Banjo chicks," says Jimmy. "Chicks who go for guys with banjos." And shakes his head.

"How about just The Five?" you say.

"The five what?" says Robbie.

"Let them figure it out."

"Just look around the room," says Jimmy. "Maybe something'll just come up."

"The Couch," says Santos.

"The Rug," says Robbie.

"The Acoustic Tiles," says Eddie. "The Acoustics."

"Two of us are fuckin' electric," says Jimmy.

"This is phony," says Santos.

"Rosita," says Eddie.

"Santos is right," says Robbie. "This ain't gonna work."

"Why do we even need one," Eddie says.

"For that damn program," says Jimmy.

"Who else is on it?" says Robbie. "Besides the Troubadours doing Tom Dooley for the millionth time? The fuckin' Madrigals? The Glee Club? That string quartet?"

"How should I know," says Eddie.

"That chick with the cello," says Jimmy. "Man."

"How about those twins with the wood flutes?" says Eddie.

"The Guineveres. God."

"Hey," says Robbie. "Wait a minute."

"What."

"How should I know," Robbie says.

"Know what?" says Eddie.

"The name," says Robbie. "You just said it."

"I did?"

"Yeah," says Robbie. "How should I know. When I asked who was on the program."

"Say what?" says Jimmy. "What'd he say?"

"How should I know."

"You just said you did."

"No. How should I know. For a band name."

"Hey," says Santos. "Maybe."

"That's not a name," says Jimmy.

"Yeah," says Robbie. Leaning forward off his chair. "That's the idea. Just think about it. It doesn't say jack shit. It's like not even having a name."

"Yeah," says Santos. "I like that."

Everyone's suddenly focused. Eddie folds up the issue of Downbeat.

"Yeah," you say. "People ask us what our name is, and we say how should I know."

"That's cool," says Jimmy. "That'll piss 'em off."

"I think it sucks," says Eddie. "You always wanna piss people off."

"Okay," says Jimmy. "It won't piss 'em off. It's just a cool name."

"It still sucks. It doesn't make sense."

"Let's take a vote," you say. "Robbie."

"Yeah."

"Jimmy."

"Yeah."

"That's three with me," you say. "Santos."

Santos watches Eddie. He takes a look at you but then looks back at Eddie.

"Eddie. How come you don't cut your fingernails?"

Eddie's head shoots his way. The next thing you know he's looking at his fingernails like he's never noticed them before.

"Why?" he says.

"Just curious."

"What if it's none of your business?"

"Then it ain't. That's all."

"Cuz every time I cut 'em, soon as they're cut, something comes up that I needed 'em for."

"That's easy to fix," says Jimmy. "Just pick your nose before you cut 'em."

"I'm not talking about my nose," says Eddie.

You don't know what Molly does with the way your mother reaches down inside and takes her heart and turns it inside out and shakes it empty and then hands it back to her. You know for Molly it isn't rage. Just this crushed accepting silence in her face. At Robbie's there's always the sense of dread that moves like a slow wind across the raw surface of your stomach. That you're here on borrowed time. That your brothers and sisters are home. Home on the other side of the bridge you travel from there to here and back. The bridge where nothing travels with you, in either direction, not when you cross it from home or when you cross it heading back. It's them you come home for. Where you know they're okay. Molly and Roy and Maggie. Karl too. Where the wind in your stomach dies in the still of their faces.

In the morning, before class, the four of you walk into Mr. Frank's office. His huge hair-backed hands are at work on a chart spread across his desk. Across the top of the chart it says Seventy Six Trombones. You think what the hell. Only two guys in the whole school play trombone and neither of them are guys you'd put on stage. His cold pipe's off to the side in its grimy China saucer.

"Mr. Frank?" says Robbie.

Mr. Frank lifts his rawboned face and looks up through his heavy glasses shocked and then furious to find you standing right there at his desk.

"Back off a step," he says. "What do you need?"

"We got a name."

"What is it?"

"How Should I Know."

"What?"

"That's the name of our band."

"What's the name of your band?"

"How Should I Know."

He looks more closely at each one of you. Then he says, "Tell me again."

"How Should I Know," says Robbie.

"I'm sorry," he says. "That won't do."

"That's our name," says Jimmy.

"Did you hear me? It won't do. It's not a name."

"Yeah," you say. "We know."

"Get out of here."

"Honest," says Eddie. "That's what we named ourselves last night."

"How Should I Know," he says. "I waited two weeks for this."

"Sorry," says Eddie.

"Well, there's not a chance in heck I'll put that in the program. My Funny Valentine by How Should I Know. Tell me how that would look to the people I work for."

"Cool," says Jimmy.

Mr. Frank stares at him until the grin melts off Jimmy's face like ice into the water it came from.

"I'll come up with something," he says. "Leave it to me."

He looks down at his chart again. You stand there thinking that'd be a cool name too. Leave It to Me. Or maybe Leave It to Us. Mr. Frank looks up again and sees the four of you still standing there.

"Is there anything else?"

"Yeah," you say.

"What?"

"That's our name," you say. "For our band."

Eddie and Robbie and Jimmy look at you. You keep your eyes on the dark fierce hairy fury of Mr. Frank's eyes behind his glasses.

"You mean that?"

"Yeah."

"Well, boys, then it looks like you won't be playing, thanks to your friend here."

"Suits me," says Robbie.

"Me too," says Jimmy.

"Eddie?" says Mr. Frank.

"We worked real hard to come up with it, Mr. Frank. Why can't we just have it? Who's it gonna hurt?"

Mr. Frank looks at Eddie. The lines in his face go soft to where you can see the musician he used to be. Imagine him playing dinner music on a grand piano with some guy with a standup bass at a fancy place like the Hotel Utah Skyroom.

"You kids are serious," he says.

"Sure," Jimmy says. And looks at his shoes.

Mr. Frank takes his glasses off and rubs his face with one of his hands before he looks back up at you.

"You're really gonna do this to me."

And then you're looking at your shoes too before you look back up and find his naked rumpled looking eyes.

"Yeah."

"How Should I Know," he says. The start of a smile. "Go away. Get some practice in. It's coming up fast."

CHAPTER 23

SOMEWHERE along the way they came up with Family Home Evening. They suggested Monday. There was already Mutual and Scouts on Tuesday, Primary on Wednesday, Relief Society on Thursday, and on Friday people needed to hang out on their own. Your father snatched it when it came along. On Mondays he gathers you all together in the living room. He starts things off with a hymn. Sometimes when your mother refuses he sits at the piano himself and plays it. Hymns are all you've ever heard him play. The rest of you crowd around and sing the words off the hymnbook propped on the shelf above the keyboard.

The hymn depends on him. A hard charging hymn like The Spirit of God Like a Fire Is Burning where all of you sing your lungs out. Or a slow reverential one like More Holiness Give Me where all of you try to give it the hushed rubato your father plays the melody with. Sometimes, your mouths open, your faces busy singing, you look at each other with the blank eyes of howling strangers.

After the hymn you take places around the living room. Your father his corner of the sofa. Your mother her armchair. Molly takes the other one and pulls Maggie up on her lap. You take the wooden chair by the patio door. Karl takes the flagstone hearth of the fireplace. Roy climbs up into the vacant corner of the sofa. Then, the Book of Mormon and the Family Home Evening lesson in his lap, your father asks each of you how things are going.

You know what he's after. Some evidence in what you did all week that your lives are guided by the gospel. You're the oldest so you're first.

"I did my interview with Bishop Wacker for my Individual Achievement Award."

"Excellent. How many will that be now?"

"Five."

"I'm getting my second one." Karl copying you. Taking the easy way out. You wonder how he fielded Wacker's question about abusing himself. If he knows about it yet. Your father looks at Molly. She scratches the side of her leg, glances at her mother, puts her hand back in her lap.

"Mrs. Aller showed me and Sally how to make brownies today."

"That's Sister Aller," your father says. "That's nice. What else?"

Molly looks at him and catches on that the everyday stuff like making brownies won't do. She thinks for a minute. "Last week in Mutual," she says, "Sister Holman talked to us about chastity."

"So." Your father brightens up. "I hope you paid attention. You're on your way to becoming a young lady now."

"Yes, Harold," your mother says. "That's very nice."

The edge of menace in her smiling singsong voice. Molly looks down and puts her arm around Maggie. Your father hears it too. Behind his broad smile, you can hear the muffled clacking of his back teeth, see the rhythmic twitch of muscle in the skin of his jaw. His more wary gaze moves to Roy at the other end of the sofa. Your kid brother picks at something on the knee of his pajamas.

"What about you, young man?"

He keeps on picking. Your father reaches across and pulls his hand off his knee. Roy raises his blank and defenseless face.

"Learn anything in Primary?" your father says.

"Yeah," says Roy.

"What?"

"Why I didn't get baptized till I turned eight."

"Why is that?"

And now Roy's face goes proud. He knows this one. "Because that's when you're old enough to know the difference between what's right from wrong."

"What about before then?"

"You're not smart enough yet."

"Very good," your father says. "But why do you have to know right from wrong to be baptized?"

Roy looks at you. He's out of answers. You're not supposed to help him.

"Baptism is to forgive the sins of your childhood," your father says. "The ones you aren't accountable for. That's why you don't have to repent before you're baptized. Can anybody tell me what happens after that?"

"Once you're baptized, you're accountable." In the face of your father's restless appetite to have this be what he wants, the words come to you too easy, leave your mouth like a cheap gift. "If you commit a sin, you need to repent before you can be forgiven."

"That's correct," he says. "Does everyone understand that? Roy?"

"I guess so," says Roy.

"After you're baptized," your father says, "there's no forgiveness without repentance. Remember that. Now. How about you, Maggie?"

"So, Harold. She is only six."

"Does that mean she has nothing to share with her family?"

"Yah." Your mother goes sharp and indignant. "Why don't you ask her about the Celestial Kingdom. Or the birthdays of all the twelve Apostles."

With a sudden happy smile your mother looks around the room for someone to share her insult with. Molly looks down. All of you know your father's way of sending birthday cards with notes inside them to the Church Authorities.

"Why don't you shut up," you say.

Her smile goes. She stares at you. Hard shock turns to liquid hurt. And then she turns to your father.

"Now you see, Harold. Now you see what I have to live with."

"Your mother was only joking," your father says.

"So was I," you tell him.

"Telling your mother to shut up isn't a joke."

"I didn't hear anyone laugh at hers."

"Yes, Shakli." Your mother gives you this weary smile. "Sometimes it would make me happy just to die."

"All right," your father says. "That's enough." He looks at Maggie. "Can you tell us something you did this past week, sweetheart?"

Maggie snugs her head against Molly's chest.

"Tell him about the turkeys we made," Molly says.

Maggie looks out around the room from her hiding place up against Molly. "We made turkeys," she finally says.

"You made turkeys?" your father says. "Just how did you make turkeys?"

"Out of paper," Maggie says. "They're for Thanksgiving."

"It's not Thanksgiving," Karl says nastily.

"It will be in two weeks," says Molly.

"In two weeks maybe. But not now."

"What's wrong?" you ask Karl. "Think they'll spoil?"

"Can we have a look at them?" your father asks.

"They're a surprise," says Molly. "They're for Mama."

"Yes, children," your mother says. "That will be nice."

"Well, I can't wait to see them," your father says.

Molly and Maggie look at each other proud.

"Paper turkeys," says Karl. "Stupid."

"You piece of shit," you say.

"So! That's enough!"

"Sorry."

"So, Mother. How about you."

"Oh, Harold," she says, her worried little laugh, embarrassed and shy. "It's fine for the children, but don't make your wife do this."

"Everybody has a turn," he says. "Mine is next."

Your mother looks around the room like Molly and Roy and Maggie did.

"Oh, I have nothing special to tell," she says. "I'm too busy raising five children." Her voice resistant and pleading like a girl's. You look at the carpet between your shoes. Think of the wagon waiting down in the garage. Of following its headlights down a road you know keeps going.

"I'm sure you can think of something, Mother."

"Only that I went to Relief Society." With a shrug like she's not up to what your father wants. You look down again. "Oh, yes. Iris Lake has asked me to play a solo for the Thanksgiving program." You look up at the sudden brightness and pride in her voice in time to have her look your way for admiration.

"Know what you're playing yet?" you ask.

"No, Shakli. I haven't had time to think about it."

"Chopsticks," Karl says.

"That is very funny, Karl." she says.

You see your father hide a smile.

"How about one of your Broadway songs?" you say.

"Oh, Shakli. I don't know."

"I'll help you pick one out."

"Yes, Shakli. That is very nice." She gives you her church smile. In her voice you can hear the news that she won't be asking you. She turns to your father. "So, Harold. You tell us something."

Your father's ready. He begins by shaking his head with a disbelieving smile. "Do any of you remember Bishop Blankenagel?"

You remember the name. "Yeah."

"Yes. When we had our first new home in Rose Park." He stops and shakes his head again. "Well, I got a call from his lovely wife last week, telling me that he finally passed away, and asking me to speak at his funeral."

"She still knows you?" you say.

"Of course. We've stayed in touch over the years."

"She asked you to speak, Father?" your mother says.

"That's right. Don't ask me why." Your father turns to the rest of you. "He was very highly regarded in the Church. I'm certain that his widow could have had her pick of several General Authorities. Perhaps even one of the Apostles. But for some reason she asked me. One of the least deserving and least accomplished friends her husband had. I tried to tell her this. But she wouldn't listen."

Your mother's lips go tight.

"That's pretty cool," you say.

"I tell you, Shake, I'll need to work night and day on that speech. I'm not an authority by any means. I have to think of those people who will see me at the pulpit and wonder what business it is of mine to speak on behalf of Bishop Blankenagel."

"Congratulations."

"Thank you. Now. Let's get on to the lesson."

The lesson is about the purpose of fasting. Of going without breakfast one Sunday every month. Of putting the money you saved from not eating breakfast into a little brown envelope and handing it over at church. Of having Testimony Meeting that day instead of Sacrament Meeting, right after Sunday School instead of in the evening, so people can get back home to break their fast with a roast or turkey or meatloaf. In Testimony Meeting, there's the opening hymn, and then the bread and water of the Sacrament, and after that, Wacker throws the meeting open to the congregation and sits back down. People stand up on their own to bear their testimonies. The Teachers run the microphones back and forth. Sometimes people break up and cry they're so grateful for something the Lord has done. Sometimes minutes pass where the only sound is the distant bawling of babies from the insulated cry room. You sit there at the Sacrament table with Lilly or West or Jasperson or Keller or Doby or Strand or Yenchik. Your stomach rattles and growls like an empty cement mixer left running. On the table are trays with leftover shreds of Wonder Bread. You could polish them off if you weren't on exhibit. From being a Teacher, cleaning the trays afterward, you know that nothing tastes better on Fast Sunday than leftover Wonder Bread. The one Sunday it tastes like it's actually blessed. The one thing you'd stand up and say you were grateful for.

Your father ends by asking all of you to kneel around the coffee table for family prayer. He pushes the table out away from the sofa to make room for all of you. Molly keeps Maggie at her side. Your mother gets on her knees. You fold your hands and close your eyes and bow your head as he starts to pray. A minute of silence to set the mood. And then his voice. Our dear Father in Heaven. He prays in a monotone, quiet, solemn, earnest. He starts by listing everything he's grateful for. Then he petitions God to bless his family. You hear your name. From there he moves out to the relatives. From there, like ripples from a rock, his prayer moves out to the members of the ward, to people he knows are sick or otherwise need help, then to the Church Authorities, and from there to the starving and suffering people around the world. After a while, to give your eyelids a break, you sneak a look around the coffee table from underneath your forehead. From the other end your mother is staring at your father's head. Your father's asking God to guide the missionaries to all the people wandering in darkness thirsting for the Gospel. The loathing and fury in her face are so powerful it amazes you how her hair stays combed. You feel like you've just walked in on something naked and raw between the two of them. Karl's looking too. And Molly, and Roy, even Maggie, from under Molly's arm, and then you know your mother doesn't care who sees her.

When Family Home Evening ends, when everyone echoes your father's amen, there's the moment where you all get up and find yourselves standing face to face around the coffee table. And then you're released. Released to go watch tv or to your room.

You close the door. The room goes dark. The window becomes a dirty gray rectangle, backlit by distant stars and the one high streetlight out of view of the window up by the Leatham's house. You won't be going anywhere tonight. Family Home Evening is going on all over the neighborhood, and like Thanksgiving, there's a shared agreement that everyone stays home. You switch on your desk lamp. On your desk there's a half-done parallelogram problem with cleanly ruled lines and angle arcs and carefully penciled equations. You sit down and look at them. You can't find where you were. At your elbow there's a library copy of The Call of the Wild with the bookmark almost to the back cover. There's the book report to write once there's not a reason for the bookmark anymore.

You stare at the spine. The creased black cloth with tiny library numbers written in white paint across the bottom. You pick up the book and open it to the bookmark. You read a sentence and don't know what you've read. You switch off the lamp, get up, put your elbows on the white tiles of the windowsill, your face to the gray glass. Light in the curtained windows of the houses around the circle gives them the hollow look of pumpkins made out of bricks. Why. The word is suddenly so wild and huge your lungs ache. Why it won't leave you alone to just be a regular family. Why it has to have everything. Why it has to make your father so desperate and your mother so obedient. Why it has to listen and watch from behind the walls in all the rooms and closets. Why it has to make your brothers and sisters scared that they won't know the words that will make them the kids they want your father to have. Why no matter what you think or feel it has to be there.

And then hate seizes you. Goes racing around inside your head. Hate for Bishop Wacker. For his football bullshit and his bored face on the podium while below him your mother works her way through a Chopin prelude. For the way he stands there waiting, happy as a pig in shit to be himself, while your father works overtime to find a new way to pay him a compliment. For your mother's mocking and spiteful face. For how sad and scared it makes you feel to know what your father wants. For how you can't relieve him. Hate. For everything you think of. Ache in your lungs. Fire in your throat. The back of your mouth raw. An engine in your head whose wailing rumble fills your ears. But there's no Hudson. No Pontiac. No Ford. Nowhere to go. Nowhere. Out the window the circle stays empty and the houses haven't moved.

CHAPTER 24

MY FUNNY Valentine. Linda may be there. And maybe her mother. Or maybe a guy. Back in the rows of faces and heads in the dark auditorium. Her Mona Lisa friend would be easy to spot. You'd have to work hard not to see her. Keep from looking at the audience at all. Just play to Santos and Robbie and Jimmy and watch Eddie play his solo while you're clacking the claves together. But the song will be for Linda when you play it. Your part anyway. Your part will have her name on it. And it will come from some other guy.

The hard rapping on the window right next to your ear startles you. It's Robbie's face and teeth and knuckles and a folded sheet of beige-colored paper. "We did it, man!" His breath is smoke in the bright cold January air. "We're official!"

He's found you out in the parking lot behind the school, with Quigley in his Hudson with the engine and heater on, just back from lunch at the Dairy Queen. You crank down the window. "What?"

He opens the back door, bangs the side of his head on the chopped roof, jumps in and thrusts the folded paper past your shoulder. "Look!" You crank the window up and take it. There's a drawing of a grand piano with other instruments sketched in around it like they're playing themselves.

"Open it!"

"Okay." And when you do, there are the Troubadours, the Madrigals, the Guineveres, the names of the girls in the string quartet, and How Should I Know.

"I remember this guy," says Quigley. "He's your drummer."

"I'll be damned," you say.

"Ain't it something," says Robbie. His breath on the back of your ear.

"We're on the program," you tell Quigley.

"Program for what?"

"The February Concert."

"We got a name for the band," says Robbie.

"Yeah?" says Quigley. "What?"

"How Should I Know," Robbie says.

Quigley turns around to look at him. "So how the fuck am I supposed to?"

"That's it," you say. You show him the open program and point to the line.

"How Should I Know." Looking at you. "That's a fuckin' name?"

"Yeah," says Robbie.

"That's what you guys call yourself?"

"That's what Mr. Frank calls us."

Dragging State Street looking to race or maybe score. Installing a set of ported heads on an engine. Doing basketball games at other schools to pick fights in their parking lots. Robbie's the coolest friend you've got. But he's about as foreign in the back of Quigley's Hudson as a kangaroo. Quigley takes the program and looks at the cover.

"February Concert," he says.

"Next Friday," Robbie says. "You gonna come?"

"Them Troubadours make me puke blood." He's got the program open. Looking up and down and back and forth across the pages. "My Funny Valentine. How's that go?"

"Want me to sing it?" you say.

"Yeah."

"You're gonna have to come."

"I'll bring Sue," he says. "Cheaper'n flowers."

"Cool."

The big domed bell on the back of the school sends a long clattering ring out over the parking lot the way hail used to hit the tin roofs of the ranch sheds. Quigley grins when he hands you back the program.

"Yeah," he says. "She'll ask where we're goin' and you know what I'll tell her?"

"What?"

"How should I know," he says. "Just how the fuck should I know."

"That's good," you say.

You pass the program back over your shoulder to Robbie.

"Where'd you get this?"

"Mr. Frank's got a box of 'em in his office."

That night, when you show your mother and father the program, it's out of duty. You already know they won't take the invitation. You just need to get them through their reasons. And then you'll be free to catch a ride with Robbie.

"That's us. My Funny Valentine."

"Oh, Shakli," your mother says. "That's such a nice song."

"Where's your name?" your father says.

"Right there." Pointing. "It's just the name of the band."

"How Should I Know?"

It makes you want to laugh that you made him say it.

"Let me see, Harold."

"Well, I see here where the string quartet all has names. Why don't you?"

"Mr. Frank just asked us for a band name."

"Maybe because the string quartet is playing a classical piece," he says.

"It's next Friday," you say. "Seven to nine."

"Yes," he says. "I see. It's just too bad that you're at the end of the program. I have to meet with Bishop Wacker at eight o'clock."

"Why do you suddenly have to meet with Bishop Wacker, Harold?"

"Because I happen to be the Ward Clerk," he says, the familiar bedeviled ridges quick to form across his forehead. "I have to report to him. By golly, Mother. Can't I do anything without an interrogation?"

"You could have told me, Harold," she says, the familiar quiet injury in her face. "That is all I meant."

"Maybe I could get Mr. Frank to put us earlier," you say.

"It's a little late, by golly, with the programs already printed. I'm sorry."

"Maybe you could see Bishop Wacker some other time."

"He's a busy man."

"How about you, Mama?"

"Oh, Shakli, you know I can't drive."

"You could ride with me and Robbie."

She looks at your father for help before she takes the only course she knows.

"Oh, Shakli, don't ask me to ride in that old junker of a truck."

"That reminds me," your father says. "The Soderstroms are expecting us. Come. We have to make our February visit, by golly."

Like you expected, when Karl became a Teacher, your father started taking him ward teaching. What you didn't expect was the way he didn't let them assign you to some other man. The way he just took on four more families so he could take you both ward teaching.

The chair Brother Soderstrom brings in from the kitchen for you is new. Red naugahyde and chrome. He got a job. Consolidated Freightways. He sold his broken Freightliner. He's not an independent any more, but with the cash from selling his truck, they were able to catch up on their tithing without the loan she talked about. God stepped in at the last minute and helped them. That's what they tell your father.

"Thank you for praying with us," Sister Soderstrom says. "That was what made the difference. When things turned the corner for us."

"I'm sorry," your father says. "I can't take the credit."

"Don't be so modest, Brother Tauffler. I've never heard a more beautiful prayer."

"I'm just the messenger, by golly."

"Well," Brother Soderstrom says. "That was some message."

Your father gives them the lesson for the month. Chastity. You watch the Soderstroms listen while you sit there on their new chair and wonder who thought it was a lesson they'd ever need. After the lesson, Sister Soderstrom gets up, picks her way through her three little kids and their toys, leaves the living room. She's carrying a heart-shaped box of chocolates when she comes back in. She heads straight for your father.

"This is for you," she says. "You're my Valentine this year." She laughs. "Don't worry. I'm not going to steal you away from Elizabeth. And it's okay with Fred." And then she says, "It's just my little way of saying thank you. I hope it's not too fresh."

For a long minute your father just looks at the cellophane-covered deep red cardboard heart he's holding. Brother Soderstrom watches from the sofa. Sister Soderstrom threads her way back through her children and sits down next to him. You watch a slow incredulous humble bliss move into your father's face. His head start slowly turning side to side.

"By golly," he finally says. For a second you see his face go red and rough like he could cry. "I'm just speechless."

"I don't need a speech, Brother Tauffler. Happy Valentine's Day." Sister Soderstrom puts her hand on her husband's knee. He puts his hand on top of hers and pats it. In her sleep suit, one of their little girls gets up and waddles across to where your father's holding the box and reaches up for it, opening and closing her little hand. Sister Soderstrom, right behind her, scoops her up. Your father hardly notices. His eyes are glistening. You've never seen something move him like this.

"What about you, Shake?" Sister Soderstrom says. "Do you have a Valentine?"

You're their way out of this awkward place, you realize, and smile back at her. "No. Not yet."

"Well, you've still got a few days, son." Brother Soderstrom's voice is rough with what his wife just did. "Better get started."

"I'm playing in a Valentine's concert at school," you say. "Does that count?"

"You play an instrument?" Sister Soderstrom says.

"Yeah." You glance at your father. "Trumpet."

"I had no idea," she says. "Did you, Fred?"

"No, Shirley. I didn't."

"For how long?"

The heart-shaped box still in his hands, on his lap now, he's looking out into the middle of the living room. Bliss is still there but he looks lost, his face furrowed with bewilderment or regret, thunder gone off in his head like he looked in the garage that Saturday when he asked about your trumpet and told you his favorite song. Mrs. Soderstrom glances across at him.

"A little over four years," you tell her.

"I'd love to hear you play," she says.

"What do you play?" says Brother Soderstrom.

"Jazz mostly. Blues."

"You're kidding," he says. "I love jazz. It's all I listen to on the road. When I can find it, anyway."

"You do?"

"Sure. Count Basie, Charley Parker, Duke, Coltrane, Bill Evans, you name it. You have a band?"

"Yeah." Aware of your father sitting there. "Five of us."

"That's terrific."

"When's your concert?" Sister Soderstrom says.

"This Friday at seven."

"At the high school?"

"Yeah."

"Your band?" Brother Soderstrom says.

"We're on the program," you say. "At the end."

"What are you playing?"

You look at your father. His power of prayer has been recognized but he sits there numb with a heart-shaped box of chocolates in his lap.

"My Funny Valentine."

"Good song," Brother Soderstrom says. He's taken a look at your father too.

"Can we come?" says Sister Soderstrom. "Is that okay? Can we get tickets?"

"No tickets. Just come."

"We need to call Janice to babysit."

"I'll do that tonight," Brother Soderstrom says.

"Well, that's it," Sister Soderstrom says. She turns to your father. "I guess we'll see you and Elizabeth on Friday."

Your father moves in his chair and looks at her.

"Yes," he says. "Yes. We've taken enough of your evening. Let's join in prayer, if you don't mind, and we'll get out of your hair."

After the State Fair, through the fall and into winter of your junior year, you did what you could to avoid her. Found out where her classes were and the routes she would likely take between them. Used the upstairs or downstairs hallway, sometimes the parking lot, to detour around them during breaks. Surrounded yourself with buddies, yucking it up, when you knew she'd be coming up the hall with her Mona Lisa friend. Had lunch somewhere besides the cafeteria. Headed for Wally's Burger Bar or the Frostop with Yenchik or West or one of your auto mechanics buddies. Ate in one of their cars or in Robbie's panel truck out in the parking lot with the engine and heater on.

And then you felt her let you go. You remember knowing when it happened. Not the exact date. Just somewhere in December. It was just a day when you suddenly couldn't remember what it felt or sounded like when her mother said your name.

You were free then to roam the halls again. Start going out with other girls. Not that you asked them. Picked them out and tracked them down the way you had with Linda. But that they came to you. That they asked one of your buddies for an introduction. She thinks you're cute. She wants to meet you. Maybe go out. Okay. Or that they found some other way. Looked at you bashful but sly out of a group of their giggling friends. Winked at you and smiled. Then came asking. Okay. Sometimes they were popular. Sometimes innocent like Linda. Most of the time pretty. Once an Attendant to the Snow Princess. Sometimes one of the expensive-looking girls from the rich kid crowd. Once one of the Madri Singers.

Okay.

You play dumb. Keep it friendly. Make them laugh. Talk to them like you're some hick who wouldn't know romance from a cow turd. Sometimes one of your auto mechanics buddies shows up at your locker with one. One with her books held bashful across her chest but with this look in her face like she knows you. Like you can't fool her. Like you can act as hick as you want and she won't let go. And so you talk. And then it gets to where everything's been said and there's nothing left for anyone to do but walk away or bring up going out. And what you're standing there wondering is what's wrong with her. Maybe bad breath. Eats with her hands. Shaves her legs and armpits with her father's razor. Farts when you go to kiss her. You don't know. You just wonder.

"Maybe we could go to a movie sometime," you finally say.

"Sure. I'm free Saturday."

"Okay. I'll see if I can get my dad's car."

And sometimes you do State Street. With Quigley or West or another buddy with a car worth putting out on State.

You practice like Mr. Frank said to. With the band at Robbie's. On your little stage up on the hillside, where your foot taps out the cadence, easy and unhurried, on snow you've packed from coming here. My funny Valentine. Sweet comic Valentine. You make me smile with my heart. Linda. This is the only place you have where you let yourself remember her. Up here where things are high and open. Where nobody would want to look for you. Here in the cold heart of winter, the only place you know where she's in the booth with you again, where she sings along with the radio in the station wagon, where she exposes her eyes to the porchlight and shows you the possibility of a place for you behind them where she does her dreaming. Linda. The only place you know. January gone. February now. The only place where you let yourself hope she's got herself a Valentine. Your looks are laughable. Unphotographable. The words. You wonder if she knows them. When you go into the solo you'll be playing, you'll hear them in your head, hear her sing them, and there's something pitiless that comes into your playing then because you know the words were never meant for you. Don't change a hair for me. Not if you care for me. Your foot moves. In front of your eyes, out of the ragged tips of the fingers of your cloth gloves, your fingertips work the valves without you thinking, on their own. Stay little Valentine stay.

PART 4

STATE STREET

CHAPTER 25

"DOING ANYTHING?"
"Nope."
"Wanna do State?"
"Sure."
"I'll be over."

Just down the short hill from the State Capitol Building is where it starts for real. Where the arch of the Eagle Gate Monument spans the street and holds a huge bronze eagle with its wings spread wide. From the red light there, where the joke is not to let the eagle crap on you, State Street begins to lay its four broad lanes of traffic down. Four broad lanes that go like a spear through the four-block heart of the city's downtown, and then keep going, straight as a runway through the city's outskirts neighborhoods as far as you can see. In the daytime it's this bleak ragtag promenade of tire places, parts shops, furniture outlets, repair shops, hundreds of one-story businesses that go for miles before they peter out in unfarmed fields and scrap yards and random houses. But at night, starting on Thursday, going through Friday and Saturday and trailing off on Sunday, the stretch of State from Eagle Gate down to Twenty-First South and sometimes as far as Thirty-Third comes alive. Everyone comes out. Everyone cruises. The underside of the city. The side you don't see from a tour of Temple Square or a night at the Utah Symphony. Hot rods. Custom cars. The howl and smoke of tires when a light goes green. Dragging State. Taillights going one way. Headlights coming the other. From the red light at Eagle Gate, waiting for the green before the eagle takes a crap, it lies out there in front of you, two currents of an aqueduct of light that flow against each other. Red against white. Starting at Eagle Gate, cruising south, turning around at Twenty-First or Thirty-Third and coming back, everyone restless, looking to race, get drunk, fight, cop a feel, show off their wheels. Four lanes of traffic looking to connect. In the dark neighborhoods back off

State Street the houses have their doors locked and their windows dark against the savage invitation to come out this time of night.

"Busy," says Quigley, grinning, rapping the steering wheel with his fingernails, waiting for the light at Eagle Gate to let him through.

"Saturday."

The pipes of the flat black Hudson rumble through the floor. Under the hood rides the big 7X racing engine you and Quigley pulled out of a wrecked Hornet and then detuned with a milder camshaft for the street. The big loping sixbanger with its dual carbs and fat valves and deep stroke and its reservoir of torque trembles in the low body of the car. In the long aqueduct of taillights ahead of you are possibilities that have started running up and down your nerves. Above the lights the sky is black where you don't have to see the iron of the overcast.

"So whaddaya feel like?" says Quigley.

"Whatever comes up."

The light goes green. Quigley lets the clutch up easy. The Hudson slides across North Temple and slips like a dull black submarine under the surface of light. You've been here before. With West in his Pontiac where he's watched its reflection in the windows of stores to see how his spinners look. With Doby in his mother's Impala where the hula dancer lights her brakelight eyeballs up for anyone behind you. With Keller in his Bugeye where a redneck in a high-riding pickup truck poured Coke all over him in the driver's seat. Quigley's different. Serious. Like Porter and Snook. A guy with nothing to lose but a fight. In the driver's seat his grin is the cut of a thin blade deep into his face. He keeps the Hudson in the inside lane to give you a shot at the possibilities on your side. A bashed-up green Plymouth with its sides raked dirty white with winter salt, its door mirror busted off, the faces of four girls through its windows. You're good by now at this passenger stuff. You crank the window down. The window goes down in the back door of the Plymouth. Her face is chubby. Greasy strands of brown hair skate across her forehead in the January wind.

"Hi," she says.

"Hey."

"Neat car."

"Thanks. I'll tell my dad you like it."

"Your dad." And then she says, "How you guys doing?"

"Better than you."

"You think so, huh?"

"Wanna prove us wrong?"

"That depends."

"On what?" you say.

"If you guys got any vodka."

"If we got any vodka depends on what you got."

She pulls her face back in. For a minute it looks like she's fighting with the other girl in back. They're switching places. And then the other girl is there with her sweater and bra pulled up and her naked boobs pushed up between her elbows out the window.

"Quig," you say. "Take a look."

"Nice," he says.

She's got her face there now. "Sorry," you tell her. "We're all outta vodka."

Quigley backs off the gas to let the Plymouth slide ahead where you can see it's got a taillight out. A finger out the window comes your way. Four guys in a silver Buick go tearing past and cut in front of you for their shot. At the next light, two guys are leaning out of the passenger side of the Buick, yelling at the closed windows of the Plymouth.

"They ain't horny," Quigley says. "Just thirsty. Too fuckin' broke to buy their own."

"Yep."

"Probably too broke to get treated for crabs."

"Yeah."

You've been here before, with Robbie in his panel truck, not to drag State but to look for clubs where you could think of playing. See what you could tell from their signs and the way they looked at night and the kind of crowd they had out front. Now, in the Hudson, you roll with the traffic across Ninth South. Past the usual shops and lots and places with their windows dark. Past South High. A club called the Indigo. At Thirteenth South you watch a white 57 Chevy and a purple 49 Ford rev their hammering engines and take off laying rubber just before the light goes green. You drop the window to clear the smell of toasted rubber out. At Twenty-First South you do the turnaround. Make a left, hook through a parking lot, come out on the northbound side. Quigley sticks to the outside lane this time for his own shot. Far ahead of you, at the head of State Street, the lighted dome of the State Capitol Building hovers over the red and green gates of the traffic lights and the long burning flow of taillights. You've come out behind a Corvette, a red one, a white stripe up its trunk, its white top up, snug against the cold.

"Maybe we got us one," says Quigley.

"I don't think so," you say.

"No?" says Quigley.

"Naw. They're not here to race. They're just goin' home."

"Old farts," says Quigley. "Oughta be drivin' a Packard."

You pass a used car lot where a crowd is always congregated for a break from dragging their cars. Heads follow the Corvette. You think of Hunt and his lawnmower engine voice and his Hawaiian wife. Some heads follow you. Bottles flash as they're lifted.

"Check it out," you say.

On Quigley's side there's a new Ford Fairlane sawing back and forth in the lane along the Hudson. A girl's face in the passenger window looking his way. A State Street smile. Another girl's face in the driver's seat. Quigley gets his window down. Cold air comes rolling around and chills the back of your head. The Fairlane's got its window down. Hair so dark it looks black is gathered in the girl's hand.

"Hey," says Quigley.

"Hey," she says. "Like your car."

"You're welcome to a ride."

You know what she's looking at. Quigley's good guy grin with all the evil out of it. The girl pulls her head inside for a conference with the driver.

"We got 'em," says Quigley, before she comes back to the window.

"Okay," she says. "A quick one."

"Okay," says Quigley. "You park. We'll follow."

He drifts the Hudson back to let the Fairlane in front. Through the rear window you can see their heads. You've been here before, on State Street on your own, in the borrowed ride of your father's Chevy wagon. Not to drag State. Just to pretend like you're some guy on his way home from somewhere. Some guy passing through. You've gone down as far as Forty-Fifth South to turn around where nobody would see you, south far enough that you wouldn't be matched with the same cars coming back, wouldn't give yourself away. You follow the Fairlane into the dark side lot of a shop called Stan's Radiators. Watch its taillights and then its brakelights go out and then both its doors come open.

Here it is, you think, and it feels irreversible, like pushing off the top of the water slide at Lagoon, like having the guy who runs the Hammer latch the door shut.

"They're gonna want the radio on," says Quigley, reaching for the knob, watching the girls get out of the Fairlane while the radio warms up and then fills the Hudson with Wake Up Little Suzy. In the Hudson's headlights, the driver's blond, her hair a teased ball with a flip that rings the bottom, wearing a white car coat that doesn't give her boobs away, a light blue skirt that doesn't give her knees away, light blue loafers. Her passenger's wearing a car coat too, dark like her hair, a pleated skirt that's plaid instead of solid blue, dark loafers where you catch the glint of coins. They both shield their eyes from the headlights when the Fairlane's locked and they come your way.

"They look rich?" says Quigley.

"A little. Yeah."

"Shit. Which one?"

"You choose."

You're thinking shit too. Here it is and you don't know where it's taking you. Out of all the paint and rubber and chrome and noise and light of State Street it's not just a face in a passing window. You get out, let the girl driving get up front with Quigley, close the door on her, open the rear door, follow her passenger into the deep back seat and close the door behind you.

"Hi," she says, settling in, tossing her hair aside, her face right there. "That's Jeanette. I'm Sandra."

On the cold air she brought in with her rides her warm breath sweet with a fresh stick of Spearmint.

"I'm Shake."

"Shake?"

"That's it."

"Like milkshake?"

You give her a grin. "Nope," you say. "Like Shake."

"Yeah," she says, her own grin quick. "Like a raspberry shake. Hi, Shake."

Quigley backs the Hudson off the parking lot and eases it out into the river of traffic again.

"So where would you ladies like to go?" he says.

"You decide," says Jeanette, scooting more toward Quigley. "You're driving."

From the back seat you watch Quigley throw his good guy grin at her. "Okay. So we'll just cruise. Till I hear a better idea."

And so you do. She goes to East High. She's a senior. She plays flute in the marching band but she'd rather play classical guitar. She's danced ballet since she was eight but she'd rather do modern dance or maybe paint. She played Dolly Tate in the senior production of Annie Get Your Gun but she would have made a better Minnie. She used to go with a basketball player but he moved to Florida last summer. She's in the ski club but all she can do so far is snowplow. Next fall she's going to the U but she can't decide if she'll study history or business. And then there's psychology because people are always coming to her for personal advice.

You sit there thinking East High. The school whose kids are drawn from the city's old neighborhoods where names can be traced clear back to the pioneers. More snobby than rich. More stuck up than cool. What they think they're doing dragging State Street. Why they'd take on two guys in a dull black lowered Hudson with its caged engine and chopped roof and its windows cut low like the malevolent black narrowed eyes of evil. What makes her think she can sit back here like you're having tea. Think she can come down here and not be hurt. Gab about every-thing she's doing but how she'd like to be doing everything else and not be hurt. You've seen Quigley's grin burn down to ashes and leave this flickering restless desperation in the face of the same inane and dither-ing stuff you're getting. You've reached the head of State. You've made the turnaround. You're through Eagle Gate again and headed south and she's talking about some uncle now.

"You're really pretty," you finally say. "I'm a junior."

She looks at you. Like she's just noticed. Like she's talked enough of her world away to get to where she can see that she's wandered into someone else's. She looks down at her lap. In the dark you can tell what she's thinking. Which way she should go.

"This car feels really powerful," she says.

"It does okay," you tell her.

"Do you guys ever race it?"

"Sometimes."

"Do you win?"

"Always."

"It's warm in here. May I take my coat off?"

"Tauffler. Check this out." Quigley's grin is gone and his profile's grim.

"Sure. Take it off. Don't spill your tea."

You move over to where you can see around the blond ball of hair up front with the flip like a rain gutter around the bottom. Ahead of you there's an old beige-colored Ford wagon with bruises of rust in its bumper and body rot along its tailgate. Next to it, in the inside lane, there's a brand new dark blue Pontiac Bonneville. The guy in the pas-senger seat has his arm out the window and a claw hammer in his hand. The driver keeps bringing the Bonneville close to the wagon where the guy can rake the claw along the side. The wagon keeps slowing down and swerving toward the curb. The guy driving the wagon looks small. Young. Knows he can't stop. The girl across from him in the passenger seat is crying. In the shifting shine of light off her terrified wet face you can tell she's Mexican.

Quigley hangs back. You watch the Bonneville move in again, the hammer reach out like a meathook, the wagon swerve, the claw connect and rake the metal when the wagon gets trapped against the curb, when it pushes up against the curb so close the rims leave sparks and the tires leave gouts of rubber on the concrete. You watch the Mexican girl open her mouth. Watch the Bonneville move back into its lane. Watch the two guys inside turn and laugh into each other's faces like crazy theater silhouettes. Watch the driver lift a bottle and knock back a slug. The

East High chick in front, Jeanette, sensing trouble, sensing what she left
her East High house to come here for, slides back across the front
bench toward the door. Quigley opens his window, looks back, waves
the car behind the Bonneville back, slides the Hudson into the lane behind the Bonneville. You watch the driver's head tilt up to check the
change in his mirror. Then the passenger's head look back. Quigley revs
the engine hard. Just once. You're used to it. You helped build it. But
the East High chick who'd rather play classical guitar jumps up and
yelps when the sudden snarling thunder of the engine cracks the street
wide open. The Bonneville driver's head jerks up again. The passenger's
still got his head turned looking. The guy driving the wagon has his face
turned too, Mexican like his girl, scared. Quigley revs the engine again.
Puts on his brights and lights up the guys in the Bonneville. Your gut
lets you know they're rich. Rich and mean. From the new East Bench
neighborhoods whose decks look down on the city. The driver's head
comes up again. He flips a bird at his mirror but guns the Bonneville
past the wagon and moves to the outside lane.

"I wanna get 'em south a ways," says Quigley. "Outta this traffic."

"Yeah."

You slide over, put your window down, put up your thumb to the
Mexican guy when you pass him. And then Quigley brings you even
with the driver of the Bonneville. You're smiling by the time he turns
and looks at you. The long bland snot nasty face of a rich boy.

"Hey. Must be fast."

"Fuck you," he says. "What's the fuckin' idea?"

"We're just lookin' for a little race. Whaddaya say?"

The guy looks through his windshield for a second. Then looks back
and forth along the Hudson. Then back at you with a sneer in his rich
boy face.

"That fuckin' antique? Can't even afford a paint job? You got it."

"You care which lane?"

"Inside. You're gonna need the fuckin' slow lane."

"Okay." You look down the street. "Next clear light we get. Okay?"

"You're on. You and your fuckface friends."

"Hey," you say. "Don't be so fuckin' profane. Please."

Quigley drops back to let the Bonneville cross over, then crosses the
Hudson over to the outside lane, pulls even with the Bonneville again,
motions to the passenger to hold back, let traffic pull ahead. Jeanette
turns around and does some face talk with her friend Sandra and turns
forward again. Suddenly Sandra's hand is on your leg. Without her coat
there's this white ski sweater with Norwegian stuff across its chest. Her
hand comes up and takes your head and pulls it next to hers where you
can smell her East High perfume in her hair. Across her shoulder, out

the side window, the lights of State Street run like colored water along the gleaming body of the Bonneville. Quigley's got the radio off again.

"Touch me," she says in your ear.

"Not now," you say back.

She finds your hand and brings it up and holds it pressed against her boob where you feel the give of wool and cloth with nothing under it but flesh.

"Not right now." Not knowing how to extricate your hand from under hers without making her feel like shit. She moves your hand down to where her sweater ends and guides it up her bare skin to her boob again. Most of what you feel is the thick stitched cloth of her East High bra. You're wondering if she'd rather have you hold her other one.

"Squeeze it," she says, Spearmint on her breath, and suddenly, insanely, you're thinking what her boob would sound like if you did.

"Later," you say.

"No," she says.

"Okay," you hear Quigley say up front. "We got us a light."

"Shit," she says.

Her voice is hoarse but she lets you go. You sit up straight while she pulls her sweater down. There's a traffic light ahead just going yellow. The light at Thirteenth South. A block of clear asphalt, two clear lanes, before the taillights start again.

"We'll take 'em south a few more blocks," says Quigley.

The cross light turns yellow. The guy driving the Bonneville runs the engine up. From its whining strain you can tell it's automatic, in drive with the engine revved, him standing on the brake to hold it back. You cringe at the hydraulic demolition going on inside his torque converter. Quigley brings the Hudson's engine up. The light goes green. The Bonneville chirps its tires and goes. Quigley keeps the Hudson close but gradually lets the Bonneville slip ahead.

"I thought you said you always won."

You ignore her. The Bonneville slows up and lets the Hudson come even. The passenger guy is out of his mind. His face all rich boy teeth.

"Hey," he yells at Quigley. "How's that fuckin' smoke taste, asshole?"

"Like shit," Quigley says, grinning. "Bet you can't do that again."

"You shittin' me? We could do it all fuckin' night."

"Then let's go," says Quigley. He checks his mirror. "From here."

"Right here?" Looking for a light a few blocks down. Twenty-First South.

"We got room."

The passenger guy says something to the driver. The driver nods. The passenger guy turns back to Quigley. By now you've sized him up.

Bigger than you, a bully, a guy who thinks he can come down here to State and not get hurt.

"Deal," he says

"You say when," Quigley says.

From a dead stop in the middle of some block on State the passenger guy chops his hand down. Quigley does it again. Lets the Bonneville slide gradually ahead. Lets it slow back down when it's won to where it pulls even with the Hudson.

"Still taste like shit?" says the passenger guy.

"Yeah," says Quigley. "But I'd just like one more taste."

"We're headin' back. You're not fuckin' worth it."

"Come on," Quigley says. "See if your daddy's car can make it three for three."

The guy looks at him like Quigley just sucker punched him.

"Fuck off," he says. "You fuckin' hillbilly moonshine motherfucker hick."

"Just one more," Quigley says. "Come on."

From the light at Twenty-First South where half the traffic takes the left turn lane to do the turnaround back north. This time, when the cross light goes yellow, Quigley opens the carbs and runs the engine up into its savage range where the unobstructed throats of the big exhaust pipes split the air of the street. In the Bonneville the face of the passenger guy goes suddenly alert.

"Sit back," you tell the East High girl who had you squeeze her boob and is probably already thinking she wanted you to squeeze her other one instead. At the change of the light Quigley dumps the clutch. The engine digs in and breaks both tires and hunkers the Hudson down and rockets it forward. The East High girl shrieks and grabs your arm. You turn and watch the smoke-hazed headlights of the Bonneville fall back. The tires find traction. Quigley hits second and breaks them again. Out the chopped back window, the Bonneville's half a block back, running hard.

"That girl's face," yells Quigley, and you know he's saying the Mexican girl in the old Ford wagon, and you know he's saying Remember the Alamo, but you don't need reminding, because it's what you've been thinking too. Her please don't hurt us face.

"I got the hammer guy," you yell back.

"Here goes."

He slams the brakes and drifts the Hudson sideways with all four tires shrieking. The East High girl gets thrown across your legs. When the Hudson stops it's jackknifed across both lanes. Quigley's out, running straight into the headlights of the Bonneville, into the howl of its tires trying to haul the big car down before it broadsides the Hudson. You're out behind him, watching the Bonneville start going cockeyed on its locked tires, judging which way it's going. When it stops, Quigley's already there at the driver's door, pulling the guy head first through the window.

The passenger door comes open. You finish opening it, and when the passenger guy comes stumbling out, slam it hard and catch his leg. He yells, recovers, hops and stumbles back to size you up, size up where he wants to land the hammer, but he goes to swing it and you're there, catching its head and handle, twisting it, walking him back around into the headlights of the Bonneville, backing him up against the grill, pushing him back across the nose of the hood. One hand keeps letting go of the hammer to pop the side of your head. You keep your focus on the hammer. "The hood ornament!" he yells. "It's fuckin' stabbin' me!" His hold gives. You've got it. You jump off the hood and back away for room. He comes after you. You raise the hammer high, let him reach for it, let him get his arms up, then swing it low and bring it up into his gonads. He rises high, folds, goes down moaning. You look around. Quigley's got the driver pulled out of the window now, pinned against the door, both arms going. Two lanes of headlights are stuck behind the Bonneville. Both lanes on the opposite side of State are stopped. Guys and girls hollering. Pounding car doors. Two guys in a topless 32 roadster with a supercharger mounted on a monster engine and flames that run from the firewall back along the body lift their beers when you look their way. Horns start blaring farther back in both directions. Breathing hard, you think of taking the headlights out, leaving the hammer buried like a hatchet in the hood of the Bonneville, but you know better. The passenger guy's still on the street with both hands buried in his crotch. You can hear a siren.

"You fuckin' asshole," he says.

"That station wagon back there?" you say. "The one you were taking the hammer to?" Stopping for breath. "That was my sister. You need to apologize."

You watch him look confused and then bare his teeth when he remembers.

"Fuck your spic sister," he says. "Fuck her with a rubber hose."

You haul back your foot this time and let him have it in his undefended stomach. He coughs, howls, coughs. You hear girls cheering and guys hollering and think back to playing Summertime.

"We can do this all night," you say. "Or you can say you're sorry."

"Asshole. The cops are coming."

He's holding his stomach now. So you haul back your foot and let him have it in the crotch again. He howls and reaches one hand for his gonads.

"Okay. Okay." Coughing, taking his hand off his stomach, raising it. "I'm sorry."

"Her name's Lupe."

"All right," he says, his breathing ragged. "Lupe. I'm sorry."

"Stay the fuck off State."

There's a song still playing on the radio of the Bonneville. Too much other noise to hear what it is. You look for Quigley. Watch him hold the driver up and tell him something and then let him slide across the door and then roll off the fender.

"That chick, man," says Quigley. "I was about to rip my eyeballs out to shut her up. East High. Jesus Christ."

Remembering getting back to the Hudson when you heard the siren, the engine still running, all four doors wide open, the East High girls gone.

"Wonder where they went. We had to be fifteen blocks from where they parked."

"Think I fucked my hand up."

On Highway 89 you're rolling north through the dark of the outskirts home toward Bountiful. You watch him take his right hand off the wheel and flex his fingers.

"Yeah. My ear's sore."

"Wonder what that guy's gonna tell his daddy about that window."

"You busted it out?"

"He had it closed. The door locked."

"Wonder what my guy's gonna tell his girlfriend about his gonads."

"You let him know who it was for, right?"

"Yeah."

"You always gotta let 'em know that. Who it's for."

"Yeah," you say. "I know."

"Even when it's just for the hell of it," says Quigley.

"I know that too."

"That was just for the hell of it. You gotta tell 'em."

"Who'd you tell him?"

"Pocahontas. You?"

"My sister Lupe."

In the light of the Hudson's dashboard Quigley grins. You'll tell him some other time about almost copping your first feel. An East High girl. If that even counts. Her bra.

"I'm hoping nobody got your plate," you say.

"Don't worry. My dad's a cop."

"You're shitting me."

"Nope," he says. And then grins and says, "Like I'm gonna be."

"You're gonna be a cop? For real?"

"Shit, man, you play trumpet."

"You just decide that? Being a cop?"

"Fuck, man. I dunno."

CHAPTER 26

NEMESIS. A fancy word you learned in English for what Strand used to be for Brother Rodgers. And now it's the word for what Yenchik is for Brother Hunt. In Priesthood class, with you and Doby and West and Jasperson and Yenchik and Strand and Keller and Lilly and some of the older Priests slouched out in the creaky folding chairs you've used the last five years, Brother Hunt gives you the lowdown on polygamy. Out the window, two rows out, you can see his latest Corvette, the top down, the red paint blinding in the summer morning sun. In a month you'll be a high school senior. You've sat in this chair too often, Sunday after Sunday, to remember what it was like when you were twelve, a kid, where its backrest must have reached your shoulders, where your shoes must have barely brushed the floor. These days it hits you just below your shoulder blades and your shoes reach the floor with leg to spare. You've grown into it. Not always the same chair. But then all the chairs are always all the same.

Since class started today, Brother Hunt has been coasting along, running neutral, free to go on talking without having Yenchik throw a sudden steep upgrade in front of him.

"After death," him saying, "every contract made under earthly law is void. That includes any marriage outside the Temple. The only marriage that'll survive the resurrection is marriage in the Temple. The Temple's the only place you can enter into the new and everlasting covenant of eternal marriage."

Something he's been fiddling with down in the bottom of his pocket all of a sudden gets his interest. He pulls out his hand and glances down at his fingertip and goes back to his lecture. You didn't see anything. Maybe a sliver under his nail.

"Why'd the Lord think it was necessary to include plural marriage in the new and everlasting covenant?"

Jasperson puts his hand up. Brother Hunt ignores it and goes on to answer his own question while Jasperson's hand comes down pretending it was reaching up to smooth his hair.

"There's only one way you can enter the highest degree of the Celestial Kingdom. That's through the covenant. As man and wife, sealed together for all eternity. There are good single people who'll also enter the Celestial Kingdom, but they'll only be angels, or ministering servants to those who've made the covenant."

When he pauses it's to give the wall over Yenchik's head a distant look. A look like he's waiting to see what Yenchik may do with something he just said.

"Those angels will be people who've lived every one of the Lord's commandments except the everlasting covenant. People who never had the opportunity to marry in the Temple. Many of them will be women. Through no fault of their own. Maybe the right man never asked them. Maybe they weren't so blessed in the looks department. The Lord didn't see that as fair. So he created a way for them to have that opportunity. That opportunity is plural marriage."

Brother Hunt turns, takes a couple of steps across the front of the room, head down, contemplative, like he's talking to himself. Sometimes you get the feeling he's using the class as practice for when he's a coach. Like a locker room.

"What does plural marriage mean? It means that a married man can open his marriage to another woman. Or to several women. Through plural marriage, he can reach out and include other women in the new and everlasting covenant, make them his wives, and enable them to enter the highest degree of glory."

You thought you knew all about polygamy. How God revealed to Joseph Smith that worthy holders of the Priesthood could marry different women. How Joseph was getting married all the time himself. How they had to get rid of polygamy in the 1890s so that Utah could become a state. How the Church had to get rid of it. What you didn't know is what Brother Hunt is saying now. How it isn't gone.

"In the early days, the Church was able to give women that opportunity here. But the laws of man prevailed. And so we aren't allowed to practice it right now."

"What do you mean right now?" Yenchik finally says.

It still catches you off guard. You're going along okay, listening to Brother Hunt, and then Yenchik says something in his huge deep foghorn voice, and you suddenly hear how high and strained and overworked the voice of your teacher is.

"Right now. On Earth. Here in Zion."

"I don't get it," says Yenchik. "If it's one of God's commandments, how could they turn around and just get rid of it?"

"It was against the law of the United States. It stood in the way of Utah gaining statehood."

"But it was God's law."

"We have to live within the laws of the land. It's also God's law that we obey those laws. You know the twelfth Article of Faith?"

"Sort of."

"Let me hear it."

Brother Hunt strolls over toward the window with his hands in his pockets and takes a look outside. He knows he's got time. You watch him take a long look at his red Corvette, look across the rest of the parking lot, turn around again.

"Louder," he says to Yenchik. "I missed it."

"It's the one about having the gift of tongues," Yenchik finally says. "Right?"

Jasperson and Lilly both shoot their hands in the air.

"Go ahead, Mike."

"We believe in being subject to kings, presidents, rulers, and magistrates, and in obeying, honoring, and sustaining the law."

"That's the one," says Yenchik. "That's it."

"What does it mean?"

"What it says." Yenchik shrugs. "Obeying the law."

"You don't look satisfied."

"Well, if polygamy was God's commandment, shouldn't they of kept it anyway?"

"Sure. And have the whole membership of the Church in jail."

"People used to get killed for following God's commandments. You know. Crucified and burned."

"Those were different times."

"But what if the United States made a law that said everybody had to smoke?"

"That's not about to happen."

"It could," says Yenchik. "Like if a guy with a cigarette company got elected president."

You sit there knowing only half of Yenchik is being funny. Knowing his other half is just looking for things to make sense to him.

"A president can't make up a law all by himself. But we're off track here. What you need to remember is that polygamy is a permanent and sacred part of the gospel. I don't even like to call it that. Plural marriage. God's plan. Just because it's been outlawed doesn't make it a crime. Or something to joke about. We just can't practice it while we're here."

"What if it wasn't outlawed?" says Yenchik. "Would we still be doing it? Like could you go back to Hawaii for another wife?"

Brother Hunt narrows his eyes at Yenchik. But Yenchik's playing it too dumb for Brother Hunt to get it. "All I can tell you is that it's still very much a part of the gospel," he says. "Still alive and well."

"You mean in heaven."

"Sure. In the Celestial Kingdom."

"So ugly women can get in."

Brother Hunt looks at his shoes. Starts working something in his pocket again. Looks back at Yenchik.

"I never used that word. You'd be smart not to use it either. And that's only one of the Lord's reasons for it."

"Sorry," says Yenchik.

"You do know that one day you'll have the opportunity to be a god yourself."

"Yeah."

"With the power to create worlds of your own."

"Yeah."

"And populate them with your own children."

"Yeah. I guess."

"How many children do you think one wife can give you?"

"I dunno. Maybe twelve."

"So you're going to create an entire world for just twelve children."

Yenchik sits there stumped. You're thinking what if there were only twelve people on the whole Earth. Who they'd be. Who you'd pick.

"You know how many children it takes to populate an entire world?"

"Not exactly," Yenchik says.

"Well, for a planet like the Earth, it takes billions. You think you can ask one wife to give you billions of children?"

"Well, if it's eternity, maybe."

"How long does it take a woman to have a child?"

"Nine months?"

"So if you can only have one child every nine months, how long do you think it'll take to rack up, say, just the first billion?"

"You need a wife to have children? In heaven?"

"Of course you do. What did you think?"

"You mean . . . like making babies?"

"That's exactly what I mean. How do you think you're going to get, say, a billion spirit children? Just snap your fingers?"

"I thought God just made us."

"You boys are big boys," says Brother Hunt. "So here's how it is. The same bodies we have now, we'll have then, except they'll be immortal. But they'll work the same. We'll use them for the same things and in the same ways. We'll still use our lungs to breathe, noses to smell, eyes to see, feet to walk. That goes for procreation too. You won't be making babies out of mud. Or pixie dust. You'll be making them the old-fashioned way."

Everybody just sits there thinking without giving anything away. But it's still showtime for Yenchik.

"But they're spirit children," he finally says. "Not real children."

"You still make them the same way."

Nobody but Yenchik can look at Brother Hunt. The rest of you stare at the floor.

"Okay? You boys all got that?"

And that gets you to look up at him again.

"By the time you've progressed far enough to be worthy of god-hood, you're going to have thousands of wives to bear those children for you."

Nobody says anything. All of you get it. It's just Yenchik who still wants to have it all spelled out for him.

"So every time you want a spirit child, you've gotta get one of your wives pregnant."

"That's the way it works here. So that's how it works there."

"Where are they all gonna come from?"

"They?"

"All the women?"

"They'll be there."

"But there's about as many guys in the world as girls. If there's supposed to be thousands of wives for every guy, then I should be the only guy in Bountiful High."

Even Brother Hunt laughs.

"That's assuming every guy is worthy of godhood," he says. "The truth is that not very many will achieve it."

"I thought that everybody who lived the commandments got to be a god."

"That's true. But there are millions of men who won't live them all. Who won't measure up. And there'll be millions of women who will."

You're thinking Brother Hunt could have as many as he wanted to right now. Starting with every girl in the ward. Or go back to Hawaii like Yenchik said for the next one. A matched set. End up driving his demo Corvette around with a different wife in the passenger seat every day of the week. A Sunday wife and Monday wife and from there all the way to a Saturday wife.

"So in heaven," Yenchik says, "I'll be a polygamist."

"You'll have the opportunity and even the obligation to have many wives. That all depends on you."

"If I get to the Celestial Kingdom."

"The highest degree of the Celestial Kingdom. And that's just the start."

For a minute, Brother Hunt and Yenchik just look at one another, almost like two guys playing that paper and rock and scissors game.

"How about God?" Yenchik says. "Is he a polygamist?"

And now you see Brother Hunt start catching on that Yenchik could be playing him.

"I'll give you a word of advice. Don't ever make fun of the new and everlasting covenant. Don't ever turn it into something dirty. In the eyes of God that's blasphemy."

"I wasn't."

"I'm dead serious. It's the most sacred covenant you'll ever make. All of your mothers understand and accept it. When you boys get married in the Temple, your wives will too, or you'll have to make them understand. That they'll need to make room in their marriage for other wives. They may be the first. But they'll only be one of many."

Brother Hunt looks down at his polished shoes for a minute, like he's taking a break and looking for a way to shift gears, or wondering what his fingers are working deep inside his pocket.

"I know we've grown up in a monogamous society. We're conditioned to think that monogamy is the natural order of things. One man. One wife. It isn't. It's a fabrication of man. Men aren't made that way. A woman can only give birth every nine months. A man can conceive a child just about any time. And God gave him the appetite to go with that ability. And that's the problem. Monogamy tries to put a limit on that appetite. Which is why we have prostitution. Adultery. Immorality."

And then Brother Hunt goes on to give you a history lesson. How the nations in all of recorded history that have lasted the shortest, that have fallen the quickest, have been the monogamous nations. How the Roman Empire was one of them. How the founders of Rome were robbers, and stole women, and wanted all the women to themselves, and made laws that promoted monogamy because women back then were scarce. How the Romans spread their monogamous system from Rome through all the Christian nations. How monogamy caused the Great Apostasy. How the Roman Empire fell because monogamy led to prostitution and adultery, and prostitution and adultery led to disease and wickedness, and disease and wickedness led to the decay at the root of all the institutions of the Christian world.

"Rome was where it started," says Brother Hunt. "The whole system of monogamy. Celebrated by the Catholic church and other Christian churches as a holy sacrament. It was all set up by a pack of robbers and womanizers."

He looks at you with this smooth and easy salesman look like he's just described how a Corvette can run circles around a Ferrari, even with its emergency brake on, and how he's got the test results to back it up. And then he looks right at Yenchik, but Yenchik just sits there, lets him look for all he's worth.

"This is all historical fact," says Brother Hunt. "You're not gonna read about it in your history books, and you're not gonna hear your teachers talk about it, because if historians and teachers put that fact out there, the world would have anarchy on its hands. But you'll read about it in the teachings of our leaders. Brigham Young. John Taylor. Prophets of God and Presidents of the Church. Men who communed with God and Jesus Christ. George A. Smith. Orson Pratt. George Q. Cannon. All of them Apostles."

And now Yenchik's hand goes up.

"I figured," says Brother Hunt. "Go ahead."

"So Caesar was a robber?"

"You don't think Caesar and other Roman Emperors had all the women they wanted? How do you figure they got them? By making sure every other man in the Empire only got one."

"What if one's all you want?" says Yenchik. "My dad doesn't want more than my mom. You saying that's wrong?"

Brother Hunt looks at him for a minute, like he's waiting for the echo of Yenchik's big voice to die out, like he's wondering what part of himself he'd trade for Yenchik's voice.

"Okay," he says. "A while ago I talked about a man's appetite. I'm sure your dad's a good man. Faithful to your mom. What you probably don't see is the will power he has to exercise to keep that appetite under control. That's what's wrong. God gave us that appetite for a reason. To replenish and multiply the Earth. And our own worlds, when the time comes."

"I thought he gave it to us to test us," says Yenchik.

"God gave us plural marriage as a way to exercise that appetite. The Romans took it away. So it's a false test. A test of man. And it's just not healthy. Apostle Heber C. Kimball tells us that a man who only allows himself one wife will soon begin to wither and dry up. A man who enters plural marriage will always look fresh and young and sprightly. Apostle George A. Smith tells us that men who chain themselves to the law of monogamy and live their entire lives under the dominion of one wife are narrow-minded and pinch-backed. These men were free to engage in plural marriage. So they know what they're talking about."

Yenchik's got his hand up again.

"No, son," says Brother Hunt. "I'm not saying it's healthy to go out and fornicate. You wait till you're married."

"That's not what I wanted to know."

"What?"

"Nothing."

And now Strand raises his hand. You've been feeling skepticism come off him like oil smoke off an exhaust manifold.

"Yes," says Brother Hunt.

"What about Jesus Christ?"

"What about him?"

"He's the Son of God."

"Yes?"

"Mary was his mother."

"That's right."

"And God was his father."

"Right."

"So you're saying that Mary and God . . ."

"Go ahead."

"So they conceived Jesus the way regular people do."

Brother Hunt just looks at Strand. "Of course."

"By having intercourse."

Brother Hunt stops and clears his throat. You think the way you always do that it's going to open up his voice. It never does.

"The Catholics and a lot of other churches put out this doctrine they call immaculate conception. God said some magic words, and bingo, Mary was pregnant, and nine months later, there was the baby Jesus. The virgin birth. That's not how the body works. That's not what we believe. That's not the natural order. Even God has to abide by natural law."

"Wasn't she married to Joseph?"

"She was."

"So did Joseph know what was going on?"

"God spoke to Joseph. Told him why he needed Mary. Of course Joseph knew. It was okay. This was the Son of God they were talking about. The Savior. Someone who would save the world. You think Joseph would stand in the way of that?"

"God and Mary had intercourse?" says Yenchik.

Brother Hunt looks at him. Shock passes quiet and quick through his tan face. Down in his pocket his fingers stop working.

"That's right," he says.

"Where? Like in the stable? Where was Joseph?"

"We don't know where. The stable is where Jesus was born. I've heard that God took Mary to a special place. Listen. It was a sacred and divine act. If you want to make it something else, you need to get on your knees and tell God you lost your testimony."

"It just feels creepy," says Yenchik.

"You think this is about how you feel? What you feel doesn't mean squat. You can't expect the gospel to ask how you feel about it."

He pulls an empty folding chair off the front row, spins it around, puts his foot on the seat, leans forward. Both hands are out of his pockets now, crossed on his knee, and you can tell he's mad, his face hard. You can smell the locker room. He isn't selling a Corvette. In his high tense labored voice he's telling off his football team.

"You have any issues, feel like making any jokes, go home and read Section 132 of the Doctrine and Covenants. See what the Lord thinks. See what he thinks of people who want to ridicule his new and everlasting covenant. It's gonna take you thousands of years to purify your thoughts to where you'll even be able to understand the covenant."

CHAPTER 27

FOR THE LAST several weeks West's Pontiac has been stinking like something crawled in and took a crap and then died somewhere inside it. West's tried everything he can think of to get rid of it. Taken out the carpeting and scrubbed it with shampoo and disinfectant. Looked up under the dash. Taken the cage of the heater blower apart to see if a mouse got up inside it. Taken all the seats out. Hung three cardboard pine trees off his mirror and radio knobs to override the stench. Even sprinkled Elsha cologne all over the interior. And then it just smelled like something sweet had died. A few days ago it started getting better on its own. Like it just wore itself out. Almost to where West can start using the Pontiac to go out on dates again.

You and your buddies haven't talked about a Sunday School or Priesthood lesson for a long time. This one's new. This one gets you going. That Wednesday night is oil change and lube job night at Steed's Texaco. It's after eight. The station's closed. In one of the two bays, up on the rack, the engine of West's Pontiac is bleeding a thin twisting column of black oil into a big red pan on a pole. Out in front, in the dark with the sign and the pump lights off, Doby's Impala and Yenchik's Ford and Keller's Bugeye are waiting for their turn. You've got your father's Chevy wagon out there too. Inside, the dirty black radio on top of a black tool cabinet belts out Fabian, Elvis, the Everly Brothers, the Shirelles, one request after another. Doby's standing with his head in the blast of hot air coming from the heater hanging off the ceiling. Keller and Yenchik are standing around drinking cans of Olympia beer they got out of the fridge.

"All those wives," says West. "What the fuck."

"Yeah," says Keller.

"That's a lotta windowpeeking," you say to Keller.

"I'd almost rather peek on 'em than be married to 'em." Keller says.

"It'd be weird," Doby says. "I'd feel more like their boss or something."

"Like having your own cathouse," says Yenchik.

"If you got a thousand of 'em," says West, "you'd never get tired of any of 'em, cuz by the time you get around to the first one again, like two years later, she'd be like new again."

"They don't have years in heaven," says Keller, taking a slug of his Olympia.

"You guys put some money in the cup for those beers?" says West.

"Yenchik didn't," says Keller.

"Yeah I did," says Yenchik. "You're the one who didn't."

"Yeah? Go look. There's only enough in there for one beer. Mine."

"Screw you," says Yenchik. "That's my money in there."

"Wanna check for fingerprints?" says Keller.

"To prove you picked it up after I put it in?" says Yenchik.

West's underneath his Pontiac with the grease hose, greasing up the little nipples in his suspension and drive shaft joints, letting the engine bleed all the way out. Now and then, the air compressor kicks on, and you've all got to holler to hear yourselves over the hammering putter of the pump.

"You believe that stuff Hunt was telling us?" says Doby.

"The polygamy stuff?" says Keller.

"Yeah, that, but—"

"You could marry every pig at school and call it Yenchik's pig farm."

"Screw you. You couldn't get a real pig to marry you."

"How come he got all pissed? Nobody was making fun of nothing."

"I meant the part about God and Mary," says Doby.

"Yeah. Pretty weird."

"I'd rather believe in that immaculate conception thing. Man. Just thinking about God doing it is weird."

"Yeah. Especially with Mary."

"I wonder what Joseph did."

"Just sat out in the living room. Took a walk. I don't know."

"I wonder where they did it."

"Yeah. God's not the kind of guy who can sneak around exactly. Go to a hotel and say he's Mr. Smith."

"Why not? He's God. He can be any guy he wants."

"He wouldn't sneak around. He'd just tell Joseph. This is what's up. I'm gonna commit adultery with your wife."

"If Joseph said okay, maybe it wasn't adultery."

"I know what my dad'd do. He'd tell him to go screw himself. He wouldn't care what it was for. He'd say no way, Jose."

"Mine too. He'd say go find your own. He wouldn't put up with it."

"My dad too. He'd say you're God. Go make yourself a woman if you want to knock one up."

"Yeah. Why'd he have to pick one who was married?"

"I dunno. Maybe so Jesus would have a regular dad."

"Yeah. But he wasn't his dad."

"My dad wouldn't have to say anything," Yenchik says. "My mom'd do it. Just tell God she had a headache."

"How's he doing?" says Keller. "His new shop?"

"Good," says Yenchik. He sucks on his beer. And then says, "He's doing good. Yeah."

"He like being by himself?"

"Hell yeah. He hated where he was at. Hated that asshole."

"What kinda stuff's he doing?" says West.

Yenchik shrugs. "Parts mostly. Parts you can't get anymore. Guys with these old cars, you know, Model Ts, that kinda shit, wanna keep 'em stock, they bring him their busted parts, he makes 'em new ones just like the busted ones. You can't tell the difference."

"That's gotta cost," says West. "He charge 'em good?"

Yenchik looking at West for a minute. Trying to read what he's saying from the way he's focusing on squirting grease into his front end nipples. "He's kinda got a monopoly," he says. "They're rich anyway. They could give a shit."

"I'd like to see what he does," says West.

"He's not big on company when he's working," says Yenchik. "Says that's how people get hurt."

"I'm not saying I'd talk to him. Just watch."

"Same thing," Yenchik says. "He don't even like me around."

"Wasn't Mary supposed to be a virgin?" Doby says.

"Yeah. I heard that. So Joseph hadn't even had a shot at her."

"Like they hadn't even had their honeymoon."

"Jesus H. Christ!"

Everyone looks. West drops the grease hose like a live snake and comes exploding out from under the Pontiac. His eyeballs are scared so huge they look like they're trying to outrun his head. He goes flying past you. Yenchik pulls his beer can back out of the way. West doesn't stop until the wall across the bay does it for him.

"Holy fuck! Holy fuck! Holy fuck!"

And then he's just standing there, doubled over, his hands on his knees, gulping down air like someone's just told him there's no more Saturdays.

"Hey, man," says Doby. "Calm down."

"Oh, Jesus! Jesus Christ!"

"What happened?"

"Go look!" he says.

"Look where?"

"Behind the front wheel." Panting now. "On the driver's side."

"What is it?"

"I found where the smell's been coming from," says West. "Oh, Jesus."

The four of you wander over underneath the Pontiac to where the drop cord's hanging where West left it, off the steering column, throwing light up into the complicated heavy trusswork of the frame and suspension.

"What?" says Yenchik.

"Holy shit," says Keller. "Look."

And there it is. Just sitting on top of the frame, just back from the front wheel, like someone glued it there on purpose, the dirty head of a brown cat, nothing left but its fur and skull and teeth and the sockets where its eyeballs were.

"Jesus," says Keller.

"Just its head?" says Doby. "How the hell'd that happen?"

"How'd it get up there?"

"How'd it stay there?"

West's back, standing behind Yenchik, taking another look himself.

"That was it," he says. "That's what was stinking up the car."

"You wanna leave it there?" you say.

"You fuckin' nuts?" he says.

You take the drop cord off its hook and hold it up close to the ravaged head. It looks wild. The teeth bared and parted in this permanent hiss and the skin pulled back from the sockets and the ears laid down from weeks of facing into the wind underneath the Pontiac. The fur matted and plastered with water and dirt from the wake of the tire. But otherwise clean. Clean of flesh. Clean of maggots. Clean like the flattened carcass of the coyote you found one day in the fields off the ranch. You reach up and take hold of it. It's stuck. You work it back and forth, feel the crinkling give of the skin, and it finally breaks loose from the frame. Everyone backs away when you bring it down.

"Fuck, Tauffler. How can you fuckin' touch it?"

You're turning it around, looking it over, your buddies leaning in to see themselves. It's as light and hollow as a Christmas ornament.

"It's just bone and fur."

"That's how come it stopped stinking," says Keller.

"Here. Hang it off your mirror."

You toss it at Keller. He jumps out of its way. It goes skittering and rolling across the floor like a ball of yarn until it hits the steel edge of the lift in the other bay.

"Think someone planted it there?"

"Nobody hates West that much."

"Less maybe some girl."

That summer your father trades the Chevy wagon in on a new car, a Plymouth Valiant, what they call a compact. It's a smaller wagon with a slant six engine. He gets it white with a red interior. He gets it with a stick because you make the case that a stick is cheaper on gas than an automatic. It comes with a floor shifter. A long hook of a steel rod that comes looping up from the transmission hump and puts a white plastic ball right there where your hand is. You take him out and teach him how to drive it. Stay with him until he gets a rough idea of the way the gas has to work with the clutch to keep the engine going. One day, when it's home and he's out doing church work with another man from the neighborhood, you tint the inside of the dome light red the way West did Doby's Impala. Just enough to get away with. Just enough to where he can live with it without getting it replaced.

Keller's the only guy who ever brings up all the wives you'll have in heaven. You've just replaced his brake pads, run his Bugeye Sprite into Salt Lake, up the road past Hogle Zoo, up Emigration Canyon and then Little Mountain for a test drive. You stop and get out on the dirt clearing up on top of Little Mountain, walk to the edge where it falls away, look down where the winding road goes down the other side, a gray vein along the hills all the way to where it meets the highway that comes down Parley's Canyon back into the city. Far below you, a semi the size of your thumb is using its diesel engine to hold it back, keep it from having to use one of the runaway lanes down the canyon.

"I wonder if you can just have one," he says. "You know. If that's all you want. If God would say okay."

"I know," you say. "Like the one you married here."

"Yeah," he says. "You know. Just the one you bring with you."

He's thinking of Cheryl. The girl from Clearfield he's been going steady with for more than a year now. The brown-haired chesty freckled daughter of a Clearfield cop.

"Did Hunt say it was a commandment?"

"I don't remember."

"I think it was more like a privilege."

"I mean what's she supposed to think? We get there and I start marrying these homely chicks. That's not right."

With the sun warm on your back where you're standing, where the dirt and weeds of Little Mountain start to fall off and the long descending bowl of Parley's Canyon opens the hills below you, you're thinking of your mother. What she'd do if your father came home with another wife. How he'd even handle more than her.

"Yeah. I know. It's not right."

"I don't care how holy you make it."

"No."

"Think of it the other way around. If a woman could have all these husbands instead. Man, I'd feel like shit, knowing she was doing it with all these ugly guys."

You're thinking how it could never be the other way. A woman can only have one kid at a time no matter how many guys she does it with. Twins or triplets if she's lucky. How long it would take her to populate a planet. How one guy could get a thousand babies going at a time. But you know what Keller's saying. How you'd feel, one of a thousand husbands, waiting for your turn to come around.

"It sucks for women," you say.

"Does it ever," says Keller.

"It's a long way off," you say. "We don't need to think about it now."

Keller doesn't say anything. You can't make sense of it either. Maybe there are men who can. Who love the idea. You see yourself with just one girl. Your face for her face, your eyes for her eyes, your hands for her hands. Not like the big brown moth-eaten bull they had in La Sal. Not with a factory of women.

"Yeah," says Keller finally. "Downhill time. See how your brake job does."

And the next hot late August night, the next time your father goes back to the office after supper and out your door and down the hall your mother lies there naked on her bed, you wonder what your father would do. If you were Jesus Christ. If your mother were Mary. If God had to fuck her to have you. What your father would say. Sure. Go ahead. I'll just go back to the office. Let me know how else I can help you. Mother, maybe you could call me when you're done. You look down the hall and imagine God on top of her. Imagine them doing what you saw your aunt and uncle doing that night so long ago when you heard the busy springs of a bed and took a peek through the crack of the blankets they hung up for walls in your grandfather's basement.

CHAPTER 28

YOUR SENIOR YEAR, all around you, everyone signs up for all the different clubs. The Key Club, the Forensic Club, the United Nations Club, the Rifle Club, the Ski Club, Future Teachers of America, the Aviation Club, Future Homemakers of America, the Red and Gray Bowling Leagues, the Twirlers and Banner Carriers, the Letterman Association, the Dance Club, the Drama Club, the Modern Dance Club, the Wachatawa Pep Club. And all the music groups. The Bountiful High School Orchestra. The A'Cappella Choir. The Concert Band. The Pep Band.

"We could use you in the Jazz Club," says Mr. Frank.

"I'll think about it."

"You and the other boys."

"I'll tell them."

"We could use your stuff. We could help you."

You're standing there thinking you've already got the best musicians in the school. You think back to when you didn't think you belonged with them.

"Okay," you say.

"I can tell you're saying no," Mr. Frank says. "Just think it over. I'm asking you. You and the other boys. No audition."

"Okay."

West joins the Madri Singers because in his white tuxedo jacket and pink tie he figures he can croon girls into his Pontiac. Doby and Jasperson join the United Nations Club and the Rifle Club without much of a reason except for an extra picture in the yearbook. Strand signs up for the Debate Club and goes around debating other schools. Keller goes for the Key Club where you razz him for thinking he's shit in his navy blue blazer with a pocket patch. Eddie goes for the Aviation Club. Someone tells Yenchik that with his voice he should go for the Drama Club. He lasts for the first meeting, and then goes for the Madri Singers, and it pisses West off, because there's Yenchik in his own white jacket and pink tie and pink crepe paper carnation, booming out the bass parts like a foghorn.

"What the fuck?" says Robbie. "The Aviation Club?"

"We get to go for a plane ride," says Eddie. "We get to fly it."

"Naw," you say.

"What?" says Eddie.

"Jolene Hunter's in it. That's what you signed up for."

"The braces?" says Jimmy. "The glasses?"

"Yeah."

"Why? She wanna be a stewardess?"

"That's a dirty lie," says Eddie. "I signed up before she did."

"So maybe she signed up cuz of you," says Robbie.

In Robbie's basement you watch Eddie check his reed. Wonder how this shapeless disorganized guy can have the stuff he's got inside him. The stuff on his sax. The way he took to playing congas. Like an African. Like a Cuban. Even Santos said so.

"Just don't grow a moustache," says Jimmy.

"Why?"

"Cuz you'll end up getting it stuck in those braces."

"You're all assholes." And then he says, "That's why it stinks so bad here all the time."

You don't join anything. Mr. Frank asks you to join the Jazz Club two more times before he gives it up. Robbie and Jimmy and Eddie don't join either. You don't know why. Just this feeling of another harness. Another name. Member of the Jazz Club. Something else just in the way of playing. The Dance Club asks you to play for them when they learn the samba and the tango. Mrs. Gill, their director, teaches them the sweeping heel-cracking moves on the hardwood floor of the stage in the auditorium. One of the girls who dances while you play is Susan Lake. Santos drives his pickup truck out from West High after school to play with you.

"Keller tell you what he wants to do?" West asks you when it's you and him and Doby one night at Steed's Texaco.

"What?"

"Put a mirror on the floor of his Bugeye. The passenger side."

"Yeah. He tried it. It's so tight down there he couldn't see it from the driver's seat."

"What for?" Doby says.

"Jesus, Doby."

"Oh. Yeah. Okay."

"More like something Yenchik would do," West says.

"He's got room," you say. "That big old Ford. Lots of open floor."

"Yeah. He could sing to 'em while he's lookin' up their dresses."

Word of the band keeps taking you farther and farther out from home. You figure it's the name. Something people can pass along. Jimmy gets business cards made. How Should I Know. An International Jazz Ensemble. Robbie's phone number since that's where your headquarters is.

"An international jazz ensemble?" says Eddie. "Are you kidding?"

"You say it onsomble," says Santos.

"I meant the international part."

"Hey," says Jimmy. "Shake's from Switzerland, Santos is Mexican, Robbie's half Mexican, and we can do all this African and Cuban and Brazilian stuff. Why not?"

"Cuz we're a friggin' high school band," says Eddie.

"Oh yeah," says Jimmy. "And you're Polish. I forgot. We do polkas too."

"We're in friggin' high school."

"Yeah? So? You gotta be a certain age to be international? Look at Unicef. That's all little kids."

You can tell from the look on their faces that Santos and Robbie think it's stupid too. But business cards are business cards. If they're not set in stone then they're the next most permanent thing.

"I think it's cool," says Robbie. Like he figures too that you can't just throw away five hundred business cards. You've got to go by what they say until they're gone.

"What's this ensemble mean, anyway?" says Eddie.

"Onsomble," says Santos. "It's just a fancy word for a bunch of guys playing together. Like a band."

You're playing against bands from all the other schools. A couple of bands from the University. You're playing for money too. Places in Salt Lake. Clubs. Places that make the five of you get your underage cards from the State Liquor Commission. The Sojourner. PJ's. Places sometimes that make you all wear shirts and pants the same. Places along State Street and out toward Redwood Road and up toward the East Bench. The Crow's Nest. The Staircase. The Indigo. Places south as far as Spanish Fork, north toward Ogden, out west across Skull Valley in Tooele, where the guy who thought you looked like Mouseketeers last year thinks you look okay now. A place off Dugway Proving Grounds where Army guys hang out and dance slow in their uniforms with their neckties loose with women who show up from Tooele and God knows where else. A club out in Wendover, the Nevada border town out past the Salt Flats where you got three bucks of gas one night, where Air

Force guys bring girls in from the whorehouses on the Nevada side of town.

Always the Salt Lake clubs. Club Cabana. The Black Bull. The Library. Club Manhattan. Clubs where there are signs outside that say How Should I Know. Where women and men sit back in their silhouettes in the blush-colored dark at little tables with bottles of liquor and glasses and packs of cigarettes and ash trays on them. Where you can cut into a ballad and suddenly pull men and women you didn't even know were there from the dark recesses of the room up to the dance floor. Where they come up and ask for songs and drop coins or put dollar bills in the glass on Jimmy's amp. Where there are stages and spotlights. Where you play in shafts of light that tint the skin of your fingers and knuckles blue and red and sparks and spears of blue and red run up and down your trumpet. Where sometimes you wonder if this is what it was like for Joseph Smith in the shaft of light in the Sacred Grove when God and Jesus Christ and the Holy Ghost appeared, the knuckles of his folded fingers in the blazing light.

Since you're playing for money now, you're down to a couple of afternoons and nights a week at Servus Drug, sometimes a Saturday shift where you clear up the basement banquet room, where you know the women now who leave heavy smiles of lipstick on half-finished drinks, bright smears on the cigarette butts in the gray dust of the ashtrays. In her waitress outfit, old Gladys lights one up herself, waiting for you to clear glasses and little plates and utensils off a tablecloth.

"Tom and me want to come hear you sometime," she says.

"Okay. You like to dance?"

"Oh, my goodness. Always."

"You know the Indigo?"

"The place on State?"

"I'll tell you next time we play there."

"You do that, honey. You make it soon."

Christmas comes to the house and up on the hill where you practice. Your mother lets Molly and Maggie hang their yellow and red construction paper angels but makes it clear that they ruin the rest of her ornaments. That they have to come down whenever company's expected. Karl uses a candle to singe their feet off. You can tell it was a candle from the streaks of greasy black that run up their paper dresses from the ashes of their ankles. And then your mother takes them down for good. Molly's known for a long time that you don't cry without being ridiculed for crying. Maggie knows now too. Knows from Molly that they had it coming for wanting their angels on the tree to start with. Up on the hill you play Little Drummer Boy and What Child Is This to the distant strings of Christmas lights that map out the streets below you without showing you the houses.

That winter you get another interview from Bishop Wacker for another annual Individual Aaronic Priesthood Award. You've got five of them racked up now. Five fancy certificates signed by the Presiding Bishopric of the Church and by the bishopric of your ward. One for every year you've had the Priesthood. For doing all your Priesthood jobs. For giving at least one talk. For working on church projects. Stickers for good attendance. You're here to get approved for number six.

His desk stands between you. Selling Fords part time. Your father's never bought a car from him. You never will. Especially a Porsche. If he sold them. If he was the last man on earth who sold them. Even if he was selling them like Almond Joys for a nickel apiece.

"Pay your full tithing last year?"

"Yep."

"Attend tithing settlement?"

"You were there."

"Live the Word of Wisdom?"

"Yep."

"Didn't do any smoking or drinking?"

"Nope."

"Kept your thoughts clean?"

"Yep."

"Fondled yourself?"

Fondled. It throws you. The way he's always asked if you've abused yourself before.

"Nope."

"I understand you're playing in night clubs."

"Yep."

"You act like you don't think there's anything wrong with that."

Feeling him want to reach deep down and pull out everything. Your trumpet. Robbie and Eddie and Jimmy and Santos. Mr. Selby and Mr. Hinkle. Mrs. Harding. The way people dance out in front of you.

"Nope."

"Nope what?"

"Just nope."

"Maybe one of these days you'll grow up. Make your dad happy for once. Me, I don't see it happening for a long time."

"You know best."

And wherever you play there are girls. At the clubs, the youngest ones are college girls, and even the college girls are way too old for you, and from the way they look at you when you're on break, you know that what they're looking for doesn't have anything to do with you. Without your trumpet they'd look at you the way they look at a cloud or at a city bus. Even Robbie knows it's just the music. That's what you come looking for and end up taking home. The chance to play for them. The way it gets to them.

At the high schools you play, the girls are more your age, more your speed, and sometimes they're like Linda was. They want to see you again. They want to know if you can come back sometime to see them. To get a ride, you ask if they've got friends, and then let Quigley or Porter or Snook in on them. And then you're rocketing down Highway 89 in the Hudson around Point of the Mountain through Orem and Provo to towns like Springville. Into Salt Lake and down State Street in Porter's Mercury to one of the back street neighborhoods where South High draws its girls from. North to Clearfield in Snook's Chevy. Your buddies from auto mechanics who belong to a club you can't just sign up for. The club that hangs out in the parking lot. Greasers. Hoods. No application. No faculty adviser. No planned activities you could invite your mother and father to. No group pictures in the yearbook. Just a car. Or something else to offer. Like playing jazz. Like knowing girls you can introduce them to, so that you can catch a ride to see the girls you want to see again.

"Go ahead."

"Sure it's okay?"

"Yeah."

"Which one?"

With your nose in her ticklish sweet hair you can feel the soft giggle of surprise in her warm breath up against your ear.

"Which one?"

"Yeah. Which one."

"I don't get it."

"The right one or the left one?"

"Both of them. Silly."

And in the back seat of Porter's Mercury you get what your mother said you got the night you rode the Ferris wheel with Linda in the dusk a year and a half ago now. Not what they sound like. But what they feel like. Not through a bra but soft and warm and naked in your bare hand.

Bishop Wacker. Like a hundred other men you've watched and listened to all your life from a bench or chair in one or another chapel. A hundred other men you've been told to respect and obey no matter what. During the week they're just men. Men who climb telephone poles. Fix radios and televisions. Teach Driver's Ed. Fill chuckholes for the State Road Commission. Sell kitchen appliances or men's suits at Sears. Men like your father who work in offices and do what their bosses tell them. Come Sunday they change. They wake up possessed. Nobody tells them what to do. They put on the look and come to Priesthood Meeting full of their own eternal godhood like Presidents or Kings who can tell you what you have to do to keep from being sent to Outer Darkness. The men who've always been your father's army. Who look at you like they wish they could ask you why you can't shape up for once and make your father happy. Except for Bishop Wacker they never ask. They just give you the look to let you know. That they can see through your look. That they'd like to reach inside you and pull out everything you are that isn't one of them.

That year Molly starts changing. Doing what they call developing. At twelve years old, the buttons of her little nipples have stopped looking like a guy's, have started swelling out like when a guy's get twisted, and you know from talk around the house that she's started growing hair between her legs. Your mother still braids her hair on Saturday on a stool in the kitchen, braids it into two dark blond coils that crawl from her temples back across and down the sides of her head, tight enough to where you can sometimes see Molly flinch and tears roll off her eyes while you're sitting there eating Cheerios. And she still wets her bed. Every night while she lies there sleeping. While she lets it go not knowing. While the pool of urine the rubber sheet on her mattress keeps puddled around her body rekindles the fiery rash from her waist to her knees. You see it sometimes in the morning, when you see her running for the bathroom, holding her soaked flannel nightgown up away from her burning skin, while your mother goes out of her mind because she can't think of words that are savage enough to measure up to what Molly's done to her.

"You tramp! You are worse than a tramp! You are filth! You disgust me! You think you are turning into a woman? Pfui! A woman doesn't wet her bed! Your friends would have nothing to do with you if they knew the truth!"

You see it and hear it and it fills you with this ruthless hunger to hurt someone so bad they'd rather be dead. You just don't know who.

CHAPTER 29

THE BANDS from the downtown high schools are the tough ones. Especially West High, where Santos goes, where the kids are drawn from the city's Mexican neighborhoods. You beat them mostly on technique, and on versatility, where you go light on the latin stuff and dig into more of your straight-ahead mainstream repertoire. South High, the poor school that draws its kids out of the neighborhoods just off State Street, where you can tell the kids work hard on technique, practice like there's no tomorrow, play raw like there's nothing they've got to lose.

"Close your eyes," says Santos. "So you don't see all the dancing. Just listen."

You're sitting there in the hard chairs of their gym, watching this band on a portable stage, guys making these electrocuted jerks and recoils like they're hooked into their amps, rocking and bopping, ricocheting off the drum beats like they're being punched, throwing their butts and heads and legs and elbows around like some jamboree for spastics. You don't need to close your eyes. You can strip away the spastic stuff and hear the music on its own. Hear what Santos did to tighten you guys up. Especially Robbie.

"Yeah," you say. "I know."

"That's what the judges do," he says. "Just look down and listen."

The bands from East High, the school whose kids come from the city's old established neighborhoods, not as rich as they are snobbish, not as cool as they are conceited, bands that are into behaving like they're playing more than they are just into playing, bands that play like they're drinking tea on stilts with chopsticks up their butts.

"Fuckin' music stands," says Robbie, sitting back in the auditorium with you and Jimmy, watching them set up.

"Yeah," says Jimmy. "Like they're playin' the fuckin' Messiah."

But the bands from the rich new high schools are the gravy. Highland and Olympus. Up on the East Bench. Where the guys on State Street with their Bonneville were from. They play like they deserve to win just for showing up and having the most expensive instruments. Play just enough to where they can get away with telling girls they're musicians. The lazy half-bored way they nod to the beat like they're doing the audience a favor by staying awake. Like every note they play sends diamonds showering out across the auditorium.

When you play against them you play their faces off. Leave them standing there stupid and mean and looking cheated because some hick band from Bountiful named How Should I Know, a name that's not a name, just a question without a question mark, came in and had the nerve to not stand back and let them win. Their mothers pissed and yelling at the judges while they hang behind them looking hurt and mean and stunned. Their girls ignoring them. Their girls sneaking looks your way instead. Sly. You not sure if they're mad or curious.

"Don't take them up on it," says Robbie.

"How come?" Jimmy says.

"Fangs. Bloodsuckers. They don't leave hickies. They leave these little holes."

"Speaking from experience?"

"Take my word for it."

With the kids at West and South it doesn't matter if you lose or win. It's like all of you are one huge band. One band where you get together afterward and show each other stuff you heard each other do. With the kids at East what you see is why you didn't want to join the Jazz Club. With the kids at Highland and Olympus, who pack their gear up afterward in their showroom cars, their new Corvettes and their Thunderbirds and their Triumphs and MGs and Healeys, what you find is what you couldn't find at home. Who it is you want to hurt so bad they'd be happier if you just killed them.

You don't know why. Why they can look at you and send sparks racing up and down the muscles in your arms. Maybe because they look at you worse than they'd look at a dog turd. Like you're the stain a dog turd leaves when it gets picked off concrete. Sometimes afterward, when you and Robbie and Eddie and Santos and Jimmy stop for a Coke and Robbie sits there stirring cream and sugar into a thick white cup of coffee, you see them in the booths of East Bench places like Marie Callender's, toying with slices of mud pie, where their placid eyes let you know there's nothing they need from you or anyone else beyond the allowance they'll never have to reach the bottom of. Not the Mormon Church. Not the Priesthood. Not some testimony. Not a mission to some godforsaken place like Finland or Tennessee. Sure as hell not the city they look down on from the patios and decks of their East Bench houses.

And so you go back. You have to. Not for their bands but for their basketball games. Not with Robbie and Eddie and Jimmy and Santos, but with Quigley and Porter and Snook, guys who see the same thing you do, who get the same sparks running their itching lines up and down their arms, who want to take their fists to it, after their games, in their parking lots. You park your cars along the distant backs of the lots with their lowered noses out. Where the high yellow lights can barely catch the chrome of their bumpers and grills and the glass of their head-lights back in the dark. Just enough to where they can tell you're back there.

"Let's go," says Snook.

"No," says Porter. "We're not starting anything. Let them come to us."

"Who says they're gonna?" Snook says.

"Watch."

"They act like we ain't even here."

"Yeah," says Porter. "They're funny that way. Give 'em time."

And sure enough, after every game, once the kids with the parents leave, and the teams and the cheerleaders, once the lot is mostly empty, slow, with weapons, the rich kids make it over. Brass knuckles. Fist pipes. Bats. Equalizers. Stuff as new and unused-looking as their in-struments. Sometimes there's small talk first. Got a problem? You guys lost? Your mom know you're here? Enough to pick out a face and see what he's got for a weapon. Enough to see what the chicks who trailed along behind them could be carrying aside from their fingernails. And then, to make up for your size, hit first, hit second, keep it in their face, fight crazy like a wolverine, protect your mouth. And afterward the way they stand there, back behind their chicks, their faces oily black with sweat and blood, holding their mouths together, looking at you mourn-ful and resentful like you didn't understand you were supposed to let them win again, while you bat away the clawed arms of their chicks and laugh at the names that come shrieking like bats out of their sneering bare-toothed faces.

"You hick piece of Mormon shit!"

"Go back to your hick little town, you candyass fruitpicker!"

"Yeah! Go pay your fucking tithing!"

"Yeah! Go play with your fucking little Mormon titties in your stupid Chevy!"

A couple of times the blood yours. A couple of times your head sore, your face like it's been burned, your side where someone got you with a bat, your stomach raw on the ride home afterward. And then one night, in the parking lot at Olympus High, fighting some guy who makes you feel like you're fighting Eddie, this big disorganized bear of a guy, and all of a sudden he grabs and holds you and the back of your head explodes. You break loose, spin around, and this kid with curly blond hair and hate smeared all over his face like mustard is coming after you again, brass knuckles gleaming off his fist. The rich kid version of Eddie tries to grab you from behind to hold you for another hit. Porter comes charging. Tackles the kid with the knuckles. Takes him down. And then he's on top of him, taking his arm, stretching it out on the asphalt, pinning his wrist there with his knee, the kid's fingers still wearing their gold harness of hard brass loops.

"Go ahead," Porter tells you.

"Go ahead what?"

But the rich kid version of Eddie still wants to pin you from behind. When he feels you reach back for his crotch he lets you go. The whole back half of your head hurts like it's coming back from being frozen.

"Snook!" Porter yells. "Get over here!"

"What!"

"Here!"

And before you even know what Porter wanted you to do, Snook's there, and he brings up his leg, takes aim, and brings the heel of his engineer's boot down hard on the kid's hand. You hear this howling wail come bawling out of the face between Porter's knees. You watch the kid's fist spring open. Watch his thumb and fingers work to wiggle the hard rings of the knuckles off. And then Snook's heel comes down again and stays there while Porter talks to the kid.

"Knuckles? Fuckin' brass knuckles? You ain't got your own fuckin' knuckles?"

The rich kid version of Eddie just stands there quiet next to you. You reach for the back of your head, feel your hair wet, see blood all black and oily on your fingers when you bring your hand around. The parking lot goes quiet. The air goes out of all the fighting. Guys come gathering round. It's not the cops. It's the blond kid bawling. It's the same for everyone. This sound you never heard before.

"That's good," says Porter.

Snook twists his heel down one last time. Porter gets off and stands there. The kid stays down. Just curls on his side and doesn't move his hand, leaves it on the asphalt like something he doesn't want to know is his, just lies there bawling quiet now. You don't look. Don't want to see what the knuckles did. You can see just from his face. From the faces of his rich kid friends across from where he's lying. Bad enough to be permanent maybe.

"Never from fuckin' behind," says Porter. "Never with a weapon."
And then he says, softer, "Hope you wasn't planning on being a piano
player."

Porter looks at you. Looks down at your hand. You watch the blood
he sees there register in his face.

"You want his knucks?"

"I don't need 'em."

"Souvenir?"

"Nah."

Porter looks at the guy's hand.

"Just as well. Don't know if I could even get 'em off."

And then he turns around and takes a step toward where the rich
guys and their chicks are standing. The rich guy version of Eddie made
it over there, to their side, without you knowing.

"Who's next?" says Porter.

Not even the chicks say anything this time. All of them just stand
there watching Porter. A couple of them turn around. Start walking off.
You watch it spread. Watch more of them turn slow and start going off
like if they go quiet and casual enough you won't notice them. Like it's
their turn now to be a stain where a dog turd used to be.

"Take your fuckin' friend here," Porter says. "Take him home. Jesus
Christ. What the fuck's wrong with you people."

One Saturday night at the Indigo a tall blond haired woman in high
heels and a sleek red dress comes across the dance floor. It's January.
You're lucky this time of year to have a steady gig. You're getting ready
to play again, your last set, Jimmy tuning his bass against Santos tuning
his guitar, Eddie lapping at his reed to get it wet again, Robbie adjusting
his cymbals.

She touches your hand. It's you she wants. She's older. Where she
puts her head in the column of light from a spotlight her hair is this
fierce coarse wiry blond that comes off her scalp in brittle shimmering
waves down to her freckled shoulders and the thin straps of her red
dress. Where the spotlight grazes her face it turns her skin translucent.
The shadows it cuts are brutal and make her face look ravaged. There's
this hope in her smile that makes you wish you were already playing.
Playing so you wouldn't have to talk to her. Because the hope scares
you. Because you can see how beautiful she was. Because you can tell
that what she's hoping for is for nobody to hurt her.

"You know," she says.

You stare at her. "Know what?"

In one of her hands is a folded dollar bill that you watch her slip into
the wine glass on Jimmy's amp.

"You just know," she says. Then she says, "I can tell."

"Okay," you say. And while you stand there, her smile turns a shade more serious, and she takes her hand and puts her palm and fingers up along your cheek.

"You don't know it yet," she says. "But you know."

"Okay."

"When you're done playing," she asks, "can I see you?"

You don't say anything. She smiles.

"Just for a minute," she says. "I have something for you."

You say okay. And then she lets your hand go, takes her face out of the savage light, turns away, goes back across the floor, then disappears in the dark recess past the bar where the tables are. Jimmy steps up.

"Who was that?" he says.

"I don't know," you tell him.

"You sure?"

"Yeah. How should I?"

It's never made sense to you to introduce the band at the end. Like saying hello when you're saying goodbye. After the last song of your last set, after you've introduced Santos and Jimmy and Eddie and Robbie, she's there, waiting on the dance floor off the stage while you take your mouthpiece out and put away your trumpet. This time she's wearing a long black shiny coat over her red dress.

"I'll be right back," you tell Santos.

You don't wait for him to look up and see what's going on. On your way off the stage you hear him say to take your time. The woman hears it too and smiles.

"Come with me," she says. "Just for a minute. Please. Get your coat. It's cold."

She leads you to the door. At one in the morning State Street has barely started winding down. While you hold the door for her a white Corvette and a dark blue pickup truck go hammering past wide open. The raw noise makes her wince as she steps outside. While the noise recedes down the block and the street returns to the normal flow of its steel and rubber current she takes you across the parking lot to an old Ford sedan in the corner. In the deceptive yellow parking lot light you can't make out the color. But the paint is faded and hazed and blistered off in places down to primer. She unlocks the back door on the passenger side. It groans when she pulls it open. When the dome light bathes the interior you're startled at what it illuminates.

Clothes. Books. Magazines. A green plastic radio. Shoes. Record albums. A cardboard box half full of plates and silverware. A frying pan. Sheets and blankets. Photographs and pictures in painted frames. A toaster. The whole back seat and the passenger seat up front are piled to the window sills with stuff that belongs in closets and drawers and cabinets and on walls and counters and in rooms. The only open seat is the driver's. Everything she owns. You feel like you're looking inside her life. You look away. She crouches down at the open door, reaches her hands into the pile, starts groping for something deep inside it. You hold the door and look out at State and watch a cop drive past in a convoy of suddenly obedient cars. You glance down at her brittle hair and look away again. She finds what she's looking for. Works it out from deep inside the pile. Gets up and has it in her hands. A lamp. Small and ornate with a stained glass shade. She pulls the rest of the cord free from the pile, straightens the shade, holds the lamp out to you. Some of her hair has come loose into her forehead.

"This," she says. "This is for you."

"I can't take it," you say. "It's too nice. You should keep it."

She laughs lightly. "Where would I keep it? On the dashboard?" And then she says, "It's for you. I want you to have it. Please."

She tosses her head to clear her face of hair. Away from the spotlight, out here in the cold, in the gentler bath of the yellow light across her face, it's easier to see that there was a time when she was beautiful, beautiful like Mrs. Harding, and everybody knew it.

"Don't you live somewhere?"

She smiles. "Don't worry about me," she says.

Shame turns your face hot and makes you glance away. There are other questions. Why you. If she lives in her car. Where she came from. If she's even from Salt Lake. Who did this. Who did what you're looking at.

"I'm sorry," you say.

"Don't be. Please. Just take it. It's a gift. I heard you play Someone to Watch over Me. I enjoyed the way you played it. That's all. I'm not looking for anything." And then she says, "I'm just saying thank you."

When you take it out of her hands she smiles and puts her hands together. It's heavy for its size. You hold it up where the yellow light gives you a better look at the glass facets of its shade. You can't tell what colors the facets are. But you can see the carved bronze of its base.

"It's beautiful," you say. If she's heard you play here before. If she'll come here again so you can ask her what she'd like to hear. "Thank you."

"It's not a magic lamp or anything," she says. "It's just a lamp. It's really pretty when it's on. Red and green and gold and blue. You could keep it on your nightstand."

Why she makes you think of Mrs. Harding when Mrs. Harding's hair was dark when she was young. If she sings.

"Thank you."

Out on State Street there's the splitting explosive crackle of a big engine being revved through the unmuffled throats of its straight exhaust pipes. A wince goes through her face again. Where she'll be going when she leaves here.

She looks at the lamp in your hands. Then at you.

"I'm so glad you took it. Thank you for playing." She closes the door. The light goes out on everything she owns. "Good night."

CHAPTER 30

RIDING HOME sometimes, home to Bountiful in Robbie's panel truck from playing, in Quigley's Hudson from fighting some nameless kids you'd never recognize in daylight, in Porter's Mercury or Snook's Chevy from seeing some girls you know in some other town, in Yenchik's Ford or West's Pontiac or even Doby's Impala from dragging State, you look out the window and suddenly there it is, out there in the dark, this deep nervous fear that things are going too fast. Like you're leaving things behind you haven't ended. Like you're outrunning things you need to stop and wait for. You don't know why. You just feel it. This dark and anxious mystery of fear, deep in the back of your head where you can't reach it to understand it, in your shoulders, down in the bottom of your stomach. You're doing everything they want, everything you're taught, and there's this fear, and the closest you can come to understanding it is that you're moving through things too fast to give them time to be forgiven, that you're leaving things behind that you haven't been forgiven for.

"I got it figured out," Quigley says one night.

You're in his Hudson, coming south down Highway 89, home from seeing a couple of girls you met in Brigham City, the windows up, the heater going, the radio on, the resonant even rumble of the 7X engine through the steelpack mufflers in the floor.

"What?"

"There's three kinds of girls."

"Yeah?"

"Yeah. First, there's the kind that won't talk to you. Period. No matter what."

"Okay."

"Then there's the kind that won't talk to you unless you talk to them first."

From out of nowhere Linda. Like something you just saw come into the headlights, the sudden blur of an animal in the smeared current of the highway, you turn away, toward the window at the passing dark out through the glass.

"What's the third kind?" you say.

"The kind that will."

"Like Bonnie North."

"That's my kind," says Quigley.

Through the windshield of the Hudson you can see the black truss-work of sticks that form the rickety hills of the roller coaster at Lagoon. Home. You're almost there. You used to ride your bike this far. Molly. What kind she'll be. The look on her face when she looks at other girls. Not jealous. Not lonely. Not sad. Just through a window hungry.

"There's a fourth kind," you tell Quigley.

"What?"

Home to Bountiful. At the top of the hill when Quigley turns onto your street you'll see the porchlight on and feel the night go ugly in your stomach. You'll go inside. And there she'll be. It's never like the first time. It doesn't need to be. She doesn't need to say it. Just stand there and you'll know. The pulse of the tires on the joints of the concrete highway makes you crazy. The radio makes no sense. Your fist clenches. Wrings itself in the dark against the door panel.

"I don't know," you tell Quigley. "Just sometimes wish."

The night at Olympus High, after the blond guy gets his fingers mangled, after two of his friends get him to his feet, after his knuckles fall off his fingers and chime when they hit the asphalt, you ride away in Porter's Mercury, between Porter and Snook, your feet on the hump of the tranny, your knees up, the radio set to KNAK smack in front of you, Sam Cooke doing Chain Gang from behind the speaker grill. Wasatch Boulevard. The long boulevard that snakes along the foothills of the East Bench up above the length of the city, the city quiet from here, this vast quiet wilderness of light that hovers like the surface of a night ocean on the pitch black nowhere of the valley.

Snook's got a Pall Mall going, keeping it next to the small wing window, cracked to suck the smoke out and let him tap the ashes off. A fancy coffee shop and restaurant place goes by. Kids inside the windows in their booths with their bottomless allowances. Kids out front with cups and cigarettes not bothering to look around at the rumble of the Mercury's laker pipes. Two chicks in their cheerleader outfits.

Olympus lost. South won. Bountiful wasn't even playing. What were you doing there besides looking for someone you didn't know to hurt, someone you didn't know to hurt you back, hurt you with something real, something you could take and show a doctor. It hurts good. Chain Gang ends. The radio goes to the Everly Brothers doing Cathy's Clown. Under the skin of the simple melody you can hear the moving bones of its simple chords.

"You didn't wanna take State?" Snook finally saying.

"Naw," Porter saying, looking to his left, through his window, down at the lighted city, back at the windshield. "The scenic route tonight."

Snook taking a hit off his Pall Mall.

"We get his right hand?" he says.

"Who?" says Porter.

"The kid with the fuckin' knucks," says Snook.

You've had him on your mind too, since you left Olympus, since Porter headed his Mercury up Thirty-Ninth South, toward the mountains, instead of down into the city to see what was happening on State. The long wail you've never heard come out of someone human. Infinite. A river. If he played piano. Suddenly sick of trying to hide it from your band, from how you play, from Mr. Selby when your mouth gets hurt, from your mother when there's blood. You watch the road. Keep your breath shallow in the sour smoke of Snook's Pall Mall breath.

"Yeah," says Porter. "His right."

"Gonna have to learn to jack off with his left one," Snook says.

"Or have his chick do it."

"Or one of his faggot buddies."

Traffic merging onto the boulevard now off the highway out of the open mouth of Parley's Canyon. Wasatch Boulevard changing to Foothill Drive. Cathy's Clown ending. The radio going into Teen Angel.

"This song makes me fuckin' wanna puke my lungs inside out," says Snook, after the first few measures.

"Yeah," says Porter.

"His girl gettin' killed by a fuckin' train. Cuz she goes back for his fuckin' school ring. He thinks it's something to sing about."

"Yeah."

"Them finding his ring in her fuckin' hand."

"Turn it down if you want."

Snook reaches across your knees, takes the volume knob, turns it down to nothing, sits back and hits his Pall Mall again.

"Clutched in her fingers tight," Snook says. "Sounds like he's about to puke himself, the way he fuckin' sings it."

"Yeah," says Porter.

"The guy gets her out of the car and then lets her go back. What the fuck. Just lets her go back knowin' a train's comin' at her. He can't stop her? He's crippled? He should fuckin' kill himself. Not sing about it."

"It's just a song," says Porter. "Nobody died."

"Know what I wanna know?" Snook saying. "I wanna know where they found her fuckin' hand."

"Yeah?"

"Yeah. I mean, they found his ring in her fingers, but where'd they find her hand? She had to be scattered all over hell."

"It's a song," Porter has to say again.

"Hey Tauffler," says Snook. "What's with you?"

"Just thinking," you say.

"About what?" says Porter.

About doing this. How it doesn't get more stupid. How this is it.

"You guys jumping in," you say. "Thanks."

"Shoulda got there sooner," says Porter.

"Soon enough," you say. "Any later, I'd be selling my trumpet."

"Yeah," says Porter. "He was going for your mouth."

Snook reaching forward, putting the butt of his Pall Mall in the open crack of the wing window, letting the wind take it.

"Good fuckin' reason not to play one," he says.

"Anyway," you say, "I'm done."

Snook looks around. "Done what?"

"What we just did."

"What?" he says. "Fight?"

"What'd we do it for?"

Snook turns and looks out the windshield like the answer's out there in the headlights.

"The hell of it," he finally says.

"Too many of 'em are just for the hell of it."

The light green where the road from Emigration Canyon comes down across Foothill Drive. Porter cruising the Mercury through the crossfire of headlights waiting. Following the long downhill bend of Foothill past Fort Douglas and the signs for the University and then down into the streets beneath the lighted surface of the city.

"That song's gotta be done by now," says Porter.

"Yeah," says Snook. "Turn it back up."

That month you quit your job at Servus Drug. You're tired of riding your bike, negotiating rides, giving one or another waitress a buck for gas for a ride home, working with the belly of your teeshirt always soaked and cold from washing pots and pans and spraying food off plates before racking them for the dishwasher. Tired of working a job your father says builds character. Tired of learning what he calls humility from cleaning up for kids you have to see at school. You're making more money playing anyway. Frank the soda jerk shakes your hand. Dolores lights up a cigarette. Old Gladys gets tears in her big wrinkled eyes and takes your face in her thick soft waitress hands and kisses you. You've told her fifty times when you're playing at the Indigo. Her and Tom have never made it. As spring comes on, and business follows it, it isn't long before you're playing elsewhere, old places like The Sojourner, The Crow's Nest, The Staircase, Club Manhattan, new places out in the valley towns, north and south along the mountains, out on the desert again. Tom and Gladys. A couple of times you thought you saw them dancing. But they turned out to be other people.

"Are you going anywhere tonight?"

"I don't think so."

"Can I borrow the Valiant?"

"Why? Where do you plan on going?"

"There's a concert at the University."

"On a Thursday?"

"Just a small one. In the Music Building."

"Why haven't I heard about it?"

"Nobody has. My teacher told me about it."

"You can't get a ride with someone?"

"Nobody I know's going."

"Then why are you?"

At the head of State Street, waiting at the red light under the Eagle Gate Monument, sometimes it's the Impala or the Ford or Pontiac, the Hudson or Snook's Chevy, the engine loping at a restless idle, the fractured rumbling raw through the long steel throats and flared tips of the scavenger pipes under the rear axle. Tonight it's you. You in his driver's seat. Your hands on his steering wheel. Your gas in his engine. It's only Thursday, but through his windshield, the long moving aqueduct of red and white opposing light of State Street is out there. The carloads of Mormon kids who venture out for a look. How easy they are to spot. Their eyes round, their faces like they're at the zoo, their cars borrowed, trying to understand what it's like to have a thousand wives, enough wives to populate a planet, here to see what State Street has to offer. Tonight it's your eyes. Your face. Your father's Valiant wagon. No Utah Symphony concert. Just the woman in the red dress with her face in the light from the spotlight.

You know.

No I don't.

You know. You just don't know it yet.

Just you tonight. When all you know is why you're here at the light at Eagle Gate with State Street out ahead of you. You're here to look for her. The light goes green. Not find her. Just to look for her.

CHAPTER 31

ONE SATURDAY in March, down to weeks away from graduation, you wake up to the smell of something in the weather. Not where you catch for that one first day the smell of spring. That day's already come. Today it's something mean. Out your bedroom window you see it in the color of the sky. Pale blue stained the weak yellow of poisoned tea. Your father's out there, on the high side of the yard, pulling the shark-toothed rake through the yellow grass, raking out the deep suffocating winter dinge so the yard can come back to life in April. A job that's yours. From the line of dead gray grass that trails in a long and shaggy tail from the curb across the yard to where he's raking, you can tell he's been out there a while, done maybe thirty feet. One of the garbage cans is out there, to haul the grass out back, dump it in the field. You dress, pull on a sweater, take a pee, catch the smell of the smoke from the club last night when you get your hair straight with your fingers, run out the door.

"Sorry."

He's wearing a long-sleeved flannel shirt. His face is ridged and sweating.

"I had a few minutes to kill before leaving for the office."

"Let me have the rake."

The smooth stick of the handle warm where you take it.

"The gloves too?"

"Sure."

Warm and soft and baggy on your hands. He uses a flannel sleeve to wipe his forehead.

"What time is it?" he says.

"Almost nine."

"Yes. I have to go, by golly."

"You have to work all day?"

"I should be home by early afternoon."

"Okay."

You pick up where he left off, thrust the rake hard into the grass, pull low to keep the teeth deep, feel the dead and knotted stuff let go, then pull it through the patch again until the teeth pull easy. Move to the left and start another patch. The garage door opens. The Valiant backs up the driveway. You wave. Go on raking. The sky keeps its stain of poison yellow when the pale sun crests the mountains. This could be it. The kind of storm West's been waiting for. You're supposed to do some jamming with the band this afternoon at Robbie's. You'll have to see. You take your sweater off. Across the circle, on his porch, Woody Stone's got his head turned up, his hand to his forehead like he's saluting someone in the sky. Nicky Bird's laying out a tarp around her mailbox post.

Not long and you're hungry. Your mother should be up, browning slices of Cream of Wheat from the batch she made last night and put in the fridge to get stiff enough to slice and fry. You lay down the rake, drop your father's gloves, grab your sweater, head for the door. When you get there you can hear it. Your mother screaming. Too weak with the door closed to travel out across the circle and get Woody Stone and Nicky Bird looking. Someone crying. Molly. When you open the door the noise comes out around you like heat from a furnace door. You close it quick behind you.

Roy's in the living room with his scared face looking down the hallway. You can make your mother out down by her bedroom door. Her back to you. And just past her your brother Karl.

"Yah! Teach her to wet her bed! Teach her!"

And on the floor, in her nightgown, Molly, curled up, and it's then that you get that the two of them are kicking her. You let it happen. Throw your mother out of the way against the wall, step over Molly, take Karl off his feet back into your mother's room, slam him on his back, come down on him.

"Are you fucking nuts!"

He tries to scuttle out from under you. You slam down your hold. His fingers look for your eyes. You get your knees on his arms. He tries to claw your ankles. You slap him one across his face. Hard as you can.

"Are you fucking nuts!"

He bucks and twists underneath you. His legs fish like crazy for your head. This crazy fear and crazy hate in his face like he'd have to kill you to get rid of it. One of his groping hands finds a high-heeled shoe and swings the point of the heel at your face. You're way ahead. Rip it loose. Throw it out of reach. Crack him across the face again with your open hand.

"Your sister! Jesus Christ!"

Behind you Molly crying, your mother shrieking, clawing your tee-shirt, pulling your hair. You swing an arm around, hit her somewhere, hear her yelp, feel her go. Take another slap at the scared fierce nasty hate in Karl's face where it's trapped between your knees while his hands grope the floor for anything to hurt you with. You smell ammonia. Molly. Feel a crack across your back, hard and sharp and hot, across your shoulders, a familiar crack that lets you know your mother's gone and got her rugbeater. "There!" The side of your head. "There!" You can hear the spit. "There!" You let it happen. The hunger to slap the meanness off the face between your knees, every doll whose hair he's ripped off, every paper angel whose feet he's torched, every nasty look he's ever used to wither and crush his sister, every scowling sneering thing he's ever said to take the light out of her eyes.

When he finally knows enough to guard his face you stop. The rugbeater keeps going. "There!" Karl cracks his hands back off his face to see. "There!" Still hate, but he's looking up past you, at your mother, and he's more scared than anything.

"Your sister. For god's sake."

He looks at you. Tries one last sneer. You crack him quick across the mouth and then there's nothing there but shock. And then pain races like electricity from your scalp down through the bones in your ears into your neck. "There!" You raise your hand. "There!" Pain races from your fingers down your arm and turns your crotch to ice and fire together. You jump up, spin around, yank the rugbeater out of her hands while she cowers back, her arms up, her mouth open, caught off guard too quick to howl.

"This fucking thing!"

You brace the rugbeater across your knee, yank hard, and the bamboo twists of the handle splinter. Fibers still hold it together. But it's useless now as a broken leg when you bring it up and hold the dangling bamboo pretzel in front of her.

"Try it now!"

Her eyes shift. What hits your head feels like a pickaxe. You spin around. See the high-heeled shoe in his hand again. You grab the shoe and shove the fractured handle of the rugbeater into his stomach. He grabs the handle. You put your knee into his crotch. He lets everything go. Your mother's on your back again, slapping you, shrieking.

"So! What is going on here!"

The boom of your father's voice like a bomb in the hallway.

"Harold! Stop him! He wants to kill his brother!"

You glare at Karl. He looks at you bewildered, out of breath, like you didn't know his crotch was off limits. You drop the shoe and rugbeater. Turn around. Your father comes around your mother.

"Now! Tell me what's going on!"

"They had Molly on the floor. Kicking her."

"That is a lie! Liar! Pfui!"

"I saw you. You know it."

"That's enough!" your father shouts. "Why aren't you outside raking?"

"I came in for breakfast."

"Yah! He came in to hurt his brother! See! See how Karl's face is red!"

"He was kicking Molly around. So were you."

"Is this true, Karl?" your father says.

"Leave him alone! He did nothing! He was helping me!"

"Helping you what?" Your father turns to her. In the crowded hallway it makes you sick to hear his back teeth going.

"To discipline Molly! Because you weren't here to do your job!"

"My job is to support this family! And this is what happens when I leave! Three children in the basement crying—"

"—Because of him!" Your mother wheels her look on you again.

"You started this!"

"You liar!"

"You know it! You're the liar!"

"Let me have him!" Trying to reach around your father's head. Her fingers scratching the air. Your father's face wild.

"A Priest doesn't call his mother a liar!"

"Yah! Tell him, Harold!"

"Hush, Mother! Now! Everybody settle down!"

"Yah, Harold. He pushed me! He didn't care if he hurt me! His own mother!"

"You tried to hit your mother?" he asks.

"I took the rugbeater away from her. That's all."

"Yah! Look what he did to it! Now I have to send away to Switzerland for—"

"So you can keep beating the shit out of your kids?"

"So!" your father yells. "I won't have that language!"

"What do you expect from a liar!"

"Let's get to the bottom of this," he says. "Let's go ask Molly."

"No. Leave her alone. She's scared enough."

"Yah! Because you terrified her! Beating up her brother!"

"Hush, Mother!" Your father turns to you again. "All that Molly has to do is tell us the truth. Why should that scare her?"

"Because she knows they'll take it out on her."

"Oh, Harold, I wish I had never given birth to him."

"What will they do to her?"

Your father asking you. His face so close you can smell the still fresh smell of toothpaste. And there it is. The small almost laughing turn in his attitude toward ridicule.

"They'll figure it out. You know they will."

"Maybe you're the one who's afraid. Of what Molly will tell us."

"You're not gonna ask her."

"Don't tell me what I can and can't do with my own children."

"You're not asking her!"

"We're going to ask her! But first you're going to apologize to your mother."

"Apologize."

"For pushing her. For hitting her."

You look at him. "You're crazy."

"Apologize to her."

"She can pick shit with the chickens."

"So! Now apologize!"

"You want an apology?" You look at him hard enough to see things take a stumble in his eyes. "You got it." You look over his shoulder at her. "I'm sorry you're—"

The doorbell stops your father cold. Thunder in his head. While it goes through its eight little turnaround chimes you watch fear flood the hate off your mother's face.

"Oh, Harold."

"Wait here."

Your father turns and heads for the living room. You hear the door pull open.

"Why, Mr. West!" Your father's booming and jolly voice. "To what do we owe this pleasure?"

West. To take his Pontiac to the sandpit.

"What is he doing here?" your mother whispers.

"We had plans," you say.

Her eyes go blank like she's lost you. Then she smiles, turns, shapes her hair while she heads up the hallway.

"Yeah, my dad's home for a couple of weeks," you hear West say.

"He's a lucky guy, by golly," your father laughs. "I have to keep my nose to the grindstone. In fact, I'm just on my way out the door. Please tell them hello for me."

"Hello, Bobby," your mother says. "How are you?"

"I'm fine, Sister Tauffler, thanks." He looks at you. "You ready?"

"Yeah."

Your mother looks at you, and the look is hesitant, fretful, across a distance she knows she can't cross. "But don't you have to finish the yard?"

"There's a storm coming. It's gonna be here any minute."

"Ah." Clutching her throat.

"I'll get the tools cleaned up."

"Yes, Shakli."

"Okay then," your father says. "Let me get what I had to come back home for."

CHAPTER 32

RAIN. THE WAY your geography teacher back in eighth grade said it always came. From the west, hundreds of miles across the desert with nothing in its way, riding a wind that ran unresisted ahead of it, a wind that since California and all the way across Nevada swept salt and dirt up off the desert floor and raised it high to feed it to the clouds. And then it hits the Rockies, the only thing for hundreds of miles in its way, and the Rockies turn it back into itself in hard-edged currents that are fierce and hard enough to lift dirt off the hills and pit the windows of houses. And then the clouds come in behind the wind, butt up against the wall of the Rockies too, too heavy with water and salt and dirt to lift up over them, and so they stay, stay and get crowded in, and then it rains. And the salt and the dirt in the rain is what leaves all the cars white when the clouds have rained themselves out enough to lift up and over the Rockies and let the sun come out again.

You're up here for the wind. From the ridge of the sandpit you stand next to West and watch. Watch the clouds come in across Skull Valley. A high gray solid wall of them just coming off the desert. Behind you, out on the floor of the sandpit, his Pontiac is parked and ready, ready to have its yellow and white paint blasted so he can get State Farm to paint it metallic green. He's got the spinners off to keep them from getting pitted. Just the black rims. He didn't take the bumpers off, or the other chrome, because State Farm would have wondered why the paint underneath where they were was pitted too. And then they would have figured everything out. So West has to take his chances with what the wind and dirt will do to the chrome.

"This is gonna be good," he says.

"Think so?"

"Yeah."

You can see the wind before it reaches you in the charged and dirty yellow light it gives the air above the valley. Then you start to feel it.

Gusts begin to slap your teeshirt around. Dirt starts to lift around your legs and tear away in quick and crazy twisters from the ridge around you. You've been here before, practicing, in the sandpit and well up the side of the hill above it, your back to the wind to keep the dirt out of your trumpet. You watch the clouds as they start to move into the valley. The way they sense the barrier of the Rockies just ahead of them. Watch them start sending their long thin crooked stilts of lightning down to the valley floor like the feelers and legs of mile-high insects. The crack and then the rumbling tail of their thunder. Gray sheets of rain start falling through the poison yellow light in places out across the valley.

"Let's go," says West.

"Give it more time."

The sandpit. Where you played soldiers and cowboys and indians and cops and robbers. Where you fried beetles with magnifying glasses and shot Blackwell's rifle at the big steel hoppers for the whanging sound of the ricochet. Where you learned how to play your trumpet. You know how the dirt can sting. You know it better than West. The way it behaves in a windstorm.

"Why's the side of your face so red?" says West.

You're thinking of Karl. You used to play up here with him.

"It is?"

"I'll say. Like fuckin' welted."

"Guess I slept on it funny."

"Looks like you slept on a stove," he says.

He turns again to look out across the valley. You watch his trimmed hair bristle in the wind.

"What're you gonna tell State Farm?" you say.

"I got caught driving in a sandstorm."

"Like they're gonna believe that."

"It's not like I'll be lying."

"You're parked, man. You're not driving."

"Close enough."

And from where you're standing on the ridge you can see the circle of houses where you live, the tar and gravel roof of your house, the yard behind it with the clothesline, the incinerator barrel and the field. You look out across the valley again.

"How about now?" says West. "This shit's blowing."

"Nope."

And a few minutes later the wind is finally where it needs to be, hard enough to send you sailing and slogging down off the ridge through sand up to your ankles, out across the harder dirt of the sandpit floor toward the Pontiac. West takes the driver's side. The wind comes from everywhere, an invisible circle of big rich kids around you, wheeling you around, shoving you back and forth, hurling dirt in your face.

"Throw it up in the air," yells West. "Along the sides."

"Get back farther," you yell. "Give it room to pick up speed."

And then you're on your knees in the blinding dirt, scraping it up with both hands, hurling it into the air. In the dirty howl of the wind you can hear this sifting noise, this fizzing noise, and take it for the sound dirt makes when it's cutting paint. You keep going, crabbing back and forth, scraping dirt up off the ground, sending it blind to do its job along the door and fenders, around the back. Dirt whips around inside your teeshirt and crawls up your pants legs. You keep going. Through thunder starting to explode around you now. Through the first fat stinging drops of dirty rain.

"That's it, man," you hear West yell. "Let's get outta here."

And then the rain is pelting you, exploding in dark wet pocks on the dirt, spattering the Pontiac. You jump in and slam the door. West starts the engine, pulls the Pontiac into gear, fishtails out across the dirt toward the road, the little cardboard pine tree dancing off his radio knob. He turns the wipers on. The first few strokes leave a rainbow film of thin white mud before the rain starts really coming down.

"You really think your paint job's gone?"

"Not gone, man, just pitted." And then he says, "I can't live with that."

He swings the Pontiac onto the paved road out of the sandpit. The rain turns the roof into a metal drum.

"Save it for State Farm," you say.

"I'm supposed to be happy with it. That's their job."

"To make you happy."

"Yep."

"When do we take all the chrome off again?"

"Soon as State Farm okays the claim."

And then you're coming down the hill and turning left and then right into the circle. Rain makes the asphalt glisten, black and alive, like it's swarming with a million drowning black grasshoppers. Your house. The yellow grass you were raking dark. The concrete path to the porch shining. The stubbed and naked branches of your father's rosebushes black. Karl. Molly. Roy. Maggie. Getting through a Saturday afternoon that will end at five o'clock with hot dogs sliced into a steel pot of dark gold lentils. Your house. Your stronghold of a house where nothing is ever finished and nothing heals. Where you'll sit there in this hard and festering anger with your bowl of lentils and little wheels of hot dog slices and still smell polish on your fingers from the family of everyone's polished shoes lined up on the floor in front of the washing machine for church tomorrow.

"You waiting for it to let up?" you hear West say.

The wipers whacking back and forth. The Pontiac parked idling at the curb. West with his foot on the brake pedal. You remember Karl saying he liked drums. The mean uncertainty in his scared face when you told him about the rattlesnake in the mouth of the cave.

"I need a favor."

"Sure."

"A ride over to Robbie's."

"Your drummer?"

"Yeah. Let me grab my trumpet first."

"You guys playing tonight?"

"Yeah. Later."

"Where at?"

"The Indigo."

"On State?"

"Yeah."

"I gotta get one of those underage cards."

"You still couldn't get in."

"How come?"

"You need to have a job there."

"You don't have one."

"Yeah I do. I play. I'll be right out."

You run the distance to the front door. You're dripping when you get inside. Your mother comes out of the kitchen.

"So, Shakli." Her voice flat and melancholy like she's had to forgive you for something again. "You are home."

"Just to get my trumpet."

"Where are you going?"

"To practice."

You head for the room just past yours where Molly and Maggie sleep. Your mother follows you. On the rug between their beds your sisters have their painted tin saucers and teacups arranged between them. Maggie looks up happy. Molly guarded. You wonder who they're pretending they are. With your mother there, her attitude still riding a razor's edge, you know you can't ask them.

"How you guys doing?"

"Okay," says Molly, but her watchful eyes look past you, then down again.

"Good," you say. "I'll see you for supper."

"Okay."

You leave your mother standing there. Head into your room. Grab your trumpet case. She's waiting when you come back out.

"Where are you going now?"

"To find Karl."

"Why do you need to find Karl?"

You reach the stairs. She's behind you.

"Just something."

And then she's behind you down the stairs. Karl's stretched out with his pillow and blanket the length of the naugahyde couch. The sound of gunshots and an orchestra of hard-driving violins comes from the tv set. Roy's watching from the Navajo rug on the floor. He's got his pillow and blanket too.

"What're you guys watching?"

When Karl doesn't move, Roy rolls half over, looks at you, behind you at your mother, at Karl, back at you.

"Some cowboy movie," he says. And then he says, "Just waiting for Larry."

Larry Rowley. His buddy. The freckled kid he races bikes with in the dirt track in the weeds back in the field where you showed him how to race a couple of years ago. Like you and Blackwell used to.

"He's coming over?"

The orchestra doing the movie explodes in a tantrum of dizzy violins and horns and kettle drums. You put up your hand to Roy to let him know to wait it out.

"He's coming over?" you say again.

"Yeah. When the storm stops."

"Cool." Then you say, "How about you?"

Karl gives it a minute to see if there's someone else in the room you could be talking to. You wait for him. Knowing he's got no friends except maybe the one whose mother takes the two of them to school and back.

"What?" he finally says.

"You doing anything?" you say.

"Nope."

Still his brushoff attitude. But you can tell he's rattled and scared and doesn't know what to think or do about what happened.

"Wanna come to a jam session?"

"Look out." Your mother moves forward, comes even with you, and you can hear her hurried breath. "He could be tricking you."

"Sure. I'm gonna take him out in a field and kill him."

"What's a jam session?" he says.

"My band. We just play. Try new stuff. Come see for yourself."

"Don't trust him," your mother says sharply.

"You sure?" Karl says.

"Yeah," you say. "You can play the congas."

"What're they?"

"These huge bongo drums. They make you feel like a midget. We'll show you."

"Where's it at?"

"My drummer's house."

He gets up off the couch. Looks at your trumpet case.

"How we getting there?"

"West."

"Am I dressed okay?"

Standing there in a plaid sport shirt and blue corduroy jeans.

"Yeah. Get your shoes on."

"When will you be home?"

You look at your mother. She's riding that edge again where things could turn and go screeching off the other way. But you can tell she's done. It's used up for today.

"For supper."

"But I have to do my grocery shopping this afternoon."

"Papa can take you when he gets home."

"But how will you get home? If Bobby takes you—"

"I said we'll be back for supper."

"You have a home of your own, Shakli."

You wait for this sudden crack of thunder to let go of the house and chase off through the ending rain.

"I'll do the shoes when I get back."

CHAPTER 33

KARL RIDES between you and West. The rain lets up. The roads go from glossy to damp. The overcast starts lifting. You can look down the valley and see where the clouds are rising like a receding inverted flood up the slopes of the mountains. Out west there's a thin line of blue. Karl looks back and forth across the dashboard, out the windows, his first ride in a car that isn't stock. Like you got with Linda, there's this feel of a life there next to you, in your trust, and when you listen close you can hear him breathing, away from the house, taking things in. Out in the valley, where two roads cross and there are fields more than there are houses, West pulls up to a stop sign. You can sense the worry come off your brother that you've tricked him. That maybe you've brought him out here to finish him off in the mud of a middle of nowhere field.

"Show him what you got," you tell West.

West looks at you and grins.

"Deal."

He takes a quick look both ways, more for cops than cars, slams the pedal, dumps the clutch, and on the damp asphalt the back tires break, hissing and squealing. Karl's head rocks back. His hands grab the lip of the seat. West hits second. The tires break again, and this time, West's working the wheel back and forth, keeping the Pontiac headed straight. You look at Karl. This small scared grin in his face now. West hits third. This time the tires hold but you've never come down this road this fast. Finally West lets off.

"Whaddaya think?" you say to Karl.

"Holy crap." And then he says, "How fast was that?"

"Crossed a hundred," West says.

"Miles an hour?" he says.

West laughs at the question. "Never gone that fast, huh?"

And then you're coming down Robbie's road. While West is dodging puddles, you're looking for Robbie's house, and then you're looking for his panel truck, and it's there, and Jimmy's Indian motorcycle too. No Eddie yet or Santos. West drops you off and heads home to see how good a job the dirt did. Karl follows you up the steps of the porch. Through the porch you can hear Jimmy and Robbie going at it down in the basement. Robbie's father opens the door with an Olympia in his hand and his flannel shirt open and red hair all over his white chest and stomach. He looks at Karl.

"Lemme guess," he says. "This is either Rattle or Roll."

"Naw. My brother Karl."

"Hi, Karl. Come on in."

You show Karl the stairs and follow him. Open the door at the bottom and nudge him through. Robbie sees you and stops. Jimmy looks at him, and then looks where he's looking, and then he stops too.

"Hey." he says. "Now we're talking."

"Saw your bike," you say. "You didn't ride it over in the storm, did you?"

"Naw. Got here before. You look like you got it, though."

"Yeah."

"Who's that?" Jimmy nods at Karl.

"My brother Karl."

"Hey, Karl."

"Hey there, Karl," says Robbie.

Karl just stands there, everything paralyzed but his eyes, busy darting around, taking in the room, the drums, the furniture, the old piano, Rosita on the wall.

"That's Robbie," you tell him. "That's Jimmy."

"You play anything?" says Jimmy.

"Sing?" says Robbie.

"Talk?" says Jimmy, smiling.

"Speak up," you tell him.

"I don't play anything," Karl finally says.

"Well, sit back, then," says Robbie.

You take your trumpet out. Set the case on the floor.

"I promised him a conga lesson," you say.

"Cool. Santos called. He'll be here in a while."

"How about Eddie?"

"Haven't heard."

"What were you guys doing?" you say.

"This new tune," says Robbie. "All the Things You Are. Know it?"

"What's it called?"

"All the Things You Are."

"No."

You slip the mouthpiece in and blow a couple of warmup scales.

"Here's the chart," says Jimmy.

You take the chart, hold it where Karl can read it too, while Robbie starts laying down a beat and Jimmy starts plucking his bass. You are the promised kiss of springtime that makes the lonely winter seem long. You hand the chart to Karl to hold, bring your trumpet up, bring the melody in. You are the breathless hush of evening that trembles on the brink of a lovely song. You stop just shy of the bridge.

"Nice."

"Ain't it," says Jimmy.

"You know what Eddie's gonna say when he sees it."

"Yeah. We need a singer."

"Fuck him," says Robbie. He looks quick at Karl. "Sorry. We got this sax player who keeps trying to turn us into a friggin' orchestra."

Karl just standing there. Still holding the chart for All the Things You Are. You take it out of his hand and set it on the nearest music stand.

"Oh, yeah," you say. "It's Karl's birthday."

"It's not my birthday."

"We missed the last one. This is makeup."

"Okay," says Jimmy.

Robbie gets it going. Jimmy comes in, and then you, and you play Happy Birthday straight the first time, and then go off where all there is left from the song are the changes. Karl doesn't move. Just stands there the whole time watching your band play, not looking you in the eye, just your instruments, until you finally bring it back and end it.

"Happy birthday, Karl!" Robbie yells, the way he does when you play it for someone at a gig, and does a flourish all over his drums and cymbals. Finally this guarded but helpless smile breaks through Karl's face, his eyes round, like the Mormon kids on State Street.

"Man," he says.

"Hey," says Jimmy. And gives him a little bow. "Happy birthday late. Or early."

"Thanks."

"Come here," says Robbie. "Let's get you goin' on these congas."

And then Karl's looking at you. Like for permission for something he's not supposed to have.

"Go on," you say.

"Over here," says Robbie. "Behind 'em."

"Go on."

You watch him cross the room and work his way in behind the congas where Robbie's waiting.

"Ever hear of Afro Cuban music?"

"No."

"Okay. Here's your basic three two clave."

"What?"

"Claw vay. It's just this simple rhythm. That's what they call it."

From across the room they're standing side by side, Robbie with his crazy black curly hair and his teeshirt, Karl with his short sleeved shirt tucked into his corduroy jeans, Robbie's face wide open, Karl's pinched and scowling, and there's that urge again, the dart of a lizard across the red surface of your heart.

"Okay. Two measures. The first one. Bop a two bop three a bop a. And then the second. One a bop a bop a four a. Okay? Hear that?"

"Sort of."

"Let's put 'em together. Bop a two bop three a bop a one a bop a bop a four a."

"Still sort of."

"Okay. It's a four four beat, but we're gonna use eight beats. Eight beats a measure. That'll make it easier. Okay?"

"Okay."

"So we'll go bop two three bop five six bop eight. And then one two bop four bop six seven eight. On the one and four and seven, and then the three and five. One four seven and then three five."

"Yeah."

"Take the other drum here. Hands like this. We'll play it together."

Karl lets Robbie put his hands right. You can see them trembling.

"Nothin' to be scared of," Robbie says. "We ain't in the Mormon Tabernacle Orchestra. Just my basement."

"Sorry."

"Relax. Watch my hands. Do what I do. Like this. Slow. Bop a da bop a da bop a da da bop a bop a da da. Good. Again. Bop a da bop a da bop a da da bop a bop a da da." He stops. "Okay. Hold on."

And then he's stepping behind Karl, reaching up, working the saddles between Karl's shoulders and neck, working down his arms, shaking him back and forth, and Karl's looking at you with this mix of being scared and being angry and in the middle helpless.

"Man. Stiff as a fuckin' scarecrow. You gotta loosen up, man. Start from your toes, up through your knees, your shoulders, down through your arms."

And then Robbie's back at Karl's side at the other conga. "Okay. No counting this time. Just feel it. Like this."

It takes him time. But soon he's matching Robbie, hit for hit, and soon his hits are harder, more confident, like the hollow thump of his conga matched to Robbie's is letting him know it's okay. And then Robbie starts easing up on his, until finally he's lifted his hands off the skin, and Karl's on his own, starting to lose it, looking doubtful now.

"Keep it going," Robbie says. "I'm gonna add some more rhythm. And then Jimmy's gonna come in. And then your brother. You just keep going. You're the rock. You're the foundation here. You quit, it's all gonna fall apart."

"Okay." Not taking his eyes off his hands or his concentration off the still fragile hold he's got on the rhythm.

"We're countin' on you."

Robbie gets on his stool. Uses a stick on the rim of a snare to play the beat with Karl till Karl's okay again. Then starts laying another rhythm on top. Soon he's adding his high hat, bringing his bass drum in, using his cymbals, knocking on his cowbell. You and Jimmy watch. Karl keeps going. He's got it. And then Robbie nods at Jimmy, and Jimmy puts his bass in, and Karl looks scared still, scared and mean about doing his part, more mean than scared now, daring the world to stop him, screw up his part, make him mess things up for the rest of you. You've got him off the hill again. Out of the mouth of the cave four years ago and away from the diamond rope of the rattlesnake you watched slither past your shoe. Your brother. Watching him now, your brother, you know. You wet your lips, get your trumpet up, wait for Jimmy to bring it around to one again to bring the line of the melody in.

Part 5

Soldier Boy

NOBODY'S TALKED about it much because all through high school it's been so far away, something out there, past the horizon, out past the curvature of things you cared about or could see, something you took for granted would come along and happen on its own, like growing pubic hair or going on a mission. Now, in the closing weeks of your senior year, it comes up more and more. Military service. What everyone plans to do. The Army. Wait to get drafted. Figure a way to get out of it. Sign up for the Air Force or Navy or Marines instead. Which one you should take care of first. Your service to your country or your mission. Either way, in the end, it was a tossup. Either way, when you added them together, it came out to at least four years. And then one day at school you get word about this deal the Army has. Recruiters are coming that night to talk to anyone who's interested.

You catch a ride with Keller in his Bugeye. They hold the meeting in a geography classroom with the usual roll of roll-down maps racked above the blackboard. Maybe thirty high school senior guys show up. Gus and Cleverly and Reinbeck and Korbuck and Mouse and Boon and Jackson and West and Quigley. Two men are there from the Army, in their thirties maybe, dressed in army fatigues, silver bars on their collars. Lieutenants. Bands of white cloth above their shirt pockets name them Borg and Tanner. The deal they put to you is the Army Reserve. You've never heard of it. Join the Reserve. You'll do six months active duty. Come home and do a weekend every month, and two weeks every year of summer camp, for another three and a half years. And then do four more years of inactive reserve where all you do is keep your uniform hung in your closet in case they have to call you up. Eight years total. But only half a year full time. Most all of the rest of it belongs to you and to what you want to do with it.

The recruiter named Lieutenant Borg is short, with a smooth tanned face and a blond crewcut, and his army fatigues are tailored and ironed to where they fit him like a lightly faded khaki paint job. He does most of the talking. He doesn't waste much time or motion. Just tells you flat out, not arrogant but with the attitude of a teacher who doesn't mind letting it show that he's smarter than all of you, that he's offering you the deal of your life and you'd be nuts to turn it down.

Without being tall, Lieutenant Tanner is taller, less meticulous, more easygoing, happier to be there, more in gear with you and your buddies. He brings up going on a mission. The time you'll serve on your mission, he says, will count off your four year stretch of inactive reserve. And then he lays a schedule out. Sign up now. Do your six months active duty out of high school. Be home for Christmas. Do a weekend a month at Fort Douglas and start knocking time off your active reserve while you're waiting for your mission call. Take some college while you're at it. Then go on your mission. Come home a returned missionary. Do three more years of summer camps and weekends and all you'll have left is a couple of years of inactive reserve. In the meantime you can live your life the way you want to. You take it from there. Get married in the Temple to the girl of your dreams. Pick up and finish college. Start the kingdom of your family. Die and become a god. Marry a thousand more women. Create and populate a planet somewhere in the universe.

"What if a war comes along?" says Gus.

"They'll use the Regular Army," he says. "The boys they've drafted. The Reserve is just in case they run out of boys like you to draft."

"That'd be a big war," says Reinbeck.

"That's right."

"So what if everyone took this deal?" says Quigley.

"What do you mean?"

"Signed up with you guys instead of getting drafted. There wouldn't be much left to draft."

"There's a limit on how many guys the Reserve can take," says Lieutenant Borg.

"What about Cuba?" says Cleverly.

"What about it?"

"President Kennedy's been talking about fighting Castro."

Lieutenant Borg smiles. "The Regular Army can take care of Cuba."

"What if Russia helps them?"

"Russia's not going to."

"Yeah? Khrushchev's pretty crazy."

"Don't worry," says Lieutenant Tanner. "That won't happen."

"What about that place in Asia?"

"You mean Vietnam?" Lieutenant Borg says. "That's nothing. That's not our war."

"We got soldiers there."

"They're not soldiers. They're advisors."

"What about the South?" says Quigley.

"Right," Lieutenant Tanner says. "South Vietnam. That's what we're talking about."

"No. Here. All the stuff the Negroes are doing. They've got soldiers down there."

"That's the National Guard."

They tell you the different kinds of jobs you can sign up for. Radio. Radar. Mechanics. Artillery. Cooking. Infantry. Not as many choices as the Regular Army has. No band for one. But one of the choices grabs you. Armor. Your hand goes up.

"Yes."

"Does armor mean tanks?"

"Yes," says Lieutenant Borg.

"We can sign up for tanks?"

Lieutenant Borg gives you this little smile. He's got you. He knows it. You don't care. He lets Lieutenant Tanner take your question.

"Absolutely."

"We get to shoot them?" says Keller.

"You'll get to do everything," says Lieutenant Tanner. "They'll be your babies."

"Drive them?" says Korbuck.

"Right into a ditch. And then back out again."

"Wait a minute," says Quigley.

"Yeah."

"You're gonna let us play around with tanks."

"They're weapons," says Lieutenant Borg. "We'll train you how to use them."

While you feel it catch on around the room, fire your buddies up, you remember the tank at the ranch, in the dirt and sagebrush of the junkyard along with the army trucks. The barrel was gone. So was the breech of the gun. So was the turret. Someone had taken the turret and left an iron crater in the iron center of the tank. There was a toothed ring all the way around the crater. The iron floor of the crater had given way to rust and dirt and weeds. In front, nested in the nose between the tracks, the hole where the driver sat, the levers he used to steer it, litter and busted bottles down around the pedals. When the meeting ends, you sign up, and Keller and West and Quigley and Gus and Korbuck and Boon and some other guys sign up along with you.

A tank. Who needs a car when you've got a tank that could crush any car you ever thought of wanting. This time it comes with a gun.

You get your physical done at Fort Douglas in one of the old brick buildings up on the hill above the University. The room is a regular old office room with filing cabinets and wooden desks and benches, a bank of gray lockers on one of the pale green walls, tall windows with crooked Venetian blinds. You sit on a bench in your shorts in front of the locker you hung your clothes in. The doctor who puts the stethoscope on your chest uses a round stool on little rubber swivel wheels. He takes a long look at you.

"I know you," he says.

He lifts the stethoscope off your chest. You look at him. An older man with small gray eyes behind round glasses with clear plastic frames, cheeks full of holes that look like they were made by nails, a forehead wrinkled like paper wadded and straightened back out, thin brown hair going gray. In the pocket of his shirt where his smock hangs open there's the torn top of a pack of cigarettes. He sits there thinking. You don't know if you're supposed to talk.

"Wait," he says. "You play trumpet."

"Yes Sir."

"The Officers' Club. You and some other kids."

"Yes Sir."

"There was that song you played." And he hums the opening notes while you catch the smell of warm meat and cigarette smoke on his breath. "Know that?"

Her eyes get gray and cloudy, you think. Then the rain begins to fall.

"Yes Sir. When Sunny Gets Blue."

"That's it." He snaps the fingers of his other hand. "God damn. I've been beating my brain to death, trying to remember."

He's moving the stethoscope around your chest again like he's playing checkers on your skin. "Like the wind that stirs the trees," he's singing, and then he's humming again, like he forgot the words from there. Wind that sets the leaves to swaying, you're thinking, like some violins are playing, wondering if you should tell him what they are.

"I used to play clarinet," he says.

"Yes Sir."

"Hold on here."

His forehead goes wrinkled like it's been wadded up again. He stops the stethoscope.

"We've got a little murmur there."

And then he's moving it around like a checker jumping everything again while you're wondering if it's the Holy Ghost he heard, its disapproving murmur, here in this Army office on this wooden bench in your underpants.

"No. I'm wrong. Just a truck or something."

"A truck?"

"Yeah. Outside somewhere." He raises his head and rears back off his stool. "Hey!" he hollers. "God dammit! Can somebody keep the windows fucking closed around here for a fucking change!"

And then he's moving the stethoscope across and up and down your back like he's jumping every checker on the other team. And hold her near when Sunny gets blue.

"Welcome to the Army," he says. "Breathe in. Okay. Out."

You graduate. Leave Bountiful High School to Karl, just out of his sophomore year, out from under your shadow when he heads back for his junior year this fall. You get your orders from the Army. You've got a month to kill. The other members of the international jazz ensemble known as How Should I Know graduate too. The drummer. The saxophonist. The bass player. The guitarist. Robbie keeps talking about joining the Navy because of all the foreign places he can play. Jimmy signs up for the National Guard because he doesn't want to get shipped out of Utah. Santos just figures he'll take his chances for now with the draft. Eddie's looking to get a deferment because he's got too many bones in his ankles. You'll be the first to go. You'll be going in July. Fort Ord in California for basic training. Then to Fort Knox in Kentucky for four months of armor training. Tank school.

You fill the time playing, all you can, because you can feel it moving, moving too fast, rushing past you out some passenger window while you play, and there's nothing you can do to slow it down because you're not the one who's driving. There's a new club down on Second South just off First West, Sammy's, where they open the stage on Tuesdays for jam sessions. Anyone who shows up with an instrument and knows how to play it can take a turn on stage. Most all the guys who come down and play are from the University. Since you quit Scouts, handed it off to Karl, you've got Tuesday night open. Usually it's you and Eddie and Santos who go to Sammy's. Robbie tries it once but he doesn't like using their drum set. For the first time you get to watch Eddie and Santos from the audience. See how they do with other musicians. See how you do with them.

At a table at Sammy's one night, you and Santos and Eddie, Santos drinking a Coke, you and Eddie water, a skinny guy on stage strumming a big acoustic guitar, howling some three-chord folk song for all he's worth, everyone else in the place talking.

"You taking your horn?" says Santos.

"It's the Army, man. I can't."

"They take musicians."

"If you sign up for two years, maybe."

"Get a bugle," says Eddie. "They use bugles."

"Six months, man," says Santos. "You won't play for shit."

"I'm taking my mouthpiece."

"Yeah," says Santos. "That could work."

CHAPTER 35

WHEN YOU'RE not playing, taking the money you earn and dividing it up after tithing between spending money and money for your mission, you knock off the few requirements you've still got left on your Duty to God Award. The big award. The exit award from the Aaronic Priesthood. The gateway to the Melchizedek Priesthood when they make you an Elder once you turn nineteen. You've been knocking off the requirements since you turned twelve. Given all your talks. Done all your Priesthood duties. Gone to all your meetings. Memorized everything they've asked you to. The Articles of Faith. The Ten Commandments. The blessings for the bread and water. Passages out of the Doctrine and Covenants. You've gone to the Stake Patriarch to receive your Patriarchal Blessing and have yourself adopted into the Tribe of Ephraim. Met with the Stake President, Dwight Christensen, for an interview. Taught Family Home Evening lessons to your family in the living room. Visited the hospital to see Sister Soderstrom when she had her stomach operation. Played at enough old folks homes to give your buddies each a bunch of them for their own requirement to visit the sick and elderly. Done a couple of bowling nights for the Priests. Learned how to bear your testimony in German.

Whatever they've asked. Whatever they've said you needed to do. It was just a thing of knowing what they wanted. You've set goals for yourself, and for every goal you've set, and then gone out and made, you've asked the questions you've been told to ask. How it would help you on your mission. How it would help prepare you for the Temple. How it would strengthen your testimony. How it would help you serve the Lord.

Every goal except one. One you take care of now. If you play an instrument, you're supposed to play it in church, at least once, to get your Duty to God Award. And so you get together with Sister Avery, who can sing like an opera singer with a country singer's appetite for ending each line on a little heartbreak of a yodel, and Sister Johansen, who plays the harp like she's got four arms and forty fingers, and work out an arrangement of a religious song you've heard your mother play and sing at home. He Walks with Me in the Garden. You get the okay from Sister Lake, the choir director, that the song is in keeping with the standards of the church. Iris Lake. Susan's mother. The girl you fell in and then out of love with and she never had a clue. Like a butterfly that landed on the back of her dress and stayed for three or four years and then took off again unnoticed.

You divvy the song up. First verse and chorus. Then a solo for harp. Second verse and chorus. Then a solo for trumpet. You write the trumpet solo out and help Sister Johansen do one for her harp. A simple string of notes and chords she can turn into a waterfall. You rehearse in Sister Avery's living room where all the furniture is western from the wagon wheel chandelier to the wood-framed couch and easy chairs. A painting of a tired cowboy on a tired horse hangs above the fireplace. You haul Sister Johansen's harp inside from her station wagon amazed by how light it is. How even the breeze the short distance from her wagon to the door gets this nervous little hum going in the strings.

You play in Sacrament Meeting. Sister Avery stands in front of the congregation and belts the song into the microphone like she's singing to the entire United States Navy wherever they're stationed around the world. You stand off to her right and let her go. Don't even try to put any phrasing in because Sister Johansen, over on the other side of Sister Avery, is playing like a rainstorm. The louder Sister Avery sings the harder Sister Johansen makes it rain. You have to look away and remember that you need this. You keep your solo simple, close to home, to where you don't scare anyone, because you know that's what they're listening for. For you to stray out of their reach. Sister Avery keeps breaking in. Can't follow the changes the way you taught her. Doesn't know where the song is. Stage fright. Each time she breaks back in, and catches on, she looks more mortified and sorry.

When your solo's done and the song comes back around, you make sure to put a closing sound on it that she can't miss. And then let Sister Avery and Sister Johansen bring the last verse and the chorus home. At the end, in the silence that washes across the astonished congregation, it gets awkward. You're in church. Sacrament Meeting. No applause allowed. You expect to see their hair blown back by the blast of Sister Avery's voice. Soaked from the rainstorm of Sister Johansen's harp. Nothing. Just astonished faces. Sister Avery and Sister Johansen look bewildered, not knowing what to do, naked as deer caught in the sudden glare of the silence. Sit down, you think. Just walk away and sit back down. They don't know how. You finally step forward, take in the congregation, hope you don't run across your father's eyes, extend your arm.

"Sister Judy Avery on vocals!"

She turns and looks at you confused and scared. Finds you smiling. Catches on. Turns back to the congregation and takes a deep country western bow. People start laughing.

"Sister Jill Johansen on harp!"

Sister Johansen revives, works her way out from behind her harp, stands up, takes a modest bow more like a curtsy. And now everyone's laughing. Because laughing is allowed when it's an evident joke and it meets the standards of the Church for laughing in a chapel. And then Sister Avery's putting out her arm toward you.

"Shake Tauffler on trumpet! Let's hear it for Shake, folks!"

And then, like a watermelon reaching the end of a silent freefall off the roof of a ten-story building, the place explodes. Everyone's clapping. Sister Avery's bowing like Miss America at a square dance festival. Sister Johansen stands there like a bashful big kid, grinning, her hand up to her mouth, like if her grin falls off her face she'll be ready to catch it. You can feel the loathing from Bishop Wacker behind you warm your back like sunlight. As you lift your trumpet high you can sense your father's eyes out in the congregation trying to get you to look into their crosshairs.

When you've checked off the last requirement, when you see Bishop Wacker for your interview for your Duty to God Award, he looks unhappy. You know why. There won't be anything he can find to keep from recommending you. He takes you through everything. Has you recite the Sixth Article of Faith. The Eighth Commandment. Verses 33 through 44 of Section 84 of the Doctrine and Covenants. Goes through your paperwork twice. Stares at signatures where you needed them and got them. Nothing's missing. Nothing on paper anyway.

"I don't see where you've spoken at a Stake Conference," Bishop Wacker says.

"It's in there." The little form you had the Stake President sign. "I was a Teacher. Seven minute talk. How a Teacher can always watch over the church."

Whatever else is missing is deep somewhere in the mystery in the back of your head. It can't be counted. Can't be used against you. Because it can't be reached. Because you've got the look locked down to where he can't see through it. He finds the form and looks at it like Dwight Christensen's signature will vanish if he just looks hard enough.

"Then that's it," he finally says.

If this is how he admits he lost a football game.

"Yep."

You watch him let a little meanness through his eyes. The way they draw this bead on you, harden, then rest there. Like you can do with a rifle when you know you've got your target cold. You let some through yourself. Because you've got him too. Go sell a Ford, you think. A used one. To your quarterback. To your wide receiver. A couple of Sundays later you're wearing it, your Duty to God Award, a lapel pin, a silver cattle skull the size of your thumbnail, in the right side lapel of your suit.

The last time you play at Sammy's you come off stage with your trumpet and take your usual place, next to a column out of the way of the tables and the bar, to watch the other musicians. You're not happy with how it went. The piano player got lost in your changes. You had to pull him like a trailer to where you finally had to uncouple him and take off on your own. You're clearing your spit valve into your handkerchief when a big Japanese guy with a sketchy black beard and little round spectacles without rims comes up and leans against the other side. You know who he is. You've seen him play. You can tell from the guys you've seen him play with, the guys he sits at tables with, that he's from the University. His hook for his sax hangs on a strap down off his neck. He's holding a mug of half-gone beer.

"All Blues," he says. "Nice. I heard what you were after."

"Thanks." And then you say, "You too."

"Thanks," he says. "You want a beer?"

"That's okay. Thanks."

"That big kid on sax. Calls himself Nails. He says you play together."

Nails. So Eddie's been telling people that's what his name is. He's been clipping them ever since the night you named the band and Santos asked him why he never clipped them. Robbie's been calling him Nails since he started clipping them. Nails Meservy. The other thing he's famous for is being the kid who threw up on his plane ride and quit the Aviation Club in high school.

"Yeah."

"You guys really still in high school?"

"We just got out."

"Coming to the U?"

"Yeah." And then you say, "In January."

"Look me up. My name's Art."

He's not from here. From his playing you'd say maybe California. He doesn't know. The woman whose face you saw in the heartless slash of the spotlight would know he doesn't know. He doesn't have to. He can just be a regular guy.

"I'm Shake."

"Shake?"

"Yeah."

"You think you're hot shit, don't you."

You look at the stage. A girl standing front and center in a black turtleneck sweater, long brown hair, microphone in her hand, waiting for the guy at the piano to finish messing around with the head to Embraceable You. Hot shit. You wonder if he's suddenly stupid enough to be looking for a fight. You look back at him.

"Not really," you say.

"Start thinking that way," he says. "You're good." And finally smiles.

"Thanks. Thanks, man."

You've never heard her before. But the piano stops and in the silence you look to the stage where she's standing with the microphone in her one hand and her other hand up under her hair along her neck.

"Embrace me."

She sings in just a whisper, just breath with the music inside it, and then she stops again, and looks down, and waits another minute.

"My sweet embraceable you."

And there it is again. Inside her breath the line of her musical voice floats out across the smoke-hazed room on a lone thread of pure silk that finds you. Just her. Just you. Not an orchestra of anonymous musicians with one eye on their music stands and the other eye on the conductor. Just her. Just for you. Not for a thousand other anonymous people in the Tabernacle where you feel lost to all the furious business on the stage. Just her and what's inside her. Just you and what's inside you that answers her.

"Embrace me."

The piano player lets her go again.

"My irreplaceable you."

And then joins in quiet underneath her voice. You stand there and watch her. She knows. So does he. And before you get to know them, you're gone, on a Trailways bus, out of the depot on West Temple where your father drops you off on his way to work. In the Valiant wagon, parked at the early morning curb, he tells you to always remember who you are.

"I will."

They told you to travel light. Pretty much just what you need to wear to get there. You take your mouthpiece with you through Skull Valley and the Salt Flats and then across the Nevada desert west.

CHAPTER 36

YOU GET ASSIGNED to a barracks, and a bunk inside the barracks, and issued all kinds of clothes that smell like turpentine and mothballs. You get a footlocker and an M1 rifle. For the second time in your life you watch a barber shear your hair away in rolling shelves and leave you with a mousie. That night, your first night at Fort Ord, in your stiff fatigues and unwrinkled combat boots, you take a table together in the mess hall with your trays, you and Gus and Keller and Quigley and West and Korbuck and Mouse, start joking around the way you always have. Real soldiers patrol the tables. Soldiers with stripes on their faded sleeves and the faded brims of their hats pulled down on their roving eyes.

This time it isn't just you with a mousie. This time it's your buddies too. Their tans run up their foreheads and then, where their scalps take over, their skin turns this death-hazed white where they all look sick. Ears like handles. Skull bumps that make their heads look like sacks of rocks. And then you get them started playing like they're lepers or polio victims or inmates in a nuthouse. In the middle of cackling back and forth across the table, all of a sudden there's this grim-faced soldier standing on the other side, right behind Keller, looking right at you, square and hard enough to shut you up. Keller's got his tongue stuck out the side of his mouth. Smacking his forehead with the back of his spoon. The soldier stands there calm while your buddies one by one catch on. And when he finally talks it's to you.

"Maybe if you used your mouth and hands to eat, soldier, we could close the mess hall before midnight."

"Yes Sir."

He stands there a minute longer. Until your face and ears go hot and you get it in your head to pick your knife and fork up. And then he turns and walks away. Still riding high on the spastic retarded leper you were playing, your buddies watching, you put your fork and knife back down, bring up both your hands in double birdies, send them winging at his back. Across the table Keller's face falls open horrified. Before you have time to wonder why, before you can bring your hands down, you're lifted by your armpits off your chair, your chair gets pulled away, and when you're let back down, on your feet, you're turned around, face to face with two of the most pissed off looking soldiers you've ever seen.

That night, after the bugle plays taps on the loudspeakers, you report to the back door of the mess hall and tell this mountain of a Negro cook smoking a cigarette outside that you're there to scrub his garbage cans with a toothbrush. He gets you a toothbrush and a can of Ajax and shows you where the hose and the garbage cans are.

"What you so fuckin' happy about?" he says.

"Cuz I'm not dead, Sir."

"Why?"

"I made an obscene gesture, Sir."

"Flip the bird?"

"Yes Sir."

"Who'd you git?"

"This soldier in the dining room."

"One a them orderlies?"

"I guess."

He looks at you. You hear this quick burst of sound from deep inside his chest.

"You got balls, kid. Lemme tell ya."

You don't say anything.

"They mean motherfuckers. But ain't nobody gonna kill ya over flippin' a bird."

You get to work. Think about the garbage cans at home, half the size of these, and the big brush you get to use to scrub them. Think about the last time you double birdied somone. Think about the Jeep when it went rolling over. Think about what Doby would say about the power in your finger now. Glad you've still got the hands you need to get twenty or thirty cans scrubbed clean. Around you, except for a high security light here and there, insects doing their death dance with the naked bulb over the back door, Fort Ord goes quiet and dark. You run tunes through your head. You think about your balls. You're down to four cans left when a soldier comes out of the dark and takes on form at the edge of the light from the door bulb. From his stripes you know he's a sergeant. On the wet cement platform off the back of the kitchen you jump to your feet and salute him.

"Time to quit, son."

"I'm not done, Sir."

"I'm not an officer, son. Don't salute me. I'm not a sir, either. I'm a sergeant."

"Yes Sir, Sergeant."

"Yes Sergeant," he says. "Now let's go. It's three in the god damned morning."

"I'm not done."

"I'm saying you're done."

"I know. I just don't want anyone to—"

"I'll tell 'em. Don't worry. Now git."

"What should I do with the toothbrush?"

"I see about twenty garbage cans. Pick one to throw it in."

At breakfast, the soldier you birdied is patrolling the mess hall again, hands behind his back, head roving. You eat your scrambled eggs in silence. Your buddies are quiet too. You wonder if he knows you left the last four cans. If he knows you were ordered to. When he catches your eye from a couple of tables away you glance down quick. And then something you saw there makes you look back up. He's still looking. He gives you just enough of a wink so that nobody else will know. And then goes back to patrolling the tables.

And so you learn the first lesson the Army has to teach you. Not that if you fuck up you get punished. But that once you've paid for it you're done. It's over. No residue. No buildup of dark reproach in the back of your head where it can't be reached. At home you could follow every commandment they threw at you and still never feel like you'd done enough. Never feel finished. Never feel released. Here it happens every time you finish doing something. Done. Released at the end of every day. And then you love the Army. Then you're on your way.

You start to learn the rest of what the Army has to teach you. At reveille every morning, lined up with guys from everywhere, you're one of them, just another guy, here from scratch. Here at the same starting point. Here with the same sick looking mousie. Here in the same fatigues and combat boots and field jacket. Here with the same big M1 rifle. All of you come from somewhere. And so it doesn't matter where you come from. All of you have a past. And so it doesn't matter what yours is. All of you did your hair a certain way. And now it's gone. All of you take a dump with your elbows on your knees and your boxer shorts around your ankles, so it doesn't matter if you're in the open, on a throne in a row of twenty thrones, lined up with nineteen other guys.

You love the rules. The way they're in the open where you know them well enough to follow them. And from there the rest is easy. It's just you. Not a churchhouse full of the men of your father's army. Not

Bishop Wacker. Not the look. Not the buildup of unforgiven things you can't slow down enough to be forgiven for. Nobody here knows your father. No iron sky. No white haired old faceless man in a suit and no stale shit smell where his face should be. Just you, from scratch, like every other guy.

You take hold of it for everything you're worth. Calisthenics. Rifle practice. Hand-to-hand combat. Obstacle courses. Full gear marches. Bayonet training. Running in formation along the rolling two lane roads around the fort through the morning fog from the ocean singing marching songs that would turn your father's ears to salt. If I die on the Russian front, bury me with a Russian cunt! Inoculations from airguns that leave trails of blood down your arms. Guard duty. Kitchen police. Everything they throw at you. You ride to the ranges in the covered beds of big trucks like the ones in the junkyard in La Sal whose dashboards you gutted of their instruments. Every time your fatigues come back from the laundry they're a shade more faded. A shade less green. I don't know but I been told, Eskimo pussy is mighty cold! On the roads around the fort, station wagons drive past, mothers rolling the windows up to protect their kids. At night, released to be themselves, the guys in the barracks start to fall into their ways. Play cards and checkers, read magazines, keep journals, write letters, tool wallets out of leather. You start to bring your mouthpiece out. Outside the barracks after taps with a guy who plays harmonica. Late at night on the head. On guard duty, by yourself, patrolling some parking lot or the perimeters of the mess hall and other buildings in the dark. Wherever you've got the time and nobody around to bother.

You start getting letters from your father. Out of hundreds you've seen or heard him type, on the big electric Royal in his den, the only thing he's ever typed for you was the note with the scripture warning you not to be a hypocrite when your mother gave you back your trumpet for your birthday back when you turned twelve. For the first time now you've got a different address. And for the first time you're treated to the amazing stuff you never knew he was writing. Stuff he's been writing for years. Stuff you can see him thinking up and phrasing between his bursts of keystrokes. The seamless weave of personal anecdote and scriptural counsel. The sense of speeches. The sense of words you'd read in a magazine or book. The sense that it might be meant that way because in the end it feels like the letter a model father would write to a model son. One comes every week, in a big manila envelope taped and double tied with string, filled with things to read. The Church News. The Improvement Era. Other church publications. Brochures about the First Vision and Temple Square and the Tabernacle Choir. Leaflets of The Spoken Word. Clippings from newspapers talking Salt

Lake City up as the greatest place on Earth to live and get an education and raise a family, clippings that leave you feeling uneasy, like you're a runaway, like he has to coax you back, like it isn't the place you already call home. Typed quotes from the Church Authorities. A reminder to find where the fort holds Mormon services and attend them. You know you should. But you're here from scratch.

For the first time you're face to face with Negroes. From Saint Louis and Los Angeles and Detroit and Omaha. All you've seen them in are photographs. You see them now in the barracks and the showers. It never struck you they'd be brown all over, all the way down, round and round, or that the palms of their hands and the soles of their feet would be this honey pink. You train with them on the rifle ranges and obstacle courses and practice fields. You eat and laugh and play cards with them and wash windows and polish floors and clean latrines and do kitchen police with them. You're captivated by the way they look at things. You have to keep telling yourself not all of them are musicians. One of them is Jeff Taylor, a cool looking guy a couple of years older, a couple of inches taller, more filled out and beefy than you are. He's from San Jose. Regular Army. Going for Airborne the way his father and his uncles did in Korea and World War II. After you're done with basic training he'll head for Fort Bragg while you head for Knox. He teaches you how to use deodorant pads to put a mirror shine on the hard black toes of your boots. You teach him how to aim and think about something else while he's squeezing the trigger to keep from expecting the shot and jerking his aim off target. He teaches you how to work Barbasol into your face and use a razor. You teach him how to take butter after doing pots and pans and work it into his hands to cool down the burning from the soap. He steers you away from the misfits. He teaches you what it feels like to be a little brother. Late one night you're in the head, sitting on one of the thrones practicing, when he shows up in his shorts to take a late night leak.

"Mouthpiece?" he says from the trough.

"Yeah."

"Trumpet? Trombone?"

"Trumpet."

"Hey. You don't need to hide it from me. What kind of stuff you play?"

"Mostly jazz."

"Hey. Me too. Bass and congas."

"No shit. We had congas in our band."

"Congas in Utah?"

"Our guitar player had 'em."

From then on most of what you talk is music. All the guys whose re-cords you grew up playing to. Your band. His family. Most of his rela-tives musicians. One weekend in August he invites you to his house in San Jose. His family's having a barbecue. A big one. Early on Saturday you catch a Greyhound north together.

"You brought your mouthpiece, right?"

"Always."

"Got my Uncle Paul bringin' his old horn."

"We gonna play?"

"Hell yeah."

"How many people're gonna be there?"

"Shit. You're scared."

"No I'm not."

"Sure you are, man."

"They know I'm white?"

"I don't recall saying."

CHAPTER 37

HIS FATHER Bill's a mechanic. His mother Bernice teaches second grade. Jeff loans you one of his Hawaiian shirts. There must be a hundred people there. Most all of them Negro like the negative of a photograph of the church barbecues back home. It's the first time you've seen a fifty-five gallon drum, turned on its side and cut in half, hinged like a casket, placed on a four-legged stand of angle iron, and filled with briquettes. The first time you've seen a turkey get barbecued. The first time you've seen a turkey and it hasn't been Thanksgiving. The first time you've eaten turkey in a back yard and tasted oysters in the stuffing and seen so many bowls and dishes full of different food. Ham. Pork roasts. Big bowls of dark beans. Macaroni and cheese. Sweet potatoes. Collard greens. The first time you've had to ask what the dishes are. The first time you've seen Negro men and women kiss. The first time you've sat on a picnic table bench and seen, across all the food on the table, the way sunlight brings out the deep and luminous sheen of rose-colored honey in the brown skin of a girl's face and arms and shoulders. The first time you've heard and watched your name spoken in the frame of a Negro girl's voice and smile.

"Shake."

"Yeah."

"Are you serious?"

When she gives you this skeptical smile where the sunlight gets to them you wonder if you've ever seen whiter teeth.

"Yep." You smile too. "What's yours?"

But she's not done with yours yet.

"What kind of a name is Shake?"

"My kind," you say.

And now she looks at you with her mouth pursed up like you're the last guy on earth she'd ever trust with even a lollipop stick she was looking to throw away.

"So what's yours?" you say.

You watch her decide if she should even keep talking to you. Watch her face give in and then her hand reach out to touch the petals of a big pink flower in a glass of water on the table.

"Cissy." And then she says, "With a C."

"Nice name."

"It's okay, I guess. Better than Priscilla."

Cissy. Jeff's little sister. Just out of high school like you. The baby of the family. You remember Jeff telling you that after his sister was born his mother couldn't have another kid. She's dressed in a pure white top and shorts with a wide ribbon of blazing white cloth tied across her lush hair. Everywhere you look, everywhere you expect to see white blue-veined skin, everywhere she's exposed, her skin is this rose-colored honey brown that celebrates the sunlight. Her stomach and back and shoulders and arms. Her legs and the backs of her knees. The veined backs of her hands and the tops of her feet. Everywhere. But it's her bright and frank and easy smile. It's the quick grace in the way she moves her lean hands, sits up with her head back and moves her arms and hands when someone calls for sweet potato pie from another table. It's how her big dark eyes don't dither about letting you know what she's feeling. It's how you watch across the yard while she holds the gathered and laughing circle of her five tall uncles captive with some story you'd give anything to hear. Her five big Airborne uncles who parachuted into Europe and Korea.

Garbage cans get filled with paper plates. Coffee goes around. The call starts going out for music. Jeff brings out his congas. Two other guys haul a couple of snares and some cymbals into the yard and set them up on a patch of bricks in a fenced back corner. Extension cords get run from the house across the grass. Guitars and amps come out. One of her uncles plays trombone. Two more get out their harmonicas. Another one his sax. Uncle Paul brings you a battered old trumpet case.

"Jeffy tells me you know what this thing is."

He's got this easy light musical mischief in his laugh after he says it.

"What you got in here?" you say. "Howdy Doody?"

"Howdy Doody," he says. "Heh heh."

He stands there while you open it. The way it lies inside in its worn velvet cradle takes you back to the first time you opened your own. The feel and heft of its pipes to the way you've done this every day for years. You look for the make engraved in the bell. Olds. You slide your mouthpiece into the tarnished pipe. Check the valves and slides. Light and quick and oiled. Run a quick riff there in the sunlight. Astonished to hear the sound, full and clean and huge, after weeks of the insect buzz of your mouthpiece.

"Yeah," says Uncle Paul. "Look like Jeffy was right."

Jeff comes wandering over while Uncle Paul goes ambling back across the yard toward his folding chair.

"Okay?" he says.

"Okay, Jeffy," you say.

"Make that the last time you call me that," he says.

"I'm gonna sit out for now. See what you guys are up to."

"The hell you are. Come on."

Blues. Standards. Gospel. Soul. Latin. Neighbors line the chainlink fences that separate the yards. Some come around and join the party. Women take their shoes off and pull their men along and dance in their nylons or barefoot in the grass. Kids dance with themselves in circles. One of Jeff's aunts sings Amazing Grace. Another woman gets up and sings Ain't Misbehavin. A little girl sings Soldier Boy. And on and on. A white guy, a neighbor from somewhere, shows up with a cooler full of Budweiser and wine, with a flute, and then you're playing off him too. And then Jeff's father is hollering from his folding chair.

"Cissy! Git up there and sing!"

From where she's been dancing in the grass with her sandals off, with a little kid in a red shirt and black bow tie, she lets go of his hands, lets her shoulders fall.

"Aw, Daddy."

"Come on! You know the one!"

And then people are turned her way and clapping and calling her on.

"Daddy, don't you ever get tired of that old song?"

"No, baby! You know I wore that record through to the other side! Only way I got left to hear it now is you!"

"All right. Just once, though. Okay?"

"You do it once," he says, "I'll let you know."

And then she's making her way toward where you're playing, watching the extension cords in the grass, taking the microphone the guy on rhythm guitar is holding out to her.

"Key of D!" her father yells. "D major!"

"We know, Pop," says Jeff. He's got his bass on now. Working on tuning one of the strings.

"She sings low now!"

"Yeah, Pop. Like we never done this before."

Then Cissy turns toward the guys in this loose makeshift cobbled-together band that plays so full of open room.

"I want him to do the intro," she says. "Just him."

Everybody nods. The guy on sax does a little head bow your way. Then Cissy looks at you.

"That okay?"

"Yeah. D. Right?"

"That's it."

"One more question."

"What?"

"What's the song?"

She's looking at you amazed. And then everyone in the band starts laughing.

"Pop, you old fool!" Jeff yells. "You make a request, you gotta tell them the song, not just the damn key!"

"Shoot," his father says. "Everybody knows that song! Only one I ever ask for!"

"Since I Fell for You," says Cissy.

"Got it," you say.

You let her turn back around to where you're looking at the way her white cloth headband pulls the soft furiously curled roots of her black hair up off her smooth brown neck. It's her turn, not yours, her uncle's horn, and so you play the intro that way, someone there just to announce her, while her body picks up the beat she's imagining. At the end of your intro, she brings up the microphone, and the snares come in, and Jeff, and then the guy on rhythm, and then you're only there to lay in some phrasing when the song lets her breathe. She does it through once. And then she lets the microphone down, and turns, and she's looking at you, smiling, letting you know she's handing you the song. Jeff's bringing the bass line around to one again. The guy on the congas is doing a turnaround. You've already thought of some places you'll take her, places far away, places you'll know how to get her home from, home to where you can set her down gently again in front of her mother and father, gently and untouched. Trust me, you think, giving her smile back, because we're going places, and you know she will.

Things finally wind down. Not that you or anybody else is out of music. But the sun's down low on the tile roofs and the tops of the palm trees and there's cleaning up to do and leftovers to package up. You blow Uncle Paul's horn out one last time. Slip your mouthpiece out and put it back in your pocket. Take out the slides to shake them clear of your spit. Put the trumpet back in its case and take it over to where he's talking to one of Jeff's other uncles with a can of Budweiser in his hand. He sees you coming. Makes his eyes big and his face scared. Starts backing away.

"Don't you bring that devil horn over here!" he says. "You keep it away from me!"

"What?"

"You put the devil in that horn, boy!" he says. "You can't give it back now!"

You stop. Jeff's other big uncle just stands there grinning. So you start toward Uncle Paul again with his trumpet case. He turns around, starts this scared little bent-kneed scamper across the grass away from you, hands going like these little paddles at the ends of his long arms, looking back over his shoulder scared.

"I mean it!" he's saying. "Don't you come near me with that devil horn! You keep it! That horn all yours, boy!"

When he's maybe twenty feet away, sees you've stopped and you're laughing, he stops too, turns around.

"You heard that, Mont!" he calls back to the big uncle he was talking to. "You heard him put the devil in that horn! Tell me I'm wrong!"

"Nope." Uncle Mont shaking his head and grinning. "He did! Boy's good!" And then he looks at you and brings his can of Budweiser up an inch or two in a salute.

"Thanks," you say.

"I told you!" Uncle Paul says. "That horn's done! It's got the devil all through it!"

"Lemme have it," Uncle Mont says, laughing. "I'll see he gets it back okay." And then he says to Uncle Paul, "I think he blew the devil right out of it. Right out the end!"

That night, after the yard gets cleared and the garbage cans filled and all the relatives and friends sent off with their trays and bowls washed and with wrapped packages of leftovers, you and Jeff and his mother and father ease back in a circle of low-slung lawn chairs in the yard. Cissy's gone to her cousin's house. The residual smell and heat of the barbecue drum occasionally wash your way. Paper lanterns hang glowing in the night air. All the army stories have been told. How Jeff taught you to shave. How you taught Jeff to use butter for his hands. Jeff and his father each hold a can of Pabst Blue Ribbon. You and Jeff's mother hold tall glass tumblers of iced Pepsi. The cold tumbler leaves a wet circle in your pants where you're resting it on your leg. You listen to insects grind out their high relentless hankering.

"I'm sending you back with some Cornhuskers," Jeff's mother says. "Real lotion. Butter's for cooking."

Jeff sits there. Contemplating bringing a bottle of hand lotion into the barracks where a sergeant will find it in his footlocker. You can already hear the nicknames.

"Thanks, Ma."

Sitting there still feeling how alive the yard was all afternoon. Thinking back to the barbecues around your own neighborhood where your neighbors stood and sat around not doing much but talking or throwing or kicking a ball around. Not eating much but hot dogs and burgers and potato or macaroni salad. Hawaiian punch. Wishing you could be there now to give them some new ideas. You listen to the whisper of one car and then a second cruise past the front of the house. Listen to Jeff's father start the conversation off again.

"Cissy gonna be stayin' over Stella's tonight?" Jeff's father says.

"She might. You know how those two are when they get together."

"Too bad. I think our guest here woulda liked the company."

"Bill!"

"I seen how he looked at her. And she was lookin' too."

You figure you were probably obvious. The way your eyes kept coming back to her. The way you always knew where she was. No matter how hard you worked to hide it. But the other thing. That she was obvious too. That she even cared. That she'd even look at you like that. That one never crossed your mind. And now you look at it as just her father's thing. Something he couldn't be more wrong about if she was here to tell him.

"Go on, now," her mother says. "You're embarrassing the boy."

"What's there to be embarrassed? They young."

"You're impossible."

"Shucks. Makes me wish I was Mormon."

"What?"

"You know. Them harems. All them wives."

You bring the tumbler up, take a long sip off the top of the Pepsi, leave the glass there against your bottom lip, let your top one rest on the liquid chill of a floating cube of ice.

"That's ridiculous, Bill."

"No it ain't. Cissy could be head wife. That's good!"

"Oh, hush, Bill!"

CHAPTER 38

AND LATE that night, Jeff and his mother fold out the Early American couch in the family room, make up a bed for you. Jeff's mother leaves a towel and washcloth on the armrest. Jeff hangs a short sleeved dress shirt on a hanger on the doorknob. The next morning, wearing a shirt of Jeff's for the second day, walking to church with the family, you follow Cissy's mint green Sunday dress along a sidewalk of one-story stucco houses painted pink and pastel blue and white and landscaped with palm trees and the thick dark leaves of desert plants. Her mother's got a Bible and a hymn book. Her father's wearing a brown hat. Along the way somewhere Cissy drops back to where you and Jeff are bringing up the rear. You walk on the strip of grass along the curb to give her room between you.

"So," she says. "What'd you think?"

What she put into it when she sang. You made me leave my happy home. You knew from yesterday it was maybe the happiest home you'd ever seen. One she'd never have to leave. But the way she sang it was like she'd been made to burn it to the ground along with everyone she loved and everything she owned for love. You remember watching her father, the way he kept poking her mother in the side with his elbow, pointing at her, nodding, like the song was about him, like it was her who made him leave his happy home, her the reason he had such misery and pain, her the reason he got the blues most every night. But that was just what you were watching. What you heard was how she knew the song. What she did with it. How she knew what was possible in every word and every chord change. How she could turn her voice from heartbreak to anger to hope to desolation and back and always stay in the lamentation of the melody, still in love, still the hope there. How she turned to you with her head down and then lifted her face when she was done. How you knew she wanted you to solo. How you knew your solo had to do what she'd just done. How she stood there and watched you play it through except when her eyes would close. You detour into the street to get around a fire hydrant.

"Nice," you say.

How you don't know what else to say without giving her or Jeff some reason to think you're after her.

"Just nice," she says. And looks down at her white Sunday shoes and where she's putting them on the sidewalk.

"Who's your favorite singer?" you say.

"Smokey Robinson," she says. And looks at you like she's daring you to know him.

"Shop Around," you say. "I meant female."

"Mary Wells," she says. And now she really looks at you.

"The One Who Really Loves You."

And now she looks impressed.

"Better than her," you say.

"What? Me?"

"Yep."

This time she's looking down with this big pleased helpless smile where she tries to keep her lips from coming open.

"Who's your favorite trumpet player?" she finally says.

"I'd have to say me."

And now she turns her face toward you and brings up her fist and gives your arm a slug so quick you just have to let it happen.

"If you were that conceited, you wouldn't be that good."

"That hurt."

"Miles Davis," she says.

"Okay," you say.

"Better than him."

You sit in a pew next to Jeff and listen to the choir sing Nearer My God to Thee. You watch Cissy sing in her turquoise robe. You listen until you can isolate her voice. The minister's a gaunt Negro in a white robe a lot like the one you wore for graduation. He tells the story you've heard in Sunday School about Jesus keeping the crowd from stoning the prostitute. You glance at the faces around you. They're nodding. You see the same devout attention to the minister's words that you've always seen in your father's Sunday face since as early as you can remember.

After church you eat a turkey sandwich Jeff's mother makes and help yourself to some collard greens and macaroni and cheese and wash it down with a tumbler of iced lemonade. After lunch Jeff and his father take you out to the one-car garage where they're keeping Jeff's yellow 58 Bel Air. They show you the tri-carb setup and other engine stuff they've done. Jeff fires it up to where the floor's about to open and the roof's about to blow off and his father stands there listening for engine things inside all the revving thunder like his ears are stethoscopes. That night, when his father drives you and Jeff to the depot for the ride back to Ord, Cissy comes along.

On the Greyhound, next to the chattering window, the steady complaining growl of the engine in your ears and the hard metal sill against your shoulder, you rock and sway with the bus as it grinds and lumbers and bucks its way through the outskirts of San Jose to the freeway. Jeff takes the bottle of Cornhuskers lotion out of his gym bag and puts it up in the overhead luggage rack.

"Someone'll give it a good home," he says.

"Yeah."

Jeff smiles, says, "Sorry, Ma. I'll stick with butter."

And then nestles back into his seat, stretches his feet out under the seat ahead of him, folds his arms across his chest.

"Wake me up when we get to Ord."

In the dark of the bus you feel his head touch lightly and in the buoyant and accidental way of sleep on your shoulder now and then. You just ride. Ride with your eyes open and with this nervous hunger for your own family in your chest and let whatever comes go past the window. The questions don't stop turning. The lights of neighborhoods you'll never know pass like armies of tiny comets across the glass. There are no answers. There are only the questions and the hunger pangs they leave. A small explosion of yellow light comes off the ceiling of the bus a few seats up ahead. You smell a cigarette. You look at the window again. What her father said. And she was lookin' too. What her mother said to him. You're impossible. In the tea-colored overhead light from the aisle, on the flat hard surface of the glass, the window holds the image you know is your face, black where the light can't reach it, like coal where your mouth and nose and eyes are. You sit there listening to the turning growl of the engine somewhere back behind you.

CHAPTER 39

A WEEK LATER, the week before you finish basic training and get shipped across the country to Kentucky, your name gets called at mail call. It's an envelope with a card inside. Cissy Taylor and her address in handwriting you realize is hers. Thinking of you, the card says, and inside the card, there's a note and a wallet-sized photo of her face. Hi Soldier Boy. I never said how nice it was to meet you. I hope you're not getting sick on that Army food. Maybe Jeff can bring you to see me again sometime. Your friend Cissy. P.S. You can throw away the picture if you want. It's not the greatest. P.P.S. I have one of you already. My Aunt Milly took it when you weren't looking. P.P.P.S. But I could always use another one. P.P.P.P.S. This is getting silly. Tell my brother hi for me.

You sit there on the lid of your footlocker with her card and note and envelope and photo in your hands. Your heart pounding. Your head racing. You put the photo back inside the note, the note inside the card again, the card back in the envelope, the envelope in the pocket of your fatigue shirt. Walk out of the barracks. Keep walking, out across the yard where you form up for reveille and taps, out across the drill field, stop when you get to the fence for the yard where they keep the big trucks that haul you out to the rifle range. And then you stand there. Just stand there in the soft California sun with the breathtaking news of her handwriting and her photo in your pocket.

That night, after supper, you walk down to Jeff's bunk, where he's sitting on his locker in his teeshirt, shining up his belt buckle with Brasso and a cotton ball.

"Hey Jeffy."

He doesn't look up. Just stops what he's doing and puts his hands on his knees and looks down. And then starts turning his head slow back and forth.

"Cissy said to tell you hi."

And now he looks up. You take a seat on the locker at the end of the next bunk over.

"What?"

"Your sister says hi."

You sit there and watch his face go through what's going through his head. Watch this big grin move into his face like sunrise.

"No shit," he says.

"Yeah."

"She wrote you."

"Yeah."

"She took to you."

"I don't know."

"What'd she say?"

"She sent me a photo. Like a yearbook one."

"Hot damn. That little scamp. Right under my nose."

What she wants from you. What you're supposed to do back. Write her. What to say. How you'd be fine the way you've been all week with just this weekend dream of her. With just her memory. How you're supposed to deal with something you never even let yourself think could happen. What you should do with this fire inside your heart. Stuff you can't ask Jeff. From back behind his grin, from back inside his eyes, he's looking at you this whole new way, sizing you up, fitting you out for this different guy from what he's used to, maybe looking for what his sister saw.

"You gonna write her back?" he says.

"Is it okay?"

"You're asking me?"

"You're her brother."

"Yeah you're gonna write her back."

"Sorry."

"You're gonna send her a picture too."

"She said she's got one her aunt took."

"One with hair. One with your own shirt on. Get one from home."

"I got my army one. In my dress greens."

"Naw. She's not into that. One from home."

Who from. Not your mother or father. Not Karl. Maybe from the studio in Bountiful where they took your last yearbook photo. Maybe they've still got the negative. It hasn't been that long. Maybe Robbie or Jimmy could get them to make one up for you.

"Yeah." And then you can't help yourself. "You're sure."

"Sure what," says Jeff.

"Maybe she's just being friendly."

"Yeah," he says. "She's being friendly. About as friendly as she can get. What the hell's the matter with you?"

"Sorry."

"That's for sure. You're one sorry motherfucker. Now go write her back."

And so you tell her, on a sheet of stationery you get off a guy named Harkinson who owes you for showing him fifty times how to break his rifle down, how nice it was to meet her too. What a good time you had at the barbecue. How you meant what you said about Mary Wells. How you didn't know how bad the food in the Army was till all the food you tasted at the barbecue. How you want to send her a photo of you with hair. How you're shipping out in a week and there won't be time till you get to Knox. How she shouldn't write you back till you've sent her your Fort Knox address because you might not get it if she does. How Jeff says hi back. How she should tell her folks hello, and Uncle Paul, and Uncle Mont, and Aunt Milly, and the other people you remember.

And then you get to where you need to sign it. Soldier Boy, you think. Your Soldier Boy, maybe, and then you drop that idea like a rattlesnake you just pulled out from under a rock, and finally you just write Shake. And then you think that maybe you should have said Your Friend the way she did. Harkinson gives you another sheet of his stationery so you can write it over. You put the letter in for the mail that night. When you get to Fort Knox you'll give Robbie a call about getting you the photo.

The first letter you've ever written to a girl. And for the next four days you can see it in her hands, her face while she reads it, and you write it over again a thousand times, right in front of her eyes. The next time you hear Soldier Boy it's on a radio someone's playing in the barracks. You're on a ladder, using a ball of crushed newspaper to buff the streaks off the glass of one of the windows. Be my little soldier boy. You catch yourself at the smell of barbecued turkey, at the high voice of the little girl who sang it with her hair done in rows of tiny braids, at seeing Cissy watching from back in the yard with one of her aunts.

In the morning, two days ahead of you, Jeff will be shipping out for Fort Bragg. That night the two of you head for the PX. He takes a six-pack of Schlitz and brings it to the counter. Sorry, the guy at the counter says, no stripes, no beer. Jeff tells him it's his last night and he's going to Airborne School in the morning. The guy takes his money. The two of you climb the long rise up away from the barracks that levels out to another drill field and some windowless buildings scattered off to one end. Jeff carries the bag. From the top of the rise you're out of sight of the barracks. You're looking west. Not far enough to where you can see the ocean. But close enough to know that the smell in the air is salt from the water where the sun has started leaving the blazing red trail you can still remember rippling out toward the horizon from when your family all came to Disneyland.

You sit on the grass. Both of you tougher now from when you got here eight weeks ago. Both of your fatigues faded and broken in the way the soldiers had theirs the night you got lifted out of your chair. Both of you soldiers too. Your scalp tanned. Jeff uses his little pocket opener to cut two holes in the lid of a can of Schlitz. Hands it your way. You think about it. He knows you're Mormon. It won't be your first beer. You take it.

"Thanks."

And then you tell him the story about giving the soldier in the mess hall the double birdies and what happened afterward. He sits there laughing quietly, mostly smiling to himself, the way you do when you're looking back on something you've come to the end of.

"I heard about that," he says. "That was you?"

"Yeah."

And then he tells you how he showed up for reveille the first morning with his field jacket on inside out.

"That was you?"

"Yeah," he says.

"Go Airborne," you say.

"Go Armor," he says back.

You've never known what it is about beer. Half sour and fuzzy and foamy when you wash it back into your cheeks. Like half of it is air and the other half oatmeal. But it's cold and wet, and Jeff's last night at Ord, and you smack your cans together.

"Done with this place," he says.

"Right behind you."

"Down to day one. Packing tonight."

You've got two days left on your own eight-week calendar. Tomorrow night you'll be packing too.

"I got guard duty tonight," you say.

"Where?"

"Motor pool."

And then both of you sit there and contemplate the walk you've both done, around and around the dark perimeter of chainlink fence, guarding the Jeeps and trucks and other vehicles inside, keeping an eye out for communists coming out of the hills around Monterey Bay in this scary part of California.

"Talked to my folks this afternoon," he finally says.

You don't move. Just keep sitting there with your legs stretched out and your combat boots out there at the end of them.

"They doing okay?" you say.

"She got your letter," he says.

You wait. Finally look over at him and catch him squinting and smiling into the orange light of the low sun.

"What's it worth to you?" he says.

"You prick."

You watch him laugh. See his teeth in the sun the way you saw his sister's. He takes a slug off his beer and licks his top lip.

"I'm just asking," he says. "How bad you wanna know?"

"I already do. She threw it away."

"That what you wanted her to do?"

"That's just what she did."

He takes another minute.

"Pa says she's been impossible. Ma says she's got a grin she's worried might take surgery to get off."

Your heart comes up into your face. You sit there glad he's talking to the sun instead of you. Because he'd see your heart right there in your face. Beating so hard and wild you can't get your mouth down over your teeth for the third time in your life. The first time the night you got a band and first rode home from school in the back of Robbie's panel truck when it was still his father's. The second time when Summertime made the gym explode. Jeff sits there like he knows you need some privacy.

"She's got that picture Aunt Milly took up on the wall in her room," he says. "You playing Uncle Paul's trumpet. Wearing my shirt." He laughs. And now he turns and looks your way. "And that convict haircut."

You nod, smile, know you still look stupid, take yourself another slug of beer, try to hide everything behind your beer can and the hand that's holding it. He turns his face out west again.

"Soon as I get to Knox I'll get a picture," you say. "I told her."

"I hear she's counting the hours."

And then you sit there. Just sit there getting used to it. Cissy. Cissy and her family. Jeff takes another beer out of the bag, works it open, holds it your way.

"Ready?"

"Not yet."

He takes a couple of long drinks off the fresh can.

"I'm gonna miss you," he says. "Don't know the fuck why."

He reaches his can across. You bring yours up and slap it against his again.

"Me too."

"Just be careful," he says.

"You're the one who's gonna be jumping out of planes," you say.

He laughs. And then he says, "I mean with Cissy."

This quick rustle of fear in your chest that gets you looking at him a whole new way.

"Be careful how?"

He takes another drink. And then he says, "I don't want her hurt."

You sit up. Stare at him. "Are you fucking crazy? Hurt her?"

"Whoa. I never said you would. I said I didn't want her hurt."

"What the fuck are you saying?"

"Shit," he says. "I knew I was gonna screw this up."

"Shit what? Screw what up? I'd hurt her?"

"Shit, man," he says. "I got trouble knowing how to say this."

"What? Say what?"

He brings his knees up, puts his elbows on them, looks at his beer can like he's reading the label.

"What?" you say.

"Nothing." And then he says, "What your church says about us."

"About who?"

"About us people. Negroes. Black folk."

You just look down and let it happen. Let this wild convulsion of humiliation come flooding up like silt from the pool of everything you've learned. Let it set your face and ears on fire and swamp the air out of your chest and up your throat and leave you numb and clumsy with nothing you know you could say and the wet silver top of your beer can on the grass between your legs the only thing you can look at. Next to you, you can hear Jeff talking, and then there's his hand on your shoulder, but you can't hear what he's saying because he's too far away, because of everything roaring around inside you, and then his hand's gone too, because of everything inside you moving too hard and wild, and you just need time to ride it out, to where you can look at the silver top of your beer can, bring it up to your mouth, take a drink with your mouth to the hole Jeff knifed through the metal, where things are cold and hollow and still. How you could be so stupid. How you didn't even think about it. How you just went to their barbecue.

"You think that's how I think."

And when you don't hear anything you take a glance at Jeff and look away.

"Fuck no," he says.

"Fuck no what?"

"Fuck no you don't think that way."

"Then what the fuck," you say. You can hear it in your voice, this high shiver, all through you, how all the wild stuff inside you wants to take you off again.

"I didn't mean it," Jeff says. "Not that way."

"Then fucking how?"

"I know what you're supposed to believe," he finally says. "What they want you to believe about us."

Amazed that the sun can hang so perfectly still in the low sky out where you know the ocean is. How its heat on your face can be so even.

"You're saying I believe that."

"I'm saying they want you to."

"What do you want me to do."

"What do you mean?"

"With your sister."

"Jesus Christ," he says. Takes a deep breath.

"I'd never hurt her."

"Fuck, man, you think that's what I'm saying?"

"You're saying you don't want her hurt."

"She's right there. All you gotta do is reach out and take her. Get married. Have a hundred kids. Uncle Jeff. I'd like that. I'd love to have you in my family. I'd love you to live in San Jose with all of us." He goes quiet for a minute. Takes a quick slug off his beer. "I could use a brother. I'd love us to start a real band."

"But."

"But?"

"Yeah. There's a fucking but in there. I heard it."

"There's no but."

"Yeah there is."

"All right. Maybe this is it. I grew up with a Mormon kid. We ran track together in junior high and high school. We were best pals. Later on in high school he wanted to convert me. Wanted to get me baptized. I looked into it. I know what you're up against. All that stuff about us not fighting hard enough in some spirit war. Being chickenshit or whatever. Coming from Cain. I could look at it and laugh. But it had him. I could tell. It was all through him. There wasn't nothing he could do about it."

"There's nothing all through me."

"Just let me tell the story."

And then he sits there quiet for a minute.

"Nothing," you say.

"He used to swear up and down he wasn't prejudiced. Didn't have a prejudiced bone in his body. Said it was just the way it was. Like that spirit war where all of us were chickenshit was the truth. Said you can't be prejudiced when something's just the truth. I used to tell him maybe the truth isn't the truth. That's what always stopped him. Like I'd put a brick wall in front of him. He couldn't go no farther. The truth was the truth."

He takes the last slug off his beer. Holds the can out, upside down, shakes a dribble of foam out of it. Out of nowhere you smell the cigarette on the dark bus back from San Jose. You wait for him to reach for another can. But he sits there holding the empty and starts talking again.

"Then he went off on this mission. Like you're gonna do. Then he got back. I figured maybe we could pick up wherever we left off. While he was gone I did some college. I was working with my dad then. He used to come over and work with us sometimes. We could still joke around. Not like we used to. But some. I just had to watch my step. But he could look me in the eye, and in the same breath where he could tell me I was descended from Cain, he could tell me he wasn't prejudiced. Same fucking breath. I'd look him back in the eye and there'd just be this look there. Like the windows of a house where there's nothing home but the goldfish. Like I could've stood there and pulled faces at him all day long. Swore my head off at him."

You know the look. Just hearing Jeff describe it, you can feel it, this reflex, wanting to crawl into your face. Jeff brings the can up to his mouth. He gets that it's empty. Reaches into the bag for his third one. You take a slug off what's left of your first one.

"It scared me," he says. "What happened to him. It was like he was blind. Like I didn't matter. Like he didn't either. He came back with this smile. Like some blind people smile. I'd never seen it before. Not on him. It was always there. On his face. But it wasn't his."

You know the smile too.

"What happened to you guys?"

"He started in hard on me. How he had the Holy Ghost and wanted me to have it too. How he had this memorial or something—"

"Testimony."

"Yeah. How he knew everything was true beyond the shadow of a doubt. How he had this burning inside him. I'd stand there wondering if whatever was burning inside him wasn't a fuckin' cross."

You look at the grass down between your legs.

"I didn't mean that," he says.

He gets up and walks a few feet off.

"You think I look at you like that."

He brings himself around.

"Fuck, man. Never in a million years. I don't even know where I'm going. I just wanted to say I didn't want Cissy hurt."

"You think I look at Cissy like that."

He looks down at his boots and then up at the sunset. "This is fucked up. This is like telling my fuckin' minister not to steal my Bel Air. I just know that shit can get inside you. I saw it happen."

And then you're pissed, and you're up, and you're putting yourself in his face, eyeball to eyeball.

"Why'd you bring me home? Why'd you even fucking bring me?"

"I wanted to."

"If you knew I had all this shit inside me? If I was some fucking Trojan Horse full of all this shit you were bringing home?"

He looks at you startled.

"You got it wrong, man. Trojan Horse. That's fuckin' nuts."

"I don't got a fucking thing wrong. You could of said all this before. What you think I got inside me."

"I'm tellin' you. You got it wrong."

And now you can see the hard glare move into his eyes.

"Look hard," you say. "See somebody home besides fucking gold-fish?"

"I know what they want out of you."

"I'm not your track buddy. You know that?"

"I know you can't pick and choose, man. I know you're supposed to believe every bit of it. Including me being a chickenshit in some fuckin' spirit war."

You look down, at his neck, at the bumps on his neck he told you once were ingrown whiskers, whiskers that coiled round and round just under his skin. You feel instantaneous shame for seeing them. Glance off over his shoulder to where the soft California sky has started going hard.

"You think that's inside me. That you're a chickenshit."

"You're going on that mission, right?"

"Yeah. I am. That a problem too?"

"Okay," he says. "Okay." He backs off a step and brings up the palms of his hands. "Try this. You go to Knox. Finish out tank school. Then say fuck it. Take a left turn. Tell everyone you've changed your mind. You're not going. You're moving to San Jose instead. We can help set you up. You can go to school here. UC's got a great music school. One of my uncles teaches there. Uncle Joe. You got a family. You got Cissy. You got a life. Ready made."

"The trombone player uncle?"

"Yeah."

You know what he's putting in front of you. How the last eight weeks have been you. Just you. For the first time. Nobody knows your father from a million other men. Nobody knows your mother from a million mothers. Nobody knows your neighbors. Nobody gives a shit about your churchhouse or Clark or Rodgers or Bird or Hunt or Bishop

Wacker. Or the way you break up a slice of Wonder Bread. Or anything they taught you. Or your Individual Achievement Awards or the Tabernacle Choir or the Crossroads of the West or Temple Square or anything under that dead sky. Just you. Almost like you got here naked. To start from scratch. Just you. This place the place you could start from. Your head goes wild again to where you can't say anything. Just stare at him.

"Walk away from it," he says.

"You're daring me."

"I'm seeing if it's there."

"You're fucking daring me."

"Walk away," he says.

"I got my little brothers and sisters. Two brothers and two sisters. All looking up to me."

"They why you're going?"

You look away. Just long enough to know you shouldn't have. See how low and red and fat the sun is.

"Yeah."

"Then that's a good reason."

"I'll never hurt Cissy."

"I know you won't." He brings his hand up to the back of his neck. Lowers his head and turns it side to side. "I'm sorry. This got way outta hand."

Off in the distance a long formation of jogging soldiers moves like a dark snake rolling along one of the roads that rise and fall with the low hills. The cadence of their boots floats in and out of hearing range like dirty drumbeats with the marching song they're chanting.

"Your folks know?"

Your question brings Jeff's head back up.

"Know what?"

"About Cain. All that shit."

You can tell from the way his eyes change. How you ate their food. How you slept on their couch. How you looked at their daughter. How you went to church with them.

"I brought you home," he says. "That was all they needed to know."

"Your dad knew about all the wives."

"Shoot. Everybody knows that."

"What should I do."

"What you want."

"No. With your sister. Tell me what you think I should do."

"I told you," he says. "Whatever you want."

"Look. I never figured on it anyway. That she'd be interested. So no big deal."

You hadn't. Just made a dream of her so you could fall in love with her without her knowing. And that was fine. He looks at you. Turns and walks off. Stands there with his back to you and drains his beer can. Then, where you can't see him do it, where all you can see is his shoulders and elbows work, he takes both hands and crushes it, lets it fall, starts bringing down his boot on it, over and over, quiet and methodical. And then when he's done he picks it up and heaves it. You watch it sail on a high wobbling arc into the sky where its rumpled metal skin catches sparks of fire off the sunset. You watch him pocket his hands and stand there, kicking the grass, kicking for rocks that aren't there.

"Hey," you say.

He stops. "This got away from me. I never wanted to fuck it up."

"It's cool."

He turns toward you again.

"Look. She's interested. You're interested. Fuckin' go for it. Both of you. Fuck what I said. Fuck the whole story I told you. Fuck that asshole. That's all he was. Just a fuckin' asshole."

You don't say anything.

"We came up here for a couple of beers. To say goodbye."

"We got two left," you say. "One each."

He looks at you, long and even, to where you get feeling awkward looking back.

"You'll always be my brother," he says.

"Same for me."

"Fuck, ten years, twenty years, fifty. Till one or both of us is dead."

"Same here."

Out of nowhere he steps in, brings up his arms, takes hold of you. You put your arms around him the way you watched his uncles do. His chest up against yours. His big shoulders in your hands. Yours in his big hands. The grizzled skin of his jaw against your skin. It doesn't last long. Before it's over you've thought of Cissy. Thought how this is as close as you'll get to her.

"I'd never hurt her," you say.

On the way to letting go he slaps you twice on the back. You do the same. The way you stood there and watched his uncles do when they let each other go.

"Let's crack those beers," he says. "Put the sun down on this bull-shit."

CHAPTER 40

THAT NIGHT the stuff in your head won't rest. If she'd wait for you. Like they teach the girls back home. Wait and then get married in the Temple. If she'd wait till you're done with yours. Until you're finally done with everything. Until you could move to San Jose and marry her and make Jeff an uncle a hundred times. In the meantime she could write you. You could write her. If she'd wait. The possibility so mythical and huge it makes you think the two of you could make it happen. You calculate the time from now, tonight, to when you'll be coming home for good, a returned missionary, and the answer turns you cold. What you'd give her for a reason. Because you couldn't give her the reason the girls back home had. Couldn't marry her in the Temple. Couldn't even get her in the door.

That night, by the time you're on guard duty, marking off the asphalt from one dry puddle of dirty light to the next one, you already know. Know you can't ask. Not to take that time and spend it waiting. Waiting while you knocked on doors. While you spread the gospel. While you baptized people who could go to the Temple any time they wanted. White and delightsome people. People who would look at her and see a Fence Sitter. A girl with skin this breathtaking glow of rose and gold and brown because she needed to be punished.

The guy Jeff knew. The guy who looked at him blind. While you pace off the chainlink fence around the motor pool you rake through everything. Everything you saw and heard and tasted and smelled at the barbecue. Meeting Jeff's mother and father. Watching the yard fill up with Negroes. If what you were watching was a yard fill up with the seed of Cain. If you thought that. Cissy across the yard at the center of the circle of her Airborne uncles. If somehow you watched them and thought chickenshits somewhere in the dark mystery just out of reach in the back of your head. Uncle Paul and his trumpet. If somehow the way it was tarnished and old made you hesitate to use it. Cissy singing Since I Fell for You. If somehow you watched her from behind and felt more valiant, more valiant than the girl who stood in front of you, more valiant than the girl your heart had been turning circles around since the minute you first saw her. The fresh blue sheets and the hands that took them to make a couch into a bed. If somehow you had trouble sleeping. The shirt Jeff loaned you. If it felt weird to wear it. The bacon and grits you had for breakfast. On the walk to church the small translucent buttons on the back of Bernice Taylor's blouse. In church the way they nodded and murmured and sometimes cried out when the minister was talking. The turkey sandwich they made you for lunch. If the meat tasted like dust. The lemonade you drank. If the glass tasted dirty. The backs of Bill Taylor's hands on the yellow fender of Jeff's Bel Air. If you looked at them too long. The ride on the night bus back to Ord. The orange flare of the match a few seats up. The smell of the cigarette. The repeating growl of the engine from the stinking dark of the engine compartment somewhere back behind you. Fence Sitter. Fence Sitter. Fence Sitter. Fence Sitter. Was it in there? You listen harder. Try to isolate it. You can't. Jeff's head bobbing off your shoulder. The lights of the locked neighborhoods out the window.

In the end you come up empty. Nobody you looked at. Nothing you smelled or tasted or heard or thought. Just this wild doubt that just because you came up empty doesn't mean it wasn't there. Maybe it was too far back. Back too far in the dark in the back of your head. Too deep back there in the dark of everything to isolate from everything else.

Zanni comes wandering out of the dark with his rifle hanging off his shoulder to relieve you. From under his helmet all you can see is his nose.

"Dint hear ya playin," he says. "Dint know where ya was."

"No gig tonight."

"Spot any commies?"

"Just the usual ones."

You head for the barracks, dress down to your underwear in the dark formation of all the bunks, get in your own, lie there below the sagging wirework of the bunk up over your head where you can hear Spainhower whistling in his sleep. You didn't need to be relieved. You could have walked around the motor pool all night. You'll be awake anyway till the soldiers come charging and bellowing through to get everyone up for reveille.

You've been here before. When you drove into Linda Bowen's neighborhood and stood in her living room wondering if you belonged there. When you had to dodge her in the hallways afterward. You know how it works. How to do it. How it's going to feel. What to expect and where to expect it and how to get through or around or over it. You just need to stay awake for it. Let her go. Let go of the possibility. Of her face and her eyes and her teeth and voice. Of the quick and alive and easy way she had with everyone like a ballad was playing inside her. Of her skin. Of the possibility of bringing her smile out where you could see it and she let you know that it was you who put it there. Of her rose gold arms and shoulders and legs and face and hands and feet. Of the lush black wilderness of her hair. Of her mother and father. Of her circle of uncles. Of her life. Of the possibility.

Through what's left of the night, you lie there and make the fierce and desolate journey out of love, and by dawn, she's back where she was, someone you never had a shot at in the first place, someone just to dream about and have her take your breath away when you do. And then she's gone. Just you. You and your underwear and the bedding and the raft of the mattress. And rage. This howling rage when you thrust your bayonet into the heart of a hanging heavy canvas sack of sand you're supposed to think is your enemy, no head, no arms or legs, no face, just the torso of this hanging beast of sand, just your enemy, just where its heart is, the blade turned sideways to get through where its ribs are to its heart, over and over and over and over, until the lights come on and the soldiers whose job it is to get everybody up for reveille come storming down the center aisle, banging their sticks on the pipe frames of the bunks.

CHAPTER 41

ART TATUM. Clifford Brown. Coleman Hawkins. If the negro men on Mr. Selby's wall could see you through the paper eyes of their photographs they'd look at you and you'd know what they would tell you. They'd ask you to back off a step. If there was a red velvet rope in front of the wall they'd want you to stand behind it. Dexter Gordon. Wayne Shorter. Charlie Parker. If the negro men who played on Mr. Selby's albums could hear you they'd stop and listen and it would be okay with them that you wanted to play like them. As long as you never thought you were one of them. Or could ever be.

In the heavy air of the dawn outside the barracks Jeff comes down the stairs for reveille in his dress greens and his dress hat carrying his duffle bag. The toes of his black dress shoes are gleaming. He looks like an officer. Two other guys in their greens are with him, headed like him for Bragg, for Airborne training.

"Hey," he says.

"You're lookin' sharp."

"Think so?"

"Yeah," you say. "Even got your shoes deodorized."

To see that quick grin he shares with his sister.

"Yeah."

"How come your jacket's inside out?"

He's not quick enough to stop the reflex of a quick glance down.

"Shit," he says. "Got me."

"You make it easy."

"Don't count on me to write," he says. "I don't do that."

"Okay."

After he's gone you take her photo and put it in the secret compartment in your wallet where you still keep your underage card. Two days later, wearing your own dress greens with the toes of your dress shoes deodorized, you're put on a bus for Los Angeles and the airport, and then on a plane to Kentucky. It's the second time in your life you've been on one. You were too young the first time to still remember it. This one's a jet. You're astonished at the force, at the way the cushion of the backrest gives, when the engines come full throttle and lift you out of California. How to keep from hurting her. On the flight to Louisville you figure how to do it. Make it her idea. Make her wonder what she saw in you. Once you know your address you pick together some change and call Robbie. You write Cissy to tell her you're here. A week or so later you get an envelope from Robbie with a wallet-sized print of your yearbook photo. You send it to Cissy.

At Knox, you come face to face with a tank again. This time it has a gun, and an engine that works, and there are men who are ready to teach you how to command and fire and drive it, and get you to where they can trust you to put it in your hands and walk away. You've never been trusted with anything bigger than a borrowed car and an M1 rifle. And so you throw yourself into Armor School the way you did at Ord for basic training.

You learn everything there is to know about an M48 Patton tank. How to sit down in front in the driver's seat in the nose of the hull between the tracks and prime and fire up the big engine back behind the turret. How to handle fifty tons in motion. How to use opposite lock to turn it in place, on a dime, the tracks working in opposite directions. How to ford it through water. How to lock down the hatch and drive through the periscopes. How to rack a 90 millimeter shell into the breech and lock it and get back out of the recoil path, up against the side of the turret, to give the rear of the main gun the room to come slamming back when it's fired. How to sit next to the main gun up inside the turret in the gunner's seat, put your eyes up to the binocular rubber of the optical rangefinder, crank in the right windage and elevation, and lob a 90 millimeter projectile across a valley into a target on a distant hillside. How to sweep fire the coaxial thirty caliber machine gun mounted in the turret next to the main gun. How to take it apart and clean it and assemble it again. How to command. How to load and fire and take apart and clean and assemble the big fifty caliber gun up on the commander's cupola. Boresighting. Maintenance. Kentucky Windage. Tennessee Elevation. Radio. Headset. Conduct of Fire. How to read maps. All kinds of tactical and parade formations. How to work with a foot squad using the tank for cover. How to escape if you're hit.

You get issued a forty-five caliber pistol and learn what a blunt and sloppy gun it is and why it's made that way. Close-in fighting. Blowing the arm off an enemy soldier to get him off your tank. Stopping him cold with a hole through his chest you could put your arm through. Sergeant Pharris, your platoon sergeant, a wiry little guy with red hair, is strict and tough and loud, profane when you do something wrong, or screw around, but you always know you're okay, the way you always knew you were at Ord. Sergeant Lamb, the tall fierce-looking Negro who's boss of the firing range, shows you how to swear in the middle of a word. Guaranfuckinteeya. Unfuckinbelievable. Kenfuckintucky. Tennefuckinsee. Outfuckinrun. That Eustace kid could outfuckinrun a gazelle. I guaranfuckinteeya. I seen him. Just unfuckinbelievable. But he can't shoot to save his fuckin' nutsack from a housecat. Still don't know his Kenfuckintucky from his Tennefuckinsee.

You get your own set of stationery just for Cissy. You answer every letter she writes. If you can figure out what made her fall for you. Then you can gradually take those things away to where she'll wonder what she ever saw in you.

My girlfriend Loreen wants to set me up with a blind date. I told her I'd think about it. Have you ever been on a blind date?

You see her sitting next to some guy in the back seat of someone's car and let go of what it takes to see her there, laughing, not knowing what she's laughing at, not hearing what her laugh is like. You let go of everything else you want to write. And then you write and tell her you went on a couple of blind dates too just for the fun of it.

I know this club on Stimson Avenue that has a jazz band every Friday night. They play mostly new jazz like Miles Davis. Maybe we can go when you can come on leave.

You see her in the audience out in front of some other trumpet player and let go of what it takes not to look out past the gold bell of your trumpet and see her there. You let go of everything else you want to write. And then you write and tell her you'll get there when you can but you don't know when but she should go in the meantime anyway and enjoy the music.

What did you do for fun back home? Did you go out on weekends? Did you have a band? Sometimes I try to picture what you're like when you're in Salt Lake City with your friends.

You see her walking next to you on a downtown sidewalk on a bright winter afternoon, in boots, in a coat whose upturned fur collar is the white nest of a flower that holds her breathtaking face. You let go of what it means to have her point at the gray spires of the Temple and ask you what the funny castle is. You let go of everything else you want to write. And then you write and tell her you used to have a little band but it was just a high school thing.

I just got off the phone with Jeff's friend Mike. He lives around the corner. He asked me if I wanted to go see The Day of the Triffids. I told him I had to wash my hair and couldn't go.

You let go of what it takes to see her lush hair, the high wet lathered stack of her hair, lather in accidental little rivulets down into the dark skin of her forehead, her shining surprised embarrassed smile when she turns around from the sink and sees you standing there in the kitchen. You let go of everything else you want to write. And then you write and tell her if she sees the movie to let you know if it's worth it.

I really want to see The Miracle Worker. If I had a choice I'd like to go see it with someone like you.

You see her next to you in a theater, shoulder to shoulder, the color of her fingers laced through the color of your own, and let go of what it takes to be a choice she wouldn't want. You let go of everything else you want to write. And then you write and ask her how her folks are doing.

Let go. Let go. Let go. Let go of all the things you want to keep a hold on. The things you could have. Let go of everything else you want to write. And then write her back the lamest stuff you can think of. Sometimes you spell words wrong on purpose. Screw up the grammar to let her know that along with being lame and dull you're not too bright. Sign every letter Your Friend the way you did the first time.

It makes you sick. It makes you avoid the shaving mirror in the bathroom and the full length mirror in the lobby. It leaves dirt in your mouth whenever you send a letter off to her. And in the next letter there she always is. Still there to reach out and take the way her brother said you could. You still with this hold on her where all you have to do is close your hand around her hand. There at the end of your duty at Fort Knox. There at the end of a plane ride home to get your trumpet and your other stuff. To tell your father you won't be going on a mission. To drive your mother into town to close out your joint bank account and take all the money you saved for your mission and get a car with it. To say goodbye and then head for San Jose. Goodbye to Karl and Molly and Roy and Maggie. And then you see their faces again in the brakelights of the Buick that night your mother ran away with an empty suitcase. And then you let go of that possibility too. Of telling your father to take your mission and go on it himself. Of leaving Karl and Molly and Roy and Maggie there in the house where they have to live while you run off to San Jose.

One day toward the end of October they put you on alert for deployment to Cuba. The Russians are building missile bases there. Kennedy's going to war with Khrushchev and Castro.

"What the fuck," says West.

"What?"

"They told us we didn't have to sweat Cuba."

"Yeah," says Mouse. "What's with the Regular Army?"

"What," says Korbuck. "You guys scared?"

"It's not that," says West. "A deal's a deal. They said no Cuba."

"You're scared shitless. That's what the fuckin' deal is."

You spend the whole night up and dressed and ready, your duffle bags packed, waiting for the order to come through, the trucks to pull up outside. You feel for the first time like a real soldier. Advancing a tank down the narrow street of a Cuban village. Shutters slamming shut. Historic old buildings in the crosshairs of the gunsight. In your hands the handles that sweep the turret back and forth and level off the barrel. The triggers under your fingers. Women like your mother was in Switzerland, terrified, running with their baby buggies down the street ahead of you.

All around you guys are busy writing letters to their girlfriends. Hollering back and forth about how you spell Castro and Cuba and Khrushchev and Communist and Russian. Names you can't keep from spelling in your head when you hear them hollered. You're charged too, with things you want to write, and to keep from looking lonely like some of the other guys, guys playing solitaire on their foot lockers, you write a letter too.

Looks like I'll finally be your Soldier Boy for real. As soon as I get home let's go on that blind date. Pretend we never met before. Your friend Loreen can introduce us. Let's go see The Miracle Worker. Let's go see Day of the Triffids after you wash your hair. Let's go to that jazz club on Stimson Avenue every Friday. Maybe they'll let me sit in. I love you. Spell every word right. I love you. Write it again and again and again. And while you write you can see where she'll hold the letter while she's reading it, the hand she'll be holding it with, its color, the coffee honey color of her hand while she turns the letter over to keep reading. I love you. In the morning Sergeant Pharris comes in and stands you down. The crisis is over. Krushchev chickened out. You're not going anywhere. You or the letter you wrote where you never wrote Dear Cissy at the start.

In November, at the end of your training, you take an Individual Proficiency Test. Go from station to station to see what the testers want and show them what you've got. Map Reading. Weapons. Boresighting. Main and Auxiliary Engine Operation. Turret Operation. Driving and Maintenance. Tank Gun Ammo. Conduct of Fire. At the end of the test, at the last station late in the afternoon, you hand your scorecard to the last tester, get on your knees, wait for him to tell you go, take a thirty caliber machine gun apart and put it back together, stand back up and face him. He snaps his stopwatch off and takes a look at it.

"Time to spare," he says. "Good work."

He looks your scorecard over.

"Holy shit," he says.

You haven't looked at the card yourself, just kept it folded, in your pocket, taken it out at each station, taken it back, put it away again. He looks you up and down, and for a minute, you get that old feeling that he'd be happier if you were someone else.

"What?"

"You maxed the test," he says.

"What do you mean?"

"You got a perfect score. Every station."

"I did?"

"Motherfucker. I never seen this done before."

You turn out to be the seventh soldier in the history of the Armor Training Center to get a perfect score. The seventh guy out of thirty thousand something guys who've been through here ahead of you. Three other guys in your platoon come one point short of perfect. Keller and Korbuck and Jackson. Guys who came from Bountiful to Ord with you and then from Ord to Knox. The Stars and Stripes does a writeup with a photo of you in your dress greens. The photographer poses you with Captain Helmlinger, the company commander, shaking your hand and handing you a blank sheet of paper because they don't have a certificate for what you did. Sergeant Pharris stands there grinning like the proudest father in the world. Your company holds a ceremony of its own in the street out in front of the barracks. You stand there, in front of all the guys, the big guys, most all of them bigger than you, and it embarrasses you to hear yourself described as an example of what a tanker is. You look at the roof of the barracks across the street because, at attention, you can't look at the ground, and the pride coming off your buddies is something you can't look in the eye. Captain Helmlinger presents you with a Zippo lighter engraved with your name and your company and brigade and battalion and what you did. Seventh out of Thirty Thousand. Everyone cheers. Sergeant Pharris gives a little speech. His voice cracks when he calls you tankers. He gets hauled around in the air on the arms of the guys he trained.

That night they bring cases of beer and bottles of whiskey into the barracks and let you tear the place apart. For the first time, with the permission of the United States Army, you and West and Keller and Korbuck and Gus and the rest of your buddies get drunk. Pillows and mattresses and shaving cream and blood end up everywhere. The fire extinguishers get emptied. Korbuck goes tearing around the barracks naked and ends up sitting in his bunk cradling and talking to his whiskey bottle like it's a teddy bear. You keep looking for Sergeant Pharris, on his chair at the front of the barracks with a glass of whiskey in his hand, looking to make sure things are still okay, but he just sits there grinning like it's Christmas and you're all his kids. Quigley turns all the showers on full blast and goes dancing and singing naked around the shower room like a ballerina in a rainstorm. You and Eustace turn the main hot water off. Quigley isn't fazed. He's too drunk. And so you turn the hot back on and then turn off the cold. By the time he's as pink as baloney and the shower room's all steam, he gets it, and blames the shower heads, and tears them one by one out of the tile walls. West falls asleep in the driver's seat of a Jeep he's too drunk to steal. Most everyone's thrown up before it's over.

In the morning they let you sleep it off till noon. And then they have you clean up everything that doesn't take a plumber or carpenter or painter or tile guy. And then they take you to another barracks for a shower. The next morning, a month and a half to go before your discharge, they move all of you to another company to make room for another round of trainees. Sergeant Pharris still has this grin on his face, this fierce pride, when he shakes your hand goodbye. You paid attention. You earned his trust. You did your job. It was that easy. It still amazes you.

You need to let your father know. Since you left home for Ord, and then Ord for Knox, he's been sending you his package once a week, double tied with string, packed with things to read about the Church and Salt Lake City, like you need to be reminded where you're from, like you need to be sold on the place you already call home. It still leaves you restless. It still makes you feel like you don't belong here, where you are, where you've started like everyone else from scratch. Now, with the clipping from the Stars and Stripes, you've got something you can send him back.

You send it folded in a letter that adds what the Stars and Stripes left out. The humility you know he'll look for. The requisite credit to him and how he raised you. You leave the Church out. A week or so later he sends you a small return clipping. It's from the Church News. Priest Wins Honor at Fort Knox. You go cold at being called a Priest in the headline. Colder when you read the clipping. Shake Tauffler. Active

Priest of the Bountiful Utah 13th Ward with six Individual Priesthood Awards and a Duty to God Award. Before they even get to what you did from scratch, on your own, at Knox.

A letter from Cissy makes it to your new address, the address she wrote scratched out by someone in a mailroom somewhere, the new one scrawled in next to it. Jeff called, she writes, to tell us that you were in the Army paper. Wow. That's really something. You must really be proud. Congratulations. Cissy.

You catch yourself at the thought of her father's hands on the yellow fender of Jeff's Bel Air. The buttons down the back of her mother's blouse on the walk to church. The mistake she knows she made of her dazzling smile. You wonder if this is it. If this is the one you don't have to write a lame and lying answer to. You put it away.

On weekends you start to catch the bus into Louisville and walk around downtown. The weekend after Thanksgiving all the Christmas stuff comes out on the streets and in the windows. People come out, shopping, and you get in the spirit too, and buy a shawl and a Johnny Mathis Christmas album for your mother, a book on the History of the Armor Training Center for your father, presents for Karl and Molly and Roy and Maggie.

Sometimes you take a room for Saturday night in a downtown motel and then go looking for a jazz club. One rainy Sunday afternoon, wandering through a clothing store not knowing what you're after, you buy a yellow Hawaiian shirt. On the way to the bus station in the rain again a woman starts yelling from a pile of clothes and blankets on the sidewalk across the street. You're the only other person on the street. From across the wet gloss of the street, when you can find what looks like her face, she looks like the oldest woman you've ever seen. Her voice is hoarse and toothless. But you can tell from the way she tries to make it sound beguiling that she's offering to fuck you. A theater marquee in the rain above your head reads Lolita. You dodge the water coming off it. Keep going. The voice across the street turns shrieking. Metherfecker! Heh! Lil sumbitch! Think yer too good fer me! Heh! Metherfecker! Git outta here! Piece a shit! Git away from me! Empty cans rattle and skate across the wet street after you.

CHAPTER 42

THE NEW COMPANY has it in for you. All of you. Nobody knows why. Maybe because of your scores on the Individual Proficiency Test. Maybe because you're from the company that got into the Stars and Stripes. Maybe because you tore a barracks apart. Maybe they want to put you in your place. It's clear from the start you won't be bringing out your mouthpiece. The Master Sergeant is this hulking bear of a World War II and Korean War veteran named Kedso with a white brush cut and a face cut deep and dull with a thousand years of hate and an attitude always looking to be crossed. He reminds you of Mrs. Brick from Webster Elementary. He wanders back and forth across the backs of the overheated classrooms like he's on patrol, waiting for a head to nod, a pencil to stop moving, any other sign you're a communist, so he can come up from behind and slap you hard enough with a hand the size of a catcher's mitt to knock you three chairs over.

Going into December there's a cold spell where the weather goes down below zero and stays there. The heat goes off in the barracks. In the coffee cans nailed to the posts for cigarette butts the water freezes up and stays that way. They turn the water off in the head to keep the showers and sinks from freezing. Guys show up for reveille with their faces scraped and bleeding from shaving dry. They turn the toilets on for half an hour in the mornings and then off again.

In the heart of the cold spell they take you out on bivouac where you wake up at dawn to the canvas ceiling of your pup tent coated with ice from your breathing. Frost you're used to. This is ice. A coating of ice that is thicker every morning. They have you work on tanks and heft rounds and shells and casings barehanded. Your fingers keep sticking to the metal. They send you on marches and have you play war in the brittle woods without earmuffs or liners in your field jackets. Your fingers stick to your helmet when you reach up to set it straight. They stick to the grip and trigger of your forty-five. You remember the cold in your knees from the winter you spent in the sandpit. A week later, after two of the tanks freeze up and some of the guys end up with frostbite, they truck you back to the barracks.

The heat's still off. The butt cans still frozen. The air the same bone cold as it is outside. You've never gone this long without heat. The cold is so deep in your back and your bones it feels permanent. A couple of the guys complain. And suddenly the heat goes up to where the butt cans can't thaw out fast enough. To where you can barely breathe. To where guys are waking up to nosebleeds with their pillows bright red with blood.

Nobody complains at first. And then someone does. And one night, you don't know when, they get you up, tell you to put on your boots, take you outside in your underwear. For the second it takes to leach out all the heat the bitter air on your bare skin feels fresh as spring. By the time you're formed up on the street your skin is nubbled and hard with goose bumps. They run you around the barracks four times. And then they form you up again. In his overcoat, Sergeant Kedso stalks back and forth in front of you, his breath these ragged pulses of steam like cold exhaust, pulses that twist and shrivel and disappear as soon as they hit the air. In just your boots and shorts, it's the first time you've been out-side without Cissy's photo where you could reach for it.

"Fuckin' bunch a Goldilocks!" Kedso yells. "It's too cold! It's too hot! Do I look like yer fuckin' mommy? Fuckinest bunch a pussies I ever seen! Yer a fuckin' insult to the Army! Ya stink like pussy! Stop fuckin' shiverin'! Yer at attention! Anybody wanna fuckin' bitch about the heat now?"

"No Sergeant!"

"I think yer a bunch a fuckin' liars!"

"No Sergeant!"

"A bunch a faggot pussy stinkin' liars!"

"No Sergeant!"

"You tellin' me I'm wrong?"

"No Sergeant!"

"Then lemme hear ya say it! I'm a faggot pussy liar!"

"I'm a faggot pussy liar, Sergeant!"

"I fuckin' love it hot!"

"I fuckin' love it hot, Sergeant!"

"I fuckin' love it cold!"

"I fuckin' love it cold, Sergeant!"

"I fuckin' love it in the pot nine days old!"

"I fuckin' love it in the pot nine days old, Sergeant!"

"I'm just a fuckin' pussy Goldilocks!"

"I'm just a fuckin' pussy Goldilocks, Sergeant!"

"Now git yer fuckin' pussy Goldilocks asses to bed! Dismissed!"
"Yes Sergeant!"

At reveille a couple of mornings later a Jeep pulls up and a major gets out. He looks and walks and acts like an accountant or some other office worker. But Sergeant Kedso and his platoon leaders clop their heels together and salute him like their arms are mousetraps. He gives them back a little wave off his head like he could give a shit. And then he calls four names. You and Keller and Korbuck and Jackson. He orders all of you into his Jeep. A corporal drives you through the fort to a quiet street lined with huge trees and yards the size of parks and then stops in front of a quiet old red brick mansion you could never find your way back to the barracks from if they paid you all their stored gold.

A sign out front tells you it's the Headquarters of the First Armor Training Brigade. The major takes you through rooms and hallways where guys should be wearing suits instead of fatigues to a big old-fashioned office where you stand in front of a wooden desk the size of a dining room table. The man you salute, the man in the upholstered office chair across the desk, is a colonel. Just a regular looking middle-aged guy, most of his brown hair gone or going gray, running to paunchy, looking like he'd be more at home in a ratty old sweater than a starched fatigue shirt with silver eagles on the collars. He doesn't get up when you salute him. Just does a little flip off the side of his head the way the major did like he's had it with being saluted. You stand there with your fatigue hat in your hand, at attention, wondering why you're here. Whatever it turns out to be you figure you'll do what you've always done. What you're told to. Put anything else that matters behind you to do what's in front of you.

"You soldiers did an outstanding job on your proficiency tests," he says. You're surprised at how soft and relaxed his voice is. "That's why we picked you. Figured you were bright and responsible. We're looking into some rumors we've heard about your company. You're here to help us. I want you to go with the major here. You'll be under his command for the time being." And then he looks at Keller.

"Don't worry," he says. "You boys are fine."

The major takes you down a hall to another big room with tall windows and a conference table surrounded with armchairs. Four big glass ashtrays are the only things on the table. The major tells you you're going to be spending the next day or two in here. Writing. Writing down everything you can remember from the time you first got moved to the new company until this morning when he came to get you. Everything out of the ordinary. Everything that didn't sit right. Every incident. Every officer. Every detail. Every fact.

Shit, you think, and then you and Korbuck and Keller and Jackson are looking at each other.

"No," says the major. "You're not rats. You're not here to squeal on anybody. You're not being insubordinate. You're here to tell the truth. You're under orders to do this. This is your mission."

You're ready.

"Each of you take a seat on a different side of the table. No talking to each other. Sergeant Gollard will be with you the entire time. You'll get breaks every couple of hours. You need anything, got any questions, ask the sergeant. You ask each other, this is over. Understood?"

"Yes Sir."

"You'll be billeted here for the time being. We've got a room for each of you to sleep in. I don't want you talking to each other until everyone's done. Inside or outside this room. I'm afraid you're stuck with the same fatigues you're wearing for the duration. But we'll see that you get fresh underwear and socks every morning. We'll issue toothbrushes and shaving gear too. We've already picked up your footlockers and emptied your wall lockers. Your things are safe. Anything you need?"

You think of your mouthpiece tucked back in the bottom corner of your foot locker. The letters from Cissy tucked there too. But Korbuck and Keller and Jackson have already told the major no.

"Anyone want coffee?" he says.

"I'll take some coffee, Sir." From out of nowhere.

Keller looks at you. And then he says, "Me too, Sir."

And then Korbuck and Jackson go for coffee too.

"Any of you boys smoke?"

"No Sir."

"Sergeant, get rid of these ashtrays here. See that these boys get coffee and breakfast. And then put them to work."

The major leaves. Sergeant Gollard goes for coffee. The four of you look at each other and then around the room and then back at each other again. Korbuck's first to break the rule about not talking.

"This is different," he says.

"What're we supposed to write?" says Keller.

"I don't think I like this," says Jackson.

Sergeant Gollard comes back with a tray and four white mugs.

"You're under orders not to talk," he says. "Now shut up."

The four of you spend the next two days across the table from each other writing to the sound of your pens, your chairs creaking, pages ripping off your pads, while Sergeant Gollard reads newspapers and magazines in an easy chair in the corner. By supper the next day you've got everything written down. Keller and Jackson and Korbuck wrap it up too. Sergeant Gollard collects your pages. Says you can talk again.

None of you has much to say. They keep you there that night, and then the next day, and then overnight again and into the next afternoon. Let you sit around and read and listen to music and play cards and write letters and play ping pong. Let you try to sort out what's happening on your own. And then, in the middle of a card game called Fuck Your Buddy, the major comes in and takes you back to the colonel's office. The colonel gets up this time, reaches across his desk, shakes hands with each of you.

"Thank you, men. You've been a real help. You've conducted yourselves like soldiers. I'll be putting a letter of commendation in each of your files. Now. Your company's ready for you again. Dismissed."

Back at the barracks you find your mouthpiece and the stack of Cissy's letters where you left them. But things have changed. There's a whole new company command. Everyone wants to know where you've been.

"They're gone?"

"Yeah."

"Where?"

"Kedso got busted to private. He's back in Korea. Until he retires or dies."

"What about the company commander?"

"Shexnaildre? He's out of the Army. He coughed up his commission. His pension too. They wiped out his whole record."

"You're kidding."

"It was that or a court martial. His choice. A court martial would of landed him in prison. Hell, this way, he can still learn how to cut hair or something. Start a new career instead of sitting out his life in Leavenworth or someplace."

"What about the rest of them?"

"Gone. I'm tellin' ya. We got a whole new command. All the way down to the platoon leaders and mess cooks. They're great, too. What'd you guys do?"

"We just wrote stuff down for two days. And then we sat around."

"What kind of stuff you write down?"

"Just the stuff they were doing. They made us."

"Man. Whatever you wrote, it worked."

A hand in getting the guy busted and sent back to Korea who clobbered Eustace so hard it made his ear bleed. A Master Sergeant. A World War II veteran. Busted to your rank. The stripes ripped off his sleeves and shot up his ass so hard he landed in Korea. A hand in getting a company commander kicked out of the Army so hard it was like he'd never been there. Like they'd even taken away the stories he could have told his customers while they sat in his barber chair and watched him trim their hair in the mirror. Your hand. The enormous possibility. The taste of coffee. The United States Army.

You remember the colonel's handshake. Not the handshake you expected. Gentle. A handshake with nothing to prove.

That night you dig out the letter you got from Cissy. The last one she wrote you. The short one about the story in the Stars and Stripes when you got the perfect score. The one congratulating you. The one that was over almost before you could tell you were reading it. There hasn't been an answer to the one you wrote her back. It worked. You never wanted it to. But it looks like it did. Like you did it. Got her to look at you and wonder why and then keep on looking. The wall above her dresser blank like you were never there. Kept your word to Jeff. Nobody hurt. For a long time, you sit there on your locker, her letter this dead thing in your hand, and the last thing you care about or pay attention to is everything going on around you. Finally you fold the letter up, slip it back in its envelope, put the envelope back with the rest of them, put on your field jacket and walk out into the night air.

Walk. Walk till you're out of sight of any barracks. Walk on the crisp grass under a thin moon out to the middle of a dark parade field. Take a look around. Off to one side there's a tank pool, one you've guarded, the hulks of the tanks lit by the high lights at the corners of the fences. You look for the guy walking guard. You slip her photo out of the secret compartment of your wallet. Take out your Zippo, loaded up with a flint and fluid, ready to fire, the way they gave it to you. You flip the lid back and give the wheel a quick turn with the edge of your thumb. The soft flame flares and weaves up off the wick out of its little windproof cage. You can see your hand. Feel your face light up. You bring her photo up to where you can light her face up too. Catch the quick reflex of shame her smile has always sent like a startled animal across your heart and up your throat.

Soldier Boy. And then you just look at her, not for long, just long enough to let her share it, her smile for your humbling pride, maybe as long as it would take to light a cigarette, not long enough to draw a holler, long enough to leave her imprint, before you flip the lid back down and kill the light. And then, not done, for another minute, long enough to light another couple of cigarettes, for a couple of buddies who came along. And then the night air comes cold through the legs of your fatigue pants. It's time to move. You kill the light for good, drop the Zippo in your pocket, slip her photo back in its place inside your wallet.

PART 6

COMING HOME

CHAPTER 43

SO THIS is what it's like. It nails you as soon as you step through the door onto the steel landing of the staircase they've wheeled up to the plane. You put your dress cap on. The crack of air in your nostrils. The unexpected cold that makes all the sunlight fake. The pale blue iron skin of the sky. The light makes you reach for the sunglasses you got in a Louisville drugstore. Out past the teased-up hairdo of the woman starting down the stairs ahead of you, across the city, the mountains and canyons of the Rockies vault up off the valley floor so abrupt and close behind the city that their foothills take the back neighborhoods up with them. The rich neighborhoods. Halfway up their flanks they turn white with snow along a horizontal line that runs even and straight across them like the line of an overcast.

For an instant, you see the mountains for the first time, the way they are, not stark and magnificent like the Tetons, just these hulking big-shouldered homely thugs of mountains, and then they find their imprint. Where you grew up. Where you're from. The Shadow of the Everlasting Hills. The stuff that didn't matter in the Army.

Across the asphalt from the plane a cluster of people are gathered behind a chainlink fence in the bright cold, waving and pointing, and at first it's just another arm and hand, the arm and hand of a kid, and then you recognize Karl, more with your gut and heart than with your eyes. Your father's there too, next to him, but he keeps his hands in his overcoat pockets until you're through the gate and it's time for him to shake your hand and slap your shoulder.

The pride all over his face is helpless. In the cold-flushed skin of his jaw you can tell he's got his back teeth going. You shake Karl's hand. The scowl you forgot about is there, more defined and permanent, but you can tell he's proud too, eager to have you home. You go inside the terminal with reunions going on around you. You can see your father work to keep what he's feeling off his face. He starts talking business.

"So, by golly. Do you have luggage besides your gym bag?"

"Yeah. A duffle bag."

"Do you have to wait for it?"

"Yeah."

This restless half-bewildered way he looks at you and then looks off and then looks back again. Having his kid come home from the Army. He's not sure how it's done. It's the first time for you too. You keep your sunglasses on. On the way to the luggage area you tell him you almost got deployed to Cuba. He tells you he watched the standoff between Kennedy and Khrushchev on the news. And then he apologizes, says he has to get back to the office, shakes your hand again, heads across the terminal for the blazing front glass door while you and Karl go wait for your duffle bag. Christmas is four days off.

"So how do we get home?"

"The Valiant."

"What's Papa driving?"

"Some guy's car he borrowed at work."

"I don't get it."

"I got my license back in October."

"I know. What's the deal with the car?"

"Papa rides to work and back with Ron Whipple."

"Who's he?"

"This guy who works at the press. Out in the bindery. He lives in the Twelfth Ward."

"It's Saturday."

"Yeah."

"So you get the car all day?"

"Me and you. For school and work and stuff."

"You working?"

"Yeah. At Union Furniture. In the warehouse."

"Like after school?"

"Yeah. Me and Rast."

You stand there, watching suitcases and bags come in, getting used to being with Karl again, feeling the pull that makes you brothers.

"So how you doing?" you say.

"Fine."

"Going out with anyone?"

"Nah."

"How come?"

"I don't care about that stuff," he says. "What's that medal for?"

"Marksman," you say. "With a rifle."

"Where'd you get it?"

"Fort Ord."

"Is that the highest you can get?"

"No. I screwed up. All the way through training I always did expert. Then the day they tested us I just lost it. I couldn't hit anything."

"That sucks."

"Yeah. But look at this."

You reach down in your pocket, pull your Zippo out, hand it to him. He stands there with his head down reading the stuff engraved about you in its chrome-plated face. He already knows the story.

"They gave you this?"

"Yeah."

"Does it work?"

"Try it."

He pulls back the lid once he sees the way it's hinged.

"Spin that little wheel."

He uses both hands to hold it. His finger to spin the wheel. And then he watches the flame while you look him over, his hair grown out, parted down the middle, combed back, straight and gleaming like he's using Brylcreem now himself.

"How do you put it out?" he says.

"Just close the lid."

"That's it?"

"Yep."

He opens the lid again to see for himself. Then closes it and hands the Zippo back.

"Why'd they give you a lighter? You start smoking?"

"No."

"What's it like to drive a tank?"

On the way out of the terminal, out into the hard cold absolute lock the sunlight has on everything, you tell him. Where you sit, down low in the front of the hull, between the two tracks, the long barrel of the big gun over your head. The steps you take to get the engine primed and fired. Not the two levers like the tank in the junkyard at the ranch, but a little steering wheel, shaped like the wheel of an airplane, that turns the tank by braking the track you turn it toward. How you could drive it up and over a car and flatten it and blow its tires out and keep on going.

He leads you through the parking lot to the Valiant. The fenders and sides are splashed and streaked and crusted dirty white with salt. So it's already snowed in the valley too. Just melted back to the snowline along the mountains. He offers you the keys.

"Let's see you drive," you say.

And then you're leaving the airport, heading up the four lane highway of North Temple, where you can look ahead into the small downtown heart of the city and see the six gray spires of the Temple and the massive turtle-backed dome of the Tabernacle nested in among the downtown buildings. Again that quick loose restless pulse. That this is your first time here. And then the Temple finds its imprint. And then the highway. The highway you used to come back from the desert on. With Robbie. With the band. One night by yourself.

"So what's new?"

"Grossmama kicked the bucket."

"I heard."

Motherless Child, you remember thinking, reading your father's letter, how it might be time to play it for him finally. Behind the wheel, Karl's showing you his stuff, riding up on cars and trucks in the inside lane, yanking and hammering the Valiant out around them, this angry sneer for anyone else on the road, this wicked snicker when he gets someone to honk at him. It's your first time in a car in half a year. You're not used to how light and quick it feels. How out in the open you are. How the interior is red enough in the sunlight to tint the air around you red.

"So what else is going on?"

"I got a flute."

"A flute? Cool. You taking band?"

"Nope."

"Got a teacher?"

"Nope."

"I can find you one."

"I got a book I'm using."

Your first book, the thin book you used to lay out on the cold dirt of the sandpit floor, the rocks you used to hold the pages back, the pebbles you brushed away before you got on your knees to read the notes. The number Mr. Hinkle wrote in pencil on the cover. The Professor. Mr. Selby.

"You need a teacher," you tell him. "Trust me. There's stuff a book can't teach you."

"How do I find one?"

"Leave that to me." And then you say, "You go out at all?"

"Not much."

Sitting back, letting Karl drive, you catch up on other stuff, stuff on the surface, the stuff you know you can talk about while you watch things go by out the window. The fairgrounds. West High. Wasatch Springs. The streets are dingy with salt. The gutters lined with the eroded and pitted skeletons of dirty snowbanks where they were left by the plows. Again that restless pulse. Your first time here. How this could be any American city. You head north on Highway 89 through the industrial outskirts and scarred gray foothills of North Salt Lake. Onto the sudden smooth slab of the new freeway. Past the Phillips 66 refinery and the red barns and cattle pens of the Cudahy stockyards. Off at the Fifth South exit for Bountiful. Any town on a sunny day in winter on the shabby outskirts of any city in America. Soldier Boy comes on the radio. Along Orchard Drive it finally ends. And then up the long hill through the ranked houses of your neighborhood, the corner at the top where Karl turns left, toward the house on the circle.

"Oh, Shakli! Look at you! A soldier! Children! Look!"

Molly and Roy and Maggie follow you up the stairs from the base-ment. Your mother's there, at the top of the stairs, in her apron, her Swiss accent, her damp hands and fingers on your face like she's look-ing at you blind, Johnny Mathis singing Silent Night on the record player from the living room.

"Is that the album I sent you?"

"Oh, Shakli, I haven't stopped playing it since I got it. He sings so beautifully, doesn't he? Like an angel! Thank you so much for thinking of your mother!"

You wander into the living room. The Christmas tree is up where its tinseled branches fill the picture window. The flagstone wall of the fire-place is shingled with Christmas cards. The mantel is ranked with your mother's little Hummel figurines of chubby angelic sugar-faced girls and boys in farm clothes with flowers in their hands and around their shoes. She's added a few to her brood. On top of the piano, to the left of the center lamp, the old nativity scene, the baby Jesus with its chipped head. All is calm, sings Johnny, all is bright. You turn around. See Karl there with the rest of them now with his flute case.

"I'm home," you say. "Jesus."

"Yes, Shakli, you are home again. Home where you belong. Are you hungry? Yes, you must be! Come! Let me make you something!"

And then she's pulling you into the kitchen. Karl and Molly and Roy and Maggie right behind you.

"What would you like, Shakli? Some crepes? I know how much you love them! Here! Let me make you some!"

"Thanks, Mama. I'm okay."

"Oh, Shakli, please let your mother make you something!" And then with this sudden hushed conspiratorial surprise she says, "I have some frozen raspberries!" She opens the freezer, looks, plunges her arm in-side, comes out with the red and white carton, filled with the purple red half liquefied berries, the heavy syrup, the precious dessert she saves for special occasions, or sometimes just springs on the family out of no-where. "Look! I can thaw them! It will only take a minute in some warm water! Come, Shakli! You can have them with your crepes! I know how you love them! Come!" And then she looks at Molly and Roy and Maggie. "Oh, children! Look at your handsome brother!"

You turn around and look at them, huddled together, their wide eyes watching the carton, their faces quiet, trying not to let it show.

"Whaddaya think?" you say. "You guys want some?"

"Yeah," says Roy.

"Come on. Sit down." You take off your uniform jacket and hang it across the back of a kitchen chair. "Crepes and raspberries."

Your mother shakes off her brief reflex of resistance. "Yes, children, come!" she cries. "Crepes for all my children!"

While your mother makes the batter, while Molly brings down the old pale turquoise melmac plates and hands them around the yellow table, while your mother calls for one plate at a time when each crepe is ready, while all of you sit there in the afternoon sunset spooning frozen raspberries out of a stainless steel bowl, you tell them what you can about the Army, stuff you think they can understand. You pass around your Zippo. Watch them wipe their hands before they take it. Karl takes the silver tubes of his flute out of their dark blue velvet racks, assembles them, picks his way through a few hoarse notes of London Bridge. Roy tells you he's taking piano lessons now from Iris Lake.

Afterward you roll up your sleeves and wash the dishes. Have Molly dry. In your hands, they're like toys next to the stuff you washed in the Army, the two yellow sinks like shallow pans compared to the deep steel tubs of the mess hall kitchens. They're done, out of your hands, handed off to Molly, dried and put away before you know it.

Afterward, in your room, you close the door and dump your duffle-bag on the Navajo blanket bedspread you've had since La Sal. Fish your mouthpiece and Zippo and wallet and change out of your pockets. Set them on the desk. Change into clothes you call civvies now. Relish the almost barefoot feel of your tennis shoes and the soft second skin of levis and a sweatshirt. Stuff the gym bag full of presents back in your closet along with your combat boots and dress shoes. Hang your uniform. Shake out and hang your field jacket. Fold your fatigues and army shorts and socks away in the bottom drawer of the chest. Take your shaving kit, set it on the chest, and for a second look at your drawing of Rufus. And take your trumpet case down off the closet shelf, lay it on the desk, pop the latches, lift back the weathered lid.

CHAPTER 44

AT FIRST, lying in its cradle on its side, it looks old, and unfamiliar, its pipes bruised where you had nothing to do with the bruises. You lift it out and for the first time since July slip the mouthpiece in. Let your hands find their place on their own the way they've always held it. Recognize from where your fingers fall that some of the bruises are yours now. Put it to your lips, keep them closed, just feel it there, watch your fingers work the stiff valves, let things come back to your hands and arms and shoulders, the line of sight past your fingers out to the flare of the bell. Put it back in the case. Not now. Take your time. Close the case and set it on the floor. Sit at your desk. Just sit there. Pick up your Zippo, turn it over in your fingers, read the inscription, set it back down next to your desk lamp. Let it sink in. Out the window the circle. Let it come back. On your nightstand the stained glass lamp. The parking lot of the Indigo. The woman. State Street.

That night, when your father gets home from work, you pull up a folding chair next to him in the den, give him the money you've taken out of your army pay the last six months for tithing, show him the piece of notebook paper you used to track your pay, hand him an extra six bucks for the monthly fast offerings you weren't around to make. He's the Ward Clerk. The bookkeeper for the congregation. You're giving it to the right man.

"Yes," he says. "I'll take care of it."

You catch scraps of the wet fat garlic smell of baloney on his breath. Wonder where he's hidden it. See traces of gray in the hair off the sides of his forehead.

"I'm proud of you, son."

"That's good to hear, Papa."

He puts everything back in the envelope you had it in, pulls out a drawer of the filing cabinet that holds up the end of the door he uses for his desk, slips the envelope in front, slides the drawer closed.

"What are your plans now?"

"Get a job. Take a couple of quarters at the U. Wait for my mission call."

"Why the U?"

"Why not?"

"Why not BYU?"

Your ears go hot. You walked right into it. In the unforgiving white glare of the two fluorescent tubes of his desk lamp you should have seen it coming. Because I don't want to play hymns with some sanctimonious musicians. Because I'm a hypocrite. Because all I'm out to do is disappoint you. And then you look down to stop yourself. The renegade stuff you came home wanting to avoid. The cruising. The fighting. Taking things too far too fast. You look for a practical reason to give him for not going to BYU.

"It's down in Provo. Forty miles. It's a long drive every day."

"You could live there. On the campus."

"I don't have the money."

"We'll help you."

"What do you mean?"

"With tuition. Living expenses."

"You're serious."

"Yes. Your mother and I have talked it over."

"You can afford it?"

"We'll find a way. Just think. You won't have to work except for pocket money. You can devote all your time to your studies."

"The U's cheaper. I can live at home."

"It's not the right environment for a holder of the Priesthood. You know that."

"It's a university."

"I'm not telling you you can't go there. But you can't expect us to support something we know won't be good for you. You can't ask us to compromise our principles."

"So you're saying BYU or nothing."

"You can go anywhere you want. Nobody's trying to run your life. But the only school we can help you with is BYU. By golly. If you choose to go elsewhere, I'm sorry, but yes. You're on your own." And then he says, "That offer goes for all our children."

You look at him. This eager to keep you on track, erase everything else about you, he's ready to offer up his hard-earned money, to work nights. Under the heavy flesh and in the weary hoods of his eyelids you can see what you've always been to him. Your first day home. This morning you were in Fort Knox. On a bus through Louisville to the airport. From somewhere else.

"Thanks for the offer," you say. "I'll think about it."

West comes home to his 57 Pontiac with the metallic green paint still fresh from back in spring. Keller to his bugeye Sprite. Quigley to his monster flat black Hudson. You go to church the next morning in your suit with the silver cattle skull of your Duty to God Award still pinned to the lapel. West and Keller show up in their dress uniforms.

"Where's your uniform, soldier?"

West asks it like he's been promoted to general just for coming home. Like you've been demoted back to your first raw day at Ord.

"Wake up," you tell him. "We're home."

You finally make the trophy case in the churchhouse lobby. In a thin black frame the photo from the Stars and Stripes where you're shaking hands with Captain Helmlinger. The clipping from the Church News where you're headlined as a Priest. Everyone welcomes you back. Tells you how proud they are. Bishop Wacker has to do it from the pulpit. Strand is gone. The Air Force transferred his father to California back in the fall. Doby's going to the U. Jasperson's going to LDS Business College. Yenchik's working in his father's machine shop, making stuff out of steel, tin, aluminum, brass, his fingernails lined black, his knuckles hard and raw and gray in Priesthood and Sunday School. Like Keller and West and you, they're in limbo too, waiting for their mission calls, looking for something to do between now and then, something not too permanent, something they know they'll have to stop and put on hold. Lilly is already off. Knocking on doors in Mexico. Rodgers and Clark and Bird and Jensen and all your other teachers starting from when you were twelve are still around. Scoutmaster Haycock and his wife.

A new guy teaches your Sunday School class, a guy just back from his mission, named Elder Oliphant, a Priest when you were a Deacon. Susan Lake's got the glow that tells you she's unavailable, out of circulation, on her vigil, waiting for a missionary to come home and take her to the Temple. Doby tells you it's this guy from another ward named Kent Boxleiter who'll be knocking on doors in Oregon the next two years. Julie Quist and Ann Cook and Brenda Horn sit there on the girl's side of the classroom and look itchy in the glare of her waiting radiance.

Hunt still teaches your Priesthood class and sells Corvettes. For the first time you and Karl sit in the same class. For the first time you watch him break slices of Wonder Bread and hand trays off to the Deacons. Hear his amplified voice come down off the rafters when he recites the blessing for the water off the card you used to read yourself.

On Monday you call around to the rest of them. Porter's going to Trade Tech to be a certified auto mechanic. He's working at a transmission repair shop out in Woods Cross. Snook got made a cop instead of Quigley and had to marry Bonnie Baker. When you call Mr. Selby he invites you over at two on Christmas Day. Robbie's home when you call. Eddie's there hanging out. Jimmy's somewhere in Missouri getting his basic training for the National Guard. Santos took his congas off to join a new band. You take the Valiant down the empty roads through the dead fields to Robbie's to see what the remnants of How Should I Know are up to. In the driveway Robbie's dirty panel truck looks tired. Eddie's old Volkswagen sits canted out front on a bank of hard snow.

"Here," you tell Robbie first thing. "For the photo. Thanks."

"What photo? Oh. Right. No. Wait. It didn't cost ten bucks."

"That's what it was worth."

Eddie and Robbie are taking classes at the U. General freshman stuff and a couple of basic courses in the Music Department. A new professor, a guy from California named Fisher, just started a new Jazz Program. Eddie's delivering bread and pastries to hospitals. Robbie's got a night cook job at a diner on Redwood Road.

"You? Cook?"

"Yeah."

"What?"

"Mehican. What you theenk I cook, gringo?"

"Mama's recipes," you say.

"Si. Rellenos, huevas rancheros, enchiladas, you name eet."

"What happened to the Navy?"

"It's still there," says Robbie. "Back of my head."

"You guys playing any gigs?"

"Naw," Robbie says. "Not with working nights. I do all my playing at school."

"I go down to Sammy's," Eddie says.

"So How Should I Know is history."

"Bands fall apart," says Robbie.

"So do international jazz ensembles," says Eddie.

It takes you a minute to remember Jimmy's business cards.

"Still not over that, huh?"

"That's why bands fall apart," Robbie says. "Sax players and their fuckin' attitudes."

Robbie's seeing some girl from Cheyenne who's studying opera at the U. Eddie's after a candystriper at one of the hospitals he delivers to. You show them the Zippo. Tell them what you did for it. They don't much get it, the writeup in some Army paper, so you hold back the story about sending a sergeant to Korea and a company commander to barber college for Mr. Selby when you see him tomorrow. You hold back the story about the barbecue too. Keep Cissy in your wallet.

From there you toss your common stories back and forth. The night at the Indigo when the big Samoan guy kept paying you five bucks a pop to play Stormy Weather and then pulled a gun on the manager when he came around complaining. The night out at Wendover when the Air Force pilot tried to take a leak in the bell of Eddie's sax while Eddie was playing his Waltz for Debbie solo. The night this. The night that. The basement hasn't changed. Just taken on the bleak feel of a night club in the daytime when sunlight gets inside it. A place where you wanted to live once. Rosita. Like a tired woman now on the far side of feeling like she's beautiful. Of going out and doing what's behind her smile. Like all she wants to do now is change her clothes. Cook supper. See how her kids and animals are doing. Three guys sitting around telling each other stories. Two of them like they've got all the time in the world when all you've got is six or seven months.

You still love this place. But you get restless. Enough to finally need to get up and grab your jacket. For a minute you look at the trophies you got from beating high school bands where they stand on top of the old piano.

"One day there's gonna be this big plaque," you tell them. "Out by the front door. Birthplace of How Should I Know."

Even Eddie laughs.

"Buses full of tourists. Like Lagoon."

"Like Temple Square. Parking meters."

"Yeah. With those signs that say out of state plates only."

"Your dad giving tours."

"My mom serving nachos."

"It's gotta say international jazz ensemble too," says Eddie. "The plaque."

"You gotta sign up at the U," says Robbie.

"I'll see you up there," you say.

"Cool," says Robbie. "We'll get together."

"I can't believe you let Santos go."

"I can't believe you didn't bring us back some bourbon. You were right there, man."

"Sour mash," Eddie says.

CHAPTER 45

BACK HOME from Robbie's that afternoon, you unpack the gym bag, wrap up the stuff you picked up in different stores in downtown Louisville the last few weekends, put them under the tree, pass them out that night on Christmas Eve.

Roy runs his toy tank back and forth across the carpet. Karl puts on his Army teeshirt with Armor Training Center stenciled in black across the chest. Tears the paper off the souvenir Louisville Slugger bat you got him. From the wicked look in his face and the way he slaps it into the palm of his hand you figure you should have seen how close it was to a nightstick. Molly holds up the gold charm bracelet like the one Cissy wore on her wrist, studies the little gold animals and bells and stars, needs her fretful mother's help to latch it. Maggie sits there holding her little stuffed Kentucky Derby horse like it's a baby. Your father leafs through the big picture book of the history of the Fort Knox Armor Training Center. Your mother holds up her gold and crimson and silver striped silk shawl and tells you it's too expensive.

You sit there on the flagstone ledge of the fireplace with Johnny Mathis on. You're home. Home for Christmas with the only people who could ever be your family. The tree going. The lights outside. Your chest this wilderness of relief and sadness and love. Under their hopeful and apprehensive scrutiny you open the presents they bring you. Karl a Chet Baker album. Molly a small wood box with painted flowers for your valuables. Roy and Maggie a tiny gold bugle.

You make a big fuss. Take one of the pairs of Gold Toe socks your father and mother gave you and put them on like long hand puppets to get your mother to laugh and call you a fool in Swiss. Tease her about wanting to take Johnny Mathis off and hear the album Karl gave you. Put your Zippo and change in Molly's box. Put the tiny bugle to your lips and pretend you're playing it. Roy stands there grinning big and proud and unashamed with the tree lights on his face.

Christmas Eve. Your family just your family for one night, one night where everything else has to stay outside, one night where the colored lights along the roof and railings hold everything else at bay, one night where nothing can touch just the family you are. One night where you set yourselves free of the family you're supposed to be. Your father jokes and laughs like the man he'd be if you stripped him down, away from here, hearty, powerful, restless, the son who became the man who brought his family all the way here from Switzerland.

Most everything else has been opened when you watch Molly dig a white-wrapped box from under the tree. Your guard goes up when she walks it with both her hands in front of her to where your mother's sitting on the sofa. It's her big one. That's why she saved it almost to the end. You watch your mother open it while Molly stands there, her hands together behind her back, her fingers working at each other. She tells your mother it's from her and Maggie.

You watch your mother take both hands to lift it out of the box and hold it up. A little white statuette of two girl angels with their folded wings tipped with gold. Not a Hummel. Not by a long shot. The kind they sell at Servus Drug in the gift section. Take it, you think, watching your mother. Just take it. Tell her it's perfect. Just what you always wanted. Just take it.

"Oooh," your mother says. "Two little angels! How beautiful they are!"

You watch her hold it by the base, turn it back and forth admiringly, and then look in this liquid smiling panic around the room for help with what to say and what to do. And then suddenly she holds it out toward Molly.

"Here, sweetheart," she says, eager and bright. "Why don't you put it in your room! I have so many already! Just look! I don't have room for any more! You can take this one!"

"Can't they go on the piano?" says Molly.

"Oh, I don't think so, sweetheart." Her voice this fretful little sing-song protest. "I already have so much to dust in here."

"Can't you put them in your room?" says Molly. "They're for you." And then she says, "I'll dust them."

"Oh, sweetheart, I don't know." You watch her lay it back in its nest of tissue in the box while Johnny Mathis sings White Christmas. Set the box on the coffee table in front of Molly's knees. "We can decide later. Now! Let's see who is next, children! We still have presents left!"

Your mother looks back and forth at everyone but Molly with this lunatic lively delight all over her face. Nobody moves. Like the pools of wrapping paper and presents around everyone's feet are quicksand. Like Molly herself is glued to where she stands in front of the coffee table and the glue that holds her there is this paralyzing shame. For a minute the only thing going is Johnny Mathis singing about children listening for sleighbells in the snow.

"They'd look great on the piano," you say. Careful to sound cheerful.

Your mother looks your way. Takes a minute to find you. Another minute to know who you are in the face of what you said.

"Oh, Shakli," she says. "I don't know."

You get up, careful not to step on anything, reach around Molly and take the box off the coffee table.

"Won't hurt to try. Come on, Molly. Help me out."

Around the back of the sofa, at the piano, Molly points to the blank place up on top where she thinks it should go. You hold the box out to her. She reaches in, picks up the statuette, reaches up and carefully sets it on the piano your mother brought from Switzerland.

"How's that?" you say.

"Oh, children." Your mother's voice this complaining lament that you know could still go either way.

"Yeah," says Karl. "Good."

"It looks pretty there, Mama," says Maggie.

"Looks good to me," says Roy.

"It's perfect," your father says. "Don't you think so, Mother?"

But your mother's already up, and in the dining room, and you can hear a drawer pull open in the big buffet, and then close, and then she's there at the piano, breathless.

"Not without a doily, children!" she says. "Lift it up, please! Before it scratches!"

Molly lifts the statuette off the wood so your mother can slide the doily underneath it. And then your mother puts her hands on top of Molly's hands to set it back down again, turn it back and forth, get it to where she likes it.

"There, sweetheart," she says.

Your mother and Molly stand back where they can look at it. Your mother's hand comes up and strokes the back of Molly's head. Molly nests herself against her side.

"That's where they belong," your mother says. "Look! Look how beautiful they are! Thank you for such a beautiful present!"

That night, when it ends, Molly and Roy and Maggie take their Christmas stuff to their rooms, your father heads for the den, your mother heads for the kitchen to put leftover food away that's cool enough now to go in the fridge. You and Karl pick up all the paper and ribbons, take them out back to the dark edge of the yard, get the incinerator blazing to where sparks the size of fire bats go flying skyward, to where the bricks and the dark windows across the back of the house turn orange.

"What kind of music you want to play?" you say.

"What do you mean?"

"Jazz, classical, rock, what kind?"

"I guess classical. Why?"

"So I'll know what kind of teacher to look for."

"What kind of stuff did you shoot at?" he says.

"In the Army? Targets. Sometimes old trucks. Old tanks. Whatever they had."

"How far away were they?"

"Half a mile. A mile."

"What happened when you hit one?"

"Depends on what you hit it with. There's different kinds of rounds. Armor piercing. Anti-personnel for enemy soldiers. High explosive."

Across the barrel, his face underlit from the dying flame, you see if he's staying with you.

"There's this plastic antitank one that's pretty nasty. You shoot it at a tank, it sticks to the turret like this glob of putty, and then goes off."

"Yeah?"

"This shock wave goes through the turret and breaks off these big flakes of steel. They fly around inside the turret and carve the crew to pieces."

You look to see how he's doing. The flames are down and their glow too weak to be sure. Cold starts to flood back in around you. Cold and dark. But he's looking back at you.

"Holy crap," he says. "Like a blender."

"That's why they call them rolling coffins," you say.

"What?"

"Tanks."

"How do you shoot one?"

You take him through Conduct of Fire. One. The driver positions and holds the tank. Two. The commander selects the target and type of round. Three. The loader slides and locks the round inside the breech, stands clear, gives the signal. Four. The gunner aims, figures Kentucky windage and Tennessee elevation, fires, puts the round into the target at its center of maximum vulnerability.

"What're those?"

"What?"

"Those Kentucky and Tennessee things."

You tell him. How Kentucky's how you adjust the aim for wind or a moving target. How Tennessee's for the way you adjust the aim for how far away the target is.

"What's that maximum thing?"

You tell him. The point on a target where you can do the most damage. The center of maximum vulnerability on a tank is the turret ring. The ring where the turret meets and rotates on the hull.

"A good hit there and you'll blow the turret right off the tank. Turn it into a convertible."

"Yeah," he says. "Without a gun."

"That goes too. If the hit's a lucky one, on top of being good, it'll set off the racks of shells inside the turret too. And then you've got a convertible with fireworks."

"What could you do to a house?" he says.

"A house?"

"Yeah. Like ours."

You tell him. How you could take a tank and drive it up the path through the front wall, control its measured fall through the floor into the basement, bring it up the other side again, keep the tracks pulling so you don't get mired. How you could roll one down into the circle, set it out in the center where the seagulls chase pieces of bread the kids toss out, and from the gunner's seat control the slow turn of its turret, use the gunsight to bring the long barrel to bear, load and aim and fire. Feel the tank rock back from the recoil. Watch through the gunsight while the smoke clears off the end of the barrel to show you what your hit did. Load and aim and fire. Seven times. Seven rounds. Turning each basement around the circle into a dumpster for the rubble of its house. And then put the order through the driver's headphones to move out again. A renegade tank.

"You could've done Mrs. Harding's house with one shot."

You remember the steam shovel clawing away the second story of her house. The way the house gave up the upstairs bathtub.

"Yeah."

Across the remaining glow from down inside the belly of the incinerator barrel he listens. All you can see of his face is what the last of the ashes light from underneath. The cuts of the shadows up from his mouth show you how deep the scowl has started nesting in the muscles there. More mean than tough. More scared than cruel. Center of maximum vulnerability.

From inside the house comes the faint but violent choir of your mother screaming and your father yelling. Neither of you looks at the lighted yellow box of the kitchen window. Both of you listen. Your father wants to go to the office in the morning. Your mother can't believe he wants to work on Christmas day. It isn't real work. He needs the adding machine to do some church work. Under his old blue parka

Karl's still wearing the teeshirt you brought him from Knox.

"You ever shoot anything live?" he says.

"Like what?"

"I don't know. Like a cow."

"Come on." And then you say, "I never saw a cow. The whole time there."

"They got horses. How about a horse?"

"Horses?"

"Yeah. The Kentucky Derby."

"Wanna listen to my new Chet Baker album?"

He looks at you like you're nuts.

"No. Down in the garage. On my old record player."

"It's gone," he says.

"What do you mean?"

"Papa cleaned out the garage. He threw out all the old stuff."

You look at the empty kitchen through the lighted window. The night you stood out here and watched your family eat comes back to you. How easy they would have been to a stranger with a twenty-two to kill.

"No problem," you say. "I'll just get a new one."

On Christmas morning you're up early enough to hear the front door latch. You look out the window into the cold dawn shade of the circle and watch your father in his overcoat climb into an old white Chrysler with a headlight out. You figure it's Ron Whipple. You shower, get dressed, make your bed the way you've made it now for the last three days, the corners squared, the sheets and blanket tight to where they'll bounce a quarter. You get your trumpet out, find your cleaning gear, grease the slides, oil the valves, push the coil of the cleaning brush through the tubes, wash the mouthpiece.

After breakfast you look through the classifieds in yesterday's paper. Simple jobs, like your buddies have, jobs you can learn in an hour and then quit six months from now. You circle a few you can call in the morning when places are open again. Today you've got Mr. Selby to see at two. Late in the morning you put on your combat boots, your field jacket, the wool liners for your Army gloves, your sunglasses, grab your trumpet, head out the door.

After the muted light at Ord, and then at Knox, you're still not used to sunlight this bright and cold at the same time. Your combat boots make the climb up the first hill to the sandpit easy. You cross the sandpit past the big black hopper. The steam shovel sits there idled by the fact that the dirt it's supposed to work is frozen. You know how to operate it now. As rusted and shabby and old as it is they'd use it at Knox for target practice. You catch yourself checking it out for its center of maximum vulnerability. The tin cab. You climb the back cliff and then head up the hillside.

Your place is still there. Still well below the early winter snowline. Dead weeds cover the hard dry slick dirt where the patch of the hill fell out of the hillside and formed the small platform you practice on. The weeds don't find their imprint. They're new. And then you understand. You were the reason they never grew before. Your shoes. The way you kept the dirt too packed. You take a look around. The dead marshlands out toward the Great Salt Lake where the long black vein of the railroad tracks runs north toward Ogden. The long black desolate ridge of Antelope Island out in the lake. The needle of the Kennecott smokestack off in the distance where the Oquirrh Mountains come down black to the valley floor.

You play middle C. Just to hear how it sounds, how loud it is, how it sets the hard air ringing and then takes its piercing flight off the hillside. A few more notes, hesitant, not knowing what will happen. You wonder how you used to play up here, wide open, reckless, unconcerned. And then you get into your warmup. Some long notes, some tongue work, some harmonic arpeggios, some Arban exercises.

The hesitation gradually lets go. The grip of the worry loosens. All the notes are where you left them. All the scales are still in your fingers when you skate high into them and then come skating down. All the keys. All the progressions when you take a run at some songs. Take Five. My Funny Valentine. All Blues. Scrapple from the Apple. All the Things You Are. Moonbeams. Stella by Starlight. Harlem Nocturne. Your chops are rough. The notes at the top of your range have this squeal to them for not coming deep enough from your lungs. This burr from your lips. Notes that crack when you bend them. You don't care. You know you'll get things back. You throw in some Christmas tunes in case the Leathams or anyone else is listening. Little Drummer Boy. What Child Is This. A hymn for your father. Lead Kindly Light.

CHAPTER 46

WHEN YOU come up the steps into the shade of his porch Mr. Selby has the door open. The same feel of the boards under your shoes. The same gray eyes and the same mix of reserve and delight in the way they take you in. The same high forehead. The same beard. The same comfortable smile nested in his white whiskers. The look the same. Sweater vest, long sleeved shirt, crazy tie. Oatmeal and chocolate chip. You can tell where the smell comes out the door around him.

"First time I've seen you come here in a car," he says. "On your own anyway."

"Yeah. I guess so. It's my dad's."

"Come on in."

He escorts you inside. You stand there with your case the way you always have. Theo comes trotting out of the kitchen and goes for your legs. Everything in the room finds its instantaneous imprint. The model fighter plane hanging off the light fixture in the ceiling. The grizzly bear on the mantel. The bowl of ball bearings. The wall of photographs. Its arrangement of frames so fixed in your head you can tell the change immediately. There's a new one. The Stars and Stripes photo. Captain Helmlinger and Sergeant Pharris. You in your dress greens. On the wall with all of Mr. Selby's framed musician friends.

"Where'd you get this?"

"Oh, I have ways."

"Where?"

"One of my students brought me a clipping. I made some phone calls. You forget I was in the Army. Still know some people. But here. You need to autograph it."

Mr. Selby takes the frame off the wall, walks to his desk, turns it over, pulls out a couple of pins that hold the backing in place, slides the photo out from between the glass and the cardboard, lays the photo face up, picks up a fountain pen and hands it to you. The same deliberate way of moving. You remember the shrapnel up against his heart. How you saw the Holy Ghost that way against your own.

"What's the matter?" he says. "Never been asked for your autograph?"

"No."

"Great. I get your first one."

"What would you like?"

"How about to the best trumpet teacher I'll ever have. I could live with that."

You sit down in his cushioned desk chair, at his desk with the Valiant out through the window in the sunlight, take the pen and use the lightest part of the photo. To Mr. Selby. The best trumpet teacher I'll ever have. And then you write, underneath it, because it just comes, I owe you everything I am. And sign your name. And put Christmas 1962 because you've seen how his other photographs are dated.

"How's that?" Handing it to him. Looking away when he reads it because of the quick little flex his jaw makes underneath his beard.

"Dandy," he says.

You stand up and wait while he blows the ink dry, slides the photo back between the glass and the cardboard, slides everything back in the slots of the frame, puts the pins back in, goes over and hangs the frame back on the wall among his other photographs. You remember when you used to wander back and forth and look at them without thinking. Look sometimes in shame at their mostly negro faces. Read what they'd written. And then you met Cissy and learned to keep your distance. Mr. Selby adjusts your frame a couple of times till he's satisfied the way it hangs. And then he turns and looks you up and down.

"A tanker," he says.

"Yeah."

"You look tough. Lean. Older. Let's see what the Army did for your playing."

And so you play. Together. Like the old days. Like every week from five years ago. Your case roped to the bike rack. His albums in the leather pouch. Side by side, two trumpets going, the music stand there when you need it, and he treats you less like he's a teacher now, more like Eddie, you and Eddie playing off each other, handing things back and forth. After a time you move to the piano where he plays behind you, where you watch his familiar hands, the way they voice the chords, the chords he substitutes that open up new paths for you. He finally looks at his watch.

"My," he says. "After three. Over an hour."

"That was great."

"Your playing's changed."

"Six months without it."

"No. I can hear that. I mean something else. I'm not hearing anything I already know. I'm not hearing anything borrowed. I'm not—"

"Borrowed?"

He looks at you alert and then with deliberate care. "Let me finish," he says. "You remember the people who taught you how to play."

Clifford Brown. Louis Armstrong. Bird. Wayne Shorter. Chet Baker. Miles. Coltrane. Gordon. Bud Powell. Your portable record player.

"Of course."

"I used to hear them," he says. "All the time at first. Then less and less. But they were always there. That's fine. That's how we learn. It's how I did."

"So I sounded borrowed."

He gives you a tolerant smile.

"First of all," he says, "you should be proud you were good enough to know what they were doing. Borrowed? No. You sounded like you were them sometimes. That takes a darn good player."

You remember seeing Mr. Selby appear at a back table at the Indigo. At the bar at the Staircase or the Sojourner. And then be gone before the set was over. You want to go back and play every gig you've ever played again. Have all the same people there. Show them.

"I know what you're thinking." he says. "Forget it. It takes a good ear to hear where you sounded that way. A trained ear. Nobody you played for probably ever knew. If they knew, there's nothing wrong with paying homage to the men you learned from."

"Okay."

"If you'll stop interrupting me," he says, "here's the second thing. They're gone."

"Gone."

"Gone," he says. "All of them."

"What do you mean?"

"Everything I just heard was you."

You're looking into the level and steady hold of his gray eyes. He finally smiles.

"You were a phenomenal player. I saw you stop conversations cold your first three or four notes. You were young. An apprentice." And then his smile goes. "What I just heard? I heard something I've never heard before. I heard your voice."

What it sounds like. What makes it different. And then Cissy. The photograph of her face in your wallet. What she had to do with what you're hearing. If he heard her there. Mr. Selby breaks his eyes away and turns his head and then walks across the room to the wall of his photographs.

"A player who knows who he is," says Mr. Selby.

"Okay."

"You want to know what I heard, don't you. You don't have a clue."

"I can take your word for it."

"I hear you playing more inside the dimensions of a song than I used to. Sure you could go outside. And people know you could. But there's more insinuation. More restraint. More strength. More reserve. They listen for that. You know that. I know you do. I just heard it. A lot of musicians get to be old and never learn that. They can't get out of the way of the song. They're all over it. They dress it up like a Christmas tree to where you can't even see the tree itself."

"I didn't play for six months."

"You went away," he says. "Apparently you grew up some."

"But—"

"A break is always good. Speaking of that."

He goes out to the kitchen. You pull the typewriter board out of his desk and bring the piano stool across the floor. He comes back and sets the tray with its plate of fat brown cookies and two tall glasses of milk on the board.

"You think you're too grown up for these," he says. "Well, you're not. But you're too grown up for me. You just graduated from the Selby Conservatory. Just passed the final exam. Congratulations. Here. Have a graduation cookie."

You take one. But you just sit there and hold it while it turns the tips of your fingers warm.

"What are you saying?"

"You're done here. I heard what I needed to. It's time to move on." He takes a bite of his cookie, smiles at you while he chews, like what he's saying is somehow supposed to be good news.

"I'm done here?"

"I'm out of lessons," he says. "Things to teach you."

You stare at him. A man it never crossed your mind to think was anything but infinite and inexhaustible. To think you could ever get to the end of. All the years you've sat here and watched him try to keep crumbs from catching in his beard.

"But you're a professor."

"Yes. I am. And most of my students graduate in four years. You've had at least five."

"So this is it."

"We'll be seeing each other," he says. "Like I told you. My students are my kids. My private students. This is your house too. Just call first. And stop looking at me like someone just died. It spooks me. It could be me. Eat that cookie."

"Sorry."

And for the time it takes to eat it, and wash it down with half a glass of milk, things are quiet. Theo comes wandering in. His sleepy yellow eyes follow your hand for a minute, and then Mr. Selby's hand, and then he turns and leaves.

"There's a saying. You need to close the door behind you to open the one in front of you. That's all we're doing."

Outside, from the copper stain in the white paint of the Valiant waiting at the curb, you can tell the sun has started sinking into the reservoir of haze west of the valley.

"So what do I do now?"

"What do you want to do?"

"Get a job. Go to the U." And then you say, "Until June or July."

"Why June or July?"

"I'll be going on a mission."

"Ah yes," he says. His eyebrows tighten just enough to bring out the familiar choiring of lines in the skin between them. "Okay," he says. "We've got two quarters before that. I want you to sign up for a couple of classes. Jazz Harmony and Jazz Composition. Time to start doing some composing. There are prerequisites but you won't need them. I'll talk to Bill Fisher. You know a lot of the stuff they'll teach you. They'll show you another way to know it."

"When are they?"

"When? You'd have to look at the schedule."

"Day or night?"

"Afternoons. Two or three afternoons a week."

"So I should probably get a night job."

"I worked as night watchman for a warehouse in Queens. A restaurant supply place. Just me. Guarding Italian food." He smiles. "A whole warehouse of Italian food. That's where I did all my practicing."

"They didn't care?"

"They didn't know. Now. Tell me about the Army. The story behind that autographed photo over there."

And so you do. The test you aced. Jeff. The barbecue. The borrowed horn you played. How you played with Negroes. How you played with this singer and then watched her sing in her choir. While you're telling him everything, everything but the one thing, you can't stop thinking how you'll tell him.

"I fell in love," you finally say.

"You did? Now that's something. Who's the lucky girl?"

"The one I did Since I Fell for You with."

"A singer. Well. You're in for an adventure."

"Want to see her?"

"Of course."

And there she is. The photo, curved from your wallet, cupped in his hand where he can look at her. Where she's smiling at him instead of you. Like you just introduced her.

"My goodness," he says. "What a beautiful girl. Just look at her."

"You think so?"

"Does this incredible girl have a name?"

"Cissy." And then you say, "With a C. For Priscilla."

"Did she fall in love too?"

"Yeah."

He looks up. His eyes are grave but he's smiling.

"You're in for more of an adventure than I thought," he says. "The two of you have plans?"

Double dating. A jazz club on Stimson Avenue on Friday night. The Miracle Worker. Her in the kitchen lathering up her hair.

"No."

"She's got kindness in her. I can tell that. You'd be safe with her. Where'd you say she was from?"

"San Jose."

He hands you the photo back. You put it away without looking. He sits back, lays his sleeved arms on the armrests, and then just looks at you, this curious little worried smile like all your hair just turned to lint and you don't care.

"What?" you finally say.

"What are you doing here?"

"Where?"

"Here. In my house. In this town."

"What are you saying?"

"What are you doing here?"

This time there's no smile. Bewildered, you look at the tray between you, the plate with two cookies left, two glasses, this room that you always knew was here where you could always count on everything. Jeff's face. The dying California sunset on his skin.

"I should go to San Jose?"

He studies you.

"I'm saying what are you doing here."

"Yeah."

Because you don't know what else to say. You look away. Down at your hands because your throat goes thick and you don't know how to tell him it's too late for anywhere but here.

"You wouldn't know a good flute teacher, would you?"

"You don't get it," he says. "I really mean it."

CHAPTER 47

YOU'RE HIRED by Hiller Heavy Construction, a heavy equipment rental and construction outfit on Thirty-Third South out by the freeway, to watch their yards at night. The big dirt yards are filled with dozers and graders and loaders and tractors, haulers and pavers and harvesters, scrapers and backhoes and excavators, drill rigs and generators, big flatbed semis to haul them out to the sites and back. Most all of it is Caterpillar yellow. The service shop is a huge tin-sided hangar with a long wall of tall overhead doors. Other shops and sheds are scattered around the yards for parts and tools. The man who hires you likes how you just got out of the Army. Likes how you're a tanker even more. Offers you an apprenticeship as a mechanic or operator. Your choice. Tells you how much more money you could make.

You tell him he'd be wasting his time and money training you because you're going on a mission. He agrees. He reaches for a cigarette. You've seen it before, when you bring up the Church some way, the way guys who aren't Mormon will reach for a cigarette. He hires you anyway. Tells you he'll pay you extra to plow the yard if it snows on your watch. Gives you a flashlight and shotgun. Just to scare people off, he says. Tells you to make the rounds every hour or so. Check the perimeter of the high chainlink fence. Open the gate to let the road guys in, the night mechanics, the guys who go out to construction and excavation and mining sites to work on the big machines at night when they're not being used. The rest of the time just stay awake. Midnight to six in the morning. He gives you a walk around. Shows you where keys and switches and all the alarms are. Shows you an old black bike you can use when you don't feel like walking. The tires are gone. From the way the rims are banged and dented and muddied up, you realize that's the way you're supposed to ride it, on its rims.

"Most everything's in the yard now," he says. "Stored up. March gets here, the ground thaws, this place'll start to empty out."

"Okay."

"You'll start seeing mechanics come in like four, five in the morning, looking for coffee."

"I'll make sure it's ready."

"You don't have a problem with that. Being Mormon."

"No. It's okay to make it."

He's a skinny guy in an old Pendleton shirt with slick black hair and a thin face carved deep with savage lines. He walks with a tender limp like he's hurt. He's maybe in his fifties. Tells you he's got arthritis bad. Shows you the huge knobs of his knuckles. Asks you what else you do. You tell him you play trumpet. He tells you he played sax for a couple of years in junior high. You ask him if you can use the time between making rounds and letting the night guys in to practice.

"Why not. Some noise'd be good. Let people know there's someone here. Case anyone actually gets it in their head to try and steal a dozer."

On the bright hard cold afternoon of New Year's Day you gather down at Steed's Texaco for a round of oil changes and lube jobs. Keller and Doby run out in Doby's Impala to the Frostop for burgers and fries and malts. They come back with bags from Wally's because the Frostop and every other burger joint down Highway 89 was closed. West's got the trash barrels blocking the pumps to let people know the station's closed. West's Pontiac and Keller's Sprite are done and back outside. Jasperson's here with his hand-me-down Rambler. Yenchik's 40 Ford is on the hoist. West raises the other hoist just high enough off the floor for a bench and lays out a fender pad so you don't have to sit on steel. The big blast heater going in the corner of the ceiling has things warm enough for teeshirts. You pull chairs out of the dingy office to form a loose circle with the padded hoist. Then, while you're eating, Yenchik tells you.

"He bought you a new engine?" says West.

"Yeah," says Yenchik. "And a tranny."

"What'd he get?"

"A 39 Ford three-speed. But a floor shift instead of a column."

"I mean engine."

"Same thing. Flathead. Just newer. Bigger. Wants to bore it out to maybe 276."

How you helped him build the old one. How his father bored the cylinders and stroked the crank and you and Yenchik torqued new connecting rods around the polished wrists between its counterweights.

"Why you doing another flathead?" says West. "Why not an overhead?"

"My dad wants to keep it kind of stock," Yenchik says.

"Why bother?" says West.

"I know," says Yenchik. "He's talking about blowing it."

"A blower?" Keller says.

"Yeah. New carbs too. Three Carter 97 two-barrels."

"Why's he doin' all this?" says West. "What'd you have to promise him?"

Yenchik shrugs. "Nothing," he says. "He just started doing it one day. I asked him. He told me not to look a gift horse in the mouth."

"What's it gonna put out?" says Keller.

"He wants to crack four hundred."

"Holy shit," says Keller.

"Anyway," says West, raising his malt cup, "Happy New Year."

You put up your malt cup and throw your Happy New Year in.

"There's beer in the fridge," says West.

"Anyone hear from Lilly?" says Doby.

"How'd he end up in Mexico anyway?" West says.

"All that Spanish he took in school," says Keller.

"Where's he at in Mexico?"

"Mexico City, I think."

"There any other cities in Mexico?"

"Tijuana."

"Maybe he's there."

"What're you gonna do with your car?" Doby asks West.

"Block it up," says West. "Take the wheels off."

"Me too," says Keller.

"Mine's going to my little brother," says Doby.

"I'm gonna store mine too," says Yenchik.

Six feet in the air the fat tires and shaved treads of his big red Ford hang like the paws of a lifted dog out of the housings of their fenders.

"With a new engine?" says West.

"It'll be here. Ain't goin' nowhere. My dad'll start it now and then."

"What'd Lilly do with his Renault?"

"I think junked it."

"Naw," says Keller. "It's behind his house."

Their cars. The way this conversation has always gone without you. The way you tried to keep your arm off the windowsills in summer, out of the sun, because it was your right arm, because the guys you always rode with always had their left arms tanned.

"Any idea where you're going, Jasperson?" says West.

"Wherever they need me."

"I think you get to tell them where you'd like," says Keller. "Three choices."

"Doesn't mean they have to care," says Doby.

"I'm gonna say Hawaii," West says. "All three times."

"Yeah," says Doby. "You and a hundred thousand other missionaries."

"Maybe I'll throw in Tahiti."

"Finland," says Yenchik.

"Finland?" you say.

"My mom's from there."

"England," says Keller.

"You going to Switzerland?" Jasperson asks you.

You're thinking New York. Doing your mission among the musicians on Mr. Selby's wall. You're on his wall now too. You could give them all the Priesthood.

"I can't," you tell Jasperson. "I'd get drafted."

"You're already in the Army," says Yenchik.

"I'm still Swiss," you say. "They don't care what other army I'm in."

"That'd be crazy," says Yenchik. "The Swiss Army. You seen their knives?"

"I thought they were neutral," says Doby. "What do they need an army for?"

"I guess to stay that way."

"Know what I've always wondered?" says West. "How come your parents got accents but you don't."

"So if Switzerland's out," says Jasperson, "then where?"

"I don't know. Maybe Austria."

"Who's goin' next?" says Yenchik.

"Me," says Keller. "February."

"March," says Jasperson.

"April," says West.

"What you all got planned between now and then?" says Doby.

"Not a thing," says Keller. "I haven't even got two months."

Doby looks at Jasperson. "So what're you doing? Between now and March?"

"Working with my brother," he says.

"Me too," says Yenchik. "With my old man."

"I'm gonna make a couple of quarters at the U," says Doby.

"I'm gonna get as much nookie as I can," says West.

Doby looks alarmed. "You gotta stay cherry. Technically."

"I will. But two years, man. The closest I'll get to a girl is if I baptize one. I gotta store up."

"You scared you'll rape somebody if you run out?" says Yenchik.

"Why don't you try storing up some spirituality," Jasperson says.

"I never thought of that," says Yenchik. "Storing up something."

"Shit," says Doby suddenly.

Everyone hears it in his voice. Everyone looks. Doby's got his big heart in his face.

"Yeah," says Keller finally.

Miles Davis. Giving him the Priesthood. You look around the suddenly hushed circle of your buddies. It hasn't been that long since they could have laughed about it. Maybe they still could. You're not so sure. Somewhere along the way they stopped cracking jokes about all the stuff you'd been taught in Sunday School and Priesthood class. Doby stopped talking about the power your middle finger had to turn over a Jeep full of high school football jocks. Keller stopped talking about the house where Brigham Young lived with his wives and the windowpeeking bonanza it must have been. Yenchik stopped talking about Jesus wearing a Stetson. Somewhere along the way it got to where it started to make them nervous. Started turning what Jasperson called sacrilegious. Like everything they'd been taught was closing in on them. Spreading its way across the sky in a weatherless iron overcast. Like cracking jokes had been a way of thinking they could hold it back, and then found out they couldn't, and then started giving in to it. Like the Holy Ghost could blow their hearts wide open if they even listened to the wrong joke. You don't know. Just that they started taking on the look. Happy to shake your hand. This nervous chiding tolerance when you cracked a joke too close to where the iron sky ran out for comfort.

Like giving the Priesthood to Miles Davis.

And then Duke Ellington.

And then Clifford Brown.

And then John Coltrane.

Art Blakey. Sonny Rollins. Thelonius Monk. You could do them all right here in the circle of your buddies. A chair in the center. Jasperson could interview them to make sure they're responsible. And then you could take the power you've given them to play with them. You shake it off. You know without looking that nobody's in a joking mood. This could be the last time all of you circle up like this.

You stand up and stretch.

"Hey Bobby," you say to West.

"Yeah?"

"The offer for that beer still good?"

"Sure is. Hell, might as well bring me one."

"I'll take one."

"Me too."

"Yeah. Hell with it."

"How about you, Jasperson?"

CHAPTER 48

THE MUSIC BUILDING is on the old part of campus, the long U-shaped drive around which the stately academic buildings stand, flank to flank, old brick and stone buildings three or four stories tall. Anthropology. Mathematics. Chemistry. Physics. Home Economics. Kingsbury Hall where they do Swan Lake and the Nutcracker. At the top of the drive the building where you register for Jazz Harmony and Jazz Composition.

A long and lazy plantation porch spans the front of the Music Building with tall stone columns and maybe twenty or thirty shallow steps you'd look stupid or crippled climbing if you took them one at a time. Right inside there's a concert hall with a makeshift stage and the floor cluttered with hundreds of folding chairs. You follow old brass railings up the stone staircases and stone floors down the hallways. The classrooms are shabby and beige and plain, the windows tall, old blackboards across the front wall, a battered grand piano in the corner. Faculty offices with frosted windows in their wooden doors line the west end hallways of every floor. Mr. Selby's is on the second. You learn that the building was built and used for the student union until they built the new one up on the hill where the modern buildings are. The concert hall used to be the cafeteria. In the hallways of the basement are the practice rooms, small windowless bare-walled rooms that come with music stands, folding chairs, old studio pianos. Through every door comes music. Violin. Cello. Clarinet. Guitar. Flute. Piccolo. Piano. And horns. English to French to tuba to trombone to sax. Oboe. Bassoon. All the instruments Mr. Hinkle played and then some.

The first time you go inside you're caught off guard. You've been here. You've spent time here. Whatever you did had enough of a bite to have found soft metal in your memory, machine its light and smell and sound and feel and look there, deep and permanent and exact enough to slide and lock into position, like a piston into a cylinder, an intake valve into its brass seat. The building itself has an imprint. Some earlier place. At first you don't know when or where. And then you do. It never was a real place. It was the place you patched together in your head when Mr. Selby started you on Arban's book of exercises. When he told you about the Conservatory in Paris where Professor Arban taught. The place where you used to imagine yourself when you closed your eyes and practiced his technical exercises. Here it is for real. Plaster and paint and stone and brass and wood and desks and blackboards. Air warmed by spitting radiators crusted with old beige paint. Even the space defined by the vault of the dingy walls and the high gray ceilings. Its feel of discipline. Of practice. Of work. Of taking stuff that looks impossible to learn at first and making it not only possible but part of you. Diligent and patient and over and over again until you've got it to where it can never be taken away. And now the building too.

You catch on quick, your first day there, from what you hear from the classrooms and the practice rooms and concert hall, from the students you see in the hallways, that classical music rules the place and almost all its students. That the building is mostly a training ground or holding pen for the Utah Symphony Orchestra. And then, what you sense in the building you put together in your head, in the music, in the students, is your father. Another face of his army, its orchestral face, they look like they already know he's out there in the audience, in the Tabernacle in his season ticket seat, his big hands primed to clap for them no matter what they play. Rachmaninoff. Chopsticks. Farmer in the Dell. In the hallways they always look first for your instrument case. Trumpet. A jazz student. For the first few days you're new enough to smile or nod or say hello. And when all they do is look, or look away, you're new enough to let yourself be ambushed by the hunger you remember from junior high when you haunted the music room and trailed the kids with instrument cases down the hallways. And then you catch yourself. You're going. You don't have to care. And then what they think of you is gone, smoke off fire, water off a waxed car hood.

A fierce little guy named Professor Rodriguez teaches your Jazz Harmony class. He's got the hard good looks of a bandit, an attitude quick as a switchblade, slick black hair. He wears a bolo tie where the slide is a silver cattle skull that looks like your Duty to God award. What matters most to him is that you never take your eyes off him. While he lays out the hard-driving bebop style of Bud Powell and shows you the way Powell harmonically freed the right hand from the left, while he demonstrates the more introspective rubato style of Bill Evans and shows you how Evans used modal harmonies like Debussy, you can see his hawk eyes on the hunt for anyone he can kick out of class and as far away as possible from thinking they've got a shot at jazz. Guys who disagree with him. Guys who pick their noses or look at their wrists for the time. Guys who look at anything else in the room. Guys who happen to turn their heads if a delivery truck backfires out the window. Before they even look back they know they're dead. And then he goes after them with a flurry of insults about everything from their posture to their attitude to their talent to their weight to their clothes and hair to their mother. You can tell he's watched them because what he picks by way of insults is right on target. Center of Maximum Vulnerability. Some guys fight back. Some guys beg. One guy starts crying. One guy tells him he's a piece of wetback crap who needs his ass kicked back across the Rio Grande. You hear about guys who were kicked out of class so hard and far they went and started majoring in chemistry or math. For you it's simple. Fall back on what you learned in the Army about rules and doing what you're told. Keep your attention on him. Look like you know jazz. Like you are jazz. Keep the way you're going on a mission to yourself.

"Today he told this guy to give his bass to his mother to keep her snake collection in."

"He told this one guy if he wanted to improve his flute playing to jam it up his ass and eat a burrito an hour before practice."

"He went after this guy once for bringing a dead cat to class. The guy asked what cat. Zorro told him the one on his head. He meant the guy's hair."

"Can't he get canned?"

"He knows more harmony than the rest of this place put together. Times ten."

"Plus all these great players."

"Did you know he's really from Brazil?"

"He is?"

"Yeah. Everybody just thinks he's Mexican. It's ignorant."

Professor Fisher teaches your Jazz Composition class. The man who came here from California to start the Jazz Program. He's lanky and relaxed with a face as placid as a cow and strands of dark hair streaked with gray pulled across the crest of his big forehead. Nothing bothers him. You can pay attention to him or you can sit there and pick your nose till it bleeds or punch your eardrums out with your pencil or find another way to go to hell. He doesn't care. All he pays attention to is what he's there to teach. Everything else in the room is furniture. Like someone between a mechanic and a jigsaw puzzle wizard, he takes apart one compositional form after another, lays out its pieces, gives all the pieces names, shows you what makes them what they are and how they work, and then reassembles them. Sometimes he shuffles them around. Mixes them up. And then puts them all in motion. You come to see where Mr. Selby taught you flight, and now, Professor Fisher, the hollow bonework and the intricate articulations of ligaments and tendons that are the mechanics and mathematics of the way jazz flies.

The students call him Benny. Nobody knows where it started or why. Two theories are that he's a perfectionist like Benny Goodman or that he's hung the way Jack Benny is. He can play anything. Sometimes he'll borrow an instrument off a guy in class, play it like it's his, then give it back, and leave the guy who owns it looking like he doesn't want to admit it's his. Sometimes he'll sit at the big black grand at the front of the room and use the keyboard to illustrate what he's saying, talk about modal harmony, lay out the difference between the ionian and aeolian modes and how they sound over a melodic minor, and before long he's not saying anything, just playing, and then he'll look around like he's in some jazz club, this look on his face like he's wondering what kind of club would have desks instead of tables. You take him on too. Take his assignments, little compositional pieces, and do them at night in the office out at work. And then do something extra with them, because doing them straight is never good enough.

Your family arranges things so that the Valiant is mostly there for you when you need it. In half a year they'll have it to themselves again. Till then your father will ride to work and back with his friend Ron Whipple in his one-eyed Chrysler. He has to prove to you that it can work, his logic, not needing a car of your own because there's always someone else with one. You take them up on it. Drive from Bountiful to your classes at the U. Find a place to park along the established tree-lined streets just off the lower campus where professors live and where the fraternity and sorority houses are. Head home for supper. Head for work at night where the big machines wait in the yards to be watched over, guarded from giant thieves, where you park the Valiant in the lot inside the gate, till six, when you turn the yards over to the day guys and head for home again.

Some mornings, coming home in the dark at half past six, following the headlights of the Valiant up the hill through your neighborhood, you can see the one bright headlight of Ron Whipple's Chrysler coming down the hill the other way. Some mornings they haven't plowed, and in the unmarked snow you have to slip the Valiant past the one-eyed Chrysler in this slithering fender-to-fender dance where the Valiant's headlights set white fire to the salt-streaked flank of the Chrysler, where the Chrysler's headlight swerves and rakes your face white, where you wonder if your father can see you, working the steering wheel in the quick white slash of his friend's one headlight. Some mornings you park out in the circle and shovel snow before you bring the Valiant down the driveway. You wait while Molly and Roy and Maggie gear up for school and then come back to sleep. Before noon you're up and ready to go again. Tell your mother thanks but you don't have time to eat. On Highway 89, on the way out of Bountiful, stop at the Frostop and grab a burger and Coke on your way back to the Music Building.

Keep to yourself. Don't go looking for friends. Don't let yourself wonder about the Greek letters above the doors and over the porches of the fraternity houses. Don't let yourself think that anything you do will be permanent. You're going. It's been there every time you looked at the other possibility. With Jeff the time on the hill when you first considered it. When Mr. Selby asked you what you were still doing here. You're going. You're not from Louisville or San Jose or some other American city. You're from here. Jeff and Mr. Selby didn't get it. You should have told them. You didn't know how.

Around the halls, between classes, you hear stories about Professor Fisher the way you hear them about Professor Rodriguez.

"One day Benny got to playing and the bell rang for the end of class. The noise made him look up. He saw us up and moving around with our stuff. So he got up and welcomed us to class and told us what he'd be teaching us today."

"You're kidding."

"It was the same stuff he'd just taught us. How modern classical music gets into jazz. How Gil Evans would use stuff from Debussy and Ravel."

"What'd you do?"

"Just sat down. Pretended like we were just getting there. Most of us didn't have another class."

"Nobody told him?"

"Hell no. You get a bonus class from Fisher, you don't screw it up. Even if it's a repeat. It's always different. The stuff he knows, the people he knows, man, it's amazing."

One day, down in the hallways of the basement, looking for a vacant practice room, you hear a line, a line you recognize, a blues line, guitar and bass, and you follow it down the hall and down some stairs you didn't know were there, down underneath the basement, down into the stone foundation of the building, where bundled black ropes of electrical wiring run along the ceilings, where huge leaking pipes make the air damp and drip what they're leaking into thin puddles on the concrete floor. Three guys. A girl.

"Let me guess. Trumpet."

"Yeah."

"I'm Lenny. Where you from?"

"Bountiful. It's north of here."

"I'm from Fresno."

"I'm from Wisconsin. Steve."

"I know Bountiful. I'm Roland. This is Sandy."

"I'm Shake."

"I remember you," the girl named Sandy says.

CHAPTER 49

YOU AND KELLER and Korbuck and Jackson and West and Mouse and Gus and the rest of you come home from Knox to an Army Reserve unit that has changed from Infantry to Armor. They want to be tankers too. They've managed to get their hands on some tanks, old Patton tanks like the tanks you trained on, and are looking to you to train the rest of them. In January, on your Reserve weekend, in your fatigues and combat boots again, that's what you start to do. Catch a ride with Keller and West to Fort Douglas and teach guys from the captain on down through the ranks the stuff you learned at Knox. How to command them. How to load and fire them. There isn't a firing range around, so you teach them how to load and fire dry, with the breeches of the big guns empty, waiting until you go on summer camp in June for a couple of weeks of the real thing.

"I heard we're going to Yakima," says Mouse.

"Where's that?" says Korbuck.

"I dunno. Washington I think."

"I won't be here," says Keller.

"Mission?" says Mouse.

"Yeah."

"I heard Fort Irwin," says Gus.

"Where's that?" says Boon.

"Out in the Mojave somewhere. Between Vegas and Barstow. Closer to Barstow."

"The Mojave Desert?"

"Yeah," says Gus. "A whole desert to run around in."

The property that makes up Fort Douglas lies around the eastern and southern sides of the University. Sometimes the boundaries between them aren't clear. Some of the old one-story barracks are used by the University for student services like health and special testing and career counseling. You teach the guys in your unit the sequence for priming and firing up the engines. And from there you teach them how to drive the big machines. For now, for the winter, with the fields above the fort into the foothills blanketed in snow and the fields themselves frozen, you're limited to roads. The pads on the tracks are rubber, not cleated steel, so you can use the roads around the fort without shredding up the asphalt. From the tank commander's cupola up on top of the turret, your helmet on over your headset, you give the guys down in the driver's hatch instructions over the intercom. You take them out on roads around the fort. Sometimes out on roads you aren't sure you should be using. Sometimes you know you've wandered onto university roads, roads lined here and there with dormitories, roads where occasional students in their winter coats and boots step back against the plowed snow and watch you clank and rumble past. Sometimes, for kicks, you look down and salute them. Sometimes they salute back. One girl puts her mittened hand on her heart. One guy flips you the bird. He's quick to fold it up when you grin and lay your hand on the fifty caliber machine gun swinging in its yoke on the commander's cupola.

From January into February the yards at Hiller are dead. Under the tall yard lights, sometimes under moonlight, snow crests every surface of the big yellow idled machines, and the hoods and roofs of the semis and the maintenance trucks. Out past the fencelines are vacant fields with random piles and ridges of bulldozed dirt, other industrial places guarded by dogs whose occasional barking gives them away as dogs you wouldn't mess with, and to the west the long dike of the freeway, where all you can see of the big dark roaring semis that have the lanes to themselves this time of night are the upper running lights of their cabs and trailers.

You practice to bulldozers and road graders and payloaders that gather round in the dark. You wander the packed dirt and snow between them and stop to play to them like they're quiet tables of customers at a club. You take requests. Sometimes the dogs get barking from the neighboring yards. You use the wool liners of your Army gloves to keep your fingers warm and workable. This time you do it right. Only cut the tips off the right hand fingers. And then just the three you need for the valves. This time, when you walk the frozen dirt, you do it in combat boots instead of galoshes.

You do your written homework at the battered desk in the small office where they hired you. A small electric heater keeps the air warm to where the mostly naked blondes on the posters around the walls won't freeze. Sometimes you fire up one of the payloaders and spend the night pushing snow. You always take the radio the way you were told to. Always the flashlight. Sometimes the shotgun. Sometimes you use a semi on the freeway, the way the sound of its engine deepens after it passes you, to practice bending notes.

At the end of January Keller gets his mission call. He's going to England. The father who adopted him has ancestors or relatives there. They schedule his Missionary Farewell to take the place of a Sacrament Meeting two weeks into February. He gets to make up the program. Decide on everything from the hymns to the speakers to the musical numbers to the men who will give the opening and closing prayers. And then get the program printed. The night of his farewell you drop a couple of twenties through the slot in the top of the cardboard contribution box on the table in the lobby, have an usher hand you a program, take a seat next to Doby in the chapel. Keller's up on the podium in one of the cushioned theater chairs between Bishop Wacker and the First Counselor. Relatives and friends come up to the pulpit and brag him up and down while he sits behind them not knowing where to look. One of his Key Club buddies from high school, a guy named Herman Walsh, does his tribute to Keller wearing his Key Club blazer. A woman the program says is Susan Huber plays Ave Maria on a violin. A man named Orville Wall with a belly like a hippopotamus and a voice that goes with his belly belts out Ode to Joy from the Ninth Symphony while your mother plays the organ behind him. Both choices leave you clueless.

At the end, Keller gets up, thanks everybody, says a few words about how worthless and undeserving he is, testifies that he knows beyond a shadow of a doubt that the Church is true and that President McKay is a Prophet of God. He promises he'll work hard for the Lord and for everyone in the congregation while he's off in England.

"How much did you give him?" you ask Doby on the way out.

"None of your business," says Doby, offended, like you've asked him what size bra his mother wears.

"I gave him forty," you say.

"Forty? Holy crap."

"Too much? Not enough?"

"Too bad you won't be here to give me forty."

"So how much did you give him?"

"None of your business."

And on Monday Keller's gone to do a week in the Salt Lake Mission Home for instruction and conditioning. And then, the last day, a visit to the Temple, where he'll go through the ceremony and make his everlasting covenants with God and wear jockey shorts for the last time. Then on from there to England. This is what it's like. The road. It ends. You're gone. Just gone. Not for an interlude of months. Not where your place can be saved. But for years. Heading for class that day, taking the Valiant past the stockyards, past the refinery, this is what you need to keep remembering. The road runs out and you're just gone.

Two of the students who make up the Jazz Program are girls. One named Debbie who plays jazz violin. The other one Sandy, who sings, the girl who sang Embraceable You the last night you were at Sammy's before the bus ride out across the desert to Fort Ord. The first time you wandered down the stairs into the stone foundation of the Music Building she took your breath away for the second time. Not because she was singing. She wasn't. But because you remembered what her voice felt like. And somehow she remembered you.

The blond-headed guy who played piano that night behind her was down there too. Lenny. The guy from Fresno. Once she told him who you were, where they'd heard you, he lit up, remembering you too. A trumpet. All Blues. You shook hands with Steve. He had an acoustic guitar on his leg. You shook hands with Roland. A standup bass. And then you shook hands with Sandy. Her hand was small and soft and her grip was just with her fingertips.

"Where'd you find that piano player?" Lenny saying.

"Piano player?"

"The guy who thought he could play with you."

"I didn't know him. He was just there that night."

Lenny with this constant smile going, like something good or something funny is always just around the corner, this ready contagious laugh he throws around you and Sandy and Steve and Roland like Hawaiian flower necklaces.

"That guy was clueless," he says. "He didn't know what the hell you were doing."

"He said he knew the tune."

"Yeah. Until then you started throwing those curveballs in."

"He got mad," you saying.

"Mad?" Lenny saying. Laughing again. "He got killed. Serious. He hasn't been back."

"Where have you been?" Sandy looking at you. "We kept looking for you."

"You did?"

"Yes."

"I had to do the Army."

"So you're back now?"

"Yeah."

"Still know how to play?" Lenny saying.

"I think so."

"Here."

Handing you a sheet of music paper, chords written in, the notes of a melody, lyrics for Sandy to sing, a title written in capital letters across the top.

"Refrigerator Blues?" you saying.

"Yeah," him saying. "Why not?"

"Just asking."

Sandy smiling. "Lenny's got this problem with his landlord."

CHAPTER 50

KELLER GONE. Inside the turret, on the floor along the back wall, within easy reach of the breech for the main gun, there's a row of racks that stand and hold the big ninety millimeter rounds. Back in the turret overhang there are secondary racks. The racks on the floor are for primary fire. You tell the guys in your unit that in combat they always need to make sure they keep the floor racks stocked from the racks in the overhang.

Sometimes you look at the racks on the floor and see your buddies lined up there like tank rounds. Tall brass shells. Thick tapered steel-cased heads. The first rack is already empty. Lilly's already gone. Loaded and aimed and fired off at the mission field of Mexico. And now, from the racks that hold your buddies, round number two. Keller aimed and fired off to England.

At the end of his farewell, when you shook his hand and said good-bye, his face was gone already. The old Keller face. What was there instead was the look, gone to steel now, soft and silver and blank, his face encased in it, the steel-cased head of a ninety millimeter round. The smile cased in steel too. The same steel-cased smile that people in Mexico see when they open their door and find Lilly standing there in his dust-hazed shoes.

When you look at the racks now, it's Jasperson, the next round up, ready to be slipped into the breech and locked, ready to be aimed and fired. All he needs is a target. A letter from the President of the Church to make the call. Then West. Then you. Austria maybe. Just not New York or Switzerland. Doby in the rack behind you. And behind him Yenchik.

On the Saturday afternoon of your Reserve weekend in February, on the asphalt out behind the old Fort Douglas building your unit uses,

Lieutenant Tanner dismisses you for the day. Guys in their fatigues and combat boots head for their cars under the dark overcast of the winter afternoon. Small flakes, random and fitful, float in the air around you like they're scout flakes, testing the air for the big flakes. You're talking to an older guy named Hadley, one of the guys on your crew, and to West, about snow coming, about getting the Pontiac home before it starts coming down for real, when Lieutenant Tanner comes up to you.

"I hear they gave you a special lighter at Knox. That true?"

"Yes Sir. A Zippo."

"I'd like to see it. I'm sure the other guys would too."

"Engraved or something?" says Hadley.

"Yeah," says West. "Seventh out of thirty thousand."

"Bring it tomorrow," says Lieutenant Tanner. "Okay?"

"Sure thing, Sir."

You haven't seen the Zippo since Christmas Eve when you put it in the box that Molly painted with flowers and gave you. It felt safe there. Locked not by an actual padlock but by the hand of her guardian angel. When you open it that night, there's some change, your arrowheads from La Sal, the tiny gold bugle Roy and Maggie gave you. You try to remember taking it anywhere. To show the guys at Hiller's. Eddie and Robbie. Mr. Selby. You didn't want to show it off. That wasn't what it was. It was only when someone asked for it. You check the pockets of your pants and jackets. Your desk, your nightstand, the four drawers of your chest, your closet. Under your bed. Behind everything. Molly's box again. Rifle the change around like your Zippo could hide like a penny under another coin. It's gone. On the stove a steel pot of lentils simmers under its canted steel lid. You find your mother in the dining room with the ledger book she uses to put together all your ancestors.

"No, Shakli. When was the last time you saw it?"

"Christmas Eve."

"Are you sure you didn't take it and forget to put it back?"

"I'm sure," you say. "Don't worry."

Karl. The way it got his attention in the airport. The way he played with lighting it. His thing for fire. You find him watching another cowboy movie in the recreation room.

"Did you borrow it? Forget to put it back?"

"No. Honest."

"You should call that flute teacher."

"Okay."

In the den your father's using his cork-backed steel ruler and a red pen to draw a line like a knife would leave in skin under a line of print in a fat book spread wide open on his desk. You close the door behind you. Half the paragraph is already underlined in red. His portable radio plays classical piano music low. On its wheeled metal stand his big Royal typewriter hums away in neutral. You stand behind it where he can see you when he turns his head.

"Where's my Zippo?"

He gets another line of the paragraph underscored with a razor's line of blood before he puts things down and turns your way.

"Zippo?"

"The lighter they gave me in the Army."

"What about it?"

"Where is it?"

"I got rid of it. Why?"

"What do you mean?"

"I threw it out."

"When?"

"On Christmas Eve."

Him knowing you put it in the box that Molly painted. Knowing you left the box in the living room that night. Waiting you out. Sneaking the lid open. Your Zippo in his thieving hand. You wonder if he paused somewhere in there to admire Molly's handpainted flowers.

"Tell me where it is."

"Tell me what purpose it had besides lighting cigarettes."

The men who gave it to you. The reason they did. Cissy's face in the light of its flame. Everything the Army meant. You motherfucker, you think.

"Where'd you throw it? Where the hell is it?"

"Settle down. It's gone. You can't get it back. You'll have to accept that."

"It can't be gone. It's where the fuck you threw it. Tell me where."

"This is my house. Don't tell me what to do. And don't use that language."

"Then tell me the Swiss word for fuck."

"That's enough."

"I don't even smoke."

"It doesn't matter. In this house we have to avoid even the appearance of evil."

"It's an award."

"It's a tool of the Devil."

"It's what they gave me. For something I did."

"You could have given it back. Asked for a nice plaque instead."

You look up, at the shelves of his books behind him, suddenly alone, on the night highway back from Wendover again, listening to voices out of the night comfort each other on the radio, crying for them, crying for their comfort too.

"But you were proud of me."

"Of course."

"You put me in the Church News. You put me in the trophy case."

"Yes. I was very proud. But I take more pride in one of your Individual Achievement Awards. And you have six of them. Do I see them among your valuables? Do I hear you bragging about them? Or your Duty to God Award?"

"You haven't heard me brag about the Army."

"No. But I see you put a tool of the Devil in a box for your valuables. What example is that for your brothers and sisters? Treating a cigarette lighter as a valuable."

"They see me wear my Duty to God Award."

"Yes. But think of Molly. All the trouble she went to, making that box for her older brother. And he puts a cigarette lighter in it."

"And her father comes along and steals it."

His face goes hard.

"You were in the Army. You should have learned some respect."

"Don't act like you care what I did in the Army."

"Tell me how many times you went to a church service."

"Not once."

"Then don't expect me to care what else you did."

"I learned how to play Motherless Child."

His face goes rough, from doubt, from some memory. He drops his eyes to the carriage of the big gray Royal. The sheet of paper. The steel keys in their cradle angled and machined to strike the same steel gunsight of the slot where the paper waits. He looks up.

"While you were away?" he says. "Your trumpet was here the entire time."

"Back when you told me it was your favorite song."

"I told you that?"

"Yeah. In the garage. Remember?"

"Why would that song be my favorite? When I have a few hundred hymns to choose from?"

You stare at him. It's what he has to say. Every book on the raw pine shelves behind him is written by a General Authority. The commanders of his army ranked and harnessed in his den where the furnace suddenly lights off behind the steel wall his door of a desk stands flush against. His army waiting while he holds your own harness out to you. His weary scolding resentment from being the one to always have to do this, come forward and stand there in front of his army embarrassed again, because you're his son, and it's his house, and it's his job to strip you of your Zippo. In front of them it's what he has to say. This hungry fire rages underneath your skin like you're being burned from inside out. The steel wall of the furnace shudders as the blower comes on. Johnny Mathis singing Twelfth of Never gets pushed by heated air back up through the heating ducts. From the recreation room you hear the crack of gunfire and the drumming sound of horses galloping on dirt and an orchestra racing them along. You can't avoid it. This house you left and then came home to knowing how to blow to smithereens. Your Zippo. Your eyes burn while you stand there and finally let the fact go howling through you, cold and raw through the place where your Zippo was.

"It's gone, isn't it."

"And you should know why."

"It was all I had, Papa. For something good I did."

"You have a big newspaper article. And a clipping from the Church News."

"It was something I could hold. Something I could show people if they wanted."

"Well, you'll have to show them something else."

He gives the keyboard of his idling typewriter a glance. Everything he has the way he wants it. Motherfucker, you think. You had your Zippo. At Knox you could reach into your pocket and there it was. You could run your thumb across its face and feel your name and what you did in the letters cut into the steel. Seventh out of thirty thousand. The first time in your life you were good enough. Motherfucker. That's what you had. What you brought home. Fuck your church, you think. What lie you'll have to tell Lieutenant Tanner tomorrow for your father.

"Don't ever touch my stuff again."

"I'm sorry," he says. "but it's my house."

Looking down at the concrete floor where he's got a big flat plastic pad for the rollers of his office chair. What you could do to his house.

"Okay then," you say. "Guess I'll remember that."

PART 7

THE HIGHWAY NOW

CHAPTER 51

TRAVEL LIGHT. Stay loose. You're passing through. Soon the road will end. Where you'll just be gone. Lift your head too quick and you can see where it will happen. Where the blacktop will run onto roadbed, and the roadbed onto dirt, where the barriers and arrow signs will shunt you off, and so you keep your head down and your headlights low so all you see is the onrush of the blacktop right in front of you. Keep the place where it ends in the dark.

The stuff you learned from Mr. Selby. The musicians whose songs and solos and moves you learned from Mr. Selby's records. What you learn in your classes now is how to look at what's inside them. The logic and structure and sense in their phrases and harmonies and chords and melodies and rhythms. When they're trapped and held still they all have names. Antecedent and consequent phrases. Compound lines. Guide tones. Modal and tonal and chromatic approaches. Transformations and inversions and reharmonizations. When you let them go again they shed their names like husks. It doesn't take long to understand that it's stuff you already know. Stuff you know as soon as you hear it played and put to flight.

There are guys in class you recognize from Sammy's. Guys ahead of you in school. From the desk you take toward the rear you let them do the talking. You're the new guy. You take the names they teach you, learn them and give them back on tests, leave it to the other guys to toss them back and forth in class, the guys who've learned how to play them in the improvisational solos of their long and elaborate sentences.

At night, in the office at Hiller's with the heater keeping the poster girls warm, you use the names to do your written homework. And after you're done, when you walk the yards with your trumpet to play what you've written down, what you play is nameless. You keep it that way. So that the line of sound is clean and agile with flight when you send it out among the silent yellow hulks of the nameless machines they use to build roads.

In February somewhere, from the yards, you start to see light to the east toward the end of your shift. Not much. Enough to start to bring the long familiar rolling shoulders of the mountains into silhouette. In March the big machines start disappearing from the yards. The man who hired you was right. You never know when you get to work which ones will just be gone. The night mechanics start showing up at the gate in their maintenance trucks, back from their work sites, from four in the morning on. They've radioed in to let you know they're coming. You've got their coffee made. They sit there in the office and have a cup with a cigarette and tell you where they were and what they fixed that night and what stories they picked up. How some clown managed to tear a track off a dozer. How some other retard managed to dump a grader off a bank. How a blast of dynamite found a fracture in a hill they didn't know about and the hill got away from them. They smoke Lucky Strikes and Pall Malls and Chesterfields. Most of them light their cigarettes with Zippos, Zippos they haul out of their pockets, flip open, strike and hold till they draw smoke, snap closed, put away again. Sometimes, listening to their stories, you sit there thinking you could be one of them. Start as an apprentice. Tag along on their night adventures out into the wilderness of some road they're building somewhere. End up with your own truck, your own tools, your own work orders, your own stories to bring back and tell the night watchman, your own Zippo. You open the gate again to let them out. On your own ride home, on the street up the hill through your neighborhood, houses start taking on form around their lighted windows, and the oncoming body of the Chrysler starts to take shape around its single headlight.

The nameless hunger you found waiting when you got home from Knox. The headlights low and your foot light on the throttle. You keep doing your job, turning in your homework, invisible in class and silent, until the day Professor Rodriguez calls your name. Calls you up front.

"No. Bring your trumpet."

If he wants to make an example out of you on your way out the door to a major in engineering. The new guy. When you get up front you can see the whole class thinking it. When Professor Rodriquez is done with you he comes back from the corner.

"That's what I was after," he says. "Okay? Everybody get that?" And then he looks at you. "You forget where your desk is?"

As your classes move through March, as word comes back that Keller's doing fine in England, Professor Rodriguez and then Professor

Fisher keep calling you up front to help them illustrate a way of phrasing, some harmonic overlay for a blues chord or modal progression, whatever they're teaching. The guys in your classes turn out to be okay with you. Talk to you in the halls, show you their homework, ask you to join their groups when Professor Rodriquez and Professor Fisher break you out for session work. You start hanging around the Music Building deep into the afternoons. Winter quarter ends. You sign up for spring for the next level of the same two classes. Snow thaws back from the banks you piled up at night along the fencelines of the yards at Hiller's. When you catch the Chrysler coming down the hill, there's enough light now to have its headlight off and see Ron Whipple's glasses, the steel glint of two silver dollars in the shadow of his face.

Jasperson runs out of road the end of March. When they ordain him an Elder, slide him into the breech, get him locked and loaded and ready to receive his mission call. He's hoping for France. Hoping the Lord will take a hint from the year of French he took in high school. A week later, when his letter comes, it's West Virginia. He's not thrilled. Wherever the Lord needs him, he says, but he acts morose and looks gypped.

His farewell in early April is more of a homespun thing than Keller's was. Everyone on the program is right out of the congregation. He has Brother Clark and Brother Rodgers and Scoutmaster Haycock speak. Scoutmaster Haycock talks about the time Jasperson spent at Charlie Belnap's bedside in the hospital, holding the hand of a man who kept calling him Lucy, before the old man finally died. He has Sister Johansen and Sister Avery do a harp and vocal duet of I Believe. This time Sister Johansen doesn't come off like a cloudburst in a jungle and Sister Avery tones down the country western stuff. This time they perform muted, almost like they've been chastised, for having been excited, for having drawn applause. You wonder if Wacker had a talk with them. Jasperson has your mother play the first movement of the Moonlight Sonata on the organ.

At the end, Jasperson himself gets up, thanks everybody, testifies that he knows beyond the shadow of a doubt that God the Father and Jesus Christ and the Holy Ghost appeared to Joseph Smith in the Sacred Grove, and says what a blessing and humbling honor it is to go forth and spread the glorious message of the restored gospel to the good people of West Virginia.

"You give Jasperson forty too?" says Doby afterward.

"None of your business," you say.

"He got forty too," says Doby. "Didn't he."

"I'll leave you forty," you say. "I'll leave it with Karl."

"You expecting forty from me?"

"Did you ever hear Jasperson say glorious before?"

"No," says Doby. And then he says, "I knew something sounded weird."

On Monday the order to fire when ready goes to the gunner. The tank rocks back with the force of the recoil. The breech of the gun comes lunging back into the turret smoking. The loader steps up and opens the breech and pulls out the smoking shell with his oven mitts. The warhead named Johnny Jasperson is gone. To the Mission Home on its trajectory to West Virginia. The next round in the rack is West. And the next one back from West is you.

Cold still takes back the nearly empty yards at night. But you can make your rounds with the liner out of your field jacket. Practice without wearing the liners of your gloves. All the road guys know you play. They see your trumpet standing on the desk when they come in for coffee and a cigarette before heading home. Most of them have heard you. Most of them have asked if you know one or another song. Some of them have sung along. You know them all by name. You know how they work. Show up at a construction site at night when the big machines have been retired for the day. Set up their lights around the machine they'll be working on. On desert sites, sites in the middle of nowhere, walk around the machine with a crowbar, banging and yelling to chase out the rattlesnakes that crawled up inside the engine bay and running gear, looking for warmth for the night.

One night toward the end of April you let a guy named Frank in through the gate and sit there while he sips his coffee and smokes a Chesterfield across the desk. He's married and has a kid. He's learning how to play a guitar his wife got him for Christmas. Johnny Cash songs.

"Hear what happened to Larry?" he says.

"No."

"Truck's gone. All his tools."

"What happened?"

"He was down there with me last night. Working on a grader. Took him all night. By the time he's wrapping things up and putting away his tools the guys are showing up for work. I'm already done and gone. He gets his truck loaded and heads out. The service road is this cut they bulldozed down the side of this little canyon. It's rough. All boulders. He's picking his way down this road when he feels something under his butt. He's got one of those ventilated cushions on his seat. There's nothing right under his butt, so he reaches under the cushion, and feels something, and knows right away what it is."

"What?"

"A rattler." Frank takes a long pull on his Chesterfield, holds it, then exhales through this expanding smile. "He bails. Right out the driver's door. Lucky for him it was the uphill side of the cut. Not so lucky for the truck. It goes off the downhill side. Right off the edge."

"Jesus."

"Here's the good part. Larry gets his head together and climbs down to look his truck over. It's totaled. All his cabinets are trashed. He's got tools scattered from hell to breakfast. He looks in the cab. The snake's still in there. Laying in the roof cuz the truck's upside down. It's dead. But not from the accident. It's been dead from the start."

"Somebody planted it."

Frank sits there looking at the ash of his cigarette. Nodding.

"He walks back up to the site. The guys who did it thought it was hilarious. So they've been telling everybody. By the time Larry gets there, the story's all over the place. A bunch of the guys are laughing. He acts cool. Doesn't say who he is. Just gets the story. Two guys got to work that morning, killed this diamondback they found, coiled it up under his cushion. He gets their names. Then he heads straight for the contractor's trailer. Tells the guy in charge what happened."

"What'd he do?"

"The two guys are gone. They got kicked off the site so fast they probably went into orbit. Hiller's getting a new truck, rigged out with a whole new tool set. Actually Larry is. Compliments of the contractor. Hell. He coulda been killed."

"That's a lotta money."

"Shit. The tools are what cost. You could probably buy five trucks for what some of the tools were worth."

"What'd they do with the old truck?"

"It's still down there. Belly up. Wheels in the air. I saw it last night when I drove up. What a mess."

"They gonna pull it out? Salvage it?"

"They may just leave it. Hell. Hiller doesn't have to care. It belongs to the contractor now."

"Where's Larry?"

"He's off till he gets his new truck. With pay. That's on the contractor too."

"Nice."

"Yeah. Fuckin' nice is right. Makes me wish they'd put a rattler under my cushion. For a deal like that, hell, I'd sit on a live one."

CHAPTER 52

ONE NIGHT back in March, at Sammy's, you met a girl named Katy. A girl with sleek brown hair and sleek brown eyes and a wide sly slice of a killer smile and a street way of holding your arm to where she keeps her breast pushed up against it. A boots and levis and sweater girl from South Salt Lake. She isn't Mormon, but she's been around enough to know what a mission is, and to understand that when you say you're going on one, you're going. And so she knows. Knows this is just for now. She's a receptionist for a heating and plumbing company. She drives an old blue Studebaker Hawk her uncle gave her. You take care of getting its oil changed and chassis greased. Flush the radiator. Install new plugs and an air filter. Fix a burned out taillight. Tighten up its steering. She comes to Sammy's to hear you play and be your girl. You meet her on campus sometimes, sometimes a place downtown, and sometimes you park on the hill below Ensign Peak, up high behind the State Capitol Building.

The lights of the city below you spill out for miles on either side of the infinite spear of light of State Street, quiet from here, the noise of its engines and tires and voices lost in the vast murmur rising from the city, in the chirping of crickets in the weeds around you. You come here to make out. You don't use the Valiant. Its windows are too big. It's a family car. Other parked and darkened cars flank the Studebaker. She has you take the driver's seat. It's the way you're both used to having it. Sometimes she lets you underneath her sweater to spill her breasts out of her bra.

And then one night she says, "Want me to wait for you?"

You pull back from her face and look at her. See just enough edge to her eye and nose and mouth to tell she's smiling. The way she sounded.

"You're nuts."

"Isn't that what I'm supposed to do?"

"Somebody else beat you to it."

It sits her back to where she can tell you're kidding too.

"Okay," she says. "I'm a good loser."

On a Sunday morning toward the end of April, at Priesthood Meeting, West has his father and four of his father's friends escort him down the hall into a classroom and ordain him an Elder. Later that week he gets his letter from President David O. McKay, addressed to Elder West, calling him to be a missionary, to labor not in Hawaii or even Tahiti but in the mission fields of British Columbia. He's in the breech now too, looking down the long gleaming tunnel of the gun tube, target selected, ready to aim and fire. And then something jams. The breech can't close and lock. He isn't seated all the way. At the last minute, he got hold of something with his toes, hooked them in, and now he won't let go. Everything else is ready. He quit his job at Steed's Texaco. Had the Army put him on inactive reserve. Put his Pontiac on blocks, took off the wheels, hung his spinners on the wall.

You don't know if it's Connie, or this girl in Kaysville he just started on, or just that he hasn't stored up everything he thinks he needs yet. You can't find out because you can't get hold of him. He's holed up. His mother says he's fine but can't come to the phone or door. He doesn't come to church that Sunday. His mother's there, her usual cheerful self, her glossy hair bunched up like a thousand black Christmas bows, a walking demonstration of her gift for doing hair. Everyone knows. You know from the way they treat her, gently like she's breakable, like West's been in an accident or diagnosed with polio.

"You talk to him?" you ask Doby.

"I tried," says Doby. "You talk to Connie?"

"I can't talk to her. Not the way I know about this Kaysville chick."

"You think maybe he knocked her up?"

"Which one?"

"God," says Doby. "Either one."

"Shit. Both."

What worries you is what West's problem means for the timing of your own departure. How long you'll have to wait till they've cleared the breech. Either fired him off or pulled him out and marked him as a dud.

"He chickened out," says Doby.

"Naw. He doesn't do that."

"I meant his mission."

"Wanna bet on if he goes or not?"

"Lemme guess," says Doby. "Forty bucks."

In April, when they're thawed and dry enough, you start using the long sloped fields of the foothills above Fort Douglas, off the mouth of

Emigration Canyon, across the road from Hogle Zoo to run your tanks. On its rise of a shallow hill just up from the road stands the monument they call This Is The Place. Where you told Yenchik you played trumpet and then told him you never felt the burning of the Holy Ghost.

For the first time, the guys you're teaching are facing open country, rough terrain, uneven ground, the topography that tanks were built to run and do battle on. It's Saturday morning. You've brought the tanks up from the motor pool. They stand in a row in the dirt and weeds on the downhill apron of the sloped fields, their turrets turned backward, their long barrels bracketed back over the engine grates in travel lock. The guys are standing or squatting around Korbuck and you in their fatigues with their helmets in their hands. There are things about driving a tank you need to teach them. The way a tank will handle on rough terrain. The way a string of dunes and gullies, run at the right speed, will start to amplify the lift and dive and rebound the way a diving board or trampoline will a person. How they have to break speed or the rebound can get to where it's out of hand. You ask them if they get it. They say they do. If they have questions. They don't.

"Just take it slow at first," you tell them. "Get a feel for the way it rides."

"Yeah."

"I'm serious."

"Yeah."

For the rest of Saturday, and then again on Sunday, you and the guys who did Knox with you are riding herd on a bunch of lunatic kids. Especially the officers. Especially the two who showed up at school that night and recruited you. They don't want to hear about breaking speed. From down in the driver's hole they just want to race. They're in a tank. They're indestructible. They don't care about sending its nose in a hard vault eight feet off the ground to where all they can see is sky, diving it down into its shocks so deep its nose is almost scooping dirt and weeds and boulders, vaulting it higher off the next dune, deeper into the next gully. All they want to do is beat the next tank over, another tank doing the same thing, lunging down the long slope off the foothills, wide open, engine howling, another tank bounding alongside yours like fifty tons of jumping dolphin, where you can look across and see Korbuck doing what you're doing, riding his own big dolphin off its roiling wave of dust, braced in the commander's cupola up on the turret, hanging on for everything he's worth, yelling into the intercom the way you are.

"Sir! Slow it down!"

With the turret turned backward so the gun can ride in travel lock, with the overhang in the way, you can't look down and see Lieutenant Tanner's helmet in the driver's hatch.

"Sir! Slow down! God dammit!"

Cars park on the dirt shoulder along the road that leads into Emigration Canyon between the shoulders of its yellow hills. Families stand along the fenceline looking. People line up along the rise where the monument stands with their backs turned to the statue of Brigham Young. Nothing comes back on the intercom. Your headset stays dead.

"Sir! You're gonna lose it!"

Nothing.

"Sir! You're gonna throw a track!"

Nothing.

"Sir! You're gonna blow the shocks out!"

Nothing. Nothing from the driver's hatch. Nothing from the guys down in the turret, the loader and the gunner, banging around blind, too busy hanging on to reach for the intercom switch. Nothing. And nothing you can do but ride it out. Because the guy down in the driver's hatch, Lieutenant Tanner, is an officer. Because you're only the acting tank commander. Because like some temporary weekend god, you're the seventh out of thirty thousand, and they know you'll keep them safe. Because it's your job to yell. Yell while families watch and kids wave their arms from the rise of the monument and the fenceline along the road.

CHAPTER 53

LENNY RENTS a house with a couple of other guys on G Street in the Avenues, an older house, like the neighborhood where your grandfather had the house in whose basement you and your family and all your relatives lived at first, in rooms whose walls were blankets.

There's a baby grand in his living room, along with a caved-in corduroy sofa and easy chair, a wobbly coffee table scarred with the circles of old drinks, a bookshelf painted blue, furniture they carried home from curbs around the neighborhood. There's an old refrigerator with its cord and plug taped to its side and its wire shelves empty except for a box of Wheaties, a bag of noodles, some cans of Campbell's soup and Del Monte beans. Milk and other stuff that needs to stay cold goes out on the small back porch.

Lenny does stuff you've never seen anyone do on a keyboard. The first time you're here you realize that his accompaniment to Sandy that night at Sammy's was an engine running on maybe one of its eight cylinders. You've never heard anyone play with more technique and more invention. Bridge tunes into other tunes. Ellington into Brubeck. Debussy into Bill Evans. Bach into a chorus of Killer Joe. He'll start off playing some Brahms piece like a rhapsody. You'll grab your trumpet and soon what you're playing is Sibelius jamming with Charlie Parker and Thelonius Monk. Other musicians drop by to play along. Art, the sax player, the big Japanese guy with the sketchy beard and the rimless glasses. Other guys you recognize, from Sammy's, from class, from down in the foundation of the Music Building.

You've been coming here since February thinking you could live here. Not in the secret way you did with Robbie's house where the thought alone brought you up against the untouchable privacy of his family. This time for real. Because you could be just another guy who pays his share of the rent and bills and lives here. Because there are dishes you know how to cook that Lenny and the other guys would like. Because the Army taught you how to pick up after yourself so well you could make it like you'd never been there. Because you know how to keep toilets and windows clean. Because you could keep their old cars running.

Soon Lenny and you are writing tunes together, in his living room, in Sandy's key with lyrics. Soon, out in his driveway, you're changing the oil in his Volkswagen, putting a new muffler under his roommate's old Dodge. Soon you start using the concert hall in the Music Building when it's not being used by some string quartet or other chamber group that has to page its way through Mozart or some other piece that needs a music stand. Soon other students start dropping in and taking chairs along the back wall. Sometimes with cello and violin cases. Sometimes with flute and oboe cases. Sometimes with English and French horn cases. Soon you're walking the cracked and buckled plates of the side-walks of the tree-lined streets where professors live, where the sorority and fraternity houses are, and Lenny and Sandy and maybe Art are there with you, on the way to the house you can't help from feeling could be where you live.

Late in April you tell them. You're going. You're not sure when. Sometime in June. You don't know where. Lenny at his piano listening with his usual expectant smile, Sandy standing back from him, looking serious, listening hard, like you're telling them you've got relatives in Siberia you need to see.

"Wait a minute," says Lenny. "Those guys in suits. On bikes. That's what you're saying? That's what you're gonna do?"

"Sounds like it."

"I used to see them in Fresno," he says. "Wow. That's wild."

"I need to hear it again," says Sandy. "I think I missed something."

You try to tell them why. They don't get why you're going but they get why you're telling them. So they won't get in with you too deep. So they won't come to count on you. They don't care. In time for rent for May, the landlord finally takes the old refrigerator out and slots a newer one, a smaller one, into the hole the older one leaves in the kitchen.

Buds are fat enough now to start breaking skin on the branches of trees on the streets on the walk to Lenny's house. In the morning, when the day crew comes in, you turn the yards over in daylight. Coats no longer hang off the backs of chairs in your classes. Windows start com-ing open. Music trapped inside all winter explodes through the open windows now when you come up the walk and then up the shallow steps where students sit back in the sunlight, next to their instrument cases, eating and reading and talking and sometimes looking to say hello, mostly just looking, seeing your trumpet case, hoping to nail you with a stinging look of classical disdain. But you've got it turned around by now. Take every chance you get to stare them down. Stare them down with this hard thin outlaw smile like there's a foldup bazooka in your trumpet case. Stare them down to where their faces lose hold and they have to look off. Where they have to admit they're scared to flat a fifth or sharp a ninth or substitute a chord because it isn't written down that way. Because the only roads they know are the roads that were built for them by Beethoven or Mozart or Rachmaninoff or Stockhausen or Ives. One day you hear this joyous bebop parody of Springtime in the Rockies from one of the open windows. You look down at the walk to keep your smile private. Lenny. Lenny letting them know.

One afternoon you hook up with Eddie and Robbie at Ed's Café for a burger. You haven't seen them since Christmas. They're only in the Music Building in the morning, for one class, and the rest of the day they're off to other parts of campus. A couple of hours of catching up and Coke glasses and plates greased with ketchup and littered with the stubs of fries occupy the little table you're gathered around by the window.

"Classical students are fuckin' snobs," Robbie says.

"We know," says Eddie. "For the hundredth time."

"Like they're all from East High."

"They are."

"Like even their farts belong in a safe deposit box."

"For the hundred and first time," says Eddie.

"Why?" you ask Robbie. "What's up?"

"I tried asking out this cello player," Robbie says. "She looked at me like I was trying to sell her a set of secondhand encyclopedias. In fuckin' Chinese."

"When?"

"Just last week." And then he says, "She's not even that hot."

"You're a drummer," says Eddie. "You play jazz. That's two strikes right there."

"I just figured she'd be easy," says Robbie. And then he says, "She's already used to having her legs apart."

"That's just ugly," says Eddie. "Strike three."

The rickety glass door shrieks. Two dark-haired girls in bright spring sweaters take a quick look on their way to the counter. Sorority chicks. Probably from one of the houses just down the road past the Music Building. The guy behind the counter gets off his stool to see what they want him to do.

"Here's strike four," says Robbie, smiling, picking the crusted stub of a french fry off his plate, cracking it with his teeth. "In my next life, I wanna come back as a cello."

Eddie ignores him. Looks at you. "You still going on a mission?"

"Yeah."

"When?"

"This summer. Don't tell anybody."

"Why would I?" says Eddie.

"Because you would," says Robbie. "You don't need a reason."

"How come you don't want anyone to know?"

"I just wanna be a guy for now."

"You gonna take your horn?"

One girl orders a cheeseburger with a voice like a violin bow dragged hard across two untuned strings. The other one wants a slice of cherry pie with ice cream. Her voice has the sound of what she's ordering.

"Nope."

"Why the fuck not?"

"Hey," says Robbie. "He's a missionary. Watch your mouth."

"That's why I don't want anyone knowing," you say. "I don't want anyone having to watch their mouth."

"What about your chops, man?"

"I'm taking my mouthpiece."

"Great. The kazoo. How long?"

"A couple of years. Maybe two and a half."

"That's it," says Eddie. "You're dead."

"Naw. I got my whole life after that."

Robbie's been dreaming, about the sorority chicks at the counter, but now you've got his attention too.

"Two and a half years? You shittin' me?"

"I'll be back before I know it. That's what they say."

"I'll be a junior by then," Robbie says.

Eddie looks at him. "You'll never last that long," he says.

"Not if I get famous first," says Robbie.

You check the Pepsi clock up on the back wall. Just after five. You need to get going.

"You guys are gonna wait for me," you say. "Right?"

"Long as you don't come home playing church music," says Robbie.

"Just make sure you take your mouthpiece," says Eddie.

The thought of home lights off this fuse of worry the way it always has. Now it starts burning its way through the nervous late afternoon light toward the time you need to leave. None of this can come with you. Not Ed's Café. Not Robbie or Eddie. Not the stuff you caught up on. Not your composition class earlier this afternoon where Professor Fisher had you play your ostinato. Not Lenny or Sandy. Just you and the family car. You look at Robbie. Wonder what rhythm he's got in his tapping fingers and bouncing knees and the way he's watching the girls at the counter.

"You're not moving, are you?"

He looks at you. "Moving?"

"I mean your family. They're not moving."

"No. Unless you know something I don't."

"Like in the next two or three years."

"My dad's got his business."

"Okay. I need a favor."

"What?"

"I need to keep my trumpet at your place while I'm gone."

"Sure." And then he says, "Why not your place?"

Because at your place you can't trust things to still be there. You look at Robbie sitting there. Wish to God you didn't have to lie to him.

"Little brothers and sisters," you say. "You never know."

"Yeah. Sure. I understand."

"Thanks, man. I'll bring it over before I leave."

Sometimes you sense him while you're out practicing in the yards among the big machines and along the fenceline. In the lull of a quiet stretch between traffic on the freeway the noise will go away and leave room for just the shade of his smell or sudden presence. Like always he stays off the center of your line of sight. Standing off the back of a drilling rig or excavator or out on an open area of the yards where he's mostly in silhouette and only has substance when moonlight and starlight give his white hair the glow of ghost hair or the passing lights of a semi up on the freeway rake out across the dark. In winter when you cleared snow off the yards the payloader's headlights sometimes grazed his dark suit. In the yards he keeps his distance. He never shows up in the office or the other buildings you patrol. Sometimes he'll make part of the ride home with you, on the passenger side of the Valiant, where you could reach out and touch him if you were crazy enough to want to, if you didn't know why he was there. He never talks. Just rides and listens to the radio.

CHAPTER 54

IT TAKES WEST a couple of weeks to come around, let his toes loose where they can get him slid into the barrel, get the breech locked behind him. He shows up for Priesthood Meeting his usual self. Like it's about time. Like where has everybody been. He's ready to go. He's got that look of steel now, that faceless look, that blank steel look of a warhead at the top of a ninety millimeter shell. You and Doby figure he just needed time. You let it ride because his eyes have this edgy look to them like his attitude is thin, thin and fragile as ice on an April morning puddle, to where if you put too much weight on him you could send him back into holing up again.

They hurry and get his farewell organized and scheduled. He asks you to do him a favor and sit with Connie. You and Doby plant her on a bench between you like her bodyguards. One of West's uncles talks about the way salesmen run in the family. How West will put that family trait to work in the sales territory of the Lord. Two of his high school buddies from the Madri Singers do an a cappella version of The World Has Need of Willing Men in their white tuxedo jackets. Kent Steed, the owner of Steed's Texaco, talks about the way he's watched West mature around the station the last few years into an outstanding young man the entire congregation should be proud of. A girl whose name the program says is Patricia Franklin plays Clair de Lune on the piano.

West gets up at the end, thanks everybody, testifies that the Holy Ghost has let him know beyond the shadow of a doubt that the restored church is the one true church on Earth, says how eager he is to start knocking on doors to prove it, and sits down, and they do the closing hymn and the benediction.

Connie cries through all of it. Sometimes out loud. She looks drained when it's over. In the lobby she tells you and Doby that West didn't look her way once. You tell her it was probably too hard for him because he knows he won't be seeing her. Doby jabs you in the ribs for reminding her, but it's too late, because she's already bawling again, heading for the door. You and Doby follow her outside into the afternoon sunlight and watch her trot with her head down toward the parking lot in the dress and shoes she picked out that afternoon to have West remember her by.

"I can't believe he did that," Doby says.

"Did what?"

"That girl that played that piano piece?"

"What about her?"

"That's his Kaysville chick."

"You sure, man?"

"Yeah. I saw her with him once. At the Redwood Drive In."

"You sure it was her?"

"Ask him who he took to see Lawrence of Arabia," says Doby. "While you're at it, ask him what it was about."

You can't. Because early Monday morning the gunner pulls the trigger and West is off. And when the big gun recoils back into the turret, and the smoke clears, and the hot shell comes out of the open breech, the next round in the next rack is you.

The day you take over the Music Building for real comes in May. For the last few weeks, when it's been available, you and Lenny and Sandy have been using the concert hall in the afternoon for session work. You've heard grumblings and rumors around the halls. Seen dirty looks from students who crack a door and take a gander at the stage. Some of them come in and take a chair in back. The afternoon the takeover happens you're working on a tune you wrote with Lenny. A ballad called You Were Beautiful While It Lasted. Sandy singing, Lenny on piano, Roland on bass, Art on sax, a guy named Gene on drums. You on trumpet. Roland's plucking through the second chorus of his bass solo. Lenny's dropping in some counterpoint stuff. The rest of you are counting things off, tracking the changes, when two of the back doors are hurled open, crash back hard into the wall, leave Professor Rodriguez standing there. The students listening from the chairs in back give him their full attention. Two of them reach for their cases. Jazz students. The rest of them look like they'll stick around. Classical students. They know who he is. They know he's not here for them.

"Shit," Art says.

Roland and Lenny stop playing. For a minute Professor Rodriguez stands there in the dust of the quaking doors like Pancho Villa at the Alamo. And then he comes charging for the stage. You reach out for Sandy's arm to step her back. He doesn't come on stage. Just stops when he gets to the edge, stands there three feet shorter than the rest of you, his brown face hard and mean.

"What the hell are you doing?" He says it slow and level.

"Practicing?" Lenny finally says. You wish for once he could keep himself from smiling. Professor Rodriquez just stares him down.

"You're cute," he says. "A real Shirley Temple. You know that?"

"Actually—"

"Shut up. I just had a visitor. The head of the music department. He wanted to know what the hell was going on. You guys practicing in here. I couldn't tell him. Why do you think that was, Miss Temple?"

He stands there waiting. You try to think of a way to explain to him that Lenny's got this problem where he can't talk unless he's smiling. But then he turns to Art.

"You there. Hirohito. Why couldn't I tell him what was going on?"

Art looks up from his sax. "Because you didn't know," he says.

"That's correct. I didn't know. Anyone know why?"

And before he can come up with a name for you, or for Sandy, you say, "Because we didn't tell you."

"Everybody hear that? What Little Boy Blue here had to say?"

"Yeah," says Art.

"Yes," says Sandy.

Zorro, you stand there thinking, your ears on fire. Zapata. Pancho Villa. Every Mexican bad guy from the Alamo and every other movie you've seen and book you've read. You could give a shit if he's really from Brazil.

"Let me hear you say it," he says. "All of you."

"Because we didn't tell you."

And then he's glaring at you again.

"This was your idea," he says. "You and Shirley Temple. This is your band."

You're going. Nothing to lose if you take the hit for something you and Lenny came up with together one afternoon.

"Just mine," you say.

"Either way," he says. "It has you all over it."

"Sorry."

"You people need to ask," he says. "You need to tell me. I got a real problem being ambushed. I don't like it."

"Nobody was using it," says Art. "We just figured—"

"Don't figure nothing. You should have got permission. We got enough trouble here with all these candy ass Mozarts running the place. Anyone say anything to you?"

"No," says Roland.

"Figures," he says. "Chickenshits."

You stand there quiet.

"Well, you got permission now. Me and the head of the department reached an understanding. I got you booked three afternoons a week. Monday, Tuesday, Thursday. Three to five. Anybody says anything, you send them to me."

And then he stands there waiting.

"Act like you heard me."

"Thanks," says Lenny, and then the rest of you say thanks.

"You're welcome. Now. Play your butts off. Don't embarrass me."

He whirls around. You can almost see the flare and swish of a black cape. On his way back down the center aisle he stops and looks at the students who haven't slinked out the open doors while his back was turned.

"You ladies and gentlemen enjoying this?"

They look at him out of faces that look like they're trying to burrow deeper into hiding places that don't exist. A couple of them say yes.

"Got any requests?" he says. "A favorite love song?"

He looks at a girl with short brown curly hair whose round glasses take you all the way back to Carla and her violin case in junior high.

"How about you?" he asks her.

There's a flute case in her lap. She glances down and looks back up.

"My Favorite Things?"

Professor Rodriguez turns back to face the stage. "Hey! She wants to hear My Favorite Things! Got that?"

"Got it," you say.

You look at Sandy. She's smiling. She looks at Lenny.

"E minor's fine," she says.

Sometimes at supper you look around the table at the night ahead for Karl and Molly and Roy and Maggie. Some homework. Some tv. Some storm cloud moving malevolent and dark through your mother's head. Sometimes you think you should stay home, spend time with them, be there when the storm breaks open. But you can't. This nervous fear you can't name is running underneath your skin and lifting it off the underlying tissue. You tell them good night from the door of the recreation room where their faces turn your way in the flickering bath of gray light from some tv show whose name you don't want to know. Sometimes your mother begs you to spend a night at home. Soon you'll be gone. You tell her in the bullshit way you've heard your father use. You can't. Sometimes he's there with them. Sometimes you hear his typewriter through the closed door to his den. Sometimes he's already taken the Valiant and gone.

CHAPTER 55

LOAD. LOCK. Aim. Fire when ready. Lilly to Mexico. Keller to England. Jasperson to West Virginia. West to British Columbia. In May, when your reserve weekend rolls around, you figure the guys in your unit have had their fun. That they're ready to settle down and learn some serious handling. You couldn't be more wrong. This time they're experts. This time they don't even wait for the day's instructions. Just head for their tanks like they're bumper cars at Lagoon. You're the guy who takes their tickets, tells them to hold on and have fun, throws the switch.

Lieutenant Gerald Tanner down in the driver's hatch. Somewhere in his thirties, pushing forty maybe, he's one of the coolest guys you've ever known from the generation of guys somewhere between you and your father. Friendly without looking for anything. Outgoing without being pushy. Athletic without being a jock. Confident without it depending on putting you down. Tough without showing muscle. Like Lenny, always this ready smile, this expectant eager readiness to laugh, like a man standing in a river relishing the way the current just keeps coming. Married. Six little girls. A sportswriter for the Salt Lake Tribune. Mormon. So he wears the harness too. He just wears it lighter than any man you've ever known. Not like he's pulling a wagon loaded with boulders across the Rockies. More like he's just running with the harness on, not under load, no big deal, like the wagon he's pulling is light as light itself. You never see it. Just know it's there. Because you sense this quiet and deep respect for it no matter how easy and light he acts like he's wearing it, with this good-natured smile and this infectious magnetic force that draws out of you the things that make you the same kind of guy he is.

You don't know why he likes you. Why he always wants you on his tank. Just that he does. So this time you say go ahead. Blow the shocks out. Throw a track. This time, from the cupola up on top, braced in and hanging on, riding fifty tons of lunging steel down off the hills again, watching the tracks come spooling off the front sprockets, watching the nose come bounding up and then dive down again so deep the whole tank groans and stumbles, you don't bother. Leave your radio switch alone. Let him have his ride. Because he knows there's nothing you can do to stop him except climb down and put a bullet in his head with the forty-five you can't get bullets for without his signature.

Released from winter, spring comes on with its usual explosive force, and around the circle your neighbors come out with their mowers and garden tools to hold it back, harness it their way. The roses are out on your father's bushes. Sometimes you come home for supper to find him on his stomach, picking shoots of weeds out of the dirt around them, repairing his little moats around their trunks, his portable radio going on the grass. On Saturday Karl takes your mother shopping. You still help mow the yard and edge and trim the grass and hose the driveway down. But now it's Roy who's out there, taking the lead while Karl's gone, then Karl once he gets your mother home. They can handle this without you. They figured it out last summer and fall while you were in the Army. And now you're going away again. Molly and Maggie extract the roots of petunias from the soil of their wooden flats and hand them to your mother to plug into holes in the flowerbeds. You know it makes sense. You're going. But you still feel sidelined. Nudged out of the place you've had since you were twelve in the ruthless Saturday momentum of the circle.

It's been daylight enough for weeks to make out your father's face behind the windshield on the passenger side of Whipple's Chrysler in the morning on your way home from Hiller's. Clear enough to see the rough impatience to get his Valiant back. To finally have you gone. But you're caught off guard when he tells you he's scheduled an interview the following night with Bishop Wacker to clear you for your ordination to the rank of Elder. Another interview with Stake President Dwight Christensen the next night to confirm that you're worthy of serving the Lord. You're still eighteen. It's only halfway into May. Your birthday isn't for another month. He tells you there's no fixed rule that says you have to be nineteen. Just close enough and worthy.

When you get to his office Bishop Wacker gets up from behind his desk a changed man. Not like he's lost a hundred pounds or grown a thick head of wild hair or lost the smooth and tanned and placid look of someone happy to be who he is. What puts you on guard is that he acts like he's glad to see you. He's never got up before when you've come in.

Now he comes hustling around his desk in his pale blue golfer shirt and shakes your hand and slaps your shoulder, all big and grinning, like you just scored a touchdown against Davis High, like you just paid asking price for a used Thunderbird at Larson Ford. He has you sit down, then sits back down himself, still smiling in the afterglow of your arrival. You wonder what you got away with. In the drapes behind him you can see the nebulous burn where the sun hangs close to setting in the sky. He won't stop smiling.

"That was a heck of a thing you pulled off in the Army," he says.

"Thanks."

He wants you to tell him about it. And so you do, except for the Zippo, except for the night you got drunk and tore the barracks up, except for the photo in your wallet, answering things he wants explained along the way. And then he wants to talk about himself. He tells you things you never needed to know. Why he'd never own a Ford. How he hopes his son will never play football. How it still makes him laugh the night you got Sister Johansen and Sister Avery going in Sacrament Meeting. How he never had the chance to serve his country because of a heart murmur.

"Maybe it wasn't a murmur," you say. "Maybe it was just a truck."

"What do you mean?"

And so you tell him what happened to you.

"That really happened?" he says.

"Yeah. Maybe that's what happened with you."

"That's a heck of a story," he says. "But mine's real. I've had more than one doctor tell me."

After he's run the course of what he has to tell you, he just sits there, then looks at his watch and says he's got somewhere else to be. You look at him. The man you got to sign your yearbook three years ago so Doby and you could forge his signature on the swimming requirement for First Class Scout.

"That's it?"

"That's it. Tell your dad you're ready."

The following Sunday morning, your father puts together his posse of friends at the churchhouse, and for the fourth time walks you down the hall to a vacant classroom. You sit there with the warm and soft and twitching weight of their hands on your head while your father ordains you an Elder and gives you the keys to the Melchizedek Priesthood. For the fourth time you use the muscles of your neck to keep the shifting stack of their hands balanced on your head. The power to minister and baptize and bestow the Holy Ghost. The power to anoint and heal the sick. The power to pass the Priesthood on. Except to guys like Jeff and his five big Airborne uncles. You see yourself surrounded now by them instead of your father's friends. Imagine the weight of the hands on your head is theirs. Ordaining you a Negro. Turning your skin the color of Cissy's. Giving you the keys to the Airborne Priesthood. Your father says Amen. You go around the circle shaking hands. Elder Tauffler. Thanks. The look locked into place on your Airborne face.

It comes in the mail near the end of May in a letter from the Office of the First Presidency of the Church. When you get home for supper late that afternoon, Molly and Maggie are setting the dining room table with china and silverware, and your mother has a batch of breaded pork chops simmering in spaghetti sauce in two frying pans, your favorite supper. Your father asks you to show him how to adjust the height of the blades on the power mower. Yes, he says, he knows he never mows the lawn, he just wants to know how it's done for the time when all his boys are gone. Nothing, your mother says, when you ask her what's going on. Karl gives you this wicked sneer. Roy wanders off. When your mother calls everyone for supper there's an envelope on your plate.

Steam rising off the bowl of pork chops and spaghetti sauce, off the platter of snarled white spaghetti next to it, while you read the return address, open the envelope with your table knife, fold the letter out, start reading it.

"Read it out loud," says Karl.

"Let him read it himself first," your father says.

Dear Elder Tauffler. You are hereby called to be a missionary of the Church of Jesus Christ of Latter Day Saints to labor in the Austrian Mission.

You look up. "Austria."

Your mother gasps. Her hands fly to her mouth.

"Where's Austria?" Molly asks.

"Right next door to Switzerland," your father says. "Now let him read, by golly."

Your presiding officers have recommended you as one worthy to represent the Church of our Lord as a Minister of the Gospel. It will be your duty to live righteously, to keep the commandments of the Lord, to honor the holy Priesthood which you bear, to increase your testimony of the divinity of the Restored Gospel of Jesus Christ, to be an exemplar in your life of all the Christian virtues, and so to conduct yourself as a devoted servant of the Lord that you may be an effective advocate and messenger of the Truth. We repose in you our confidence and extend to you our prayers that the Lord will help you thus to meet your responsibilities.

"Take all night," says Karl.

"That's enough," your father says.

The Lord will reward the goodness of your life, and greater blessings and more happiness than you have yet experienced await you as you serve Him humbly and prayerfully in this labor of love among His children. We ask that you please submit your written acceptance promptly, endorsed by your presiding officer in the ward or branch where you live.

It's signed by David O. McKay. The President of the Church. The Prophet himself. The man who speaks with God. The signature is basic penmanship, each letter drawn with the obedience of someone learning how to write from letters on a blackboard, and shaky, the way a second grader would write drunk. And then it strikes you, for the first time, how old and feeble he must be. You hand the letter to your father.

"What did it say?" says Karl.

"That I've been called to the Austrian Mission."

"What else?"

Everything you've been taught for seven years about being called to be a missionary and going on a mission. Except this time it's you they mean. We repose our confidence in you. You. The Lord will reward the goodness of your life. Your life. The phrases keep repeating themselves where you can see and hear and almost hold them. They're for you. It will be your duty to live righteously. Your duty. You can feel this warm and powerful welling in your chest. The Holy Ghost, coming out of his long and troubled slumber, rising, stretching his arms, finally starting his morning campfire in your bosom. The sheep awake. Jazz playing.

Your mother finally reaches over and takes the letter out of your father's hand. He lays his forearms along either side of his plate and looks up. And then you can see the shine of water pooled in his lower eyelids. He lifts his face, to the chandelier above the table, to keep tears from breaking. And then he lowers his head and looks the length of the table out to the living room, through the flagstone wall of the fireplace, through the wall of the house, and from there out past the circle, the neighborhood, the town of Bountiful, the everlasting hills, the distance in his eyes so vast it could be infinite, across space and time, maybe all the way back to Switzerland when he was a guy your age. Your mother finishes the letter. She goes to put it in Molly's waiting hand. Karl reaches out and grabs it.

"Oh, Shakli," she says, her hands on her cheeks, looking at you with the naked adoration of a little kid. "Our first missionary!"

"What's it like in Austria?" says Roy.

"Oh, it's beautiful, sweetheart. Just like Switzerland! And Vienna! Oh, Shakli, the City of Music! The music capital of the world! Beethoven! Strauss! Mozart! Oh, how I wish you had let me teach you piano!"

Karl finishes the letter. "Holy crap," he says. "President David O. McKay signed this."

"Let Molly have a look," you say.

"Say something, Harold! Your first missionary!"

Your father gives his head a slow shake. And then you see it happen. This soothing liquid light that spreads through the flesh of his big bewildered face and leaves it smooth and radiant. His church face. His Utah Symphony face. The first time you've seen it in the house and there hasn't been company.

"By golly," he finally says, lowering his gaze to the plate between his forearms. "You'll have to forgive me."

"Yes, Father. We forgive you."

"This is the proudest day of my life."

"Yes, Father. Come now, children. Let's not let our special supper get cold. Shakli! Let me have your plate!"

You watch Molly read the letter while she holds it with both hands. Watch what you can see of her lowered face while you hand your plate across the table where your mother already has a dripping pork chop in her ladle.

"Please, Mother. This is an opportunity I never had for myself. I've waited all my adult life for this moment. Let me just enjoy it."

"Nobody is stopping you, Harold."

He turns your way. The look in his face makes you look away. You reach for the pitcher of apple juice in front of you like it's what you had in mind.

"I want all of you to know how proud I am of your big brother," he says. "Yes, we've had our share of disagreements, our growing pains, but this is where he becomes a man. Your grandfather dedicated himself to the Church. Unfortunately, I had a family to raise, so I never had the opportunity to follow in his footsteps. Now your brother has been called to fill his shoes."

You wait till he's finished to pour juice into your tumbler. Molly looks up for the next person to hand the letter to. Your mother finishes ladling sauce on your spaghetti and hands your plate back. You take and set it down.

"It doesn't say when I'm going."

"First we have to give them your written acceptance," your father says. "Then they'll let us know when. It will happen fast. We'll have to start planning your farewell."

"I've still got summer camp to do. With the Army."

"Yes. You'll have time for that."

"Oh, Shakli, when you get home from summer camp, we'll have to go on a shopping spree! Suits, and shoes, and some shirts and beautiful

ties! We'll go to Arthur Frank's, yah? We'll make you a handsome missionary!"

"He'll need some garments too," your father says.

"Oh, yes! They make nice ones now for summer, you know! A nice
cool polyester blend, where you won't have to sweat so much!"

"Thanks, Mama. This looks great. Thanks for making it."

"Oh, Shakli! Our very own missionary!"

CHAPTER 56

LIGHT ON THE GAS to keep from running too fast through time. At night, in the yards, you don't hold back, because sometime after midnight there's a point when time just lifts away, when the massive machines that are left in the yards for repair are timeless, when the red and yellow running lights of the semis that roll past the yards out on the freeway move only through distance, when the line of sound you send out moves only through the space of the timeless night.

The night you discover them, back in early May, you're walking along the back fence. Beyond the fence are the fields that surround the yards. You can feel them first, in the sudden uptick in your heartbeat, before you can see or hear them. You stop playing. Let the sound of the trumpet clear out of your ears and the last notes scatter out across the yards and vanish. Stand there, tensed and relaxed, your head cleared of everything to give your senses full attention. The hard smooth tubes of the trumpet in the fingers and palm of your left hand. The cool still air through your teeshirt. While a semi approaches and then recedes you use your eyes to scan the yards and the few machines in the thin starlight and the pale mist of light rising off the city. Nothing. Turn your head to look back at the maintenance shops. Nothing from here.

It takes forever for distance to finally carry the semi out of the range of hearing. For your ears to get used to the stillness again where you can listen for things you know aren't part of the usual haze of sound out here at night. Nothing. You look toward the fence, and through it, out across the rubbled and bulldozed fields. With the snow off them, the fields are dark now, where nothing is immediate, where you have to just keep looking and wait for things to reveal themselves on their own.

You start walking. And that's when you see them. Dark figures just through the other side of the chainlink fence. Two of them move. The way they move you can see arms now, arms coming down, hands letting go of the fence. Behind them the dull sheen of starlight off lines that define the hood and roof and trunk and fenders of a car. From the gleam off the hood ornament you recognize the chrome-plated head of an Indian chief with the long blade of its chrome-plated headdress out behind it. A Pontiac. For a second you wish you'd brought the shotgun. Think of going back for it. And then you see two of the figures turn, the rest start moving back, hesitate, this nervous indecision in how they move.

You keep heading toward the fence. Leave the flashlight in its holster on your belt. You can see them now. Four guys. Two girls. One of the girls thin with straight blond hair in a simple housedress and open sweater. The other one heavier, in pants, a stack of dark curls rising from a headband. The guys are high school maybe. The bulky Pontiac out in the field behind them an old one.

Who goes there, you want to say, like they taught you in the Army. You give the fence a look for any cuts in the wires.

"How you guys doing?"

Nothing. Nobody runs. Nobody gives ground. The girls whisper. The thin one points an arm your way. What they're up to. If they're here to drink. Make out. Break in. Start a fire. If there's a set of cutters in someone's pocket or up against someone's leg. If you're about to see a gun or knife.

And then a voice says, "We were just listening."

You look for the guy who said it.

"To what?"

"Your trumpet there."

"I told you," you hear one of the girls whisper.

You can make out the guy who's talking now. A tall thin guy in a black or dark blue teeshirt. Dark straight hair that fits his head like a sweatshirt hood. The light off the side of his face makes it look long and rough and gaunt. Older than the rest of them.

"You live around here?" you finally say.

"No. We were headed home."

"Where's home?"

"Magna."

The outskirts town out west across the valley along the foot of the Oquirrh Mountains. In the shadow of the Kennecott smelter and its smokestack. The mining town. Their fathers miners who work the tiers of the huge copper pit up in the mountains. You know why you lost the sense of threat when they appeared out of the dark. Miner kids. The trailerhouse kids in La Sal whose fathers mined uranium. Jimmy Dennison. Susan Morrow. Roy Pierson. Rough kids. Poor kids. Here they are grown up. The thin blonde reminds you of the girl who pulled and ate her hair down to where it was fuzz too short for her fingers to get a hold on. In the dark, looking at her long hair through the chainlink fence, it's almost like she got over it and turned out fine.

"So you're just here listening."

"We heard this music. Wondered what it was. So we came in for a look."

"Actually we came to listen," the girl with the headband says.

"Yeah," says the guy. "That's right." His thin arm swings up toward his face. A fuzzy sudden point of red light flares up and lights his knuckles and the long ridge of his nose. In their sockets his eyes pick up the gleam while he takes a quick hard drag off his cigarette. He drops his arm again. "Just listen."

"You're kidding."

"Nope."

"You play crazy," the girl with the headband says.

"Where'd you hear me?"

"Out on Thirty-Third. At a red light."

"I heard you first."

One of the other guys. You can't tell who in the dark. He says it rushed and eager like the conversation might run away and leave him.

"Yeah," says the thin guy. "Billy heard you."

"I made 'em pull over. Get out and listen."

"We just followed it," says the older guy. "After that."

"Yeah," the girl with the headband says. "Like a treasure hunt."

"Are you famous?"

A new voice. One of the two guys left who hasn't said anything.

"No."

"How come you're in there?"

"I work here. Night watchman."

"Where's your gun?"

You walk up to the fence where the tall guy doing most of the talking is standing. "My name's Shake."

You watch him dip his head, switch his cigarette to his other hand, come up to the fence too with his hand out.

"Walt," he says.

The best you can do for a handshake through the fence is touch fingers. The other guys are quick to come up too, their names ready, their hands out. Billy. Luke. Chaz. The girls hang back but call their names out. The one with the headband Maria. The blond one Jenny.

"We been here before," says the guy named Luke. "This is the first time we seen you."

"Shhh!" says Jenny, quick as a snakebite, harsh as the caw of a crow, enough to make you glance her way.

"What?" says Luke. "We didn't hurt nothing."

"Still! He don't need to know!"

You look back at the older guy named Walt.

"You been here before?"

"Just a couple of times," he says. And then he says, "We liked what we heard."

"Chaz wants to know if he can play along," another guy says.

"Who's Chaz?"

"Me." He raises and drops his arm.

"What do you play?"

"Harmonica."

He stands there and lets you look him over. He's a short big-shouldered kid in a white teeshirt with the ends of his levis rolled up in big cuffs around the tops of his black engineer boots. Tough kid stance. Ready to fight if that's what it comes to. But there's nothing tough in his face. Not asking for anything. Just hoping you'll say yes.

"I can't let you in," you say to Walt.

"We know that," he says.

"I can't come out there either."

"It's just a fence. No big deal. Won't bother us."

"You play anything?"

"Guitar."

"Billy's already been playing along," says Chaz.

"You been out here playing? What? When?"

"Look. Show him, Billy."

The guy named Billy brings something out from behind his back. Two circles at first, ghost white, one smaller than the other one. A set of bongos.

"Tonight?"

"Yeah," says Billy. "Quiet, though."

So that was what drove your heartbeat up. What you heard. What you stopped hearing once you stopped playing.

"You sound like you could show us a thing or two," says Walt.

You look them over through the diamond wirework of the fence, looking back at you, waiting, not saying anything. You wonder how they got together. What they share to make them hang with each other. Get in the Pontiac and drive across the dark valley to the lights of the city. Street kids. Kids from the same street out in Magna. That's all you can figure.

"Got your guitar?" you say to Walt.

"In the trunk."

"Go get it."

CHAPTER 57

THEY DON'T know much. Walt some three and four chord songs he picked up from the radio. All of them the same slow haunting tempo, filled with space, some melancholy country western ballad. Chaz knows some melodies and licks he made up out of nothing. In the dark, the way he plays, you can tell how raw he is, just this raw and unapologetic kid, this kid who wakes up every morning torn in half because that's how it is. Billy beats his heart out on the bongos. Since that first night, they've been showing up around half past midnight every night, except for one, when Walt had to take someone to the hospital. Sometimes it's just been Walt with Billy or Chaz or maybe both of them. The girls have either been there together or not at all.

You play some of the songs Walt knows at different tempos. Show Chaz how to open his air flow. Soon you're teaching them some blues progressions. You bring Walt a set of guitar scales from one of your friends at the U. Roll the pages up so you can pass them through one of the diamonds in the fence. Hold your flashlight so Walt can see what you're talking about while you explain them. He catches on quick. Chaz too. You give them the names of some blues and jazz guitarists and tell them to get their records. You show Billy some latin rhythms.

Around half past midnight you're there when they come across the field, the headlights out on the Pontiac, come piling out of the doors eager to show you the licks they've picked up and practiced. In a few nights you've got them doing some blues tunes. Maria hums and warbles along. Jenny stands there dancing, dancing in place, wheeling and swaying and tossing her ghost blond hair in the thin light of the stars and then the moon when it starts to come round again. They bring a couple of camp stools, one for Billy and his bongos, the other one for Luke or one of the girls or sometimes Chaz and his harmonica. The girls bring popcorn. You tell Chaz not to eat before he plays or while he's playing.

Always the fence. Always in the dark. Luke shows up one night with an old electric bass without an amp. Always a couple of hours before they have to get back in the Pontiac, close the doors soft, head back across the field again, wait till they get to the road before they turn the headlights on.

That night, after the celebration dinner in the dining room for your mission call, your father takes you downstairs, where your letter of acceptance is already half written in his typewriter. Bishop Wacker's waiting. Your father's already called to let him know you're coming. You and your father finish the letter together and drive to his house for his signature. This time you watch Bishop Wacker sign his name himself.

You still can't figure out what happened. Why he took you in and told you everything he did. If he did the same thing with your buddies. If he sent Lilly off to Mexico knowing his bishop had a heart murmur. Keller off to England knowing his bishop hated the cars he sold. Jasperson to West Virginia knowing his bishop's favorite constellation was Andromeda. West to British Columbia knowing his bishop ate himself sick once on a pound of olive loaf. If he was saying you were men now. If he's ever had a conversation with your father like he had with you.

You wonder what casual secrets your father would share. The way his wife calls him fat and mocks him when he prays. The way he has to hide snacks in the back of his filing cabinet drawers and his soda cans in the shelves that hold his church books. Your father says he'll put your letter in the mail from his office in the morning. That way, mailed from the city it's going to, they'll get your letter one day quicker.

They talk about hanging out with you, during the day, away from here, from the fence and field and yards. Invite you out to Magna where they can show you their stuff. Luke says his father's building a dragster. Maria wants to introduce you to her cousin. Walt says he's got an old motorcycle he's rigged and stripped for offroad riding. He can take you up into the Oquirrhs to this ridge where you can look down and see the bowl of the copper pit and how deep it cuts into the mountains. He tells you it's something. Like looking into the guts of the earth.

One way or another you tell them you can't do it. You've already got a girlfriend. School. Time to sleep. A practice session. Homework. You don't give them the real reason. How you need to travel light. How this is where you need to keep them, here, after midnight, where the night goes timeless, on the other side of the fence, where you haven't had to think about the way things are ending either.

That night, your acceptance letter signed and in your father's briefcase, you finally stop kidding yourself. You're going. When they show up that night you tell them you're quitting a week from Friday. You're going away.

"What the fuck," says Chaz.

He walks off around the other side of the Pontiac.

Billy stands there holding his bongos. Walt sets his guitar on the dirt in front of him and leans the neck against his legs. He strikes a paper match and lights a cigarette. And then stands there smoking like this is something he understands.

"Where you going?" he says.

"I gotta do two weeks with the Army. Summer camp."

"So we'll take two weeks off," says Luke. "We'll come back."

"After that I gotta go somewhere else."

"Where?" says Jenny.

For a minute you don't know what to say.

"You know what a mission is?"

Walt looks at you. In the dark you watch him drop his cigarette and use his shoe to twist it in the dirt.

"Sorry," he says. "I didn't know."

"The smoke?" you say. "Screw that."

"What's a mission?" says Billy.

"That's why you didn't hang out with us," Maria says. "That's why you always had some excuse."

"Maria," says Walt. "Shut up."

"What's a mission?" Billy says again.

"It's a Mormon thing," says Jenny crossly.

"What kind of Mormon thing?"

"God," says Jenny. "It's where you go somewhere and convert people."

"From what?"

"Maria," you say. "You got the wrong idea."

"No," she says. "You're too fucking good to be seen with us. Too fucking ashamed. Too scared they'd kick you out," she says. "God," she says. "I hate this fucking city and its fucking Mormon shit."

"Maria," says Walt. "Watch your mouth. That ain't it."

"Yeah it is," says Jenny.

"It ain't," says Walt. "It explains it, but it ain't it."

"Then what is it?" says Billy.

You look at him not knowing what to say. The way you used them maybe. To stop time. To keep the road from ending. The way you held them here to keep from seeing it.

"He didn't want to get too deep with us," Walt says. "Figuring he'd be going."

You can feel Maria's eyes all over you.

"Bullshit," she says. "He coulda told us."

"Why?" The word comes like a bark out from behind the Pontiac. "Stop acting like he fuckin' owes you. He don't owe you jack shit."

"Fuck you, Chaz," says Maria. "He coulda told us."

"No. Fuck you. He don't even have to be here. He don't have to do nothing. You're always telling people what to do."

"He coulda told us. Not string us along."

"And now he did. And what fuckin' difference does it make."

"A big one," says Maria.

"We're wasting time," says Walt.

"He wouldn't of wanted your skank cousin anyway," says Chaz.

Maria reaches down, grabs up a handful of dirt, gets up and flings it. You can hear it spatter and ping off the glass and metal of the Pontiac.

"Hey," says Walt.

"I wanna go now." Maria slaps the dirt off her hand on her leg. "Just take me home."

"Me too," says Jenny.

"You wanna go home," Walt says, "then get out there and put your fuckin' thumb in the air."

"Come on, Jen."

"I didn't know for sure till today."

Walt looks at you. Maria stops and looks at you and folds her arms across her chest.

"Know what?" says Walt.

Chaz comes back from around the Pontiac.

"When or where," you say. "I just found out today. Honest."

"You knew you were going somewhere," Maria says. "Sometime."

"Is that what he coulda told us?" says Chaz to Maria. "That he was going somewhere sometime?"

"Where you going?" says Walt.

"Austria," you say. You look around. Look at Luke. Why he hasn't said anything. And then you say, "So. You guys ready?"

You get another letter from the Church in answer to your mailed acceptance. They've scheduled you to start at the Mission Home on the Monday a week after you get back from summer camp. Bishop Wacker sets that Sunday night aside for your farewell. You get a haircut, put a part in your hair for the first time since you sat in the barber chair at Grant's Hair Styling, put on a tie and suit with your Duty to God Award in the lapel, get your mission portrait taken. Apply for a passport. Sit down with your mother and father in the dining room one night and plan out a program of speakers and musical numbers.

It's their show as much as yours. Half their choice and half yours.

You want outsiders. Evidence to put in front of everyone of your life outside this neighborhood, outside this congregation, outside this young Priesthood holder, outside the harness of this guy you are to everyone at church. You've already asked Lieutenant Tanner if he'll speak. Sandy and Lenny if they'd do a song. You spell out their names so your father can write them down.

"Who is this man, Shakli?"

"A lieutenant in my Reserve unit."

"A lieutenant?" your mother says. In her nervous singsong voice the question is about more than just his rank.

"Yeah."

"Why would you have a lieutenant speak at your farewell?"

"Because he's a friend."

"Why would a lieutenant have you for a friend?"

"Why not?"

"Isn't he a grown man?"

"Yeah," you say. "He is."

She looks at your father with the vexed and watery and helpless and half-wounded smile of someone innocent of where her thinking is leading her.

"Is he LDS?" your father says.

"Yes."

"Who are these other two?"

"Friends of mine. From the U."

"What do they plan on singing?"

"I'll have to let you know."

"It has to be soon," your father says. "I have to get these printed while you're away in the desert."

"I'll find out."

"Yes, Shakli," your mother says. "You have lots of friends, don't you."

CHAPTER 58

SIDELINED when it comes to yardwork. At church lately it's been the same way. They've learned to handle things without you. Younger guys shred the Wonder bread and read the blessings off the reversible card at the Sacrament table. One of them Karl. Young kids have been standing at the chapel doors where you and Doby used to stand. Still younger kids have been walking Sacrament trays up and down the aisles and re-laying them along the benches. One of them your brother Roy. After seven years you're another guy out in the congregation. Another head out there with a face. Singing hymns. Taking your piece of bread and your paper cup. Listening to kids give their little talks. Women their musical numbers. Men their speeches. It's the way you've seen things go. They were busy holding Keller, and then Jasperson, and then West in the spotlight of their hopes and prayers and expectations, celebrating them, sending them off. They left you alone. Alone to do about any-thing you wanted to. They always knew you'd be there, in the rack on the floor of the turret, in easy reach, not going anywhere. It's been okay. It's only been your father where you've had to feel impatience.

And then West left. And then things began slowly to swing around toward you. From the women these quiet and admiring smiles. Back-slaps from some of the men. And then you started going to the Elders' Quorum where they welcomed you like someone they'd been waiting for. And then word got out that your mission call had come. And now you're here, in their raw hot blinding spotlight, where your neighbors come up to you admiring and proud and unashamed and take your hand, so close they put their faces in the spotlight too, so close you can see where their lipstick doesn't follow the line of their lips but the line of what they'd like their lips to look like. Where the woman that night at the Indigo comes to your mind, her red dress, the unforgiven shimmer of her blond hair, the shadows the blade of the spotlight cut down her face, there at the edge of the stage to tell you that you know. You know enough to want to look for her again. Enough to not draw back from her this time. Enough to not draw back from the smiling faces of your neighbors, but stand your ground, squeeze their hand back, match them smile for smile. A hundred women are your mother.

"I'm so proud of you. Just so proud."

"Thanks, Sister Holman."

"I've watched you grow from a young boy into a young man."

"Thanks, Sister Jeppson. It took long enough."

"I know you'll make a great missionary. I know how proud we'll be of you."

"Thanks, Sister Bangerter. I'll try my best."

"Just look at you. How thrilled your parents must be."

"They're pretty happy."

"I still remember that brave little boy who knocked on my door to ask if he could help me with my yard."

"I forgot about that."

"Ron still tells me you were one of his all time favorite Scouts."

"He does?"

"I always knew the Lord had great things in store for you."

"Thanks, Sister Maxwell."

"How does it feel? To be called to the harvest?"

And as many men for fathers. You tell them great. Great to be going. Humbling to be called to work for the Lord in Austria. And then Doby and Yenchik ask you what it's like. You tell them the same thing.

"Hey," says Doby. "Tell us for real. I'm next."

"Okay. Like I'm about to be sacrificed. Like some Aztec guy."

"You scared? Like West was?"

"He wasn't scared. It was just bad timing."

Now that you're going you've started to feel this warm expansive calm in your chest like cream of mushroom soup. This calm you don't know how to trust.

"What's the Elders' Quorum like?" says Yenchik.

"It's carpeted," you tell him.

"I've seen the room. Dickhead."

"Hunt's in there too."

"Priesthood Hunt?" says Yenchik. "The Corvette guy?"

"That's gotta be weird," says Doby. "Being in the same class as your teacher."

"Yeah. Guess who else. Bird."

"Bird," says Yenchik. "Holy crap."

"Hey," says Doby. "Pipe down."

"He still hasn't figured it out," says Yenchik. "What you did."

"I guess not," you say.

"He's still busy proving he's not a pervert," says Doby.

"Wish my birthday'd come up," says Yenchik. "I've had it with being a Priest already."

Your classes end. You tell Professor Rodriguez thanks. He says he'll see you next year. You're on your way out of Professor Fisher's room when he calls you out. He wants to see you in his office. You wait for him to get there first. At his desk the window behind him is raised on a million shimmering mint-colored leaves and the racket of birds at the brink of summer. You knock on the door jamb. It takes him a minute to find you.

"Tauffler," he says. "Come in."

He has you sit down in the chair across the desk from him.

"On second thought," he says, "let's take a walk."

You come down the shallow steps of the Music Building into the bright warm sunlight side by side with the lanky distracted man who heads the Jazz Program. He takes them one by one and so do you. Students look up from where they're sitting. When the steps run out he shields his eyes and looks around. Takes his arm and points out toward the park that makes up the interior of the U-shaped drive.

"Over there," he says.

You wait for a truck to go rumbling past. Then cross the drive and pick up a path toward a bench. He sits and motions to you to sit next to him.

"Where'd you learn how to play?"

The light breeze makes the mint-colored leaves all around you quiver. You don't know what he's looking for. What answer he's expecting to hear. So you just tell him plain.

"In a sandpit."

"A what?"

"A sandpit," you say. "Where they dig up sand and haul it off."

"Like a quarry, you mean."

"Yeah. Except it's not rocks."

"A sandpit. No kidding."

"Yeah."

You watch him lean forward, put his elbows on his knees, look straight ahead.

"You're the best trumpet player this school's got."

You've heard it but never let yourself come close to admitting it. To hear it now, from Professor Fisher, makes your ears hot and alters the shiver of shadow and light on the concrete and grass around you.

"Thanks."

"I didn't think that would come as a surprise to you."

"I wasn't sure."

"I've been in this business almost thirty years. Mostly on the coast. You know. The mecca for musicians."

He looks down at his hands. You do too. Notice how big and quiet they are the way his fingers are loosely woven through each other.

"I can't remember hearing a better trumpet player. For a guy your age."

And then you just sit there. He turns his head and looks at you.

"Every time you play I hear something I've never heard before."

And now your whole head is on fire.

"Thanks."

"Nothing to thank me for," he says.

He turns his head toward the Music Building across the drive. The skin on the back of his ear looks gray and dusty.

"You don't belong in school," he says. "You're wasting your time."

"I've got a lot to learn," you finally say.

"You don't have a summer job, do you?"

"No."

"Good. I want to send you to Los Angeles for some studio work. Recording sessions. See how you like it." And then he says, "See how you do."

You've heard how he does this. Singles a student out to work with real musicians. Musicians who make records. Records whose jackets have your name and instrument on them. Shake Tauffler. Trumpet. Records whose tunes have your solos on them. Los Angeles. A ride on a bus from San Jose. Everything Jeff said.

"I won't be around."

You say it quick to where Professor Fisher sits up, leans back against the bench, turns his head, looks you in the face. You've never seen him this close up, his face this big, this sharp focus in the pupils of his pale eyes.

"What do you mean? Did Selby get to you first?"

"No."

"Talk to me. I've already lined things up. What's going on?"

"I'll be in Austria."

"Europe?"

"Yes."

"What's in Austria?"

"A mission."

"A mission? A religious one? You mean Africa."

"No. Austria."

And so you tell him. And then he just studies you.

"I've heard that you people do that," he finally says.

"Yeah."

"What do they pay you?"

"Nothing."

He turns away. Leans forward with his elbows on his knees. Looks at his hands. Turns them over. You watch a crooked vein in his temple flex.

"How long did you say?"

"Two and a half years."

Just the flick of a smile in the side of his face. Two and a half years. That's nothing. I'll keep the offer on hold. Just get in touch when you get back. We'll pick it up from here, from this bench, from a day just like this. I'll ask what you've got planned and you'll tell me nothing. You're available. Free to take me up on what I'm offering. No big deal. You look down at your knees. Hold your eyes shut for a minute.

"There's no way I can change your mind," he finally says.

"No," you finally say.

He studies his hands for another minute.

"That's a shame."

He puts his hands on his knees and pushes himself to his feet. Looks down at you.

"I've got some calls to make. Nice talking to you."

You get up too. To shake hands. To tell him thanks. But he's already walking off, like he was just out walking, came across a bench, sat down, then got up and kept on walking. He gets to the drive and looks back and forth for traffic. And then looks ahead again.

You pick up your trumpet case and notebook. It's okay. You've had your six months. That was the deal. You try not to look too obvious to the students on the steps across the drive, in the sun on the steps of the Music Building, like the conversation you had with Professor Fisher was no big deal, a conversation you can walk away from too. You follow a path away from the bench like you know where you're going. Like you already remember where you left your father's Valiant parked.

CHAPTER 59

AFTER THE NIGHT you tell them, the girls stop showing up, but Walt and Chaz and Luke and Billy still keep coming every night. There's not much time. You want to give them everything you can. Pull hard for them while you watch them try to sort it out in the dark on their instruments. And you can feel it. Every time you bring your trumpet up to show them how something goes. Every time you set the rim of the mouthpiece home. Every time you send the first note out into the night. The difference. The sudden strike and uptake, rich and clean, immediate and sure. How far ahead of them you are. How far you've come from the sandpit.

They hear it too. You can tell in the shadows of their faces when you bring the trumpet down. They don't say anything. Just stand there facing the impossibility of the distance. You know. You had the sandpit. They have this place to start from. From here the way the road will just keep opening. Stretch after stretch. All they have to do is just keep moving. You wish you could show them. Not your road. But the first stretch of their own. The possibility of their own road across the scary impossibility of the distance.

"Guys," you say. "It's no big deal."

"Doesn't sound that way."

"Believe me, Luke. Just stick with it. It's gonna happen. It can't not happen."

"Sure."

"I'm gonna come back and you're gonna tell me I was right. It's no big deal."

"Two and a half years," says Walt. "You're sure about that."

"Long as you stay hungry. Yeah. No question."

You clean out your room for Maggie. You can sleep on the basement couch when you get back from summer camp. You pack up your albums and music and clothes and books and Molly's handpainted box for your valuables in cardboard boxes. Make sure that Cissy's letters are tucked away in the big red battered Arban book your mother has never touched. Pack the boxes out of the way in the backs of the shelves in the garage. Store the uniforms you won't be taking to the desert in the winter closet next to the door to the garage.

Karl wants your sterno-powered steam engine and the new record player you bought yourself. Take them. Molly wants the lamp with the stained glass lampshade the woman gave you that winter night outside the Indigo. Take it. For keeps. You didn't know she liked it. Roy wants your Navajo blanket and your picture book of jazz musicians. Take them. Just hide the book from Papa.

Nobody wants the models of the cars you built. You load up the incinerator and burn them. You hold out the model of the 40 Ford you customized and painted red and then upholstered in red corduroy to look like the rolled naugahyde Yenchik did his bench seat in. He's seen it. You call him. Tell him it's his.

"That's okay," he says. "Thanks anyway."

"You sure?"

"Yeah." And then he says, "You doing anything right now?"

"Nothing much."

"Mind if I come over?"

"Sure."

"I'll be right up."

"I'll be here."

It isn't long before you hear the tight crackling rumble of his Smitty steelpacks coming down the street into the circle. He's had his new flathead engine in for a while now, running things in slow, taking it easy, letting the bearings wear in and the rings cut their seats in the cylinders before bolting the supercharger on. He hasn't asked you for help. Hasn't said anything when you've asked if he needed it. Just stayed quiet and sideways until you caught on that this was between him and his father and that it wasn't up to him. But he's told you at church what they've done. The Mercury crank with the four inch stroke. The ported and polished Offenhauser heads. The way they relieved the exhaust ports in the block. The Jahn pistons and the hotter Isky cam. The high flow Belond headers. The floor shift tranny.

The Ford sounds different. Tighter. More urgent. This mean whine to the engine. You can hear it when Yenchik pulls the Ford to the curb and revs it. A long silver air scoop rides like a polished big-mouthed fish through a hole in the red hood. As soon as you're in the passenger seat you feel it. Everything trembling from this tight and nervous power. You look at him. Remember the way he wasn't at church last week. In the driver's seat, wearing a teeshirt streaked with oil, he's still got the big raw knuckles where his hand cups the shift knob, still got his big wild bush of copper hair, except now, for the first time, like a fire spreading, the start of a moustache across his mouth, whiskers off his chin.

"A blower. You did it, man."

He slips out the clutch and idles the shivering Ford around the circle back out to the street again. From the complaining scrub of one of the tires in the tight turn out of the circle you can tell that he's still got the rear axle locked.

"Yeah," he says, his big voice flat and sheepish.

"What kind?"

"Weiand."

"This is wild."

"Wanna go anywhere in particular?" he says.

"Yeah. Where you can show me what you got."

"Sure."

He coasts the Ford down the long hill out of the neighborhood in second gear, braking with the engine, retarding the valves, letting un-burned gas into the headers to detonate in backfires.

"All set for your mission?" he says.

"Yeah."

"Got all your shit?"

"Yeah. Mostly."

He makes a right onto Orchard Drive, away from Bountiful, toward Centerville, just idles it around the corner, goes up through the gears with the engine still running low, not much above an idle.

"So," he says. "Your big mission."

"Yep."

"Must be excited."

"Excited," you say. Trying the word on. "Yeah. I guess."

The Ford feels strange. Old. Even with the raw new whistle of the Weiand blower. Even with the engine eager to reach down into the deep reservoir of its power. The dashboard and instruments. The visors and headliner. The feel and smell of old car dust despite the pine tree dangling off a radio knob. And then you get it. Yenchik. The way he's driving. Like a retired math teacher driving a Rambler wagon loaded with crates of apricots to a church canning function. He makes a left onto Page's Lane. Robbie's road.

"So what's wrong, man?"

"Not a thing."

"Tell me we're out here so you can show me your blower," you say.

"Wanna see it?"

"Tell me that's why you had to see me."

"Just wanted to see you."

"That's where my old drummer lives."

"Yeah," says Yenchik. "I used to drop you off there."

And then you're past Robbie's house, the passing echo of the Ford's exhaust rumble, Robbie's panel truck parked out front.

"Come on, man. What's wrong?"

"Not a thing. Like I said."

You look out the side window. Along the roadside and in the vacant fields the sunflowers are coming on while the weeds are starting to lose their spring shot at being green. You decide on another approach.

"The sunflowers look lovely this time of year, don't they, dear."

"What?"

"My goodness. Just imagine how big they'll be in another week."

"The sunflowers?"

"I'll be able to make that sunflower pie you love so much."

"What the fuck?"

"Maybe we'll have the kids and grandkids over."

"Heat get to you?"

"I just love these little drives in the country, dear. Just the two of us. Like the old days. We should do more of them."

Yenchik slows the Ford to a stop in the middle of the unstriped road. Lets it sit there for a minute idling. Works the long gearshift into first. Keeps the clutch down. Hits the gas pedal. The engine comes unleashed in this eager hammering shriek that splits the day wide open. Through the windshield the air scoop twists sideways from the torque. Yenchik holds it for a second at half throttle. Then pops the clutch and jams the rest of the pedal down.

The engine isn't fazed by the sudden load. It takes the Ford, twists it, shakes it, rears its front end up, breaks the big tires loose, puts the rear end into this squealing fishtail. Your feet come off the floor. Your arms float up. You're back against the seat so hard you can't even think of sitting up. Just try to keep your head straight. Yenchik works the wheel to keep the shuddering rear end behind you. The tires start finding traction, lose their squealing howl, let you start to think of sitting up. That's when Yenchik hits second and breaks things loose again. And then hits third.

The sunflowers are a streak of yellow. The road this blurred gray spear of baked out asphalt. In the back of your head, from when you used to ride your bike out here, the road runs out of asphalt somewhere up ahead. You're not sure where. You look at the speedometer. The needle is pegged past the hundred twenty mark. Yenchik's face looks carved it looks so grim. And then you come rocketing off the asphalt onto rutted dirt and the Ford is getting slammed and yanked around so hard its glovebox door drops open and tools and papers spill out onto your knees. You don't say anything. Your mouth got you into this. Just ride it out. Yenchik finally gets off the gas and on the brake and starts wrestling the Ford back down to something sane. You start picking his papers and tools off the floor. And then close the door of the glovebox.

"How's that for sunflowers?" he says.

"Pretty good."

"We aim to please," he says.

"Look, man. You wanted to see me. Maybe you'll get around to telling me why before hell freezes over."

"I ain't going."

"You ain't going."

"Nope."

"What. Where."

"On a mission."

"Don't fuck with me. That's not funny."

"See me laughing?"

"For real."

"Yeah. I mean no. I mean I'm not going."

"You gotta be kidding."

"Nope."

"Pull over."

He banks the right side of the Ford off the road and holds it there.

"Shut it down."

The hood shakes as the engine lurches and then dies. And then the quiet makes your ears feel hollow. Yenchik sits there looking at his horn button like there's something there he hasn't already memorized. You look at the knob on the glovebox door the same way.

"What're you talking about?"

"I'm not going."

Still looking at his horn button. But there's nothing grim left in his face. Just this look you've seen before. Before the big bush of dark copper hair. Before the whiskers. Before all the bones grew out and forged his jaw and nose and forehead into the anvil shape of his face for good. Before the big voice. The crewcut kid with the unformed face who peed in the big round font where they baptized you for dead people. Sitting on the back curb at the Frostop looking at his paper-wrapped burger the same way. The same gutted look.

"Why not? What happened?"

"You wanna see my mission?" he says.

"What do you mean, see your mission?"

"Come on. I'll show you."

From your side of the Ford you follow him around to the grill. He reaches down, pops the hood latch, lifts and then pushes the big red wobbly nose of the Ford into the air. Hot air laced with oil vapor comes welling out from under it. He steps back from the grill to give you all the room you need to look it over.

On top of the engine, big and polished and ribbed, the twin-barrel housing of the supercharger stands up off the manifold like the menacing head of some monster robot desert reptile from a science fiction movie, the long ribbed snout off the front that ends in the pig's nose of the pulley the wide flat belt rides on. Off the top of the supercharger stand his three linked Carter 97 carburetors. Off the top of them the long flat silver fish of the polished air scoop. The name Edelbrock cast in a circle between the polished fins of the cylinder heads.

"There it is," he says.

"What? You blew your mission money on a blower?"

"No." And then he says, "my dad bought it. All of it."

"Then what're you talking about?"

"My dad says he needs me around."

"He can't hire somebody?"

"Yeah. Same thing I was stupid enough to ask him."

"Stupid why?"

Yenchik jams his fingers to their knuckles in his pockets, looks down hard, starts working the toe of his shoe in the dirt, leaves you looking at his big red thunderhead of hair. You drop your eyes to his teeshirt, to the name Giovannoni, to the half-naked windblown woman riding the camshaft through the sky.

"I thought he wanted you to go," you say.

"Yeah. So did I. For seven fuckin' years he talked about it. So I do fuckin' everything. So now he tells me no. And buys me this fuckin' engine and all this shit to make me feel better. Like some fuckin' consolation prize. And a fuckin' blower. You fuckin' believe that? And then makes me help him put it on. And be happy. And all I'm thinkin' is I'm boltin' my fuckin' mission on top of my fuckin' engine. I been boltin' my mission on this fuckin' engine all spring. Seven fuckin' years and I end up with this fuckin' car I can barely drive in the rain."

And then you're in that place again where there's nothing to say or do that won't be stupid. You can still see him, years ago, using the butt of his hand to wipe off his tears, still look off across the parking lot where Susan Lake and the other girls are yukking it up around the picnic table. Yenchik steps forward and reaches for the hood while you take a last look at what used to be his mission. Finland. Where his mother's from. Where he wanted to go. He brings the hood down careful to pass the air scoop through the trimmed hole in the steel, puts his weight on the nose till the latch clicks into place, and then stands there, his hands still on the hood, his mouth working at something it doesn't know the taste of.

"What if your dad didn't have a choice?" you say. "What if you just got drafted?"

"Yeah," he says. "Well, he's got a choice."

"Can't you just hold off? Go later?"

"Fuck that," he says. "It'll never happen."

"No. Older guys go all the time."

And then all of a sudden he's there in your face, yelling, this wild bewildered furious look and big voice that steps you back from the fender into a couple of sunflowers.

"Look! I've already fuckin' thoughta everything! Talked to him about it! I ain't fuckin' going! I ain't ever going! I'm workin' my ass off tryin' to swallow it! Okay? Fuckin' help me! Don't stand here and fuckin' tell me to think about going! I ain't!"

He stares at you fierce and seething with his mouth still open. And then he spins away, walks out into the road, looks up and then down it, turns and comes walking back, swinging his arms, shrugging his shoulders.

"He told me my mom's dying," he says. "Told me she's the one who needs me." And then he looks at you. "The talk about the shop was all bullshit."

"Jesus Christ."

"Yeah. Jesus Christ." He spits it back at you with this twisted smile. And then wheels and walks off and stops at the ruined wire of an old fence held up more by sunflowers than its posts, his back turned, giving you time, time the way his father probably walked away to give him time, leaving you there with the engine ticking with heat behind you. The orphan kid at church. Where the parents of your buddies were always there. West with his hairdresser mother and drug salesman father. Doby with his schoolteacher mother and water department father. Keller with the parents who adopted him. Just Yenchik's parents missing, because his father smokes cigarettes and his mother drinks coffee and both of them drink liquor, because they don't pay tithing, because they don't want to hear about Joseph Smith. You look at him. The million times he's had to sit in Sunday School and Priesthood class and hear them talk about how his family could always be together. Know how he's wanted to be like the rest of you. Why he took Strand's place as the class mouth as soon as there was an opening.

He's giving you time to make his mother real. Because he knows. How nobody's real unless they come to church. And so you do. In her kitchen. The only place you remember her broad face calm like a blond meadow and her strong wrists when she put lemonade and slices of cantaloupe in front of you with your hands greasy from working on Yenchik's car and she told you not to worry. Grease wasn't going to kill you. Reindeer sweaters in winter and teeshirts when it was hot and you had to work to keep from stealing looks at the unleashed swing of her breasts and the bumps in the cloth of her teeshirts that couldn't be anything but nipples. The way her easy laugh turned into Yenchik's foghorn voice. Always the smell of coffee.

"Why?" you say.

You watch Yenchik turn around. Squint when the sun hits his eyes.

"Why what?"

"What's she got?"

Yenchik looks off to the foothills where both of you live and then comes back from the fence to where you're standing.

"Her heart. Some disease. My dad said what it was. I can't remember. Look at that. I can't fuckin' remember what's making my mom die."

"When? I mean—"

"Maybe a year." Yenchik looks down. "She's been dying half a year already. And my old man couldn't tell me. Just kept buying shit for my car. Just let me keep thinking I was going on a mission."

"Fuck a mission," you say. "You gotta stay here."

For a second he looks at you like he doesn't know who you are.

"Half a year wasted I coulda been nicer to her."

"She wouldn't of wanted that."

"The fuck you say."

"Yeah. Okay. The fuck I say."

And then for another second that look through his eyes where you could be anyone standing there from Gandhi to President Kennedy. He looks away.

"So that's it," he says. "That's what I wanted to tell you. That I ain't fuckin' going."

"Lots of guys don't go. Look at Hess. He didn't go. He's fine with it."

"Hess is a fuckin' hood."

"Quigley ain't going either."

"Don't bullshit me. You know what it's like. Those guys who don't go. Like dropouts. Like fuckin' cripples. Like Bowles. Pathetic. Everybody feelin' sorry around him. Everybody with their dirty rumors. Even us guys."

Don Bowles. The guy who didn't go. Who did the Army and then got married in the Temple and had two kids but still had that big thing missing. Like all his back teeth were gone. Like somewhere he'd stepped in shit. Like he probably knocked his wife up early.

"We were assholes," you tell Yenchik. "Bowles is a good guy. Always was. We were just assholes."

"Easy to say now."

He's got his head down looking at the ground. You're looking at the top of his head again. At the wiry swirls of dark copper hair with the stupid thought that a lizard could hide in it. You take him by the shoulders. His head comes up, and there's his face, still gutted looking.

"I'm sorry, man. This has gotta be killing you."

"I don't know what to do," he says. "Honest to God I don't."

"I wouldn't either."

"All those years. All the stuff they taught us all those years. I don't know what the fuck to do with 'em now."

"What do you mean?"

"I don't know what to do with 'em. I just don't know."

"You mean like you wasted 'em or something?"

"I don't know, man," he says. "All that Priesthood shit. And I don't know what to fuckin' do with it. Like I don't even have it."

You let your hands down off his shoulders.

"Fuck that. It don't matter."

Yenchik gives you a long look, close enough to where his eyes keep switching back and forth between yours, and you can see the canyon he's standing at the edge of, the long way across to the haze of your bullshit on the other side.

"Yeah," he says.

From the front yard, from her knees, her round straw hat, her long forked crabgrass puller in her hand, your mother looks up and around when Yenchik brings the Ford into the circle. She gets to her feet. You wave at her. At the curb, Yenchik knocks the gearshift into neutral, leaves the engine running, keeps his foot on the brake while he straightens his leg and goes into his pocket, pulls out some folded bills, separates two twenties out. The air of the circle fills with the loping concussive thunder of the idling engine out through the scavenger pipes and the whine of the Weiand blower.

"Doby said you were giving everybody forty bucks. Here's yours."

"You're not gonna come to my farewell."

"Nope. Sorry."

"You're not gonna come to church any more."

"I don't know." And then he says, "Not for a while."

"Yeah."

"Don't tell anyone. Promise."

"Sure. Promise."

"I wasn't even supposed to tell you."

"I get it."

"Thanks for seeing me," he says.

"Thanks for seeing you? Like a doctor?"

"Yeah," he says. "Here. Take it."

"That's fine," you say. "Hold on to it. Thanks anyway."

"Just fuckin' take it."

"Okay. Thanks."

"Don't mention it."

"You wanna hang out?" you say. "Go somewhere?"

"No."

"I'll call you tonight."

"No."

"Tomorrow."

"I need to figure this out," he finally says. "I need to figure out what to do."

You don't want me to call you."

"No."

"You gonna call me?"

"Yeah. I'll do that." Looking past you. "I gotta go. Your mom's got that crazy look."

PART 8

SINCE I FELL FOR YOU

CHAPTER 60

THE LORD will reward the goodness of your life. Greater blessings and more happiness than you have yet experienced await you. The lines from the letter that called you to labor in the Austrian Mission keep circling, serene and high and patient, in your head. The road is ending. Striped barriers are shunting you off where the blacktop runs out and the dirt hasn't been graded yet into level roadbed. Day after tomorrow, when you leave for the desert, your family will get the Valiant back. You pack your dufflebag that afternoon. Call Robbie and tell him you'll drop your trumpet off in the morning, early, on your way home from work, around six thirty. He tells you to leave it on the passenger seat of the panel truck. He'll take it from there.

That night, after Walt and Luke and Billy and Chaz have come and gone, for the hour or two you'll have before the night mechanics start coming in, you'll play it for the last time. And then, on the bench and in the big steel sink in back where they clean and rebuild fuel pumps and injectors, you'll disassemble it, wash and dry it, grease the slides, oil the valves, close the lid on the case. Take the mouthpiece home with you so you can take it to Austria. The Lord will reward the goodness of your life. If you work hard, serve prayerfully and humbly as his instrument, maybe Professor Fisher will remember you when you get back.

That night, your last at Hiller's, you make your first round to make sure everything's in place, shut down and locked the way it should be, then walk out to the fence, start playing, wait for them. Soon you see them, the car in the distance following its headlights slow along the dark road, coming almost to a stop, killing its lights, nosing up across the dirt curb onto the edge of the field. You watch it ride across the rough dirt of the field, the slow rocking and bucking motion of its heavy round body in the moonlight, the rolling and lumbering ghost of the Pontiac, come close enough to where you can catch the glint of the Indian chief ornament off the hood before it pulls up and stops. Walt waves as he kills the quietly running engine.

Maria gets out. The four guys and Maria. The doors close. Maria without Jenny. You don't ask. It's not your place. Nobody says anything. Walt goes around back and pops the trunk. Chaz brings a shovel over toward the fence and starts looking at the ground. He ignores you.

You feel yourself tense the way you did the first time you came across them. The shotgun in the office. Where the shells are. What other tools they brought. What you'd tell the cops. What you'd tell the boss when he found out they'd been out here every night. The kids who torched the place. The kids who took a payloader through the gate without bothering to wait for the chain to pull it open. And then shake your head to clear out what you're thinking. Because you know it's crazy.

"How's this?" says Chaz, over his shoulder, like you're not standing almost right in front of him.

Walt comes walking over.

"Good. Just back a couple of feet. Yeah. There."

Chaz sets the blade of the shovel, stands on it to drive it in, starts to dig.

"Keep it shallow," says Walt. "Half a foot. Coupla feet across."

And then Billy bringing out the camp stools. And Luke with a sack of something. And Maria coming away from the trunk with another sack. And then Walt coming back with something round made out of wire.

A grill. A grill off a barbecue.

"I'm gonna toss this over," says Billy. "Just let it drop. Don't try to catch it."

And with that he winds up and wings a foldup stool high into the air. High enough to clear the three strands of barbed wire across the top. On the way up it comes open. On its way down on your side of the fence you start to get what they're up to. Chaz pulls the shovel back. Walt holds the grill over the hole. "Got it," says Chaz, and when Walt takes the grill away, starts digging again. Walt looks through the fence at you.

"Have a seat," he says. "It's your party."

You pick up the stool. Bring it over and set it where your knees are up against the fence. Luke takes the sack and tumbles briquettes into the hole. Walt squirts a revolving stream of lighter fluid over them.

"Not too much," says Luke. "We don't want no blaze."

"Hold that tarp up, Billy. Luke, Maria, help him out."

Billy and Luke and Maria fold out a tarp and hold it up to where it forms two curtained walls around the pit to hide it from the main roads to the south and from the freeway. Walt strikes a paper match, lets it get a flame, and tosses it. You stand up. Watch the flames flicker and crawl across the round backs of the briquettes, find one another, flare up in a common blaze that comes two feet out of the pit, throws its stark red light across the dirt where Chaz stands with his boots crossed leaning on the shovel handle, where Walt stands back against the fiery red fender and hood of the Pontiac with the matchbook in his hand, where Billy and Luke hold up the ends of the suddenly orange walls of the tarp, where Maria, holding the center where the two walls make a corner, has it held up to the neck of her orange face. All of them have their faces on the fire. And then you do too. Let its heat build up and then recede as the fluid burns itself down to some flickers deep inside the briquettes.

"Okay," you hear Walt say. "Now I can't see shit."

"Me neither," says Chaz. "Fuckin' blind as a bat."

"You guys can drop that tarp now."

"Already did," says Billy.

"We'll just let it set," says Walt. "For now. While we get our night vision back."

"You guys are nuts."

"That the night watchman?" says Walt, looking at you. "Shit. We're dead."

"You just let me handle him," you hear Maria say.

And that last night, while the thin light of the night sky comes back to your vision, while the heat spreads itself in this glowing red moss through the pile of briquettes, you tell them what you want them to do while you're gone. About Sammy's. Where it is. What happens there. About the U. How there are guys there who'd be happy to take them from here. Tell Walt about a guitarist you know named Tully who's looking for students. Give him Tully's number. Maria finds paper and a pencil in her purse and writes Tully's name and number down. You tell Billy to get himself a used set of real drums. Tell him what congas are. Maria writes down Robbie's name and number too.

"Where does he live?"

"Out in Bountiful. He'll tell you."

"I don't got a license yet."

"I'll take you," says Walt. "Long as it's Tuesday or Saturday."

"I been thinking about picking up a sax," says Chaz.

You tell him about Eddie. How Eddie could find him a good cheap used one and give him lessons. Maria writes down Eddie's name and number. You ask him if he can drive yet. He says he's got a license and an old Lambretta scooter. You tell Luke to get himself a used amp and a new set of strings and talk to Lenny about a bass teacher. Maria writes down Lenny's name and number. You tell them to practice. Get their hands on records. Play together every chance they get.

"Should we start a band?" says Luke.

"Why not? You've got a singer."

"Her?"

"Fuck you," Maria tells Luke. But smiles.

"What should we call it?" says Billy.

"Anything you want."

"It's gotta have something to do with here."

"No. Not really." And then you say, "Just call it Magna."

"Magna's stupid," Maria says. "A stupid town."

"I got it," says Billy. "The Copperheads. You know, like the snakes. Cuz of the copper mine."

"Sure," says Luke. "We could all dye our hair red."

"Then you think of something," says Billy.

"The Moonlighters," says Chaz. "Cuz that's how we got started."

You don't know if they'll do it. Any of it. You think of Karl. You haven't heard him play his flute since back in winter when you first got home. It's up to them.

"Coals are ready," says Walt. "Let's eat."

"Sounds good," says Chaz.

"Hope hot dogs are okay," says Walt. "We couldn't figure how to get burgers through the fence."

"We got eclairs for dessert," Maria says.

"We got pop and beer," says Chaz. "We can throw it over."

You watch them clean up afterward. Chaz shovels the dirt back over the glowing coals and levels the ground. Billy and Luke fold the tarp back up. You fold up the stool and throw it back across the fence. Maria bags up the leftovers. They load up the trunk. Walt brings the lid down. And then they come back to the fence. To say goodbye.

"Didn't get any playing done tonight," you say.

Walt shrugs. "Wasn't the idea," he says.

"Here," says Billy.

He's threading a long thin tube through one of the diamond holes in the fence. He gets it halfway through when it sticks on a ribbon tied in a bow around it.

"Shit," he says.

"Just take the ribbon off," says Walt.

"What's going on?" you say.

"It's a present," says Chaz.

"A present. You're kidding."

Billy gets the ribbon slipped off the far end and finishes sliding the tube through the hole. "Here," he says. "Take it."

It's a rolled up sheet of paper maybe two feet long. Thick like art paper. Without the ribbon it starts to come unrolled.

"Open it," says Chaz. "Roll it out."

A drawing. A big one. Maybe three feet tall. You hold it out to catch the angle of the moonlight. Most of it is shaded. In the dark it takes you a minute to make out what it is.

"Jenny drew it," says Maria.

"Is she okay?"

"She's fine. She was scared you'd hate it. She didn't want to be here if you did."

A night sky. You can tell from the points of white that are meant to be stars. In the center, a guy, drawn in profile, his head down, playing a trumpet. A couple of low dark hulking shapes in the background.

"Oh god."

It's all you can say before you feel your voice want to skate off on its own. They stand there in the dark and wait while you look at it. While you ride it out. The way they see you. Where Jenny ran a thin eraser in crossed diagonal lines across everything to make the diamond wires of the fence. Pale diamond scars across your face and hands.

"You okay?" Walt finally says.

"Yeah. Fine."

"We tried to get her to leave the fence out," Walt says.

"Yeah," says Luke.

"She said it'd be like lying."

You stand there nodding. Thinking it was how you saw them.

"He hates it," you hear Maria whisper.

"You don't know," says Chaz.

"It's that fence," she says. "I knew it."

"Hush," says Walt. "Let him be."

"What should I do with the ribbon?" says Billy.

"I'll take it."

You roll the drawing up. The rest of them stand there and watch while Billy pushes the ribbon through a hole into your fingers.

"You tell Jenny," you say. And then you look down for a minute and get your breath. "You tell Jenny," you say, and have to stop for breath again. From their dark faces they just look back at you.

"You like it," Walt asks.

"God, Walt. Jesus."

"That's a yes," Walt asks.

"Yeah." And then you say, "The fence too. Tell her."

CHAPTER 61

THE NAMELESS HUNGER you came home to from Knox. It has a name. Back in the office you spread shop rags out across the bench and take your trumpet apart and wash the parts and snake the tubes under running water in the sink and set them on the rags to dry. It has a name. Cissy. It has her face. Her voice. Sun honey on her skin. Sparks off her teeth. Black fire in her hair. The name it always had. It stuns you now to where you have to stop your hands and stare. Every time you've been off guard. In the opening note of Sandy's voice where Lenny or you have played the head for her. Cissy. Her imprint everywhere. In every solo you've taken all the way across the white ocean of the night desert to San Jose and had the audience trust you to bring them home.

Now you're going for real.

Just to tell her.

Not in a letter. For real.

That you ever let anything fuck with what you had.

That you ever could hurt her.

The sudden weight you shuck now that you know you're going. The coward you didn't know was there until you feel it go.

Not to be forgiven.

Just to tell her.

Leave the parts to dry while you go out and make your rounds. Check the locks on the service hangar and all the shops and sheds, open the lids on the dumpsters and shine your flashlight in, flash it across and underneath the few machines still in the yards, walk the fences, the diamond scars of the wires where Jenny cut them through your face with the knife of a thin eraser.

Back in the office you oil the valves and grease the ends of the tubes and work them back and forth until they slide smooth without scratching in their sleeves. Put the snake and grease and oil and assembled trumpet in the case and the mouthpiece in your pocket. Put away the shop rags. Look through the drawers of the desk and the filing cabinet for road maps, find Nevada and California, overlay their flimsy edges to where the highways match, mark off the mile scale along the edge of an old envelope, inch it along the route, round it off with the curves to around eight hundred miles, memorize what you can of the desert towns and the towns down into California before you fold the maps back up.

You make coffee sometime after three. And then make your rounds again. And then finally see headlights at the gate. Frank comes in, takes his usual cup, his usual spoons of sugar from the can, his usual dose of milk from the bottle in the little fridge, his usual seat in the busted naugahyde office chair across the desk, and lights his usual Chesterfield with his Zippo. You're glad for the company to keep you from looking at the clock at every twitch of the second hand. But you could give a shit while he talks about the dozer whose hydraulic lines he had to fix. He lights another cigarette and picks a magazine off the windowsill. You look at the clock where its hands are moving up on four o'clock.

San Jose. Soon as you're out of here.

That you ever let anyone tell you she's black because she sat on a fence she wasn't supposed to sit on once.

"Fuckin' crazy." Frank shaking his head.

"What?"

"This monk. In Vietnam or some godforsaken place. Yeah. Vietnam. Lightin' himself off like this. You see it?"

The monk sitting Indian style in the daylight of a city street. Fire all around him. Flames trailing off his back and shoulders and head in the long shreds of sails behind him. Eight hundred miles. Maybe fourteen hours. An hour off for the time change. Sometime tonight around eight or nine you could be there.

You see it, Frank wants to know, like it hasn't been on tv and on every magazine the last two weeks.

"You'd have to be blind or live in a cave not to see it."

"Yeah," he says. "There's the fuckin' gas can sittin' right behind him. Right there in the street. How could you do that to yourself?"

"Maybe he had another monk douse him."

Just to tell her. Just to set the record straight. Tell her who you are. How you love her. How it was never her.

"I don't care who doused him," Frank says, like you've got all night to care yourself. "It was his idea. Look at that. The way he just sits there. Like he's a million miles away. Like it's nothin' but fuckin' crepe paper."

And then turn around and come home. Because she may not even be there. Because she doesn't owe you anything. Because you don't have anything coming. Because the morning after tomorrow you've got to catch your ride to summer camp with Boon and Korbuck.

"You know why he did it?" says Frank.

"I think some problem with the government."

"I heard some ugly shit about that place. We got some advisers there or something. Heard Kennedy plans on getting them all the hell outta there."

If she's not home. If her parents aren't. If nobody is. If you'll wait down the street, the headlights off, where you can see her house, where you can see her coming home.

Either way. You'll be there.

"Yeah," you say. "I heard that too."

How you'll say it. If she'll even care enough to listen. It doesn't matter. Just to tell her, in your own shirt this time, the yellow Hawaiian shirt you bought in Louisville.

Frank rinses out his cup and shakes your hand goodbye. You let him out the gate. Larry comes in. Another pot of coffee. More small talk. And soon the rest of the night mechanics have brought in their trucks and hung around and said goodbye and then headed out the gate for home. You do your last round. There's gray in the sky above the headlights on the highway and the yellow lights of the yard. The next time you look at the clock it's almost six. Your fingers drum away the last few minutes. You pick up the phone. Yenchik's father answers. You tell him who you are. He doesn't wait for you to ask. Just tells you he'll go get him.

"Hullo."

"I know you told me not to call."

"Tauffler. What's up."

"I need your car."

"Sure."

"Now."

"You mean now."

"In half an hour. I'm at Hiller's."

"The hood's off. We're gonna louver it."

"It'll still drive."

"When do you need it till?"

"Tomorrow. Sometime tomorrow."

"Tomorrow? What for?"

"San Jose."

"Jesus Christ!"

You hear the quick twanging cry of bedsprings. See him sitting up now, hair crazy, looking across his room at the poster of an Art Arfons dragster blowing fire out its headers, spooling smoke off its slicks.

"Yeah. I know."

"Tell me again."

"San Jose."

"The one in California."

"Yeah. Don't ask why."

"Jesus Christ, Tauffler."

"I'll take good care of it."

"Yeah. It's okay. When'd you say?"

"Now. Half an hour."

"Okay."

"How about the rear axle? Is it good for that kind of ride?"

"We unlocked it."

"You'll have to run me home so I can drop my dad's Valiant off."

"Sure. Okay."

"I'll take good care of it."

The door opens and the day guy comes hobbling in. Ray. The guy who hired you and who pays you the end of every week out of the cash box he brings in with him. You wave. He nods and heads for the coffee pot because he can't count your pay without a cup and a cigarette going. Pay you don't need to wait for today because you've always had a pocketful of it since you stopped putting it in the bank account where you need your mother's signature to get it out. Just give your father ten percent and stash the rest. She could cut her right hand off.

"It don't matter," Yenchik says. "Just look out for rain."

CHAPTER 62

TRAVEL LIGHT. Outrun the dirty name of everything they've taught you. The name of everyone who'd call what you're doing wrong. Run to where the sky runs out of iron. You head the Ford out of Bountiful south on Highway 89, stop at Slim Olsen's to top it off with ethyl, thread it through the neighborhoods west of Temple Square, head west past the Fairgrounds on the highway past the airport and keep on going, the windows barely cracked in the cool wind. Except for the open engine and the tall shaft of the floor shift it's what you remember from when Yenchik let you drive it. The way it rides low and hard on its dropped front spindles and the shackles you put in the springs in back to drop the rear end down. What the steering wheel does. The feel of the brakes. By the time you pass the airport and then the stack of the smelter it's almost yours. The faceless man rides with you in a dark blue suit on the passenger side. You don't have to look. You can feel and smell him there, the place where his face should be a cesspool of all the things you've never been forgiven for, fresh with what you're doing now.

You keep it steady along the high black dike of the tailings of the copper mine, along the dirty fly-infested shoreline of the lake, past the caved-in piers and Russian buildings of Saltair, everything still in the shadow of the mountains you're leaving behind, the shadow of the everlasting hills, the highway bare out past the supercharger and the air scoop and the red dolphins of the front fenders. Route 40. Two lanes that take you out through Skull Valley and then lead straight as a spear across the white brine dirt of the Salt Flats. When you break the shadow of the mountains the low morning sun catches fire in the blinding silver of the air scoop and the supercharger and lays the long shadow of the Ford out on the highway ahead of you. You pass the sign for Bonneville where they break speed records on the salt.

In the seat next to you, the faceless man in the suit rides erect, faced straight forward if he had a face, his dry white scaly hands on his legs away from where they'd ruin the creases of his trousers. He looks suited more to black limousine leather than the hotrod red rolled naugahyde of Yenchik's upholstery. But this is his job. You hold the big Ford steady, keep the rods and levers of the linkage out on the carburetors still, keep the eager rumble of the scavenger pipes at an even pitch. In Wendover, the border town where the Stateline Hotel sits right across the line and sells burgers and malts on the Utah side and liquor on the Nevada side, you stop on the Utah side and buy some sunglasses. And then talk for a restless minute back outside to two guys with their heads in the engine compartment before you can fire the engine again, back out through the dust the scavenger pipes kick swirling off the parking lot, and cross the Ford into Nevada. He's still there. You didn't ask if he needed anything. He didn't say.

That your dad?

No.

What's with his face?

Face?

Travel light. Keep where you're going in your head. Your Hawaiian shirt in the trunk, Jenny's drawing tucked behind the seat, your trumpet case on the floor next to his shoes. Once you're through Wendover you're where you've never been before. Where you follow the line of Route 40 you memorized off the map on faith. Where you turn the ink line of the highway real, mile after mile, two lanes of scabbed pavement across the rise and fall of the desert floor, the steady pulse of telephone poles, the dark roadbed of a rail line snaking away and close and away again along the highway. You hold the Ford to seventy. Keep an eye on the water gauge. Ride with the windows open now to the blast of the wind and the raw and steady growl of the scavenger pipes. Follow the highway on faith through low mountains with their ridges black and their shallow flanks still morning pink. On faith past isolated stands of distant trees. On faith across stretches of desert flocked gray with sagebrush where maybe twenty or thirty or forty miles of highway are there out the windshield ahead of you and the horizon shimmers liquid in the distant heat and the thin trembling ribbon of Route 40 looks like it dissolves into the sky but keeps on going, keeps turning real, by the time you get there.

As long as you keep going.

In the passenger seat the faceless man gets restless. Starts to fidget in his suit. Maybe he's got a speech to give, about the seed of Cain, about Fence Sitters, if a man with no face could give a speech. Maybe he hoped that the line on the map was a lie.

Oh ye of little faith.

He doesn't say anything.

You hold the restless Ford slow through the bleak heart of a town called Wells where Larry the night mechanic told you there were whorehouses and the casinos stand in morning sunlight already so harsh it's hard to tell if their neon signs are off. You stop for gas again and use the restroom while the attendant scrubs bugs off the windshield. You come out and the passenger seat is empty. You look down the street to see if he's there somewhere with his thumb out for traffic heading the other way. Maybe he caught a ride already. Maybe he knows a whorehouse. Maybe he's looking to buy himself a Stetson to match his suit. Hoping you'll change your mind while you wait for him. Too far from home. Too far to go. Out on the desert again you start picking off the traffic you picked up in Wells, passing it like fire through gasoline, just a stab of your foot to open the throats of the carbs and the sudden hunger of the engine and the long hot throats of the scavenger pipes. Semis blow their air horns. Other drivers put their thumbs up while kids with their faces warped in the wind gawk out the side windows. They don't know where you're going. You keep your head low and your face forward.

In the distance and sometimes close off the side of the highway are stretches where they're working on the big new freeway. The Caterpillar yellow of the bulldozers and graders and earthmovers you spent the winter guarding. Long dikes of graded dirt and long gashes carved out of the low hills to make the desert level. You wonder how fast it will be. How much time you could save if you could use it now. You make the slow light-gated crawl along the main drag between the hotels and casinos of a town called Elko. You watch the Ford move like slow chrome and rippling fire across the windows of a building. Cowboy hats and sunglasses turn and follow you from the naked sunlight of the sidewalks. You stop for two Snickers bars and a Coke and two packs of Spearmint before you're out on the desert again.

A town called Carlin.

A town called Battle Mountain.

The desert towns. Counting them off. Turning them real. Driving the long bright tunnel of your secret where only Yenchik knows where you're going. Out of Battle Mountain you start to feel fatigue. With the sleepless night. With the long desert. With the droning ride of the tires on the baked patchwork surface of the highway. With the raw hammering pitch of the scavenger pipes and the blazing spears of sunlight off the polished back of the air scoop. A million tremulous snakes of heat ride off the engine now. And somewhere out of Battle Mountain Mr. Selby starts to ride along with you, there in the passenger seat, in his sweater vest and his white beard and his peacock tie, side by side with you the way he used to teach you, the way he always kept you calm and levelheaded no matter how bad you played because in his steady attitude and tempered smile you always knew that if you stayed with it you'd get there. You feel the deep response you've always felt around him. The promise of your possibility. The faith to go after it. You sit up. Throw off the fatigue of having been up since yesterday.

This is quite a car.

I borrowed it.

Whatever it takes.

You let Mr. Selby do the waving when the air horns honk and the thumbs go up and the faces of kids shriek into the hot wind. You just drive. And then miles out of Battle Mountain you're shunted onto brand new pavement. Signs tell you to use both lanes. Across a strip of desert two other lanes bring traffic the other way. The new freeway, its lanes as smooth and level as a ballroom, flanked by broad shoulders, the line of ink on the map a powerful freeway that doesn't care about the desert. You can feel the Ford want to come unleashed, want to run, and then sit back and settle in, lose its little orchestra of groans and rattles, lose everything but the relaxed and steady breathing of the flathead engine, eager to run steady and even and smooth the rest of the way to San Jose. You settle in too. Stretch your fingers. Roll the stiffness out of your shoulders and neck. It doesn't last. Signs appear that tell you the freeway's ending. Barricades move you to the right and then shunt you off the freeway, onto the punishing face-to-face lanes of Route 40, in time for the outskirts motels with their air conditioning signs and then the main drag of another desert town.

The road ending.

A town called Winnemucca.

Sun on the dashboard now. Sun on your hands. Somewhere in the afternoon. Out of the highway wind the main drag of Winnemucca is a slow river of hot exhaust that floods through the windows. You wonder how Mr. Selby's handling it in his sweater vest. Engine heat wells up around your feet at traffic lights.

We'll get there. You know that.

Yeah. I know. Aren't you hot?

It's the desert.

Yeah. I forgot there for a minute.

And then somewhere out of Winnemucca you're on another stretch of freeway. This time you know not to trust it. Just use it as long as it lasts to pull you that much closer that much faster. You're shunted off again in time for a town called Lovelock. A yellow Plymouth with a blower and a rack of carburetors stuck up through its hood pulls up next to you. Hey punk. Hey. You. Utah boy. The steady little smile on

Mr. Selby's face that says this is good this far from home but you can take it farther. You take in the Plymouth. Look at the guy in the passenger seat with his sunglasses on and his black hair dolled up high and his mouth pulled back off the broken glass of his teeth. Nice, you tell him. You win. And then, like Mr. Selby, look ahead again through the windshield, because you're too far from home with still too far to go. Well fuck you Sir. Asswipe. And your Ford too. Let them go. You don't care. You're only passing through.

She must be something.

She is.

I hope to meet her someday.

You will.

And then out of Lovelock there's another stretch of freeway, and then another one before you crawl through a town called Sparks, but you can see the rising ghost of the mountains of California now, the mountains the map called the Sierra Nevadas, and you can feel their pull as you head into downtown Reno where a sign on an arch across the street calls it the Biggest Little City in the World. Through Reno you cross into the state she lives in. Start the long corkscrew climb of Route 40 through forests of tall-trunked pines into the mountains. Through a town called Truckee where signs for Tahoe point you off the road and billboards want to take you to casinos. You keep going. You watch the water gauge again but in cooler air the engine pulls the switchbacks like they're kid stuff. You crawl along behind semis until you get the openings to rocket past them.

You cross Donner Pass where a group of snowbound Mormons and other pioneers ate their dead to stay alive. Where cars are parked at overlooks and people stand in jackets along rock walls with nothing but sky to photograph. You keep going. Across the barren summit of the mountains where pockets of snow lie in the gullies of rock formations. Coming down the other side where the mountains in places fall away and the long rags of rained-out clouds lie on a table of air below you and long lakes of mist lie in valley beyond valley and you can see so far west you wonder if the ocean is out there in the haze of the horizon. In the same state with her. Late afternoon. The sun in your eyes now. Its blinding ricochet off the air scoop through your sunglasses.

In the same state.

Keep going.

Count on it.

Mr. Selby wearing the tie this time with the colored fish on it. Wearing sunglasses himself. You come down off the mountains into warmer air again through endless bright green fields and then strip motels that line the highway into Sacramento. Through Sacramento you follow the signs for a town called Vallejo. The last town you memorized. Through Vallejo the sky is hazed so red in the low late afternoon sun it looks like its back neighborhoods are burning. The cars that pull up next to you now, looking to race, looking to see what you've got, are California cars. Cars jacked in ways you've never seen. The guys in the windows not the mouthbreathing dolled up hicks of the desert towns, but slick and cool and silent, their eyes and their smiles thin and admiring and mean, because they can't believe that what they're looking at has a Utah plate on its butt. You smile too. Like you give a shit. Like you'd like to stick around and do the aimless shit they're doing in this burning town. But you're just passing through to where you're going. Across a trestle bridge and they're gone. Along with Vallejo. The last town whose name you care about. Until San Jose.

A town called San Jose.

Across the trestle bridge it happens. Where you've come far enough to have run the sky out of iron. Where you've outrun all the names except the names that matter. Where you can smell salt on the air through the open windows. Where the passenger side is empty now because you can do the rest of this alone. San Pablo. Richmond. In the low sun the air scoop and the blower housing are made of pale gold and the iron weight of all the names lifts off your shoulders. You turn the headlights on and light up the row of Stewart Warner instruments across the dash. Signs for the Bay Bridge to San Francisco. You don't look. In the dusk and the taillights you keep heading south through towns that are one long muddled strip of gas stations and stores and motels and places to eat and buy tires and watch movies. Their lighted signs lift into the dusk blue of the sky now in this pale balance between going and coming light. The mingled balance of your trumpet and her voice. Burgers. Hot dogs. Tacos. You're not here to eat off a tray hung on your windowsill. Keep heading south. Spears of colored light blaze off the ribs of the blower and skate along the polished back of the air scoop like stage lights off your trumpet. Alameda. San Leandro. Names that mean nothing because there's nothing heading south to name and the only name you care about is San Jose. And in the cradle of San Jose the name of the street where her house is.

San Jose.

A guy with crazy Robbie hair and a banjo case across his back. Walking along a sidewalk. You pull over. He leans in through the passenger window. You ask where the Greyhound station is. He stands back and looks at the Ford before he leans back in.

"What the hell you need a bus for?"

"Just picking somebody up."

"Hoooee. This is some ride."

"Thanks."

And then he tells you how to get there.

"Thanks."

Inside the station, the station you remember from being here with Jeff, you ask the man behind the counter for her street. Easy. Up this way. Then left on Santa Clara. Up past the college. Look on the left.

Cissy.

Go slow down her street. By the time you see her house, it's almost dark, but it's there like you saw it yesterday, its imprint so quick from the day you walked to church with her you can see the back of her mother's blouse. In a lighted driveway down the street some kids are playing basketball. A couple of houses short you pull over, kill the engine and the lights, watch the gauges drop and go black, hear the racket of insects flood the sudden raw vacuum of your ears where you've heard road and wind and engine noise all day. You strip off your tee-shirt, tuck it under the seat, get your Hawaiian shirt out of the trunk and put it on still warm with desert heat. Start the engine again. Idle the Ford to the curb of her house. Shut it down.

Lights in the downstairs windows, in one of the upstairs windows too, in the silhouette of the roof against the clear dark turquoise of the sky. Someone home. The porchlight off. Not left on for someone who's gone out. Cissy. Could she be home. You rake the comb of your fingers through your hair. Get out. Nudge the door with your knee until you feel it latch closed. A dog barks from a yard. When you stretch and inhale the air is mild, like medicine in your desert lungs, sweet with flowers you couldn't name. You come around the Ford and the ticking of its cooling engine, stroke its fender, walk the path to the porch and the door, find the doorbell, hear its chimes go off inside.

Just to tell her. Tell her face to face so that she'll know it's true.

The sudden harsh bath of the porchlight just over your head. And then the door pulls open.

CHAPTER 63

FOR THE SECOND you stand there in the light, looking to tell her who you are, you're still crazed enough from the road to be caught off guard by the color of her skin, but you can hear her quiet voice again, chiding her husband Bill that night when the barbecue was over, telling him he was impossible.

"Shake? Oh my Lord! Shake! It's you!"

"Hi, Mrs. Taylor."

The Taylor muffled because her hands come up and take your face and cradle it, warm and soft, like medicine the way you can feel them pull the wind out of your skin.

"Bill!"

She reaches down and finds your hands and takes them while her eyes dance back and forth across your face and keep finding your eyes again. You look down at her dress, at thousands of tiny blue flowers on the white field of her dress, because the light burns your eyes like head-lights coming your way, because you still feel like everything's moving even though you're standing here. And then suddenly her husband's there behind her, his broad and easy face, his hair still going gray around his ears, a fresh black teeshirt, the mechanic, the joke about Cissy being head wife, the big hands on the yellow fender of Jeff's Bel Air.

"Shake! What you doin' here? Bernice! Let the boy in!"

"I'm sorry. Come on in, honey!"

She pulls you through the door into the living room and puts her arms around your waist and holds you tight, long enough for you to reach around her shoulders and hold her too, long enough to feel the generous round strength in her shoulders, smell flowers and smoke in her hair, something she washed it with and something she cooked. When she lets you go you shake hands with Mr. Taylor. See Jeff in his big face and his big open suddenly serious grin.

"That yours out there?" he says. "That what you come in?"

"The Ford? Yeah."

"So glad you came, honey," Mrs. Taylor says. "So good to see you!"

"It's good to be here."

"Utah?" her husband says. "Is that right? You drove that thing from Utah?"

In the short hallway from the room you're standing in, toward the kitchen where you sat and ate grits and bacon in a borrowed shirt that Sunday morning, there's the alcove where the staircase starts to go upstairs. You try hard not to look that way.

"Yeah."

"How long'd that take? About eight hours?"

"I don't know. Maybe fourteen. Since seven."

"This morning?" says Mrs. Taylor. "Good Lord. Did you eat?"

"Kind of."

"You know Jeff's not here, honey," she says, alarm riding on her gentle breath, lines of worry rising in the skin between her eyebrows and around her mouth. "He's in Georgia."

"I know."

You say it gentle too. Then, your ears still raw with road noise, the blower whine still running through your nerves, you watch it dawn on her mother who you came here for.

"I just need to talk to her," you say. "Not long."

"Cissy?" Mrs. Taylor finally says. "You're here to see Cissy?"

You watch Mr. Taylor just stand there and stare at her.

"That little peanut?" he says. "Hell, Bernice, from Utah? I don't know I'd even cross the street for her."

"Hush, Bill."

"Yeah," you say. "If she'll see me."

"I think seeing you will be just fine with Cissy," Mrs. Taylor says. "But you need some food, honey." She turns and takes a step toward the hallway. "Cissy!"

The thousands of times you've said her name and she hasn't answered. So it doesn't surprise you when you listen for her answer now.

"Must have her door closed," Mr. Taylor says. "Talkin' on the damn phone."

"I'll be back," says Mrs. Taylor. "Bill! Get him something to drink!"

You watch her start up the staircase.

"You want beer?" Mr. Taylor says. "Soda pop? Lemonade?"

"I'm not thirsty. I could use your bathroom, though."

"I guess you could. Remember where it is?"

"Yeah."

"I'll be outside. Lookin' that ride over."

Outside, in the last trace of turquoise, in what reaches the Ford from the porchlight, you tell him what you know. The original flathead you and Yenchik built. The new one with the relieved and polished exhaust ports. The Edelbrock heads. The Isky cam. The big Weiand. The Carter 97 carburetors. The Belond headers. Four hundred horsepower. Who Yenchik is. You can hear wind in your voice. You can see your fingers tremble when you point things out. From driving. From nothing having called you wrong for coming here. You don't know. Mr. Taylor shakes his head, asks things, listens to your answers, puts his hands on the fender to look in close, stands back again.

"Wish I'd made it an hour earlier," you say. "You could've seen all this."

"Don't worry," he says. "I could be blind and know what I'm lookin' at."

"Bill!"

Mrs. Taylor standing there, the front door open, the light of the living room behind her.

"Yeah!"

"I'm getting you something to eat! Cissy's changing!"

From being here and having Cissy changing.

"Fine," says Mr. Taylor. "You give us a holler when it's ready."

You join him for a walk around the car. Tell him about the dropped spindles. The shackles in the back springs. He gets down on his hands and knees to look under the rear end at the flared tips of the scavenger pipes.

"So he let you bring this big boy all the way to San Jose," he says. Brushing off his knees and then his big hands. "Must trust you."

"I helped him build it."

"Figured you had some payback coming, huh."

"He doesn't owe me anything."

"First Utah plate I ever seen. That I remember anyway."

"I see enough for both of us."

"Where's the hood?"

"Him and his dad are gonna louver it."

"I gotta hear this thing," he says. "That okay?"

You look up and down the quiet street where some of the houses have porchlights on and a couple of yard lights flood out onto the asphalt.

"You sure?" you say. "It's pretty loud."

"The neighbors?" He laughs. "Hell. They like Bernice's barbecues too much."

"Okay."

You get in, pop the tall stick into neutral, pull the handbrake tight, tap the gas pedal, hit the key, and at the first hint of the starter cranking, the engine shakes and catches fire. You rev it, let it settle down, get out, stand next to Mr. Taylor at the fender.

"It wants to run," he says.

"Oh yeah." Remembering the ride you took with Yenchik.

"Mind if I run it up a little?"

Breaking the calm. Asking for trouble. Letting everyone know that this is where they can find you, here where the tunnel ends in the light of its secret, here where they'd call you wrong, here on this street in San Jose where the girl you made the drive from Utah for is changing so that you can tell her what you're here to tell her.

"Go right ahead."

Mr. Taylor reaches up across the fender for the linkage. Brings it back slow toward the windshield. The engine stumbles, then catches on, then settles in and starts to climb as Mr. Taylor feeds it, slow, steady, the whine of the blower rising, air starting to whistle through the air scoop, the rumble going raw and loud and howling, this thunder deep in your chest and down inside your ears and all around you. Mr. Taylor keeps going, his hand on the linkage steady, his head cocked, listening with his stethoscope ears, taking it high and holding it at this high-pitched savage scream while you wait for the roofs up and down the street to start blowing off the houses before he starts to bring it down again, steady and slow, holds it a couple of times on its way back down to the idle it started from. And then gives it two quick shots, hard, two blips that twist the engine in its cradle, two lunatic howls that go rolling in waves across the dark neighborhoods and leave dogs from blocks away barking in their wake.

"That's what I'm talking about," Mr. Taylor says.

"Yeah," you say.

"Go ahead and kill it," he says.

You turn the key and the engine stumbles once and goes quiet.

"It's tuned for Utah," he says, when you're next to him again, the light from the porch steady now where it catches the blower and the silver hull of the air scoop. "Little rich for here. That's what you're hearing there. First I'd lean it out. Then maybe change the cam. Don't know if it's right." And then he looks at you and says, "But you're goin' back."

"Yeah."

He starts to raise his arms and then stops himself.

"I'm used to a hood," he says. "I was reaching for a hood that ain't there. Old fool."

You both laugh soft in the quiet air of the street.

"How's the Bel Air?" you ask him.

"The Bel Air? Hell. Way Jeff talks, it'll be ten, twenty years before it sees the road." He looks at you. Then at his house. "He wants to be an officer now."

You look at the house too. Remember the way Jeff talked about being your brother.

"He'll make a good one."

"Yeah." Mr. Taylor shakes his head and looks down at the palms of his hands. "Them damn uncles of his. They got to him."

"Could do worse."

"Yeah. By the way. I saw that story in the Stars and Stripes. What you did at Knox. Nice work."

"You saw it?"

"Jeff sent a copy home. Hell. I think Cissy still got it on her wall."

"Her wall?"

"Hell yeah. Right there in her room." He looks at you. Finds you staring back at him. "Hell, boy. What you think?"

That she keeps you in her room where she can look at you. Soldier Boy. That you've driven all the way here this stupid. Just to tell her. You reach for your wallet to show him what you think. Then, in the sudden imprint of her voice, the question it makes of your name.

"Shake?"

CHAPTER 64

STANDING THERE, the edge of the porch, just ahead of the porch-light, just the silhouette of her, except the white skirt, except the honey of her bare shoulders, except the fiery tumble of her lush black hair.

"Shake?" she says again. And then she says, "Is that really you?"

"I were you," Mr. Taylor whispering, "I'd say yes."

"I got this." Letting your wallet go. Walking up the path to where you can start to see the contour of her face, lighted from behind, like the way you played behind her while she sang, to where she can see for herself that it's you. Eight hundred miles. Stopping when you get half-way to the porch so that she can have the distance to get used to what it means to have you standing here.

"Hi," you say.

"It's you." She turns her head aside, throwing her face into profile in the light, the skin of her forehead rough the way it suddenly draws to-gether, a sudden smile of disbelief and maybe everything else against having you standing here. And then, just as quick, she looks down and then turns and raises her head back to you again. "It's really you."

"Yeah." And then you say, "You too."

Not knowing what to do except stand there and let her look at you. Let her look at you and square what she remembers, what she's let her-self imagine, with what she's looking at. Try to leave yourself wide open. Standing there you almost wish you'd left your teeshirt on instead of a phony Hawaiian shirt from Louisville.

"You've got hair," she says.

"Yeah."

"Why are you here?"

"To see you." And then you draw a breath and say, "To see if you'll let me talk to you."

"Talk to me?"

She steps forward. You take a step toward her.

"If you'll let me."

"Food ready, peanut?"

The way he says it you can hear the same attention to her that he paid to Yenchik's engine, listening with his stethoscope, looking for some little glitch hidden deep inside the rich confusion of all the power coming off of her. You step aside for him. Feel him put his big arm across your shoulder. Recognize that he's listening too for something inside your own confusion, to everything pounding and turning wild and blind inside you too.

"No, Daddy. I'm taking Shake out. Mommy knows already."

"Let's go inside for a minute, then."

Where you can see the yellow top she's wearing, sleeveless, two broad bands across the saddles of her shoulders, the way it fits her snug enough to show her upper body, the way the color amplifies the buried glow in the dark honey of her skin, the dark full red of her lipstick, her hair pulled high off her neck and forehead in this eruption of black curls. Where you can sense her grace again, frank and bold and gentle, in her large eyes and the smooth contours of her breathtaking face, standing there in the living room with a beaded yellow purse in her left hand. Where you still have the road instead of carpet under you. Where you stand there like her driver in the California uniform of your yellow Hawaiian shirt.

"Cissy's taking you out," her mother says. "We'll have the couch made up by the time you get back."

"Nothin' wrong with Jeff's room," her father says. "He can sleep there."

"I can't stay," you say. "I wish I could. I'm sorry."

"Why? Where else would you go tonight?"

"Home."

"You makin' that drive tonight? Why?"

"My friend needs his car back."

"The car that was making all the racket?" her mother says. "That's not yours?"

"Yeah. No."

"Well, there's something to be grateful for," her mother says. "My Lord. What a noise. The whole world knows when you come calling on Cissy."

"That wasn't no racket," her father says. "That was music. Wasn't no trumpet playing, maybe, but music all the same."

"Darn you, Bill. Now I have to do a barbecue just to calm the neighbors down."

"Honey, these kids don't need to stand here listenin' to us bicker."

"You're right." She and Cissy hug and lightly kiss each other's cheeks. "We'll see you later, baby. You two have a good time."

"We will, Mommy."

And then Mrs. Taylor gives you another hug.

"You come back any time you want, honey," she says. "Take the bus next time. So you don't have to go running home."

"I will. I promise."

"He's promising, Bill. You heard that."

"So don't keep him out too late, peanut. You take care drivin' home, Shake."

"I will."

You trade another handshake with Mr. Taylor.

"You need anything," he says, looking at you but talking to his daughter, "you know to call."

"Yes, Daddy."

"Don't forget your sweater here," her mother says. "We'll leave the light on."

You hold the passenger door of the Ford while she steps in, lets herself down on the rolled red naugahyde bench, brings her other leg inside, gets herself seated with her knees together and her white skirt straight and her purse and sweater in her lap.

"Would you like the window closed?"

"It's fine." Looking your way smiling. "I can always close it."

You check to make sure the door will clear her arm, bring it closed, go around the back of the Ford, get in the driver's side.

"What do you feel like eating?" she says.

"You look beautiful."

"What do you want to eat?" she finally says.

"I'm not hungry."

"Okay."

"Unless you are."

"We ate. Before you got here."

Thinking where you were while she was eating. Vallejo maybe where the sky was burning. Crossing the trestle bridge into the long muddle of all the nameless towns.

"I'm okay," you say. "I just need to talk to you."

"Want to go where we can talk?"

"If it's okay."

"We can go over to campus."

"Okay."

CHAPTER 65

YOU TRY to fire the engine quietly. Idle the Ford away from the curb and down the one-way street. Turn right here. Okay. Turn left here. Got it. While she gives you directions you sense the astonishing presence of her life, a life made up of all the things she told you in her letters, the things she shared with you, the things she wanted to have you there to share with her. Washing her hair. A club where they play Miles. The Day of the Triffids. Your band. You and where you're from. And now you're here, where you can smell her perfume through the smell of flowers and salt, where you can see her long dark arm rise toward the windshield, her hand point toward the next turn. All the names outrun. Just hers. In a lighted parking lot, where lawns and the canopies of trees are spread across the windshield and a path leads into them, you kill the engine.

"What's this?" she says. Turning her knees aside, leaning forward, looking down.

"My trumpet. Sorry. I forgot I had it there."

"Can I look at it?"

"Course you can."

She lays her sweater and purse on the open part of the bench between you, wrestles the case out of the footwell, sets it across the lap of her white skirt.

"Here?" she says, her thumbs where you pull the little knobs to snap the latches open.

"Yes."

She looks at it where it lies in its cradle of worn blue velvet. Her fingers trace its tubes and valves without touching them.

"Can I take it out?"

"Sure."

"I don't want to smudge it."

"Don't be crazy."

And then it's in her hands, across her palms, and suddenly you're in his store again, the first time you held it in the scraped palms of your own hands, Mr. Hinkle there across the counter. You watch it turn in her fingers.

"Where's the part you blow into?" she says. "The mouthpiece?"

You arch up, reach into your pocket, hand it to her, show her where it goes.

"Like that?"

"That's it. You want to play it?"

"No, silly." And she turns her face your way and smiles. "Just asking."

"You can if you want."

"How do you hold it?"

You go to take it away from her, to show her, but she pulls it back.

"No. Show me where my hands go."

One hand at a time you guide her fingers into place around the valves and where they join the tubes, brass and skin and pale pink fingernails, the first time you've ever touched her, and when all her fingers are in place you let her go and watch her bring the mouthpiece up toward her face.

"Did you come from playing somewhere?" she says. "Is that your band shirt?"

"No. Just from my job. This is just a shirt."

"You take your trumpet to work?"

"I didn't take the time to drop it off."

"What's your job?"

"Night watchman. I keep big machines from getting swiped."

"Big machines?"

"Bulldozers. Road graders. Payloaders. That kind of stuff."

"So what do you do?" She looks at you and the flash of her smile comes on sudden and bold and playful the way you've memorized it. "Play to them?"

"Just to you."

"Shake," she says.

And her smile goes slowly closed and her eyebrows draw together and raise fine lines of bewilderment in the smooth dark skin between them. You look away.

"I'm sorry," you say. "That was way ahead."

"Do you feel like going for a walk?" she finally says.

"Yeah. I feel like I'm still doing seventy, sitting here."

You lock the Ford so she can leave her sweater and purse there, put the trumpet in the trunk, set off on the path through the trees. Under the trees, along other paths, around the fronts and backs of buildings, you let her tell you everything she wants. How this is where she goes to school. How she'll be a sophomore in the fall. How she doesn't know yet what she wants to major in. Not teaching like her mother. Maybe History. How she thinks about Biology. Sometimes Political Science or English in case she wants to go to law school afterward. When you come across the library she tells you she shelved books there last year. When you come across other buildings she tells you about the classes she took in their rooms and the professors she took them from and the friends she came away with, friends she studied and partied with, friends with names like Josie and Sue and Betty and Maria. She doesn't mention any guys. You listen mostly. Ask questions to keep her stories going. To keep having her take all the things she does and open them and make them real, the way her letters did so you could be there too, watching her wash her hair, listening to jazz with her. You keep an eye out for a building where they might teach music. Here and there, people come the other way, alone or in pairs, and sometimes couples like the two of you, and some of the windows are lighted in some of the buildings, and sometimes the paths are lighted, where you can see her face while she's talking, until finally she stops and says,

"So tell me about you now."

And so you tell her. Your classes. Your professors. Sammy's and the other places. Sandy and Lenny. Robbie and Eddie and Jimmy and Santos. Mr. Selby. Playing to the big machines at Hiller's. Racing army tanks down off the foothills. The kids at the fence. And she does what you were doing, keeps your stories going, keeps making the things you've been doing things she can hold and look at like she did your trumpet, things she can put herself in the middle of, at the heart of, where you've always kept her. Summer camp in the Mojave Desert the next two weeks. And then where you're going after that. Not the word, because it's your father's word, and she'd hear it in his voice instead of yours, and you don't want your father inside a million miles of her. Just that you're going to Austria to knock on doors. She nods. She gets it. And then, in the soft light from two second floor windows in the back wall of another building, she reaches down and takes your hand, not to hold it, just to stop you, have you look at her.

"You could have called."

She says it playful. Where her smile lifts into the dark panels of her cheeks but her eyebrows are pulled together again and the lines in the skin between them and the way her eyes are set are meant to scold you. You think back to Walt and Luke and Maria and Chaz and Billy. The fence across your face.

"I didn't know I was coming till early this morning. I didn't want to wake you up."

"You don't call this waking me up?"

"I know. It just happened this way. I'm sorry."

She sets her lips and gives you a look like you've just tried to tell her that grass is red and you're the king of Poland. And so you tell her.

"I thought you might leave if I told you."

She keeps looking at you. And then she folds her arms and glances off and smiles.

"I almost went out. You don't know. Then out of the blue I just didn't."

"Where were you thinking of going?"

She looks back at you. "Someplace you'd like," she says.

You don't ask. You've had to read about too many places. And now you're here where it's time to tell her what you came to tell her.

"Those letters I wrote," you say. "Those weren't me."

Her smile slowly goes. She tries to hold your eyes while all the things you know you've made her feel come up and ripple openly across the smooth surface of her face. She finally looks down. And after a minute raises her face again.

"Who were they then?"

"Just . . . just this guy who let himself get scared."

"Scared."

"Scared he'd . . . end up hurting you. Without knowing it. Or how."

She keeps her face smooth and expressionless this time and her eyes hold this tender and sad curiosity.

"You hurting me," she says.

"I know how stupid it sounds."

She just looks at you while everything ripples across her face again.

"You wanted me to stop wanting you."

You look away, down the path, ashamed at the frank simplicity of what you thought you could get away with, wait for the heat to leave your face before you turn back to her.

"I didn't know a better way."

"Maybe there wasn't one."

"Maybe there was."

A quick smile skates through her lips like the shadow of a small bird, a passing bird that her eyes seem to want to follow off before she brings them back to you.

"What about me?" she says. "Did my letters mean anything?"

"I'd read them till it felt like I was here with you. Till here I was." You stop yourself. "Jeff knows. Ask Jeff."

She pulls her lips together, quickly looks down, brings up her face again, looks off in this wild confusion across your shoulder.

"Jeff." She makes a quiet laugh you can see in her shoulders, shakes her head, brings up her hand to reach across and hold the elbow of her other arm. "I did."

"Did what?"

"I asked Jeff," she says, looking up again. "And he told me."

"Told you what?"

"Oh, Shake." She turns her head from side to side, takes a long deep breath, lets it go. "What happened, Jeff? Did he find somebody else? Why's he doing this?"

She looks off again at something.

"He finally told me. The talk you guys had. What he said. About his friend." She looks at you. "By then you were home again. Back in your regular life. It just felt too late."

You stare at her.

"Don't hate him. He feels horrible. He was just being my dumb big brother."

"He was scared." And then you say, "He's my brother too."

"That's what he calls you."

"The stuff I wrote was the opposite of everything I wanted to write you."

"What did you want to write?"

"Things that would make you want me," you say. "Maybe love me."

You're staring at her hand where it moves slowly and unconsciously up and down her other arm. You look down and run into her shoes. You look off at a shrub. And finally you work up the nerve to look at her where her eyes were waiting all the time.

"Jeff's friend," she says. "He was strange before he went away. He didn't come back that way. He was always strange."

"I know that now."

"You're not like them. Don't you know that? Smiling like they're the best friend you could ever have when they don't know a thing about you? That's not you."

"I know."

"I'm sorry. I know they're your people. Sure, it bothers me, knowing how they look at me, thinking where I come from. But you look at the stuff they preach, like all those wives, and you'd be silly to even care."

She stops, just looks at you, and the skin of her forehead goes coarse again.

"Except I fell in love with you," she says. "So I had to care. That's when I had to think that maybe that was why your letters were so . . . strange." She drops her eyes to your chest. Looks up again. "And then I knew it wasn't," she says. "Because I turned you every which way and it wasn't anywhere."

In the light from the upstairs windows you look her in the face. The way it holds tenderness and sadness in the coffee honey color of her skin. The way anyone could call skin this astonishing a curse. Her astonishing cursed skin. The shit they've handed you. The shit they've put in your head and left to you to make sense of, slug out with your conscience while you look her in the face, her face flush with negro blood, blood the underlying blush of rose in her lush smooth astonishing skin, blood the rich dark bottomless wellspring of all the feeling rippling in the surface of her face. The girl you love. Charged with negro blood. With rich pulsing powerful loving blood where the shelter of her heart stands wide open. This is where you could hurt her. This is where they've taught you to hurt her. She wouldn't even see it coming.

"Shake?"

Her open lips when they turn your name into a question.

"Give me a minute."

To look away. To let this fierce black wind and the million black wings of its shrieking birds go the rest of the way through you for the way you ever let anything fuck with this. You look back at her and keep your voice calm.

"They're not my people."

But it steps her back the way you say it.

"How can you say that?"

"Because they're not."

"Who is?"

"Everyone but them," you say. "Everyone else. You." And then you say, "You more than anyone."

She looks at you startled. Steps back, turns her face down, shakes her head, brings her hands up to hold you back from doing something you don't know you're doing.

"No," she says. "Don't."

"What? Don't what?"

"Don't. Just don't."

"Don't what?"

Her head stops shaking but her hair still spills over her downturned face and the palms of her hands still hold you back from coming close.

"Just don't."

"I won't. Just tell me."

And then her face comes up, wet and shining where the light of the windows grazes it, and she turns the palms of her hands around and wipes back her cheeks with them.

"What?"

"Don't tell me that. Okay? Don't just show up and tell me I mean more to you than anyone. I can't take it. Not right now."

"Come here."

At first when you take her bare shoulders in your hands you can feel her want to pull away.

"I'm sorry."

She puts her own hands flat on your chest. She gives you her face but keeps her eyes down, hooded by the dark smooth skin of her eyelids, shielding what you know from the naked set of her mouth would be resignation if she looked at you. With her eyes still down she gives you the pulsing warmth of her breath and the scent of rain it carries.

"You're going away again."

"I'm here now."

"I know you're here." You can feel her go tense and then restless. "I know. Just out of nowhere. Like the first time. Then nothing. Till you're here out of nowhere again."

"I'm sorry."

"I could understand before. I could understand those letters. I didn't know why it had to be that way, but I could understand that it had to be. But to have you here?"

"I know."

"What did you think?"

"I didn't know."

"And now you're going away again," she says. "And I can understand that too."

"Just to finish something I started," you tell her.

"You started this too," she says.

"Something I started a long time ago."

"I know. I understand."

"Please look at me."

In the skin between her eyebrows you can see longing and hope and reluctance argue with each other. And when she raises her eyelids the tempered crossfire of tenderness and resignation in her eyes.

"You're going away tonight," she says.

And she lays her face against your shoulder and your face is in her hair and your hands move around her back to hold her.

"Not for long," you say. "And then I'll be here for good."

"I don't want you to."

"I don't want to. Look at me."

She lifts her face off your shoulder and gives you her eyes again. And suddenly you're looking through them, through the shining dark defenseless way she holds them open, to where she's made a place for you, not just the possibility of a place, but an actual place for you, the two of you, where she's hung all her clothes in the closet but left half of the rod for you, half of the dresser drawers, half of the medicine cabinet, where she's kept herself to one side of the bed and kept another pillow on the other side, a place where she's already thought of curtains, already hung the Hawaiian shirt you're wearing, a place where you walk in the door made out of desire and hope and longing. A place she can't help but show you. A place she can't hide when she sees in your face how you've seen it, when she falters, when she lowers her eyes and then raises them again, and you can see that tears have pooled again in the curves of her lower eyelids.

"You're here. Standing here with me. I'm not looking at some picture. Just the way you played I knew I could love you." And then she says, "I could tell you wanted me."

"I did," you say. "I still do."

"Just no more pictures," she says.

And then, when her hands move up your chest and slowly push your arms aside so she can move her fingers up around your neck, up the back of your head, you understand what's coming, and your hands move too, up her shoulders and up along her neck and into the coils of hair where her neck gives way to the back of her head, the fierce lush tiny coils you saw while you stood behind her in sunlight and listened to her sing the song her father wanted her to sing.

CHAPTER 66

YOU KNOW to take it slow, both of you, to stay lost in each other's touch and taste and smell and warmth, in the sound of each other's breathing, in the way your mouths find out about each other, in the way you use your mouths to read each other's faces, every fraction of an inch of skin, every feature, every contour, hungry but slow to savor as long as you can the exhaustion of your long hunger. Slow to kiss away each other's pictures, slow to make each other real, searching and slow and lingering in your hands and fingers to memorize all the shapes and textures of each other, learn where things are soft and where they harden over bone and cartilage, learn where you can close your eyes and cup your hands and there she'll be and there you'll be, slow to say I love you into her hair and slow to hear it back again, slow to let your noses loiter in the scent of a certain place, slow the way you hold your bodies close to let them memorize each other too, you the way her breasts feel soft against your chest, her the way your chest must feel against her breasts, slow so that what you make each other feel right now can root itself inside you, slow to make sure the imprint is deep and lasting because neither of you knows how long it will have to last. No more pictures. You don't know how long you stand there. You don't know who opens the window up above you and a minute later closes it again. Who walks past and takes the grass around you. But you know together when you've run the hunger out. When you pull your faces back. When you lean apart in the cradle of each other's arms. When she exhales and leans her head into your chest again.

In Yenchik's Ford you turn the dome light on and the rearview mirror her way. She sits high on the edge of the bench, uses her hands to bunch and shape her hair, takes lipstick out of her yellow purse and strokes it lightly back and forth across her lips.

"They hurt," she says, surprise in her laugh as she turns her face to look over her shoulder at you. "I can't believe it."

"Mine too."

"Oh, Shake. It's all over your face. And your shirt."

And when she's done and sitting back again, her sweater and purse in the lap of her white skirt, you fire the engine, hit the headlights and light up the row of gauges, reach up and turn the dome light off, set the mirror back to where you can see the split rear window, start to back out when you're startled by movement in the mirror. You hit the brakes. Lit up in the sudden red of the brakelights, it's a guy and a girl, hustling out of your way. Cissy turns to see what's up and then watch them go. Leaving the parking lot she gives you directions again for the streets that lead back to her house.

"Turn down there. Left."

"Okay."

"You're sure you have to go," she says quietly.

Finding your way out of San Jose. Running up through all the name-less towns again toward the town called Vallejo. You don't want to think about the rest of it.

"I need to get the car back."

"I mean . . . knock on doors."

Street lights travel along the back of the air scoop and flash in the polished ribs of the blower. The restless rumbling of the scavenger pipes off the dark river of the asphalt underneath the floor.

"Yeah. I do."

"Make a right there," she says.

"Okay."

"Jeff said it was a voluntary thing."

Yenchik. Like a defective round. A round they've had to take out of the rack because his mother needs him there to watch her die.

"They call it that," you say. "It's not the way it really is."

She slides across the bench up next to you with her knees deflected to the side to clear the floor shift. Lays the side of her head on your shoulder and her hand on your upper arm but light enough not to mess with your shifting.

"It couldn't be," she says. "Or you'd be here."

"I will be."

"You need to turn left up there."

Another turn. Each turn one street closer to the porchlight of her house.

"Okay."

"Do you know why you're going?"

"My family."

"They want you to go?"

"They need me to."

The way you say it keeps her from going on. Out past the headlights the street you're on runs straight in the light of the moon and the metered gates of its street lights. At the cross streets all the stop signs are the other way. Nothing to slow you down. Your lungs have that hollow tired feel you got sometimes at Hiller's when you were deep into your shift before the night mechanics started coming in. You start to wonder what you'll have to do to make it all the way home this tired. The windows down. Gum. No food. Her hand moves on your arm. You lean the side of your face into her hair.

"I love you."

"I love you too," she says, and all of a sudden she's off your shoulder, over toward the far side of the bench, straight up, her voice urgent. "Stop the car. Just pull over."

Like maybe she's sick. You don't waste time. Hit the brakes, cut the wheel right, bring the Ford to a stop along the curb. And then wait while you hold the brake and the clutch down. Wait while she doesn't move, just sits there, her face down, her hands in the white lap of her skirt where she has her sweater, where you can see the luminous pink shells of her fingernails while her fingers nibble at the label sewn into her sweater's neck. Where the light from the row of the gauges reaches her, you can see a hundred wild things at work in the skin of her quiet face.

"Are you okay?"

"I can't let you go like this," she finally says.

You leave the engine running. Just push the light switch in one notch to kill the headlights and leave the parking lights and taillights on. Slip the gearshift into neutral and let the pedals up and stare at the water gauge into the possibility of what she means. It's been on your mind too. You feel it move up your back and spread into your shoulders.

"I don't want to go like this," you tell her.

She nods slowly like she knows too. "What happened back there," she says. And then she says, "I don't want anyone else to ever . . ."

"I know."

She glances around at you then, quick, just the flash of her eyes, and then just as quick out her window, and then down at her hands again.

"Just you," she says.

"Me too."

"You too," she says.

"Just you."

She looks up into headlights coming the other way. Lets the light take her face and show you everything up to the last harsh instant when it suddenly goes dark again. And then for a minute you sit there with the restless loping idle of the engine and the smell of unburned gasoline in the exhaust.

"I won't know how to go home," she finally says. "Face my mom and dad." She laughs quietly. "Church and everything." And then she says, "I know I'll have to."

"I won't know either," you say. "Just that it won't matter."

"Turn right up there," she says. "There's a park we used to play in."

CHAPTER 67

YOU FIND AN OPEN gas station coming out of San Jose and ask the old guy in the pale blue teeshirt who fills your tank what time it is. He tells you sometime after two. Coming north from San Jose the streets of the nameless towns are close to deserted. You listen to the pipes. Follow the streets and let the colors of the neon signs run in streaks off the air scoop. Most of the lights are green. Some are set to flash yellow to keep you moving through the dark neighborhoods with their doors locked against strangers this late at night. Vallejo ahead of you. In the cool air through the open windows, you ride easy, awake, alert, knowing you're fine, knowing you could drive like this if it stayed night forever.

Cissy still there in the passenger seat.

How she put her hand on the dashboard and her pink fingernails were there when you took the turn. How after another couple of turns you came to the darkened block of a park she used to play in. How she turned you into the park on a gravel road barely wide enough for the Ford, rocks whanging out from underneath the tires, deep into the park, the leaves and branches of trees as they parted off the windshield and swept along the roof and sides and tried to reach you through the windows. How she finally had you stop where there were leaves across the windshield too. How the smell of exhaust came in through the windows when you killed the engine and all the lights and suddenly couldn't see a thing.

What's the matter?

I want to look at you. I didn't know it would be this dark.

I can turn the light on.

No. We'll get used to it.

Okay.

Across the trestle bridge into Vallejo. The street through its neon-spangled heart deserted now and the burning back neighborhoods extinguished and dark in the moonlight. Long black howling stripes of rubber laid deep into the intersections by cars that were looking to race you earlier tonight. Vallejo. Here now where you saw Mr. Selby for the last time. Here now where things want to start to pick up their names again. Except for the signs that keep you headed toward Sacramento you hold them off. Cissy.

I'm scared. I've never

Me either

How you could feel her look at you. If she could believe you.

It's true

So we're both

How you didn't want to say it either. How you said amateurs instead.

So neither one of us

Guess we're in the dark that way too.

How you held and kissed each other first to make sure in the dark you were there. How finally your eyes could see light where it filtered through all the leaves from the moon and from houses around the park. Not much. Enough to tell shape from nothing. How you could see her start to pull her yellow top up, hesitate, then pull it over her head and face and hair and there was the luminous white of her bra on the startling dark of her skin. How you took your shirt off. How she faced you while she reached both hands behind her back and then brought in her arms to catch her bra when it fell away. How the breasts you hadn't dared come close to with your hands were there then, in the dark.

Can you see them?

I wish.

How she picked up your hand and guided it and held it flat against the giving flesh you knew was one of them.

Can you feel my heart?

God. There it is. How about mine?

Yeah. Wow. Is that for me? The way it's beating?

Where the motels of Sacramento start thinning out you stop for gas again for the dark climb up and then across the back of the Sierra Nevadas. Coming out of Sacramento you run the deserted lanes of Route 40 across the dark ocean of endless fields with the high beams on and the speedometer on seventy. Isolated lights in the distance move with the stillness of big ships. In the night sky high above the fields the stars are locked in place. But in the long throw of the headlights the streak of the highway keeps going as it starts to rise now into cooler air toward the mountains you know are there ahead of you. You run with the high beams on. Cissy still there in the passenger seat where you can barely see her.

Where can we put our clothes?

On my side. Here.

How when both of you were naked you took it slow again, went slow to make the rest of your bodies real, memorize what you felt like skin to skin, learn with your hands what you couldn't see, where all you could see was the play of light and dark and light and dark of your moving hands on each other's skin. Where you stayed away from the places you knew you'd be getting to, because both of you were nervous, because both of you knew you wouldn't be turning back once you did, because both of you knew it would start the way the night would end.

I love your back

I love your legs

I love these

I love everything

Ahead you can see the jagged shadow now where the mountains have started to lift their vast black hull into the night sky. And then soon the sky is gone. In the headlights the highway takes one of the canyons of the foothills. The blind and restless engine starts the long pull. You drop the speed of the big Ford for the curves. The cold gets serious now. You roll the windows up but leave them cracked for the air to stay alert. You don't turn on the heater. Leave the radio off. Keep an eye on the lighted face of the water gauge. Look for the luminous eyes of animals caught by accident in the headlights. Shift down for the harder curves where the headlights rake sudden walls of blasted rock or shoot out into open space and vanish high above barely visible points and clusters of light from the fields you barely remember crossing a while ago. Cissy. Still there but you don't want to take your eyes off the road to look at her.

I can't wait any longer

I can't either

How you finally touched each other there, and then just stayed that way, just held each other, listening to each other breathe. And then how she wanted something under her and you found your shirt and she arched her hips so you could slide it under her and spread it smooth across the naugahyde before she let herself back down. How she guided you. How she winced and held her breath and then said okay okay and then winced again for a minute and then said okay okay again. How you cringed from every time you hurt her till she had you all the way inside her. And then how both of you held still while you held each other tight and listened to each other start to breathe again.

Cissy

It feels so good

I know

Let's just stay like this

Okay

How in the dark your hips were cradled in her legs and your stomach warm against hers while her hands floated without sense or direction up and down your back. How inside her you could feel her quivering.

Just for now

Forever

That's good too

How you finally started moving because it came to both of you that it was what you were supposed to do. And how slowly nothing started mattering because you got lost in each other after that to where you couldn't tell anything apart, hand from hand, arm from arm, mouth from mouth, face from face, blouses from shirts in the closet, panties from shorts from socks in the drawers, pillow from pillow, mingled together in bed in a place you both called home. How you cried out jesus god I love you Cissy when it happened and clung to her for life and let her hold you tight while she said honey honey and started moving faster, more urgent and powerful and scared, sensing now how it was going to happen for her and scared she would lose her hold on you before it did. How you moved with her. How she cried out then from under you and then it was your turn to let her cling to you while you held her tight.

Oh god Shake help me help me help me oh please please

Cissy Cissy Cissy

The highway keeps climbing. Sweeping the headlights across the trunks of pines and the flanks of rock formations and sometimes nothing. You work the steering wheel and the gearshift and clutch and keep the big Ford moving on the easy power of the engine Yenchik and his father built. Sometimes you get the sudden slash of headlights going the other way. The cold deepens. You close the windows all the way. Heat from the engine through the firewall wells around your feet and legs. There are places now where the deep shoulders of the mountains fall away and you can see moonlight on their ridges and starlight on the air scoop.

Does anyone live up here?

Just bears. Lions and tigers and bears.

It must be beautiful in the daytime.

Are you warm enough?

I'm fine.

How afterward you just held each other there in the passenger seat and let your sweat evaporate and the heat leave your mingled skin and then started to fall asleep and finally knew you had to go. How you had to turn the dome light on to tell your clothes apart. How for the first time you could see each other. Everywhere your skin was white was the continuous dark rose sheen of her body while you ran your eyes from her face to her breasts to her stomach to the shining black curls in the deep cradle of her hips down her gleaming legs to her knees while she looked you over too. How you took her hand and laced your fingers through hers and sat there looking. How she was looking too, at how things were separate again, your fingers from hers, your shirts from her blouses, her panties from your shorts, together still but in their places now. How she reached out with her other hand and gently touched your left arm.

It's all sunburned.

Yeah. Look at that.

How you finally had a driver's sunburn, not a passenger's, even if it felt like it was borrowed too.

Ouch. Does it hurt?

No. Not really.

How come your other arm's not burned that way?

This one was in the sun. From driving across Nevada.

Oh oh. I think I need a tissue.

How she took her hand and dropped the glovebox open. How Yenchik's papers spilled out onto her naked knees. How you helped her pick them up.

I'm sorry. I was looking

That's okay. Use my shirt.

Are you sure?

Yeah.

How she sat there for a minute naked, holding and studying a card, and you realized it was the registration for the Ford.

Melvin Yenchik. Is that your friend? Is that how you say it?

Yeah.

This is his car?

Yeah.

How she sat there and studied it some more and then smiled.

Yenchik. Is that a Mormon name?

It's just a name.

Yenchik. It's kind of fun to say.

Where you crest the mountains and see signs for Donner Summit and Donner Pass the meadows are white with starlight and the pockets of snow in the gullies of the rocks are incandescent.

Oh my God. Shake. Look. All the stars. I've never seen so many up so close.

A quick look up. Wow. Yeah. And then back at the turning road in the headlights.

It's like we're out in space with them.

How when both of you were dressed, you in your teeshirt this time, she had to borrow the mirror again, and when she was done you fired the engine and set the leaves trembling on the windshield. How you left the headlights off and eased the clutch up to back the dark Ford out of the branches. How you touched the brake to hold back the nervous pull of the idling engine and suddenly the brakelights set this dull red fire to all the leaves behind you, thousands of them, instantaneous and startling, close enough to make you jam both pedals down in panic.

Cissy. Look.

Oh wow. Look.

I forgot they were there.

It's like fall up in the mountains.

How she finished giving you directions to her house. How the windows were dark and in the porchlight you could see her downturned face in profile as she sat there next to you.

You be careful going home.

I will.

Make sure you pull over if you get sleepy.

I'll call you. I'll write. Real letters.

No. No. Not now. I need it like this for now. I need this to be the last thing. Just for a while.

How long?

I don't know. Not long.

I'll be in the Mojave Desert for the next two weeks. Close to Barstow. I get next weekend off. Maybe—

No. That's too soon. How she glanced at her house and then turned and took your hand. I'm sorry.

I'll just send my address. I'll send it to your folks.

Okay.

How you knew then that even if you had the time you couldn't stay here overnight. How you had to go. How you looked at the steering wheel and saw the ride home for the first time. At how far you'd come and how far you had to go. Vallejo. Sacramento. The mountains. And then the summit. Where the highway starts to bring you down the other side you can see the razor cut of sharp gold where the sun has started setting its thin line of morning fire to the Nevada horizon. Truckee. By the time you leave California, leave the state she lives in, there's enough daylight to look across the car if you wanted and know now that she's gone.

You try to keep her there while you ride alone through the grim dawn of downtown Reno where last night's neon looks exhausted in the rising light of the desert sun. By the time you get through Reno, the sun is off the horizon, all the way up, already blazing and stark and unforgiving the way it will be all day, its punishing light like fire off the air scoop and the blower, like grit and ash together in your tired eyes. You don't care. You stare it down. Because nothing can hurt you now. You roll the windows down to let the wind and noise back in.

You're shivering

How you knew. What you didn't know was if it was hunger or sleeplessness or what just happened.

I'll be okay

I love you

I love you

Lovelock. Winnemucca. The desert towns home. Two nights without sleep. The long desolate grind of the stretches between them where all there is to do is hold the speedometer on seventy, check the steady needle of the water gauge, keep the Ford in its lane on the endlessly vanishing highway that endlessly replenishes itself out of heat and dirt and sagebrush. Where the raw fatigue of two days awake wants to turn the long blast of the wind and the growl of the engine and the pulse of the telephone poles and the blaze of sunlight off the air scoop into a long tuneless lullaby and the driver's seat into the warm cradle of Cissy's naked arms. Where you stretch the stiffness out of your fingers and tap out tunes of your own on the steering wheel and chew the rest of your gum. Where vast lakes of silver water lie spread across the desert and their glistening shorelines keep receding just always out of reach ahead of you. Where tall distant shimmering black ships turn with infinite slowness into the chrome and paint and glass of semi trucks as they approach and then go roaring past you in a wall of wind. Where you keep hearing music and voices no matter how often you twist the knob to make sure the radio's off. Where the telephone poles remind you of Brother Rodgers and in the sleepless heat you see him climbing them. Where you start in the endless blinding sunlight off the supercharger to see men hung from the crosses of the poles. Men you know. Who've always told you what to think and how to live. The soldiers of your father's army crucified and left in the desert heat to be picked apart. You shake your head, rub your face, look away before you see your father.

Past sleep. Past hunger. Keep going no matter what. Count off the desert towns and the stretches of desert between them.

And then somewhere out of Battle Mountain he's there again, in the passenger seat, the faceless man in the dark blue suit he was wearing yesterday, wearing a dark blue Stetson now to go with it, and this time you're glad for the company, because nothing can hurt you now, because having him here takes your mind off the long fatigue in your stomach and lungs, and there are a thousand things you want to talk to him about. The fence in the pre-existence. What it looked like. How tall and long it was. If it was chicken wire or chain link or a picket fence or more like the fence you used to sit on with your spear and wait for the crack of the rifle and the whip of the steer's head and the slow stumbling slump to its knees. If it was more like a wall. If barbed wire ran along the top. If there were places to sit. Why God picked such an astonishing color for a curse.

Nothing can hurt you. You want to tell the faceless man how you know he talks to God. How you'd like him to talk to God and tell him it's okay with you if he strikes you dead but you need to get Yenchik his car back first and drop your trumpet and Jenny's drawing off at Robbie's. How God can have you then. How he'll know where to find you. How you could even meet somewhere. How if he'd rather show his mercy he could satisfy his wrath by cursing you instead. Turn your skin black. Make you Negro. Make you Cain. You catch yourself. Decide to be conversational because you need the company.

Good to see you again.

He doesn't say anything.

You know how God said Missouri to Joseph Smith?

He doesn't say anything.

Think God's ever said Winnemucca?

He doesn't say anything.

Sorry I had to leave you stranded yesterday.

He doesn't say anything.

I didn't know where you were. I had to keep going.

He doesn't say anything.

Nice hat. Hope you had a good time.

Nothing. You almost smile. Knowing he can't talk without a mouth. To either you or God. Knowing nothing can hurt you.

I sure did.

And then you just ride. Ride the long hot stretch of desert to Carlin and then toward Elko. And on the highway coming out of Elko you catch a whiff of smoke. A hard quick pulse of panic brings you all the way awake. You check the gauges. Look out at the engine and then at the fenders for tire smoke blowing off the wheelwells. Check the rear view mirror for oil smoke. Look over at the faceless man to see if he smells it too before you realize without a nose he can't smell anything. And there it is. Wisps of smoke off the place where his face should be. Wisps of white smoke that dance wild and vanish in the wind. And then flame. Hard to see in the sunlight but licks of transparent flame that do the same wild dance in the turbulent wind. He doesn't move. Stays erect and immobile in his Stetson and keeps his hands on his trouser legs away from the creases.

You look back at the highway. Keep going. Keep your breathing light because the smell that wants to flood your lungs and empty stomach is bad enough to make you want to puke. You look across again. Flames lick off the sides of his head and move through his thin white hair and catch the brim of his Stetson. The tops of his ears are burning. He hasn't moved. You look ahead again. Come up on the back wall of a semi trailer. Drift the Ford out to where you can see the oncoming lane clear and then rocket the Ford out and around it. The honk of the air horn. You keep going. The next time you look across the Stetson is blazing and flames have eaten their way down along his legs and started to lick off the backs of his hands. The passenger side of the Ford is this swirling fire and wind. You look ahead. Signs and billboards for the town of Wells. You stop for gas for what you hope may be the last time before you fill the tank to give it back to Yenchik. Go inside to buy a Coke and another pack of gum and see from a clock on the cinderblock wall above the cigarette rack that it's just after one o'clock. And when you come back out the attendant's waiting there.

That old guy you got with you.

Yeah.

He's on fire.

Yeah.

You gotta do something. Get the hose or something.

No. He's okay.

You sure?

Yeah. Let him be.

Smells like shit burning.

How much for the gas?

Out on the highway, where the wind can feed it again, a hurricane of flame engulfs the faceless man, fills the swirling interior all around you, gets pulled out the windows in long transparent shimmering red streamers you can see behind you in the mirror. You look ahead. Keep going. Put your faith in what the needles of the gauges tell you and the steady rumble of the sightless engine that knows you're heading home. Cissy. The girl you love. The girl you belong to. Her place your home. Her blood your blood. Your blood hers. Red and thick and mixed and impossible even for God to tell apart. The border town of Wendover where you check the gas gauge and cross to the Utah side. The fire comes with you. Until your burning passenger is gone. Until the faceless man is gone. Until the cesspool where his face should be is gone. Until all the shit they've wanted you to learn is burned away. Until Karl and

Molly and Roy and Maggie and their faces that night on the street in the brakelights of your father's Buick are the one clean reason left for going where you're going. Until everything you've never been forgiven for is smoke. Until the wind has cleared the smoke away and the desert air makes you start to cry for how sweet and fresh and cool it is. Oh Cissy. Your tears burn the tired skin of your eyes. On the Salt Flats out of Wendover you start to see in the distance the long low walls of the coming mountains under the iron sky where the desert ends and the road runs out. You don't care. It doesn't matter. Nothing can hurt you. Cissy I love you. I'm going Cissy but I'm coming back and I know the highway now.

Part 9

Where You're Going

CHAPTER 68

YOU SPEND the next two weeks in the Mojave Desert, in southern California, somewhere north of Barstow, somewhere near Death Valley. The flat vast bottom of the world. Sand and dirt mottled with dry sage and dead weeds and most of all nothing for miles all around you. Cliffs and ridges baked different shades of red and brown and orange rust. Blackened hills and low mountains so far in the distance they go liquid in the heat like mirages you could never reach. The cracked floors of lake beds bleached with salt. The silent and immense and lawless kind of place where they make science fiction movies. Where anything can happen. Where anything is possible. A place called Fort Irwin. An outpost, some barracks and buildings in the dirt, fuel and ammo and water depots, motor pools and tank yards. A hundred forty in whatever shade you can get from the side of your tank or underneath its belly. Hot enough inside the oven of the turret to sear your throat and nostrils if you take in air too hard.

Live ammo. Bullets for your forty-five. Long belts of thirty and fifty caliber cartridges for the machine guns on the turret. Big ninety millimeter rounds for the main gun, the brass so hot when you pick them off their pallets in the sun of the ammo depot you have to wear oven mitts to carry them to your tank, hand them up the turret and down through the loader's hatch, lock them in their racks. The same mitts again when you bring the casings back in the afternoon, empty shells, their warheads fired off across the desert at conjured targets in the burned hills, shells with names on them like Lilly and Keller, Jasperson and West, the names of other guys from your unit, other guys you went to Knox with, guys who aren't there in the desert because they're off on their missions already. You've seen places as desolate and vast and lawless. From cars. From highways that cross them. From the run to San Jose. Never from smack in the middle of them where the roads you make are your own. Never from inside them.

You know why you're here. To knock one summer camp off your Army Reserve obligation before you go to Austria. Lieutenant Tanner takes the job of tank commander and rides up in the cupola in radio contact with the other tanks in your formation. A guy named Hadley the gunner. Logan the loader. You do most of the driving. You run tactical, a hundred or more yards apart across the desert floor, twenty tanks in an arrow or wedge or frontal line, and from the top of the turret, riding along on the commander's cupola or on the loader's hatch, you can look to either side and see them, dark charging hulls with their barrels out like stingers, columns of desert dust rising in pale red thunderheads behind them. You run tactical, spread out, in case of a bombing run or incoming artillery from an imagined enemy. That way a single bomb or round can only take out a single tank.

There are dunes. And gullies that lie hidden in the liquid heat across the floor of Bicycle Lake or some other flat and infinite floor of sand and sagebrush, gullies and dunes that have the regular rhythmic cycle of ocean waves from the wind that shaped them. And so you have to watch your speed, make sure to keep the rise and fall of the tank from matching the rhythmic rise and fall of the land, from amplifying the rolling cadence of the desert in its suspension as it dips into the gullies and rolls across the dunes. A tank travels fastest when it travels flat. Twenty miles across the desert an imagined army hides in the low black hills. The flatter you run the faster you'll get your gun there, in reach of their imagined tanks, their imagined trenches and bunkers, their imagined howitzers, their imagined ammo and fuel and water dumps.

Sometimes along the way you see a tank start to veer off course, the guy in the cupola hunched over his fifty caliber, dirt erupting in a raking line a few hundred feet off the front of his tank, and you know they're doing a strafing run on a snake or turtle or gila monster or some other desert animal they've flushed out of the sagebrush. Sometimes you'll see a buzzard lift crazily out of nowhere while bursts of dirt do this furious dance around it.

You know why you're here. To blast the crap out of the desert. Take the battle to the enemy. North Africa. Rommel. The Desert Fox. His battalions of Panzer tanks. You can make up any enemy you want in this much heat and space because everything is illusory already. You get within range and Lieutenant Tanner tells you to take position. You look for a shallow gully, a dip behind a dune, to protect the hull and turret ring of the tank and still leave Hadley the line of sight to aim and fire. You drop your seat down low. Reach up and swing the lid to the driver's hatch in place and bring it down and lock it.

Up behind you Lieutenant Tanner looks through his binoculars, picks out an outcrop of rock or some other target, turns it into a Nazi tank with an iron cross on its turret, helps Hadley sight in on it, tells Logan to load. You can feel the turret pivot and twitch behind you as Hadley does the final lineup of the gun. Feel the round slide home and Logan lock the breech in place behind it. Down in the hot dark hole of the driver's compartment you're blind. All you can see through the hazed and dirty glass of the periscope is the dirt you've hidden the tank behind. You sit back. Wait for the ready command. Wait for the blast and the recoil to rock the tank.

Sometimes Lieutenant Tanner has Logan or Hadley do the driving. You ride along on the turret, in the loader's hatch, next to Lieutenant Tanner, high off the desert floor, dirt roiling off the flanks and rear of the tank, and watch the rest of the formation. Sometimes you watch them fire. Watch the blast of smoke come snaking out of the barrel behind the round. Watch the tank rock back. Watch the shock lift the dust off the hull and turret like the red ghost of the tank itself rising off the shape of its dark steel body. Then hear the crack of the round. Then look forward and wait for the hit to appear, a silent flash of fire and bloom of smoke and dirt off a distant ridge or hillside, then wait again for the concussion and sound of the hit to travel back to you.

Sometimes, down inside the hatch, waiting for Hadley to pull the trigger, you think of the places you've filled with sound. The sudden jolt of Robbie's drums. The opening pulse of Jimmy's bass. The sudden command you take and the sudden way the place will change. The sudden unexpected strike of your trumpet. You wonder what it would take to fill this place with jazz. What it would be like to play out here.

In the desert Lieutenant Tanner learns what you've tried for months to teach him. Travel flat. Don't let the roll of the tank come into phase with the rolling swells of the gullies and dunes to where it starts to porpoise. You never know what's out there in the heat and sagebrush. Don't take anything for granted. You still have to fight him. He tells the crew you're heading back to one of the ranges to shoot off what's left of your ammo. You're leading the formation. The point tank. Taking a course around a ridge of some blackened hills to the right. You prime and fire the engine. Turn the tank around and start across the lake bed. The other tanks fall into place, off either side behind you, and form the two cutting edges of an arrowhead.

The bed of the lake is flat enough to go full throttle. Around the hills you come off the bed onto less regular terrain. Sagebrush and weeds. Thick dust churns out and catches the wind and streams off the leading edges of the fenders. You feel for the way the gullies and dunes are spaced. For the way the tank rolls over them. When you feel it start to pitch and dive you back off the speed to where it's rolling level and loose again and you can see things coming. And then Lieutenant Tanner comes on the radio.

"Driver."

"Yes Sir."

"We've got some tanks out here who want to know why we're slowing down."

"For the terrain, Sir. They know that."

"I told them my driver knows what he's doing."

"You're right, Sir. He does."

"I won't tell you what they had to say to that."

"Thank you, Sir."

"But I can't let them get away with it, either."

"I don't copy, Sir."

"Speed it back up," he says. "Let's show these guys."

You know from the way the tank is hitting the gullies and dunes and ridges and rolling over them that this is where you should be.

"This is optimum speed, Sir."

"What do you mean?"

"We'll lose speed if we try to go faster."

"That still doesn't make sense."

"It's how it works, Sir."

"Floor it. Let's go."

"We don't know what's out there, Sir."

"That was an order."

Through the static and the howling roar of the engine and running gear and tracks you can hear him smiling. But he doesn't say it kidding.

"Yes Sir."

You put the pedal down. Hear the engine open up behind you. Feel the speed pick up. Soon you can feel the tank start to move into phase with the roll of the dunes and gullies. Start diving down and pitching up. Hear the engine lug and rev and then lug again with the push and release of the load.

"Sir, I'm telling you. We need to back off."

"I'll worry about that."

"Roger, Sir."

And then you need to warn the gunner and loader inside the turret the way you were trained to do in rough terrain.

"Logan. Hadley. You guys hang on."

"Got it," you hear Hadley say.

"Sure thing," says Logan.

"Take the gun up too."

"How come?" says Hadley.

You wonder what Lieutenant Tanner's making of you talking to his crew like this.

"Trust me. Raise it. All the way. Over."

"Roger."

You watch the end of the barrel steadily rise. Good. Out of harm's way. Soon the nose of the tank is pitching high enough to where all you can see is sky, diving deep enough to where all you can see is dirt and sagebrush rushing up at you, where the shocks squeal and bottom out, where the suspension groans and the torsion bars twist up, where the engine lugs down hard to push the tank off the sudden thrust of the new dune, where the torsion bars release the force that twisted them, where the shocks rebound, where the engine revs when the tracks are left clawing at nothing much more than air. You keep your foot down. Watch the heavy end of the barrel out over your head sag up and down and up again. And then the tank comes diving down off a rebound where all you saw was blue, where you were trying to keep from floating out of the hatch, and it keeps on diving, and suddenly you're looking not into a gully, but deep into the dry ravine of a riverbed.

The tank slams hard into the bottom. The barrel spears the dirt on the opposite bank. Dirt explodes around you. You come flying up out of the driver's hatch. Your helmet goes. On the way out you get your arms around the barrel. The tank shudders, comes rearing up, slams you down on its nose. You can feel it want to claw up the other bank on the blind momentum of its fifty tons. And then you can feel it start to stagger, wallow, give out, and you scramble back through the hatch, grab the wheel, find the pedal, put it down. The engine howls. The tracks start pulling. With enough momentum left they don't break traction. The end of the barrel rakes clear of the dirt. You bring the tank up the slope and crest the ravine and then rock the tank forward onto level ground. Dirt sifts off the high end of the barrel. You keep the tank rolling. Because you don't stop till you're in control and clear of danger. Because when you stop you're child's play for a bazooka or antitank gun or dive bomber. Dirt blows off the nose of the tank. You get your headset on again. You can smell raw gasoline. There's dirt all over the instruments, the controls, the floor. There's a sagebrush jammed in the left headlight rack with its roots up. You hit the radio switch.

"Everybody there?"

"Jesus fuckin' Christ! Jesus fuckin' Christ!"

"Logan?"

"I think my fuckin' shoulder's busted! Jesus motherfucker it hurts!"

"Hadley?"

"Yeah. I'm good."

"Drop the gun. All the way. It's full of dirt."

"Got it."

You slow the tank down hard and then stop it easy. It stands there shaking with the engine breathing hard and idling hoarse. More dirt sifts out of the end of the gun tube. You can still smell gasoline. You gun it a couple of times to clear the overload of fuel. Leave it running. Turn around for a look into the turret. Logan's leaning against the back holding his shoulder.

"Move your arm!" you yell.

He looks at you with this quiet almost bawling anguish in his face.

"Try it!" you holler.

Slowly his arm comes up. He's shaking but he's fine. You turn back around. Just sit there. Catch your breath. You're shaking too. Remembering all the way back to the ranch. The way the steer that would feed the ranch for the week would go down when it was shot. The way when the rifle cracked it would sink to its knees and then try in this bewildered awkward pawing way to get to its legs again and then sink down for good. The way the tank felt down in the bottom of the riverbed. When it started to wallow not knowing what was happening. You hit the radio switch.

"Lieutenant!"

Nothing.

"Lieutenant!"

"I don't see him," Hadley says.

"No?"

"He's not in here. The cupola's empty."

"Empty?"

"I tell ya. I'm lookin' at daylight."

Motherfucker. You pull your headset and goggles off. Climb out of the hatch around the barrel and up onto the turret. Hadley's helmet is coming up out of the cupola. You look around. The other tanks are stopped, spread out, back along the other side of the barely visible line in the dirt and sagebrush that marks the riverbed you came across. You can see guys out on their turrets and engine decks. Some on the ground at the edge of the riverbed.

"Shit," says Hadley.

And then you see him too. Coming up out of the riverbed like a man rising out of the floor of the desert. Walking slow. Limping. Carrying two helmets. Heading your way.

"We're rolling," you tell Hadley. "Tell Logan."

Back in the driver's hole you put your goggles on, wheel the tank around, run it back across the desert toward him. He stops when he sees you coming. Waits. You bring the nose of the tank right up to him. The lowered barrel right across his shoulder close enough to make him think about stepping back. His fatigues are more dirt than cloth. His face is smeared. He looks at the helmets he's carrying. Holds yours out. Through the dirt smeared all over his face he's smiling.

"I think you dropped this, soldier."

A joke. You don't say anything. Just reach out and take it. He dusts off his chest and arms a couple of times. Pulls the sagebrush out of the headlight rack and tosses it aside. And then stands there across the nose of the tank and looks at you.

"How's my crew," he says.

"They're fine, Sir."

"How's the tank."

"We need to clean the gun out."

"Fine," he says. "Then we will."

He takes a look up at the turret. Nods his head. You figure it's Hadley up there. Maybe Logan too by now. He looks back at you for another minute.

"Okay," he finally says. "You're mad. I get it."

You don't say anything. Just sit there holding the brake down with the engine running neutral. He looks down. His hair is crazed with dirt. Back across the line of the riverbed the other guys are watching. He looks up at you. He isn't smiling. There's a whole new look in his face.

"You've got a right to be," he says. "You tried to tell me. I was too stupid to listen."

He looks up over your head.

"Hadley. Get on my radio. Tell everyone to stand by. My order. We'll move out in a few minutes."

"Got it, Sir."

And then Lieutenant Tanner looks back at you again.

"So go ahead. Tell me off."

"You're an officer," you finally say.

"I could've destroyed a tank. I could've hurt people."

"You're an officer."

"A round could've broken loose."

You've thought of that. Now you think of it again. A high explosive round. Breaking free of the rack. Hitting its nose on something. Setting off everything else. The turret going up like a beanie on top of the monster head of a fireball. The four of you vaporized. Red ash. You watch him wait for you to say something.

"I'm sorry," he finally says.

"Yes Sir."

"It won't happen again," he says. "I've learned my lesson. Believe me." And then he says, "Is that good enough?"

"Yes Sir."

He turns around and takes in the tanks lined up along the other side of the riverbank. The other guys watching and waiting. He turns back around. He's grinning.

"Looks like we won," he says.

Won. Unbelievable. When you almost wasted a tank and maybe four guys and made morons out of yourselves in front of the rest of the unit. For a minute you just stare at him. The certainty. The confidence. The way he can say something and grin and then that's the way it is.

"Yeah," you say. "We won."

"That was one heck of a finish line," he says.

"They're still not across it," you say.

"Okay. Tell me what I need to tell them to get them over."

"Raise their guns. Keep 'em out of the dirt."

"Okay," he says. "What else."

You think. Tell them to look for a shallow place. A place where the bank on the other side comes up smooth instead of a ledge that can kick them over backward. Go down easy. Get to where they know they can roll across the bottom without burying the nose. Then goose it. Keep it goosed the whole way up the other side until the tank makes level ground again. You look at them standing there back across the other side of the riverbed. You can feel the grin start coming.

"Let them figure it out," you say.

Lieutenant Tanner looks at you.

"Like we had to, Sir."

And then he breaks out with his grin again. With all the dirt on his face it makes him look like a little kid.

"Now we're talking," he says.

At the end of the first week, on Friday afternoon, you bring the tanks in to the fort, hose all the dust and dirt out of them at the water depot, open the grill doors on the engine decks, hose out the engine bays. Then you're on pass for the weekend. The guys who drove their cars down use the same wash pads, the same hoses, to get the dust off them. The guys they're taking along to Vegas or Los Angeles help out. They wash them in mud. Dry them in the dirt. Change into Hawaiian shirts and sunglasses and head back down the road toward the highway thirty or forty miles to the south. Most of the single guys head for Vegas. Most of the married guys for Los Angeles. Red dust comes out of their wheelwells and up from under their bumpers and swallows them before they're out of sight.

You stay in the desert. In this naked and silent place, where the sun is inescapable, you get them to let you use a Jeep for the weekend. On your rides out through the desert you come across things you don't see or have to look for from a tank. The aluminum frame of a lawn chair caught in a drift of dirt against a sagebrush. A bathtub with its bloated iron bullet-riddled belly and iron feet up in the air. The back seat of a car pecked and shredded by buzzards down to the steel of its springs. A tumbleweed wound up in a dress bleached pink and white by the sun. People leave things here, things they don't need, and keep moving, and the desert just takes them.

Late Sunday afternoon, the guys start showing up again, out of the same red clouds that swallowed them on Friday, their cars all hazed the color of rust again. They come back sunburned where their helmets and fatigues kept their skin white, looking dazed and crazy, with souvenirs, with shot glasses, with pens with naked ladies floating up and down inside them, with triangular flags and Mickey Mouse ears and watches. On Monday, without anyone knowing, you turn nineteen. You take your tank and head back out for your second week out on the desert.

CHAPTER 69

SOMETIMES you'll climb the side of a tank or grab the headlight rack to hoist yourself up the nose and suddenly she'll be there. In the steel where she left her imprint the first time you ever climbed aboard a tank at Knox. In the steel of the tank she's so vivid you have to say her name. Cissy. Steel that got so cold at Knox your fingers froze to it. Steel that gets so hot in the desert here that it can sear your hands. Cissy. It stuns you to where you have to stop where you are, just hang there for a minute in the middle of your climb, let the steel scald your hand, hold on while you drop your head and close your eyes and let her go through you, this sudden scuttle of paper across the headlights, a rush of light or air through your heart. And then you can keep going. Because she loves you. Because she said it was okay.

You know why you're here. When the day ends, when you're done with maneuvers, when you've got the tanks parked for the night, parked tactical, hundreds of yards apart across the dirt and sagebrush, when you've had chow, when your ears come clean of the hammering roar of the tanks and the shock and blast of the rounds, when the sun goes low and takes the heat along with the light out of the air, when all the sound goes out of the desert too, you find ways in this vast blank timeless place to spend time by yourself.

Mr. Selby called them doors. You've looked at them like roads. Out here it doesn't matter. There are no doors or roads. There are just things. The things you're here to think about, make yourself okay with, and then leave here.

Sometimes at sunset you bivouac close enough to the post to where you can hear the tenuous sound of the bugle across the desert, deliberate and slow and solemn, each note struck and held and given time to have the desert to itself. Taps. Played straight, note for note, no improvisation. Just lips and tongue and air flow and the harmonic leaps you discovered in the sandpit because on a bugle there are no valves.

On Friday they bring you in from the desert for good. You wash down your tanks again. Turn in your water cans and radio gear and sleeping bags and leftover ammunition. Shower. Eat a real supper in the mess hall. Half the guys show up in their sneakers and sandals and levis and shorts and Hawaiian shirts. In the morning, after breakfast, they'll release you to head back home. You'll know why you were here. If there were doors you'll have closed them. If there were roads you'll have let them go dark behind you. If there were things, then you'll head home through Vegas, St. George, north through Utah, and you'll be clean of them.

"Doing anything?"

You're sitting out on the barracks steps, in your fatigues, to catch the way the air gives up its light and heat and the desert its sound. Lieutenant Tanner. There in a Jeep in his own fatigues. The windshield down. His grin on. His helmet off. Dust settles back down around the tires where the Jeep sits idling.

"Nope."

"Feel like a ride?"

"Sure."

With your helmet off and cool wind in your hair he tells you the Mormon Battalion came through here back in the eighteen hundreds on its return march from guarding San Diego. Over the mutter and whine of the engine and running gear and the creak and groan of the suspension he has to keep his voice loud. The tracks of tanks go off in all directions through the dirt and out across the desert. He tells you how the Army tried camels here a hundred years ago to see how they did against horses and mules for desert transport.

"Where'd they get camels?"

"Egypt. They bought around seventy and brought them across the ocean up through Texas. They brought an Arab along too. To teach our guys how to handle them."

"You're kidding."

"They used the one hump ones for riding. The two hump ones for cargo."

"How'd they do?"

"Real well. They could carry around five or six times what a horse or mule could. They could carry it longer. They could go ten to twelve days without water. They could eat anything that grows out here. Horses and mules couldn't do that."

"Sounds pretty good."

"Best part was," he says, "they scared the heck out of the Indians."

In every movie you've seen the United States Cavalry used horses. You've never seen them going after Indians riding camels.

"So what happened?"

"They were nasty. You couldn't get along with them. They'd bite and spit and make nasty noises. They tried. It just never took. They finally just let them go."

"Let them go?"

"Cut them loose."

"Out here?"

"Somewhere out here."

"Are they still around?"

"You'd think so. They should've thrived out here."

"Maybe they were all male. Or maybe female."

"Could be," he says. "The Army's done dumber things."

You don't know how far you've come when he stops the Jeep and shuts the engine off. Maybe ten or fifteen miles. You're parked on the vast floor of a dry lake. With the heat out of the air, without the illusory shimmer of heat, the crests of the black hills and mountains in the distance are cut low and sharp against the deep sky. All you can hear is the burble and tick of the cooling engine. If you listened hard enough your breathing probably. Across the dropped windshield and the faded hood and the faded white star painted on it you're facing the sun. The stalks of the scattered weeds that can live out here cut long crooked knives of shadows across the salt-crusted dirt.

"You don't mind if we sit here for a while, do you?"

You can talk normal now with the Jeep still.

"No."

"I love it out here," he says.

You look at him. In the driver's seat he's smiling off across the desert at the sun. You follow his lead and look out across the desert too. Why you. Why not some guy his age. Some guy who could talk about sports. Some guy who had a wife and kids like him. Another officer maybe. It's a question you've had since you got home from Knox and he singled you out for his tank. What he wanted. What he saw in you. So you could know where you stood and what to give him. Now, out here, it doesn't matter much. You can feel how he's never wanted anything.

"What I love," he says, "is that there's nothing but God out here."

You think about what to say. God and maybe some old camels, you think, and he'd probably laugh if you said it.

"Yeah," you say. "That's what it feels like."

"You know," he says, "I'll bet this is where he comes when he wants to get away from everything. When he just needs to think things over."

You can feel how the distance out in front of you and to your right and left goes all the way around you.

"Maybe that's why he made it this way," you say.

"Yeah?" he says. "What way?"

"Hot and dry. So nobody would want to live here. So he could have it to himself."

"I never looked at it that way," he says.

And then you sit there quiet, thinking this is where some other guy, some guy his age, would bring up sports, or kids, or house payments, or other things men like him talk about.

"So," he finally says. "Tell me what I don't know."

When you look at him, he's got his face turned your way, smiling, this gentle but direct attention that holds you there.

"About what?"

"You."

"Like what?" you say.

He laughs. "That's what I'm asking."

So that's it, you think. You're out here to be interviewed. You wonder how many he's done. How many athletes and coaches. What he'd write about a trumpet player.

"What do you want to know?"

"Whatever you care to tell me."

"Stuff you can say at my farewell?"

"I already have that down," he says. And then he says, "Just anything. What you think about. What you like. What you do on a typical day."

"Anything?"

"That's the idea."

You look down at his hand on the gearshift. The silver sports ring. The way the sun has browned the backs of his fingers. Browned his knuckles and left the skin inside the wrinkles white. He knows you're looking and holds it still. And there it is. His way of letting you know that this is how he is. And there it is too. His easy way of drawing out of you the way you are. You look up at the lowered windshield flat on the hood where the panels of glass are silver from the sky.

"I play trumpet," you say.

"Trumpet?" he says. "Since when?"

You tell him. And you go from there to other things. Things you've never talked about to anyone. Because once they were behind you they didn't matter. Because you were always moving through them. Because you were always letting stretches of road go dark. He stays with you. He keeps you going. By the time you catch yourself, and look away, the sky has gone to red and copper and bronze. Bright lines of fire follow the ridges of the distant hills and mountains and the desert floor is this sheen of almost metal blue.

"Sheepherder music," he finally says. "That's what you went looking for."

"Yeah."

He knows about Mrs. Harding but not about her tennis court. About the sandpit but not about the cold. About the horns of the freight trains but not about the engineer. About How Should I Know but not about Rosita. About Mr. Selby but not about the musicians on his wall. About the clubs but not about the woman dressed in red. About the backyard barbecue in San Jose but not about how all of them were Negroes. About Lenny but not about his house. About the Zippo but not about the box that Molly painted with her flowers or the lie you told him for your father. About the Music Building but not about Professor Fisher. About the night yards at Hiller's but not about Walt and Chaz and Jenny and the rest of them. About Katy but not about the girl you love or where she lives or what her name is. You look at your hands. Notice that they're brown too while this hunger howls around inside you for all the things you've told him and for all the things you haven't.

"We should head back," he finally says.

"I've got a question," you say.

"Fire away."

You know the minefield you're about to set foot on.

"All of it has to be true," you say.

"You mean the gospel?"

"Yeah. All of it has to be true. Or none of it is."

"You'll have to give me more to work with."

You can hear the way he's out on the minefield too.

"You can't . . . you can't take one thing out and believe all the rest of it."

"It's all God's word," he says. "I guess if you let yourself doubt one part of it, there's no reason to keep you from starting to doubt the rest of it."

The answer you've always been taught.

"It's all God's word," you say. "You're sure about that."

"I see what you're saying," he says. "Something could have slipped in. Something that wasn't from God." And then he says, "I've wondered about that too. I think everybody does. Some of it can be hard to swallow." You look at him. See his eyes narrowed against the low sun and his face hazed red in its light. He looks at you.

"Why?" he says. "What part has you troubled?"

You look away. At the sunset off the silver red panes of the windshield where it lies on the hood. Cissy. Her skin flush with negro blood.

"Different stuff. It just happens sometimes."

"Tell you what," he says. "Let's stretch our legs."

"Okay."

It feels good to walk. Hear and feel the hard scuff of the lake bed underneath your boots. Maybe a hundred feet out in front of the Jeep he stops and turns to you. He's got this easy and eager smile like he's just thought of some quick game to play out here.

"Listen," he says. "Mind if I say a prayer for you?"

He holds his smile. You can see in his eyes where it took him guts to ask you. Where the cloth lieutenant bars on the points of his collar don't mean a thing out here.

"Here?"

"Why not?" he says. And then he says, "It's just us and God."

"Sure."

"Come on."

He uses his boot to scrape a place clear for his knees. Gets down on his knees in front of you. You scrape a place clear too, get on your own knees in the dirt, face to face with him. He brings up his arms and places his hands on the saddles of your shoulders. You can tell from his face that he wants you to follow his lead again. Under your hands and through his shirt you can feel where the muscles of his neck and shoulders run. He gives you a wink. And then bows his head.

"God."

And then he waits. Not like he's organizing what he wants to say. More like he's giving God time to drop whatever else he's doing, show up, sit down, give the two of you his full attention. His hands on your shoulders are still.

"You know this young man here on his knees with me. You know everything there is to know about him. What's in his heart and soul. His strength and courage and intelligence. You know that everything you've ever asked of him, he's done, with the spirit of a champion. Everything you've ever asked him to take on faith he's taken. I know how proud you are of him."

You've never heard anyone just come out and talk to God. Calm and easy and with this quiet confidence. Like God's just some regular guy. Out here, in this place where anything can happen, where nothing has to have a reason, God has a hundred ways to remind him that he's God. You want to stop him. Tell him all the things you didn't tell him, all the other things God knows, before he pushes God too far, before you hear God's big mocking laugh fill the desert around you while both of you turn to salt. You keep still.

"Sometimes I can see shame in him. And that saddens me. I know there's nothing in him that would give you cause to put that shame there. You know that too. The shame I see is shame that was put there by men. It has no place there. You need to let him know that."

Under your hands the crude fabric of his fatigue shirt. And under the fabric the still muscles and tendons of his neck and shoulders. And under his hands you try to keep your neck and shoulders still.

"This young man kneels here, at the doorstep to his mission, ready and willing to give you more than two years of his life. So I want you to look at him. I want you to look at the way a young boy recognized the gift you'd given him in something he heard on the radio. At the way he pursued it on his own. Knowing it came from you. Knowing it was his responsibility. I want you to look at the people who've had their hearts filled and their spirits lifted by his music. I want you to look hard at what he's putting aside for you."

He stops and waits again. Maybe to give God time to say something back. Spikes of dirt with nowhere to go have started to feel like needles in your knees. Light gusts of restless sunset air play across your neck and ears.

"Now it's your turn. You know your responsibility to him. I do too. I know you won't disappoint him. I know you'll watch over him. In Austria you'll give him what he needs to do your work. You'll see that he gets good companions. Hard-working companions who'll know how blessed they are to work with him. I know you won't waste his time."

You can hear emotion make his voice waver, make him stop and clear his throat, make him shift his hands on your shoulders some.

"You bring him home safe. You bring him home and reward his work and sacrifice. See to it that his life will be here, ready and waiting, as if he'd only missed a single day of it." He stops for another minute. "So here he is. I put him in your hands. In the name of Jesus Christ, Amen."

You say Amen. You open your eyes. You need more time. Time to just look down at the dirt where the scrape marks from the sole of your boot are still visible in the light left in the sky. Time to breathe. Time to trust where you are in the still fire that rims the desert all around you. Lieutenant Tanner doesn't say anything or move. Just keeps his hands on your shoulders and lets you keep yours where they are.

CHAPTER 70

YOU COME HOME to the last few days of leaving. To sleeping on the basement couch while Maggie keeps fixing up your room her way. To another round of Sunday meetings. To Doby, an Elder now himself, called to serve a mission in West Germany, there with you in the carpeted classroom of the Elder's Quorum.

"Nice tan," he says afterward.

"Thanks. Like I could help it."

You're standing in the morning sun outside the glass door off the classroom wing of the churchhouse. Cars are pulling into the parking lot. Families dressed for Sunday School are getting out. Mothers with the wrapped and shrouded trophies of their latest babies. Girls Molly's age with the smiling shields of their Sunday faces in place and raised into the sunlight. It used to be all of you out here. Keller and Jasperson and West and Lilly and sometimes Strand. You wonder how Yenchik's doing.

"It looks good," says Doby.

"It's just from the neck up."

"It's all you need," he says. "You're gonna be wearing a tie from now on anyway."

"Elder Doby," you say. To try it on.

"Yeah," says Doby. "Elder Tauffler yourself."

"When's your farewell?" you say.

"Two weeks after yours."

"Germany," you say. "We'll be pretty close."

"I was thinking," he says. "Maybe we could work it out to get released together. We're only gonna be two weeks apart. Tour Europe together a little."

"Yeah. Sounds good. Bring a couple of Porsches home."

"Only thing is it'll be winter. Cuz of that extra half year."

"We'll learn how to ski," you say. "You seen Yenchik?"

"He hasn't been here. Maybe he's been sick."

"He's never sick," you say.

"Maybe he didn't want to be a Priest all by himself."

"Yeah. Maybe."

"So next week, man," says Doby.

"My farewell? Yeah."

"Think you're ready?"

"I can't remember when I wasn't."

You don't need the long laudatory sendoff of a farewell. It reminds you of the long introduction you'd sometimes get from the owner of one or another club while you and Jimmy and Robbie and Santos and Eddie hung back itching to get going. How Should I Know. It wasn't who you were. It was what you did. All you need to do is go. You watch the Valiant pull into the parking lot, Karl driving, your mother in the passenger seat, Molly and Maggie in back. You remember when it used to be your job to go home and fetch your family after Priesthood Meeting. Now, with Roy a Deacon, just the women need fetching.

"You scared yet?" says Doby.

"Nope. You?"

"Ever since I got my letter."

"Try praying."

"I been doing that," he says. "Praying my nuts off."

You watch Molly come around the back of the Valiant to catch her little sister's hand when Maggie gets out the other side. In her pink and white dress she keeps her eyes down. Doesn't look for you. Doesn't raise her face into the sun to look around. Nothing shields what you see there. The way she's coming through the ranks herself. The ranks they have for girls. Beehive. Mia Maid. Laurel. Obedience and chastity and hope. You watch her step out of Karl's way like she should have known where he'd be headed. You want to tear his face off.

"Then just sit back," you tell Doby. "Let it happen."

Your father has to ride to work with Whipple one last time. You and your mother take the Valiant to spend the day in Salt Lake, in the shops and department stores on Main Street, where she helps you pick out two dark suits, a set of white dress shirts and dark ties, two pairs of shoes, socks to go with them, a London Fog raincoat with a zip-out lining of soft thin fur that converts it to a winter coat, five pairs of temple garments for underwear, a big gray Samsonite suitcase to carry everything in.

The salespeople all know what you're looking for. Your mother's breathless excitement and animated accent and contagious pride in shopping for her missionary son, her firstborn missionary son, leave them smiling. The next day, the Valiant back in your father's hands, you ride your bike down to Main Street in Bountiful to pick up other supplies. A briefcase and toilet kit. The toiletries to go in the kit at Servus Drug. A notebook and pen and airmail envelopes at Carr's Stationery. A big red English German dictionary. You ride it all home in the basket bracketed to the handlebars and on the rack behind the seat where you used to lash your trumpet.

You save your last night, the Saturday night before your farewell, for Katy. Your father needs the Valiant to take your mother to the Temple where they'll go through the endowment ceremony in the names of two dead people they don't know. Katy drives out to pick you up. You come down the walk past your father's roses to her idling Studebaker Hawk and in the light through the windshield see that her face is white.

She drives you back to Salt Lake. You try not to think, in the passenger seat, how easy this is, how much you can take this for granted, the time you've had with her. You take her to dinner at a place called the Polynesian. The place is made up inside like an island jungle. Tiered up off the main floor, half hidden in palms and vines and other jungle plants, paths lead to private booths that are sheltered with grass roofs. An island canoe with an outrigger hangs from the rafters. Perforated water pipes run overhead through all the vegetation. Every twenty minutes there's a storm. The place goes dark. Lightning starts flashing from random places. Hidden speakers crack out wind and thunder. In the rafters the canoe starts rocking back and forth. You can hear pumps start to chug. Rain start coming down. Hidden gutters keep it off your heads and carry it away.

Katy reaches out and lets her hand get wet. You try not to see Cissy's hand. Try not to see her face across from you in this shelter from this manufactured rain. At the peak of the storm a large tree keels half over. The rain starts letting up. The pumps shut down. The storm moves on. The lights come up again. A cable hoists the tree back into place for the next storm. You eat your island food through one storm and then another one.

Afterward you head for a spot the two of you have used before, in Memory Grove up City Creek Canyon, a patch of mowed grass shielded by trees from the road and the rest of the place. You head there because she's driving. Because you don't know what to say or do. Because none of this is her doing or her fault. You throw down the blanket she keeps in the trunk. Lie on your back when she tells you to. Feel crisp blades of grass through the wool. She straddles you. Opens her blouse and pulls it off her shoulders. You look for a way to stop her that won't insult or hurt her. In the moonlight that gets through the leaves her swollen bra is there. And then she takes it off.

You've been here before. Felt the weight of her body ride on her breasts on your bare chest with blades of grass in your back. The heat between her thighs. Once the edge of her pubic hair before she tightened her thighs and gently pulled your hand back. Roman hands and Russian fingers. That's what she said you had. Now everything seems foreign, not Roman or Russian and not the way she meant them, but only half familiar, a place that should be yours but with different furniture, the rugs worn where you didn't wear them, a bowling shirt in the closet, a cowboy hat on the shelf above it. This sadness now when you look at her, her breasts just bare, no other imprint, none of this her fault. You reach up and gently keep her from laying herself on top of you. She doesn't fight you. Just lowers her face to where you inhale the damp heat of her island breath. Then sits back up, unbuttons your shirt, pulls it back, and you don't know what to do to stop her.

"Whoa," she says. "That tan sure comes to a screeching halt."

Her finger traces the line across your throat where the neck of your teeshirt was when you were in the desert.

"I should've worn a tie," you tell her.

"It would've had to come off," she says.

You look up at her. Up past her breasts where her hair falls forward and forms an alcove for her shadowed face.

"I need to take it easy tonight," you finally say.

"I want to do it tonight," she says.

"Do what?"

"Don't act dumb."

"I'm supposed to lose my papers tonight?"

"Not just you," she says. "Me too."

"I can't, Katy. Jesus. Not tonight."

"Why not?"

In the dark where her face is hidden you can tell from her teeth the shape of her teasing smile.

"You know. Tomorrow. My farewell."

"I know. We'll trade papers. Nobody loses anything. I'll take yours and you can have mine. That way we'll both still be virgins."

The way you smile back at her feels like it's stitched to your teeth.

"You gonna wait for me?"

"Are you asking me to?"

"Would you if I did?"

"Two and a half years?"

"Soon as I'm gone you're gonna start hitting the country bars."

"I hate country."

"Give it a chance."

"That's not country."

"Sure it is."

"So what do you say? Mine for yours."

"I'll come home, you'll be married to some cabinet maker, a couple of kids."

"A cabinet maker? Gee. Thanks a lot."

"I don't know. Some rich guy then."

You look up at her while she looks away, smiles at the distant possibility, her breasts bare for a guy with a closet full of expensive suits and golf shirts.

"So come on," she finally says. "Let's call it a goodbye present."

"I won't have enough time to repent before tomorrow."

"You're kidding."

"Yeah. But still."

"I want you to remember me. All of me."

"I will. But I can't."

"We don't have to tell anybody."

"This is crazy."

"I put perfume on it and everything."

"Perfume," you say.

"Ambush," she says.

"I'll smell it then. But that's it, Katy. Sorry."

She rolls off you onto her back. Arches her butt off the blanket and pulls her jeans and her panties down together. Waits while you do what you said you would, face to face with it, careful not to look at it longer than you need to get your nose there, careful not to touch it, even when it nudges up to touch you. The smell makes the back of your head feel like it's gone, open suddenly to the night air and the island storm. You pull your nose away. Roll onto your back on the blanket again.

"So?"

"Like heaven."

"I'm sorry too," she says. Her hand down there now where your nose just was. "I just need to do this."

It takes a minute for all the wild things to calm down again to where you get it.

"You can either watch or take a walk," she says.

"What would you like me to do?"

"You could hold me." Her voice already low and trembling some. "That'd be nice."

And so you do. Roll up against her side. Put your arm across her stomach. Close your eyes. Keep them closed when it happens, when the muscles of her stomach tighten, when her head comes off the blanket, when she cries out jesus twice, when you know you shouldn't be here. You stay with her. You remember your father standing that night in the doorway to your room. Remember the shame. You stay with her afterward. She rolls her body up against you, slow and heavy and soft, puts her face in your shoulder.

"What about you?"

Her hand moves down your leg. You feel your blind pud want to meet it. Say here I am. You gently nudge her hand off course and hold it there.

"Now who's got the Russian fingers," you say.

"This is a tough way to say goodbye," she says.

"I know."

Riding home, in the passenger seat, you listen to the radio, watch the highway in the headlights, ride with her smell still in your nostrils. She takes the Fifth South Exit she knows and won't be using again.

"Pull over."

"Where?"

"Anywhere. Right here."

"Why?"

"I'll tell you after."

Where your nuts ache so hard from getting worked up and then not getting there the pain is like one long constant kick. Where there are only two things to do to make it go away. The first is jacking off and finishing the job. The second is lifting something that's impossible to lift. She slides the Studebaker in against the curb across the street from the Queen Theater where you've seen South Pacific with your mother and The Blob and Bridge on the River Kwai and a shitload of other movies with your buddies.

You get out. The lighted sign across the street on the theater says The Birds. Tippi Hedren. There's a woman behind the window of the ticket booth. There's a parking lot full of cars but nobody else around. You hobble around the front of the Studebaker, square yourself against the grill, squat down, grab hold of the low bumper, take a deep breath, and let a car pass by while the hood ornament stares you in the face from the metal field of the dull black hood. Heat from the running engine wells around your ankles. In the windshield Katy's face shows curiosity. You hope she holds the brake. You lean hard into the grill and lift with everything you've got. The nose of the Studebaker comes up moaning in your hands. You hear the fluid surge through the shocks. Watch Katy's mouth go open through the windshield and her hands grab for the steering wheel. Don't be scared, you think, hold still, wanting to cry when you feel the ache go out of your groin.

CHAPTER 71

SHE DROPS you off. You watch her taillights on her way out of your neighborhood. When you go inside the house, the lamp in the living room, set on low, lets you know your mother and father aren't home from the Temple yet. You head toward the hall for the bathroom. Maggie's standing there in her nightgown by herself. In her face a look you know. Karl, you think, going after Maggie now, the youngest one, downstairs in bed, sleeping off whatever he did to her. You get on your knees, put yourself face to face with her, but in your head you're already down the stairs, already busting into his room.

"What'd he do? Where's Molly?"

"She ran away."

"Where? Why?"

"They took her lamp away," she says.

Where her face was sad it goes all of a sudden scared. Something she sees in your face. They. Your father and mother. The way this suddenly goes a hundred times more serious than Karl. You take a slow breath. Look down and take her hands where they come out of the puckered little ruffles around the wrists of her nightgown. Look at her again.

"The one I gave her?"

"Yes," she says. "The pretty one."

You think back. You left before they did. The honk of Katy's Studebaker while your mother was wandering around the house in her slip and nylons. Things were fine. Molly and Maggie were out on the patio doing something. So it happened after that. Before they headed for the Temple with their little suitcases filled with their secret clothes. Maggie's trying to pull her hands back. You've been rubbing the backs of them with your thumbs without knowing how hard.

"I'm sorry," you say. "Do you know how come they took it?"

The bottom half of Maggie's round face comes unglued and starts to quiver. She looks down at her hands.

"It's okay." You catch her chin. "Look at me."

"Mama called her a bad name."

You don't need to ask. You don't need to hear Maggie have to say it. You already feel it crawling up your back into your neck.

"Okay. Where'd she go? You know?"

"Maybe her place."

"Her place?"

"In the orchard."

"Her place in the orchard?"

Maggie hears it the same time you do. Her face goes scared again. The creak of the Valiant's suspension crossing the hump at the top of the driveway. The hot rough whisper of its engine. The ratchet of the emergency brake. The next thing you'll hear is the driver's door. Then the garage door. Your father in the headlights, swinging it up, your mother behind the windshield watching him, her mouth stitched tight, thinking God knows what in her nasty nervous appetite to cut anything about him down. How stupid with tools. How bad a driver. You rub Maggie's shoulders.

"Go to your room," you say. "Close the door. I'll find Molly."

"Promise?"

"I promise."

You wait in the living room. For the car doors to thunk shut. For the garage door to come down. For the door to the basement to open. For the mutter of their voices. For their shoes on the steps. In your head, while you wait, you take your mother's chubby little Hummel kids off the mantel, one by one, stand back, pitch each one of them hard into the scorched maw of the brick fireplace. A pile of splintered white ash from a porcelain fire. By the time they approach the top of the stairs you're holding one of them. A little girl with flowers in her chubby fist. Your mother appears first, in her gray Sunday dress, carrying a little gray evening bag. Your father rises behind her, in his gray suit and a tie that matches the sudden red of your mother's lipstick, carrying their little suitcases. Your mother sees you. What you're holding. Your father throws a look into the living room and heads the other way, down the hallway toward their bedroom, where they keep their suitcases on the closet shelf.

"Yes," she says. "You are home." Her voice pale. Her smile glazed with having walked into something unexpected. A feeling you know.

"I need to talk to you."

She comes into the living room on her high heeled shoes.

"Yes, Shakli. Your father and I have had a nice evening."

"The lamp I gave Molly."

"Yes. It is time for bed." And then her face and voice go bright with an attitude of duty. "We have a big day tomorrow!"

"Tell me what you did with her lamp."

"What are you doing with my Hummel?"

"Where's the lamp."

She sets her bag on the armrest of the sofa. Closes the distance between you, her face angelic, looking at her missionary son.

"Yes, Shakli. Let's put it back. So we can all go to bed."

"Where's the lamp."

"We took it from her."

"Tell me why."

"Because I won't let her turn her room into a whorehouse."

"A whorehouse."

"It was the lamp of a whore," she says.

"A whore."

"Yes. Now let me have that. So we can go to bed."

You look down at the figurine in your hand. The brittle cheeks of its chubby face. The brittle painted flower in its fist. Its brittle high-topped shoes. Its brittle painted farm dress. And then you look up calm.

"Tell me where it is. Or this goes in the fireplace."

Terror takes all the composure out of her own painted face.

"Harold! Harold! He wants to smash my Hummel!"

Your father's still wearing his suit when he comes out into the living room. She backs away and steps aside to give him room. He comes as far as the end of the sofa where her bag sits on the armrest.

"So. What's going on here, Mother. We have sleeping children."

"Your son wants to smash my Hummel! Show him!"

You look at your father. "The lamp I gave Molly."

"Yes," he says. "What about it."

"It's gone, isn't it."

"That surprises you?"

"You don't just throw stuff out! When will you people learn!"

"So! We are not people! We are your parents!"

"You agree with her? Your daughter's a whore?"

"Of course not! It's a figure of speech! You don't have to take it so literally!"

"Yah!" Your mother steps back up and puts her face in yours. "You would know what a whore is! You smell like you just came from one!"

"And you'd know the lamp of a whore!"

In her Sunday dress and high heeled shoes she shrinks back, lipstick on her teeth like blood, this wounded look like your hand should hurt from slugging her. You set the Hummel back in its place on the mantel. Look down at your shoes to burn out the rage and pity and heartbreak.

"I need to go find her."

"Find who?" your father says.

"Molly."

"She isn't in her room?" your mother says.

"She ran away."

"She ran away." Hand to her mouth. Her voice this hoarse hushed hopeless resignation like running away was one more thing she'd expect from her daughter whore.

"Her mother called her a whore. You. For the love of God."

"I'll go with you," your father says.

Here where you've run out of road. Where you've let go of everything. Where all you have left is them. Molly out there, wherever she is, shame crawling all through her, nowhere to go where she can get away from the faceless smell of her shame this late at night.

"No. I'll find her. You stay away from her."

You find her after crashing through the orchard with your forearms up like bumpers to keep from getting whacked by branches. Just a girl moving, in the moonlight, arms out for balance, picking her way in starlight across the rocks and boulders down the slope off the downhill side of the orchard. Molly. Headed away. Not fast. More like she already knows she'll be run down but doesn't know what to do except keep going. You clear the orchard yourself and stop so you won't spook her. Molly. Off to your left the silver lake of the parking lot in the moonlight and the churchhouse like the sudden dark sinister hull of a battleship. She reaches where the slope ends and the ground smoothes out and keeps on going, not running, more like hurrying, more out of fear of being hurt than being caught. It isn't long before you're right behind her. She stops and stands there with her back to you and her head down. A dress you know. A simple one with buttons up the back. You stop behind her. Shame. It comes off everything. The back and buttons of her dress. The puffs of the sleeves on her shoulders. Her plain brown hair with the yellow braids long gone. Her arms and elbows. Her legs. Down to her shoes. Shame. If shame was something you could smell you couldn't have gotten close enough to catch her. Molly. You move around in front of her. Her eyes come up but not her face.

"You're not what Mama said."

And now her eyes go down.

"You're not."

It has no smell. It's just shame. So you're able to hold her and then a while later slowly lead her up the dirt road around the orchard home.

CHAPTER 72

"For behold, I am endless, and the punishment which is given from my hand is endless punishment, for Endless is my name."

– Jesus Christ to Joseph Smith, 1830

FROM A BENCH toward the rear of the chapel, out of the way, you look at the program you were handed by the young kid at the chapel door. A Farewell Testimonial. On the cover a color photo of the Salt Lake Temple, a Hawaiian-colored sunset behind it, the silhouettes of the spires hit with floodlights. On a center spire, high enough to catch the fire of the setting sun, the gold statue of the Angel Moroni playing his long gold horn. Inside the cover of the program a list of missionaries in the field. Elder Michael Lilly. Elder Chip Keller. Elder John Jasperson. Elder Robert West.

On the facing page a black and white portrait of a young man in a dark suit looks up at you. Elder Shake Wilford Tauffler. Pinned to his lapel the small silver cattle skull of his Duty to God Award. The knot of his dark tie stands off the collar of his white shirt. His head is canted slightly down, a President Kennedy haircut, a young face, his eyes direct and friendly.

Shake. A nickname that may have stuck. He's on the stand, in one of the cushioned theater seats up there, shouldered in between two big imposing men. Earlier you heard a woman behind you say how nice to have his two bishops on either side of him. At the organ, a heavy man with thick brown hair and a graying beard runs the deep smooth current of the prelude under the clamorous babble of happy chatter while benches fill in around you.

So this is what it was like for Keller and Jasperson and West. Why they looked the way they did. Why West never looked at Connie. Why you couldn't catch their eye. Why even afterward they looked at you like they were working overtime to keep you from really seeing them. They were scared. They had stuff to hide. They had stuff you knew about.

From your seat on the podium, held there between the shoulders of Bishop Byrne and Bishop Wacker, what you see is astonishing. They've opened the massive folding doors that make the back wall of the chapel and set up rows of folding chairs across the gym. People by the hundreds are entering the chapel, holding the small brochures of your program the ushers handed them, looking your way while they fill out the benches and chairs. You've surrendered the armrests to Bishop Byrne and Bishop Wacker. Your arms are crowded in against your sides. You keep your hands off the creases in the trousers of your new missionary suit. You've got stuff to hide too. From all your neighbors. From people from your father's job. People back as far as when you lived on Brewery Hill and in Rose Park. Your father's and mother's immigrant friends from Switzerland. People you don't remember or never knew. Mothers who may have held you naked. Brother Rodgers and Brother Hunt and Earl Bird. Susan Lake, her sainted face, her waiting for her missionary face. Brother Clark. Sister Avery. Hide from everyone. Because this is all for you. Walt Hanks at the organ to let your mother get the full measure of the show. The Priests at the Sacrament Table with the bread and water ready underneath the tablecloth. One of them Karl. The Deacons in their benches ready to relay bread and water trays back and forth along the benches. One of them Roy. Scoutmaster Haycock and his wife. Doby and his mother Jennie. Sandy and Lenny on the front bench a couple of steps away from where they'll perform.

You keep your eyes moving. Like a dragonfly chasing insects too small to see. Keep them from lighting anywhere on any face. Because their smiles are ready and in the naked blaze of their pride and admiration you'd have to smile back. You know. You tried. You smiled back at Sister Jensen and your smile took off like a chipmunk all over your face before you could catch it. Your mother in a beige dress on a bench a few rows back. Her hair black and her church smile red. Molly there, stuff of her own to hide, hidden so deep her face is blank of everything but its features. Maggie between them. Your father behind you, a couple of seats to your left, in the second row of the podium. Everyone ready. Everyone's shoes polished.

Bishop Wacker gets up and welcomes everyone. Iris Lake gets up and uses her white baton to take the congregation through all four verses of the opening hymn you and your father settled on. Onward Christian Soldiers. Marching as to war while you share a hymn book with Bishop Byrne. Forward into battle while hundreds of voices thunder and howl their way through verses you've sung with your chest swollen and your heart pounding since you were a kid. Your Uncle Klaus gets up and gives the invocation. Iris Lake gets up again. This time the congregation listens while she leads the choir through the Sacrament hymn you let your father pick. Lead Kindly Light. Lead kindly light amid the encircling gloom while Karl and two other Priests get to their feet behind the Sacrament table and fold the white tablecloth back off the bread trays. Lead thou me on. The night is dark and I am far from home while Karl picks slices of Wonder Bread apart. Lead thou me on. Karl gets to his knees and reads the blessing for the bread into the microphone. Roy and the other Deacons take the trays they're handed to their benches. And then they do the water. And then they're ready for the real show. The show they've come here for. Where you're their hero. Where you're their soldier going off to conquer Austria.

What they hear is a bragfest. After the Sacrament it's Bishop Byrne who gets it started. He pats your knee with his big hand, his rough eroded painter's hand, pulls himself up, and talks from the pulpit about watching you grow from a twelve-year-old boy to the fine young man who sits on the podium today. About the seven Individual Achievement Awards you've earned. About the day you helped Scoutmaster Haycock replace the clutch in his Volkswagen bus. They hear two women, your mother's friends, play a violin duet. They hear Lieutenant Tanner talk about what you did at Knox. How what you achieved proves that you'll also achieve great things in Austria. How he put you in God's hands on the floor of the Mojave Desert.

At the pulpit again Bishop Wacker thanks Lieutenant Tanner and introduces Sandra Lynch and Lenny Stockton and the number they'll sing. Lenny takes a seat at the grand piano and sizes up the keyboard. Sandy brings a microphone stand out from behind the piano and adjusts it in front of the waiting congregation and turns it on and says hello to test it. And then there's her voice inside your churchhouse.

"I know the program says that Lenny and I are doing You'll Never Walk Alone. That's been changed. I hope it's okay."

In a long black gown that bares her white shoulders she takes a step back and smiles Lenny's way. Lenny opens with a couple of chords in whose dissonance you can hear a woman's broken inconsolable longing. Sandy turns to the congregation. Lenny lets up to let her take the song.

"Sometimes I feel like a motherless child," she sings, and there it is, her breath with the music inside it, the way it was at Sammy's the first night you heard her sing. "Sometimes I feel like a motherless child," she sings again, and there it is again, inside her open breath, more reverent this time for the sorrow and resignation in the lyrics that her voice floats out across the congregation on the line of the melody. From their suddenly arrested faces you can tell she's reached them and let every one of them feel singled out. "Sometimes I feel like I'm almost gone," she sings, while Lenny stays back and lays in traces of the changes just to let them know where the song is going. You look down in case your mother tries to find your eyes. You wonder what's going on in the row behind you. If your father feels it too, singled out, like the song is just for him, like the girl who's singing it knows what it means to him, understands why it's his favorite song. "Sometimes I feel like I'm almost gone." After the second verse, she takes a step back again to give the song to Lenny for a solo piano runthrough, then steps up again to close with the last verse. "A long ways from home," she sings, "a long ways from home," and in the hush of the chapel after her last note, you hear women crying softly, noses blowing into handkerchiefs.

After Sandy and Lenny finish, and the mood of the chapel gets back to business, the people who came to your farewell hear a white haired man your father knows from Switzerland named Bishop Pletzler talk about your famous grandfather and how your calling to harvest the mission field of Austria is a continuation of his great and courageous work. They hear Bishop Wacker talk about the first time he heard you play trumpet in the high school gym. How he knew you had a gift. How he wished it had been for football instead because he could have made you a real hero of a quarterback. They hear Walt Hanks play an organ piece your mother chose, a Brahms piece, a piece called My Heart is Filled with Longing.

And then it's your turn. A response from the departing missionary. The last thing on the program before the closing hymn and the benediction. On the podium, from the row behind you, you can feel your father's nervous worry like heat off the supercharged engine idling in the engine bay of Yenchik's Ford.

The young man you're here to help send off to Austria doesn't need an introduction. Like you, everyone's been following the program, ticking off the list of names, waiting for him. You watch Bishop Wacker and Bishop Byrne roll their shoulders back to release him from his seat. At the pulpit he pulls the microphone down. A man behind him on the podium shifts abruptly in his seat.

In a voice that starts out shaky, a voice in which you can hear his nervous awe that this is all for him, he starts by thanking you for coming. He talks about the journey that has brought him here. Singles out and acknowledges the people along the way. Clark. Rodgers. Haycock. Name after name, something to say about each one of them, something they did to keep him straight, something he'll always be grateful for. Bird. Hunt. Tanner. Sometimes there's humor, sometimes nostalgia, and sometimes a reverent laugh or empathizing sigh from the congregation. He saves his mother and father for last.

And then gets down to business. About his debt to you. About how hard he'll work to make it worth the time and effort and faith and hope you've selflessly and for so long entrusted to him. How he knows beyond the shadow of a doubt that the gospel he's bringing the people of Austria is true. His testimony is fervent, deep, authentic, engaging. He keeps it light, quiet like it's just for you, the way the girl did the song.

He says Amen. And then the chorister gets up again, a spirited woman with a head of scalloped and flared red hair and a smile with the blood red and startling white of a bitten apple, waits while the man at the organ plays the opening and the congregation get their hymnbooks open, and takes them through the closing hymn. A call to battle. Zion's army. Children of the promised day. Hope of Israel. Rise in might. With the sword of truth and light.

Your Uncle Charlie gives the benediction. You shake hands with all the men on the podium. Your father hangs back. Waits his turn. When you shake his hand his eyes keep skating off, away from yours, and in his big confounded face you can see him working hard to keep what's going on from going public. You come down into a waiting swarm of people. A woman you don't know tells you with an accent like your mother's how she used to change your diapers back in Switzerland. The Soderstroms come forward. He presses a bill into your hand while she tells you you're still her favorite Ward Teacher. Doby comes up to watch and maybe remind you of the deal you struck to call it even on the forty bucks.

Sandy and Lenny are there. Their first venture into this part of your life and they look at you now like they're wondering if they know you. Sandy kisses your cheek. Scoutmaster Haycock steers his wife forward. Lenny does a double take when he turns around and gets a look at what bumped him.

"You've sure got lots of friends," says Sandy.

"Thanks for the song," you tell her. "It was beautiful."

"You take care of yourself," she says. "See you when you get back."

"Yeah," says Lenny. "Keep those chops up."

"I will. Thanks."

Chapter 73

EARLY IN the morning on his way to work your father drives you to the Salt Lake Mission Home. The first of July. Sunlight floods the red interior of the Valiant. In the cool morning air you feel like you're riding in an inferno of red light. The air you breathe is red. A new striped tie and the bright bib of a new white shirt and the legs of a new charcoal suit fill the lower field of your sight like stuff you're floating in.

Your father hasn't had much to say since your farewell. He doesn't say much now. He still doesn't get along with the stickshift you talked him into buying. Still too sudden with the clutch. Violins and cellos play like dizzy wasps through some furious piece of classical music on the radio. Your new gray Samsonite suitcase rides in the seat behind you like some important man from out of town in whose presence your father can't talk about anything personal. Looking out the window, taking a last look at the stockyards and the refinery and other places you know you won't be seeing for a long time, you know he won't be mentioning the song. You follow his lead. Try to keep everything you're feeling harnessed. Let him drive. Wait for the highway to clear and the piece on the radio to end before you speak.

"How do you think the farewell went?"

"Very nice," he says.

"Think the program worked out?"

"Of course," he says. "Why would you ask?"

"It's hard to have people talk about you."

"Yes. I can understand that. Just don't let it go to your head."

"I won't."

"Humility is the most important virtue you can have."

"I know."

"Now you have to prove that everything they said is true."

"Maybe they were already true."

"That's what I mean by humility," he says. The usual uptick of a victory in his voice. "A humble person doesn't take the nice things people say as a compliment. He takes them as a challenge. He continues to look for his faults and improve on them."

"So what are my faults?" you say.

He looks across at you and finds you looking through the windshield at the rear end of the Edsel you've been following.

"You'll have to discuss that with your Heavenly Father," he says.

He drops you off on the corner of Main Street and North Temple. New missionaries and their families and girlfriends and suitcases crowd the sidewalk in the morning sun in front of the old mansion that serves as the Mission Home. He shakes your hand in the Valiant. Waits for the back door to slam once you've pulled your suitcase out. Revs the engine and pops the clutch. The Valiant stumbles forward. You lug your suitcase through the crowd and through the door and up the stairs to the second floor to find the room they give you the number to.

Go in humble. Look inside the compliments people give you for your faults. The last piece of advice he had for you. You go in scared. But on your own it isn't long before you feel released from six long months of having had to run with the headlights low. Your life is on its way again.

You spend the next few days in the Mission Home with more than two hundred other missionaries. More than two hundred guys and a handful of girls who were celebrated at farewells just like yours and then had the trigger pulled. They're here from everywhere. Idaho Falls. Cheyenne. Vegas. Phoenix. Seattle. They're headed now for London. New Orleans. Toronto. Berlin. Samoa. Louisville. Manila. Sidney. Buenos Aires. Their hearts on fire, their bosoms burning, their knuckles itching to knock on doors, armed with the same introduction in forty or fifty different languages. Hello. We're two missionaries from the Church of Jesus Christ of Latter-Day Saints. We'd like to speak with you.

The same inexhaustible fire in your bosom. The same itch restless in your knuckles. The same shared sense of purpose you loved about the Army. Early every morning you put on the uniform of a tie and suit like it's permanently Sunday. Head down to the basement cafeteria for breakfast at long tables under fluorescent lights recessed into the acoustic tiles of the vast ceiling. Eat surrounded by the shrill brilliance of more than two hundred white shirts. You share the two sets of bunkbeds in your room with three other Elders headed for Vienna.

"Hi. Elder Hatch."

"Elder Wissom."

"Hi. I'm Elder Clayton."

"Elder Tauffler. Hi."

The same quick big confident smile. The same resolute handshake. In the Army of the Lord this is how they salute. Your squad of four. All of you with things you've put on hold. Shut down for now. Hatch, the jock from Idaho Falls with a year-round job at Jackson Hole as a lift operator and a lifeguard until he got his call to a place he had to be told was Austria and not Australia, his brown hair washed almost blond by sun and chlorine, the acne scars in the sunburned hollows of his cheeks this dry and savage red. He's kissed off a swimming scholarship to some college in Texas. Wissom, the gangly guy from Granite High, slick wavy black hair and a death-white face that strikes you as sinister until you learn he was studying accounting when he got his mission call. Clayton, from a farm outside a town in Central Utah called Salina, big and blond and chubby, big round head and perpetually happy Pillsbury Doughboy face except for the permanent look of some volatile panic in the hard brown beads of his pupils for having to leave his cows or his mother or someone else at home. All of you fresh from the limbo of having waited all this time. Of having known it was coming. All of you finally here where you're supposed to study and pray and memorize the lesson plans together. Where you're supposed to call each other Elder. Elder Wissom. Elder Clayton. Elder Hatch. Elder Tauffler. None of you can do it with the names. And so you leave them off. Just call each other Elder because it's weird to put your names with Elder when you're just four guys.

You're herded through a daily round of lectures and discussions by Church Authorities and other specialists on missionary life. All of them wear suits. All of them are men who look as natural in suits as the officers at Ord and Knox looked in fatigues. All of them talk with this smooth and easy and smiling fluency that reminds you of the way cream plunged and then rose to the surface when the night mechanics out at Hiller's poured it in their coffee. You're told how to have a tailor patch the crotch of your pants to keep the seat of your bike from wearing through. How to change your monthly check to foreign currency. How to budget. How to live and eat cheap. How to get along with your companion. How to stay close to the Lord. How a person looking to hear about the gospel is called an investigator. How knocking on doors is called tracting. When to get up and how to schedule your day.

Rules come at you as fast as you can field them. Pray with your companion morning and night. Never leave his sight. Write your family once a week. Be valiant. Never waver. You're soldiers in the Army of the Lord. Never underestimate the Devil. Never forget that he's there, invisible but powerful, his power in his invisibility. He'll use every tool at his disposal to work his way inside your testimony. Magazines. Radio.

Television. Newspapers. Books. Parties. Sports. People who'll want to be friends. Your feelings. Discouraging times of doubt and loneliness and homesickness and longing and frustration. You'll have them. Pray them away. Times when you'll want to criticize or argue with your companion. You'll have them. Pray them away. Never complain. Don't phone home. Stay away from the agents of other religions. Stay out of their houses of worship. Immerse yourself in your mission twenty-four hours a day. Keep your thoughts and words and actions pure. Always stand apart. In but not of the world.

At night you're herded down to the basement for supper. After supper you're back in your room for study and prayer with the guys you'll be flying to Vienna with. Wissom writes everything down, all the rules, in a leatherbound notebook with a blue and silver Schaeffer fountain pen he keeps fueled up and ready.

"How many pages you got so far, Elder?"

From the one small desk in the room, the rest of you seated together on the two bottom bunks, Wissom gets the idea that Hatch is talking to him.

"A few," he says.

"There's an easier way," says Hatch.

"What's that, Elder?"

"One rule," says Hatch. "Don't do anything."

"I haven't heard anything I don't already do," says Clayton.

"Wait till they give you the girl rule," says Hatch.

You love the rules the way you loved them in the Army. Do what you're told and you'll be okay. They won't let you telephone anyone. They discourage visitors. You're way ahead of them. You've said all your goodbyes. Nobody out there expects to hear from you. They won't let you leave the Mission Home except in the custody of someone they can trust you with. And only then for a reason related to your mission like going to a doctor for a shot you didn't know you'd need or to Deseret Book for an English-German dictionary. You've got yours already. Through the open windows you can hear the city right outside the walls. Its engines and horns. Sometimes its sirens. Snatches of voices passing on the sidewalk. The general hum of its energy as prevalent as weather. You're here now. You're clean of it. This is just another army. Where all the recruits are white except for a guy who looks like he's from Hawaii or some other South Pacific island. Where nobody smokes or drinks or cusses or plays solitaire. Where nobody uses deodorant pads to turn the toes of their combat boots to black chrome. Where nobody gets issued an M1 rifle or a forty-five.

What they issue instead is a little black pocket-sized notebook whose pages contain the six lessons you'll use to convert people to the gospel. Each lesson reads like a play between two actors. One of them named Elder and the other Mr. Brown. They read like the Socratic dialogues you studied back in high school. A question followed by an obedient and inevitable answer followed by another question.

The first lesson leads Mr. Brown to acknowledge that there can only be one church that has the authority of Jesus Christ. From there, the answers Mr. Brown hears from his own mouth lead him to acknowledge the necessity for the Great Apostasy, almost two thousand years where God withheld his presence, while the Catholics and Protestants flourished under the reign of Satan. Having come this far on the stepping stones of his own obedient answers, what Mr. Brown hears next is the story of Joseph Smith, the First Vision, the restoration of the true Church of Jesus Christ. The first lesson ends with your testimony. It's written out too, the way the questions and answers are, but you're told you have the liberty to improvise.

In the questions you hear Brother Clark. Your Priesthood teacher back when you were Deacons. In the answers you hear your buddies in their folding chairs.

You thumb through the next five lessons. The story of the Book of Mormon and the appearance of Jesus Christ in the Americas during the three days between his death and his resurrection. The Plan of Salvation. The three Kingdoms. Eternal marriage. The Word of Wisdom. Not the hard and mystifying stuff, the stuff you're not supposed to question, where Indians and Mexicans are brown because their ancestors were wicked, where Cain was turned black for killing Abel, where Negroes all descend through Cain because they sat on a fence in the War in Heaven, where thousands of wives will bear your spirit children in the afterlife. Mr. Brown just gets the basic stuff. Tithing is saved for the sixth and final lesson. Where you tell Mr. Brown that everything you've promised him will cost him ten percent of what he earns. By then he'll have had you in his living room five times. He'll have heard about the possibility of immortality for his family. He'll have heard your testimony.

You're supposed to learn all six of them by heart. Well enough to sit in his living room and give Mr. Brown the impression that all you're doing is having a casual conversation. After supper, in your room for the night, that's what you and Clayton and Hatch and Wissom do. Read lines back and forth. Repeat them. Try to recite them without looking. Coach each other.

"We supposed to memorize Mr. Brown's part too?" says Hatch.

"Yeah," says Wissom. "That's what they said."

"Why?"

"You need to know if he's giving you the right answers."

"We're gonna get this in German when we get to Austria. I don't get why we need to memorize it in English."

"This guy Mr. Brown," says Wissom. "He could be anyone."

"Yeah," says Clayton. "Like John Doe."

"So how do we know he'll actually say what it says here?"

"Maybe he's supposed to memorize it too," you say.

"Funny, Elder."

"He's right," says Clayton. "What if Mr. Brown says something else? What if he goes off on some tangent?"

"Tell him he got it wrong," you say. "Tell him to take another run at it."

"You're a regular comedian, Elder," Wissom says.

"I never thought of that," says Hatch.

You get the wrong answer from Mr. Brown, you think, you go with it. Improvise and then look to bring it back again.

"What if he starts arguing?" says Wissom.

"What do you mean?"

"Like when you tell him the Catholic Church is false."

You sit there seeing yourself in a living room in Austria somewhere, you and your senior companion, invited in, the way the Ward Teachers used to sit in your living room.

"Maybe you bear your testimony," says Clayton. "Or ask if you can pray."

"What if he says no?" says Wissom. "What if he's an atheist?"

"Maybe you change the subject," says Hatch.

"To what?"

"I don't know. Skiing maybe."

"You'll have a senior companion," you say. "Let him handle it. Just watch and learn from him."

"I think I'd leave," says Wissom. "I'd say he's had his chance."

"Yeah," says Clayton. "Stomp the dust off your shoes on his door-step."

"Come on," you say. "You don't write someone off just cuz they don't agree."

"That's what they told us to do," says Clayton. "If they reject the gospel after they've had the chance to accept it."

"It's not your house," you say. "It's his. He let you in. You don't tell him his church is the whore of the earth and then go stomping off if he takes too long to agree with you."

"So what would you do, Elder?" Wissom says.

"Play it out," you say. "See what he has to say. Get to know him some. That's what I'd do. Elder."

"Waste your time, in other words," says Wissom.

"Maybe go skiing with him." Hatch shrugs. "It's Austria."

You look at Wissom. It's no use getting pissed. Someone with a pen like his.

"Like I said. That's what your senior's for. Show you how it's done."

In the uniform of your new suit and new tie you sit in the auditorium one morning and listen uneasily while you're told to refrain from the active pursuit of Negro converts. How it's fine if they come to you. How you should go ahead, talk to them, answer their questions, satisfy their curiosity, baptize them if that's where things eventually lead. Just don't go looking for them. You're told it's not an official policy of the Church. More like off the record stuff. More like counsel you should just adhere to in your heart.

On another morning you're eating a bowl of oatmeal and a cup of fruit cocktail across the table from a guy you noticed the first time you saw him. He's tall, blond, thin, immaculate, the smooth hair of a golfer, a classy tan-colored suit he looks like he was born to wear while everyone else goes around in navy blue or black or charcoal. A light blue shirt with stripes of blue and gold in his tie. A pair of round glasses that gives his lightly bronzed face a detached look of cool wisdom. A guy right out of your father's missionary catalog. There were guys like him in high school. Guys you could never hang out with because they were guys your father would use to let you know what he wanted.

You're nervous about engaging him in conversation. Relieved when you hear his girlish voice. You figure East High. But he tells you he's from Provo. He's short on talk. Just answers what you ask him. He did his freshman year at BYU and he's headed for Tahiti now. You remember your father reading a story out of the Church News at the kitchen table one Sunday a month ago to you and Karl and Roy.

"I heard about that shipwreck they just had there," you say. "Sorry."

"Thanks," he says.

"I heard the boat hit a reef."

"That's right."

"How many people were killed?"

"Fifteen."

"I heard they were on their way back from dedicating a new church building."

"Yes."

After every answer he goes back to his oatmeal. And every time you ask another question he looks up surprised that you're still there. But you're riding on the excitement of the Army of the Lord. You like the feeling of mischief you get from making him use his voice.

"I've got a question," you say. "About Tahiti."

"Go ahead."

"The people there. They've got black skin."

"Yes. Dark brown."

"How do you know they're not Negroes?"

"They're not."

"I don't know," you say. "I've seen pictures. They're pretty dark."

"Negroes are from Africa. People in Tahiti are Islanders."

"So how come they're the same color? In Tahiti? They get cursed somehow too?"

"That's just evolution. To protect them from the sun."

"Don't they live in grass huts?"

"I guess so. Some of them."

"They don't have doors," you say. "At least not in the movies."

"That's probably because it's always warm there."

"I know. That's not what I'm asking."

"What are you asking?"

"I was wondering what you knock on."

"What do you mean?"

"You know. If they don't have doors."

"I never thought of that."

"So how do you let people know you're there? If you can't knock?"

"I don't know."

"Just stand in the doorway and yell hello or something?"

"I guess I'll find out."

"I guess you won't get too many doors slammed in your face."

"You shouldn't make fun of the Lord's work."

"So what language do they speak in Tahiti?"

"Tahitian."

"How do you say Mr. Brown in Tahitian?"

"Really, Elder."

Your ears go hot. Yes. Really. The pious look on his bland face isn't because he's immersed in the spirit of his calling or the taste of his fruit cocktail. It's because he's a prick. Some rich prick from the equivalent in Provo of Highland or Olympus High. Some prick with a rich chick girlfriend whose complacent face would go mean and profane in a second if you made him bawl in a parking lot.

You won't be asking forgiveness this time around. Because you don't care. Because all you've ever asked for is a reason. Because except for the guy who looks like he's from Hawaii all the soldiers here are white. Because Fence Sitters may be valiant enough for the United States Army Airborne but not enough for the Army of the Lord. Because God has never told you why. Because in Tahiti this prick will be looking at breasts the color of Cissy's skin. And for all the human association he'll give them they could be the breasts of kangaroos. You watch him concentrate on scooping some pieces of fruit out of his little white bowl with his little fruit spoon.

"And the women," you say. "The way they go around topless. Like in National Geographic. That'll be tough."

You've got his attention now. With a piece of pineapple and a slice of maraschino cherry and a chunk of maybe peach on his little spoon he's looking at you instead.

"What did you say?"

The lenses of his glasses round like magnifying glasses. Like you're something he has to magnify to make big enough to see. He knows what you said. He just wants to watch you say it. You keep your face stupid.

"Topless. You know." And then you say, "Maybe you'll just get used to it. Seeing them all the time. You know. Like a doctor does."

"You're kidding."

"Besides," you say, "it's not like they're white or anything. White would be tough."

"Do you want me to report you, Elder?"

"You started this."

Girls. The men who lecture you tell you how they understand. How they were boys once too. What girls can do to you. The things they can make you feel and think about. The temptations they embody. The way they can run away with you. The way they can make you lose your head. Casual and easy in their suits like they were born to wear them, in their smooth and fluent voices, they stand there and smile, sometimes wink, sometimes invoke the lifting release of a collective obedient laugh off the auditorium of more than two hundred guys.

Girls. The Devil knows. He's never had a body himself. Never known physical desire first hand. But he's been a student of desire long enough to know that the deadliest weapons in his arsenal are girls. That's why the rules against them have to be so strict. Never be alone with one. Never think of flirting. Never get within arm's length of one. Never forget that the sacred powers vested in you require the vessel of your body to remain virtuous and pure. You can get sent home for kissing. You can be disfellowshipped for petting. And for the sin of sexual intercourse, the irrevocable act of losing your virginity, the offense of fornication while you're an Instrument of the Lord, you'll be excommunicated. No questions asked. Stripped of your Priesthood. Of your membership. Everything you've worked for. Everything you've been taught to believe beyond the shadow of a doubt. Gone.

One morning on your way to breakfast you see two Elders with suit-cases in the lobby. At breakfast you hear they climbed out the window of their room the night before where their girlfriends were waiting in the parking lot. They're on their way home. One afternoon, in the audi-torium, a smooth-looking man with hair like silver fenders for his ears, a man who's introduced as a prominent Salt Lake businessman, gives yet another speech on girls. He starts to tell what he calls an anecdote. You're not paying much attention. It doesn't feel like anyone is. You've heard anecdotes all week, sudden little stories that put concepts and rules and pieces of advice in human terms, and they've started to sound alike, like they all came out of some manual for anecdotes. You listen anyway because you're here.

"I forget who the missionary was or where he was going," he says. "But I'll never forget what his mother said to him at the airport the day he was leaving. Son, she said, I love you only the way a mother can. And it's only because I love you that I say this. But I'd rather have you come home in a coffin than dishonored."

He pauses. Gives more than two hundred guys the time to catch up to what he said. Figure out what being in a coffin means. In the seat next to you Hatch sits up a little straighter.

"Now that, Elders, is the highest love you'll ever hear a mother ex-press. That's the standard all of your mothers should aspire to."

In the auditorium even time feels like it comes to a stop while more than two hundred guys do what you're doing, considering your mother, seeing her at the airport watching your coffin come out of a plane.

You hunt down the address for the Mission Home in Austria. Write it in a thank you note to Cissy's mother Mrs. Taylor and take it to the lobby where the mail goes.

On your next to last night, an Elder you don't know knocks on your door, says there's a visitor for Elder Tauffler in the lobby. Wissom looks at you with his eyebrows halfway up his forehead. Hatch grins at you. Clayton just looks scared. Faces and names you thought you'd said goodbye to chase around your head. You throw your suit coat on and check your hair and snug your tie in the little rectangular mirror nailed to the back of the door. Head down the hall and the stairs and find Lieutenant Tanner there.

"Hey," he says. "There he is."

Grinning, stepping forward, swinging his arm around to shake your hand, dressed casual in slacks and a sport jacket, a light blue shirt with-out a tie, the collar open, he makes the lobby feel alive and charged and open, like the energy of the city came through the door with him.

"Hey," you say. "What a cool surprise."

"I hope so," he says. "How's everything going?"

"Good."

"Let's go outside."

"I need permission."

He turns to the Elder guarding the lobby with his usual relaxed and confident expectation to have things go the way he wants them.

"We're stepping out for a minute," he says. "I'll take responsibility for him. He'll be in good hands."

"That's fine," the Elder says.

Outside, in the light on the front porch of the Mission Home, he looks you up and down. Looks at you with this quiet grin and this fierce admiration in his eyes. You stand there remembering his unapologetic prayer in the desert sunset. You feel the pull of State Street. The long opposing rivers of traffic from the light at Eagle Gate. The light changing. Katy's face behind the windshield of her Studebaker. Walt and Maria and Jenny and Chaz and Luke and Billy cruising in from Magna in the Pontiac. Sammy's. The feel and sound of your trumpet and the pull inside your lungs to play it. Mr. Hinkle. The smell of Mr. Selby's cookies. Lenny and Sandy. The huge wet pipes in the stone foundation of the Music Building. You stand there in your suit and tie and feel their pull, powerful and dangerous, deep inside you, the way wind will pull leaves off grass, sand off the ridge of a dune, the sudden helpless response of your hunger losing hold inside your lungs.

Yenchik staying home. Yenchik not going.

"They treating you right?" Lieutenant Tanner says. "Are you doing okay?"

"Yeah. Just that I haven't seen a guy without a tie in a while."

He laughs. "It's in my pocket. I can put it on if it bothers you."

"That's okay."

"So what's the plan?" he says.

"Tomorrow's it," you say. "They're taking us to the Temple. I leave the day after."

"I know. Sorry I can't make the airport. I've got to be in Pocatello. That's why I'm here now."

"That's fine. That's great."

"Bet you're eager to get there," he says. "Finally get to work."

"It's been a long time coming."

"I got you something," he says. "Here."

You've seen it in his hand. Wrapped in silver paper. No ribbon.

"Open it," he says.

You take the paper off. Wad it up. Leave yourself holding a book like the Bible. Soft black leather cover. Gold lettering embossed across the top half. Book of Mormon. Doctrine and Covenants. Pearl of Great

Price. The three volumes of the official doctrine of the Church in a single book of scripture. What they call the Triple Combination. In the bottom right corner your name, spelled out, all of it, Shake Wilford Tauffler, in gold letters. The pages edged in gold. A thin silk ribbon for a bookmark.

"Wow. This is amazing. Thanks."

"You like it?" he says.

"I've never had anything like this."

"Good," he says. "I was worried you already had one."

He thought of you. On his own, just a guy on the street, he went to a store somewhere and picked it out. Now, standing here on the porch, you can tell how much hope he put into you liking it, feel the treacherous pull of the city again.

"No," you say. "Never like this."

"Good," he says. "You'll put it to good use. I know you will."

"Count on it," you say.

"Excited about where you're going?"

July of 1963. The city you won't see again until thirty months from now. January of 1966. Cissy. The pull to have him tell you it's okay. You're paid up. Whatever you owed. Head for San Jose. Tell Professor Fisher you've changed your mind. Take your horn and grab a bus. I'll talk to your folks. I'll talk to everybody. Go get your stuff. I'll wait here. But he doesn't know to tell you. And in the desert you made your peace with where you're going. In the desert where he handed you to God.

"Yeah," you say. "It's finally happening."

CHAPTER 74

GOING TO the Temple. Like being baptized, you can only do it here, on Earth, with a mortal body, and you only need to do it once. The first time you go is for yourself, in your own name, and after that, you go voluntarily, like your mother and father do, like you and Yenchik did, for the dead, for the names of dead people waiting in the Spirit Prison to be liberated, to make their covenants and receive their endowments, to have their shot at the Celestial Kingdom. In the morning you're sent to the auditorium for a briefing. Told that the rites you'll be going through may seem strange. That they may perplex you or even tempt you to laugh. What you need to bear in mind is that they're the ways of God. That if you're perplexed it's because you're accustomed to the ways of man. If you're tempted to laugh it's because you haven't purified yourself to accept them in all their wonder and mystery on the faith that they're the ways of God. Which is why they're secret. Why they have to be protected from the rest of the world. Why you have to be interviewed, prove you've followed the commandments and squared your tithing up, before you're issued the Temple Recommend that will allow you inside.

After the briefing you're herded across the street to Temple Square. At the door to the Temple you show an old man the signed slip of paper that constitutes your recommend. You remember the last time you were here. The room with the golden steers where you were baptized nineteen times for nineteen long dead men. More than two hundred guys and a handful of girls each pack a brand new pair of garments. This is the day you'll lay aside the childish thing of jockey shorts. From this day forward, your underwear will be a pair of garments that goes from your shoulders to your knees, a two-foot gash in back to let you bare your butt to take a dump, symbolic buttonholes sewn over your nipples and navel and one of your kneecaps to shield you from Satan and keep you strong and healthy and mindful of your covenants. You've heard the nicknames people have for them. Jesus Jumpers. And your all time favorite. Funderwear. God forgive you for having heard it. For not knowing how to forget it.

They separate the girls out. You're herded with the guys to a locker room. Old retired men in white pants and smocks attend to you. Temple Workers. You pick a locker, strip, hang and lock up your clothes. You're handed what they tell you is a shield, a knee-length poncho made out of a white sheet, no sleeves, the sides open, a hole for your head. With the key to your locker in your hand you're herded barefoot to a tile room for the washing and anointing. You sit on a tile pedestal in a tile booth. An old man, so old you wonder how he can be alive, starts a rapid incantation you can barely understand. I wash your head that your brain and your intellect may be clear and active while his wet fingertips take a quick swipe across your forehead. Your ears that you may hear the Word of the Lord while his fingertips leave wet streaks on the rims of your ears. Your nose that you may smell while his wet fingertips run deftly down your nose. Your lips that you may never speak guile while he touches water to where your mouthpiece rides. Your neck that it may bear up your head properly while he leaves a quick cool dab of water on the back of your neck. Your shoulders that they may bear the burdens that shall be placed thereon while his hand goes underneath your poncho. Your back that there may be marrow in the bones and in the spine. Your breast that it may be the receptacle of pure and virtuous principles while he wets his fingertips and leaves fresh water in a streak across your chest. Your vitals and bowels that they may be healthy and strong and perform their proper functions.

His fingertips dart and light and dart off again like a dragonfly. Your arms and hands that they may be strong and wield the sword of justice in defense of truth and virtue. And then he goes under the poncho again and you feel his fingertips touch down in your pubic hair. Your loins, he says, that they may be fruitful and multiply and replenish the Earth, that you may have joy and rejoicing in your posterity. Your legs and feet, he says, brushing his fingertips along your thighs and down your calves to your feet, that you may run and not be weary, and walk and not faint. Another Temple Worker suddenly joins him. They put their hands on your head and recite a rapid confirmation of your washing. You sit there amazed at how nimble they are at what they do.

Water is exchanged for olive oil for the anointing. The incantation is identical and just as nimble. I anoint your head. A trail of oil brushed across your forehead. This time you're ready. This time you know what's coming. This time, when his fingertips shoot for your groin, you hold still. At the end of the anointing there's another confirmation. And then the Worker tells you your secret name. Your Temple name. The name to which you'll answer when you're called from your grave on the Morning of the Resurrection. The sacred name you're never to reveal. Peter. You're asked to repeat it back to him.

"Peter."

And then, washed and anointed and confirmed and named a secret name, you're ready for the ceremony. From the next booth over, on your way back to your locker, you hear another incantation end, and another Elder murmur Peter. You're handed a bundle of clothes. A pair of white slacks, white slippers, a white belt, white socks, a white knit tie. The rest of the bundle is unfamiliar. Back at your locker you're told to take off the shield and put on the special pair of garments they've handed you. Not your street pair, not the pair you brought with you, but a special Temple pair, called the Garment of the Holy Priesthood, a limp and flimsy pair of long johns whose legs run to your ankles and whose arms run to your wrists, open in front from your crotch to your throat, with sets of strings on either side you're told to tie like shoelaces.

You start at the bottom, careful not to catch your pubic hair in the knot, and work your way up while a Temple Worker watches you and two other Elders doing the same thing. You put on the socks and pants and belt and tie and shoes. You wear your own white shirt. You're left with a long and blousy thing that looks like a toga. A white cloth hat that looks like a cross between a baker's hat and a big beret. A long white sash. The only thing that isn't white is a small square apron, green, embroidered with leaves. Somewhere along the way you heard that the apron is meant to represent Adam's recognition of his nakedness and his effort to cover it. For the women it represents Eve and her carnal discovery. You're told you'll be putting the rest of the bundle on at various points in the ceremony.

You're herded into a simple room. Given more instructions. Reminded to be alert and attentive and reverent. Told that your endowment will prepare you for exaltation in the Celestial Kingdom. That the words and signs and tokens you'll be taught today will enable you to walk back into God's presence. Warned again that God will not be mocked. Told that you can raise your hand if you'd rather not go through with it. No hands go up. They give you another minute to consider what you're about to do while Temple Workers stand like white buzzards around the room and watch.

You're led from there with your bundles of secret clothes to the Creation Room, a room whose floor is filled with theater seats, whose walls are painted to the ceiling with murals portraying the creation of the Earth, its evolution from a lifeless landscape of red barren rock to a landscape lush with trees and plants and water, under a sky that follows its own formation from nebulous red gas through a dark and swirling sky whose clouds are tinged with fire to an atmosphere finally at peace. You're told the story of your own beginning. Your creation out of formless intelligence as a spirit child of God. The Great War in Heaven where you fought valiantly on the side of one of the favorite sons of God against his other favorite son and helped achieve the defeat and expulsion of Lucifer. At first you wonder how they know. And then you get it. They can tell with certainty that you fought with valor, because you're white, because you're here.

From the Creation Room, you're herded to another room with muraled walls between the tall veiled windows, the Garden Room, where the murals this time are the trees and plants and flowers and soaring birds of the Garden of Eden, where the walls roll into the high ceilings and the ceilings are muraled with mottled sky around a veiled and recessed skylight. You wonder how sunlight can reach this deep into the Temple. You're seated in rows of theater chairs again while men at the front of the room act out the story of Adam and Eve and their temptation and fall. Lucifer shows up with a college-educated minister he's hired. The minister tries to convert Adam and Eve to something called the orthodox religion. Adam rejects him. You get it. College-educated ministers are the agents of Lucifer whose job it is to convince you to believe in their false gospels.

Lucifer and his minister wear black suits. The other actors all wear white. Lucifer and his minister both wear embroidered green aprons, aprons the size cocktail waitresses wear, like the apron in your lap. You get it. The leaves embroidered in their aprons are fig leaves. They're wearing them because they both have carnal knowledge of their genitals. When Eve and then Adam partake of the fruit of the tree of the knowledge of good and evil, and become carnally aware and ashamed themselves, you're given a role in their dramatic awakening. You're instructed to rise, more than two hundred guys and a handful of girls, and tie your own embroidered aprons around your waists.

Soon, together with Adam and Eve and Lucifer, you're expelled from the Garden of Eden, and herded with your bundles out of the Garden Room to the World Room, a room muraled from the floor across the ceiling with more familiar landscapes, mountains and valleys and cliffs and pine trees under a sky whose color and clouds you recognize, the mortal world, where things are born and live and die, where actors and speakers again portray the Great Apostasy, the long uninterrupted reign of Lucifer through the Christian history of the world, and the Restoration of the Church of Jesus Christ to Joseph Smith in the Latter Days. With the gospel restored, along with all its rites and ordinances, you're herded from the World Room to the Terrestrial Room, the room of the Second Degree of Glory, a room this time without murals but ornate instead in the heavy white architecture of its arched doors and carved moldings and chandeliers, a room of sacred and quiet opulence, draped across the length of its front wall with partitions of white veils. You get it. The room is a waiting room for passage to the final room, the room that represents the highest Degree of Glory, the Celestial Room.

Along the way you stick with Hatch. Along the way you sit and watch actors play out other stories you've known all your life. God condemning Lucifer to a life of going on his belly and eating dust. The Apostle Peter rebuking Lucifer. Lucifer turning to the audience and telling you that if you don't live up to every covenant you make today you'll end up in his power. The First Vision. The Angel Moroni and the Golden Plates. Along the way you make covenants with God. To follow the Law of Obedience. To dedicate your life to God and devote your time and talent and means to the glorious work and wonder of his church. To sacrifice all you possess and even your life if needed to sustain and defend his Kingdom. To observe the Law of the Gospel. To avoid lightmindedness, loud laughter, evil speaking of his anointed, the taking of his name in vain, every other unholy and impure practice. Observe the Law of Chastity.

And along the way you're taught four secret handshakes whose purpose is to enable you to pass through checkpoints on your path to the Celestial Kingdom. You partner up with Hatch to learn and execute them. The first two are called the First and Second Tokens of the Aaronic Priesthood. Regular handshakes where all you do is put your thumbs on each other's knuckles. The third is called the First Token of the Melchizedek Priesthood or the Sign of the Nail. Hatch holds out his hand while you form your finger and thumb into a clamp and touch his hand, front and back, where the nail was hammered through the hand of Jesus. And then you let him do your hand. The fourth is called the Second Token of the Melchizedek Priesthood or the Sure Sign of the Nail. Another regular handshake, except with your little fingers intertwined and the tips of your index fingers on each other's inner wrists, where the second nail was hammered through when the first nail didn't hold, when it ended up tearing through his hand.

Between handshakes you learn and enact the penalties for revealing them. Three ways to kill yourself. For the first handshake, you put your right thumb under your left ear, draw it quick in a gash a knife would leave across your throat to your other ear, and promise that you'd rather have your life be taken than reveal the handshake. For the second handshake you draw the symbolic knife from your armpit across your chest to your other armpit. For the third handshake you draw the same symbolic knife across the span of your waist. Each time you make the same promise. To have your life taken rather than reveal the token. You get it. First how to cut your throat. Second how to open up your chest to have your heart and vitals torn from your body and given to the birds of the air and the beasts of the field. And third how to disembowel yourself.

And along the way you're told when and how to put the remaining pieces of your bundle on. The big blousy toga over your shoulder and around your waist where it falls like a dress half down your calves. The crushed baker's hat you tie with a string to a loop in the shoulder of the toga in case it gets windy in the Temple. The white sash around your waist to hold your toga in place. The embroidered apron over everything. Fully clothed, finally, in the Terrestrial Room, all your covenants made, you and Hatch wait for your turn to be taken through one of the veils at the front of the room into the Celestial Room.

You watch Temple Workers quietly lead hushed Elders ahead of you to one of the veil's partitions, position them against it, help them bend their right knees into it, put their faces up against the cloth. Sharp movements come from the other side of the veil like fists or gusts of wind. Crabbed old hands come through openings and hold the Elders in place. And then openings are pulled back like drapes and your fellow Elders are drawn through the veil to the transcendent place behind it, the Celestial Room, the room where God and Jesus live.

While you wait, you can't avoid the hushed wealth and holiness of the room, the heavy gravity of the covenants you've made, the warm awareness in your lungs of the sacred unquestioning acceptance of their grave strangeness and mystery. You try but can't remember who you were at Hiller's. What the ride was like across Nevada. Why Professor Fisher's offer mattered. This has been where you're going all along. And then it's your turn. The Temple Worker there to guide you points out strategically positioned holes in the veil and instructs you in the Five Points of Fellowship. Tells you to reach through two of the holes and grab the hand and shoulder on the other side. You take hold of a shoulder and hand that are mostly bone. The Temple Worker instructs you to touch the inside of your right knee to the inside knee through the veil. You fish for it and find it. Your chest through the veil to his chest. You pull up close and feel it. Your mouth to his ear. You find the side of his face. Through the cloth of the veil you feel his mouth against your ear. Things are rapidly whispered that you don't quite understand but know are urgent and important. You go through the four secret handshakes. He asks for your secret name. Remembering your promise never to reveal it, fresh from the penalties you've inflicted on yourself, you hesitate.

You hear his voice in your ear. "Say it. It's okay."

And then you get it. Here at the gate to the Celestial Kingdom, the eternal presence of God, ready to be rewarded for the goodness of your life, you've died and been resurrected. This is when you're supposed to reveal it.

"Peter."

He pulls back the veil. You don't know how old he is. But with the gentle smile and skeletal hand of a dead saint he invites you through the veil. You take his hand and go through the veil into his booth with this reverent and scared defiance. The gate to the presence of God. A presence so intense and brilliant, you've been taught, that in your mortal state, not cleansed and purified and worthy, it would annihilate you, turn your eyes to smoke and the rest of you to ash like a walk into the sun. But you've been resurrected, with eyes that can withstand the sight of him, with immortal fluid running through your veins.

And this is where he'd stop you. You just don't know how. Hand you a shining knife and your choice of the three ways you've just been taught to kill yourself. You know the rules. No fornicators in his kingdom. No mixed blood. You're ready. Cut your throat. Take out your heart and hand it to him. Spill your guts on your slippers. You'll take all three and hope you can stay on your feet till you get through them all.

"Son?"

You look at the ancient man who's pulling at your hand. A servant in the House of God. In the humble pride and fatherly sweetness in his floating eyes you can see what it means to him to work here. That this is his house too. That what you've been thinking is disrespectful.

"I'm sorry."

"Go," he says, eager for you. "Welcome to the Celestial Kingdom. Go in. It's fine."

And so you go through his booth and enter the Celestial Kingdom. The top layer of Julie Quist's banana and coconut cake. It catches you off guard. You were expecting murals covering the walls and ceiling of immortalized families. Of planets being formed by gods. Of hosts of spiritual wives and spirit children. Instead, it's a room out of a European palace, so magnificent and rich it takes your breath away, a high arched ceiling, tall ornately cased windows, massive hanging chandeliers, furnished like the lobby of a European hotel you've only seen in your imagination, settings of sofas and chairs across the field of the carpet, almost every color one or another shade of cream.

Missionaries wander the cream of the carpet in their white slippers and their togas and hats and aprons. In the vastness of the room, in the way it towers over them, they look like the miniature people in Gulliver's Travels, miniature Roman bakers who've wandered into the palace of a giant king. Some other time you could maybe laugh, but now you don't, because you've been washed and anointed, because you've made your covenants with God. Because you've just been taught three ways you'd be happy to kill yourself. Because you're here in the Kingdom of God with her blood mixed with yours. Because this has all along been where you're going. This palatial room she's not allowed to enter in this outfit she's not allowed to wear.

Cissy.

In an open field of cream behind a King Louie sofa, standing there alone, from his round glasses, you recognize the guy who's headed for Tahiti. Without his tan suit, without his pastel shirt, with his golfer's haircut out of sight inside his baker's hat, he looks lost at the wrong party, and it strikes you that alone is the only way you've ever seen him, that he's just another guy like every other guy in the room, fresh from having had his crotch touched, from having learned three ways to kill himself. And then suddenly Hatch is standing there. Fresh through the veil himself.

"Hey, Elder," he says.

"Hey."

He takes a quick impatient look around and then turns back to you with his sunburned grin.

"Man. That spooked me when I felt that old guy's hand hit my . . . you know."

"Yeah," you say. "Me too."

"So my name's Peter," he says. "What's yours?"

You just stare at him.

"What?" he says. "What?"

"You weren't supposed to tell me."

"I wasn't?"

"No. It's secret. They told you that."

"When?"

"When the guy gave it to you."

"I didn't hear it. I couldn't understand him. Just all this crazy mumbling."

"I can't believe you told me."

"What kind of trouble am I in?" He looks petrified. "What do you think's gonna happen?"

"I don't know."

"Can they give me a new one? One you won't know?"

"You'd have to tell them you told someone."

"You're right," he says.

And now he's the one wrestling with three ways to kill himself.

"I'll just act like I never heard it," you say.

"I feel sick, man."

"Maybe it's not so bad."

"Why?"

"I heard them name another guy Peter."

"You did?"

"Yeah. On my way out."

Hope starts breaking through his sunburned face.

"You think they named everybody Peter?"

Three of you. And now maybe a whole Celestial Room full of guys named Peter.

"I can't tell you that."

"How come?"

"It'd be like telling you my name."

"I still feel sick."

"Go sit down. Put your head between your knees."

You watch him look around. "It's okay to sit?"

"I guess so. They're doing it over there."

Guys and occasionally girls keep coming out of the booths where the veils are, taking things in, moving into the room slowly, almost like they're wading, feeling for rocks and dropoffs before they put their feet down all the way. The vast floor of the Celestial Room fills up. More than two hundred guys and a handful of girls all dressed alike. You're given time to meditate. Get the feel of what eternity in the presence of God the Father and Jesus Christ will feel like.

Just a few of you sit down. Almost all of you stand or mill around, in your own directions, like strangers waiting for different trains. You wonder how to meditate. What you do. You try to imagine being a god some day, creating planets, populating them with the children of a thousand wives, but it doesn't make sense in this palatial room where almost every color is one or another numbing and rich and evasive shade of cream, where Mozart could have played a harpsichord. Lilly was here. Keller too. Jasperson had his crotch anointed. So did West. Your father and mother too the night they came home with their baby blue suitcases and found you there in the living room. Like you now, under their church clothes, dabs and streaks of olive oil on their backs, their shoulders, their chests, their knees, down in their pubic hair.

They finally herd you back downstairs to the locker room. You undress, step naked into your first new pair of garments, pull them up over your shoulders. The legs ride up your thighs when you pull your pants on. You shimmy and shake to get them down again. Other guys around you do the same new dance. Outside, blind in the afternoon sunlight, numb to the sudden heat and air and noise of the city, you walk past the tended flowerbeds and out the gate of Temple Square. With a handful of girls in modest dresses and two hundred other guys in suits you cross the broad bright asphalt of North Temple back toward the Mission Home. Air goes through your crotch the way it did when you wore the boxer shorts they gave you in the Army. Cars wait for you at the crosswalk in the dazzling sunlight of North Temple behind their idling engines. You don't look for faces through the windshields.

CHAPTER 75

NINETEEN years old. The oldest of five. In the morning your father's Valiant rides the whole family to the airport. Your mother rides up front. You ride behind her, in the back seat, packed in against Molly, Maggie next to her, Karl on the far side, his face in the same hot wind as yours. Roy rides in back with your big gray Samsonite. Your mother keeps using her hand to brace herself on the dashboard. You ride past the Cudahy stockyards. Nobody moves when you ride through the stink of sulfur past the black trusswork of the Phillips 66 refinery. In the sunlight, off the top of the tall black candle, the long tail of flame is defined more by heat than fire. The radio is dead. You ride past West High. You ride past the State Fairgrounds. On the ride out, from the back seat, you catch your face in the bright wind on the sideview mirror on the front door. You look away. And then back again a couple of times before your father finds a place to park in the airport lot.

Inside, once you've shown the man at the counter your passport and told him you're going to Vienna, once you've had your Samsonite taken away and all you're left with is your new Triple Combination, you head with your family for the main terminal. Through the vaulting expanse of glass that forms the front wall, vast windows that face the runway, the shoulders of the hills across the valley are pale with their already yellow weeds. Across the polished stone of the floor the morning light of the sun is fierce and underlights the faces of your family.

Your mother takes one of the chairs up front with this shameless angelic smile that won't let go of you. You think of all the Broadway songs she's always played and sung at home to an audience your father never listened from. Families form loose clusters around the terminal, missionary families, dressed like it's Sunday, gathered with smiling adoration around their missionaries, and it's easy to tell their girlfriends, girls who stand back, already radiant with the enduring and purifying patience of the long chaste wait ahead of them, letting everyone else have a turn at saying goodbye because they know they'll get the last turn, the important goodbye, the kiss goodbye that holds the warm soft promise that the Lord will reward the goodness of their missionary's life.

You see Hatch and Wissom and Clayton with their families. Hatch's girlfriend is a sunburned restless-looking blonde in a sleek white dress who doesn't look like she'll make the wait much past a week. Wissom's is a surprising knockout, a tall dark-haired librarian-looking girl with glasses, the East High kind of poise you'd think Wissom would have to look up in the dictionary before writing it down in his notebook. Clayton's girlfriend is bigger than he is, a big round country girl probably as used to helping cows give birth to calves as she is to making sugar cookies, but even from here you can tell she's the one real sweetheart of the three, the one who'll last.

Your seats won't be together for the flight. Your mission starts the minute you board the plane. Instead of sitting together, sharing the ride, they want you to sit with strangers, go to work on them.

Your father wanders around, looks out the windows when a plane coasts by, watches other families assembled around their missionaries. You've settled the money thing with him. How you'll pay for this. He'll send you sixty bucks a month out of your bank account. When the money you've saved runs out he'll send you sixty dollars of his own. You've got enough cash in your pocket to cover two months and buy yourself a bicycle. Roy and Maggie ask your mother if they can go look at the souvenirs.

"No, children. We have to stay together now. Your brother's plane is leaving!"

"Let them go," your father says. "We have time."

Speakers suddenly crack the air with a loud announcement to board a flight. Families drift toward an open attended door at the front of the terminal.

"All right then, children. Just don't ask for money. Things are very expensive here!"

In one of her Sunday dresses Molly looks around. From her face, its empty shyness, how deep she stays behind it, you can tell she's stealing looks at other girls, girls happy and unashamed in the bosoms of their happy missionary families. Karl wanders up to you.

"You hear about Yenchik?" he says.

"What?"

"They found his car in Pine View," he says.

"Reservoir?"

"Yeah."

"What do you mean, they found it?"

"In the water."

You look at him hard and close for the quiet sneer that tells you he's got something real on you. Feel your stomach go tight when you see it.

"Don't kid me about Yenchik."

"They found the guardrail busted. So they looked in the water and there it was."

You know the road. Two lanes that snake along the shoreline up the canyon. Sunflowers in the dirt and rocks along the guardrail. Waves from the wakes of ski boats keeping the boulders along the water wet.

"His car," you say. "The red Ford. You're sure."

"Yeah."

"What about him?"

"He wasn't there. They looked. It was just his car. Nobody was in it. They looked all over."

"That's crazy. Where is he?"

"Nobody knows."

"When?"

"A couple of days ago."

"He hasn't come home?"

"Nope."

"That doesn't make sense."

"Nope."

You look at your brother close and hard again. Remember the last time you were here with him. The way he wanted to know how your Zippo worked.

"You're not making this up."

"Nope. Ask Papa."

Standing there in your suit, your Triple Combination in your hand, the still ricochet of sunlight off the stone floor, your head runs wild. Yenchik. In his driveway the afternoon you brought the Ford back. His big dry desert bush of copper hair and his anvil jaw and forehead and his grease-streaked arms and the teeshirt with the woman riding the knobbed rocket of a camshaft. Still with that gutted look. In the house his mother dying from something wrong with her heart whose name he can't remember. Where he'd go. What city. How he'd get there. The sidewalk of what street with that gutted look. Karl standing there, just watching, watching his news sink in and do its work. You can see it glitter in his eyes.

"So you waited till now to tell me."

"Like you coulda done anything."

Why you couldn't be where you could help him. Why you had to be where you were.

"I coulda got used to it."

"You're lucky I told you. Papa said not to."

"Where's his car? What'd they do with it?"

"They pulled it out. That's all I know."

The water gauge. The steering wheel and gearshift in your hands. The seat behind your back where you had to lean forward to let the wind cool your teeshirt and dry the sweat off the naugahyde. The engine in your ears and spears of sunlight off the air scoop. At seventy across Nevada. You wince at the startling crack of the speakers again and the thunderclap of a voice telling David Jensen to come to the United ticket counter.

"No blood or anything," you say.

"It probably dissolved if there was."

"Thanks for telling me."

The Lord shall reward the goodness of your life. Every silent prayer you said, morning and night, kneeling there at your bunk with Hatch next to you, was about Yenchik. Every prayer. You look for your father, find him standing at the front of the terminal, by himself, his hands in the pockets of his suit pants, gazing out the huge windows that overlook the runway, empty for the moment, looking straight into the sun. You head his way. The look on his face makes you hesitate. It's the look you would know in the dark, your father alone, not thinking anyone could be watching him, the restless contemplative look you've caught in his face a thousand times, the man who brought his family all the way from Switzerland, who lives with the constant haunting possibility of the failure to keep them together the rest of the way home. The look cut deeper now. Cut deep into his face in the blast of sunlight where even from a distance you can see the muscles flex along his jaw. You circle around to give him room to see you before you get there.

"You know about Yenchik."

"Who told you?"

"Yenchik's my friend," you say.

"Yes. It's a tragedy. He was planning on being here today."

"He was?"

"That's what he told your mother. He called and wanted to know about your flight."

"When?"

"It had to be early last week sometime."

A quick light scurry of fear through your chest when you recognize how remote from your own life you already are.

"How's his mother?" you say.

"How should I know? Why? Is something wrong?"

You look at him. Not even close to aware that he just said the name of the band he made it his mission to never recognize. To never come out and see and listen to and clap for.

"She's dying."

"By golly. I wasn't aware of that."

"Excuse me."

You walk away. Back into the terminal out of the sun. Far enough to think this out. Cash your ticket in. Empty your bank account. Find a used Porsche you can afford. A busted one you can fix. Head west across the Salt Flats with your trumpet on the other seat. You know the highway. Cissy. I have to stay home tonight and wash my hair. Sweat breaks your armpits and cuts down your sides. I know this club on Stimson Avenue that plays jazz on Friday night. Maybe we can go. You've sent her mother three addresses. The Mojave Desert. The Salt Lake Mission Home. The Austrian Mission Home on some Vienna street. I really want to see The Miracle Worker. Elko. Winnemucca. Battle Mountain. You know the desert towns. Vallejo. The Porsche painted red like Yenchik's big Ford. The Porsche red inside like the red interior of the big Ford, the red upholstered chamber of its heart, where Cissy and you were dressed, and then were naked and indistinguishable in the dark, and then were dressed again, her yellow top and her white skirt, and then everywhere the dusk rose sheen of her coffee honey skin, and then her yellow top and her white skirt once again while she fixed her hair and put on lipstick in the mirror.

You look down. Try to clear your head. On the polished floor you look like you're wading in sunlight halfway up your legs. The Ford that night. The breathtaking blush of the way you wanted each other in her face. You look up again. You can feel her in your hands now, her imprint, everything you took the time to memorize. Clusters of families, white and delightsome families, gathered in white-faced oases across the floor of the terminal, but all you can see is her, in San Jose, dressed not in yellow and white but in pink, dressed not in a top and skirt but in a dress this time, the two of you going to church, you in your charcoal suit, her in a flowing soft pink Sunday dress, both of you dressed for church where you'll pick her voice out of the choir. You see her again, the blaze of her teeth and eyes in the sunlight of her yard, her unforgettable poise, playful and bold and unafraid in the circle of her five big Airborne uncles. In the sprawling cluster of her family you can see your family there, your father clowning around, your mother chatting with Mrs. Taylor, flashing the silver hook of her bridge when she laughs, Molly with Cissy in the circle of her admiring Airborne uncles, Karl trying out Jeff's conga drums, Roy and Maggie shyly sizing up other kids their size. Cissy. In her white shoes, shoes with modest heels, white shoes she wears to church, holding a small white purse. If only you could show them.

CHAPTER 76

WHILE YOU STAND there imagining her the speakers crack with the Polynesian thunder of another boarding call. Families here and there start drifting toward the front of the terminal.

And then something's wrong. Wrong enough to scare you. Families are crossing in front of the way you're imagining her, blocking her from sight, turning to look at her like they can see her too, and when they're gone she's there again, wearing the flowing Sunday dress you're imagining her wearing, a soft pink dress that reaches down to just below her knees and leaves her calves and ankles showing, sleeves that end in flares half down her forearms where they leave the startling skin of her wrists and hands exposed, the scoop of its neckline off her shoulders deep but still modest, a cradle of pink for the sudden color of her chest where it lifts into her collarbones and then her neck and then the face you've memorized by touch and taste and smell.

In her white Sunday shoes. Holding a small white purse. Like she's really there. Like you've turned her so real she's standing there, across the terminal, where other people see her too. A soldier stands next to her in his dress green uniform and service cap. You watch her hand come up. A smile break her face. It startles you. It's for you. You've taken some trick made of sunlight and longing off the polished floor of the terminal and made it wave and smile at you.

You start across the terminal around other people's families aware of your suit. Aware of the Triple Combination in your hand. Aware of leaving your family behind to wonder what's going on. Aware of Hatch calling Hey Elder as you move around his family and cut past his sunburned girlfriend. You don't dare take your eyes off Cissy. Scared if you do you'll miss the moment when you start to lose her, when she'll start transforming into someone else, some stranger that sunlight and longing have superimposed her on the way a shining desert lake evaporates into just more dirt and sagebrush when you close the distance. But she doesn't. She just keeps turning real. The way you can see how the sleeves and neckline of her dress are bordered with lace. The way she sees you coming. The way she lets her hand down. The way hesitation vanishes from the skin between her eyebrows and happiness unleashes her smile and pleasure brings the flush of blood into her skin. She's here. Not in what your hands remember. Not in some imprint. But in your own breathless rush of blood that you know from the time you saw her standing on her porch will always unmistakably be just for her. The soldier next to her. The taste of beer in the Fort Ord sunset. Jeff.

"Hi," she says.

Her voice again. Her face.

"Hi."

And then all you can do is look at her, take in her face and eyes, and she stands there and lets you have your way until it gets embarrassing, until she has to start looking down and away, until you're aware too that there are people looking.

"You're really here," you say.

"Yeah." She looks at Jeff with a soft shy laugh. "We sure are."

"I can't believe it."

"Now you know how it feels," she says.

"You look beautiful."

Seeing the small pearls nested in the lobes of her ears. Making her smile but shy again. Looking away and shaking your head to clear out any lingering trace of mirage so that when you look back at her you can see her fresh.

"You're really here."

"Stop it now," she says.

You turn to Jeff. You've already seen the three stripes on his sleeve.

"Hey Sarge."

"Hey Brother."

You shake his hand. Still Jeff. A tougher and leaner version. All business now. Not the guy who'd fall asleep and let his head bob off your shoulder on a night bus out of San Jose. Slick in his tailored uniform.

"You look great too. All dressed up."

"She made me," he says.

"I did not," she says. "You wanted to."

"I figured you'd be in a suit," he says. "I couldn't let you show me up."

"Cool patch there," you say, nodding at his shoulder, and he turns to give you a better look, a tall blue patch, the single wing of a white bird, a white wing that carries a red sword in a white hook.

"Thanks."

"What's it stand for?"

"173rd Airborne Brigade. I just got assigned. I'll be shipping out for Okinawa once I get your girl home."

"He wants you to notice his medals," Cissy says.

"What are little sisters for," he says.

"I see them. Some collection. You've been busy."

"I've got another one coming," he says. "For driving."

"You drove here? When?"

"Last two days. We spent a night in Reno. Got here last night." And then he says, "I heard you did it straight."

"Yeah." Thinking the highway. The trip they made for you.

"He owed me," Cissy says. "After the way he scared you off."

"I'm sorry," says Jeff. "I never meant to get between you."

"I know. Where'd you stay?"

"Last night? Some motel just up the road."

"You drive the Bel Air?"

"Dad let us take his car. You look good, man. All suited up. Where's your horn?"

"Had to leave it home."

"Is that your Bible?" Cissy asks.

"Yeah. Sort of." You take another long look at her. "How did you know? About this morning? About my flight?"

"From your friend. Melvin. With the fun last name."

On the edge of the seat naked, under the dome light, her hair wild, her long back bare from her shoulders all the way down to the rumpled yellow of your Hawaiian shirt on the red naugahyde. Yenchik's registration card in her hand. Memorizing his address. In front of her brother you try to hide the memory. Fill the glove compartment with water. Flood the red interior of the Ford and everything that happened there with reservoir water all the way to the roof.

"You got hold of him?"

"I wanted to surprise you."

"When did you talk to him?"

"A couple of weeks ago the first time. He said we probably wouldn't get to see you till today."

"So you drove up."

"We're staying for the day. To see the sights. We'll head back home tomorrow."

Her in your town. You not here.

"Save some for me to show you."

"Don't worry," she says. "We're just doing the tourist stuff. Temple Square. The State Capitol. Stuff like that." She smiles. "We won't go see your band. Don't worry."

And then she just looks at you. Waits for Jeff to get it and walk a few steps off. And then you reach down and she lets you take her hand.

"I can't believe you came to see me."

"I had to." And then she says, "I didn't know how far it was. I'm sorry. I never should have let you go that night."

"It's okay. I had to."

"Did you make it home okay?"

"Yeah. Were things okay with your folks?"

"Yeah."

"I'm glad."

Nothing. Embarrassed now.

"I'm sorry."

"I love you," she says, and you feel her fingers tighten their hold on yours.

"I love you."

"I wanted to say it to your face. That's why I came."

"I love you."

"I love you."

"Can I finally write you?"

"Yes." And then she says, "I've already written you."

"You have?"

"It may already be there," she says.

"In Vienna?"

"Air mail," she says.

The speakers crack again with a boarding call. It startles her. You feel the flinch in her hand and see its quick pulse in the skin between her eyebrows.

"That's me this time," you say.

"Oh," she says. "Jeff? That's his flight. We need to go."

"Come meet my family," you say.

"Are you sure?"

"They're good people. Like yours."

"This is their time to be with you."

You look back to where you left them. Your father standing in the sun. Looking your way. Your mother on her feet now, looking your way too, and Karl and Molly watching.

"Come meet them. Look. They can't stand it."

You take her hand in hand across the stone floor of the terminal, your sweetheart too, poised and reverent and astonishing at your side. Past Clayton's family, past his own big sweetheart, who looks at the two of you with this sweet adoring benevolent smile that makes you blush the way you're so quick to fall in love with her. Past Wissom's family. Past Wissom's tall librarian, who's looking too, through her glasses out of her bloodless East High face, while you wonder what you could have seen in her. Past Wissom, whose look is blank and undisguised like you're incapable of looking back, already doing the nasty math against the possibility that she's Tahitian or Tongan or some other South Pacific Island princess. You give him a week to have the word all over the Austrian Mission that your sweetheart is the striking and unbelievably beautiful seed of Cain, the prized and beautiful seed of Negro royalty, too prized and beautiful to go alone, so prized and beautiful she's been assigned the full dress escort of a United States Army Airborne Soldier. Past Hatch, who's looking too, looking like his teeth ache, and then straight to where your father's standing, in the open, where you know you can count on him to be decent and civil no matter what you've just done to rain on his long-fought day of triumph.

"This is my dad. Harold Tauffler. Papa, this is Cissy. Cissy Taylor."

"I'm pleased to meet you, Mr. Tauffler."

She puts out her hand. You watch him shake it. "No," he says, his voice jocular, his smile broad in the ridged flesh of his broad face. "I'm afraid all the pleasure is mine, by golly."

"This is her brother Jeff," you say. "We were in the Army together."

"Good to meet you, Mr. Tauffler."

"It's good to meet you, Sir. By golly. Look at those medals."

"They're here from San Jose. They came to see me off."

"From San Jose," your father says. "That's quite a tribute."

"He's worth it," Jeff says.

"Yes he is," says Cissy.

"This is my mom," you say, where she's standing next to your father now, her church face on, smiling and angelic, but you can see where it's undermined by this questioning apprehension. "Elizabeth Tauffler. This is Cissy, Mama."

"Pleased to meet you, Mrs. Tauffler."

"Yes. It is nice to meet you too. Are you a friend of our son's?"

Cissy looks at her. "I guess you—"

"She's my sweetheart," you say.

"Oh?" Your mother looks at you. You can see her face start to cave to all the questions wanting to ask themselves. "You didn't tell us—"

"Don't you want to shake her hand?"

She looks at Cissy's still extended hand. "Oh, yes," she says, quick to animate herself, shoo away her questions like unwanted birds. "I am so sorry!" And then she says, "How beautiful you are! Shakli, did you see? Did you see how beautiful! Did you see how everyone was looking, Harold! Children! Look how beautiful she is!"

You introduce her and Jeff to Karl and Molly and Roy and Maggie. In return for their shy and quiet astonishment she gives each one of them the full attention of her lush face and the frank and easy smile you fell in love with. Karl looks at her hand while he shakes it. Molly keeps skating her eyes away from Cissy's face and back again. Roy looks up at you with this thrilled and helpless smile.

"My brother's a soldier too," Maggie tells Jeff.

"That's right," says Jeff. "A good one."

The crack of the speakers. The boarding call for your flight again.

"So, Shakli!," your mother cries. "That is the second time! Come! Hurry, children! Let's not make them wait!"

"Yes, everybody," your father says. "It's time."

"We need to go," Cissy says.

Jeff steps up to take her. You look across the terminal where Wissom and Hatch and Clayton are standing in line with their families at the door of the gate. Wissom with his head down, busy listening to a guy who could be his father but looks more like his accounting teacher, his librarian standing behind him trying not to look forgotten. Clayton and his sweetheart shoulder to shoulder, their heads together, their arms around each other's backs. Hatch and his girlfriend in the hoops of each other's arms, grinning, making a game of pecking at each other's sunburned faces. Other missionaries making the most of hugging and kissing their sweethearts goodbye. Your father already on his way across the terminal.

"Walk with us," you tell her. "Just to the line."

"Okay."

And now your arm slips around her waist and her head rests on your shoulder and you can feel the tingle of her hair on your neck and ear and cheek and smell the desert ride in there, in her hair, mingled in what she washed it with. Even in modest heels she's almost as tall as you. Her hand finds its way beneath the jacket of your suit and then leads her arm across your shirt around your back. She puts her other hand on your chest. At the end of the line, thick with families, where your father waits for his, you let each other go.

"I guess this is it," she says.

"I'll start writing a letter soon as I'm on the plane."

"I'll write you one today too," she says. Both her hands on your chest again and the skin between her eyebrows coarse while her eyes roam back and forth across your face. "Tonight in the motel. After I've seen your town."

"I love you."

"I love you," she says. "Do I get a kiss too?"

Because nothing can hurt you.

"Jeff. Here."

You take her purse and your Triple Combination and hand them to her brother. Take her face in your hands and close your eyes from there. Feel her warm lean hands on your own face. And when you kiss you still know everything. See the place where she keeps the closet and drawers and pillow for you. When you let each other go, you see water pooled again in the pink crescents of her lower eyelids, and then quietly break across and down her cheeks.

"I'm sorry," she says. "Jeff, please, hurry, I need my purse."

But he already has it open. Already has a hanky out. She wipes her cheeks. And then wipes her lipstick off your lips. The line has pulled forward, left you stranded, backed people up behind you. Nobody says anything.

"Okay," she says. "I'm ready. I'll go now."

"I love you."

And she steps away. Jeff hands her back her purse, hands you your Triple Combination, shakes your hand. "See you in San Jose, Brother."

"Count on it," you say. "You take care in Okinawa."

"Nice meeting you all," she calls to your family. "Thank you. Thank you all so much."

The line moves slowly. Family goodbyes take their time. Nobody minds. And soon it's your family's turn, at the head of the line, at the place where only empty floor stands between you and the door that leads outside to the white plane, floor you'll be crossing on your own. Your mother takes your face between her hands and kisses you on the mouth where Cissy wiped you clean. Karl steps in and shakes your hand while you use the back of your other hand to wipe your mother's lipstick off. Molly comes up. She lets you hold her, lets you have your way, the way she did the night you caught her below the orchard. "Remember what you promised me," you whisper in her ear, "about letting me know," and feel her nod her head. Roy comes up and lifts his Deacon's face and puts his arms around you. You hug him back. Feel his shoulders and back through the coarse-haired cloth of his sport jacket. How much bigger he'll be when you see him again. Maggie looks up and tells you goodbye from the shelter of Molly's arm around her shoulder.

And then it's your father's turn. Down to you and him.

"Well, this is it," you say.

"Yes."

You feel him shy back from you. Feel him want to have this over. Feel him tense, restless, almost hostile, something in his attitude like the need to settle some score with someone you've never known. You don't know. It's never felt like one thing you could pinpoint. All you know is that you've coughed up everything. Emptied your pockets. What more he wants. What it is he knows he's always kept from you.

"If you hear anything about Yenchik," you tell him, "please let me know."

"Yes," he says. "I will."

"Thanks."

You'll fly from here to New York. And from New York to Vienna. He shakes your hand. You search his face for any sign he'd call this off for you. Tell you that he doesn't need for you to do this. That you don't need to go for him. That you could just as easy go to San Jose and he'd be fine with you. And you'd say no, thanks, you're going anyway, because all along it's always been where you're going. At least you'd know. At least you'd know you were okay. But you can see where he keeps it trapped in the wilderness of the ridges of his face. You're on your own. At the rim of the cliff, Dead Horse Point, where the level ground you've come across just falls away, down thousands of feet through open sky, where the next step you take is where he'll fall away himself, and everything from there will be on your own. The way his face looks makes you turn and look out through the window at the white plane waiting in the sunlight, people climbing the staircase to its door, before you can look at him again. You feel it too. The need to have this over.

"Remember who you are," he says.

"I will," you say. "I promise."

"You're an Instrument of the Lord now."

"I know. I'll remember."

~ *to be continued* ~

ACKNOWLEDGEMENTS

Those of you who were kind enough to read and enjoy *Journey* and share your experience and enthusiasm not only with me but with your friends and with strangers on Amazon and other sites where readers gather.

Diane Cole for her exceptional reading and editing and the gift of her experience and support in showcasing the trilogy to its home audience.

Professor Sherri Van Houten for her pioneering use of *Journey* in her religion and philosophy courses. Her remarkable students for bringing Shake to life with their passion, insight, empathy, and enthusiasm.

Tim Stephenson for the friendship and faith and coaching that did so much to make this happen. Seth Ersner-Hershfield for helping me earn back the freedom and sense of entitlement to write.

My sister Margie for her always inspiring and tireless cheerleading. My brother Marv for helping me authenticate the musical and local jazz theory and Salt Lake to keep those aspects of the story real, and for his always defiant support and tireless advocacy.

Ed Wilson of the Nevada Department of Transportation for helping me sequence the construction of Interstate 80 across Nevada in the 1960s.

My original agent Michael Strong of Regal Literary who for three years guided me in getting Book 1 and Book 2 right.

John Murray for his counsel on how to place this book where you could stumble across it.

The circle of poets and writers – Nik Gruswitz, Melissa Montimurro, Carlo D'Ambrosi, Chase Talon, Bryan Straube, and others – who made up the workshop in which Shake had his genesis.

The women and men of the New Jersey Replicar Club who read my monthly newsletters and were such an important audience to write for.

Carolyn and Jim Youngs, publisher and editor of *Kit Car Builder*, who gave me the license to write what I wanted, and extended that important audience to wonderful readers of all walks of life across the country.

A trumpet player in Key West who let me know that you don't write about a kid who plays jazz trumpet without knowing how to play yourself.

Ed Selby, jazz trumpet player and teacher, who taught me how to play, and also allowed me to model Shake's teacher on him.

The people who offered to read *If Where You're Going Isn't Home* as a work in progress. The long – and daunting – draft they read would eventually be divided to become the first two books of the trilogy. More story – the third book – remained to be told. But at 378,000 words it was time to learn how the story would play to different readers. Twenty-five people, ranging in age from 18 to 77, from all walks of life, religions, backgrounds, interests, reading tastes, and regions of the country, stepped up to volunteer. In completely random order, these remarkable people are Jean Turco, George Goetz, Kim Keefer, Nikolaus Tea, Marian Murray, Marjorie Zimmer, Debra Lynn Nicholson, Lewis Turco, Helen Tobler, Alan Merklin, Paul Mossberg, my niece Sophie, Edwin Selby, John Murray, Bob Smart, my son Damon Cooper, Seth Ersner-Hershfield, Marilyn Weber, Chase Talon, Fred Simpson, Theo Mickelfeld, Joan Selby, Matt Smart, and Marv Zimmer. It is impossible to capture in words what their effort, faith, and feedback have meant to me and to the book. All I can do is thank them. Over and over. Again.

Rick and Cheryl Hughes for throwing the best surprise party of my life – my very first booksigning – in their new home.

Joan Waldron, owner and proprietor of Max's Station House, for the best watering hole a writer this side of the Hudson could ask for, and Tina Hollowich, another regular there and the inspiration for the lady in the red dress who captivates Shake in this novel.

Mrs. Whitaker, Miss Johnson, Ruth Jones, Blanche Cannon, Steve Baar, Franklin Fisher, David Kranes, Hal Moore, Richard Schramm, and all the other teachers who guided, encouraged, and championed me.

Grace Paley, Ray Carver, E.L. Doctorow, Lewis Turco, John Gardner, John Cheever, Jack Cady, and other established writers who saw promise in my work.

All the people – all my students and friends across more than four decades – who have had to wait and believe in me so long to finally see this happen. I hope you'll think it was worth it.

The Boys from Bountiful – George Baty, Bobby West, Roger Jensen, Mike Flowers, Johnny Rasmussen, Harold Zesiger, Steve Derbyshire, Bob Gardiner, and Johnny Greenwell – for giving Shake the fictional buddies to continue the journey with.

My parents who raised me and loved me and, in the end, supported me and gave me a story worth telling.

My wife Toni.

ABOUT THE AUTHOR

Max Zimmer was born in Switzerland, brought across the Atlantic at the age of four, and raised in Utah in the take-no-prisoners crucible of the Mormon faith. He earned a B.A. and an M.A. from the University of Utah and was teaching fiction, working on a doctorate in writing, when he was invited east for a summer at Yaddo, the writer's retreat in Saratoga, New York. He never intended to stay in the East. But from Yaddo he took a job teaching fiction in the Writing Arts Program at SUNY Oswego. It was there, in the summer of 1978, that *If Where You're Going Isn't Home* was first conceived, as a long love story. From Oswego, Max gravitated toward the city, lived and tended bar in Manhattan, and eventually moved to the northwest corner of New Jersey, where he married his wife Toni and settled in to write *If Where You're Going Isn't Home* from the beginning. The East had become home now. Utah had become a place he was from, a place he wrote about.

Aside from the first two novels of the trilogy, Max's published work includes poems, stories, reviews, magazine articles, short biographies, and liner notes for jazz albums. He was an immediate success as a writer. Following its nomination by Ray Carver, his first published story "Utah Died for Your Sins" was awarded the Pushcart Prize, and singled out in *Rolling Stone* magazine as a raw new voice in American fiction. Max has read at venues ranging from coffee shops to SUNY writers' conferences to the Pen New Writers Series. Jack Cady, Grace Paley, Lewis Turco, and John Gardner are among other established writers who have expressed their high regard and admiration for his work. E. L. Doctorow called Max's writing the best he'd seen in a coast-to-coast college tour following the release of *Ragtime*. After meeting him on a similar tour following the publication of *Falconer*, John Cheever enthusiastically promoted Max's work for the last five years of his life.

As a break from the long and ambitious project that *If Where You're Going Isn't Home* has been, Max still writes poetry, short fiction, and an anything-goes human interest column under the heading "Actual Mileage" – inspired by a Ray Carver story – for an automotive magazine with an international readership.

www.maxzimmer.com

CPSIA information can be obtained at www.ICGtesting.com
Printed in the USA
LVOW07s0232070815

449224LV00004B/160/P

9 780985 448158